P9-DGG-222

"A mystery that will hold you in its grip to the last page."

"*Murder at Sunrise Lake* is everything I didn't know I needed in a thriller."

The Carpathian Novels

Anthologies

Specials

RED ON THE RIVER

CHRISTINE FEEHAN

BERKLEY ROMANCE
New York

BERKLEY ROMANCE
Published by Berkley
An imprint of Penguin Random House LLC
penguinrandomhouse.com

Copyright © 2022 by Christine Feehan
Excerpt from *Shadow Dance* copyright © 2023 by Christine Feehan
Penguin Random House supports copyright. Copyright fuels creativity, encourages
diverse voices, promotes free speech, and creates a vibrant culture. Thank you for buying
an authorized edition of this book and for complying with copyright laws by not
reproducing, scanning, or distributing any part of it in any form without permission.
You are supporting writers and allowing Penguin Random House to continue to
publish books for every reader.

BERKLEY and the BERKLEY and B colophon are registered trademarks of
Penguin Random House LLC.

ISBN: 9780593439159

Berkley hardcover edition / June 2022
Berkley Romance mass-market edition / June 2023

Printed in the United States of America
1 3 5 7 9 10 8 6 4 2

For Deborah Wold Wallace,
my adventurous friend

FOR MY READERS

Be sure to go to christinefeehan.com/members/ to sign up for my private book announcement list and download the free ebook of *Dark Desserts*, which includes recipes of many wonderful desserts! Join my community and get first-hand news, enter the book discussions, ask your questions and chat with me. Please feel free to email me at Christine @christinefeehan.com. I would love to hear from you.

ACKNOWLEDGMENTS

As with any book, there are so many people to thank. This book was particularly difficult because it was necessary to get the details of gambling, climbing, kayaking and hiking correct. Any mistakes are mine and not my primary sources', who were so gracious to help me over and over. I have to thank Denise Tucker, who graciously provided help, went on research trips and spent hours going over scenes with me. Tiffani Canevari, thank you for going on the research and climbing trip with Denise to Red Rock and on the kayaking trip on the Colorado River. The two of you provided such valuable information. Jimmy Bussey, thank you for providing me with so much information on the world of gambling. Thanks to Chris Walker for double-checking my work. Sarah Hafer, thank you for editing what you could. Diane Trudeau, thank you for coming through at the eleventh hour and staying up with me for days and nights editing to get it done! This was a labor of love.

CHAPTER ONE

∿∿∿∿∿∿∿∿∿∿∿∿∿∿∿∿∿∿∿∿

Vienna Mortenson pushed her shiny key into the private elevator to take her to the floor where her suite was located. She had never been impressed with money. Never. She preferred camping outdoors to hotels, no matter how luxurious they were, and casinos were *not* her thing. Being a nurse and seeing time and again what cigarettes could do to people, she despised the smell of them. Just walking through a casino floor made her want to tell all those people smoking what was inevitably going to happen to them. Yet here she was, being impressed with this particular hotel.

The Northern Lights Hotel and Casino was owned by billionaire Daniel J. Wallin. Vienna was aware that he had partners, but Wallin had started the hotel; it was his concept and he owned the majority of shares. It was rare for a single hotel to do the kind of business that his did. It was popular, full to capacity at all times. The twice-a-year gambling tournaments drew the biggest names and had some of the biggest returns, which was one of the reasons she had decided to participate even though it required her to be there in person.

Normally, Vienna competed online. She'd built her reputation through her username *luckypersiancat*. She'd managed to pay for her mother's cancer treatments. Her mother still lived in Vegas with her partner, and Vienna paid her rent using her gambling money. She'd put herself through nursing school. She owned a nice house in Knightly, where she resided with her Persian cat, Princess. She'd put quite a bit away for retirement and invested most of the rest of her winnings. She gave a great deal of the money to the local hospital and also invested in search and rescue gear for the county she lived in. She had established a scholarship program for single mothers with children. She'd been careful to stay under the gambling radar, living and working in Knightly at the local hospital. She was also head of Search and Rescue for the county.

"Honey, hold that elevator," a voice called out.

Vienna turned. She didn't particularly like to be addressed as "honey" by total strangers, but the gentleman calling out to her was older. He looked to be about seventy, with thick gray hair and faded blue eyes. He did look fit, even though he walked with a cane. She flicked a quick, assessing glance over him to see what his injury might be. He didn't appear to have one. He wasn't actually limping or even leaning heavily on the cane. He wasn't even walking with it correctly. He did have a key to the elevator in his hand, so she held the door.

She looked past him to the man behind him and her breath caught in her lungs. Everything in her stilled. She nearly let go of the door. Zale Vizzini. The moment she saw him, she could taste him. The way he kissed. Feel him inside her. The way he moved. The way he filled her. No one was like him. No one ever would be again. Her eyes met his, and she caught the little shake of his head. It was almost imperceptible. His hand lifted to his chest and he waved her off— again, the smallest movement.

Vienna flashed a brilliant smile at the older gentleman, who was nearly to the elevator. "You know, if security is watching, I'll probably receive a visit from them."

"And rightfully so," the man said cheerfully. He stepped inside the cedar-scented elevator, hooking the cane over his arm as he did so. "I'm Wayne Forsyne. You're actually more beautiful in person than in your photograph, and I thought that was extraordinary." He completely ignored Zale slipping into the lift behind him and settling against a wall.

The doors slid shut silently and the elevator began to rise. Vienna kept her gaze steadfastly on the older man, although every nerve ending in her body was vividly aware of Zale. It was embarrassing and rather humiliating not only that she could feel his body heat when he was completely across from her but that she could feel her entire body reacting to his presence. That *never* happened around other men.

Deliberately, she sighed. "I suppose you're referring to that obnoxious wraparound photograph the hotel has of me along with the other tournament players going around and around the outside of the hotel and then in the lobby and again in the casino?"

"You look lovely, even more so in person."

"I think it's a little overdone to have us everywhere, not to mention it seems like it's miles high, but I suppose it's good advertisement for the hotel and casino."

The elevator smoothly came to a stop and the doors glided open. Forsyne waved for her to precede him, and she did so without hesitation. She didn't need to be in such close proximity to Zale. She would know his scent anywhere. The cedar in the elevator couldn't cover the way his skin hinted at first snow and fresh rain in the High Sierras.

She wanted to run to the door of her suite, but instead she turned calmly to smile at Forsyne. "It was lovely to meet you."

"If security takes you to task for helping an old man out, you call for me. I'm next door."

There were only four suites on the entire floor, and his suite was directly across from hers. She shared the elevator with Forsyne. The other two suites had their own elevator on the other side of the floor.

"I'll do that." She was very proud of herself for not looking at Zale as she inserted her gold key into the lock and the door opened for her. She stepped inside and closed the door, nearly going to the floor, her legs turning to rubber.

She had never thought she would see Zale Vizzini again. Not ever—and she didn't want to see him. She wasn't a woman to make a fool of herself over a man. He'd walked away from her without a backward glance. That had hurt. Really hurt. She knew better than to have any faith in men, but she'd wanted to think she'd mattered to him. She hadn't. So, okay. She'd gotten her heart broken just like a million other women. She was tough. She could take it. She didn't want a repeat of the process, and seeing him and feeling her instant reaction told her she was susceptible to him.

Vienna slid down the door to sit on the floor. There was no one around to see her moment of weakness. She had learned to take those moments if they came. She was decisive as a rule. She'd been raised by a single mother and they had struggled financially, though not at first. They seemed to have money coming in, and they lived in a nice neighborhood in a nice home. But when it came time for her to go to school, that hadn't lasted.

She'd had to learn at an early age not to let other people's opinions bother her. Her clothes weren't good enough. The car her mother drove wasn't nice. They eventually lived in a run-down apartment so the money could go to private school tuition. Soon, they didn't have the money for that. Vienna was grateful that they didn't have the money and she could leave that school where the girls weren't nice to her. She got odd jobs to help out, contributing the money and feeling like it was the two of them, her mother and her, against the world. They were so close, and she loved that.

Vienna took a deep breath and looked around the far-too-large-for-one-person suite. It was gorgeous, from the marble floors and grand piano, to the sweeping views and up-to-date high-tech gaming room, to the deep soaking tub, Jacuzzi, private hot tub on the balcony, walk-in marble shower and enormous far-too-comfortable bed with fireplace and views.

There wasn't anything she could possibly think of that had been left out. If she did need anything, she simply had to pick up the phone and her own personal concierge would immediately provide it for her. Best of all, it was free. Why? Because she'd been invited to play in their tournament. The one with the enormous prize at the end. How could she possibly resist coming out from behind her anonymity for a chance at millions, especially since she was already going to be in Vegas?

She'd been there for over a week, playing along with more than a thousand hopefuls trying to get a seat in the semifinals. She'd steadily advanced, one game at a time, until she'd finally managed to make one of the coveted seats.

Her phone buzzed and she glanced down. Stella Harrison. The bride. One of her best friends. "Right here, but I'm not sure I'm speaking to you at the moment," she greeted.

"Uh-oh. What's wrong? Are the other players being mean?"

"I can handle players in a tournament," Vienna said. She stood and ran her finger back and forth along the beautiful table. There wasn't a speck of dust. Not one single speck. Now she was putting fingerprints on it. She felt a little guilt over that. "Do you remember when Sam had some of his friends take us to Shabina's house because he felt it was the safest place to be when the killer had threatened us?" She couldn't make herself say the killer's name. It still hurt, after all these months.

"He threatened you specifically, Vienna, and me," Stella said. "But yes, I remember."

"I wasn't so happy about being forced to leave work by some man I didn't know. He didn't give me much choice. And he didn't talk much either. It wasn't like he explained the situation."

"As I recall, none of Sam's friends were big on talking, but then, Sam isn't either," Stella agreed. "We've just gotten used to Sam over the years we've known him."

Vienna appreciated that Stella was allowing her to get

around to what she had to say without hurrying her. Vienna wasn't certain how to explain the situation. "The man he sent to collect me was named Zale. I found him the most annoying and attractive man I'd ever met in my life. He was so damned intelligent and could actually talk when he wanted to about a wide variety of subjects."

There was silence on the other end of the phone. Vienna could almost count the breaths Stella took. "When did you ever have a conversation with him? Certainly not at Shabina's house. We were all together. I would have known you were talking to him. And afterward, when we found out Denver was dead, we were all so shocked and devastated, we just kind of stayed together for a little while and talked things out."

"I know. But then I went backpacking up into the mountains alone. I didn't want to be afraid of a serial killer coming after me. I have to be able to go into all sorts of places without being afraid. I decided I needed to just go, to get it over with. I had built up a ton of vacation and I took six weeks, packed up and went hiking. Zale followed me."

Again, there was a long silence. Finally, there was the sound of a door closing. "Sorry, someone came in. I take it you didn't send him away."

"No, he stayed with me for the entire six weeks. He was this amazing man. So intelligent, and you know how brains matter to me. He could make me laugh. And he was great outdoors. On top of that, he was dynamite in bed. He could light up the night. I had no idea sex could be like that. We didn't talk about my home life or his, because I thought we had all the time in the world. For some ridiculous reason, I believed he was as taken with me as I was with him. I mean, he didn't say so, and neither did I, but when he touched me, I felt it. So much for my intuition as a woman."

Vienna was very proud of herself for keeping any bitterness from her voice. She didn't even feel bitter. She'd been hurt, but she wasn't bitter. Zale hadn't given her false promises. If she had built a relationship between them, it had been all in her mind. He'd shown up, they'd talked. She couldn't even say he'd seduced her. The attraction had been mutual. He'd been respectful. Careful of her because they were alone out in the middle of Yosemite. He'd told her he'd pitch a tent away from her. She'd been the one to make the decision to allow him to stay with her.

"What happened?"

"He just packed up one day and disappeared without a word. I mean, I woke up, he was packing up, he leaned over and kissed me goodbye and was gone. I never heard from him again."

"Are you kidding me?" Stella sounded outraged.

"No. He really is one of the ghosts Denver was always going on about. In any case, he's clearly working some job here. He signaled to me that he didn't want me to acknowledge that I knew him. Or maybe he's married and his wife is here with him. Sheesh, I never even considered that." Now that she thought of it, she was alarmed. Horrified.

"No, he's not married. Well, at least I don't think he is. Now I'm going to go grill Sam. Zale Vizzini is Sam's best man. I had no idea you even knew him other than for that brief moment at Shabina's or I would have told Sam he was banned from our wedding. I wonder if it's too late to kick him out. I'll turn into bridezilla for you."

Vienna laughed. "You can't do that. I can handle it. It was just such a shock to see him." She sobered up suddenly. "Although if he was married at the time, I'll have to retaliate even if it's in a childish way. That would be so disgusting. I do *not* mess around with married men. And that includes men in partnerships."

"I'll find out what I can and call you back."

"Please keep what I told you confidential."

"I'm very aware you're an extremely private person,

Vienna. In any case, you kept everything about me confidential," Stella said. "I can't wait to see you in a few days."

"I'm looking forward to bouldering and some other outdoor adventures. After the tournament, I'll need to be out of this building," Vienna assured. "Don't forget to text or call me back when you know something. I don't want to be up all night feeling guilty if I didn't do anything wrong."

"Will do," Stella promised.

Vienna paced around the suite several times. She'd meant to stay in and just relax, but now she couldn't. She needed action. Something. Anything outdoors. She would have to work tomorrow, starting early afternoon, and play carefully to stay in the game. She was playing against some of the top players in that world. She'd made it through to the semifinal table, a feat she was certain hadn't been expected of her.

When Vienna first started, she'd had to borrow money to buy into her first online game. She'd won. She'd been able to borrow the money because those who knew her were aware of her uncanny ability to win at cards. It wasn't that Vienna counted cards or anything like that, she just "knew" things. She had a gift, and over the years she'd come to believe in it and knew she could trust it. Because she saw her talent as a gift, she didn't overuse it, and she made it a point to give back in some way.

She knew that when she entered the room with the other players at the semifinal table, they would all be looking for anything they could to help them get an advantage over her. Vienna had been in charge of others as a surgical nurse and also as head of Search and Rescue for Inyo County. Sometimes that would spill over to Mono County as well.

She was experienced in all-weather rescues, and could do avalanche control when needed. She'd climbed Mount Whitney several times and rescued more than one person as well as retrieved bodies when weekend climbers thought they knew more than the experts who warned them of the various hazards.

She had to make split-second decisions that could be life or death for others as well as for herself under extreme conditions. She didn't give much away unless she wanted to. She wasn't worried about the tournament. She had made it through to the semifinal table and had every confidence that she would make the final table.

Once, because she'd needed the money for her mother's cancer treatment, Vienna had made the mistake of playing in person at some of the tables in Vegas, and someone had tried to rob her on her way home. As if she'd carry cash in her pockets. What idiot would do that? She'd arrived home shaken beyond belief, needing comfort from her mother, only to end up in a huge fight with her. Her mother had been her best friend all of her life. That night had changed her life forever. Vienna had moved out, and she'd never played poker at a table in Vegas again.

Vienna gambled online as *luckypersiancat*, a totally anonymous way to gamble. No one knew who she was or how much money she made. She no longer had to borrow money to get into the ten-thousand-dollar buy-ins with the five-hundred-thousand- or million-dollar rewards at the end. She could manage that all on her own now.

Vienna decided to go running, one of the few things that could clear her mind completely. She drove out to Red Rock and parked, choosing one of the many trails that looped around. It was still fairly hot, although the sun would be setting soon enough. She made certain she was carrying enough water and had a filtration system with her just in case. She was a hiker, not a dedicated runner, and knew any injury could suddenly change everything. If she was caught out in the blazing sun without the ability to call for help with no water, she could easily lose her life. She'd seen that happen too many times not to prepare for an emergency.

Vienna had long legs, and within minutes she had hit her stride, covering ground with a steady rhythm. The sights were breathtaking. She wasn't going for speed so much as just wanting to be grounded by the beauty and peace of the outdoors. Red Rock had natural formations of rock, with various colors and unusual concretions. Red dots were scattered throughout some of the rock, while brown rock balls were dense in others. Erosion caused many different shapes, from fins and spirals to caves and arches. It was difficult not to want to stop and explore them.

Shadows fell across the rocks towering above her at times, lending them different appearances, coloring them with darker varnishes, but she kept her pace even though, again, she wanted to examine them closer. Her friends would be joining her in a week or so for Stella's bridal shower. Stella's event wasn't a traditional one. They would be bouldering first and then exploring the various scenic trails Red Rock had to offer. They would also do some trad climbing there as well.

Next—and all of them were excited about it—they would spend a day on the river kayaking, starting at Hoover Dam. They planned to find out-of-the-way coffee shops, something they all loved. It definitely wasn't the traditional bridal shower, but for Stella it was perfect. They planned to follow it up with hiking and camping the Tuolumne trail in Yosemite along the river for an additional adventure before the wedding.

Vienna felt lucky to have five such close friends as the ones she'd met in Knightly. They had been unexpected— and wonderful. Five powerful women, women who made each day count. They shared the same interests and loved the outdoors. They loved to dance and often met at the Grill, a bar where they danced, drank their favorite drinks and ate the owner's famous offerings surrounded by other locals. Had she not fought with her mother, she never would have moved and found a new life filled with friends and adventure. She detested that she'd never gotten back her friendship with her mother, but she truly loved her life.

Vienna was hot and sweaty, but felt so much better when she was once again back in her suite at the Northern Lights.

After a shower, she soaked in the deep tub, enjoying the hot water on her sore muscles. It was nice to close her eyes and relax, to feel at peace again.

Wrapping herself in her robe, her long hair in a towel, she checked her phone. Stella had messaged her back. No relationship ever. Vienna breathed a sigh of relief. She wouldn't have been to blame, but it would have left a bad taste in her mouth had she been with a married man, even through no fault of her own. She hadn't asked Zale that question, and she should have.

Refusing to allow Zale Vizzini to take up any more time in her brain, she checked out the menu to see what really great dinner she could order. Everything was first-class, including the food. She hadn't been disappointed yet.

The door buzzed and she swung around. No one knew her suite number, with the exception of the hotel personnel, Zale and the gentleman he guarded, Wayne Forsyne. Maybe security was really going to lecture her. She hadn't even told her mother where she was staying. She planned to visit her, but *after* the tournament. There were millions of dollars at stake. She didn't want anything distracting her. Well, maybe she'd go sooner. She really wanted to see her.

Fortunately, her robe was the type that had buttons instead of a belt, so she was fairly decent. Vienna went to the door and peered into the peephole to see who her visitor was. The older man and Zale were outside the door. Zale was looking up and down the hall alertly. Something in the way he did it sent chills down her spine.

She hit the intercom. "I'm not exactly dressed for company."

It was Zale who answered. He reached past Wayne to hit a button to respond. "Open the fucking door, Vienna. We need to get out of sight now."

He was *such* an ass. He was back to the man he'd been when he'd ordered her out of her place of work and into his car. When she hadn't cooperated, he'd simply abducted her.

No second chances, just picked her up, tossed her over his shoulder as if she weighed no more than a child and took her to Shabina's. He had that same low voice with the commanding purr. Not a growl, a purr. It wasn't a nice purr.

She opened the door because Wayne's face was pale. If she could have, she would have allowed him entrance and barred Zale from coming into the suite. She must have stepped into the doorway, because he put a hand to her belly and pushed her inside, closing the door after himself.

"I need you to check out Wayne for me, Vienna. I don't think he's hurt bad." As he spoke, Zale helped Wayne to the nearest couch. She trailed after them, watching the older man carefully. He carried the cane, rather than leaning on it, and even though Zale was helping him, he walked as a much younger man would.

She noted blood on Zale's shirt, a slash line on his belly and right arm. There was blood on Wayne's shirt, much more of it than on Zale's. Wayne's wound was on his left side, along his ribs. Zale unbuttoned Wayne's shirt as Vienna hurried to the bedroom to retrieve the small medical kit she always carried with her. She also got warm water from the master bath.

"Tell me what happened and why you didn't take him to the hospital," she ordered, nudging Zale aside with her hip so she could take over.

"We were outside the casino, just taking a walk. It can be difficult staying indoors so much when you're not used to it."

She understood that. She also caught the "we." Wayne didn't have to go with Zale to take a walk. He could have stayed locked in the safety of his suite. She kept her mouth shut. The knife had sliced into the skin, under the ribs, missing all vital organs somehow. The wound was shallow enough that she was certain she could close it with glue.

"Zale blocked the attack," Wayne provided. "Otherwise, I would have taken the hit right in my heart. They came out of nowhere. I think they were in the flower beds."

"They were," Zale confirmed.

Her heart accelerated for a moment before she could get it under control. More than one attacker. Zale was obviously working undercover. This wasn't a random attack, and there had been more than one assailant. She washed the wound carefully.

"Knife wounds are tricky. This isn't deep. You don't need stitches. I can glue it, but if the blade had bacteria on it, you can get an infection that could eventually kill you. You need antibiotics. I don't have those, and I really mean you should have the wound flooded with them *and* you should take them orally. I've got a topical I can apply for now, but Zale, if the two of you have access to help, get both of you antibiotics. I can see the knife cut you as well."

She finished up with Wayne and turned her attention to Zale, indicating for him to take off his shirt, although that was the last thing she wanted him to do. She remembered his body all too well. She'd mapped every single inch of him with her tongue. He was there in her mind, never to be forgotten.

Refusing to meet his eyes, she kept her gaze fixed on the wounds. Maybe it was cowardly, but she told herself she was a nurse, and she needed to make certain the laceration was cleaned properly. "Very shallow. Same with your arm. But I'm very serious about the antibiotics. No doubt the blade of the knife contained bacteria." She hoped it didn't contain poison for their sakes.

She smiled at Wayne cheerfully as she sat back on her heels. "You're good to go." Meaning they could leave her suite.

"Do you want a drink, Rainier? Rainier is a friend of Sam's as well, and you'll be meeting him soon enough at the wedding, Vienna," Zale informed her. "He's undercover as Wayne Forsyne."

She put her hands over her ears. "I don't want to know anything more. You two are obviously working on something important, and I don't need to know anything about it."

Zale ignored her and went to the bar, turning to raise an eyebrow at his friend.

Wayne sat up. "Nice to meet you as me, Vienna. Zale has assured me you know better than to break confidentiality." There was warning in his voice.

"I take it you're not seventy. I'd already guessed that. You don't walk with your cane correctly." She stood up and went to the master bedroom to change into actual clothes. Having no underwear around Zale made her feel vulnerable.

"You want a drink, Vienna?" Zale called out.

"No, thanks." She needed her wits about her. Dressing hastily in leggings and a favorite comfortable sweater, she unwrapped her hair and brushed it out, leaving it down to air-dry. She wasn't going to try to make herself look good for Zale. If anything, she wanted him to ignore her, just as he'd done these last few months.

Zale and his colleague had made themselves right at home, sitting in the living room, Rainier going through the menu. He looked up when she entered. "You sure are a beautiful woman," he reiterated. He sounded like he was stating a fact rather than flirting with her. He just looked her over and then was back looking at the menu. "You hungry?" he added. Even the voice was different, sounding much younger.

"Yes." Vienna went to stand beside his chair, looking down at the menu. "I was about to order room service when you announced yourselves. Do you think you were followed?"

"No one can get up to this floor. In any case, Zale wounded all three assailants."

She didn't look at Zale, but continued to peer at the menu as though she were really studying it. *Three* attackers. He'd managed to block the initial attack from Rainier, keeping him from getting killed, and then taken on all three.

"Won't they go to a hospital and report that they were attacked by the two of you? There must be security cameras outside of the hotel." She took the menu right out of Rainier's hands.

"I jammed the cameras for a moment," Rainier admitted, "but the fight was over in under eight seconds. Zale seriously wounded them. They don't think the wounds are bad enough to seek help, but that's classic textbook. They'll bleed out slowly without even being aware they're going to die. They're heading to a safe place to lick their wounds, but it will be too late for them."

Rainier sounded very satisfied. Vienna couldn't blame him. If someone came out of the bushes and attacked her to kill her, she would want them just as dead. She wasn't a forgive-and-forget kind of girl. That was one of the reasons she wasn't going to look at Zale. No matter what, she wasn't falling into any traps—if he even thought about going there again.

"You've looked at that menu long enough to memorize it, Vienna," Zale said, using his purring, commanding voice after Rainier gave her his order. "Hand it over." He didn't come to her. He stayed across the room in one of the two-person cuddle chairs.

A red flag went up instantly. She thought about flinging the menu at him, hoping to hit him right in his hard head. But that wouldn't go along with her calm, didn't-give-a-damn-that-he'd-left-her-and-never-contacted-her-again façade.

"Sure. I do think I've memorized it." She shared a little laugh with Rainier and then walked slowly across the wide expanse of the room to Zale. Before she reached him, she held out the menu. "I'll call it in for everyone. That way, they'll only hear my voice."

Thankfully, Rainier responded, giving her the opportunity to turn back toward him.

"That's a good idea. We'll hide out in another room when room service gets here, although they're going to think you're a very big eater."

Unfortunately, with her back to him, Zale was able to lean forward and shackle her wrist, drawing her close to him, toppling her into the seat beside him.

"What are you doing? I was going to call in the order." She did her best to sound a little surprised at his outrageous behavior.

"I need time to look this over, and you can sit here while I do it. You didn't seem to have a problem giving Rainier time. Or standing right over the top of him while you were deciding."

"You do need to eat. I think you have low blood sugar. I might have trail mix in the other room so you can snack on something while we're waiting for dinner," she suggested helpfully, starting to push up from the cuddle chair.

He didn't even look at her, but his arm swept across her like a bar, restraining her. "Just stay put. If my blood sugar starts to drop, you'll be the first person I'll tell."

She looked across the room at Rainier. "Is he always this grumpy before he eats?" She poured concern into her voice.

"I never noticed it before." Amusement colored Rainier's voice until Zale looked up, pinning his friend with a dark stare. Rainier sobered instantly.

"I'll have the steak, rare. Baked potato with everything. House salad. The roasted brussels sprouts."

"That sounds eerily like Rainier's order." Vienna took the menu out of his hands and once again made a move to go to the phone. Again, Zale blocked her.

"Are you going to look at me?"

"I have looked at you."

"You haven't."

She sighed. "I'm hungry and tired. I have low blood sugar. I just came back from a long run and I have a big day tomorrow. I can't afford any distractions, Zale. I appreciate that the two of you are in trouble. Maybe the fate of the world is in your hands, I don't know, but I have to keep myself under control. Whatever the two of you are into, I can't be a part of it. I'm not in your world and you're not in mine."

There was a small silence. Rainier broke it. "I'm sorry, Vienna. We needed medical attention, and Zale mentioned you were a nurse. We couldn't go to the hospital, and you were on the same floor. You were going to meet me at the wedding anyway, so it wasn't like you weren't going to find out I was working undercover with Zale. We didn't mean to drag you into our problems."

She felt a little ashamed. It wasn't as if she didn't want to help them, especially when they both were hurt. She shrugged. "I don't really mind helping out. It's just that I know I'm not supposed to know what you do, and I respect that. Like I said, I'm just tired and hungry. I'll call in the order so we can get our food."

Zale had removed his arm, so she took that as permission to make a break for the phone. While she gave their orders for dinner, Zale made another drink for Rainier and himself. She took the sparkling water from him and sank into the single cuddle chair across from him, putting her head back to stare up at the ceiling.

"I guess whatever you're into is dangerous. If your cover is blown, shouldn't you pack up and go home?"

"Not necessarily," Rainier said. "No one saw the attack in the parking lot. We're betting the three die before they report to their boss. They aren't going to be too quick to tell whoever they report to they missed an old man, and the lone personal protector wiped up the floor with them. At least, that's the hope."

Vienna studied the ceiling. "You're betting your lives."

"This is Vegas," Rainier said, humor once again tingeing his voice.

Vienna let the air move in and out of her lungs. Waiting. It was a bet. A wager. It didn't matter that lives were at stake, it came down to a bet. Three men were somewhere slowly bleeding internally. They were unaware they were dying. Would they call their boss and report to him or her that they had failed to kill their intended target? What were the odds? There were three of them. They wouldn't die at the same time. They each had a cell phone. The boss could call them. They'd grow cold. Weak. Would they try to call for help?

Vienna nodded her head slowly. "I do believe you have a good chance those men won't admit their screwup to their boss. By the time they realize what's happening, it's going to be too late." She knew things. How? She had no idea, only that she could bet on cards because she knew what each opponent had in his hand and what card the dealer would put down next. Bets were tricky things. "But there are a lot of variables. Their boss might just show up last minute."

Rainier laughed softly. "I was feeling good for a minute there. You just shot that down."

"That's the nature of the gambling beast," Vienna said, joining in his laughter.

"You seem to do fairly well. Did you expect to make it to the semifinals?"

"I expect to win," Vienna said. "I've been playing for quite a few years now. It isn't like I just walked in off the street. I was invited to the tournament, and it just so happened that Stella wanted to do a few fun things in Vegas, so I thought I'd come ahead of the rest of my friends and do a little work. I prefer to play online."

"Why is that?" Rainier asked.

"I'm not terribly fond of having my photograph plastered all over the casino. I like to sneak around under the radar. You should know something about that. You don't even use your real name."

Was Zale even his real name? Had she slept with someone and she had no idea who he was? Probably. She didn't look at him. She detested that she meant nothing to him at all when, in her mind, he'd been *the one*. She had never been that kind of woman. She didn't build fantasies around men.

She'd never grown up thinking she needed a man to rescue her or complete her. She worked hard and took care of her mother and herself. She was happy. Zale had been . . . unexpected.

There was a knock at the door. Zale snapped his fingers and indicated for Rainier to go to the other room. Both men were suddenly all business, expressions sober and weapons out. Zale concealed himself in the shadow of the bathroom off the living room. He left the door partially open in order to cover her.

The cart was rolled in and the dinner put on the dining room table. Plates and silverware were used, not Styrofoam takeout containers. Linen napkins were set beside each dish along with wineglasses and water glasses. When the servers left, she made certain the door was properly locked while both men took out small devices to check the room for any listening bugs.

Vienna seated herself at the table. "Interesting way you have to live."

"We don't usually live around other people," Rainier said.

She nodded. "I'd forgotten that. Sam's been away from it for quite a long time. We're used to him. He doesn't talk much, but he participates. He goes to the bar with us. Most of the time, he's our sober driver, and he gets an earful. He works at the resort and fishing camp, but he normally works alone, unless he partners with Stella."

She took a bite of her food. She'd forgotten how hungry she was. She decided less talking and more eating was in order.

"Sam just walked off the job one day," Rainier said. "He was like that. He'd make up his mind to do something, and you couldn't talk him out of it. He wouldn't argue with you, he'd just do it." He indicated Zale with his fork. "He's like that. Decides and that's it."

"What's there to argue about?" Zale said.

"There's nothing wrong with discussions," Vienna said, savoring the roasted brussels sprouts. "Discussions are fun."

"That's not the same as arguing," Zale said. "Arguments lead nowhere and usually end up in hurt feelings."

"This is good steak," Rainier declared. "As in great. Notice, there's no arguing on the subject."

CHAPTER TWO

~~~~~~

If Vienna thought her photograph was large before, gaining admission to the final table had her picture enlarged by quite a bit. She could barely stand going downstairs, where anyone could see her. There was no way she wouldn't be recognized. Her photograph was flashing outside on the building's walls along with the other players'. It was inside in the lobby, running in a pattern around the top wall. It was on the casino wall, flashing like a neon sign. She was the only woman, young and considered good-looking. Her looks seemed to intrigue everyone, as if she couldn't look the way she did and be able to play cards too.

She lay on the floor of her suite, under the piano, digging her fingers into the thick rug she'd pulled over to stretch out on so she wasn't on the uncomfortable marble. Her phone had been blowing up for the last half hour with congratulations as well as messages from her mother. She knew she was going to have to answer everyone soon, but she just didn't have anything left in her.

Cards could do that to her. Exhaustion set in and she would just lie down and not get back up for twenty-four hours. She couldn't sleep. It wasn't that kind of tired. Others became so exhilarated they would stay up and gamble in the casinos. Or party all night. She supposed she was used to solitude and the peace of Yosemite. Vienna was certain it was her "gift" that drained her.

She was hungry. And thirsty. She looked over at the menu and the phone. It was a long way away and she would have to crawl out of her cozy little self-made cave. She just didn't have the energy. She should have thought about water. She always hydrated. She could maybe call on her cell. Her concierge was the best, but then she'd have to get up and open the door.

As if just by her thinking of it, the heavy door across the room actually opened. It didn't squeak. There was no sound, but she was looking at it wistfully, and the door opened as if by magic. Her heart stuttered as she saw the legs of a man encased in trousers and soft-soled shoes. He shut the door behind him as he slipped inside.

"Vienna, what are you doing under the piano?"

She closed her eyes at the sound of his voice. Zale. In a way, she would rather he be an intruder come to rob her. Or interrogate her to get information on Zale and Rainier. At least she wouldn't feel so vulnerable.

"Go away, Zale. I can't deal with you right now."

She didn't hear him walking around or going back out, and she didn't want to open her eyes, but curiosity and self-preservation got the better of her. She peered at him through her long lashes. He was crouched down beside her, far too close, his dark eyes looking like velvet. Her sex clenched in response to that sensual look on his too-gorgeous face.

"Before you go, hand me a bottle of water. And the menu. And see if the phone reaches over here." She made herself sound as matter-of-fact as possible when she wasn't even certain she could pull air into her lungs. Her voice came out in a whisper rather than the firm, forceful tone she wanted. Still, she wasn't shaking—yet. If he stayed too close and she kept smelling fresh snow and rain, she might jump him. He'd already started a slow burn in her body and he hadn't done anything but enter the room.

"Come out from under there."

"I'm not moving."

"You're not? Or you can't? There's a difference." He handed her a bottle of water.

She contemplated that. "That's a good question. I might be able to roll out from under the piano, but then I'm on the marble floor and that's not going to feel so good. I'll just stay here for the time being. Thanks for the water, but go away, Zale. You're too much trouble right now for me to bother with."

He gave her a ghost of a smile, and her stomach fluttered. Rolled, exactly like a roller coaster. "I don't like roller coasters," she told him decisively.

Zale reached for her, sliding an arm under her knees and one behind her back. He pulled her out from under the piano, stood and carried her into the large master bedroom.

"What is the significance of not liking roller coasters?" Placing his knee on the bed, he carefully put her on the duvet, back to the headboard, with the pillows for a backrest.

She'd had the presence of mind to hold on to the water bottle. She took a long drink. It was important to stay hydrated. "You. Anytime you're around, it's like being on a roller coaster. Go away, Zale. I'm exhausted."

He ignored her request. "You need to eat. I'm going to order food. Do you have any preference?"

Vienna knew her mind was a little sluggish, but even so, alarms went off all over the place. "I'll make the call. You can't, Zale. What if you get in trouble? You have to have a place to . . ." What in the hell was she saying? Thinking? If he was in trouble, he could disappear the way he was supposed to. He was a ghost. A man who vanished. He hid in plain sight and then was gone before anyone knew he'd ever been around. He certainly didn't need her suite as a last resort to hide in if he was hunted.

"That's smart, Vienna. I doubt if it will come to that, but still, you're right. Order me the number three with everything." He placed the phone next to her hand.

"You aren't staying."

"I'm staying. I remember you telling me how drained you get after you play cards. I don't want you alone. It's no big deal to see that you eat food and stay hydrated."

She wasn't going to argue with him because she knew he didn't argue. He'd just stop talking. She ordered the food and told room service to knock once and then leave the cart outside the door, that she'd get it when she was ready. When she hung up, she put her head back and just observed him. He'd taken one of the chairs across from the bed, near the fireplace. He was brutally handsome. He'd aged a little in the months they'd been separated, but essentially, he looked the same.

"Thanks, Zale, but really, I'm a big girl. I've been looking after myself a long time. You don't need to stay." She did her best to look him in the eye. That wasn't as successful as she hoped. She managed to look at the bridge of his nose.

Immediately, the sensual lines in his face went blank, totally unreadable, and he regarded her with his dark, scary eyes. "You told me you don't like to play in tournaments in person. This one had to be a huge buy-in. What made you change your mind? Your photograph is everywhere."

She swept her hair back from her face. "I know. It's like a giant me hanging off the side of the building. You're right. Normally I wouldn't play in person like this, but I received an invitation and the buy-in was waived. That doesn't happen unless you're a celebrity with a massive following or you win a tournament that has a buy-in as part of the prize. It sounded too good to be true, so at first I ignored the invitation, but then I was contacted by the hotel and found out it was real. Apparently, my career as *luckypersiancat* has been followed, and the hotel thought it would be good advertisement for the tournament to have me in the mix. There are millions at stake, and Stella wanted to see Red Rock and kayak the river, so why not? I just didn't expect my photograph to be ten feet tall."

"Why aren't you asking me how I got in here? You should be."

She shrugged, trying to look nonchalant. "Does it matter? I doubt too many others could manage. Maybe Rainier."

"Why would you bring up Rainier?" There was a bite to his normally calm tone.

"I imagine he was trained the same way you and Sam were."

"Let's leave him out of this. Let's leave everyone else out but the two of us. We have enough problems without bringing anyone else into our world."

Deliberately, she took another long drink of water. "We have problems? I wasn't aware, Zale. What kinds of problems do we have? I certainly would never undermine your undercover work. I hope you know that. I can stay in my suite until the final tournament, if that would help." She did her best to sound accommodating.

"I interrogate prisoners, Vienna. Stop trying to pull off bullshit. I know you would never out me when I'm undercover. That's not what I'm referring to and you damn well know it. I'm talking about us."

"Us?" She raised her eyebrow. "There is no us, Zale. If you're worried I'm going to be clingy or expect something from you at Sam and Stella's wedding, seriously, there won't be a problem. It's been months since we had our little fling. Six weeks together isn't a relationship. It doesn't make us a couple. I have no expectations of you. You're off the proverbial hook."

He continued to search her face with those dark eyes of his. Eyes filled with temptation and sin. He could easily make her heart skip a beat and her sex dampen with need. Her breasts ached and felt heavy. That was his gift. He could make women want him when he hadn't said or done anything to warrant it.

"It was six and a half weeks, and I don't want to be off the hook." He made the statement quite clearly.

Her heart accelerated. Her pulse leapt and pounded frantically in her neck. It was all she could do to hold herself still, fingers curled around the bottle of water. "One round with you was about all my heart could take, Zale." She didn't care what she was admitting to him. "It was beautiful and fun and I'll cherish those memories. But not again. You'll have to find someone else for your downtime recreation fun."

"Is that what you think you were to me?"

She lifted her chin and swallowed more water, letting the cool liquid slide down her throat. "Does it matter what I think, Zale? Quite a bit of time has passed. I've got my life and I'm just fine. We were careful. There aren't any secret babies you have to worry about. I'm not crying every night and begging Sam to find you for me."

She hadn't asked Sam once about Zale. She hadn't even told Sam they'd been together. She was proud of herself for that because it hadn't been easy. She had cried at night. Not every single night, but she'd cried a lot of nights.

"Would it shock you to know that I asked Sam for updates on you?"

She froze with the water bottle halfway to her mouth. That couldn't be true. Why would he do that when he'd just packed up and left without saying much of anything? He hadn't said he'd come back. He hadn't asked her to wait for him. He'd given her nothing to hold on to. He'd kissed her and walked out of her life. Why would he ask Sam about her?

She regarded him over the water bottle and then took a slow sip of water. What difference did it make? Maybe he was in the habit of asking Sam about all of Sam's friends. It didn't change anything. He'd walked out without a backward glance. She knew because she'd stood at the front of the tent and watched him go until the trees and brush had swallowed him up. He hadn't looked back.

"What could you have possibly wanted to know?" If there was disbelief in her voice, who could blame her?

"I needed to know that you were safe. You were alive and healthy. I didn't want another man in your life. At the same time, I wanted you to be happy."

She contemplated that. "Well, there you go, Zale. I'm safe, alive, healthy and very happy. There's no other man in my life at this time. You can go away feeling very fulfilled by the news."

The knock at the door signaled the food was there. "I can get it," Vienna assured. She was weak, but it wasn't as if she were helpless. Once he ate, he could leave.

"I'll get the cart. You stay put." Zale was already up, a flowing ripple of muscle beneath his clothing, gliding across the floor straight on through to the front door. He looked through the peephole to ensure the server had followed instructions, and then he opened the door and drew the cart inside. After checking it carefully for audio and camera devices, he wheeled it into the bedroom.

The moment she smelled food, she was suddenly starving. Vienna might look as if she rarely ate, but she loved good food. The Northern Lights had the best chefs, and she took full advantage of their menu.

There was silence for a few minutes as the two of them began eating, passing condiments back and forth and automatically sharing with each other as they had so easily when they'd been together before.

"You don't want to know why I would contact Sam and not you?" he prompted when they were eating the dessert—a strawberry and kiwi tart.

"Absolutely I do *not*." She narrowed her eyes at him. "I mean it, Zale. I'm not going to be that woman you have your little holiday fun with and then disappear from for months on end. Find someone else. I know I look tough and act it, but I'm not quite as tough as you might want me to be. One go-around with you was enough."

"For God's sake, Vienna, it wasn't like that."

She leaned forward, looking him in the eyes. "It was

exactly like that. And it's okay. I was thinking one thing, making it all a fairy tale. Women can do that, misunderstand when things aren't talked about right up front. You had a few weeks off. We had chemistry that was off the charts, and I was a willing partner. For you, we fucked like bunny rabbits for your vacation, and you packed up and walked off without a word and never looked back. My guess is, you do that quite often. Most women know the score. It isn't your fault I didn't. But I didn't, Zale, and I'm not going to lie, it hurt. I got over it because I'm a big girl and I take responsibility for everything I do. That wasn't on you, it was on me. But I'm not going there again. Why would I want to stick my hand in a very hot fire and get burned all over again?"

He swore and jumped out of the chair to pace across the room and back, his restless movements reminding her of a caged tiger kept in a cramped space. "That's not how it was, Vienna. I never once thought of you like that. Not once. You meant something to me. Too much to me. I couldn't let go of you, even though I knew it was the right thing to do."

"You let go of me when you walked away without a word. It's been months, Zale."

He spun around from the inside of the doorway to the bedroom. "You think I don't know how fucking long it's been? I count the weeks, the days and sometimes even the hours when I'm lying in a bed somewhere, or on a plane or a train. When I'm trekking through a jungle. You're always with me, Vienna. I worry about you. Obsess over you. Dream of you. And yeah, that could get me killed in a hot minute—or worse, get you killed. That's the reason I contact Sam and not you. I can ask Sam using code on an encrypted line. I protected you by following you when you left to go into the forest alone, instead of going with you. I didn't want anyone to see us together. I suppose that only added to you thinking I didn't want a real relationship with you."

She didn't like the way her heart reacted to his declaration. His voice might ring with truth and sincerity, but he still worked the same job. He still needed to be able to disappear for months at a time. He would still walk away, and she wouldn't know where he was or even if he was alive. Sam had quit. It wasn't the same thing. Stella had met Sam *after* he had decided he was done with his work for the government, or whatever agency they worked for. Zale was still very much working.

Vienna pushed the dessert away and looked at the man she thought was really the perfect man for her. She hadn't thought any man would ever suit her—but for whatever reason, Zale did. Wasn't there always a major flaw?

"I appreciate that you would tell me that, Zale, when you didn't have to." She rubbed her finger along the duvet cover. The sheets in the hotel were the best she'd ever slept on. The duvet was the same brand and just as heavenly. "The thing is, you're still working for whatever company you work for. Nothing really has changed. If we hadn't met in this hotel, you wouldn't have come looking for me, would you?"

"I don't know," he admitted. "I was getting to the point where I was feeling desperate. I made a couple of mistakes on the job. So, yeah, I might have, but I don't honestly know. But I would have eventually, just maybe not right away."

"Even if you had, you have no intention of quitting." She made that a statement, watching his expression closely.

"I signed a contract," he admitted. "Sam was smart enough to quit signing them. It was far less money, but it also gave him the ability to walk out whenever he wanted. He was concerned about his father, although he didn't speak to him, but at least he had a family to worry about. I don't have anyone. That meant I just socked the money away for retirement—if I didn't die before I got that far. I knew I was locked into that contract and wasn't about to compromise you in any way. Loved ones can be used to put pressure on us. If enemies find family, they can be turned into weapons against us. Most of the time, when I was alone, thinking about you and trying to find a solution so I didn't have to give you up, most of what came to me were the worst-case scenarios."

Loved ones can be used to put pressure on us. She couldn't hear things like that. That was the trouble when she'd been alone. She was too vulnerable around Zale. She wasn't so ridiculous with anyone else. She wasn't his loved one. They'd only had six weeks together. Okay, six and a half weeks. It might have been an intense six and a half weeks, but it was still only a few weeks. Yet they were the best weeks of her life.

She was pragmatic. She might look like she didn't have a brain in her head, but she was more than above average in intelligence. She didn't need a man to lean on, or to think for her, or to make her happy. She didn't fall hopelessly in love in a few short weeks, and neither did a man like him.

"Zale." She said his name and then didn't know what else to say. She pushed the dishes away from her. She was a woman of action. She didn't sit in a bed, exhausted, barely able to lift her arms up. She climbed mountains, hung off cliffs, skied down steep slopes and planned tricky rescues into very dangerous gorges others would give up on.

He stalked across the room and cleared the bed and then his dishes as well, restacking them on the cart before wheeling it out of the suite. For a moment, she thought he was leaving, and she didn't know whether to be relieved or upset. She told herself her reaction was only because she wanted, once and for all, to be over him and they needed to sort things out. Only deep down, she knew there was no getting over him.

To her consternation, Zale came back into the bedroom and sank onto the bed, on his stomach, stretching his long body out so that his head was close to her belly. He caught one of the pillows and positioned it under his head.

"What did you have planned for your stay in Vegas? I know you're here for a good week or more. Your posse is joining you after the tournament, aren't they?" He turned his head to look up at her.

"They'll come after, yes. We're going to do some bouldering and then explore Red Rock trails. Do a little trad climbing. That sort of thing. We want to go to all the small coffee shops. It's a thing we do. And then we're taking an all-day kayaking trip on the river starting at the Hoover Dam."

"Sounds fun."

"It should be after being in the hotel, although I'll admit, this has been like nothing I've ever experienced. I could get used to these sheets. Even the duvet is amazing."

"What are you going to do before they get here? You have several days to fill before the tournament, and a couple after." His hand moved to her thigh. He just rested his palm there, but she was acutely aware of the weight of it. The heat of it. His breath on her skin through the weave of her leggings.

"My mother lives here in Vegas with her partner, Ellen." She made it a point to look at him, to watch his reaction. If he dared to make a snide comment, he was gone. Out of her room, out of her life. But he didn't so much as blink, so she decided to continue. "My mom raised me alone. I never knew my father, and Mom never told me about him. We were really close, kind of an us-against-the-world mentality. She ended up with breast cancer, and I gambled in order to pay the medical bills. They were so high, and we needed a lot of money. She met Ellen at the infusion center."

Without thinking, she dropped her hand into the thickness of his dark hair. There was so much of it. Wild with unruly waves. She'd always loved his hair. She needed the solace of touching him, of burying her fingers in all those soft, thick waves.

"Tell me, Vienna. I can feel the sadness in you. Is your mother okay?"

"Yes, she's in remission and I'm eternally grateful for that. I won a tournament. It was a pretty big win. On the way home, someone ran me off the road. They tried to rob me." When he started to lift his head, she held it down. "That was a long time ago. It isn't as if you can go hunt them down now. And how silly of them to think I'd be carrying cash."

"I'd like to hunt them down. Were you hurt?"

"Not really. Mostly scared. I wanted my mom. She had discovered love and couldn't wait to tell me. She was dancing around the house and couldn't see the state I was in. I was so upset I couldn't see the state she was in. We ended up in a terrible fight. Things were said that should never have been said by either of us. Things we didn't take back. I moved to Knightly and made a new life for myself."

"How often do you talk to your mother?"

She was grateful that there was no judgment in his voice. She judged herself often enough.

"I call her once a week, but our conversations are very stilted. I ask her and her partner to come for the holiday dinners my friends and I put on, but they always decline." She ducked her head. "If I'm being honest, it's a bit of a relief. I don't know what to say to her anymore."

"Are you sorry for the things you said to her?"

"I've apologized for the things I said, and I meant every single word of the apology every time I've said it. It was the things *she* said," Vienna corrected. "They made no sense. She was angry and she blurted out things she clearly regretted telling me. When I've called her on them, she's tried to backtrack and tell me she lied, but I know she wasn't lying."

Zale was silent, not looking up at her, just waiting for her to make up her mind to give him the entire story. What difference did it make if she shared? If he knew? Who was he going to tell? He was a ghost, one of those men who hid in plain sight, who was there for a short period of time and then vanished as if he'd never been.

"She told me that she'd given up so much of her life to

raise me and I wasn't even her daughter. The moment she said it, she tried to take it back, but I knew it was the truth. So many things fell into place. No grandparents. No pictures. No family anywhere. When I asked her later, she refused to talk about it. After that, she didn't want to be alone with me or talk for any length of time because she was afraid I'd bring it up. It was very clear she didn't want me to know who my parents were. At first, I wanted to talk to her about it, but then, when I realized I was losing her, and the cost for knowing was going to be too high, I just stopped asking. I didn't care if I ever found out. I didn't want to chance making things worse with Mom."

He rubbed his chin on the duvet while he considered the possibilities. "There are many child abductions that go unsolved."

Vienna nodded. "Yes. That was a possibility, but one I discarded. I can't see Mitzi, that's my mother, kidnapping a baby. There was money in the early days, supporting us. Then, suddenly, it was gone. I never asked Mom where it came from, or where it went. I should have, although I doubt she would have said."

"You're going to see her?"

Vienna heaved a sigh. "Yes. I'm going to have dinner with them. I'm hoping Mom will thaw a bit each time I see her and *don't* bring up anything about where I come from. I was going to wait until after the final round in the tournament, but I want to see her sooner."

"Don't you want to know?"

"Yes, but I want my relationship with my mother back more than I want to know where I originally came from. I have a friend who might be able to help me figure that out. She's good at that sort of thing. I decided I'd ask her to help me and leave Mom out of it altogether. If I never find out, it isn't the end of the world. I have a good life. I don't like that I don't have my mom or her partner in it. They should be."

"When are you having dinner with your mother?"

"I thought tomorrow evening. Somewhere away from the Strip. Somewhere quiet."

"Let me go with you, Vienna. She knows you won't bring up anything to do with your past if you have me along. It will put her at ease. I can be charming. She'll want to meet with you because she'll wonder who I am to you." He propped his head on his hand.

"That would make it a problem. She'll think you're in my life. I've never brought anyone to meet her." Why didn't she just firmly say no? Because she wanted him with her. Because spending time with him like this was wonderful even when it was heartbreaking.

"Don't you see how perfect that is? She'll be at ease and you can establish exactly the atmosphere with her you're hoping for. And just for your information, I am in your life, you just refuse to acknowledge me. I can be at the restaurant already. Then show up at your table and pull up a chair if you prefer. Would that make it easier than telling her you're bringing a friend?"

Vienna laid her head against the padded headboard, refusing to look at his face. That gorgeous, sensual face that was all angles and planes that made up perfection. It wasn't that he was so handsome in the way most women might consider, but she looked for outdoor rugged, toughness. She wanted masculine. Even his long eyelashes couldn't deter from that dark edge he had. Closing her eyes didn't help because he was branded inside her mind.

"No, Zale, it won't make it easier. Nothing about you makes anything easier and you know it."

His fingers moved on her thigh. He drew little circles and then began to write something in long looping letters across her leg. She found it distracting. Intriguing. He'd done the same thing multiple times when they were in the tent at night in the dark and she had to guess what he was writing to her. He had cheated more than once, writing his message in a foreign language.

"I want to meet your mother and her partner."

"I'm trying to repair my relationship with her. Meeting you and then having you disappear will only cause more problems."

Zale continued to write letters on her leg from her knee to the very top of her thigh. Far too close to the junction of her legs. She should stop him.

"I don't have to disappear altogether."

A painful clenching in her chest nearly took her breath away. She was a nurse and she knew she wasn't having a heart attack, but it felt like it anyway. A vise squeezing down and not letting up, the pressure nearly debilitating.

"Don't say things like that to me. You can get any woman you want to sleep with you. There's a smorgasbord of women right out that door. Go to the bar, Zale, and find somebody. I was honest with you when I said it hurt when you left. That should satisfy your ego enough that you don't have to come back for more. Find someone else."

"What did I write on your leg?"

His voice. So quiet. Gentle. Almost tender. She took a deep breath. That was a mistake. She drew him in. The scent of fresh snow. Fresh rain. The woods. Cedar and pine. He was . . . Zale.

"'You're not listening to me.' That's what you wrote on my leg. 'You're not listening to me.' And something else, but it was in another language."

"I wrote the same thing in French and Italian."

"You're such a show-off. I am listening." She wasn't. Or she was trying not to.

"Then you're deliberately not hearing me. I didn't want to leave you, Vienna. In my head, in my heart, I didn't leave you. I haven't been with another woman since, nor do I want to be. I've been looking for a way to make a relationship work between us without putting you in danger. There has to be a way, because I'm not willing to lose you. Not if you feel anything at all for me."

They can't be trusted. They lie to you. They'll say anything they think you want to hear in order to get their way. The voice came unbidden into her head. She didn't even know who told her that.

Vienna had to look at his face. Into his eyes. Would he lie to her just to sleep with her again? Their chemistry had been off the charts. Men lied all the time to get women in bed. This was Vegas. Maybe he had a bet going with his friend Rainier. She knew better. She was just afraid. It had hurt too much when he'd walked out, and she was used to protecting herself.

Zale rolled over onto his belly again, laying his head in her lap, arms around her waist. "I know you're scared, Snowflake. I don't blame you." He'd called her Snowflake because of the color of her hair. As a term of endearment, she preferred it to *baby*. Although, once or twice he'd called her *baby* as well, and in that voice of his, she hadn't minded that much.

He turned his head and pressed a kiss over her T-shirt into her belly button before resting his cheek on her again. That sent a shiver of heat down her spine.

"I don't give my word lightly. I'm telling you, Vienna, I mean every single word I'm saying to you. I left without telling you I'd be back because I had no idea if I would survive what I was walking into. I couldn't make you promises I didn't know if I could keep. I didn't realize I would feel the way I did about you when I first followed you. I only knew I had to see you again. It was a compulsion to talk to you again that had me seeking you out. You're so damn intelligent. You're good at the things that matter to me. We were out there in the woods and there wasn't a single complaint about ticks or mosquitoes. You follow the code of leaving no footprint behind. On top of that, to me, you're so beautiful, you take my breath away."

Vienna found her fingers buried in his thick hair, massaging his scalp. That had been their nights, talking together just like this. He would lie with his head in her lap, and they'd talk about everything and nothing.

"Obviously, what you're doing here in Vegas is dangerous. Is this the same mission you left to go on?" She didn't know if she should even be asking that much of him.

"No. I completed that one without a hitch. We were sent here recently. It was a get-in-and-get-out to collect information, but we aren't getting anywhere."

She heard the frustration in his voice.

"As a rule, I'm able to find the right people to talk to and get what I want from them. Rainier has a few talents as well, but neither of us has gotten a single lead that has brought us any closer to what we need to know."

Vienna frowned, that strange note of discord reacting immediately, brushing at the insides of her mind. "That isn't true, Zale. You talked to someone recently that was very close to your answer, or you and your partner wouldn't have been targets. That person had an association with the three people who tried to kill you. If their boss didn't order the hit on you and Rainier, and the three took the initiative on their own, it had to be because they were careless in some way. Maybe the person you spoke with wasn't supposed to know anything and one or all of them had been loose-lipped."

She was throwing out ideas aloud the way she did to herself when she needed to find the best chance for a rescue. She'd talk herself through every possibility until one felt right to her. Then she'd map it out and ensure it was correct and doable in every way.

She continued to rub his scalp as she puzzled it out in her mind. "Of course, it's entirely possible the boss ordered the hits. If so, that means the association leads straight to him—or her. I don't get that vibe though."

Zale scooted into a sitting position facing her, his expression serious. Dark. Almost scary. "What vibe? What kinds of vibes do you get, Vienna?"

At least he wasn't making fun of her. That was something,

but his tone and his demeanor had gone to a remote, controlled interrogator—one that sent chills down her spine.

She tried a casual shrug and looked around for the water bottle. She'd set it on the side table, and it was too much of a stretch to reach it. "Sometimes I get strong feelings. I call them vibrations because I feel them that way. I've learned that I can trust my intuition. In this case, the feelings I get point to someone you talked to associating with the three men who attacked you, rather than their boss. I have no idea what you're into, so I can't help you any further than that."

Zale's dark, enigmatic gaze drifted over her face. She had the feeling he could look right into her and see every hidden secret she had in her soul. "You already hold our lives in your hands, Vienna. You know we're here undercover. You know we were attacked outside the hotel. You allowed us into your suite. If I didn't get all the cameras, and someone managed to get footage of us, and somehow security saw us at your door, you could be compromised."

She waited while he weighed the risks of telling her more. At first, she hadn't wanted to know, because that would only tie them together further. But now, when she was contemplating gambling her heart all over again because yes, she was that big of a risk-taker, she wanted to know how much trouble he was in and what she could do to help.

"In a nutshell, we've had two agents disappear. The owner of the hotel, Daniel Wallin, contacted our employer over a year ago and reported there had been two attempts on his life. He wanted to know who was behind them and he wanted a personal protector from our agency. He had his own security, but he wanted one of our men added. Our agent disappeared. No one was supposed to know who he was or where he came from. He would never have talked to any of the other security guards around Wallin."

Vienna's stomach knotted. She didn't like the sound of what Zale was telling her. "How did Wallin communicate his request for help, do you know? Was it through a secretary? Was it private?"

"All communication was private. Wallin to our boss. No one else was privy to his request other than Wallin's friend, who is a personal friend of our boss and was able to get Wallin an introduction. A second agent was sent to look for the first and to cover Wallin. He disappeared within two weeks of his arrival. He was experienced, Vienna. Not years of experience, but he knew what he was doing."

Icy fingers of dread crept down her spine. That same boss had sent Zale to investigate. She needed her bottle of water, and this time she stretched to get to it. Her throat felt dry. There was a lump almost too big to swallow.

"Our boss told Wallin he was going to launch a full-scale investigation. He was furious over losing two men, but he wasn't including Wallin in his reports. He cut off contact. He didn't agree to send more protection to Wallin. Rainier and I came to the hotel as guests, Rainier pretending to be a wealthy man who likes to gamble and has quite the hefty bank account. If he's investigated, his background will hold up."

Vienna cleared her throat. "He needs to learn to walk with a cane correctly. I spotted he had a fake injury immediately, but I can help him with that."

"It's not his usual assignment," Zale said. "He practiced by watching tapes, although he is good at gambling and wins most of the time. That helps shore up our cover story."

Vienna took a slow sip of water while she digested what he'd told her. "You were never part of Wallin's security, and you never got close to him like the other two agents who disappeared did," she mused aloud, the way she did when she had to think things over. "Your boss cut off contact with him—" She broke off and looked over at him, pressing her finger to the strange birthmark she had on her wrist—a perfect heart. "*How* did he get in touch with your boss? Computer? Phone? How would he even know about your boss? I wouldn't. If it weren't for Sam, I wouldn't even know you existed."

"I believe Wallin and his friend go way back. His friend and my boss were old friends. The mutual friend knew how to reach out to my boss using a code indicating trouble. From there, my boss was in touch with him, and that would have been on a line that would be fully secure."

"The breakdown would have had to occur *after* the agent came to the hotel and joined the protection unit guarding Wallin," she surmised.

Zale agreed with her. "I'm certain whoever is responsible for the disappearance of both agents is in Wallin's personal security force. When our agent joined, he had to be vetted and allowed to be hired. Wallin vouched for him, so that would red-flag him to anyone that wanted Wallin dead."

That strange awareness brushed abruptly along the walls of her mind, making Vienna grateful Zale hadn't gone in as part of Wallin's bodyguard force. She dealt in percentages and placed bets accordingly. "I have to think about this, Zale. If Daniel Wallin's life is in danger, there's a reason for it. He's surrounded by security all the time, especially now that he's been threatened twice. If you wanted to get to him, how would you do it? Bribe a bodyguard, right? More than one to ensure it happens."

Zale smiled at her. His smile wasn't nice. "That's not how I would do it, but I suppose most people aren't me."

"No, they aren't, but whoever this is, is smart, Zale. Those two agents were trained in the same way you were and they're both most likely dead." She needed to point that out to him, not wanting him to get too cocky.

He pushed his hand through his hair. "I know, Snowflake. And I'm with you that more than one person on Wallin's security team has to be involved."

"So, who did you talk to that might be involved with those three men who attacked you? Because one of the three had something to do with one of the security guards."

"That's a good question. I'll bring it up to Rainier and we'll go over everyone we both spoke with. In the meantime, are you going to let me go to dinner with you and your mother? I know a nice little restaurant out of the way, nowhere near the Strip."

CHAPTER THREE

~~~~~~~~~~~~~~~~~~~~~~~~~~~~~~~~

The restaurant Zale had suggested was family owned and operated with authentic Mediterranean and Greek food. The recipes were traditional family recipes, the atmosphere casual, the dining comfortable, and the décor straight from Athens, Greece. There was a full bar with Greek wines and beer.

Mitzi and Ellen were already at the table, laughing with a waiter as he poured wine into their glasses and indicated a platter that was between them. He was clearly explaining what was on the dish.

Vienna waited until he left before she approached the table. She was very aware of Zale, his hand on the middle of her back as they crossed the room. Mitzi and Ellen looked up as they neared.

"I see you started without us," Vienna greeted as she leaned down to kiss her mother on the cheek. "That looks and smells delicious. Hi, Ellen. This is Zale, a friend of mine. Zale, my mother, Mitzi Mortenson, and her partner, Ellen Johnson. We're so happy you were able to meet us for dinner on such short notice." She sank into the chair Zale held out for her. It was the one closest to her mother.

"I was so proud of you for making the finals in that large tournament, Vienna," Mitzi greeted. "Although, I didn't realize your photograph would have to be put up everywhere. It's even on the internet, isn't it, Ellen?"

Ellen paused in the act of bringing her wineglass to her lips. "Yes, you're quite the celebrity, Vienna. I don't think anyone expected a young woman to challenge the men considered experts in their field."

"The beauty of the game," Vienna said, hoping to sound casual, "is that anyone really can win if they play the odds and know when to get out. Too many people stay in when they shouldn't."

Mitzi smiled across the table at Zale. "Where did you meet Vienna, if you don't mind my asking? She isn't in the habit of bringing too many of her friends around."

Zale covered Vienna's hand with his. She hadn't realized she was moving the silverware back and forth, exchanging the position of the fork and spoon. His thumb slid over her knuckles in a little caress and then her inner wrist, finding her birthmark. "We met a few months ago when the serial killer targeted her."

Vienna froze. She hadn't exactly disclosed that information to her mother. Mitzi paled and Ellen gasped and reached to hold Mitzi's hand, offering support instantly.

"I'm sorry, I didn't realize you didn't know," Zale said. His voice was very gentle. "You *did* know that a serial killer had been targeting people where Vienna lived, right?"

Mitzi made a fist and pressed it over her heart. "Yes, but I thought he was out in the woods or something, far away from my daughter." She indicated the appetizer. "Please, someone eat that before it gets cold. The waiter said it was to be eaten hot."

"Mom, I'm fine and the killer's dead. I want to talk about happy things. Get to know Ellen better. Find out what you've been doing. I want you to get to know Zale." Vienna forced cheer into her voice and deliberately chose one of the appetizers, not knowing what it was but hoping to take that look of horror off her mother's face.

"We'll do all that, Vienna," Mitzi assured, "but obviously, there was more to this serial killer business than I knew. You didn't tell me and don't want to, which means you think I will be *very* upset. I am your mother, and I have every right to know the danger you were in." She stuck her chin in the air and looked directly at Zale.

Vienna sighed. "I'm sorry, Mom, I should have told you. I didn't want to upset you, but you're right. I should have."

Zale smiled at Mitzi. "I can see where your daughter gets that little stubborn streak. She's strong like you. She found out ahead of time that the killer was in her circle of friends, and that a couple climbing Mount Whitney was targeted. She went up there with Sam, a friend of ours, determined to stop him. Unfortunately, they were unable to, but they retrieved the bodies and she was able to get more clues as to the identity of the killer. In the end, Vienna and her friend Stella were both targeted. Once that was found out, Sam made certain they were put in a safe house and guarded until the killer was found. You raised an amazing woman, Ms. Mortenson."

"Please, call me Mitzi, and this is Ellen. We don't stand on ceremony." Mitzi reached over to tuck strands of Vienna's long hair behind her ear. "All the chances you take, honey. I'm so proud of you, but at the same time, it's scary. And now hearing this. Anything could have happened to you."

"I train all the time, Mom. I don't take unnecessary chances with my life or anyone else's. That's why I'm head of Search and Rescue. I plan so carefully."

The waiter was back and Vienna hastily picked up the menu. Zale ordered in fluent Greek, impressing Mitzi and Ellen. He explained what everything on the menu was and gave recommendations. She ordered one of the three dishes he recommended. They all sounded delicious, and since her mother and Ellen had ordered the other two, she figured they could try a little bit of each.

"Sam and Stella are getting married, and Zale is Sam's

best man," Vienna said. "I'm in the wedding party as well, so we'll be able to see quite a bit of each other during the celebration."

"That's wonderful. Stella did send us an invitation." Ellen looked at Mitzi. "We hadn't decided whether or not to go. It's a long drive . . ." She trailed off.

"It's quite beautiful at the resort," Vienna said. "Stella will reserve a cabin for the two of you. Knightly is an hour's drive from where they're holding the wedding, so it would be so much better if you stay at the resort, unless you're going to stay for any length of time. Then I'll get you a room at the local hotel, but we'd need to do that fast."

Vienna didn't offer to have her mother and Ellen stay with her. She'd offered too many times, and her mother had turned her down. She wanted this dinner to go without any hurt feelings. She was very grateful for Zale's presence. He kept the conversation flowing anytime it began to falter into awkward silences.

Ellen was interested in knowing about bouldering. She'd watched several of the videos Mitzi had that Vienna had sent her. It took a little while before Vienna realized Ellen was playing the same role Zale was. She wanted the dinner to go well too. She was hoping to get mother and daughter back together. That felt good. Ellen was working for them, not against them. She made a powerful ally, and Vienna was grateful to her.

The evening passed with much more ease than Vienna could have hoped. She found herself laughing and slipping into old patterns with her mother more and more instead of being so on edge. Twice, her mother asked prying questions about Zale's occupation, which he sidestepped neatly. Vienna was able to change the subject smoothly both times by telling a hilarious story about her cat's disdain of all dogs. She told them how she'd done her best to make her little princess love her friends' dogs so she could walk her with them, but the cat would have nothing to do with them. In fact, her claws came out and her behavior was downright naughty.

By the time they'd finished dessert and put Mitzi and Ellen in an Uber to head back to their home, Vienna was so happy, she flung her arms around Zale's neck without thinking.

"That couldn't have gone any better. Thank you so much. I think they may even decide to come for Stella's wedding. That would be such a big breakthrough if they did."

Zale brought his hands up to her back, locking her to him before she could drop her arms. "I like them both. They're good people, Vienna. No wonder you turned out to be such a good person. Mitzi's a good woman."

"She is, isn't she?" Vienna agreed. She pulled back enough to look into his eyes. "But she doesn't look a thing like me, does she? I never noticed before."

"No, she doesn't, but that doesn't matter. She's your mother." He said it decisively.

Vienna hugged him tightly, savoring his scent and the strength in his frame. "She is. I wouldn't have wanted anyone else. I want her to know that. I could see that Ellen is on my side. She wants Mom and me to heal the rift as well."

She stepped back and he dropped his arms, allowing her to escape so they could walk to their car. They had used Vienna's car. She had picked him up from an appointed corner away from the Strip. She'd felt a little like a spy in some silly, intriguing but fun movie.

"I noticed Ellen was helping as best she could. I think she's a powerful ally for both of you."

"I don't deserve for her to be on my side. I didn't try to establish a relationship with her at first. I think I was jealous that Mom had someone else. I was like a little child, so upset that there was someone in her life other than me." She noticed that even though he walked with her in that casual, flowing way he had, his eyes were always restlessly moving, scanning rooftops of the other buildings around them. He took in everything automatically, every car, under it, the landscaping, the doorways of nearby businesses—nothing escaped him.

"I think that's understandable," he excused her, standing close as she opened the driver's-side door. He had his back to her, facing out, his body shielding hers and the car.

"You're not my bodyguard," she reminded him. "I'm not Daniel Wallin, or your friend Rainier. You don't need to stand like that."

He just smiled at her, closed her door and went around to the passenger side to slide in. He waited until she was driving through the streets of Vegas, heading back to their hotel. "You're very lucky, Vienna. I didn't have family. I never really understood what it meant, not for a very long time."

She wrapped her fingers around the steering wheel. He gave her little pieces of himself. Tiny ones. Even back then, when they'd camped for those six weeks together, when he'd told her small things about himself, she'd cherished them, knowing he didn't give them to others. That had been intuitive. After he'd disappeared without a trace, she'd talked herself into believing she couldn't trust that part of herself, not when it came to men.

"I do know I'm lucky." She had so much in her life to be thankful for. Her friends were right up there, number one on her list. She wanted her mother back. And she wanted to be friends with Ellen and was determined to make that happen. She had no one to blame for that disaster but her own jealous, childish self. Hopefully, Ellen's generous nature would allow for a lasting, close relationship. She had a full, active life, one she enjoyed. Her sassy cat she adored. Her work she loved. The man sitting beside her, who she was terrified of letting back into her life but who she was utterly relieved to know was alive and well, when there were so many nights she'd lain awake afraid he was dead.

"Do you know who your parents are?" She shouldn't ask him. She shouldn't pry. He had no problem prying into every aspect of her life, so she didn't know why she felt a little guilty asking, but she did.

"No. The agency tried to find out. They look for any dirt they can use, and I wanted them to find something, but they didn't."

She braked for a red light, frowning as she cast a quick glance his way. "You're working for them, Zale. Risking your life. Why would they want to have 'dirt' on you?"

His palm was suddenly cupping her cheek, his thumb sliding over her lips. "They find men like me. Men with certain characteristics. And they train us for jobs no one else wants. The training is brutal and it brings out those traits that would be better left alone." His fingers were gentle in counterpoint to the things he told her about himself. "Our handlers want ways to keep us under their control, I guess. As if having 'dirt' would do that. It would only piss me off."

Abruptly, he dropped his hand, his entire demeanor changing. His voice went to that rasping purr that was suddenly deadly. "And if they study us the way they're supposed to, with their fucking shrinks, they should know putting a loved one in danger would bring hell down on them so fast they wouldn't know what hit them."

"Zale." She whispered his name, aching for him. He could do that to her so fast.

"You were a shock to me, Vienna. Everything about you. I had this vague idea that someday I'd find someone, long after my retirement, if I managed to stay alive that long. I didn't think I'd feel that much for her, but still, it was something new to try, settling down, having a family. Everyone else had one. Maybe I could do it. I didn't think I was capable of real emotion." He rubbed his chest. "Most of the time, I feel dead inside." He frowned. "That's not entirely true. I'm not explaining this right."

Vienna was afraid if she said anything he would stop talking, and she didn't want him to. This was important for her to hear. To understand. Mostly, it was important for Zale to express, and he was struggling.

"I have certain friends I'm close to. I care about them. Sam. Rainier. Rush. Wilder. A very small circle, and it took me a long time to get there. Trusting anyone isn't my forte. My training didn't exactly help me there."

To Vienna's consternation, he fell silent. They were already too close to the corner where she knew he would insist she drop him off.

"When I met you . . ." He trailed off again, shaking his head. Rubbing one palm over his heart. "You changed everything I'd ever believed about myself and what I was capable of. It isn't just a small feeling, Vienna." He gestured toward the next block. "It's overwhelming. When I've never felt anything and then there it is, I know it's damn real, and I don't want to lose it because I'm not quite sure what I'm doing yet. Pull over. I'll meet you later."

He had his hand on the door handle before she brought her car to a halt. "Zale, wait, no. I'm not sure I should let you—" He was gone, melting into the darkness. She hadn't even noticed that he'd brought that dark sport jacket with him. She couldn't make him out as she pulled away from the curb back into traffic and drove to the private circle where the valet would take her car and she could go straight up in the private elevator to her suite.

Vienna couldn't help but look around the hallway suspiciously as she unlocked the door and stepped inside quickly. She was getting paranoid just knowing someone had attacked Zale. There was no one around. It was easy to see up and down the halls. Closing the door made her feel safe. The first thing she did was kick off her shoes and go to one of the very comfortable cuddle chairs so she could call Stella.

"I had dinner with Mom and Ellen tonight," she greeted without preamble. "It was a good night, mostly because I brought Zale with me. And Ellen was determined to make it

work between Mom and me. She was really wonderful."
Once again, she was talking too fast, the words tumbling
over one another.

"I'm happy for you, Vienna," Stella said. "This is the first
time you and your mother made it through an evening together in a long time, right?"

Vienna was grateful she had stayed on topic and hadn't
brought Zale up right away. "Since the fight we had. I've tried
everything to get us back together and nothing has worked.
She's been so uncomfortable around me, and I think I've
been the same way. I was really ashamed of the way I reacted
to her telling me she was in love with Ellen. It had nothing to
do with objecting to Ellen, just being jealous of her bringing
someone else into our relationship so unexpectedly."

"You have to let that go, Vienna," Stella advised. "You
can only apologize so many times."

"I know. I think both of them have accepted my apology,
but Mom's been afraid I'd bring up other things that came
out that night she doesn't want to talk about. I wanted to
make it very plain tonight that I have no intention of bringing those subjects up to her. I hope she got the message and
she can relax around me. I just want my mother back."

"How did Zale fit into all of this?"

Vienna sat tailor fashion, and the chair molded around
her. She loved the chair. She made a mental note to find out
where to get one like it.

"He offered to go with me to take the heat off so Mom
would relax. At first I was going to say no, but then I realized
it was exactly what would distract her."

"Vienna." There was caution in Stella's voice. "Tell me
what's going on."

"I'm not certain yet. He says he doesn't want us to be
over. We've been talking quite a bit and I'm listening, but
I'm not sure I want to go there again. You know how I am,
careful."

There was that thoughtful silence. Stella never rushed

judgment. She wasn't that person, which was one of the hundreds of reasons Vienna loved her. "Do you believe him?"

It was Vienna's turn to think the question over. Did she? She was certain Zale believed what he was telling her. She just didn't know how long what he felt for her would last. Admittedly, he wasn't a man who had relationships. He had no clue what that first rush felt like. Their sexual chemistry had been explosive. He could easily mistake that for something else. Once the fire mellowed, even a little, he could get bored and move on. Then what? Where would she be?

"I think he believes what he's telling me. I just don't know if he has staying power."

"Vienna." Stella's voice was gentle. "No one ever knows. It's a leap of faith. You have to decide if taking that chance on someone is worth it or not."

Vienna sighed. "I did take that chance. I invested in him once already. He packed his things and walked off, Stella. He explained, but even now, with his explanation, it's wrenching just thinking about it. I don't let people in easily. I've never let a man in, not until him."

They can't be trusted. They lie to you. They'll say anything they think you want to hear in order to get their way.

"Why is that? Have you ever thought about why you've never gotten close to a man?" Stella asked.

Stella always got right down to the heart of the matter. Not just Stella. Her other friends were the same. All of them were thoughtful and considerate, but they believed in the hard questions. They all asked and answered them with each other. Vienna had thought about it many times. She just lost interest very quickly—and then there was that voice in her head she couldn't quite get out, but she wasn't going to talk about that.

"At first, I thought I was so busy with school, trying to get ahead and make things work so I could take care of Mom. But then I realized I'd get bored just talking with someone at dinner. I know that sounds so terrible and vain of me, but it's the truth. I don't know if it's because I chose all the wrong men to date."

"We all have a type," Stella conceded.

"I didn't go for looks, I always went for men with brains. But they were all about how they were so intelligent and I couldn't possibly keep up. It always turned out just the opposite. And not one of them liked to hike or climb. You'd think that *outdoors* was a dirty word."

Stella laughed softly. "I'm sorry, I know I shouldn't laugh, but you do look like a model, Vienna. You're tall and gorgeous. Unfortunately, I think the old prejudices still remain against women with a good part of the male population. You just can't be as intelligent as they are. I did think it was mostly uneducated men, but now that you say that, I'm just discouraged."

That made Vienna laugh. "I think we'll have to stay in Knightly, where we can climb our beloved boulders and go hiking whenever we want."

"Has he quit?" Stella asked when they both sobered.

Vienna looked up to find Zale standing in front of her. Her heart jumped at his sudden appearance. He'd come right through the door, and she hadn't even heard him enter. She needed to tell the service people they should have a squeak in the door. Then again, he probably carried an oil can in his back pocket.

"No, he hasn't quit. He still works for them. He's here, Stella, standing right in front of me. I think he can float through walls."

He held up a key just like her golden one, a smirk on his face and a hint of laughter in his eyes she found hard to resist.

"I'm pretty sure Sam can do that too. We need to learn, Vienna."

"Gotta go. See you soon." Vienna ended the call and regarded Zale with a small shake of her head. "You stole my key right in front of me and made a replica of it, didn't you?"

He nodded. "You really should be more careful. You let Rainier distract you."

"I was seeing to his wounds."

"His wounds weren't that bad." He pushed the key into his wallet and sank into the cuddle chair across from her, holding out his hands for her feet.

He'd always given the best foot massages. She stretched her legs out to put her feet in his lap. She wasn't going to pretend she didn't want a massage from him, even if she kicked him out later for stealing her key.

"You acted like you were very worried."

"I needed you distracted so I could make an impression of your key."

She started laughing. "You're impossible."

"But practical. You'll need to remember that when you want to throw things at me. Preferably not the knife you sleep with."

"I didn't always sleep with it. That came after the scare." Vienna studied his face. Even just sitting across from her, seemingly relaxed, he gave little away, but she could see the intelligence in his eyes, the vigilant alertness that never left him.

He was so much like Sam. He had those same traits. She knew Sam had a master's degree in something to do with law, which was ironic considering his father was Mafia. She knew he was extremely intelligent and learned at a high rate of speed. Stella told her she'd discovered a box of medals, tons of them, ones he never showed her and she never asked about. She also found his uniforms and was not shocked to discover he'd been an officer. Considering that Zale was Sam's best friend and they'd trained together for whatever program they both had served in, Vienna thought it very possible Zale was an officer as well—or had been one. Most likely he held at least a master's degree in his chosen subject.

"I want a relationship, Vienna." His voice was quiet. "I

want you to give us a chance. Tell me what to do so you know I'm serious."

"How long would you stay working, Zale, if we did start a relationship? Your work seems dangerous, and it's obvious you could disappear for months and I wouldn't know if you were alive or dead. That doesn't seem like a good fit with me. I'm a worrier."

"We're a good fit."

He just stated it, as if it were a fact. His gaze never left hers. He acted so certain.

"You make no sense, Zale. You're a highly intelligent man. Other than that, I don't know the first thing about you and you don't know the first thing about me. You're talking as if that month and a half we had together is the same as the two years Sam and Stella had. It isn't. They had time to get to know one another. A lot of time. We spent most of our time having sex."

"I made love to you. I might not have known that was what I was doing every single time, but that was it. I knew it was different, and you had to have known it as well. Every time I touched you, it felt different. Sometimes, Vienna, I couldn't sleep. I would just lie awake and watch you sleep, breathing you in, terrified of what I was feeling for you."

"And yet you left without a single word."

He nodded slowly, thoughtfully, his expression never changing. But his eyes did. She was watching closely, and the color deepened, turned a dark chocolate, almost a velvet. She pressed a hand to her stomach to keep away the sensation of rolling. The roller coaster again. She couldn't afford to live her life on a ride at a theme park.

"I didn't know how to protect you. Or give you a promise. I had to think things through. I had to know for certain that I wasn't going to ruin your life if I inserted myself into it permanently. Men like me don't do that easily, Vienna. We have to know we can protect the people we choose to have in our world. I had to know if I could even be in a relationship and make it work. I wasn't going to insist I could and then back out later."

"You can't know that about yourself."

"I'm good at looking at my weaknesses and strengths. In my line of work, I have to be. The one thing I don't ever do is bullshit myself. I can make a life with you. I'm loyal, Vienna. That's one trait I have. And I'm capable of loving the right person. That's you. Stop shaking your head."

She might consider keeping him just for his foot massages. The entire time he'd been presenting his case, he'd never stopped rubbing her feet and calves. That felt so good. She should have been tense, but his hands kept her relaxed and mellow.

"Snowflake, you didn't date anyone else. According to Sam, you didn't look at anyone else. It wasn't like you haven't had chances. I didn't look at anyone else. We fit."

"Do you have any idea how annoying you are?" A ghost of a smile lit his dark eyes for a moment, catching at her heart. "You didn't answer me, Zale. How long are you going to stay working?"

"At least another year." He didn't so much as hesitate. He didn't look away from her either.

She put her head back and looked up at the ceiling. "If I had a job where you couldn't contact me or know where I was or even if I was alive, would you be all right with that, Zale?"

"Absolutely not."

He had that weird purr in his voice that sent a chill down her spine. She brought her head down to look at him again. Narrowing her gaze, she glared at him. "Why are you giving me attitude? You're the one with the high-risk job, not me."

"Is that so? I believe you're the one hanging off cliffs or wading through chest-deep snow to retrieve bodies. I've seen some of the videos of the rescues you've done. They're heart-stopping. The one where you rappelled down the canyon to that kid with the water rushing below you, treating him on that narrow ledge that looked like it was going to crumble any minute, terrified me. I wouldn't say what I do is half as dangerous as what you do. I can control my situations. You can't control nature, Vienna."

His expression remained the same, but his voice betrayed him. It was the first time she'd ever heard his voice shake. His eyes went diamond hard. Almost black obsidian. He looked a force of nature and every bit as scary.

"No, I can't," she agreed. "But I plan carefully. I don't leave anything to chance. I know the things that can go wrong, and I plan for those."

"While I'm away on a job, I'll have to worry, knowing what you're doing and knowing I can't get to you if something does go wrong," he said. "Just as you'll have to worry about me. I'll send you messages through Sam when I can."

Was she going to be okay with that? What was the alternative? Not having Zale in her life? She could pass up her chance of being with him because she didn't want to be home waiting for his return. It wasn't as if she was having hot date nights every night, nor would she if she turned him away. There was only Zale. Once she'd met him, she'd known no one else was going to measure up.

"You're sighing."

"Because you're annoying."

He laughed. "I'm annoying because you missed me and you don't want to admit it."

"I'll admit it. I don't want to take the chance that you're going to break my heart all over again, Zale. I'd say we need to go slow, but there's never time for us to go slow, is there? How long will you stay after Sam's wedding?"

"I have another three weeks after his wedding."

"I don't know if I can take time off. I can get friends to cover part of it for me." What was she thinking? Was she really going to start all over again with him? The idea was both exhilarating and scary—just like the proverbial roller coaster.

"Start asking them now," Zale suggested. "We need as much time as we can get."

"Are we really going to do this?"

He nodded. "We are. You aren't a woman to go through life afraid, Vienna. There's not one thing about you that says you do that."

She laughed. "Zale, how could you possibly know what I'm really like? I'm living in a town called Knightly, up in the Sierras. I ran away from an argument with my mother and avoided talking with her because I was afraid of what she might say. I didn't want us to make things worse. That's real fear right there, Zale. I don't think I can be called courageous at all."

"She's your mother, Vienna. That's a different beast altogether. If I had a mother and had grown up as close to her as you had, I would be very careful not to do anything to make things worse between us."

"I didn't do much to try to repair the damage," she admitted. "I called her and talked, but we both were so awkward when we spoke to one another, I think we just felt hurt when we hung up. She wouldn't visit me in Knightly. I always made certain to invite Ellen to come with her, so she'd know I accepted her relationship, but it didn't help. After a while, I just didn't know what to do, so it was easier not to do anything."

His hands wrapped around her feet, thumbs sliding up and into the soles. Vienna gasped at the way the massage felt. He never used too much pressure on her, it was always just the right amount.

"You never give yourself a break, Vienna. Has it occurred to you that your mother could have made an effort as well? The two of you could have talked things over and gotten the hurt out of the way. We're not doing that. If I hurt your feelings, Snowflake, you're going to tell me immediately and we're talking it out. I'm bound to make a few mistakes. It's not like I have a clue about family relationships."

"Who raised you, Zale?"

"I don't remember my parents. I'm not sure if I was ever with either one of them. My earliest memory was being cold. Really cold. I found this place in the dark where it was warm, a little hole I could squeeze into. The pipe was hot, and as long as I didn't touch it, I didn't get burned and I'd stay warm."

"How old were you?"

"I don't know, but I was in diapers."

He said it so matter-of-factly that she almost didn't understand. He even gave a little shrug, as if his childhood were of no consequence. Vienna said nothing because she wanted him to continue and was afraid if she said anything, he might stop.

"There was a bakery that sold all kinds of fresh-baked bread on the corner of the street. Below it, in the basement, were the ovens where they made the bread. The ovens were hot and the pipes ran under the bakery. I'd discovered them by accident. I had all the bread I could eat and there was a water spigot right outside the shop. No one could see me in my little space beside the pipe. Once I got rid of the diaper, I was able to run around at night and explore. I found a way into the basement and then into the bakery."

Vienna wished she could read him, but there was little inflection in his voice. He might have been telling her about another child—not a toddler—finding his way on his own in a city. He fell silent, continuing to knead up her calves.

"You can't stop there. I know you have a good education. How did you manage to go to the schools you went to?"

"The bakery. I learned by watching how to make bread and listening to people talk. I heard them reading. That was easy enough. Math was extremely easy for me. I could pick up languages. So many different people came into the bakery, and all of them spoke different languages. I stole clothes and then books. I knew the neighborhood like the back of my hand. I found out about school at a very early age and I snuck in and sat in on classes. I liked when the teachers read to everyone, but it was frustrating to me, so eventually I borrowed the books every night until I could read them all myself."

"Weren't you ever caught?"

A ghost of a smile touched his eyes. "Yeah, a few times. I had to bring papers home to my 'parents.' This sweet old lady owned the bakery. She knew I was hanging around by that time, and I helped out by dumping the garbage and doing odd jobs. I took the papers to her, didn't say a word. I think the first time, I was so little I didn't even come up to the top of the counter. I just pushed the papers up to her, didn't say a thing. She filled them out and pushed them back to me. I gave them to the teacher. I had no idea what they said at that time."

Vienna found herself a little shocked that the woman would fill out parental papers for a child she knew was living on the streets rather than report him to child services. "Why didn't she turn you in?"

"I would have run. She knew that already. We ended up having a loose relationship. I was more like a wild animal at first, and she was gruff. Had no kids of her own. I lived in the basement in a small room there and she pretended she didn't know. She bought me clothes and I pretended I didn't know, although I wore them."

"Did you continue to go to school?"

He nodded. "I learned at a very fast rate, and I *needed* to learn. I discovered the library and computers, which gave me access to the internet. That opened up a new world of learning to me. I excelled in math and languages and jumped grades. I had no real idea what that meant, and I didn't care as long as I could keep learning. I was working for Sophia in the ovens baking bread for her, and sometimes I'd go translate if she needed it. Mostly, I stayed out of sight."

Sophia. She liked that name. She liked that Sophia had taken care of him. It might not have been the care others would have approved of, but she'd done her best when others might have looked the other way or abandoned him.

"One day some men came to the neighborhood and demanded Sophia give them her special focaccia bread. She had her own special twist she put on it, and it's renowned. We were out of it, and she told them she would have the bakers make extra for them if they wanted to come back the next day. One of them, the youngest, a man of about twenty, pulled out a gun and shot her. Just like that. And he laughed. He called her a bitch and then spit on her."

Vienna's heart nearly stopped beating. She started to pull her feet back so she could go to him, but he clamped his fingers around her ankles like a vise.

"No, Snowflake, you have to hear this. All of it. You have to know who I am. What kind of man I am. I was down in the basement and I heard the gunshot. I ran upstairs and saw the car racing away. I have a good memory and recorded the license plate. I could see Sophia on the floor and I went to her. She was dying. I held her until she passed, and I promised her that I would get the bastards who killed her. Then I went to the security tape and played it. I'll never forget those faces. There were four of them. The twenty-year-old who pulled the trigger was the son of a local gangster and thought he was untouchable."

Vienna pressed her fist to her wildly beating heart. Zale's eyes moved over her face, a moody, brewing storm in their dark depths. Her mouth was suddenly dry. She wanted to wrap her arms around him and hold him to her. How easily someone had taken Sophia's life, a woman who had been kind to a little boy, giving him what he so desperately needed, a home of sorts. A place where he was safe from the streets. A chance to go to school and learn when it meant so much to him. She'd been killed for no reason at all.

"I knew who the gangsters were. Everyone on the street knew. Giovi Vella was a big man with a big mouth. He scared everyone into doing what he wanted them to do. We weren't anywhere near his original territory but he kept spreading out, claiming more and more. I guess the block where Sophia's bakery was located was next on his list. It was just his bad luck that they didn't know I lived in her basement."

He fell silent again, his fingers once more massaging her calves. At times, his thumbs pressed into her muscles just a little too hard, clueing her in to the fact that he might be sitting there looking relaxed, but the things he was telling her were painful to him.

"I hunted them down one by one. I was still in my teens, Vienna. No one really knew about me. That gave me an advantage. I found the blueprints to their homes and studied them first, and then I went in at night and killed them. Five of them. All of the men who were with the man that killed Sophia, then him, and then his father. I killed them all in one night, going from house to house. I used the same knife and then I got rid of it, breaking it up with a hammer and discarding the pieces in various places. I wore gloves and made certain I wasn't caught on any cameras."

Vienna knew he was waiting for her reaction, watching her closely to see if she was going to pull away from him. She wished she were touching him. Stroking her fingers along his calf, or massaging his foot. Anything to reassure him she understood. Sophia might not have been a mother to him in the accepted sense of the word, they hadn't lived together, but she had been all he'd had. Zale was capable of fierce loyalty, and he felt that toward Sophia.

"I'm so sorry, honey," she told him. "That must have been a terrible time for you."

He rubbed her calf much more gently. "Her lawyer contacted me through the school. She had legally adopted me somehow. Well, she had a birth certificate that appeared legitimate. She was connected to a family in Sicily, and they did the paperwork for her. They hadn't heard from her until she asked for the papers to make that happen. She left me a letter explaining what she'd asked her uncle to do for her. She left everything she had to me. The bakery, the money. Everything. She had a lot. All that was good, but suddenly I was out in the open, exposed to the world. Sophia had been murdered. Her killer had been murdered. She was connected to a family in Sicily and I was her son."

"What did you do?" Vienna asked when he went quiet again.

He looked at her again, his dark eyes pure velvet. "No condemnation for anything I told you? Vienna, I just admitted I hunted those men down and killed them."

She waved his confession away. "I'm sure you're not supposed to admit things like that. Didn't they teach you that in secret forces school or wherever you went? You're intelligent. Never admit to anything. I know you must have continued your education."

He nodded. "I did. I continued to skip grades and ended up managing to get my bachelor's in three years. As soon as I had my master's, I joined the service."

"Were you recruited or did you join? You had to have been very young."

"I was restless and I didn't know what I wanted to do. I didn't fit in anywhere. I'd sold Sophia's bakery. I couldn't look at it without seeing her lying on the floor. I didn't have anywhere to go. I needed something to do that would take the edge off. There's always been a kind of restlessness in me, and I had to find a way to explore that."

She studied his face. There had been a reluctant note in his voice, as if he hadn't wanted to share that last piece of information with her. "What happens when we're together and you start to feel restless, Zale? That could happen, couldn't it?"

He didn't so much as blink. "I suppose it could. Life is a risk, Vienna. You know that. If that happens, we talk about it and decide the best way to handle it together. I'm not that young lost kid. I can look at myself and see the things I need to work on. I see the things I want and need in my life. What about you?"

His voice was back to that soft stroke of sensual awareness, brushing over her skin so that she shivered with need. He could bring her nerve endings to instant, vivid life just with that tone of his, but when he added that hungry look from his dark eyes, she got that curious melting sensation in the pit of her stomach as well.

The last was a deliberate challenge. What about her? Everything she wanted was sitting right in front of her. "Stop looking at me like that."

He knew she'd already made up her mind. Hot flames began to flicker in his dark eyes. She felt those flames licking at her skin, tiny flicks that ignited a wildfire on her nerve endings. That was how it had started before, when he'd annoyed her by tossing her over his shoulder like some caveman.

"How am I looking at you, Vienna?"

Those dark, sinful eyes of his moved over her body as if he stroked her with a physical touch. She felt the lick of a flame on her throat, her breast, her nipple, her belly button, lower still until she wanted to moan and writhe right there in her cuddle chair.

"You know exactly how you're looking at me."

She knew she'd been doing the same thing to him—maybe worse. She couldn't stop devouring him with hungry eyes, moistening her lips with the tip of her tongue and deliberately staring at his chest and then lowering her gaze.

He put her feet on the floor and stood up, stalked to her chair and then lifted her easily. He had the caveman carry perfected like no one else. Upside down, she was laughing and trying to strip her shirt off by the time they hit the master bedroom.

CHAPTER FOUR

〰〰〰〰〰〰〰〰〰〰〰〰〰〰〰〰

Our token model made it to the final table," Art Cable said, pulling his glasses down to the bridge of his nose with one finger to peer at her. "You do know you're only supposed to be a gimmick, right, honey?"

Vienna flashed him her brilliant model smile, the one that showed off her straight white teeth, the dimple that came and went, and somehow seemed to highlight the emerald green of her eyes. She even batted her feathery lashes at him.

"How silly of me to keep winning and make it to the final table. Someone should have clued me in."

Jameson Rockefeller, another well-known gambler, one whose book she'd read before coming, snickered. "I wouldn't underestimate her, Art. She's sitting here with us, and she's earned those chips in front of her. Second-highest number of chips at the table."

"I'd like to know how that happened when no one's really heard of her," Charles Von Garden declared, his tone implying all sorts of things. "Did your sugar daddy sponsor you? What did you have to do for the money?"

She let her gaze slide over him. "You're the one with the sponsors, Charles. What did you have to do to get yours?" She smiled sweetly, but there was nothing at all sweet about her inquiry.

Charles gripped the table and nearly lunged to his feet. "What are you implying?"

Vienna lifted an eyebrow. "Why, nothing, Charles. I was just asking you the same question you asked me. You're clearly a very sensitive man."

Charles subsided, looking at the other players, all of whom were frowning at him, Art included. Art may have tried tweaking Vienna, but he didn't like what Charles had said to her.

Vienna studied the other players. There were eight sitting at the final table, with her included. These were some of the players she'd admired. She'd watched them on television. Some had written books or put up vlogs on YouTube. Others had taught master classes on the internet. For all his sarcasm, Art Cable had been the one man to help others with his videos and classes. He did charge a fee, but it was nominal and she understood that his time was very valuable.

Benny Dobsin was a ruthless player. He could be unpredictable. She had studied him closely in every video of him she could. He had a tendency to stay in longer than he should—on purpose, she was certain—and then suddenly he'd win several large pots. He constantly fidgeted, touching his face and rubbing his fingers over his eyes. He would target certain players and play against them to try to get them out of the game. She considered him a wild card.

Leo Sheldon was the oldest player at the table, in his seventies, sharp as a tack and a three-time winner of the World Series of Poker. He was a serious player, a well-known celebrity with a huge following. He had the most chips at the table, and Vienna considered him the biggest threat. He was quiet and thoughtful and gave nothing away.

Park Ables, like Vienna, played mostly online. She'd played against his online persona. He played as *onehotguy*. He was good enough to win huge tournaments. He'd outed himself deliberately, going to Vegas often and bragging about the wins when he sat at the tables. He was extremely good-looking and worked as a successful model.

Theodore Morgan traveled the gambling circuit, following tournaments and often working his way to the final table. He usually came in third or fourth but never made it into that coveted position of winner.

Light shone down on the table, and the dealer, a woman by the name of Eve, took her place. Around them, various onlookers rooting for their favorites stood behind the barrier. They were a good distance away. Vienna was used to the quiet of her room when she gambled, not a huge room with people seated at tables below them, stretching far out into the room as if they were a spectacle to behold. Maybe they were.

She cleared her mind as the cards were dealt. The first thing she did was watch the dealer as she flicked the cards to each person at the table. That well inside her opened, the warmth pouring out, encompassing everything and everyone at the table, including the cards so she was able to see the smallest detail.

Vienna knew what the cards she'd been dealt were without looking, but she glanced at them anyway to ensure she appeared to be just like everyone else. She also knew what everyone else had just by moving her gaze to each of their cards. Leo made his opening bet, which was considerable. He had a pair of twos.

She knew Art, Benny and Park would stay in for certain. Art had a pair of aces, the best possible starting hand in Hold'em. Park had the king and queen of diamonds. Benny had a pair of eights, a hand players liked to see the flop with.

The blinds started at 1,000/2,000. Art raised to 5,000 with his aces. As expected, Park called. Benny was in the big blind of 2,000, so he called the additional 3,000. All the others folded. She folded. So did James. Benny hesitated. He had a pair of eights. He stayed. Theodore folded. Art stayed and raised. There was a low murmur from the crowd at the audacity. Park wavered but remained. Leo folded.

The dealer turned over the eight of diamonds. The ace of spades. The three of diamonds. She could see Park's sudden excitement. His hand cupped his chips. His face took on a glow. Benny shifted in his chair. Art didn't so much as look up. She knew Park was going for that next diamond and he wasn't going to get it. Benny thought he had the best hand with his triple eights. He was certain he'd get an eight. He should have known better. Art had the best possible hand at the moment with his three aces and a hammerlock on the hand.

Benny checked to the initial raiser, Art, who made a small bet enticing players to stay in. Park couldn't help himself. He was a gambler at heart, and there was no way he was going to fold his flush draw with the turn and river cards both to come.

Benny, who was certain he had the best hand, pounced, pushing half his chips in. "If you're drawing, you're going to have to pay," he declared in a loud, triumphant voice.

Art, slow, methodical, calculated as always, thought it through. He knew he was calling but he wanted to entice Park into the pot as well. Without a word, Art slid half of his chips into the middle, signaling a call to the dealer. The action was now on Park.

Park couldn't help himself. "Two cards, all the money? How can I say no?" Park quickly called. With no more action and all the money in the middle, the dealer turned over the two of hearts. No help. The final card was an inconsequential seven of spades.

Art won the entire pot and seemingly never even got excited. But Vienna could see the smallest wrinkle of a smile on the corner of his mouth. It was the most emotion she had seen from him in all the hours she'd spent studying him.

She found it kind of sad to watch the desperation in

Benny, the way he played. He tried to be gracious when he lost hand after hand, making incredibly bad decisions.

The hours went by and gave her an insight into each player's personality as they played out their cards. It was her bad luck that Benny went out of the game, losing his last hand to her. He put on a fake smile and shook her hand, but she could see it in his eyes that he was upset. He was the first to go and got a round of applause, but that didn't take the sting away.

Vienna was challenged by Charles continually. Nearly every hand she stayed in, he pushed the betting, only dropping out when it was clear someone else was going to challenge her. She was careful not to buy into his deliberately misogynistic personality by appearing to look at him directly when he was aggressive. She played her cards just as she would any hand where she was confident of a win. He was trying to force her into making a mistake. Unfortunately for Charles, the more someone became antagonistic toward her, or outwardly belligerent, the calmer and more settled she became.

Four hours later, she was facing Art, Charles, Jameson and Leo. She'd been dealt a pair of queens. She opened the betting at three times the blind. Park and Theodore folded. Art was dealt the ace and king of spades. He called. Charles had the jack and ten of hearts. He couldn't resist taking the flop, so he called the bet as well. The flop was laid out—ace of hearts, queen of hearts and eight of diamonds.

Vienna made a pot-size bet, knowing Art and Charles both connected on this flop. Art raised the bet considerably, over five hundred thousand. He was sitting on two aces. Charles had a royal flush draw; the king of hearts would make his hand unbeatable. He didn't hesitate to stay in. Jameson and Leo folded. Vienna put her chips in and raised the bet another five hundred thousand. Art studied her face. Looked at the cards on the table in front of them and then pushed his chips in. Charles did so without hesitation, staring at her belligerently.

The turn was a three of clubs. That changed nothing. Vienna was still sitting best with her set of queens. Art still had top pair top kicker, and Charles was still in with a massive royal flush draw. Vienna bet big again; she knew that Art was too good to call her with just one pair, even if it was top pair. But Charles, on the other hand, was stuck. His draw was too strong in his mind.

As expected, Art studied her, studied his chips and came to the correct decision. He slid his cards back to the dealer. Charles coolly raised the bet on the river card another million.

Art sat back in his chair. "You're going for red on the river, Charles," he announced with a shake of his head. "Pretty damn ballsy."

Pretty damn stupid in Vienna's opinion. She was certain Charles wouldn't have done it had he been betting against any of the men. He seemed to have a grudge because she was in the game. She was there for the money, just like the rest of them. Vienna answered him coolly, pushing her chips in, her eyes meeting his as his eyes shot daggers at her.

The dealer turned the last card over. The eight of hearts. Charles made his flush, but it paired the board, giving Vienna a full house. Charles shoved all his chips into the middle, daring Vienna to call. She slid her chips into the middle and said, "Sorry, Charles, flush is no good. Queens full."

For a moment there was absolute silence, as if everyone in the entire room held their breath. Charles leapt out of his chair, pacing around the table, swearing under his breath. There was no recovery. He had no chips to continue. The crowd's low murmur seemed shocked at the outcome. Charles had appeared so confident.

Vienna didn't make the mistake of smiling over her victory. She offered her hand graciously. Charles nearly slapped her hand away, but in the end, he shook it, as he pretended to be civil before he left. The dealer rose, signaling they were finished for the day. It had been a grueling few hours and they were down to six players. Vienna had bumped both Benny and Charles and improved her chips by several million. She'd also made at least one enemy.

Art handed her a bottle of cold water as she stood and stretched. "I'm sorry he was such a dick. I gave you a bad time, but I didn't mean anything by it. I do that to all the players."

She took the water gratefully. "I'm well aware. I've studied your techniques for years."

Leo came up on her other side. "Art, I told you that was a bad idea, getting in front of the camera the way you do. Someone smart is going to study your every move and figure you out. Who knew it was going to be our lovely addition?" He saluted her with his water bottle.

Vienna laughed. "I don't think I figured him out. He has his timing down so perfectly, that would be nearly impossible."

"Charles is a dick," Park announced.

Leo put his hand on the small of her back to urge Vienna away from the table and the onlookers shouting at them. The cameras were still on and audio could capture anything they might say. He was used to being under the glare of the lights, having been a celebrity in the poker world for well over a decade, going on two now. He leaned down as Art took up the other side of her.

"Audio picks up everything we say," he whispered.

Vienna nodded. She had realized that immediately and gave a small shake of her head to Park, indicating the cameras. He grinned at her, uncaring, used to getting away with almost anything just by smiling. She had to admit, he was rather breathtaking. Theodore came right up behind them while Jameson led the way. She had the feeling the men were protecting her, but she wasn't certain from what. Or they were getting their airtime, afraid she would take it away from them. She didn't want it, so if that was their motivation for keeping her inside their "pocket," she was happy to stay there.

Inside the next room, there was food and drink laid out for them. Park remained close to her side as she took advantage of the fresh fruit trays. "We should do a shoot together here. I ran it by a couple of my sponsors and they loved the idea. They could send you some of their designer clothes. The lines are two of the best, Vienna."

She was well aware of the two brands he modeled. He was talking about two high-end companies selling T-shirts for well over a hundred dollars. A jacket was at least a thousand. She knew both brands were considered soft and elegant and trendy. Park looked like a million bucks walking around in the suits or the casual clothes.

"I'm not a model, Park. I'm a nurse." The fruit was amazing. Exactly what she needed. That and the water. She was exhausted and close to crashing. She needed to get upstairs and into her suite as soon as possible, but she didn't want to look like she was running away.

"You look like a model and you carry yourself like one. You could pull it off, and the paycheck is great."

"I'm hoping to score a huge paycheck very soon," she pointed out.

"You really think you can win against Art or Leo?" Park asked, leaning past her to snag a plate so he could add fruit to it.

His body brushed up against hers. She knew it was deliberate, and she stepped away from him, just enough to put space between them.

"That's why I'm here. Don't you think you can? You're a serious player online, Park. You win often. You made it to the final table because you're good. You're still here when Benny and Charles are gone, and they have more experience than you."

Park followed her to a small table with high stools. They sat down to eat the fruit they'd put on the plates. "I have to admit, I was a little shocked to make it this far. I'm good, but I'm not in their league."

Vienna lifted one eyebrow. This man was going to sit down at the final table with her in another day to play again. Would he seriously be talking to her this way? She doubted it. He seemed open and friendly, just the opposite of Charles, who was hostile. More than likely he was trying to lull her into a false sense of security so she would let down her guard and talk to him about how she played the game.

"You're good at bullshit, Park, I'll give you that."

He looked at her, a little stunned, and then he burst out laughing. "I'll bet you're a darned good nurse."

"You'd win that bet. I'm a surgical nurse, but I work in a very small town, so I take rotations in the emergency room as well. I like what I do. It requires fast decisions and it saves lives, which is very fulfilling."

Someone across the room with a camera in their hands waved at Park, signaling him to come over. He gave her a little fake apologetic smile but rose immediately and went to pose, as several flashes began going off as paparazzi gathered around him.

Theodore joined her, taking the high-backed stool Park had vacated. "I just wanted to warn you, Vienna." He kept his voice low. "I've known Benny Dobsin for years. He's well-known on the circuit and plays all over the world in the bigger tournaments. He doesn't like to lose the way he did."

He paused to take a drink. His drink of choice was scotch, and she noted he had a generous amount in the glass. He liked it neat, no ice, and when he drank it, he took a healthy swallow.

"I had the better cards. It happens."

"You're unknown. It was round one. He's a vindictive little shit. I'm not saying this to be a gossip. Everyone knows what he's like other than you and Park because you haven't been around him. He'll retaliate in some way, and it won't be nice. I'm just saying, watch your back."

Before she could say anything, Theodore slid off the stool and wandered away, as if he had just been talking about the weather. Vienna was exhausted, and she just wanted to go upstairs to her suite and get away from everyone. She didn't want to hear any more negativity. At the end of the day, she was there to play cards and win the money. The others and their personalities and motives didn't matter.

She left, keeping her head down to avoid any interaction with well-wishers or fans, and found her elevator as quickly as possible. Fortunately, their reception room was located very close to the private lift leading to her suite. The ride up was fast, the soft music soothing as she leaned against the back wall for support. She needed the peace and solitude of her room after the grueling hours of playing poker surrounded by so many people. She was used to the Eastern Sierras, where the beauty and majesty always reset and grounded her. Having so many people crowding close made her feel as if she couldn't breathe.

The elevator doors opened and she stepped onto the plush carpet of the hallway, key out, ready to hurry to her suite. To her dismay, Charles Von Garden stood in the hallway just a few feet from her door. He clearly was waiting to see which suite was hers. She hesitated, but he'd heard the elevator and turned, his expression darkening.

"You bitch."

Vienna looked up at the security camera and indicated she was in trouble. "Why do men always open every nasty conversation with 'You bitch'? It isn't very inventive. Any of the other nasty words you use for females aren't much better. What is it you want, Charles?"

She realized Charles must have one of the suites on the other side of the floor. He'd come up his private elevator and walked around the entire floor to get to her side. He took several very aggressive steps toward her.

Vienna stepped away from the elevator, moving toward the only other suite on that side of the floor. She was afraid if she tried to get back on the elevator, he would manage to get in with her and she'd be locked in with him.

Rainier and Zale were still in their undercover roles of Zale playing personal protector to the wealthy Wayne Forsyne. She could only hope Rainier was in his full mask and makeup. As a rule, he didn't go without it. The mask was extremely thin, contoured to his face and so authentic-looking it was nearly impossible to tell it wasn't actual skin.

Vienna held her hand up in a "stop" gesture, mainly for dramatic effect for the security camera. She raised her voice. "Stop right there, Charles. You're scaring me."

"You should be scared. I should beat the crap out of you."

"You knew better than to make that bet, but you did it anyway," she pointed out.

He took another step closer, and she hit her fist on Rainier's door. "Help." She had no idea if they were home, but any self-respecting woman would ask for help when confronted by a drunk out for revenge.

"You cost me the chance to win ten million dollars."

"I didn't cost you that chance. You knew better than to make the bet, but you couldn't resist because you were betting against me, not one of the others. You stopped playing the cards and you made it personal. That's on you."

She should have been placating him, but damn it all, she was exhausted, and why the hell should she have to cater to his ego? He never would have placed that bet if he'd been up against Art with those same cards.

Charles rushed her, shocking her with his speed, dipping his shoulder at the last minute like a linebacker. He was definitely drunk, but he was on her much faster than she had anticipated, knocking her to the floor with a shoulder into her midsection and driving her backward and down. She struck the side of her head on the wall and it hurt like hell, but thankfully the carpet was thick and cushioned her fall.

Charles roared something ugly into her neck, his breath reeking of alcohol.

The door to Wayne Forsyne's suite burst open, and the old man came out looking left and right, his cane swinging. His gaze fell on Charles as her drunken assailant started to sit on top of her, his fist pulled back. She was already rolling, doing her best to get out from under the big man.

"Stop, you scoundrel. Get off that woman."

Wayne limped forward, swinging his cane at Charles's head. He managed a solid hit that rocked Charles enough that Vienna was allowed sufficient room to get out from under him. She staggered to her feet.

"Stay back, Vienna," Wayne ordered. He touched the tip of the cane to Charles's side and pressed a trigger.

The cane became a Taser, delivering a charge into Charles, and the man immediately went to the carpet, rolling into a ball, whimpering. Wayne stepped forward as if he might deliver another charge into him.

Vienna gently put a hand on him. "I think he's had enough."

Two security guards emerged from the service elevator at the same time Zale did. Zale's dark gaze swept over her first, assessing her quickly. He took in everything, making her aware of her clothing in disarray, her untidy hair and the knot coming up on the left side of her forehead. His gaze moved over Rainier next, assessing him, and then dropped to Charles. That look went expressionless, but not his eyes. Zale's eyes turned even darker, flat and ice-cold. Instinctively, she felt the need to step between Zale and Charles.

The two security guards moved to either side of Charles. "You need to stand up, sir."

"They assaulted me," he complained. "He hit me in the head from behind with his cane and then Tased me."

"Stand up, sir," the security guard repeated patiently. "Ma'am, you need to press formal charges against him. We have everything on tape."

"He's drunk," Vienna said.

"That doesn't excuse his behavior," Zale said. "How often do you think he does this to other women when no one is around?"

"No, it doesn't," Vienna agreed. "And I'll press charges, but I just need to sit down for a few minutes and rest, if that's okay with everyone." If she didn't get to her suite, she would be sitting right there on the floor. She put her palm on the wall to steady herself. On top of everything else, using her "gift" in cards always drained her.

"Whatever you need, ma'am," the taller of the two security guards, who seemed to be in charge, agreed hastily. "No worries."

Vienna turned her attention to Rainier. "Thank you, Mr. Forsyne, for saving me. I was very afraid. You came charging to the rescue, and I really appreciate it."

Rainier took her hand and bent over her fingers as if he were kissing them in an old-school, gentlemanly manner. "Call me Wayne, Vienna. I was happy to help." He walked her to her door and watched as she inserted her key and went inside.

Vienna rushed across the huge expanse of a living room to the master bedroom and flung herself facedown on the bed. If she was the type of woman who could cry, she would be weeping. Her arms felt like lead. So did her legs. Her head pounded from where she'd struck it on the wall. The pain spread until it felt like it roared through her entire body. She was completely drained. She didn't want to think anymore.

Intellectually, she knew it came from using her "gift" for so long. She wasn't really the biggest baby in town, but once she was down, she couldn't get back up. She wished she'd at least kicked off her shoes. Thankfully, the duvet had that soft, heavenly feel to it, and it seemed to enfold her entire body. That's what she needed, to be swept away.

She'd been warned she'd made an enemy of Benny just by playing her cards, and now Charles. She had no choice but to press charges against him. She couldn't let him get away with assaulting her. He had her on the floor and there wasn't a doubt in her mind that he was going to punch her repeatedly. After that, who knew? He probably didn't know what he would have done, he was that drunk and out of control. If he thought he had reason to be her enemy before, once she pressed charges, he really would hate her.

"Snowflake? Don't move. I'm taking your shoes off and changing your clothes. I don't have much time. I want to stay with you, but I have to work. I've called your mother. She'll be here with Ellen as soon as possible. Hotel security will let them in. Wayne arranged everything as if he had complete authority."

"You called my mother?" She would have glared at him for interfering, but she couldn't muster up the strength to open her eyes. Her head hurt too much. She didn't even care that he was pulling off her trousers. "She's coming here? To the casino? She despises casinos. In fact, that was one of the few things we fought over. She didn't like me gambling." Her voice was muffled by the pillow.

Zale dropped his hand onto her head. "I'm turning you over, Vienna, just to take off this top so I can get you into something comfortable. The room is dark so it shouldn't hurt your eyes. Why didn't she like you gambling? You paid the bills, right?"

His hands were gentle, but it still hurt to be touched as he rolled her over and pushed the hair away from her face. He swore softly and then his fingers were deftly unbuttoning her blouse. "That bastard. He's going to pay for this."

"I hit my head on the wall, Zale. Don't do anything that could get you in trouble. He isn't worth it." She tried to open her eyes to see his face, but he stroked his fingers over her eyelids to discourage her.

"Sorry, Snowflake. I didn't mean to upset you." His voice was soothing, but he didn't sound as if he had changed his mind about hunting down Charles and making him pay.

Vienna would have tried to reason with him, but she was too tired and her head hurt worse than usual.

"Tell me about your mom and her aversion to gambling. She lives in Vegas. That seems contradictory."

"Once we needed the money, and she was too sick to make it for us, she stopped being upset over the way I paid the bills. She never said why she had such an aversion to gambling, but she didn't so much as buy a lottery ticket or come near the casinos. Not ever. I was very drawn to playing cards."

"Lifting you up to put your nightclothes on you," he warned.

Vienna clenched her teeth. Movement hurt. "I have migraine meds in the bathroom on the sink, Zale. Would you get two for me, please? I'll be fine once I take them."

Zale managed to slip her pajama top on her and lower her back to the bed. She buried her face back into the pillow. "Mom wouldn't even come to the Strip, let alone to one of the hotels." She needed to distract herself from the pain. Already she rocked her body in an effort to soothe herself.

"Vienna." Zale gently turned her into his arms and held her up as he put the pills into her palm. "Are you crying?" He used the pads of his fingers to track along her cheeks where it might have been wet. "I'll find a way for Rainier and me to get out of going tonight."

"No, really." She *wasn't* crying. She didn't cry. Her eyes might be leaking, but that wasn't crying. "I'm perfectly fine. I get weak after gambling like that. Go do whatever it is you do. I can't believe you got my mother to come here. That's a miracle."

Zale continued to hold her, his arms tight around her, one palm pressing her head to his shoulder so she was breathing him in.

"Wayne Forsyne was invited by Daniel Wallin to a party tonight. I think you were supposed to be there, Vienna. The players from the final table were going to be introduced. A couple of them are considered celebrities. We shouldn't pass up a chance to meet Wallin and the personal protectors he surrounds himself with. They'll be out in force."

"I didn't show Rainier how to walk properly with an injury. If someone knows what to look for, they'll notice."

"He's been watching videos and practicing ever since you told him. That's why he's been in the suite instead of downstairs gambling. He's a perfectionist, and your critique really hurt his ego." There was a hint of laughter in Zale's voice. "He doesn't normally take on this type of role."

"Neither do I," Vienna said, and dashed at the wet running down her face. She pressed deeper into Zale's shirt.

The last thing she wanted was for Zale to think she was weak, and yet here she was, clinging to him like a needy person. How was she going to explain it? That she had a psychic gift and it drained her to use it? That it made her cry? Had she already told him that? She couldn't remember.

He laughed softly. "Go to sleep. When you wake up, your mom will be here."

"You have to go before security catches you in here."

"Rainier is in the other room. He's having fun throwing his weight around. He's got everyone up in arms over you being attacked in the hotel right under the noses of security. If you weren't already being comped this suite, you would be after Rainier gets finished with his threats on your behalf."

"Don't let him go overboard. I don't want to have to have television interviews or anything crazy like that."

"You won't have to go to the police to fill out a complaint, they'll come here," Zale assured. "And hotel security will back you up. Wallin most likely will pay you a personal visit to ensure you aren't going to sue."

Vienna flung herself out of his arms and back onto the

duvet. "Oh, for heaven's sake, go away. Just the thought is making me ill. I mean it, go away, Zale. If you see Mom, tell her I'm ten years old again and need an ice pack for my head."

He bent over her and she felt his lips brush over the offending lump on her forehead. "I'm sorry I have to go, Snowflake. I'll be back as soon as I can. I just received a text from Rainier that security is bringing them up now."

"That was fast."

He dropped his hand into the thick silky strands of her hair. "They're worried." Abruptly, he left. She knew he just went into the other room so it looked as if he was protecting his client, but she still felt bereft.

Then her mother and Ellen were there, one on either side of the bed. Her mother sat on the edge of the mattress, stroking caresses in her hair. The moment she felt her mother's hand, the tears began again. This time she just let them fall. It was Ellen who found the ice pack to put over the lump on her forehead. She covered her with a light blanket. No one made her talk or explain anything. They just allowed her to rest and she was very, very grateful.

She had no idea how much time had passed when her mother stirred. "Someone is at the door, Ellen. Would you mind getting it?"

"Be careful," Vienna cautioned, sitting up carefully. She held on to her head just in case it decided to explode on her. Fortunately, her head stayed on her shoulders, where it was supposed to. "It could be someone else violent. Look through the peephole."

"Oh, no. I do hate these places. We should have just taken Vienna home with us," Mitzi said. "Surely they have security guards watching over you now."

Vienna had forgotten her mother's aversion to casino hotels. She looked so distressed that Vienna loved her all the more for braving her fears to come to help her. Mitzi had always had near panic attacks if she had to go close to the casinos. Vienna's gaze jumped to her mother's face. Mitzi's voice trembled. She looked very pale, and sweat beaded on her forehead. She looked close to panicking now. Looking back, it had always been that way.

Vienna slipped her hand into her mother's. "I love you, Mom. Thank you for coming to help me. I know it must have been difficult for you, and it means even more that you did."

Mitzi broke into a smile, the one Vienna hadn't seen in years. "I would always come to you, Vienna, if you were in trouble, no matter where you were. I'd find a way to get to you."

Vienna leaned her head against her mother. "I'm sorry we fought and I let so much time go by without telling you I don't care if I dropped out of the sky. You're my mother. That's enough for me, and it always will be. I have a full life with you in it. I want to be close to Ellen."

"We'll find a way to make that happen. She wants that too," Mitzi reassured.

"He says he's the owner of the hotel, Vienna, a Mr. Wallin," Ellen called out. "Daniel Wallin. He'd like to come in for a minute and see for himself that you're all right."

"He just wants to make certain you aren't going to sue him," Mitzi cautioned. "They're like that. Ellen, don't let him in. Just tell him to go away."

"Mom, this wasn't his fault. If he wants to come and apologize on behalf of his hotel, I don't mind. Maybe I'll get free coffee for the rest of my life or something cool like that." She pressed her palm over the lump, which seemed to be thumping in irritating time to her heartbeat.

"If you don't mind, then, dear, I saw that lovely bathtub, and I'm going to run you a bath while you talk to him. Ellen can order dinner for all of us. Make it very short with this man. He shouldn't take up your time when you need rest. I'll get you a robe, because you certainly aren't going to meet him in your skimpy pajamas."

Mitzi hurried to the closet and pulled one of the hotel's

luxurious ankle-length robes from a hanger and covered Vienna's offending pajamas with it.

Vienna burst out laughing. "Zale had to help get me dressed, Mom. He chose my pj's."

Mitzi was halfway to the master bath and she turned. "It's like that, is it?"

"The police are with him," Ellen reported. "They'd like to take your statement. They also want pictures of the damage."

"Just lovely." Mitzi rolled her eyes. "Ellen, would you mind staying with her while I run her a bath? I'll take a phone in with me and order us dinner. Get them out of here as soon as possible. She needs to eat, get in the bath and then rest. And watch what she says, apparently she let Zale dress her earlier."

"He had to *undress* me first," Vienna teased.

Her mother made a shooing motion and indicated to Ellen to watch over her before she disappeared into the master bath.

Ellen nodded and helped Vienna to the main room, then allowed their visitors to enter. Vienna was happy the room was so spacious. They'd sent both a male and a female officer. Wallin's personal physician accompanied them as well. Her heart sank when she was introduced to him. Dr. Miller looked kind enough, but he carried a large medical bag with him and seemed prepared to send her straight to the hospital if she blinked wrong.

Daniel Wallin was a man who looked to be in his sixties, although she knew from reading about him that he was older. He appeared to be of Scandinavian descent with his thick, wild shock of white hair falling into his faded blue eyes. He had one dimple on his left side that was barely noticeable because of the lines in his face. He was a handsome man, tall, dressed impeccably in a suit. He carried himself as if he were athletic, or had been at one time. Vienna didn't know much about him, other than he had one son, and he'd made a fortune in cards.

Wallin was flanked by two personal protectors. Both men looked as if they meant business. They openly carried weapons and looked as if they knew how to use them. They didn't smile, not even at the police officers, nor did they smile at her. They took up positions at either side of the door and just stood there, as if prepared to shoot everyone in the room if they dared to argue with Wallin.

"I'm appalled that this could happen to you in my hotel," Daniel Wallin greeted her, taking both her hands and peering at her intently. His gaze moved over her face, dwelling on the dark bump on the side of her forehead. "I was looking forward to meeting you this evening, but certainly not under these circumstances. I've brought Dr. Miller to examine you . . ."

Vienna waved that away. "I'm a nurse, Mr. Wallin. That certainly isn't necessary. I'm absolutely fine. I hit my head on the wall when I fell."

"You should have been taken to the hospital," Wallin said, turning his head slightly to give his security team a frown. "I viewed the footage several times. You hit your head hard."

"Did you lose consciousness?" Dr. Miller's tone was brisk, although his fingers were gentle as they moved over her scalp and temples.

The police officers had come close, poised to ask their questions. Vienna sighed, resigned to answer whatever was necessary to get them out of her suite so she could visit with her mother and Ellen. If she hadn't been so exhausted, she might have protested more, but as it was, she was still suffering from the terrible lethargy that overcame her when she used her gift at the card table.

The police officers took photographs of the bruising on her forehead, and after she told them Charles had used his shoulder to drive into her like a linebacker to send her to the floor, they insisted on looking at her stomach. Already, there was a dark bruise spreading across her stomach, under her breast and over her ribs. They took pictures of that as well. She was very glad when they finally left.

Dr. Miller continued to fuss over her, probing around the spreading bruise to see if she was damaged internally.

"You played your cards masterfully," Wallin said. "Twice you stayed in when others would have folded, and you ended up winning. You didn't have to show your hand because no one called you."

She laughed softly. "Is there a question in there somewhere?"

Wallin laughed with her. "I guess not. Someday, I'd like to sit at a table with you. You're difficult to read."

"Only because I'm a newcomer," Vienna pointed out.

The doctor was annoying her and she started to look at him, determined to tell him enough was enough, when Wallin took her hand again, distracting her. He turned her right arm over so her inner wrist was up. His thumb slid gently over her pulse. "I thought this was a tattoo, but it isn't, is it?"

She had a small birthmark in the shape of a heart. It was even pink in color. Few people noticed it. She'd considered having a tattoo put over it, but she never had. The birthmark was slightly raised, and when she played poker, she'd had to train herself to resist running her finger back and forth over the mark. She still did it sometimes when she couldn't quite "see" a card she needed to see.

"No, it's a birthmark. Ow." She'd been aware of the doctor wrapping her arm with a long tube and inserting a needle into her vein. She turned her head to discover the doctor taking a vial of her blood. "What are you doing?"

"Just making certain you didn't get any bacteria when you hit your head, Vienna," Dr. Miller said. "Didn't you read all the papers you signed? You consented to a blood test. We have to cover all the bases."

Vienna looked up at Ellen, trying not to laugh when their

eyes met. Mitzi was right all along. Maybe she'd signed away her right to sue and didn't even know it when she'd signed her statements for the police.

"I'm tired. If we're finished here, I really need to lie down for a while."

"Yes, of course." Daniel Wallin stood, signaling for the doctor to finish up. "I hope to see you again, Vienna. Good luck in the tournament. I'm really sorry this happened to you in my hotel. If there's anything at all you need, let me know."

"I will," Vienna assured.

Ellen walked them to the door. When they were gone, she turned her back to the door, leaned against it and regarded Vienna. "Anything you need as long as you don't sue."

They both burst out laughing.

CHAPTER FIVE

///

With six players left, Vienna felt the tension climb even higher at the table, although with the exception of Park and herself, the four other players were all professional gamblers. Art, Jameson and Leo had all won world championships multiple times. Theodore had placed at the final table in championships multiple times but had never made it beyond the third-place slot. She knew that had to be frustrating for him, but he was always gracious, always a gentleman.

They talked even more, bragging a little, teasing a bit, commenting on Park's good looks and the way he'd drawn such a female crowd. Vienna couldn't help but look at the women congregating around the barrier separating the final table from the onlookers. Park definitely had a fanatical following. The women jumped up and down, calling his name and waving items for him to sign.

Park looked resigned, giving the other players a faint shrug and his famous grin. "They're here to bring me luck."

"They make enough noise that you can't hear yourself think," Leo groused.

Art laughed. "You're just jealous because on your best day, you don't have that many women looking for the key to your room."

"Depends on whether I win or not," Leo said.

"Well," Art conceded, "there's that."

They all laughed, although Vienna didn't think the comment was that funny because she was certain it was the truth. Leo—and the others—most likely did have women vying for a chance to go to their room with them if they won.

Once the laughter faded, Leo turned the spotlight on Vienna. "I heard about what happened to you last night, Vienna. I'm so sorry. I should have escorted you up to your room, or had security take you up."

All at once, she had the attention of every man at the table. It felt as if they were all staring at the black-and-blue bump on the side of her forehead that her hair wasn't quite hiding. It was difficult to resist covering it with her palm.

"No one was to blame, Leo. Who knew Charles would get drunk and decide to assault me? My neighbor in the suite beside mine, a sweet older man, came to my rescue with his cane and whacked Charles over the head before he could punch me."

"Charles never could hold his liquor," Jameson commented under his breath, his eyes on the raised bruise on her forehead.

Art sent her a quick grin. "He did the same thing to me at a no-limit tournament at the Rio. He placed a bet he shouldn't have and he lost. He's really mad at himself, but then he drinks and wants to fight. He came at me swinging, but there were security guards everywhere, and they stopped him and took him to his suite. It was that or throw him out."

"I think he went to jail last night," Vienna said. "He actually put his hands on me. I have some bruising on my stomach where he pretended he was a linebacker and drove his shoulder into me to throw me to the ground. The cops took pictures of the bruising and of the lump on my forehead." She flashed a small smile. "I don't think the bump is going to bring me the same luck Park's frenzied fans are going to bring him."

Her attempt at humor failed because the men exchanged long looks of what had to be anger. It was Art that voiced their concern. "You have a large bruise on your stomach? He hit you that hard?"

Vienna wished she hadn't been so chatty. "It's nothing. Really. We're here to play cards, not talk about me. Did you all get a chance to meet Mr. Wallin last night?"

Leo, ever the gentleman, nodded. "Yes, he came in and made the rounds. I've met him several times. He's always gracious. There was far more security than there's ever been, most likely because of what happened to you."

"The food was amazing," Park said. "I wanted to talk to him about a couple of proposals I had for the hotel, but I didn't get more than a few minutes with him."

The dealer sat down and the mood of the crowd became electric. Vienna felt the excitement igniting through her veins. The blood rushed in a quick wash of heat and then settled so she felt the familiar calm sweep through her. At once she was aware of everyone seated around the table. The way they moved, their hands, their eyes, the set of their mouths. The way the dealer flicked her fingers as she shuffled the cards. Everything registered in her brain, cataloging down to the tiniest detail.

The cards slid to the players facedown in front of them. Art was the man to start off once the players had made the pot right. He lifted his cards with two fingers to look, his face expressionless. She'd noticed he tended to run the edge of his thumb along the cards when he intended to stay in, which he did as he dropped them to the surface of the table. He had a pair of aces. He made his bet and sat back to see what would happen.

Leo looked at his cards and folded. His move was very, very subtle. She had nearly missed it, but if he was bluffing, he slightly cocked his head to the right. Theodore took a look at his cards, dropped them down, tapped a finger on them as he always did and matched the bet. She was next. She had a king and queen of spades. She stayed. Park stayed in. Jameson folded and sat back, crossing his arms, a small enigmatic smile on his face. In the end, it came down to Art and her, as they challenged one another and the others folded.

The flop came, a queen of hearts, jack of diamonds, deuce of hearts. Art bet out, Vienna called. Turn was an eight of diamonds. Art checked, knowing his one pair, even if it was higher than the queen, was very beatable. He needed to control the pot to avoid any disasters. Vienna checked as well. The river was the king of hearts, giving Vienna the winner with two pair, kings and queens. Art bet small, trying to get the showdown for cheap. Vienna raised his bet, but knew she couldn't raise too much. Art was too smart to pay off a big raise.

The others leaned forward, just as eager as Art. None of them could read her any better than Art could. He turned over his pair of aces.

She turned over the two hidden cards. The queen of spades and king of spades. Art laughed. "That is a pretty sight. Queen of hearts on the flop. The king of hearts on the river. The river seems to be your lucky card, Vienna."

"I'll admit, I was sweating it a bit when you looked so confident, Art."

"There was no sweating that I could detect," Art said. He didn't look in the least deterred by the chips stacking up in front of Vienna.

Over the next couple of hours, she had to fold on several hands. The cards just weren't coming her way. That happened sometimes, and one had to be patient and not try to force something just to play. Park's cards seemed to be far worse, and he always played past the flop even though he should have gotten out immediately.

The third hour in, there was a fierce battle that started out between all the players with the exception of Vienna, who had been dealt a three and four. She folded to watch the others as each thought they were given potentially winning cards. The bets were enormous. Whoever won this round would add to their chips considerably.

Art was the first to bow out after the flop. Park waited for the turn and then folded. That left Leo, Jameson and Theodore. Leo raised and Jameson folded. The bet went to Theodore. He stayed in for the river. The card did him no good that anyone could see. Still, he stayed. Leo's bet was considerable. He had the chip advantage. Theodore went all in. Leo called.

Theodore had four of a kind. Four fives. Vienna closed her eyes. This was going to be painful. Who would have ever imagined? Leo turned over his cards. He had a straight flush. Low cards. All diamonds. Five through nine. Theodore sat very still for a minute and then slowly shook his head. Placing both hands on the table, he pushed himself up and extended one hand to Leo.

Leo shook his hand. "Great play," he murmured.

Theodore shrugged. "That's the beauty. You never know what lady luck is going to do." He walked away.

It had been a great hand. Any one of them would have gone broke betting on four of a kind. Although, had Theodore studied the cards in front of him, he might have considered the odds. Cards were mathematical. There was always that percentage.

She sighed. "That one really hurt."

"Now the compassion is coming out," Art said, halfteasing. "We have a chance to annihilate her."

"In your wildest dreams," she said.

Three hours later, she'd won a few smaller hands, but no one had anything to shout about. Park's playing seemed erratic to her, as if he were showing off for the crowd of women more than he was keeping his head in the game. They kept calling out to him to take his shirt off. If he stood up to stretch, they would yell for him to dance for them or to sign autographs. To take pictures with them. He didn't seem to be able to resist the white-hot glare of the spotlight.

The others around the table were amused by his rather vain posing around the spectators. Vienna didn't point out to them that he had won a couple of large hands. He might stay in longer than he should, but he had stayed in, believing the cards he was holding were enough to win. He thought he was "playing" everyone. Unfortunately, she was fairly certain he was being too clever for his own good.

She finally managed to score two cards in the pocket worth staying in, a king and ace of spades. Rubbing the pad of her thumb over the little heart on her wrist once, she blinked several times to focus on the cards as each of the others made their bets.

Leo was in first with a solid bet of a quarter of a million dollars. She was careful not to blink at the outrageous bet on the cards she knew he had. He was definitely trying to "see" who was willing to stay in. Art folded. Jameson stayed. Park stayed and Vienna did as well.

The dealer burned a card and turned over three cards: the queen of spades, the three of hearts and the ten of spades. That gave Vienna four spades. She would need to pull the jack of spades on the turn or the river in order to get her royal straight flush. One more spade, any spade, would give her a flush.

Leo looked the table over, looked at the cards and at each of them carefully. Two spades showing on the table was definitely a possible flush if someone held two spades in the pocket. He made his quarter-million-dollar bet. Jameson folded. Park stayed. Vienna raised, willing Park to stop preening to his fans and pay attention when the bet came round to him again. Leo remained silent for a few moments, looking at her face. In the end, he pushed his chips in to call her. Park did the same.

The turn was a four of hearts. Leo pushed his chips out in front of him, making his bet, a half-million dollars. Vienna raised the bet to a solid million. Park looked sober but answered. Leo studied her face again, and then once more met her chips with his.

The dealer burned a card and then turned a card over.

The jack of spades. She knew that card was going to be there, but it was still a thrill and difficult to keep her expression blank. As it was, her stomach did a somersault. She had a royal flush. That was unbeatable.

Leo bet a million and she raised. Park pushed all in. Leo answered without hesitation, certain he had the winning hand. The spectators had gone silent, the atmosphere tense with anticipation as the betting went around the table. Art and Jameson leaned in close as if they could see through the cards.

Leo and Park both called her. Park had two pair. Leo had a queen, jack, ten, nine and eight of spades—a straight flush—a hand most poker players never lose with. He'd had the nine and eight of spades in the pocket. There was a murmur of excitement as Vienna turned over her ace and king, revealing she had a royal flush.

Leo stared down at her cards as if he couldn't believe them. "My God, woman, Art wasn't joking when he said the river favored you."

Park stood up, giving them his famous grin. "I'll leave you to it." He shook hands with both of them, saluted his adoring audience and sauntered out.

"She was bluffing up to that point," Art said.

"She was playing the odds," Jameson disagreed.

"Nothing seems to faze that guy," Leo said, watching Park leave. "Did he come here to make money?"

"No one sits at a gambling table like this for any other reason," Art said. "I think half the shit he says and does is for show. I checked into him. He's the real deal in modeling. Makes so much money it's ridiculous."

"He makes it gambling too," Vienna said. "He gambles online and wins the big money."

"Why do you think he was really here?" Jameson asked. "Because I don't think it was just to play cards."

Vienna thought that over as she stood up and stretched, grateful she could escape to her room for the rest of the evening. She was an active person, and sitting for hours was difficult. Once her body got over the strange lethargy that gripped her after long hours of cards, she intended to go running. She needed to be outdoors, where she could breathe.

"You think he was here for another reason?" Art asked.

They were down to four players. The hotel had really managed to get the hype they wanted from the tournament and more. The tournament had been heavily advertised, particularly once Art, Leo and Jameson made the final table. They were huge names in the poker world, and each had their own following. Charles was a controversial player and often had eruptions at the table. Spectators watched just to see what he would do. Benny was the wild card of poker. He could be erratic, playing as if he'd thrown out the rule book, or extremely professional, following every rule. With Theodore came the drama of would he *finally* make his win? The hotel knew exactly how to build that kind of suspense.

Park was a famous model. The hotel took advantage of his making the final table by creating many opportunities for photo shoots of him with his legion of fanatical fans. Park had been more than happy to cooperate with the hotel, generating even more advertising for them.

Vienna knew she was beautiful. She couldn't look in the mirror and not see what others found attractive in her. She had classical bone structure, exceptional green eyes and a generous mouth. Her hair was thick and naturally platinum, unusual for her age. She was tall and had a figure, but never seemed to gain weight, mostly, she knew, because she was so active outdoors. Her mind was too restless to allow her to stay still for too long.

After the visit from Daniel Wallin, his security crew and his doctor, she had to laugh over the invitation to play poker in the hotel's big tournament. Mitzi had been right. There was always an ulterior motive. And why not? Wallin was in the business to make money. He'd come to her room, appearing to be nice, but making certain her injuries weren't severe enough that she could claim to a jury later that she had been incapacitated enough to be awarded millions. His lawyers probably wanted to know the alcohol level in her blood. She hadn't taken a drink, so that wouldn't help them. She didn't really blame Wallin for that either. He probably got those kinds of claims all the time.

She had given her share of interviews and posed for cameras with the other finalists, but as fast as possible, she had always made her way to her suite. She didn't like the spotlight, and she never would. This tournament only went to show her that, as wonderful as the accommodations were, online was the way to play for her. She could win big money without the glare of the spotlight.

Park, on the other hand, just like the celebrity gamblers, thrived on the attention. That continued attention from fans allowed them to be popular with the hotels—that and the fact that they were excellent poker players. Each of them had managed to create a persona that appealed to the public and knew how to use social media to their advantage.

"Good for his career," Leo pointed out. "Park probably added another hundred thousand screaming fans to his platforms."

Vienna found it hilarious that Leo knew anything at all about social platforms, but of course, he would have to.

"Good for him," Art said. "His companies most likely put up the money for him so he's not out a penny."

"I'm heading up to my room," Vienna announced. Deliberately, she touched the bruise on her head to remind them before they could protest. "I know I should go in and talk to the media, but I'm really exhausted."

"Do you want me to escort you up?" Leo asked.

She liked the man. How could she not? "I'll be fine. Charles was a one-time thing, and the hotel put enough security guards on me that I think the rest of the hotel is at risk."

Leo laughed. "At least they're taking your safety seriously."

"That they are. See you later." Vienna gave a little wave of her hand and made her escape.

The moment she was off the floor and heading toward the elevator, she was surrounded by security. She recognized the two guards who had come to her rescue the evening before. They rode up in the elevator with her.

"I didn't have a chance to thank you yesterday, and I didn't get your names, so I couldn't send you a note." She looked pointedly at their uniforms. The taller of the two had a nametag proclaiming his name to be Simon. His partner was Harold.

"No need for that, ma'am," Simon said.

"I know you don't think so, but you got there so quickly. I was scared. The man in the suite next to mine is older, and I was afraid if Charles was able to get up, he'd really hurt Mr. Forsyne too."

The elevator glided to a stop, the doors opening. Harold held the doors and Simon stepped out first, looking up and down the hallway before gesturing for her to come out. The two security guards walked her to her door.

"We're glad you both are all right," Simon said.

Harold murmured his agreement as she inserted her key into the lock and pushed open the door. The moment she was inside and the door had closed, she kicked off her shoes and stripped fast, not willing to be caught helpless in the aftermath of her card-playing fatigue. Pulling on comfortable clothes, she used the restroom, grabbed a bottle of water and the phone to set beside the bed, and caught up her cell phone to call one of her friends. She put the call on speaker so she wouldn't have to hold the phone. She could feel lethargy overtaking her, but she simply let it this time, lying back on the duvet and pillows.

"Hey, Shabina," she greeted one of the five women she counted as her family in Knightly.

Shabina Foster owned the Sunrise Café in Knightly, a popular place the locals knew to go to for the best food.

Shabina made cooking an art. She didn't offer a huge menu, and it changed weekly, sometimes daily, depending on Shabina's mood, but it was always amazing. Her mother was from Saudi Arabia and her father was American. Her father owned one of the largest and most respected companies in the world for putting out oil well fires, which was how he'd met Shabina's mother.

"I was hoping you'd call. It was all over the news that you were attacked last night. Are you all right? We talked it over and even Sam would come to watch your back if you need us."

"I'm fine. Charles was drunk and he was a very sore loser. I hit my head on the wall and got a little bruise. I think the hotel saw it as a publicity thing."

"You sound tired."

The concern in Shabina's voice warmed her. She loved her friends and counted herself very lucky. She'd meant what she said to her mother. She was perfectly content with her life. She didn't need to delve into her past to be happy.

"I'm always exhausted after I play," Vienna conceded. "Enough about me. Where are we with the plans for Stella's bridal party, or whatever we're calling it?"

Shabina laughed. "We're waiting on you to see if we can fit all the things in she was hoping to do. Have you had time to scout out everything on her wish list? If not, I can get there a day or so early with Raine and we can do it. We know you're busy."

"Tomorrow should be the last day of the tournament." Vienna was hopeful that was the truth. She didn't know if it was the long hours surrounded by so many people or the intensity of playing publicly after playing alone for so many years, but she felt drained. "I should be able to scout out the bouldering, hiking trails and coffee shops. I did already find us a wonderful kayaking trip. It's all day, and the river looks so beautiful. I'm excited about that. I know that was one of Stella's particular wishes."

"You do sound really tired," Shabina reiterated. "I can take some of this off you. I don't mind closing the café if I have to. Stella's wedding is important, and so is her bridal party. How often does one of our friends get married?"

"That's true, but I can handle this." Vienna traced the bruising on her ribs. "Do you remember Sam's friends? The ones who took us to your house and guarded us until he said it was safe?"

"Yes, of course."

"After, I took a leave of absence and went off by myself. One of Sam's friends followed me. To make a long story short, I've connected with him again. We're sort of a thing. He'll be at the wedding too. I just wanted you to know."

There was a short silence. "Which one?" There was caution in Shabina's voice.

"Sam's best man." Now that she knew Zale and Rainier had been threatened, she wanted to be cautious. "I've got to go. I am tired and need to sleep. I'll let you know what I find out about the bouldering as soon as I know."

"If you need me to help, call," Shabina said.

Vienna managed to hang up and take a long drink of water before the strange lethargy completely overtook her. She glanced at the clock. Zale was supposed to meet her later in the evening. She was becoming concerned about his safety. He had kept his distance from her in front of everyone, allowing Rainier to act his part of the elderly gentleman watching out for her. Zale was worried that an enemy might target her if they thought she was in any way involved with him.

She closed her eyes and drifted off. When she woke up, Zale was sitting on the edge of her bed. In that unguarded moment, before he realized she was awake, he looked tired and worn. He had his phone out and was looking down at the screen, a slight frown on his face, then he was rapidly typing a message.

She lifted her hand to brush the pads of her fingers over

the frown, stroking gently, as if she could erase his mood. Immediately, he captured her wrist and pulled her fingers into the heat of his mouth. Her breath hitched in her lungs as his eyes met hers. There was always that intensity about Zale when he focused on her—as if she were the only woman in his world, the only *person* in his world who truly mattered to him.

He kissed her fingertips. "I miss seeing you when I'm away from you. I never thought that would be possible."

"I miss you too. I try not to worry," she admitted.

He gently laid his palm over her belly, spreading his fingers wide so they covered from under her breasts to her ribs. "I'm not the one with a large bruise."

"I'm not the one with knife wounds," she countered.

His smile was slow in coming, but gorgeous by the time it hit his eyes. "Snowflake, I would hardly call the scratches I have wounds."

His fingers slowly began to push up the material of her flimsy top. His gaze didn't move from hers, only the intensity increased. She moistened her lips with the tip of her tongue.

"The blades of knives are notoriously filthy and covered in bacteria."

"My little nurse. I'm lucky she takes such good care of me." His tone caressed. His fingers touched bare skin, igniting flames, sending them racing through her bloodstream. It was as if he had already mapped out the large bruise, because he didn't look away from her eyes, yet he traced the outside edges before skimming the pads of his fingers over the entire interior as if painting it with a healing balm.

"Are you going to tell me what you're so worried about, Zale? I may be able to help."

"It isn't ever good to be involved in my business, Vienna, you know that."

"I understand, but I am already. It isn't as if I don't know you're working at the hotel undercover. You've told me agents have disappeared. You and Rainier were attacked once already. I get that we can't be seen together and before coming to my room you have to do something to make the security cameras glitch. I'm a nurse, Zale, so I'm used to keeping confidences."

"You could be killed if anyone connected us and knew I was talking to you."

"I'm head of Search and Rescue in Inyo County. That means I rappel down a mountainside to a victim in a gorge with rushing water or jagged boulders below me. I could be killed there too, but I do it and would every time. You don't have to tell me, Zale, but it seems to me I'm already in the know and you may as well bounce ideas off me."

He leaned over her, so for the first time she lost his eyes as he bent his head to her stomach and the dark bruising there. His hair brushed against the undersides of her breasts, a sensual slide that made her catch her breath. She couldn't help but bury her fingers in his hair as his lips skimmed over the vicious blue and purple colors spread across her ribs and belly.

She closed her eyes, savoring the feel of him there with her. It was so strange how she wasn't afraid to hike alone on trails in the wilderness, where the territory belonged to predators such as bears and mountain lions. She was confident climbing steep mountains and rappelling off them, or skiing down slopes others would never consider, but relationships terrified her.

"Zale, are we really doing this?" Vienna was really asking him if he was going to do his best to stay. She knew there were no promises. No one could do that, but she could ask for his best. She needed reassurances.

"We're really doing this, Vienna." He turned his head to one side and laid it gently on her lap, circling her hips with his arms. "I don't want to be alone now that I know what having you is like. I have to have you in my life. I want you to feel the same way about me. We can make it work, even when I'm away, working in the field. I know there's a way we can make it work."

Vienna waited until the small moment of panic in her had subsided. She brushed caresses into his hair. He seemed tired and worn when he was always so vibrant. "I told Stella about us right away, but today I told Shabina. Just in case someone might be listening in, I said I was having a thing with Sam's best man."

She felt his smile against her bare skin.

"A thing?" he echoed.

"I wasn't sure what to call us. It isn't like we're dating. What do people call what we're doing? We're not hooking up." She said that decisively. She hoped they weren't.

"We're not hooking up. You're my woman. I'm your man. We're exclusive. We're going into this with the idea that we have a future together." He took her left hand and kissed her finger. "I could put a ring here if it would make you feel more secure."

Vienna panicked all over again, nearly jerking her hand away from him. "I think it's way too soon for that, Zale. How about we walk before we try to run?"

He laughed softly and pressed a kiss into her belly button. "You're so courageous in so many ways and such a chicken when it comes to our relationship."

"You left me without a word and broke my heart." She wasn't going to pretend it hadn't happened.

He sobered immediately. "I know I did, Snowflake. I didn't know what to do to protect you. I had to think about it and figure out the best way for us."

She considered pulling his hair out by the roots. "Communication is always a good skill to have, Zale. I'm surprised you haven't heard of it in your business."

"Communication in my business gets you dead very fast, Vienna. Have we put this issue to bed, or do we need to keep talking about it? I'm willing. I want you to feel secure with me. I didn't just walk out on you. You never left my mind, not for a minute."

"Yes, the issue has been dealt with satisfactorily. I'm good. If I have a bad moment, I don't want you to think I'm panicking without merit, though. I might have panic attacks just at the thought of being in a committed relationship, since I've never really been in one before."

"This is going to be interesting, the two of us navigating our way together, since neither of us know what a good relationship is. We'll just make our own rules."

"Good. Rule one. You tell me when you're worried about something." Vienna pounced when she could.

He laughed and lifted his head, his dark eyes going velvet soft. "I can see you're going to be relentless when you want something."

"Yes. That's why I'm good at search and rescue. I don't give up until I find who I'm looking for and bring them home."

Zale pushed himself into a sitting position. "I know you need to eat. You never want to after playing poker, but you need to. You can order dinner, and while we're waiting for it, I'll tell you what I think is going on."

He wasn't exactly telling her she *had* to eat, but he put the phone in front of her along with the menu. "Would you order me a steak with the prawns this time, everything on the baked potato. Salad on the side and the brussels sprouts special. That beet thing looks good. Do you want to share it? What dessert do you want to get this time?" He paced across the room and then back again to pick up the menu and look at it a second time.

"You have it memorized," she said, trying not to laugh, because, really, he did.

"I know, but if I stare at it, items jump out at me. Look at this one. I never really noticed this one before. Grilled mahi-mahi. Some sort of lemon sauce that sounds fantastic."

She couldn't hold back her laughter. He clearly loved

food. "Should I just order one of everything on the menu? I could go down the list."

"If you didn't eat like a little bird, we could do that and share. As it is, make sure you order something I'll enjoy too, because you never finish your plate."

"How is it you don't gain tons of weight?" she demanded.

"It's called a metabolism, Snowflake. What are you ordering besides all the fruit on the menu? We need whipped cream too."

"We do?"

"Yep. I've got plans for later tonight. Serious plans, so whipped cream and a good bottle of champagne." He paced away from the bed again and then came back to peer over her shoulder. "If you get that prawn dinner you love, I'll switch to lobster with my steak."

"I might get pasta."

"You always say you might get pasta, but you don't actually order pasta. You go back to the prawns. And you love the New England clam chowder."

"Only if I can get fresh garlic bread."

"At this point, Vienna, you're the golden girl. They're afraid you might sue them, so they'll give you anything you want. You want garlic bread, if they don't have it fresh, they'll find someone who can make it for you. Hell, they might already know my background and call me on my cell to have me come downstairs to whip it up."

She laughed again. That was one of the things she loved about being with Zale most—he could make her laugh. "I'll order you the lobster and me the prawns and I'll get the chowder. It's going overboard to get the mahi-mahi too. You can order that from your room." She picked up the phone.

"Dessert," he mouthed. "Whipped cream. Strawberries."

Laughter bubbled up again as she ordered what she was certain was enough food for ten people. She let him help her up so she could make her way to the cuddle chairs in the huge living room. That way, when the food came, she could bring the cart inside the door herself.

"Did Rainier stay in the suite tonight?" She wanted to find a way to subtly bring the conversation back to Zale's problem of the missing agents and whether or not his cover had been blown.

"Yes. He normally goes down to gamble this time of night. He plays the big spender at the craps table, women hanging all over him, drinks a bit, but not too much, always the gentleman, but we were both fairly certain someone tried to kill him last night by poisoning his drink. He wasn't the one who drank it. One of the ladies at the craps table had been wrapping her arms around his neck and blowing on his dice for him. He picked up the drink and she took it out of his hands and downed it herself, smiling at him. Looking him right in the eye. She went down hard, straight to the floor. Just collapsed."

Vienna forced herself to remain relaxed in the cuddle chair. He watched her too closely, assessing her reaction, weighing whether or not he should continue. She'd pulled her share of dead bodies out of lakes and rivers and snowbanks. She'd seen young people crushed from falls while climbing rocks they never should have been on. She knew how to school her expression, and she called on that discipline now.

"I texted my people to hit the security tapes fast, because I knew that tape would be pulled to cover for whoever had attempted to murder Rainier, if they hadn't already messed with the camera, which was far more likely. I had been watching Rainier closely because I'd been worried for his safety, more so recently."

"Why?"

"I cautioned Rainier several times against asking too many questions a man in his position wouldn't necessarily be asking of security guards, but he didn't want to wait and leave it to me. He's used to being in charge. Sam, Rainier, Zyair, Wilder and I mostly work alone. You met them all when Sam needed us, and they'll all be at Sam's wedding. We trained together and we back one another up. Occasionally, we're sent in as a team, but for the most part, we work alone. Rainier just got impatient. Hotels aren't his environment. He prefers outdoors and wants to get back to it."

"At the cost of his life?"

Zale paced across the floor with fluid, restless steps that made no sound. He looked like a large jungle cat, trapped in a cage, ready to spring free at any moment. "He wouldn't view it that way. He's nearly always the smartest man in the room. He's lightning fast when he's not weighed down with all the latex and prosthetics he has to wear. It doesn't occur to him he is going to be vulnerable."

Vienna refrained from pointing out that the other dead agents most likely viewed themselves as being intelligent and fast as well. "You were watching him closely at the craps table. Did you see anything suspicious?"

"I noticed that the waitress bringing him the cocktail was one of several people we'd spoken casually with a few days earlier. We'd asked her a couple of questions, nothing that should have raised a red flag, but right after we did, that was when we were attacked by the three men with the knives in the parking lot."

"You paid closer attention because of that?"

He frowned. "I don't know if I can honestly say that. I was already in that mode, aware of everything. I'd noticed the dealer spent a good amount of time glancing up at the security cameras. That's unusual. He seemed nervous to me. I almost gave Rainier the signal to get out of there, but I didn't have anything concrete to go on, just my gut, and I was afraid he'd balk. I didn't want a scene with his security man."

"Would he do that?"

"I didn't know. He's been cooped up for a while now.

He'd sustained an injury and they'd sidelined him. He didn't take it well. Then he was given this role."

"Tell me about the woman serving the drink."

"She brought the drink on a tray, with a little napkin. She smiled at Rainier, but kind of absently, not really looking at him. She looked up toward the camera and then at the dealer. A server bringing someone like Wayne Forsyne a drink is going to expect a huge tip. He has that reputation. She should have engaged him in conversation. Flirted a little. She didn't. She turned and walked away fast. That raised red flags."

"That's when the woman took the drink from Rainier and collapsed."

"I pulled Rainier back, trying to get in there to retrieve the glass in order to send it to our people. It hadn't shattered on the carpet. Two security guards were there before me. That told me something right there. For them to get to the glass and remove it before I could get there means they were expecting someone to go down. They immediately called for a medic. I made certain to get photos of them and the dealer. I spotted the server in the crowd when I was taking Rainier to the elevator and he got one of her. Those were sent to our people. The video feed had been pulled all right, but there are backups and our people are looking into getting them. They are also tracking the server's movements to see everyone she interacted with."

"You think they'll try again."

"I know they will. I want him pulled. He says no. If they pull him, they have to pull me. I'd have no reason to be here. In any case, it would stand to reason they would think I'm an agent as well."

Vienna's heart sank. It was clear. Zale wanted Rainier safe, but he wanted to put himself in the line of fire no matter what. She studied his face. That face. Every line and angle. He wouldn't stop. He would never back down. She saw him very clearly in that moment. He was a hunter and he was hunting. It didn't matter if his prey was hunting him.

It wouldn't matter if he were called off by the people he worked for. He wouldn't stop until he found the ones who had killed the other agents. It was already far too late for her to spare her heart. Even knowing the risks he took and the compulsion that gripped him to continue to hunt, just as he had when he'd been so young that first time, she knew Zale was her choice.

"Do you know why someone would want Mr. Wallin dead? That's the real reason, right? And why don't they just shoot him? Have a sniper kill him or something?"

"Daniel Wallin is a multibillionaire, Vienna. This casino is his baby. He loves it and he nurtures it. If he comes up with an idea, that idea makes money for the casino every time. Not a little money; massive amounts of money. If he sits down to play cards with the celebrity players, it's gold time for the casino. He doesn't do it often, but if he does, you can bet it's televised and millions watch. He wins, Vienna. Every single time. He's the real deal. He doesn't cheat. He knows what he's doing. He owns seventy-five percent of the casino, which is unheard of these days. Most casinos are owned by the same corporations."

A knock on the door announced the food had arrived. Zale was gone almost before she could blink. "I don't know what I'm getting myself into," she murmured aloud as she went to the door.

She placed the cart of food between the cuddle chairs rather than using the formal dining table. She found she needed the comfort of the chairs. The chairs and the sheets and duvet were the things she would miss most about her stay.

Zale wrapped his palm around the nape of her neck. "I know the business I'm in can be scary, Vienna, but I'm trained and I don't take chances. You're good at what you do, and you have to trust that I'm good at what I do, just as you are."

She wanted to tell him it wasn't just about what he did— it was about who he was. She probably didn't have to tell him. He most likely was afraid that was exactly what she feared most—that she couldn't love him the way he was.

"You were telling me why someone might want to kill Wallin." Deliberately, she took the lids from the chowder bowls to get them started. "They did bring fresh garlic bread."

"I told you they would." He flashed a faint grin. This one, she noted, didn't quite reach his eyes. "If he dies, his shares might very well go to the rest of those investors. I have no idea how the corporation was set up, but that's a hell of a motive. He's been opposed to the idea of building a second casino, but his partners want one."

"They'd kill him over that?"

"The casino rakes in billions, Vienna."

"You just pointed out that's because of him."

"His start-up and his ideas, yes, but that doesn't mean the success of the hotel won't continue for years to come. If he's opposing them, the investors may very well have decided to get rid of him in a permanent way. It isn't unheard of."

"People die all the time."

"Wallin is very protected. After the first couple of tries, he's been completely locked down, impossible to get to. He's unaware, and so is his security, but my boss has sent extra personnel to keep him safe. They aren't going to get to him."

"Zale, you know there are at least two members of his security staff involved in trying to kill him."

He nodded. "I know who they are. I want their boss."

A chill went down her spine hearing his tone. She looked up and met his eyes. It was impossible not to see him—her Zale.

"I'm staying with you tonight. Rainier's locked in tight."

"Security has the key to your room. They could make a try for you both."

He shook his head. "We're prepared for that move." His dark eyes drifted over her, giving her chills in a completely different way. "I'm staying."

She didn't have any objections.

CHAPTER SIX

The mood of the crowd was electric as the four took their places at the final table. It could have been stifling with so many people pressed around the low cordons, but the crowd was a distance away. Still, even though the room was air-conditioned and well ventilated, when Vienna first walked in, she felt the walls closing in on her, shrinking, as if they were collapsing under the weight of so many people.

Her lungs burned. There was no oxygen, the bystanders sucking all the air out of the room with their cheering and calling out. The voices faded into the distance as her heart accelerated, and the pressure in her chest increased until it was an alarming vise-like pain. Sweat beaded on her forehead. She choked. Tried to clear her throat. Coughed.

Vienna forced her mind to work through the fog of panic. She inhaled, taking air into her lungs, and exhaled, not looking at anyone but pushing the clouds out of her mind. What was happening? She didn't have panic attacks. Her mother did. She was familiar with the symptoms because she'd grown up seeing them on a regular basis. What would cause her to suddenly experience such a thing?

It had happened before, yes. She had been targeted by a serial killer, someone she had known as a friend for years. For just a few moments she had been gripped with the same terrible fear—or maybe it wasn't fear so much as the knowledge that she was being hunted. That sent a shiver creeping down her back. Was it possible someone knew Zale had come into her room and stayed with her last night? Was he watching her now? He had eyes on her. Cameras that would broadcast to millions of viewers. There were spectators crowding around the barricades calling out to the players as they took their places at the table.

Leo, ever the gentleman, pulled her chair out for her, and she smiled up at him as she sank into her chair. "Thanks, Leo."

"The Northern Lights always puts on a good show, doesn't it?" Art said as he took his place.

No, it wasn't the crowd or the cameras. She had always been sensitive to atmosphere, even as a child. Right now, there was a feeling of malevolence emanating from someone in the crowd of spectators. The impression was especially strong on her right. She didn't look that way.

"This is the first time I've been here," Vienna admitted. "It's a little overwhelming."

"You don't play like it's overwhelming," Jameson said.

Jameson sat to her right, so it was natural for her to look that way. She turned her head to respond to him, smiling, flicking her gaze upward toward the crowd. "We'll see. It's all about the cards."

"Is it?" Leo asked. "I always thought it was about my genius play."

She'd always been a good observer, taking in details even with a quick glance. She didn't see anyone she recognized, or anyone looking particularly dangerous, but then, Zale didn't look dangerous all the time. He could fade into the background when he didn't want to be seen.

She laughed with the others at Leo's comment and turned her attention to the table. She was there to play cards. To win. She'd spent far too much of her time and energy on playing in order to get where she was to blow it because she felt someone was watching her. Unless . . . there could be a very simple answer that had nothing to do with Zale.

"Is Benny still in Vegas?"

"Sure, he's still in the hotel," Art said. "I saw him last night. He lives here, owns a couple of successful businesses, but he's staying at the hotel."

"Yeah," Jameson confirmed. "He likes to stay until the tournament is over. He never leaves until it's done. He's somewhere here." He looked up into the crowd of spectators straight ahead of him as if looking for Benny.

To Vienna, Jameson's looking for Benny in the close crush of viewers meant Benny could be the one making her uncomfortable. After the warning she'd been given, that made total sense, and she was willing to accept that explanation for the moment so she could get down to the business of playing cards.

The moment the dealer sat down, the familiar heat rushing through her veins signaled that her gift pouring into her was already strong and growing even more so. Awareness strengthened in her, intensifying and spreading outward, registering the smallest movements, no matter how subtle, of the players and dealer.

Art was in his usual position to the left of the dealer, and he started the round off with a hundred thousand. Leo raised his eyebrow and went in immediately without even looking at his cards. Jameson did the same. Vienna followed suit. She knew what she had. A pair of tens. The dealer revealed the flop. The ten of hearts. The three of diamonds. The king of spades. That gave her three of a kind.

Art glanced back at his hand, then at the flop, and decided to check. Leo cupped his fingers around his cards and lifted the edges in order to look. He cocked his head slightly to the right while he dropped them to the table and immediately doubled the bet. Jameson looked at his cards, shook his head and folded. Vienna stayed in. Back around to Art, and he quickly folded.

The turn was the three of clubs. That gave her a full house. She studied the cards and Leo's face. He was too experienced to give anything away. She absolutely knew he had nothing worthwhile, but he bet two hundred and fifty thousand with total confidence. She met his bluff and raised him two hundred and fifty thousand. If he wanted to throw money away, she was willing to take it.

Leo again stared at her face for a long time. Art and Jameson did as well. Assessing. It occurred to her none of them knew when she was bluffing or not. Leo didn't want to continue when he really had nothing at all. He wasn't that kind of a gambler. Art sometimes played a bluff successfully, but Leo was a more cautious gambler. He folded. She didn't show her cards. The disappointment at the table as well as in the room was perceivable. There was even a heavy collective sigh from the crowd.

"Are you certain you aren't Irish?" Leo asked.

She shot him a smile. "I don't think so, but far back on the ancestral tree, I could be. I know that's where you get all your charm."

Leo nodded solemnly. "I am charming. And a true gentleman, which is a dying breed."

"That's the sad truth," Art said. "But it's the times. No one wants a gentleman anymore, Leo. Women smack you in the face now if you open a door or offer to carry something heavy. You're somehow seeing a woman as less because you notice they're struggling a bit and want to help."

Vienna rolled her eyes. "You might be missing the point."

Over the next two hours they discussed the merits of equality, and she found that all three men were actually very much progressive in their attitudes about women. She liked them the more she got to know them. They were sometimes a little old-fashioned in their views, but in a good way. They were protective of women and children, but she didn't have the impression any of them thought women were less intelligent.

The cards were in play, and once again Art opened the bet with a hundred thousand. Once everyone was in, Leo pushed the bet to a half-million dollars. Jameson stayed. Vienna folded. Art folded. Vienna could see that the flop appeared to help both men. Queen, four and five of diamonds. Leo bet another half million, and Jameson stayed with him. The turn was the five of spades. The room went silent, tension increasing until it was stretched so tight it felt as if a wire had been pulled to the breaking point.

Leo doubled his bet. Jameson answered him. Leo didn't hesitate, staying with him. The dealer turned over the last card to reveal the three of diamonds. Leo bet another million. Jameson went all in. Leo matched him, calling him.

Art studied the cards on the table and shook his head, raising an eyebrow at Vienna. Jameson had a straight flush, with the ace and two of diamonds in the pocket. Leo had a full house, with three queens and two fives, two queens in the pocket.

Leo stood, shaking his head. "Hell of a play, Jameson." He held out his hand.

"Good cards," Jameson replied.

Leo offered his hand to the other two and left the table to the respectful applause of the spectators.

The very next hand, Vienna kicked off the betting with a quarter of a million dollars. Art and Jameson stayed in. Vienna was dealt two aces in the pocket. She bet a half-million dollars. Both men stayed with her. The flop added the ace of diamonds, seven of clubs and jack of spades. Vienna pushed the bet to a million. Both Jameson and Art stayed with her.

The turn revealed the queen of clubs. Vienna bet another million. Jameson matched her million and raised another million. Art looked the cards over and folded. Vienna stayed in with Jameson. He already had his straight and was certain of the win.

She was pushing her luck depending on the river card, a dangerous thing to do. That calm place she had, the energy moving in her, gave her the ability to "see" the cards before they turned over. She knew the card coming up was the seven of spades. The dealer placed it faceup. That gave her a full house, aces full of sevens. Jameson had a straight—a very good hand. She already had him beat. Still, when she went in with a million, he pushed it with an all-in bet.

With a straight? With the board pairs? She looked the cards over. She supposed it looked as if she didn't have anything and was possibly bluffing. They had all tried to see how and when she bluffed. But this wasn't the time to find out, or at least, she wouldn't have chosen to test the waters at that precise time. She called him.

Jameson showed his straight, and she showed her full house. The spectators erupted into wild applause.

"It's that river card," Art said. "Never bet against her on the river card."

Jameson stood up and extended his hand. "You've got some kind of luck when it comes to the river."

She supposed she did. It was down to Art and Vienna. The next two hands were lousy and she folded. Then he folded. Art bet a quarter of a million and she went in with him to see her cards, already knowing both of them were going to get good cards. Hers looked good. Art's looked great. He had a pair of aces. She had the queen and jack of hearts. The dealer turned over the flop. The ace of spades. The seven of spades. The ten of hearts.

Vienna studied the cards. Looked at Art's face. He gave her his little grin that said nothing and everything. She bet a million dollars. He matched her bet and raised her a million. She felt the instant ratcheting up of the tension in the crowd as she pushed her chips in to answer him. The dealer burned a card and dealt the turn. Another heart, a nine.

Art studied the cards and looked at her face as she made a two-million-dollar bet. "Are you betting on that river card?

You have to be. You don't have your hand yet. I know you don't. You and your lucky red on the river."

To see her cards and the river card, he'd have to put up another two million in chips. He certainly had it, but clearly, his warning system was telling him not to do it. Art gave her another grin and shook his head as he matched her bet.

A groan erupted from the spectators. Art didn't look up, his gaze on the dealer's hands as she burned the next card and turned up the eight of hearts. Art leapt out of his chair and paced away from the table. "No way. That's your card, isn't it? You were bluffing this entire time and the river gave it up to you."

He sank back into his seat. Vienna bet two million. Art shook his head. "I'm not crazy, Vienna. That's your card. You have a flush. Not just a flush. You have a straight flush. I'm not handing you another penny."

He'd been a good sport and he'd lost a lot of money to her. She turned her cards faceup and sent him her own little grin.

"I knew it. You do bluff."

She didn't answer. Let him decide when she was bluffing and when she wasn't. Three hands later, Art was dealt two pocket jacks. She had two pocket tens. Vienna's initial bet was half a million dollars. Art immediately raised it by another half a million. Vienna stayed in to see the flop. Two tens and a jack. That gave Art a full house with three jacks and Vienna four of a kind. Vienna bet two million. Art saw her two million and raised her two million. She met his raise.

The turn gave them an ace of hearts, which didn't do anything for either hand. Vienna bet five million of her chips. Art looked the cards over carefully and then studied her face before he matched the bet and upped it. She upped it again. A hush had fallen over the room. Art coolly pushed the appropriate chips in to match hers.

The dealer turned over the seven of hearts. Vienna bet five million chips. Art studied the cards again and then went all in. There was no possible way for him to have four jacks.

He couldn't beat her with a straight flush, even if her "gift" wasn't working. She had the stronger hand. She pushed her chips in to match his.

Art revealed his full house, three jacks and two tens. She revealed her four of a kind, four tens. Vienna had won the championship at the Northern Lights Hotel and Casino. Art, ever the consummate professional, extended his hand to her immediately.

"Amazing, Vienna. I want to be here when you play Daniel Wallin. I've asked him, I hope you don't mind. The game will be in a couple of days."

She paused halfway through the act of rising. If she were being truthful with herself, part of the reason she had accepted the invitation to play in the live tournament at the Northern Lights was that she knew part of the prize was to play poker with Daniel Wallin—a man considered unbeatable. Every top celebrity gambler did anything they could for a chance at an invite to play with him.

"Wait. What? A couple of days? I have other commitments." Her heart sank. She'd watched every single YouTube video Wallin was in, studying his every move. She was convinced he used a psychic talent of some kind. Not the same as hers, but something else. She had to know what it was. The compulsion was stronger than most things that took hold of her. Still, she'd given her word to her friends, and she didn't go back on her word.

"The winner of the tournament always plays a game with Wallin. You have to play with him." Art moved closer to her in order to be heard over the yelling of the crowd.

"Of course I want to, Art. Who wouldn't? He's considered the best there is." Then she was pulled away from him and microphones were thrust at her as announcements were made. Photos were taken. She was escorted to a room where Daniel Wallin waited, surrounded by his security and a selected camera crew to televise the prize being given as well as the speeches and her interview with the owner.

The hubbub went on so long, Vienna became exhausted and terrified that she might collapse at any moment. No matter how many times she edged toward the door in an attempt to escape, there were more interviews and more photographs. It seemed to her as if the owner of the hotel continually delayed her escape, or that could have just been in her head because she was so desperate. Thankfully, it was Art who put a stop to the crazy interviews, declaring that she needed rest. Even as she edged toward the door, Art clearing the way for her, Wallin still interfered with her escape, stopping her by standing in front of her, his security force once more surrounding them.

"We'll have our game in private rather than on the floor as we normally would in two days to give you plenty of time to rest." He sounded gracious. "I didn't like what happened to you, and I think it's best if we play it safe."

She noticed he glanced at his watch and then up at the security cameras. She just wanted to get to her room. Vienna shook her head. "I'm so sorry, Mr. Wallin. I hate to miss the opportunity to play cards with you when it's such an honor, but I have another commitment I can't get out of in two days."

Daniel Wallin's blue eyes were very sharp as he studied her. "Not tonight. You're tired and I refuse to take unfair advantage. Art asked to be one of the players as a favor, and if you have no objections, we'll include him in our little game as well." He indicated Art, who stood beside her. "Leo, of course, and Jameson. That should round it out quite nicely, and they're already here. We'll play tomorrow, then, if you think you'll be up to it."

She didn't have much time before she collapsed. She just nodded her head and continued edging toward the door. "Tomorrow, then." She gave a little wave and all but rushed out, praying she would make it to the elevator and she wouldn't have to crawl to her room once it took her up to her floor. Already, her arms felt like lead.

Vienna pulled out her phone and texted Zale. You in your suite? If so, would Wayne meet me outside just in case? I'm having trouble.

Down in casino.

That wasn't good after everything Zale had told her. Maybe the general consensus was that if Wayne didn't show up to play craps as he normally would, their enemies would know for certain Rainier was an agent. She thought the two men were playing Russian roulette and it was just plain stupid. Their enemies already knew they were agents. It made no sense that they insisted on remaining in the hotel.

As she made her way through the crowd toward the private elevator, she kept her head down to avoid being stopped by anyone congratulating her. That same malevolent feeling that had first assailed her when she'd joined the final table crept over her like a shadowy apparition, stealing into her mind to spread fear.

She stepped into the elevator, turned and surveyed the crowd on the casino floor as the doors began to close. She caught sight of Benny watching her, but there were several others she didn't know, some turning away so she couldn't register their features to take out and examine later. She just kept the impression of them as she slumped against the wall for the ride to her floor. She was extremely grateful that the elevators were fast.

Vienna fumbled for the key to her room, her fingers numb, nearly unable to hold on to it. She staggered to the door and shoved it into the keyhole, thankful the golden key made it into the lock the first time. Still, it took effort to get the door open enough for her to slip inside. Once in, the door closing automatically behind her, she went to the floor.

There was an overwhelming sense of danger that just wouldn't leave her alone. Her suite didn't feel nearly as safe as it had before. Ordinarily, she would have taken precautions to add to the security of the room, but her body was fast falling into the paralysis that followed her using her "gift." She needed to find something she could defend herself with if it came to that, and she needed a place to hide. She had only minutes before it would be too late to do either.

Her phone vibrated, but she ignored it. If it was Zale, he would know she was in trouble and wouldn't be able to answer him. Her mother would know as well. She crawled to the bedroom where her pack was. She had knives and other tools needed on the trail. By the time she opened the pack, managed to get the weapons she needed and concealed them on her person, she could barely lift her arms, let alone crawl.

Vienna still had the feeling of impending danger. She couldn't be caught out in the middle of the bedroom floor, especially if she couldn't move. She did her best to shove the open pack under the bed as she dragged her body toward the gigantic walk-in closet. The only ones who could get into her room would be the security guards, although Zale had managed. If they actually came to her room, they might expect her to hide there, but she had discovered a little space they might not be aware of. How often did security inspect the rooms?

Vienna pushed aside all thought and forced her mind to concentrate on her goal—just to make it to the closet. It seemed such a long way away, but she was determined to get there before she crashed altogether. She was positive someone was going to enter her room in an attempt to kill her. She wanted to be in that little space, in a position to at least try to defend herself if she was discovered, and she wanted to be able to identify who it was so she could tell Zale and Rainier.

The closet was built out of cedar and smelled wonderful. There was a sitting bench across from the shoe rack. On either side of it were full-length mirrors. The mirrors appeared to be built flat against the wall. Vienna had discovered that the wooden wall was a false one on the left side and that there was a space behind it supposedly to be used for storage.

There was nothing back there, and she could see no one had been cleaning or dusting the space for some time.

Vienna dragged herself to the bench and lay in front of it, studying the mirror and sliver of an opening. She had to fit herself in just right, so that if she were discovered, she would have her arm free with a knife in her hand and enough room to strike out at an attacker. It was a puzzle, and she had to figure it out so she got it right before she wedged herself inside.

Weak, barely able to move her legs, she turned her body and backed into the space under the bench, going in at an angle. Her heart began to pound. She didn't have claustrophobia. She went into very tight places as a rule. Small caves. Whatever was necessary to get where she wanted—or needed—to go. Her heart reacted because an enemy was close.

Her feet scraped against the wall. She had to go in on her knees if she could get into that position. It was a very tight fit. She was tall. She couldn't exactly fold herself into the space. She used the wall and bench to help herself into the narrow opening behind the mirror.

Vienna found herself holding her breath, as if that would make her chest smaller and allow her to fit better. It was silly, but she did it anyway. As she settled into place, the tight fit holding her upright, she heard a man's deep voice whispering. He sounded as if he was in the next room.

Her mouth went dry. She hadn't heard the door. There was no squeak. The hotel really needed to have some kind of warning, a bell, something to alert the occupants in case someone broke into the rooms. Her arm was still under the bench, the knife in her fist. She had to find the strength to pull her arm silently into the shadowy space where she couldn't be seen even if the glaring overhead lights were turned on.

It took great concentration to drag her arm across the floor, retracting it to the inside of her hiding place. She kept her fingers wrapped around the knife, although she honestly couldn't feel it in her palm.

"We only have a couple of minutes before the camera comes back on. She's in here. I saw her come in. Find her."

That was very distinct. Every word. Vienna breathed in and out, refusing to give in to the need to close her eyes. Her eyelids felt very heavy and droopy. It was terrifying to think her lashes might come down and she wouldn't be able to lift them again. She tried to stare into the bedroom through the slightly open door.

She went over the voice, every nuance, trying to concentrate on that in order to stay alert. Had she heard it before? Did she recognize it at all? She strained to hear or see if someone was in the bedroom. She hadn't been able to close the closet door, so she hadn't bothered to try. The closet was very dark. Although it was late, the balcony lights streamed through the sliding glass doors of the master bedroom so she could see a corner of the bed and a little bit of the floor.

A man's shoes and legs encased in trousers came into view. She recognized the security uniform immediately.

"Are you certain she came up here?" a voice hissed from the other room.

"Yeah, just announce yourself. Have you heard of cell phones? She's probably on her phone right now, calling for help." The shoes began stalking across the room toward the bed. The man knelt on one knee and peered under the bed. She recognized Harold, the security guard who had been with Simon when the two men had come to get Charles and then again, when they'd ridden in the elevator up to her room, supposedly "guarding" her.

Harold swore under his breath, glanced at his watch and stood up, hurrying toward the closet. "Check on the balcony. She has to be somewhere."

He flipped on the light, gave a look around, shoved at the clothes hanging in the closet and then flipped the light off again and went to the master bath to inspect the shower and tub.

"We have to get out of here. The cameras are going to come on. Move it, Robert."

Robert. Not Simon. She'd seen the name Robert on one of the uniforms just tonight and maybe a couple of other times. She'd never observed that he'd taken undue notice of her. There was no sound to indicate the two security guards had vacated her room, but the feeling of impending danger was beginning to fade.

Vienna was afraid to try to move. If she was wrong and they were tricking her, she would be helpless to defend herself. But if she didn't try to get herself out of the tight space, her body would be in a hell of a bad situation when she finally was able to come out of the paralysis.

"Don't be a baby," she whispered to herself aloud and once again concentrated on the arm that faced the opening. She needed to slide it down and out, just let it drop beneath the bench.

"Vienna? Snowflake? Answer me. Where the hell are you?"

She heard the anxiety in Zale's voice.

"Rainier, look for her. She could be passed out anywhere." Zale was already in the bedroom and practically hurling the door to the master bath off the hinges.

"Here. The closet. Under bench." That was the best description she could give, and her voice croaked like a hoarse frog.

"The place is bugged, Zale," Rainier said. "Even found cameras. We're automatically jamming everything, so we're good, but literally, every room has bugs. Someone took their time in here."

Zale swore as he flooded the closet with light and went to his knees, peering under the bench. At first, he didn't see her, but she managed to get her arm to drop into his sight.

"Vienna." He breathed her name like a benediction. As if she was his world and the relief he felt at finding her was so profound he could barely breathe. "How did you get yourself in there?"

Very gently, he opened her fingers and removed the knife from her palm. "Let's see if we can get you out of there."

Her eyelids were already drooping. He was the best sight, but even he couldn't prevent the strange paralysis that took over when she had used her "gift" for too long. "Harold and Robert came into the room after me." Her voice was that strange, hoarse whisper. If Harold and Robert were two of the men on Wallin's security force that were prepared to kill him and any agent sent to protect him, Zale and Rainier needed to know.

Zale managed to get his hand inside the small space, following her arm up to her shoulder. With exquisite gentleness, he angled her arm downward so her shoulder followed. His hand helped her shoulder through the narrow opening and then guided her head out. When he had one shoulder and her head and arm out, he waited a moment, studying how to get her other shoulder out without hurting her.

Vienna couldn't help him. She was just grateful he was there and not the two security guards.

Rainier's lithe frame filled the closet door. "Is she all right? Did they drug her?" There was a hint of something ugly, a temper bordering on getting out of control smoldering beneath the calm exterior.

She tried to open her eyes beyond the narrow slit she was managing to see his expression, but she couldn't.

"No, they didn't do this. We're going to have to check our room as well. They have access to it with their keys, and we were gone for a while."

Zale's hand slid into the opening and he once more gently maneuvered her body, turning her slightly so he could manipulate her shoulder through the narrow space. Now both shoulders were out. He caught her under her arms and pulled, twisting her slightly so she was emerging on her side to make her smaller.

She was a heavy rag doll that Zale had to carefully drag out from under the bench onto the floor of the closet. He immediately began to massage her left leg.

"Rainier, massage her arms. I'll get her legs. I don't know how long she was in there, but the space was cramped. She was hiding from the security guards. Both Harold and Robert were in here. That was all I got before she went out on me."

Rainier crouched down beside her and began to knead her right arm. "At least the bastards didn't find her. Instead, they took their time putting bugs and cameras all over her suite."

Vienna managed to make a sound of dissent, her gaze shifting to Zale, hoping he would understand what she was trying to convey. The massage they were doing was helping with the terrible sensation of returning blood to her extremities. One leg and arm felt cold and dead, the others a flood of pins and needles like flames burning through her. The more they massaged, the more the sensation receded.

Zale studied her face. "What are you trying to tell us, Snowflake? Are you saying Harold and Robert didn't put the bugs in your room?"

She tried to nod. It was incredibly difficult to find the energy to move at all, let alone direct a body part, but she managed.

Zale exchanged a long look with Rainier, but he didn't ask her if she was certain. It occurred to her that he might, since she was hiding in the closet and they had been in the suite where she couldn't see them, but she knew they didn't have time to be as thorough as Rainier indicated someone had been.

The massage was helping, not only with the terrible pins and needles but with the paralysis as well. At least, she felt it was. She was still exhausted, but the two men were driving the feeling of being unable to move back as the blood began to flow through her body.

"You good on this side, Vienna?" Zale asked.

She managed a nod. He moved to her right and Rainier switched to her left. She tried to mentally brace herself for the return of feeling to her dead arm and leg, that horrible burn that first accompanied the blood returning.

"Do you know who put the bugs in your room?" Rainier asked.

She tried her voice. "No." She thought she said *no*. It came out more of a croak than a *no*. She might have frog in her. Didn't humans crawl out of the ocean at one time? She needed to go back to school. Sheesh. Her brain wasn't working correctly.

"I think that weird noise she insists on making means no," Zale teased.

She tried a glare. Her facial muscles weren't working any better than her voice. It was going to take a little time. She had to be patient. She didn't like her body not working in front of Zale, but she detested being so helpless in front of Rainier.

"As soon as you're feeling stronger, Vienna, I'm going to pick you up and put you on the bed. We came straight from the casino to your room, which is why Rainier looks so good as Wayne. We thought it would be credible that he would come to congratulate you on your win.

"But now, we're worried that if we leave you, those guards might be back. Without a doubt, they think you're a plant because you've spent too much time with us," Zale said. "This is the reason we're careful not to involve civilians in any way. You need to get out of this hotel."

She didn't like the way he said the word *civilians*. She supposed she was a civilian. What did he mean by that? Not involving a civilian in *any* way? Not getting involved with one? Her insecurities were leaping to the foreground all over again, when she thought she'd put them to rest. She wasn't going to question him, especially not in front of Rainier. Not that she could. She could only lie there helplessly, her mind running at a million miles an hour deep inside, while on the outside she had brain fog.

"You need to call your girls and get them to start out tonight, as soon as possible. If they're ready to go, it should only take them about five hours of travel time to get here," Zale continued. "With them in your room, you can talk it up, telling them you enjoyed your little fling with me. Convince anyone listening that we were just hooking up while you were here and Wayne was the nicest old man ever. You enjoyed his company. You have to be convincing, Vienna. You don't want these people coming after you when you leave here. And you need to leave immediately."

She wished she could sit up, but for the first time, she was rather thankful for the rigid facial muscles. She nodded, showing him she understood. The blood definitely was beginning to flow into her legs and arms. She concentrated on the burn of pins and needles, setting her teeth against the terrible but necessary pain that told her in a few minutes she would be able to move again.

Her brain cleared. Her heart pumped blood through her system, relieving the paralysis slowly, inch by inch, so finally she knew she was in control again. Once Rainier and Zale finished massaging the blood flow back into her arm and leg, she would be good to go. She took a deep breath and let it out. Her lungs worked fully again.

"I'm good. Thanks, Zale. Rainier. Wayne. Whatever." Her smile was still a little crooked, but her voice wasn't a frog's. Finally. She hated when she had no control. It was so terrifying.

Zale slipped his arms under her knees and behind her back to lift her. "That was a close one. Scared the holy hell out of me, Vienna." He carried her to the master bedroom and put her in the bed, up by the headboard, so she could sit up. Retrieving a bottle of water, he handed it to her. "Why do you think Harold and Robert aren't the ones responsible for installing the bugs and cameras through your room?"

She looked from him to Rainier, who lounged in the doorway. Beneath the old-man persona, she could see the lethal man he truly was.

"If there were several of them and well hidden, they couldn't have done it. They had only minutes to search my suite for me. They entered directly behind me. I barely made it into my suite but had this overwhelming sense of danger, so I found a hiding spot and concealed myself. I wasn't all the way inside it when I heard them talking. The one called Harold reminded the other one to hurry, that they only had a couple of minutes before the cameras were coming back on. I presumed he meant the security cameras in the hallway."

"So, the cameras inside were already planted and they knew it and were jamming them as well as the ones out in the hall." Zale turned another thoughtful look on Rainier. "We're going to have to check our room for bugs, but for now, we don't dare leave her alone. We're in for a long night, at least until her friends show up, and five hours is a long time."

"We need a rig for gear and clothes for the Airbnb we rented, so someone has to drive, but Raine could hook them up with a plane. Shabina might be able to as well," Vienna said. "They'd be here fast."

"Let me tell Sam what we need," Zale said. "I don't want you texting any of the women, just in case. I want you cleared as fast as possible. I'd rather you left immediately. I suppose I can't talk you out of playing Wallin?" There was a hopeful note in his voice.

"Not on your life," Vienna said. "I wanted to play him almost more than I wanted the money. In any case, if I win, I double my win at the table."

"Do you think you have a chance?"

"There's a possibility. I suspect he has a gift. Art does. I'm not certain Art is aware of it, but he does. Mine is developed and I work at it. I think Wallin has a different one and he works at it. That's probably how he's been such a successful businessman. I definitely want to play him."

CHAPTER SEVEN

〰〰〰〰〰〰〰〰〰〰〰〰〰〰〰〰〰〰〰〰〰

The room was spacious enough, but with security and the television crews surrounding the table, it tended to cut down on what would have been a large area and comfortable atmosphere. The table was in the center of the room, and they took their assigned places. She was across and to the left of Daniel Wallin, who was directly across from the dealer. She found it interesting that she'd been placed across from him. She didn't mind because she wanted to be able to see everything he did when he played his cards. Clearly, he wanted to see what she did.

For the first time, she asked herself how he'd identified her when she'd played anonymously online. Of course, her winnings had gone to a bank account. She'd played in some of his online tournaments. The hotel certainly could have traced that account to her. Was that how he had become interested in her? She'd won every tournament she'd entered. That must have sent up a flag to someone like Wallin. It would have to her. It would have to Art.

She smiled cheerfully at those seated at the table. "We meet again. Leo, Jameson, Art, good to see you again."

"I'm not sure I can say the same," Leo told her.

Jameson laughed. "I have to second that, Vienna. But as always, you look beautiful."

She'd played up her looks, something she rarely did. She

didn't wear a dress or skirt—that would be going too far—but she did wear a deep green shirt that made her eyes appear even greener than usual. Once someone discovered her large eyes, they found her perfect bone structure and generous mouth. Her hair fell in long silky sheets of platinum down her back and around her face when she needed it to. She was tall, leggy, walked like a model when she cared to in her pencil-thin black jeans—and she cared to. She'd take every advantage she could get.

"Thank you, Jameson, you're always kind to me," she responded as she took her chair. "Unless you're pushing the bet."

There was instant laughter again. Even Wallin smiled. She looked at him last. "Mr. Wallin, it's lovely to see you again."

He sat back in his chair, regarding her carefully. "I think we can dispense with the formalities, at least while we're playing, Vienna. Call me Daniel."

She remembered that same careful, *shrewd* examination from the day before, when he'd kept her talking after she'd won the tournament. Delaying her had been calculated. She was certain of it. He'd looked at his watch several times. Was he responsible for planting the cameras in her room? If so, why would he do it?

"Daniel, then." She gave him another smile. She could be every bit as fake as he could. She planned on winning. That was why she was here. She wasn't intimidated because he was undefeated or because he owned the hotel.

The dealer sat down and an excited hush fell over the room. Vienna allowed her gaze to sweep the security. Robert and Harold were among the security guards. Simon was present. There were at least five close to Daniel Wallin. Two had come in to escort her to the game. One had been a woman, Rachel, and her partner, a man by the name of Wilder. She had recognized that name. Surely there couldn't be *two* Wilders, yet Zale had said they hadn't embedded an agent in the security company because it was too risky. Wilder didn't look at her, but rather around her, paying attention to the crowd as they walked her through the well-wishers to the private room to meet the other players. She avoided looking at him, just in case. Wilder and Rachel were directly behind her, presumably her security.

Leo opened with a hundred thousand bid. Everyone stayed, of course. Daniel didn't look at his cards, but immediately bet a quarter of a million, sounding bored. He looked directly at Vienna as he did so. It was a common enough practice not to look at one's cards until it was time to actually put one's money in. Still, he didn't look. She didn't either. Daniel had the queen of spades and the ten of hearts. She had the ten and jack of diamonds.

Art lifted the edge of his cards to look at them. Vienna didn't need to look at his expression or try to guess at what he had. The moment the dealer sat down and touched the deck, the familiar sweeping heat had rushed through her, connecting her to the cards. She "saw" them. Art had the seven and ace of clubs.

Vienna was more interested in Daniel's reaction. What was he doing? Was he studying Art? Looking at his expression? His hands? His cards? He had to have watched him play a hundred times. It wasn't the same as playing in person with someone. She ducked her head just enough that her hair fell across her face, but she kept her gaze fixed on Wallin.

Daniel was more interested in her than in Art. He wanted to see what she was doing, not Art. She fanned her lashes down and flicked Art a quick glance from under them. He made his bet. Daniel and Vienna matched it. Art had both of them beat. Leo folded.

The dealer burned a card and turned the next three cards over. The ace of diamonds, seven of diamonds and six of hearts. That gave her four diamonds. Art had two pair. Daniel had nothing. Vienna pushed the bet to half a million dollars. Art stayed with her. Daniel narrowed his eyes and looked the cards over. He folded. The turn was the eight of spades. Vienna bet another half-million dollars. Art stayed with her, although he gave her that little grin of his.

"Know better than to bet against you on the river, Vienna, especially when you want red."

The dealer turned over a queen of diamonds. Art shook his head. "Every damn time. You have it, don't you? A damn diamond flush."

She pushed the equivalent of a million dollars in chips on the line. If Art—and Daniel—wanted to see if she was bluffing, Art would have to pay.

"Not a chance," Art said as he quickly folded his cards.

Vienna took the chips and sent him a little enigmatic smile. As pots went, it set her up nicely. The next two hands, she didn't like the look of her cards and folded. She caught a pair of aces, the club and spade, on the next hand, and she opened the betting. Leo, Daniel and Jameson stayed in as well. Art folded almost as soon as the real betting took place.

The flop revealed the ace of hearts, jack of hearts and nine of spades. Leo bet a half-million dollars. Daniel saw the bet and raised to a million. Jameson folded. Vienna saw the bet and raised it another million. Leo looked the cards over.

Daniel leaned toward him. "I can see you have that look in your eyes, Leo. You're bound and determined to raise the bet and drive me right out of the game." He laughed, tying them together in that sociable way he had, putting everyone at ease. He sounded as if he and Leo were old friends.

Vienna hadn't gotten that particular vibe off Leo at all. In fact, she thought he might actually fold, but not only did he stay in, he raised, just as Daniel had predicted.

Daniel sighed and shook his head. "I was afraid you would push it." He eyed the flop mournfully, and then pushed his chips in.

Vienna made the pot right, although she wasn't quite buying Daniel's act. She knew he had two hearts concealed. Leo had three jacks. She had three aces.

The turn was a two of hearts. That gave Leo no help. That gave her no help. Daniel had his flush. Leo needed to fold.

Before he could say he was going to fold, Daniel laughed softly. "Don't do it, Leo, old friend. Don't make me put all my chips out there. You're always pushing me to my limits. I don't know how you do that to me, but playing with you makes my hair even whiter than usual."

Leo laughed with him and pushed most of his chips in.

Daniel gave a mournful sigh and matched him, then immediately raised again before turning to Vienna. "You don't want to raise again, do you, woman? Pushing an old man like me might give me a heart attack. I'm sure you should fold, not raise."

The sound of his voice tried to slide into her mind, but she was resistant to it. She did, however, realize that there was a cadence to the notes that acted like a suggestion, a form of hypnosis almost, so that the receiver did exactly what Daniel wanted. He emphasized the important words. In this case, he didn't want her to fold, he wanted her to raise. Since she had no intention of folding and every intention of raising, she could give him the impression that his "gift" worked on her. Clearly, he didn't have the same talent she did.

Dutifully, Vienna met the bet and raised. She felt bad for Leo, knowing he wouldn't survive this round. The dealer burned a card and turned over the river card. An ace of diamonds. That gave Leo a full house. Daniel had a flush. Vienna had four of a kind.

Daniel continued to talk to Leo until Leo bet everything he had on the hand. He appeared cheerful and confident. Daniel met the bet and raised. Vienna met that bet and raised Daniel back when he goaded her. Daniel looked pleased with himself as the betting went around again.

Art shook his head. "Never bet against Vienna on a river card, Daniel," he warned.

Daniel laughed the advice away as chips went into the pot as if they were penny chips. Leo turned over his full house, Daniel his flush and Vienna her four of a kind. She watched the hotel owner's face carefully as she revealed her hidden pair of aces. For just a moment his jovial mask slipped and he looked shocked. Truly shocked. He hadn't expected her hand to beat his. She knew for certain he had no knowledge of her "gift." It was that different from his.

Leo shook hands all the way around and left the table. Art sent Vienna a little grin. "I think I'm becoming superstitious about this river card and you, Vienna."

She laughed as she sipped at her water. "I thought Daniel had me. I was becoming a little paranoid. I nearly folded. I don't know why I stayed in."

Surprisingly, it was Art to go six hands later. Vienna folded before the flop. She didn't have anything worth bragging about. Jameson won two small hands, Art one large one and Daniel the largest of all. Vienna just couldn't seem to get any cards. She wasn't going to play lousy cards just for the sake of playing with the "big" boys, no matter how much Daniel subtly taunted her.

She detested seeing Art go. If there was one person she thought of as a friend, it was Art. The one thing his leaving the table did do for her was change the way her luck seemed to be running when the cards were dealt. She found herself with a pair of kings, both red. Daniel and Jameson both stayed in. Daniel had two jacks, both black. Jameson had two tens, one heart and one club.

Daniel started the betting fairly controlled for him, a quarter of a million dollars. Vienna and Jameson stayed. The dealer turned over the three cards to reveal the king of spades, the jack of diamonds and the ten of spades.

Daniel pushed the betting to a half-million dollars.

Vienna stayed in. Jameson did as well. The turn revealed a jack of hearts. That gave Jameson a full house with his concealed tens. Vienna had a full house with her concealed kings and Daniel four of a kind with his concealed jacks.

At once, Daniel began to use his voice to push Jameson into a huge bet. There was no ceiling on what they could bet, and Jameson made a five-million-dollar bet. Daniel met the bet and raised it another five million. At once, he began to use his voice on Vienna. She met the bet and raised it another five million. Jameson made the pot right and so did Daniel.

The river card was turned over. The king of clubs. Once more, the bet went to Jameson, who followed Daniel's hypnotic suggestion. Daniel raised, and before he could tell Vienna what to do or not to do, she raised again by another ten million.

Daniel sat back in his chair, his gaze on her face then dropping to the last card the dealer had placed faceup. "Son of a bitch. Art was right about that river card."

She didn't change expression. She looked at him coolly. If he wanted to know for sure, he would have to put his money up. As far as she was concerned, the play was between the two of them.

Jameson pushed his chips in. Daniel sat contemplating for a long while, as if he couldn't quite believe the predicament he was in. Finally, he called her. Vienna turned the two kings over. Daniel had four jacks and Jameson his full house. Jameson stood and shook their hands. Daniel took his hand almost absently while he stared directly at Vienna.

"The cards favor you."

She gave him her most mysterious smile, the one she knew drove everyone crazy because it gave nothing away— mostly to the men she occasionally went out on very bad dates with. "Sometimes, but all gamblers go through periods of time when cards come to them and other times when they don't. You have to be smart enough to be patient and wait for the right cards."

"You could make a fortune at this."

She laughed. "I often do. I'm a nurse first. I like my life, Daniel. I don't have any wish to change it."

He lowered his voice and leaned toward her. "Not even for the right relationship?"

She was very aware that the audio on most microphones was very sensitive. If he was trying to trap her, he wasn't going to succeed. "A man in the right relationship wouldn't ask me to change my life if I love it. In any case, I tend to steer clear of relationships. I like my freedom." She shrugged, unapologetic. "I do search and rescue, I hike and climb, and I love every aspect of what I do. Fitting a full-time relationship into my life would be very difficult. Moving, after finding the perfect place to live, is out of the question."

Daniel raised an eyebrow. "You're very decisive."

"I suppose if a man said the same thing, you wouldn't question it."

"I suppose you're right. I'm old-fashioned, but then, I'm getting old. I always think the woman will be the one to move to where the man lives and works."

"Ah, I see, she should follow him blindly and give up her dreams and everything she's worked for?"

Daniel scowled. "Put like that, I suppose it sounds quite selfish."

She sent him another smile that said nothing and everything. "I'm sure there are plenty of people who would think I'm selfish for not wanting to risk going into a relationship for those very reasons."

The dealer sat, and once more Vienna felt the rush of energy flowing through her, making her sharply aware of everything and everyone in the room. Every breath Daniel and the dealer drew into their lungs. The flick or tap of fingers, the way Daniel began to tune his voice when he spoke to the media in a little display of supposed graciousness.

Vienna knew she was going to have to play very carefully. It wouldn't matter how many chips she had in front of her, Daniel would always have the chip advantage. This was his hotel. His table. His ego wouldn't allow him to lose to her. It wasn't the money, although like for any gambler sitting at a table, that was a big incentive. Daniel was known for never having lost when it came to the big hands. He wouldn't want to do so in his hotel, and not to her—an unknown.

She was dealt the queen and ten of hearts. She knew Daniel had two kings in the hole, the king of diamonds and the king of spades. Daniel immediately set the bet at two million. She answered him. The dealer burned a card and turned over the king of clubs, the jack of hearts and the ten of diamonds. Daniel doubled the bet and began joking with her about the cards being all over the place. What were they betting on? Surely, she wasn't thinking of raising him?

Vienna did raise him, her fingers sliding over the chips easily and pushing them toward the line. The turn revealed the king of hearts. That gave Daniel exactly what he wanted. Four kings. He was certain he could end the game right there, in one hand, pushing the bet to force her to go all in. He bet ten million chips and mournfully cautioned her not to be zealous, not to try to outbid him for the sake of fame and cameras. She should fold, not raise.

Vienna met his bet and raised. Daniel shook his head, chiding a new student. The river card was the nine of hearts. Daniel eyed her stack of chips and then went all in. There was a gasp of horror from the camera crew. She pushed her chips all in, calling him.

"Very brave, but maybe a little foolhardy of you," Daniel said. "The hubris of the young." He disclosed the pair of kings he had in the hole.

"Perhaps," Vienna said, "I could occasionally be guilty of that, but not this time." She turned over her queen and ten of hearts, revealing she had a straight flush.

Daniel stared down at the cards for a good forty seconds before the knowledge hit that she'd defeated him. Adrenaline poured into his body and he leapt up, knocking over his chair, revealing he still had the moves of the athlete he'd been reputed to be. He paced around behind the table while she took a slow sip of water, watching him carefully.

He returned to the table, picking up the chair and placing it very close to her. Daniel indicated that he wanted privacy. He removed the microphone on his lapel and the one on hers and then signaled for security to remove the media. He also indicated for the dealer to leave the room.

Vienna felt very vulnerable as most of the others filed out and she was left with Daniel and his security team, none of whom she trusted. The security team moved to the back of the room. That didn't make her feel much better. She judged the distance to the door. She was much faster than most people gave her credit for. She ran every day and was in excellent shape. Still, he had a team in the room. There was only one of her.

She turned her attention to Daniel, even though a part of her mind worked on how best to survive if she should be attacked.

"In my lifetime, I saw one other man who could defeat me when we played, Vienna. He was brilliant at cards. He had a gift. No one could touch him. Playing the way you do is dangerous. Playing the way I do is dangerous. I learned to only play when it was necessary to keep the casino alive. I created a mystique around my winning. You're beautiful and a woman. That's becoming far more accepted now, but it is still resented, as you saw with Charles. If you believe players like Art or Leo are your friends, you're very naïve. They will turn on you in a heartbeat. Charles is much more honest. More to the point, the fact that you'll always win will eventually bring far too much attention to you."

"What makes you believe I'll always win?" Vienna countered, just as quietly.

"I've been playing cards since I was thirteen years old. Even younger, but seriously at thirteen. I never lost. Not once, unless I wanted to."

That didn't exactly give her an explanation for his belief.

"You just told me there was one man with a gift, someone brilliant at playing cards who defeated you every time," Vienna was compelled to point out. A part of her wanted to play the man who had managed to defeat Daniel. Had he realized Daniel used his voice to aid him in winning? Was he immune to the hypnotic suggestions as she was?

The owner of the hotel leaned even closer, his gentlemanly demeanor giving way to a much more ruthless expression as a dark mask seemed to descend on his face. "He was found in the desert after three weeks of searching, buried up to his neck in the sand. He'd been tortured and then shot, both eyes gone. In his mouth were cards, the exact hand he managed to beat me with the last game we played."

There was a hiss of malice in his voice. Venom. Vienna drew back to fix her gaze on him, trying to read him. He was very good at masking his expression, but that deep, bitter well of venom spewed like a volcano exploding out of him in spite of his discipline.

"Three aces and two jacks. I had three kings and two queens," Daniel murmured, as if it mattered what the last hand had been.

"Naturally, the police investigated. They had to think you were involved," Vienna stated. She would not be intimidated, even if what he said sounded like an outright threat.

"I had an ironclad alibi. The desert is full of dead bodies. That was nearly forty years ago. Corruption was still pretty rampant then. Not so much now."

"And you aren't threatening me in any way."

"No, why would you think that? I'm trying to warn you. People kill for the kind of money you just won. If you prove to be a consistent winner, they start thinking you're stealing the money from them. It was unfortunate that this event was televised. It wouldn't have been had I thought for one moment that you could defeat me. You will have to be very, very careful when you play from here on out."

Wallin was back to sounding like a gentleman, being kind and solicitous of her. She already knew he was a shark. She needed to get out of there, not just because she could feel the deadly paralysis wanting to invade her body, but because it made her ill to be in the same room with a man who may have actually killed someone or had them killed because they beat him in a poker game.

"Thank you for the warning. Fortunately, I don't live or work here, nor do I have any intention of doing so. I'm quite happy where I am." She stood up, forcing him to straighten in his chair, giving her breathing room. "If you'll excuse me, I have to pack up. I told you, I have other commitments. My friends arrived last night and I'm anxious to see them."

"Congratulations again, Vienna." Daniel extended his hand.

He had a very firm grip. She was very certain he hadn't congratulated her when she'd won, not that it mattered.

"I'm sending security with you to escort you to your room."

"That's not necessary." She was more afraid of his security team than she was of the crowds.

"It is very necessary. You have no idea what it's going to be like outside of this room now. Just remember, forty years ago, there wasn't the media coverage there is now when we were playing poker, and yet someone killed Liam Gram. Our game was televised. Art, Jameson, Leo and I all lost to you. Millions of people saw that happen. Overnight, you became a sensation and we became humiliated. It's possible we could allow that humiliation to eat away at us. Don't think it couldn't happen. They might smile at you and congratulate you, want to be photographed with you, but make no mistake, Vienna: they are *not* your friends."

"I get that. Just as you're warning me they aren't my friends, you might not be either." She eased toward the door, thankful the game hadn't taken very long and she hadn't had to use her "gift" too much.

Daniel signaled to his security staff and they immediately surrounded her. Vienna had to admit the owner of the hotel knew what he was talking about. The moment she stepped outside the room, she was swarmed by media. Behind them, a crowd of people looked as if they might crush her. The security team knew what they were doing, forming a diamond around her.

"Keep your head down and your hand on Wilder's back," Rachel instructed. She was directly behind Vienna.

There were two others on either side of her. Vienna didn't recognize either man and she didn't look at their uniforms. She just did what Rachel told her to do and looked at the floor as they made their way to the private elevator. Breathing deep, she matched her steps to Wilder's the entire time, blocking out the sound of reporters calling out to her.

It was difficult to process the various emotions coming at her with the energy of the massive crowd pressing so close. There were too many people. She had Daniel Wallin's parting shots running around in her head as well. The elevator doors opened and Wilder stepped aside to allow her entrance. He faced the crowd, his gaze moving over the people even as his body blocked hers. She couldn't even see around him. He was just a little too good at his job, but it did allow her to briefly process a few of the stronger emotions emanating from the crowd. One of them was a strong malevolence. That dark strain she'd felt before was radiating toward her, but this time it was much more poisonous.

The rest of the security force stepped onto the elevator and the doors silently slid closed. She knew there was a camera in the elevator recording everything they did, maybe everything they said. The ride was eerily silent after all the cheering on the floor. As soon as the doors slid open, she made a move to exit, but Rachel held her back as Wilder stepped out first, looking down the wide hallway, left and right.

He signaled to his team to allow her out of the elevator, and they walked her to the door. "When you're ready to leave at any time, call for us to escort you, Ms. Mortenson," Wilder said.

"Thank you, I appreciate it." She slipped inside her suite quickly.

Two of her friends had come at Zale's encoded message to Sam, and they rushed her as she closed her door. Shabina Foster was all of five foot four. She'd inherited her mother's incredible blue eyes, thick dark hair and beautiful skin from her Saudi ancestry. Shabina owned the Sunrise Café in Knightly.

Raine O'Mallory was an intellectual powerhouse packed into a slender five-foot-two body. She was on the extremely quiet side until one riled her, and then it was never a good idea to argue with her because you were going to lose—she knew too much. She had some hush-hush job with the military, although she appeared to be an independent contractor with them. At least, Vienna was certain she wasn't *in* the military.

Vienna towered over both women. That didn't seem to matter. They aided her to the bedroom, took her shoes off and helped her lie down.

"You didn't get any sleep last night," Shabina said. "We stayed up way too late talking. Why don't you rest for a little while? I'll finish packing your things. Congratulations on the big win. Lots of money."

"For the hospital and our search team's equipment," Vienna said. It felt so good to lie down. The weakness was beginning to invade. "I can't wait to get out of here. I'm so done with hotels."

"Even this lovely suite?" Shabina looked around her.

"Yes. I need to go camping," Vienna said decisively. Her lashes were getting heavy. "I'm getting pins and needles in my legs. I think I sat too long." The memory of Zale massaging the blood back into her legs and arms, helping to overcome the paralysis, came to her, and she hoped if Shabina or Raine did the same, it would counter the coming immobility.

"Are you really that ready to leave that hot guy you told us about?" Shabina asked, perching on the edge of the bed and massaging Vienna's left leg.

Vienna tried waving her hand. It was too difficult to bother. "So ready. Men are ultimately far too bossy for me to deal with for very long. They want to change your entire life for you. He was fun for a while, though. I'll miss certain things."

Raine laughed. "I'll just bet you will. Stella, Harlow and Zahra will meet us at the Airbnb with all the equipment. We can scope out the best rock to climb tomorrow. I looked up Red Rock online and found all sorts of great sources for the best bouldering. I think Stella will be happy. The hiking looks easy enough for all of us. Zahra won't complain."

"She'll complain," Shabina said.

All three laughed. Vienna couldn't help it. Zahra could run rings around all of them if she chose, but she did it grumbling every step of the way, as if it were a chore for her to hike a trail or boulder or trad climb. She only ran if she had a dog that was high energy. She'd lost her companion dog some time ago and hadn't gotten another one. Her friends were conspiring to find her the perfect pet to make her happy again.

Raine sank down on the bed on the opposite side of Shabina to massage Vienna's other leg. Both women had strong fingers, most likely from all the bouldering they did. They had to use their fingers in the small cracks to pull their bodies up at times as they moved up the rock. Vienna could tell the massage was really making a difference. Why hadn't she known this? She was a nurse. She should have figured it out.

"She will," Raine agreed. "But she'll out-hike us all. I don't know how she does it when she never trains."

"I think she trains secretly. Maybe in the middle of the

night," Shabina said. "I asked her once if she did. She gave me that haughty little look she gets that drives all men wild and said maybe she does."

Vienna found herself laughing again. She could picture Zahra responding just that way. She had the cutest accent, and she did have snooty little looks that were too darling to take seriously, nor did she ever mean anyone to take them seriously. Zahra was one of the kindest people Vienna knew. She was flirty, and men fell all over themselves to help her with any little thing, but she didn't date. She had been born in Azerbaijan and raised in a strict environment in a small village in Uzbekistan. She was actually quite careful around men.

"Do you want me to massage your arm?" Shabina offered.

Vienna nodded. "Thank you. I can't believe how good that feels. I haven't taken advantage of the spa here, and I probably should have. Everything in the hotel is first-class."

"You could still do that, Vienna. They'll come up to the suite," Raine said. "I've looked over all the amenities, mostly to look at the food choices. You know me, I'm all about eating."

She was the slenderest of all of them and could eat an entire pizza if she was working and not paying attention. She liked food. Shabina *loved* to cook, but she wasn't as much into eating as Raine. They often teased Raine about how much food she could actually eat at a meal. She just told them they were jealous, which Vienna thought could have some truth to it.

"Unless you two want to avail yourselves of the spa facilities, I'd rather check out tonight," Vienna said. "I need to breathe fresh air."

"If Zahra were here, no way would she allow any of us to pass up the spa," Shabina said. "She'll be ashamed of us for doing so."

"We can never tell her," Vienna said. She was feeling so much better. Her head was clearing so fast. She didn't even feel as if she had a hangover. It was impossible to tell whether it was because the game hadn't lasted for hours— she'd folded so many times and hadn't used her "gift" for a prolonged period of time—or because of the massage her friends had given her right away.

"She'll ask," Raine warned. "First-class hotel. The first thing she'll think of is, what is the spa like? She'll definitely ask. She will find you sadly lacking, Vienna."

"Harlow might even agree with her on that," Shabina said.

Harlow Frye was a senator's daughter. She'd grown up in the spotlight, having a father always in politics one way or another. A tall, beautiful, elegant woman with fiery red hair, she was also a nurse, but excelled at photography and pottery. Her landscape photos went for a fortune in some galleries, and her pottery was successful as well.

Vienna groaned and closed her eyes tight. "You're right. I'm going to get a lecture from both of them on the merits of skin care and how I sat for all those hours and should have paid attention to the needs of my body for massages every single day. Maybe twice a day."

"They would be right about that," Shabina said. "You're a nurse, which they will point out to you."

"Not you too," Vienna said. "By the time I got back to my room, I just wanted to be alone."

Raine raised an eyebrow. "Did you, now?" she asked, sounding more Irish than ever. "That's not the way I heard it. I heard occasionally some hot man snuck in for a booty call."

Vienna managed to sit up and throw a pillow at her. It wasn't a great throw, but at least she was sitting. She was so grateful her friends had been warned there were cameras and bugs in the rooms and they had to be very careful of everything they said.

"Well, okay, there was that. He made it clear he wasn't into long-term relationships, which was why I was comfortable having a couple of fun nights with him while I was here.

He's a personal protector for the nicest old gentleman. If Wayne weren't so much older than me, I might have gone for him. He's sweet and kind, and when Charles attacked me, he didn't hesitate for a minute to come to my aid. He hit him in the head with his cane and then Tased him with it."

"What a sore loser," Shabina said. "Every time the man loses at poker does he attack the man who defeated him, or is it just women?"

"Art told me Charles once attacked him after a loss," Vienna said. "I read about him, but missed that little tidbit. I knew he had a reputation for being a jerk and causing drama. I think the casinos liked him to get to the final table because it always provided so much more of a spectacle for the crowd when he ranted and raved and leapt up and knocked his chair over. To be honest, I didn't pay attention to what any of these people did *after* a poker tournament. Only during. I'd watch the tournaments online to get a feel for the way they played. Art actually gave classes online. Leo has several books on gambling."

"I look up everything," Raine said. "And I have to look up the answers from multiple sources. I never rely on just one because you can't trust the truth of just one informant anymore."

"It's so difficult to know who to trust," Shabina agreed.

"We're all so paranoid," Vienna said. "I'm feeling better. I'm going to change, put my hair up and try to change my appearance a little, and then let's get out of here."

"Did you check to see if the winnings were transferred to your bank account?" Raine asked.

"Daniel Wallin would never renege on something like that," Vienna said. "I checked when I won the first prize, but not today. That should have doubled the money. I'll do that after I transform back into the real me."

"I hate to break it to you, Vienna, but you look just as beautiful without makeup," Shabina said. "And just as recognizable."

Vienna scowled at her. "I'm sure I don't, but thanks for the compliment." She swung her legs over the side of the bed, a small experiment to see if she had her strength back. She would have to carry her backpack once they were out of the hotel. Raine would have arranged for a car to take them to the Airbnb.

She hurried through knotting her hair in a high ponytail, scrubbing her face clean of all makeup and cramming the last of her toiletries in her bag. She had minimal bathroom products to pack, so she was set pretty quickly. Dressing in old vintage jeans that had seen better days but were extremely comfortable, she pulled on her favorite pair of running shoes. She hadn't packed that many shoes either. Climbing shoes, hiking shoes and running shoes took up space. Her T-shirt was green to match her eyes, and the sweater she pulled over it had multiple pockets that zipped closed in order to secure various items she needed to carry with her.

"I'm *so* ready. We just need to call the security team to escort us out and make sure the car is right there waiting, and we're good to go."

Vienna wished she could see Zale one more time before she left, but she knew that all the trouble they'd gone to in order to convince whoever was trying to kill the undercover agents she wasn't part of them would have been for nothing. She left without looking back.

CHAPTER EIGHT

〜〜〜〜〜〜〜〜〜〜〜〜〜〜〜〜〜〜〜〜〜〜〜〜〜〜

"Shabina, you're killing us with this breakfast. We'll never be able to climb," Stella Harrison proclaimed, scooping more of the egg scramble up and placing it into a tortilla wrap. "How do you manage to make everything taste so good?"

"I just want to know how she gets up so early and has her brain cells working enough to figure out an actual entire menu," Zahra Metcalf said. She managed to sound and look exhausted even as she took more scramble from the warmers. Zahra had dark, dark eyes and hair that was cut chin length to frame her pixie face. She was the shortest of all the women and worked as a hospital administrator.

Vienna had to admit, Stella was right about the excellent food. It wasn't a normal breakfast scramble. And Zahra was right about the early morning hour. They'd gotten up long before the sun to make sure they could boulder before it got too hot.

"You're looking good, Stella. So far, the thought of marriage to Sam hasn't made you want to run for the hills and disappear. We've taken a bet on it, you know. The odds of you actually making it down the aisle aren't that great," Vienna said.

Stella did look good, with her silvery blonde hair and crystal blue eyes. "Sam says he's watching for the big runaway, and if I'm running, he's running with me. He would too. He doesn't mind not being married. Or eloping. Or just marrying quietly with only the dogs there."

"That sounds like Sam," Vienna said.

"He could track you too," Raine predicted. "In any case, you do love him, even if I think you're crazy to fall in love, so you're stuck. You may as well get over your cold feet and just marry the man. You're definitely going to stay with him. Sooner or later, he's going to knock you up and you'll have kids, and if you aren't married, when the kids go to school, there might be a bully who's mean to them. Sam will retaliate in some huge way and you'll have to live off the land in the mountains for the rest of your life."

Raine took thirds on the egg scramble without a qualm.

"Hey," Harlow protested. "I haven't had seconds."

"You're just lounging there with your feet up," Raine pointed out, unrepentant while everyone else laughed at her tale of Stella's life with Sam without marriage. "Who knew you were going to get energetic enough to actually get food for yourself?"

"There's plenty," Shabina, the peacemaker, said. "I counted on Raine to have an extra helping."

"While we're all sitting around and Raine is telling tales about Sam, I'm going to tell you about my fun stay at the Northern Lights." Vienna proceeded to tell her friends everything that had happened, including the malevolent feelings she'd gotten from the crowd. The warnings about Benny. The attack on her from Charles. She showed them the fading bruises on the side of her head and across her belly, close to her ribs. She ended with the things Daniel Wallin had said to her privately after her win.

"I don't know if he was threatening me or warning me," she concluded.

Raine already had her computer out. She could access almost any site. She had a very high government clearance, but in this case, she shouldn't need it. If what Wallin said was the truth, Liam Gram's death would have been in the newspapers. Bodies were found in the desert occasionally during certain time periods. Raine had the name and the approximate date the murder might have happened.

"Did it feel like a threat?" Harlow asked. "What did your gut tell you?"

"I wanted out of that room. After two of his security team had come to my room the day before—I was certain to kill me—I didn't want to be alone with any of them. Wallin or his security. I didn't trust any of them. I wanted to get out of the hotel. I couldn't be seen with Zale. I felt very alone and was so happy to see Shabina and Raine. I didn't even say thank you for getting a plane and coming early. I was afraid they'd overhear. The relief was tremendous."

Raine held up her hand. "I found something. Liam Gram was found in the desert by two young men riding dune buggies. He'd been missing for three weeks. He was found buried up to his neck in the sand, both eyes shot out. Cards had been shoved in his mouth and it was wired shut with his teeth clamped around the cards. When they performed an autopsy, they found he'd been tortured for some time. He was thirty-five years old at the time of his death. That was in 1980."

"Holy crap." Zahra sat upright. "This is the only man who ever beat this Daniel Wallin at a game of cards? He ended up tortured, shot and buried to the neck in sand in the desert? We need to get you out of here."

"It isn't as if Wallin never lost a hand at cards, or he didn't get bad cards," Vienna said. "No one would ever have played him if that was the case. It's just that when it was a huge pot or it really mattered, he was unbeatable." She knew, because that was how she played. Carefully, so she didn't look as if she won every single hand.

"What was the prize?" Stella asked. "How much were they playing for?"

"That's a good question," Vienna said. "Daniel was building the casino. It was in construction, and he had backers, but according to all the propaganda, he managed most of the financing himself. He was really young at the time, and no one believed he could do it. He owned seventy-five percent of the casino and a corporation owned twenty-five percent. I believe it's still that way."

"During that time, it was highly possible that 'corporation' meant one of the Mafia families," Raine said. "They were still entrenched until around 1985."

Harlow made a face of complete disbelief as she shook her head. "Where would a man his age get the kind of money it would take to build a casino like the Northern Lights? Seventy-five percent? That's a lot of cash. Even if he was gambling and winning huge pots, I can't see him making the kind of money it would take for the construction of a casino as first-class and luxurious as the Northern Lights."

"I agree with Harlow," Stella said. "Is it possible he inherited money? Raine, can you find out anything about his background?"

"I looked that up first thing," Raine said. "His father, Norman Wallin, came to the States from Sweden under murky circumstances. I say that because it looks as if he may have been escaping a scandal in his country involving a good deal of money and jewels he'd conned from his fiancée and her family. She did give them to him of her own free will, so they couldn't bring charges against him. The parents had given the money to him as an investment."

"Wallin's father was a con man?" Zahra asked.

Vienna was fairly certain the man had the ability to use his voice in the same way Daniel did. Rather than playing cards, he conned people out of their money and jewels.

"What happened when he came to the States?" Vienna asked.

"He seemed to run with the rich and famous," Raine said. "The ladies loved him. There are pictures of him with various movie stars and singers on his arm at club openings."

"Did they find out who killed Liam?" Harlow asked.

"They investigated, of course, but remember, some of the

cops at that time were corrupt. The FBI came in and did a huge sweep, cleaning up Vegas a few years after the murder took place," Raine answered.

"Was Daniel Wallin a suspect?" Shabina asked.

Vienna was very interested in the answer. Had she been a detective, Daniel would have been very high on her list of suspects, alibi or not.

Raine nodded slowly as she went back to reading the various reports. "Newspapers claim he was a person of interest but that he had an ironclad alibi. He also said Liam was a good friend of his and he was extremely distraught over his death. He had many, many interviews, really taking advantage of his disappearance and death. He knew how to turn things to his benefit even then. It will be interesting to see how he spins your win."

"Is there anything on what the prize was? It must have been news that Daniel lost such a big game," Stella persisted. She gathered the plates and took them into the kitchen.

Zahra immediately began taking the food warmers from the dining room into the kitchen. There wasn't much food left, but she scraped it into the compost container. The archway between the rooms was very wide, so they could see and hear as the conversation continued.

"I'm searching," Raine said. "That might be much more difficult than finding the facts about a murder."

"Daniel wouldn't dare have Vienna disappear and then be killed like this Liam Gram was murdered, would he?" Zahra asked. "Suspicion would fall on him right away. If the Mafia no longer has a stronghold in Vegas, he wouldn't get away with it."

"He might not think that if he's had his way all this time," Vienna pointed out. "I certainly am not going back to play anyone in person. When I play, I'll go back to anonymity and play online like I've always done. I don't know what I was thinking accepting the invitation to play in the tournament when it was in person."

Raine turned away from her laptop to look at her. "How did they know it was you, Vienna? You always played anonymously. How would the hotel know you were a nurse living in Knightly? And why would they track you down and offer the buy-in money to have you come play in their tournament?"

"I actually asked them those questions," Vienna said. "I thought it was a little shady myself. A woman who claimed she was Wallin's secretary told me I'd won a number of their larger online tournaments, which was true, and they'd paid the money I won into my bank account, which was true as well. Since they had to transfer the money I won into my account, it wouldn't be a leap that they would know the name on the account."

"I get that, Vienna," Raine persisted, "but why invite you and pay the buy-in for you? You did have to work your way to the semifinal and then the final table just like everyone else, but why would the hotel pay your buy-in?"

Vienna was a little uncomfortable admitting the truth. "According to the rumors, it had to do with my looks. The hotel thought my appearance and the fact that I'm a nurse would look good in their ads and in interviews. They thought it would bring in new viewers who would be rooting for me to win. The little working girl against the celebrities, that sort of thing."

Raine continued to frown as she drummed her fingers along her thigh. All of them knew her. When she was thinking about something, turning it over and over in her mind, she often had to do something physical to accompany the rapid rate at which her mind computed the data she viewed and rejected.

"You don't think that's the reason?" Shabina asked.

"I don't know," Raine said. "I don't like that he mentioned this Liam Gram's murder to her after she defeated him in a televised game. Everyone saw their hands. *We* were watching, Vienna. We saw you had him beat. He was almost pompous about it, so certain he had you. Don't get me wrong. My heart was pounding like crazy until that last card turned over and you had a straight flush. I don't know why you didn't fold. I would have. But you're always cool under fire."

"I honestly don't know if he was threatening me," Vienna admitted. "I hate to make all of you think he's a serial killer when someone is trying to kill him and he's practically had to go into hiding. I'm just glad I'm out of there."

"Does this Daniel have children?" Harlow asked, turning away from the dishwasher to face her friends.

"One son," Raine said. "He had him late in life with a casino employee, a woman who worked as a server in one of the club rooms. They had a son, Axel. Daniel and the woman, Miriam was her name, never lived together. Daniel was forty and Miriam twenty-two when Axel was born. She died in a car accident when Axel was five. At that time, the boy went to live with his father. He helps with the running of the hotel now," she added.

"Please tell me Miriam's body wasn't found in the desert with cards in her mouth," Zahra pleaded. "If she was, we're going back to Knightly and skipping your bridal party, Stella."

"No, she wasn't found with cards in her mouth," Raine said, laughing. "You have such an imagination, Zahra."

"I don't think it's imagination when one poor man was already buried up to his neck in the desert. I don't want to see Vienna, or any of us for that matter, buried in the sand. I'm pretty short. I wouldn't last very long."

"It wasn't quicksand, you goof," Stella pointed out.

"What was he doing upright, then?" Zahra demanded. "It seems it would be a really difficult way to put him in sand, feetfirst. It isn't like the sand in the desert would be wet. Think about the mechanics."

"You have a point," Harlow said. "It wouldn't be my first choice if I were murdering someone or even burying their body. In the meantime, Raine, did you find anything on the actual bet made between Liam and Daniel?"

"That's a really good question and might be pertinent," Vienna said. "Especially if you can find out who was backing Daniel at the time. He had to have had someone backing him. He wasn't a billionaire then. And he was young. If the Mafia still had a stranglehold on Vegas casinos, more than likely it was them. They wouldn't take kindly to anyone messing with their golden goose."

"I've got a program working on it. Nothing came up in a quick search for me, but if there was ever a record of it, the program will find it. There's no doubt the Mafia was still in business during those years."

Stella sank down onto the couch in the large open living room of the Airbnb they'd rented. "I don't know a lot about the Mafia families, only the little Sam passed on to me, but if Daniel was in bed with them to get his casino built and somehow Liam's winning threatened their business in some way, they might have killed him. Daniel had a reputation, and—Vienna, correct me if I'm wrong—the casino was built around the mystique of his ability at cards."

"That's true. He was young, handsome and very charming. In those early days he supposedly greeted the patrons of his hotel and walked through the casinos talking to players on the floor, encouraging them." Vienna now knew he used his voice to encourage high rollers to bet even more.

"Enough people won to keep coming back," Raine said, once again frowning at the data coming across her screen at a rapid rate. "The northern lights would play above machines during a big win, and at night there would be beautiful displays in the fountains and inside around the sculptures. The sculptures looked so real, as if they were made of ice, and when the lights played through them, no one had seen such beautiful sights before."

"They're still amazing and look real," Vienna confirmed.

"In spite of the fact that the FBI supposedly drove the Mafia out of Vegas," Stella continued, "it's very possible that Daniel's backers retained their share in his casino. My understanding is that many of the families are still very active but low-key, staying under the radar now. Not necessarily in Vegas, but for certain everywhere else. They could still be owners and keeping Daniel in line."

"It would be awful if Daniel had fallen in love with Miriam and didn't live with her because he was protecting her in some way from those people," Zahra ventured.

"You're such a romantic," Stella said and blew her a kiss. "But you might actually have a point. I know Sam said the men he works with were always careful not to get involved with anyone because they made so many enemies. If they fell in love with someone, that woman would always be at risk."

Harlow began to pace. She had long legs and could easily stride across the hardwood floor with its multitude of throw rugs. "Okay. For a minute, let's suppose Daniel actually fell in love with Miriam and they had a son together. Everything was fine until his backers felt threatened. Or maybe not threatened, but Daniel did something to make them really angry with him. What could have happened to make them feel that way?"

There was silence while they exchanged long looks, each trying to puzzle out the solution. Vienna loved being with the other women in situations such as this one. They were all different and brought distinctive opinions and thoughts to the discussion. All of them were intelligent and willing to listen to the others. They respected one another. She felt very lucky to have found them.

Raine, as usual, turned to her laptop. "The only thing I can find is a rumor that the Northern Lights Hotel and Casino was considering building a second casino."

Vienna sat up very straight. "That's odd. I know for a fact that a proposal was made at a business meeting recently for that very thing and Daniel was opposed to the idea."

"If he was opposed to the idea of a second casino back then, his partners could have retaliated and murdered Miriam," Shabina pointed out. "He immediately took his son under his care and surrounded him with security, but he lost the woman he loved."

"If that's what happened." Raine was the voice of caution. "Keep in mind this is just theory. Nothing else."

"Yes, but if that same thing came up, the building of another casino, and Daniel refused to consider the idea, his partners maybe did order a hit on him," Vienna said. "There have been two attempts on his life. They may think his son, who would inherit Daniel's shares, would be much easier to manipulate."

"Then Daniel would really have been warning you, not threatening you," Shabina said.

Vienna nodded. "I know that a couple of the men on his security team are the ones that came into my room with the intention of killing me. There's no doubt in my mind that that's what they were there to do. Fortunately, they didn't have the time. They also weren't the ones to put cameras and bugs in my room. They didn't have the time for that either. I think that was done when Daniel was congratulating me. He kept delaying me leaving and looking at his watch."

"Why would he put bugs and cameras in your room?" Raine asked. "That doesn't make him a good guy."

Stella's brows drew together. "Could he have been worried someone was going to try to hurt her? If he had security watching in her room, maybe he thought he could protect her better."

Raine looked exasperated. "I'm not buying it. If he was worried, *especially* if he planned to invade her privacy that way, he should have told her. For all he knew, she could parade around her room naked. And she was having fun with Zale. What if they were going crazy on the grand piano?" She suddenly scowled and turned her head abruptly to glare at Vienna. "Please tell me you respected the instrument and stayed off of it."

"What instrument are you talking about?" Vienna tried to look innocent. "Because Zale does have a beautiful one."

Laughter erupted as Raine continued to glare at Vienna. "You're hopeless. You've gone off the rails, just the way Stella has. He'd better be as cool as Sam."

"No one is as cool as Sam," Stella protested. "That's hardly fair, Raine."

"Well . . ." Vienna drew out the word. "I love Sam. You know I do. He's the brother I never had. But Zale is way cool. I'd have to say . . ."

"Don't," Stella warned. "I'd have to wrestle you to the floor, and that's so undignified. One of these terrible so-called friends would whip out their phones and record it and blackmail us by threatening to put it online."

"Yep," the others agreed simultaneously.

Vienna sighed. "Fine, then. I won't. Just know that all of you have to think Zale's awesome. If you don't, pretend you do." She glared at Raine. "Even you."

"I have to get over the piano," Raine said. "That will take some doing." She pressed her fingers to her eyes. "The image of that beautiful piano violated is burned into my brain."

"Really, Raine?" Harlow said. "Don't you like spontaneous hot sex? Anywhere? You must have seen that film with Julia Roberts . . ."

Raine put her hands over her ears. "Don't say it. I was in the movie theater and he was playing the piano and she came in and the next thing you know . . . violation is occurring. I had to close my eyes. It was just too much."

When the laughter died down, Shabina returned the conversation to Daniel Wallin. "Who is Daniel's mother? So far, I haven't heard a word about her. No one's mentioned her."

Vienna frowned. "I haven't either. I looked Wallin up when I knew I would be coming here. Mostly, I wanted to play him at cards—though, don't get me wrong, I wanted the money from the tournament win. There was no mention of his mother in any article I read."

Zahra groaned and put a pillow over her face, rolling on the couch to hide. "She was probably buried in the desert upright with cards in her mouth or something equally as horrible."

Stella swatted at her bottom with a pillow. "You're obsessed with being buried in the desert. I don't think Daniel's father played cards. He just conned people out of their money."

"Thank heavens. I was picturing multiple bodies buried upright in the sand. I had decided that I wasn't going anywhere near that desert." Zahra rolled over and pulled the pillow from her face. "You can all laugh if you want, but seeing as how Stella and Vienna barely escaped being murdered just a few months ago, and now we're talking bodies in a desert—"

"The bodies were found *years* ago," Vienna interrupted hastily. "Don't scare yourself, Zahra. Really, Liam died in 1980."

"Let's be clear, Vienna," Zahra said. "He was *murdered* in 1980."

"Okay. I'll concede that he was murdered, but that doesn't mean the same people who murdered him are still around." Vienna didn't quite cover the uncertainty in her voice.

Zahra pounced on that. "You think they might be."

"I don't know," Vienna had to admit. "But going back to where Daniel got his money, could his father have left him money?"

"No." Raine was decisive. "Norman raised Daniel, but he began drinking heavily. His charm seemed to be wearing thin with the ladies. He ended up dead in an alley." She looked over the screen of her laptop at Zahra. "No burial in the desert for him."

"Ha ha," Zahra said. "How did he die?"

"Well, he was murdered. It appeared to be a robbery," Raine admitted.

Vienna shook her head but didn't say anything. She couldn't imagine that if Daniel's father had the same gift of being able to use his voice on others, he couldn't persuade a robber to leave him alone. And what did he have on him at that point that someone would want?

"Where were Daniel and his mother?" Shabina asked.

"The mother was out of the picture and Daniel was already grown. He must have been at least seventeen or eighteen. At least he looks like it in these old newsprints." Raine turned her screen around to show them.

"He was super good-looking," Harlow observed.

"How could there be absolutely nothing said about his mother?" Vienna asked. "That makes no sense when Daniel's father ran with celebrities. He was news back then. The paparazzi followed him around just to see who he was with."

"He also ran with one of the Mafia families," Raine said, leaning down to peer at her screen and the data flowing across it. "He was often seen going into their restaurants and even, occasionally, their homes."

There was another silence while the six women considered what that could mean. Stella pressed her lips together and looked to Raine. Raine sighed and shook her head. Stella nodded.

Raine gave another sigh of reluctance. "Women in a family were often used to cement relationships or add to territories. They had little say in marriages. Their fathers often regarded them as nothing more than assets to benefit the business. If a daughter was promised to a man in another family for a reason, she was expected to remain a virgin, especially back then. If she got pregnant by an outsider, I can't imagine what would be done to her."

Zahra threw herself backward again, pillow to her face. "This is getting worse and worse. I'm beginning to really feel sorry for Daniel Wallin, and I had him pegged as a total villain."

"Is there a way to find out for certain if Daniel's mother was the daughter of a Mafia family member?" Vienna asked. "There must be records."

"Not necessarily," Raine said. "If they had promised her to someone, they wouldn't want it known that she'd gotten pregnant. They might have had her deliver and promised to keep the baby alive if she cooperated and went through with the marriage they needed."

"That would explain why Daniel was raised by his father and there was never a whisper about his mother. It might also explain which Mafia family backed him and why," Vienna said.

"I'm looking for anything I can find in records of births. Also, names of Mafia families that were in Vegas at that time and then again when Daniel would have needed money from backers," Raine said. "Those families have gone underground."

"Add in when Liam was murdered and now," Vienna suggested. "See if there's a common name. Or at least one name that fits most of those times."

Shabina went into the kitchen and began to slice up vegetables. "I'm going to make certain everything's ready for tonight's dinner. I can just put things in the Instant Pot."

Zahra leapt up. "I'll get things ready for a salad." She began pulling more vegetables out of the refrigerator. Harlow joined them.

"Here's something. It's very brief. Dr. Lars Marten rushed to the home of Angelo Bottaro to answer the call to aid his daughter, Isabella, who had fallen down the stairs and was unconscious. Isabella was doing fine, but on the way home, Dr. Marten lost control of his car on the ice, hit the bridge, spun and went into the river. This timeline fits with the birth of Daniel. It wouldn't surprise me if Bottaro ordered Marten to be killed. He wouldn't want to leave any witnesses to his daughter's betrayal of their family," Raine said.

"Is the Bottaro family mentioned in Vegas?" Vienna asked.

"Yes," Raine said. "They had a large foothold there. No mention of Isabella after her fall down the stairs. I looked for her marriage and didn't find one. She could have been married to someone in Italy or Sicily. I haven't searched there yet. I'm trying to keep to our timelines in Vegas."

Vienna began to get that feeling in her gut that told her they were on the right track. She didn't know anything about crime families or what they did or didn't do, but if they were willing to take their daughter's child from her and send her off to another man, pretending she was a virgin in order to gain some kind of political advantage, she thought they would do anything. Just how long would Isabella have been able to keep up the lie? Her husband would have discovered she wasn't a virgin. Even if she could have come up with a plausible excuse, a doctor would have known she'd had a child. What would her husband have done to her when he found out? It was so clear that her father didn't care what happened to her.

If Daniel was Angelo Bottaro's grandson, Angelo very well could have decided to build a hotel and casino with him and allowed him to be the front man.

"There's something about Daniel's father's death that struck me wrong," Raine said.

Stella glanced at her sharply. Vienna caught the look that passed between them. Clearly, Stella knew things about Raine the rest of them didn't. That was okay with Vienna. They all had things in their pasts that they would rather have stay there. Raine was very discerning when it came to murder. She had moved her screen back to the photographs in the alley where the body was discovered.

"These were taken outside the Bottaro family restaurant in Los Angeles. You can see the dumpsters here and all the boxes with the name printed on it. Look at his clothes. He used to dress really nice, in suits. Here he looks like he's been living on the streets and eating out of dumpsters. Why would someone choose to rob him?" Raine seemed to be musing aloud rather than asking any of them.

"Do you think he was there to shake the Bottaro family down?" Harlow ventured. "He needed money. He could have been desperate enough to decide to try blackmail."

"He would have had to have been very drunk or very desperate," Raine said. "He hung around that family. If he really did get Isabella pregnant, Angelo would have explained the harsh realities of life to him. He wouldn't have spared him, in fact. Most likely, he would have had his men scare the crap out of him by beating him within an inch of his life. He's lucky Angelo didn't have him killed if he really did get Isabella pregnant, as I suspect he did."

"Why wouldn't Angelo have him killed?" Shabina asked.

"Most likely, Isabella pleaded with her father and negotiated a deal for his life and the life of her unborn child. If Angelo wanted the marriage enough to someone he had already promised her to, he would have listened," Raine said.

Vienna found it interesting that Raine seemed to know quite a bit about life in that particular lane when Vienna knew almost nothing.

"All right, so we're going with the idea that Daniel is Angelo Bottaro's grandson," Harlow said.

"Was. Angelo is dead. His oldest son, Fredrick, took over as head of the family quite a while back. His grandson is a big part of it now," Raine said. "I think it's safe to say we can presume it is the Bottaro family that owns twenty-five percent of the hotel with Daniel. I'm unraveling the corporation now. That is going to be a long process, but I'm fairly certain that's who has backed him from the beginning."

"Why wouldn't the Feds have run them off?"

"There hasn't been anything illegal found at Daniel's hotel or casino," Raine said. "No matter how many times the books are gone over, there is no evidence of wrongdoing."

Vienna could see that. Daniel had no reason to launder money or use his casino for anything but making money. Angelo Bottaro had been very smart to give Daniel the lion's share of the business. If he had seen the handwriting on the wall—that eventually there would be a crackdown by law enforcement—he would want to be part of a legitimate money-making venture. Daniel presented that opportunity. The fact that he wouldn't expand might have been maddening, although had she been Angelo, she would have considered that Daniel might have a good reason for not choosing to do so when they were making so much money.

"Now, after all these years, they want a second casino again and Daniel is still saying no," Shabina said. "I get that they might want to get rid of Daniel so they can manipulate Axel, but why try to kill Vienna? Why put all those bugs and cameras in her room? That makes no sense. And if you're going to kill her, why stick a camera in there to record it?"

"That's another excellent question," Zahra said. "I'm getting hungry just thinking about it. Maybe we should stop at the coffee shop on the way and get scones and coffee before we climb." There was a hopeful note in her voice.

"You're always hungry ten minutes after we eat," Stella pointed out.

"I have a fast metabolism," Zahra said. "I feel no shame in the fact that I love food and can eat. We have time if we get out the door now."

"There is a coffee shop on the way," Raine said.

"Indulging Zahra's craving for scones is a dangerous thing," Stella warned. "But since I'm totally addicted to coffee, I say we stop."

"The temperature is supposed to be cooler today," Harlow supplied. "I'm for coffee. We did sort of get off topic," she added as they gathered up their climbing gear.

"Someone believes I'm undercover along with Zale, trying to protect Daniel, I think," Vienna said. "Whoever thinks that would be the one trying to kill me. I don't know who installed the cameras and bugs or why they did it. The two coming into my room talked about the security camera, but I had the feeling they meant the one in the hall."

"Hopefully, we dispelled the belief that you're some sort

of secret agent," Harlow said. "Sheesh, can't a woman have a booty call with a hot man without his enemies thinking she's a spy?"

"Apparently not," Vienna said. "And I look the part." She tossed her braid over her shoulder.

"I'm not sure you're James Bond worthy," Raine objected. "You've got the face, legs and body, but you don't show enough skin. Technically, your boobs should be hanging out."

"Did that happen in the recent film?"

"I don't know," Raine admitted. "I didn't see it. I kind of gave up after seeing Bond go from woman to woman the way he did. He wasn't my ideal man." She shrugged. "That should tell you about secret agents. They aren't the best bet when it comes to relationships. You end up dead, or they're over you when they're on their next mission."

Stella rolled her eyes. "Put your laptop away, voice of doom. If we're heading to the coffee shop, we have to go now. I'm marrying Sam no matter what. If you bet against me, you're losing your money."

"I bet a lot of money against you," Raine confirmed. "Couldn't you at least make a run for it and make Sam chase you so I recoup some of my money? I'll share." She closed her laptop and slipped it into a case with a special lock.

"Vienna, did you bet against me?" Stella asked.

Vienna burst out laughing. "I play the odds, my friend. The odds were strong that you would freak out, but Sam would see it coming and talk you off the ledge every time. He knows you so well, or he has a gift with you. He always seemed to know when you had a bad day. Even before the two of you were together."

Stella nodded. "He did. I'd get to the house and he'd be on my deck grilling a meal for me. He'd nod toward a cooler and there would be ice-cold beer in it. I didn't have to talk. He never expected me to. He'd just have dinner ready and then he'd leave. Sometimes he'd stay with me and we'd sit outside and he'd tell me all the names of the stars. He knows them all."

"It must have shocked you that he knew how to talk," Zahra said.

Zahra had been Stella's best friend for years. They'd been soul mates almost from the moment they'd met. No one could make Stella laugh the way Zahra could with her droll sense of humor.

"As a matter of fact, it did shock me," Stella admitted. "But his voice was sexy, and the next thing I knew, I was having all these erotic fantasies . . ."

Zahra put her hands over her ears. "Stop. I don't want to hear another word."

Vienna and her friends burst out laughing. "If we don't get a move on, it's going to be too hot to do any bouldering. Getting up before it's even light won't do us any good if we sit around talking and forget we're climbing. Especially if we're really going to make a stop at a coffee shop. You know we'll spend time there we don't have."

Zahra groaned. "I am not getting up this early again, so we're leaving immediately."

"You have to get up for the kayaking trip," Shabina pointed out with just a little too much glee.

Zahra threw one of the smaller decorative pillows from the couch at her.

"Vienna's right," Stella said. "We can come back to our little mystery of Daniel, Liam and Miriam when we get back tonight."

"We'll get it done," Vienna agreed as they hurried out to Stella's 4Runner.

CHAPTER NINE

The coffee shop wasn't yet crowded, and all the best pastries had just been put out in the cases as they arrived. They found a table as they waited for their to-go orders of mostly lattes. Even as they sat down, the door constantly opened and closed, letting in the early morning customers. Their table faced the bank of windows, allowing them to see the sun come up when it was rising.

Raine always took the seat facing the door. This time Vienna found herself sitting just to the right of her, so she could watch as well. After the attack on her from Charles, and then the two security guards coming into her room, she felt shaky inside. She hadn't admitted to anyone, or even herself, that she was more shaken than she'd realized. Daniel's warning and his grim story about Liam's murder had only added to her feeling of vulnerability.

Raine leaned toward her. "Are you feeling okay, Vienna? If you prefer to just bike first and boulder in the evening, we can switch things up."

"I'm doing fine." When Raine's blue-gray eyes remained on her, Vienna decided it was better to talk about the unexpected way she felt. "Actually, I had no idea I was so shaken up by those men coming into my room the way they did. I tell myself they thought I was some kind of secret agent or something, but it doesn't help." She gave Raine a wan smile and pressed a hand to her queasy stomach. "I don't think I'm cut out for a life of intrigue."

Vienna felt inexplicably sad. She was adventurous. She never thought she would be that woman who would fall apart because she had hidden in a closet while two men searched her suite with the intentions of killing her. She held out one hand where Raine could see it while the other women at the table laughed and talked all around her. Her hand shook.

"I can't be like this. What happens if I'm climbing a cliff to help some poor kid who went over the edge and is counting on me and I start shaking like this? I can't have someone like Zale in my life. What was I even thinking?" She rubbed her forehead as if she could erase him from her mind.

"Vienna, slow down for a minute and think this through. A few months ago, a close friend of ours turned out to be a serial killer. He targeted Stella and you both. You grieved for him, but you never acted afraid. You refused to allow yourself to consider that you were afraid even for a moment. Fear is a normal reaction. It's even necessary for self-preservation. If you hadn't been afraid in your suite and acted on that fear by hiding in the closet, you most likely would have been killed. Fear isn't cowardice."

"Do you think men like Sam and Zale are afraid?"

Raine nodded. "I know they are. Maybe not of the same things we are, but they're afraid. Someone like Zale can be as cold as ice when he goes out on an assignment and yet be terrified if his family or someone he loves is threatened. That's usually the reason they remain alone. Can you imagine what Sam would do if someone took Stella from him? Suffice it to say, it wouldn't be pretty. That's their fear. Fear is normal, Vienna."

"How come you're so smart? I'm supposed to be, but right at the moment, I feel lost and very off-balance," Vienna admitted.

The coffee shop did a brisk before-sunrise business. The early customers were mostly locals on their way to work, or tourists on their way to hike the trails or boulder like they were going to do. The little set of bells on the door continually rang to announce a group, a couple or an individual coming into the shop to head to the counter to get their coffee and pastry to take with them.

"You were cooped up in the hotel for too long. You're not used to it. I get that way when I'm away from Knightly or the Sierras too long. We're used to wide-open spaces. We've lived that way a long time now. That's how we reset. It's how we balance ourselves. Being in crowds and staying indoors too long can mess with our heads."

Vienna was grateful Raine felt the same way. "It's nice to know I'm not alone. I wanted out of there two days after I got there. The suite was beautiful. The food was delicious." She leaned closer to Raine, her gaze fixed on Zahra. "I knew if Zahra saw that suite, she'd never let us leave. The hell with the Airbnb. We'd be staying right there at the Northern Lights."

"What are you whispering about?" Zahra demanded, narrowing her dark, velvety eyes. "I know you're talking about me, Vienna, and not in a good way."

"It's impossible to talk about you any way but good, Zahra," Vienna objected. "I was telling Raine if you had seen the suite at the Northern Lights where I stayed, we would never have left. First class all the way. Food was delicious. Anything you wanted, they brought to you anytime, day or night. The spa came to your room too." She dangled that shamelessly in front of her friend, even though she hadn't taken advantage of it.

Stella pressed her lips together. Harlow put her hand over her mouth. Shabina bit down on her fingers. Raine inspected the tabletop.

Zahra sighed and slumped back in her chair. "I know darn well you never once availed yourself of those spa services, Vienna. They were wasted on you. I don't know why I can't attract a millionaire. I need to get out more. That's my problem. I really should put a little more effort into finding these hotel owners and flirting a bit with them so they ask me out."

There was instant laughter. Zahra did her best to scowl. "What?"

Stella regarded her best friend with a slightly surprised expression. "Zahra, you flirt with every male from the age of five to ninety-five. You can't help it. That's just who you are. And you've been asked out by several millionaires. *Several.* One *was* a hotel owner. If we set foot in a hotel, you get special treatment. If we hire a personal trainer, we're worked like dogs. You get special treatment. Do you not even notice these things?"

Zahra's dark brows drew together. "No. Everyone is just nice to me. Not women, they aren't very nice. And Miguel Valdez's new people at the climbing gym aren't nice either. One of them is a man."

"You won't scan your badge or wear it," Stella said.

"They know who I am. I go there all the time. I never had to do that before," she pointed out with a lift of her stubborn chin.

"The millionaires you turned down?" Stella persisted.

Zahra frowned at her. "I'm not going to date someone for their *money*. That would be awful. They were nice men. I wouldn't do that to them. They deserve someone really attracted to them."

Laughter spilled around the table. "You're such a fraud, Zahra," Vienna said. "You say you want a millionaire, but in reality you could not care less about money. That's the truth. You've had so many chances. You don't even date. Of course, there's Bruce . . ." She trailed off to give her friend time to tell them where she was with the local man she'd had hopes for.

Zahra shook her head and waved her hand. "I'm done. I gave him every chance to make a move and he didn't. I don't throw myself at men. I'm officially moving on."

Vienna felt bad for her. Zahra really didn't date, and she'd crushed on Bruce for a long time. She'd done everything she could to show the man, and he seemed to reciprocate her feelings, but he never asked her out. He danced with her when they were at the Grill, the local bar where they went to dance and hang out together. Bruce even seemed to warn other men off her, but he never pursued Zahra further.

"More power to you," Stella said staunchly. "Bruce had his chance. You deserve better. If he doesn't go after you, he isn't the right man for you."

"I'm perfectly fine on my own," Zahra said. "I've got good friends. Even if they are crazy and want to get up at the crack of dawn to go climbing around on rocks."

"And then go bike riding," Vienna reminded, just to watch Zahra's famous dramatic reaction.

Zahra didn't disappoint. She slid down in her chair with a groan.

"After we climb," Shabina said, "we can take a break and then take the bikes and go on the trail. I've mapped out some really great loops for us."

"Bikes." Zahra groaned dramatically again, this time louder. She folded her arms on the table and put her head down on her arms. "Why are you all so energetic? Did you bring my ebike?"

"No. You're going to pedal just like the rest of us," Stella said firmly. "Considering you can run rings around us most of the time with your short little legs, no one is going to let you get away with riding an electric bike."

"I'm not going to be your best friend anymore, Stella. I'm giving up the position. In fact"—Zahra sat up and pulled out her phone—"I'm going to go on Instagram and see if anyone else wants the position. You're a pain to keep up with. All this hiking and climbing and biking nonsense. Where is that app? What does it look like? I forget."

Stella burst out laughing. "No one believes you're going to give me away, Zahra. You can't post anything on your Instagram account. I have to do it for you."

Zahra groaned again. "Fine. I'll keep you as a best friend. Just so you can do the social media crap I don't want to do."

"Don't worry, Zahra, tomorrow we can lounge around the pool and rest," Shabina said. "I'll hand you drinks and fan you."

"Thank you." Zahra blew her kisses. "See, Stella, that's what you're supposed to do when you have a bridal shower. Not climb and bike and hike all over the country."

"We've got the kayaking day after tomorrow," Vienna said. "We meet the guide at the Hoover Dam Lodge parking lot at six a.m., and they'll shuttle us to the launch site. We have to have our IDs and can't be late or they won't let us launch at the Hoover Dam, so make sure you don't forget them and you get up on time. And yes, Zahra, we have to get up before it's light again."

"I suppose since I'm in a tandem kayak with Stella, I can make her do all the work for the first few hours while I sleep."

"Like I'd let you get away with that. The kayak would suddenly turn over," Stella said. "You'd find yourself in the water, dog-paddling around."

"You'd be that mean," Zahra said.

"Yes, I would," Stella said.

Vienna's phone vibrated and she dragged it out of her pocket, a little surprised. She'd taken her vacation and few people called or texted other than those in the room with her. "Zale sent me a text. He left his truck in the Blue Diamond overnight parking lot. He wants me to clean it up and get it back to the rental place for him."

"I thought you broke all ties with him," Shabina said.

Vienna heard the concern in her voice. The others looked at her the same way. She shrugged and studied Zale's text. It was clear to her that something had happened to him and Rainier. She wanted to leap up and try to find him, but she knew it would be impossible. There was no doubt in her mind that he was hurt. That "clean it up" for him meant there was blood in the truck. She swore under her breath. This was going to be her life with him.

She looked up to meet Stella's eyes. Stella knew. She was marrying Sam. This was Sam's old life. He might not participate now, but he had in the past. He'd shared little pieces of what it had been like with Stella.

"I don't mind driving his truck to the rental place for him if he doesn't have anyone else to do it. I can Uber back to the Airbnb."

"That's silly, Vienna. I can drop everyone and then follow you in the 4Runner," Stella said. "They'll have dinner put together by the time we make it back."

"Or we can all just go at the same time," Shabina said. "Dinner will only take a few minutes. You won't need to make the extra trip to take us to the Airbnb. That's just more driving time for you, Stella."

"I don't mind."

"Because you never mind going out of your way," Harlow said. "But it's only a few minutes. We can hang. On the way back we can talk about the hike to Tuolumne Meadows."

"It's such beautiful country," Stella murmured. "I'm so looking forward to that hike."

"We have the permits, of course," Raine said. "We'll park at Tuolumne Meadows and take the shuttle to White Wolf Trailhead. Hopefully, that's what you wanted, Stella."

"Exactly," Stella confirmed. "I want to start at the White Wolf Trailhead and hike to Tuolumne Meadows. We have four days. I know it's a steep downhill and then a long uphill climb going that way, but the scenery is fantastic, and this time of year there will be few people."

"The river should be high and the waterfalls really running with the snowpack so dense this year," Harlow offered.

Raine nodded. "It's supposed to be perfect weather for us too. I'm really looking forward to it."

"I am too," Vienna said. "Just the thought of getting outdoors for a few days and clearing all the cobwebs out of my head makes me feel better."

Their drinks were ready and they collected them before once again getting into the large 4Runner. Stella drove her rig out to Calico Basin, which was actually in a residential neighborhood. Used to driving in all kinds of weather, Stella was careful as she took the SUV slowly through the streets to the parking lot. They were early enough that they managed to park in the dirt parking lot, when often, they had been warned, there were so many visitors that parking had to be found on the road, and they had to be careful not to upset residents.

All the women were used to hiking distances with backpacks and thick crash pads on their backs, but the trail to the Kraft Boulders was only a five-minute approach on a fairly flat and well-marked path. There was also a long hiking trail that took off to the left of the parking lot and circled back through the boulders, which day hikers often used. The locals often walked their dogs along that left trail, but the path to the right of the parking lot led directly to the famous boulders. Since they weren't worried about weight, they loaded their daypacks with lots of snacks, chalk bags, shoes and a guidebook for the area. They shoved what they could into the two thick crash pads they brought with them, and then made their way toward the boulders.

The very first boulder they could see was the massive twenty-five-foot one called the Cube. It was a beautiful but very intimidating boulder with several very hard routes on it. They knew from the beta—information—that Raine had collected for them ahead of time that the downclimb was sketchy and hard, so they had no intention of climbing that one today. Instead, they veered left toward a cluster of boulders along the trail that were all much shorter than the Cube.

Vienna inhaled deeply, grateful to be outdoors in the early morning sunrise with her friends, crash pads on their backs as they walked single-file along the trail through the red sandstone boulders until they arrived at the black warm-up boulder. Immediately there were a variety of routes nearby, including easier ones right along the trail that Shabina might find fun to climb. She was the least experienced, and all of them wanted her to enjoy climbing, not be afraid of it. They would all need to warm up, so convincing Shabina they weren't doing easy climbs just for her as they put down their crash pads wasn't difficult.

Vienna liked to climb. She liked puzzles and she liked any activity that allowed her brain to focus wholly on one problem and block out everything else. That way, she wasn't all over the place. Climbing boulders kept her mind occupied with figuring out the best way up the surface of a rock. She wanted to center herself again after all the stressful time inside the hotel and casino.

When they needed money and Vienna suggested that she would get a job at one of the big casinos, Mitzi had told her she'd always had trouble being around large crowds and had developed an aversion to the casinos in particular. In her earlier years, like a lot of the men and women who wanted to put themselves through school, she had gone to work in one. Like most of her explanations, her mother had stopped abruptly and just said an emphatic *no*. She hadn't forbidden Vienna exactly, but at the mere mention of the hotel/casinos, Mitzi could have a full-blown panic attack. Vienna respected her wishes and stayed away from them until her mother had gotten cancer and she felt she had no choice.

Coming to the Northern Lights Hotel and Casino had been her first time back in years, and she couldn't believe how much she had disliked being in the environment. After spending the majority of the last few years outdoors in such a beautiful place as the Eastern Sierras, she almost felt as if she'd been holding her breath the entire time she'd been indoors. She hadn't even realized how much of a toll it had taken on her being inside for so long, or the stress of dealing with the threats. She inhaled deeply, grateful to be outdoors in the early morning sunrise with her friends, setting up the crash pads at the warm-up boulders where they all could climb.

Once they set their crash pads in place, all of them studied the boulders in order to choose their routes. Vienna stood looking up the rock face for a moment, drawing the fresh air into her lungs before she reached up and felt the warm sandstone. Vienna was a very strong climber with a good head, but she didn't boulder a lot. She preferred sport climbing, but this softer sandstone with lots of holds was very fun to warm up on. She quickly topped out several of the V0s along the trail, and it wasn't long before she was feeling pretty excited to try something a little more challenging. She made her way over to another boulder nearby that was just past the warm-ups. There were a couple V1s and a V2 that she wanted to try. Boulder problems were rated with a standard V scale from V0 to V15 or above, with VB meaning basic.

Stella helped her arrange the pads and offered to spot her. The climb she picked started from the left and topped out at the center of the boulder. After making sure the pads were in a good position, Vienna stepped up to the start holds. The moment she did, her mind was clear and focused. Everything disappeared but the problem she faced climbing the slightly overhung boulder. She grabbed the start holds and quickly heel hooked the outside wall of the boulder with her right foot. The pressure allowed her to keep from swinging out and made it easier to reach up with her right hand. She then found a good toe with her left to take pressure off the heel hook, and this allowed her to move it over to a new hold. She continued a repetitive pattern of heel hooking and reaching for holds as she moved left toward the center of the boulder. She then had to hold body tension as she took her heel off and repositioned her feet to go for the top jug.

The moment she grabbed the good hold she felt joy rush into her. She had it. She got her right foot up high and rocked over it to get on top of the boulder. She could hear Stella telling her good job and felt the warm sun on her face. It was the best feeling, and she decided to sit on top of the boulder for a bit to bask in it a little longer. After a little while she saw Harlow making her way toward them.

"You should try this one, Harlow, it's really fun!"

Vienna hurried down the other side of the boulder to be a spotter. Harlow was tall, and although Stella and Raine were both excellent at spotting, Vienna knew she had superior capabilities. She took the position seriously. A spotter needed to ensure the climber's head was protected in a fall first, and secondly his or her spine. When Vienna was spotting, she was wholly focused on the climber, her gaze fixed on the belt line. That way, she knew if that portion of the anatomy was dropping fast, there was no mistake, the climber was coming off the rock and she had to guide the fall.

Harlow studied the boulder and then chose a different route, a V4 with a standing start. She moved up the rock tentatively, and Vienna willed her to keep going. Several times she paused, her hips pressed against the boulder. Stella stepped close and called out instructions in a calm voice, encouraging her, telling her she could do it. That she had it.

Vienna stayed quiet, concentrating on Harlow's body language, not on the climb itself. It was her responsibility to make certain Harlow wasn't injured if she fell. Stella and the others could give Harlow the necessary reassurance to keep climbing.

Harlow came off the boulder several times, but landed on her feet without any help or guidance from Vienna. She simply looked up at the boulder, studying the rock with even more determination, and then started again. That was Harlow. She never gave up. The others gathered around, encouraging her. Cheering her on. Eventually, Harlow made it to the top, and Vienna was able to drop her arms. She'd had to move position twice, but she'd marked each position ahead of time and knew exactly what she would do if Harlow fell as she moved up the boulder.

She cheered with the others as she rubbed at her arms, genuinely happy that Harlow had made the climb. Harlow was getting better and better at bouldering and seemed to be enjoying it more. Vienna knew she preferred trad climbing. Climbers came from all over the world to take on the famous boulders just outside the town of Knightly. The iconic boulders were considered world-class climbs, and there was something for everyone no matter their climbing experience.

Vienna took out her water bottle. She looked around as she drank. The sun was up and four more climbers had come along the trail. The warm-ups were located right on the trail, and the other climbers heading toward other boulders were walking close to the boulder Harlow had been climbing. She thought perhaps they were making their way to a popular boulder called Monkey Bar. She called out to them and gave a friendly wave.

Two of the climbers looked up, smiling, returning her greeting and waving back. The other two continued on without so much as glancing her way. That was unusual behavior in the climbing world. As a rule, climbers were very friendly toward one another. They shared beta—information—on routes and helped one another out when possible. The two who hadn't looked up had ball caps pulled low over their faces, shielding their eyes, and neither carried crash pads with them. One had a daypack while the other didn't.

"Not very friendly," she observed to Stella.

"I noticed," Stella said. "Could be having a bad day."

"Or they're day hikers and were totally absorbed in their conversation." Shabina excused their lack of good manners.

"They weren't wearing hiking shoes," Raine pointed out. "One had on running shoes and the other loafers."

"That explains a lot," Vienna said. "Definitely not climbers. The other two were. Maybe they were going to get instruction."

"Or maybe they weren't even together," Harlow ventured.

Vienna took another sip of water and turned back to see

Zahra studying the boulder. Little Zahra standing under five feet. Everyone in their group loved her. She was funny and kind and extremely intelligent. She also ran the local hospital. Without her, the facility would probably have folded a long time ago, but she had managed to find ways to raise large amounts of money through fundraisers and by acquiring grants and getting enormous donations. They had up-to-date equipment and could afford to pay their doctors and nurses a good enough salary to keep them. Zahra worked very hard for the hospital. Their trauma unit was vital and the first place they could stabilize victims of accidents from skiing, climbing or any of the other multitude of sports available in the Sierras.

Zahra might complain and say everything was difficult, but she always went with them, hiking trails and climbing boulders, even if trad climbing—which she excelled at—was her favorite thing to do. If she couldn't hike the long trails due to work, she always volunteered to resupply them. She had lost her dog, Elara, who she ran with twice a day, and all of them knew she still grieved for the little half Pyrenean Shepherd, half unknown breed.

All of them were keeping an eye out for a rescue or an accident that had a dog close to the same type that they could surprise her with. She'd stopped running on her own, and when they got together with their dogs, she always looked sad. Shabina's dogs seemed to know it and always went to her, practically sitting in her lap, which made her laugh. Shabina had Dobermans and they were extremely large. Sitting on Zahra and resting their heads on her usually trapped her wherever she was.

Zahra was about to climb another VB when Stella stopped her. "You need to climb something harder than that. You've already climbed so many VBs. Get on something harder. You're so strong. You could climb a V3 easily. At least try this V1 instead." She pointed to a crimpy climb that went up the middle of the rock face.

Zahra nearly always waited for them to finish bouldering and then talked them into climbing with rope. Vienna knew Stella and Raine *really* had an aversion to rope, but they did it anyway because they loved Zahra and she nearly always came bouldering with them.

Zahra chalked her hands. "You always say that, Stella, as I land on my ass and stare up at the sky. I already see the vultures circling."

Automatically, everyone but Stella looked overhead. There were no vultures. Zahra's laughter was infectious. "You're so easy." She looked at Vienna.

"You are so ridiculous, Zahra. Just think of this as 5.10. It's easier if you talk less," Stella said with a laugh.

Zahra gave Stella a haughty smirk and turned to Vienna. "You ready to spot me?"

"I got you." Vienna had already chosen the three different places she would have to move to in order to provide the best protection for Zahra.

Zahra dusted her hands, staring up the rock face, her expression determined and focused. She was the shortest of all of them, just shy of five feet by a couple inches, which made it difficult to climb given the way many of the routes were set up. She didn't have the wingspan taller climbers had. She was extremely flexible and could smear her feet up tiny holds that others couldn't stand on. The other thing Zahra had going for her was she maintained good form. Her body always knew where her center of gravity was and seemed to keep it automatically.

Zahra stood on the crash pads for a moment and then she reached up, her fingers barely finding some small crimps to start with. She easily pulled herself up onto some tiny footholds. She pressed into the rock and reached up with her right hand above her shoulder to find the next crimp. The next move was a high step, but she didn't commit and instead jumped down. "What was that? You jumped off, Zahra," Stella said.

"I fell off."

"You jumped."

"She's just warming up. You got this, Zahra," Vienna said.

"Thanks, Vienna. Yeah, I was just warming up." Zahra smirked at Stella with her laughing dark velvet eyes.

"I think you're warmed up, girl. You got this, and Vienna and I will spot you." Stella knew that Zahra was a bit afraid, although she would never admit it to the group. She preferred to keep things light and funny. "Vienna is an excellent spotter, and you know I won't let you get hurt."

Zahra looked at her friend with knowing eyes and took a deep breath. "Okay," she said. Her whole posture changed and she approached the rock with determination. She pulled onto the same crimps, but this time with quick efficient movements and commitment. She made her way up the rock face easily, moving with natural grace. Zahra might not like bouldering, but her technique was solid and she made short work of the problem easily. Once she stood on top, she smirked at them both.

"Are you happy now, ladies?"

"Yeah, Zahra. Nice job! Now you have to try the V2," Stella yelled at her, with a laugh.

Zahra rolled her eyes at her. "You have to help me get off this boulder first. Are you going to bring the crash pad around for the downclimb?"

Even Shabina was beaming, although she sobered almost immediately. "I guess that leaves me. Are you all certain you aren't tired and want to have lunch? When Zahra comes down, we can ask her. She's always hungry." There was a hopeful note in her voice, but Vienna could see as she studied her expression that when she looked at the boulder, there was longing there as well.

"What is it, Shabina? I know you want to climb," Vienna said softly, sitting down beside her, making a pretense of holding her arms out for Shabina to massage. "You know I'm not going to say anything. None of us would anyway. We all have reasons to be afraid of something. If you didn't want to climb, we'd all understand, but it's clear that you want to. Maybe talking it out would help."

Shabina looked at the boulder Zahra had climbed and then around her at the other boulders. "I live in Knightly, where there is some of the best bouldering in the world. My best friends love to boulder, and I enjoy spending time with them more than I like to do anything else. So, yes, I want to learn to climb, but every time I look at a boulder, I get this really ugly feeling in the pit of my stomach. It takes a while to overcome it. A lot of deep breathing and meditation."

A shadow moved over the two of them and Vienna saw Shabina flinch and pull into herself, her head turning quickly and her hands going up into a defensive position. Vienna's instincts were to shield her even though she knew it was Stella and Harlow coming up behind them. The women had water bottles and the trail bars Shabina had made.

"A quick pick-me-up," Harlow said, leaning over Vienna's shoulder to hand them the goods. "Private convo, Shabina, or can any of us join? No hard feelings either way."

Shabina hesitated and then shrugged. "It's all right. It's silly really, always fighting bad memories. Stella has bad memories, and she functions fine every day. She runs a beautiful resort and a fishing camp. I'm sure all of you have bad memories," she added as Zahra flung herself on the crash pad beside Vienna.

Zahra glanced at Harlow but didn't say anything, only nodded. Raine joined them, sitting with her back against the rock, facing them. Vienna knew in Raine's job working for the government, the people around her were often vetted. Raine knew more about them than they probably knew about themselves, but she was very good at keeping confidences. That knowledge often set her apart, and Vienna sometimes felt bad for her. Often, Raine could look lonely.

"It doesn't matter what bad memories any of us have," Vienna said. "Anything can trigger someone. You can't compare like that, Shabina. None of us can. I don't think I'd ever had a panic attack, but squishing myself in a hole in the closet with those two men after me definitely gave me one. I remembered all kinds of things from my childhood."

Stella reached out and rubbed Shabina's arm. "I had so many panic attacks it's a wonder Sam wanted anything to do with me. I had them right in front of him. I'd wake up fighting, not able to breathe. It was so awful. He's so calm all the time and I was just one giant mess."

Shabina gave them one of her sweet smiles. "I love living where I do. It's so peaceful. My café makes me happy. I love to cook, and most of my customers are so sweet. There's only one or two I can't seem to win over with food. I've worked hard to find balance in my life and be on my own. I go out in the forest and bird-watch. I hike the trails. Mountain bike. There's so much I can do, but then we do this . . ." She trailed off and looked at the boulder as if it were the very devil. "It gets to me every time."

"Babe," Vienna said softly. "You don't have to climb. No one expects you to do anything upsetting to you. We love your company, but if just being around boulders is uncomfortable, we can skip it. You should have told us."

"No. That's the point, Vienna. I want to get over it. I had to work hard to learn to be out on my own. To be in a house alone even with the dogs. I don't want to be afraid. I want to keep getting stronger. I don't want to be afraid to take risks. Things others do and don't even think twice about doing scare me. I'm always telling myself, just take baby steps."

Shabina always seemed so completely self-possessed. She owned and ran the café by herself. She hiked the forest, bird-watching alone. That was no small feat. The trails she went on were often game trails and one could easily get turned around, but she had confidence in her ability to make her way home. It was true, she always took her dogs with her, but Vienna didn't think much about that. Most of the time, the others did as well.

"I had a very bad experience when I was fifteen. As you know, my father owns a company that is called on when oil well fires need to be put out. Mom and I always traveled with him. I was kidnapped and held for ransom." She spoke very matter-of-factly, but she twisted her fingers together in her lap tightly. "My father paid and the ransom was delivered, but they didn't release me. To make a long story short, I was moved around a lot and they weren't nice people. I began to think I was never going to get away from them. Finally, I took matters into my own hands and escaped. Unfortunately, they caught up with me when I was climbing up a cliff face. They were pretty sadistic men and made me climb it over and over. I have some ugly scars from that day."

Vienna was stunned. Shabina had never said a word to her about having such a horrific experience in all the times they'd gone bouldering and encouraged her to climb with them. She felt so ashamed of herself for trying to get Shabina to boulder. Her eyes met Raine's. Raine knew. Raine hadn't broken Shabina's confidence, but then she never did. It was a wonder she never shattered under the weight of all of their secrets.

"Honey." Vienna had to swallow the lump in her throat. "You should have told us how bouldering triggers those memories. It's understandable."

Shabina shook her head. "I *want* to boulder. I need to do this for myself. I really do. It's just that it's really difficult and I talk myself out of it. You all have to help me not do that."

Vienna wasn't certain she could be the one to make Shabina face her demons. She hoped one of her friends was stronger than she was.

"Then let's get this done, Shabina," Raine said decisively. "You've got this. Vienna can spot you. You know she's the best and won't let anything happen to you. We'll help you every step of the way with beta."

Shabina looked at the boulder and then at Raine. She

smiled her serene smile. "I knew it would be you, Raine. Thank you for understanding. I have to do this for me. I don't want to spend my entire life afraid. I need all of you to help me take this next step."

Vienna stood and held out her hand to pull Shabina to her feet. Shabina's family was wealthy. She would have had the best of counselors. If she said this was what she needed to do to keep moving forward, then they were one hundred percent behind her.

"This is a great boulder with an easy climb for you to start with, Shabina," Stella said, indicating the one they had warmed up on. It was overhang but with large juggy holds on it. Stella was sure Shabina would have success on it.

Shabina stared at it with great trepidation and then shook her head and indicated a tall boulder. "Maybe that one."

Vienna's breath caught in her throat. The boulder Shabina had gestured toward would be considered a "highball." In a way, she understood. Shabina was used to rope climbing. She didn't boulder or use crash pads, and the gymnastic movements that were used on overhang climbs weren't as familiar to her. The other boulder was a tall slab with pretty good holds and feet, but it wouldn't be a clean fall if you came off the boulder.

"Just try this one, honey," Stella encouraged. "It has fewer moves and is a way safer fall if you come off. You can top out easily."

Shabina watched them place the two crash pads beneath the overhung boulder before she reached up, stretching to reach the large holds to pull her body up. She found a foothold with her left foot, missed with her right and then found a little ledge to put it on.

"Keep your hips toward the wall and keep lots of body tension so you don't swing out," Vienna called out. "Now get your heel on that hold right and reach up for the jug."

Vienna stayed close, as did Harlow and Stella. The others

surrounded the boulder, calling out encouragement to Shabina. As Shabina went to heel hook the hold Vienna suggested, her left foot popped off and she was now hanging from the jugs with her feet dangling in the open air. Since the boulder was fairly short, her feet were only dangling a couple of feet from the crash pad. However, Shabina seemed to be unaware of this fact. She started to panic with real fear.

"I need to come down. I need to come down."

"Okay, we got you. Just drop," Vienna said, keeping her voice very calm.

Instead of dropping, Shabina started to panic more and kicked her feet about with a little scream. She was clearly terrified to drop.

Immediately the girls moved in closer and Vienna grabbed her waist with her hands. "We've totally got you. Calm down, we've got you. Just drop, honey. Let go."

"No. I can't. Vienna. I'm going to fall." Shabina flailed her feet around even more, panic making her voice high-pitched.

Vienna tightened her hands on Shabina's waist, casting a quelling glance over her shoulder at the other women, who were trying not to laugh. "Babe. Let go. You have to trust me. I'm not going to let anything happen to you."

With a little scream of fear, Shabina opened the death-grip she had on the rock and dropped the less than two feet to the crash pads, guided by Vienna's hands. Shabina looked shocked when she dropped softly to the ground only a couple feet. The fear melted to laughter. "I was only that high off the ground? I was so terrified. I guess I don't like falling."

"That wasn't falling, that's just letting go. You can practice that. Next time look where your crash pad is and try to fall softly with your knees slightly bent. You ready for another try? We'll help guide your hips if you come down again," Vienna said. "This is actually better for you than topping out. Like practicing a downclimb. The more you come off the rock and learn to trust the pads and your spotter, the more confidence you'll have."

"I guess so," Shabina said, still a little reluctant.

It took a lot of encouragement and Shabina coming off the rock several more times, but each time she managed her fear a little bit better and they could see a change come over her. Once she wasn't as afraid to fall, she was more focused on the climbing part of it. She was soon at the top of the boulder with a smile on her face, and they all cheered, proud of her that she'd accomplished so much.

THEIR NEXT DESTINATION was the Pearl Boulder. They made their way up to the beautiful boulder, delighted to have it to themselves. The Pearl sat right off the trail in the sunshine. The south face contained the classic route for which the rock was named, along with the V3 Clam Bumper, which went up to the right of Pearl. It was easier than the classic line, but in some ways a little more intimidating as it was slightly taller and the landing for the Pearl was better. The Pearl was Stella's current project, and since it was also her bridal shower, they had all agreed that she should get on it after they had warmed up.

The crash pads were carefully placed in the potential landing zone as Stella looked at the problem, mentally climbing each move and visualizing herself getting past the crux with the new beta Raine had recommended she try out. They stood back as she studied the rock.

Raine stood next to her and they discussed the alternative beta. Instead of matching on the nice rail midway of the route, she would use a small crimp to the left and then get her left foot up high on a small foothold. Then she should be able to lock off and pull herself up to the good hold. Stella wasn't particularly tall, where height sometimes helped on rock, but she was strong and her fingers could slip into cracks and onto small ledges and hold.

Stella pulled on her climbing shoes, attached her chalk bag to her waist and coated her hands in the chalky powder that would help keep her hands dry and create more friction while she climbed. She reached up, felt the textured rock, her left hand on the high thin crimp and her right on the much better side pull. It was warmer than she would have liked. She hoped they hadn't let it bake in the sun too long while they warmed up. Colder conditions would make it easier, but it still felt good to feel the familiar holds, and she wanted to try it. She took a deep breath and then in-stepped her left leg on a small foot and high-stepped on a small foot with her right. She rocked her body weight over the high foot, and then stood up to reach the good ledge with her left hand.

Vienna moved closer to her with arms outstretched to spot her. If Stella came off the rock, the hope was to guide her to the crash pad below and cushion her fall. Vienna was always in awe of the way Stella climbed with such confidence, her posture perfect. Climbing posture was not the same as posture everyone was constantly reminded about outside of climbing, and Vienna admired and aspired to climb with the posture Stella had when she moved up a rock surface.

Stella fought the urge to match her left hand on the good hold and searched for the crimp out left. She found it and then looked for a good foot left. She settled for the only slippery tiny foot that was in the area. This must be the foot she needed. With confidence, she committed to the foot. Her hips tight to the wall, she locked off the hold to the left, pulling her body in close as she flagged her right foot under her. The flag allowed her to counterbalance her weight and cross her right hand to the good hold directly above her. She grasped the hold, and while she felt instant relief with the knowledge she had done the hard part and the send was likely, she made sure not to relax and kept pressure through her body as she finished the last couple moves out right to top out. Everyone cheered, and Stella felt the glow of accomplishment that came with climbing a boulder she'd really wanted to experience. She was also very shocked that she'd managed to send it first go. She hadn't expected that at all.

Raine stepped up next and shook out her arms and hands before feeling the start holds. They felt smaller than they looked when Stella was on them, but they were nicer on her hands than she expected. The girls were used to climbing at the Buttermilks in Knightly, with the sharp granite boulders, so this sandstone felt pretty friendly on their fingers. Raine tried the first few moves, getting a feel for the high step and coming off a few attempts. She surprised herself by sticking the larger ledge on her fourth go, and Stella yelled at her to reach for the crimp out left.

"You're going to have to really lock off on the crimp since you're shorter than me. Get your left foot up. Yes. That's it. Trust the foot. It's good. Now flag under and cross to the jug."

Raine tried to execute the beta, locking off her left hand as she flagged her right foot under her to make the cross, but instead of smoothly grabbing the big hold, she peeled off the wall from her body weight swinging out. She felt Vienna's hands guide her hips as she landed on the crash pad. She felt the rush of excitement knowing how close she was to a good hold. It would be easy from there to top out.

"You were so close, Raine!" Stella encouraged.

The others added their voices.

In the end, try as hard as she might, Raine couldn't complete the climb. She came off the rock over and over. They had their biking to do, and she didn't want them to miss that, so she promised the boulder she'd be back another day.

CHAPTER TEN

~~~~~~

Stella had taken up mountain biking much earlier than the rest of them. She'd worked to convince them that it was a fun way to see the interior of the forest trails. Shabina ended up the first of her friends to jump on board. She biked with Stella regularly and added her voice to Stella's until Vienna and Harlow joined them on their excursions. Raine and Zahra reluctantly became mountain bikers as well. Zahra claimed she had to pedal twice as much because of her shorter legs in order to keep up with them. Raine said they were all crazy and she'd rather run behind the bikes, but she bought a mountain bike and went with them.

They drove to the Blue Diamond overnight parking lot. Vienna had never seen the truck Rainier and Zale rented. He'd sent her pictures of it and the license plate, so she shared them with her friends. They were early enough that they found it almost immediately. She found the keys hidden exactly where he had told her they would be. Collecting them, she put them in her pack and indicated she was ready to go. She wasn't going to inspect the interior now. She wanted to have fun with her friends, not worry about Zale. There was nothing she could do for him if he was injured. She had no idea where he was, and she couldn't text him. He'd been adamant about not contacting him.

They unloaded their bikes and ate a leisurely lunch at the

picnic tables. Vienna was shocked to see Benny Dobsin leading a group of mountain bikers onto the trail they had planned on taking into the desert. He seemed to be very familiar with it and rode as if born on a bike. He flashed by so fast, it took a moment to actually recognize him. The others were talking so animatedly about climbing she didn't interrupt them to tell them she'd recognized him.

Stella led the way on the single-file trail through the dirt and rock. She'd mapped out the trail she'd wanted to take ahead of time. She had told Vienna her hope was to see one of the desert tortoises, although she knew the chances of that happening were very slim. She'd chosen a trail through the Joshua tree forests where wild burros grazed. Even if she never caught a glimpse of Nevada's official state reptile, she wanted to see the burros she knew were in the desert in abundance.

Joshua trees normally had a single thick trunk and grew three to nine feet tall before branching out. The branches ended in clusters of white flowers and spiky leaves. Vienna thought the trees made the desert appear more like an alien landscape. She had read a great deal about them and knew how important they were to the environment of the desert. The Joshua wasn't an actual tree but a yucca plant, or member of the asparagus family and close relative to the agave, the plant used to make tequila.

Mountain ranges rose up in vibrant shades of earth and jewel tones. In the distance, a mountain rising on one side of them was layered with various colors of earth, clearly portraying the ages of the rise and fall of earthquakes and flash floods. Sandstone, ancient and jagged, was carved with petroglyphs. Canyons showing evidence of rapidly moving water filled the sides far above their heads. Shocking pools of water were in the middle of nowhere, tiny oases that instantly became treasures.

Vienna glanced over her shoulder quickly to make certain Raine was keeping up. Raine was in the best of shape.

She did martial arts. She ran daily—and Vienna knew Raine despised running but she still did it to stay in shape. Still, she really thought riding a bike was insane. She told Vienna that for some reason, it hurt worse than any other sport she did. She was behind Zahra, but some distance back. Zahra, either by design or because she was having trouble keeping the pace, had dropped back also. Vienna was certain she had fallen behind in order to stay close to Raine. Zahra might complain, but she never seemed to really have trouble in any sport she chose to participate in. She was a natural athlete.

Cholla cactus was in abundance, and Vienna turned her attention to the narrow trail to avoid any contact with the spines. She might admire the plant and even think the cactus was beautiful, especially in bloom, but she wanted no part of the spines penetrating her skin. Many of the plants were a little too close for comfort on the narrow trail.

There were large rocks close to the trail, as well as a few on it, so if you were pedaling fast, you had to swing around to avoid them quickly. That meant taking care not to encounter a cholla cactus when you chose which side to ride around. Vienna hoped Raine was concentrating, otherwise either Harlow or she would be picking spines out of Raine's ankles or legs and it would hurt like hell.

Suddenly, Stella, who had been bent low over her handlebars, was sitting up straighter, slowing the pace and signaling toward their right side. "Over there. Look over there. Finally." She spoke in a hushed tone that wasn't exactly quiet and she stopped moving completely, forcing everyone behind her to do the same.

Vienna found herself smiling. This was Stella's bridal shower. It was unusual and exactly what she wanted. She didn't need gifts. She wanted adventures with her friends, and they were going down her list, checking all the boxes. Vienna was grateful they had managed to run across a small herd of wild burros.

They all pulled out their cell phones in order to take

pictures. Harlow was an excellent photographer. So much so that she sold her landscapes in art galleries. She had first made a name for herself with a few of her pottery pieces, but her love of photography had won out and she began almost exclusively dedicating herself to that art. She rarely took pictures of human beings, other than the six of them when they were together. She included Sam. She used to include Denver and Bruce. Denver had proven to be a serial killer, and now Zahra had indicated that she was finished waiting for Bruce. Generally, Zahra meant what she said.

They knew to stay completely away from the burros, not interact with or feed them. The burros were wild and should be treated as such, but they all had their phones out, staying on the trail a good distance away. Only Harlow stepped off the narrow bike path and moved around the Joshua trees and few cholla cactuses to get a better angle. She was careful not to approach the small group of burros, nor did she want to startle them, but she took many pictures from various angles.

"Don't worry, Stella. I got some great shots for you," she assured, returning to the trail. "I'll send them to everyone."

"The burros were on my wish list," Stella said. "The desert has its own beauty. My first love is always going to be the Eastern Sierras, but I can definitely see the beauty here."

Vienna could see it as well. "The trips we took to Joshua Tree to see the night blooms when Harlow wanted to photograph the Joshua trees and then again in the desert during the super bloom were incredible."

"We'll have to add another trip to Red Rock in March," Harlow said. "The flowers will be out in force here. We can camp."

"Camp?" Zahra's tone was an instant protest. "No, Harlow. If you're going to take really good pictures with your equipment, you need a clean environment. I'll find an Airbnb close. Something with all the amenities. Everything you'll need. And remember, if we want Raine to come, she needs access to the internet. She has to have WiFi. I'll get right on that. We should book in advance. Stella will help me look."

"I might not," Stella said. "I'm getting married."

Zahra rolled her eyes. "Of course you will. Marriage isn't going to change things in the least. Sam is already around all the time. He doesn't mind you going on trips with us."

"What if I get pregnant or have a baby?" Stella challenged.

Zahra went very still. "You're not . . ."

"No, but it could happen . . . someday. Not right away," she assured as they all stared at her, a little in shock.

"I didn't think in terms of a baby," Vienna admitted. "I suppose that would be a natural outcome." Would Zale want a family? They hadn't really discussed that. There were many things they hadn't discussed. She was a nurse. She knew the entire biological-clock-ticking concept wasn't a hoax. The older a woman got, the less viable her eggs would become. "Do you want to have children, Stella?"

"I believe I do—with Sam. If it never happens for us, I'll always be happy and satisfied. I think Sam will be as well. He says he will and you know Sam, he doesn't say things he doesn't mean," Stella said with total confidence.

Vienna knew that confidence came from knowing Sam for over two years. Sam was steady, a man she had always been able to count on. Vienna didn't really know Zale, yet she was committing to a life with him. What was wrong with her that she hadn't sat down with him and really talked about the important things, like children?

Stella began to laugh. "You're all looking at me as if I've grown two heads. If I have a baby, that child will grow up camping, hiking and climbing. He or she will love animals. For heaven's sake, the poor thing will have Sam and me for parents. It will spend its early years being lugged around in a front- or backpack when we're climbing or hiking."

"Fine, have a baby, Stella," Zahra said. "I'm sure I'll be an amazing aunt. Be certain you have a girl. She's going to *love* spas and having her fingernails painted. I can assure you of that."

Vienna laughed with the others. She was positive if Stella had a boy, Zahra would paint his toenails as well and introduce him to the spa life early. Stella wouldn't care and neither would Sam. They'd just shake their heads and teach their child the skills needed for survival in the world and to see the beauty of the wilderness.

"Just to point out," Zahra added, "we'll need an Airbnb at first, at least while you're pregnant. Do you have any idea how many times you have to go to the bathroom?"

Another round of laughter had Vienna feeling so much better. Friends and the outdoors could push away the ugliness of the threats made. She loved these women.

"You're always so practical, Zahra," Stella teased.

"Let's get moving," Shabina said, glancing at her watch. "We don't want to be out here too late. We still have to pick up Zale's truck in the lot, clean it and get it back to the rental place before we can have dinner. We've got a few more miles on this trail to go."

Vienna didn't want to go back to thinking about cleaning Zale's truck, but she took comfort in the thought that their injuries couldn't be that bad if he was returning the vehicle to the rental agency. He wouldn't ask her to take it back if the truck was riddled with bullet holes or had massive amounts of blood on the seats.

They started out again on the single-file trail, stopping occasionally to take pictures of the various plants and rock formations along the way. They startled a few jackrabbits, but for the most part, they didn't see any other wildlife. Stella didn't get her wish to see the elusive tortoise, not that any of them really thought that was a possibility.

Vienna was tired but happy by the time they were back at the 4Runner. Observing all the others as she normally did, she could see the ride had taken a toll on Raine. That always surprised her. Raine was very fit, but the rigors of mountain biking were on a different set of muscles that Raine didn't use as often and were harder for her. She never complained, but Vienna could see the weariness on her face. She moved slower as she locked her bike in the rack.

"I'm glad we have that hot tub," Vienna said. "I'm going to be sore after all the riding. I haven't gone out on a real ride for a long time. For once, Zahra, I'm not going to complain one bit about staying at an Airbnb instead of camping."

"I'm going to agree," Harlow said. "I may skip dinner and just soak in the hot tub all night."

"Skip one of Shabina's dinners?" Zahra raised an eyebrow.

Harlow relented immediately. "I lost my mind for a minute. I'm a little tired after climbing and then biking, but the reminder was all I needed. I'm definitely eating."

Shabina laughed. "I'm really not that great of a cook. Honestly, you'd think you would all starve without me."

They exchanged looks all around. "We probably would," Vienna answered. "Or we'd eat really bad food."

"Not junk food," Harlow said hastily when Shabina gave them her raised eyebrow.

"Junk food." Raine was honest. "We'd totally eat junk food. Zahra has junk food in her backpack right now."

"I do *not*." Zahra was indignant. "Have you been snooping in my backpack, Raine?" She narrowed her eyes suspiciously.

"I was starving for chocolate. You always have a chocolate bar in your pack."

"You took my chocolate bar?" Zahra demanded.

"Only the one with peanuts. I left the other one for you." Raine sounded pious.

"Zahra, you know better than to have any kind of food in your backpack like that," Stella reprimanded. "You don't carry it when we're camping, do you? Bears can smell that stuff miles away. They'll come into our campsite and go right into your tent."

Zahra gave a little huff of annoyance. "We were going into the desert, not the forest. There weren't going to be any bears around, and I knew I could take all the chocolate I wanted to eat as long as I have cold packs, which I do." Her eyebrows came together again as she narrowed her eyes at Raine. "Unless there was more than one thief." She looked around at the others. "Was there?"

Vienna looked up at the sky, striving for innocence. The sun had set, and the sky was still streaked with various colors but was on the darker side of purple. "I will admit, I did find the craving for chocolate overwhelming. The scent was wafting from your backpack and I couldn't stop myself from peeking in to see what you brought with you. You had a salted caramel chocolate bar, which you know is my very favorite. I'll replace it . . . when we get to the store."

Zahra put her hands on her hips and turned to face all of them. It was impossible for her to look intimidating with her little pixie face, dark-winged brows and mobile mouth. "Did *all* of you find the chocolate?"

"Someone had to save you from yourself," Shabina said. "Seriously, Zahra, if you ate all that chocolate, you'd be in a coma and you know it. You'd be lying on the ground right now moaning and asking us to put you out of your misery. For the next week you'd be looking for imaginary blemishes on your face."

"Not imaginary," Zahra protested. "I always break out if I eat chocolate."

"And you get headaches," Stella pointed out. "Migraines. You aren't supposed to eat chocolate."

"Well . . ." Zahra hedged. "The doctor didn't prove that yet. He mentioned caffeine might be a cause. I can't imagine he meant chocolate. I read about how dark chocolate is good for you." Her lips formed a pout. "Did you eat all of it?"

"No. We left you one candy bar," Vienna said. "One. You need to be careful. I'm going to start checking to make sure you're not diabetic."

"Didn't you read the article on how good dark chocolate is for you?" Zahra reiterated, digging into her backpack for the last candy bar.

"In moderation. I'm not sure you know what that means," Vienna said. "Food, chocolate, booze. When you go out, you dance all night." If Sam wasn't available, Zahra was always the sober driver. She loved good food, but she ate slowly and very small portions. She wouldn't have eaten more than one candy bar and most likely brought the rest to share. Zahra was one of the most generous people Vienna had ever met, but it was impossible not to want to tease her. Her face was too expressive and her accent always became more pronounced as she feigned annoyance with them.

"I guess I've stalled enough," Vienna said. "I'm going to take a look at the truck Zale and Rainier rented to see what kind of shape it's in. Hopefully, it isn't riddled with bullet holes and the seat cushions aren't covered in blood. I'm not good at welding, but, Harlow, you are, aren't you? You can do body work and then paint over any bullet holes we find."

"I'll get right on that." Harlow tried cracking her knuckles but no sound emerged. Everyone laughed when she shook her hands. "I never could do that."

"It's gross anyway," Zahra said. "The sound gives me the creeps." She gave a little shudder just to prove her point.

"I'll go with you," Shabina volunteered as Vienna set off toward the truck Zale had left behind. Raine accompanied them, leaving the others to finishing packing the gear in Stella's 4Runner.

The truck was a Ford Ranger XLT SuperCrew. Vienna wasn't as into cars and trucks as Raine was, so she wasn't surprised when Raine whistled her approval. "They knew what they were looking for when they rented this baby. Has speed if they need it, can hit the desert with four-wheel drive, and is rugged as hell. Handles well. They were ready if anyone came after them."

"Apparently, someone did come after them *again*," Vienna

said. "This was the third time. Maybe more than that. I wish they'd just gotten out."

"Third time?" Shabina asked.

Vienna nodded. "The first time I knew about, they'd been attacked by three men with knives in the parking lot outside of the hotel. They nearly got Rainier in the heart, came out of the bushes. He was stabbed, but not deep. Zale deflected the knife. Both of them had cuts. They came to my room and I fixed them up."

Shabina shook her head. "That wasn't enough for them to know their cover was blown?"

Raine sighed. "These men don't just walk away. Once they start down a path, they keep going until the job is done."

"Or until they're dead," Shabina pointed out. "When were they attacked again, Vienna?"

"On the floor when they went gambling in their disguises. Rainier played the part of an elderly gentleman and Zale was his personal protector. A waitress brought him a drink. The drink was poisoned. Before Rainier could drink it, a woman took it out of his hand and drank it. She went down fast and hard. Security got to the glass before Zale could."

"And they still didn't leave," Raine said.

"Nope. They kept up their roles." Vienna walked around the truck, inspecting the outside of it, checking for any bullet holes, dents or scrapes that would indicate the vehicle had been involved in an altercation.

"And they think women are in need of keepers," Shabina said. "Men don't have brains to tell them enough is enough."

"It looks as if the outside of the truck is just fine," Vienna said. "Did either of you see anything? The windows look good. No cracks. The paint is fine. No scrapes. No dents. No one has even keyed it."

Vienna took a deep breath and unlocked the driver's door and then reached in to unlock all the doors. Sinking her teeth into her lower lip, she looked on the driver's seat and backrest for signs of blood. Sure enough, there were small drops in several places, smears where Zale or Rainier had hastily wiped the leather down before they got out of the truck.

Shabina inspected the passenger seat. She looked stricken. "There's quite a bit of blood on the floor mat and side of the door, Vienna. Some on the backrest, but not nearly as much."

"None back here," Raine reported. "It's clean back here. We need to wipe the entire truck down to make certain there are no prints in it. We have to remove all traces of their blood. All of it. It isn't easy to get rid of blood. Bleach doesn't cut it like you think it would. I brought a small spray bottle with me that should do the trick, depending on how much they left behind."

Shabina's brows drew together. "Raine, really? You brought a small spray bottle of something that would remove blood? Who thinks of that? Why would you even consider we might need it?"

Raine shrugged. "We're renting an Airbnb and we want our deposit back, right? I believe in being prepared. Someone is always getting hurt. Bloodstains are difficult to get out of anything, so I just mix up the miracle bottle and put it in my pack."

"I would never have thought of that in a million years." Shabina clearly admired her ingenuity. "There is a lot of blood on this side, Raine. I think Rainier might have been really injured."

"Let me take a look," Raine said.

Vienna rounded the truck to inspect the open door with Raine. Night was falling fast, and with it the light was waning. Diminishing light meant they would have to work fast. They didn't want to draw attention to the fact that they were cleaning the truck right there in the overnight parking lot.

"Do you need help?" Harlow asked as she, Stella and Zahra walked over.

"You could start wiping down the inside of the back windows. You'll need to wear gloves and do a very thorough job," Vienna said. "The inside of the doors and door handles have to be wiped down, as well as the top liner. Once that's done, finish the seats."

"I can help too," Zahra said, pulling on gloves.

"Once we do inside, shouldn't we do the outside at a car wash?" Stella asked. "We could scrub the outside of the truck and the windows."

"That's not a bad idea," Raine said. "As long as we're certain we remove all prints. They will have worn gloves and probably different prints, but still, we can't take chances."

"Does anyone have rags?" Shabina asked. "I didn't think to bring anything like that."

"I always travel light when we go climbing," Stella admitted. "So, not in my backpack, but I always carry rags and towels in the 4Runner. After Bailey was attacked, I never want to be without a medical kit for the dog or extra blankets, towels or rags."

Vienna couldn't help but remember the terrible night Stella's Airedale, Bailey, had been stabbed repeatedly by the serial killer and Stella and one of the sheriff's deputies had made the hour-long run down the mountain to Knightly to the vet's office. It had been a very long night with all of their friends gathered together, keeping a vigil as the vet performed emergency surgery on Stella's dog.

Stella jogged over to her 4Runner and pulled open the front passenger door. Between the seats was a cargo hold where she'd stored a bundle of rags. Vienna could see, although she was good about bringing medical equipment, she needed to step up her game when it came to other practical items, especially if she was going to be in a committed relationship with Zale.

Stella handed out the rags, and Raine carefully saturated part of a cloth with the contents from her spray bottle and handed it to Vienna. She did the same with another cloth and gave it to Shabina for the backrest of the passenger side. Raine began to work on the passenger door.

Vienna went around to the driver's side and meticulously went over the seat and backrest, careful to get every smear and drop of blood. She got down in the creases and wiped the sides of the seat as well. She didn't see anything on the floor mat, but she wiped it clean and then went around to get more of the cleaning product before she started on the inside of the door.

It took some time with all of the women working to wipe the entire truck clean. It wasn't easy to pronounce it finished. Each of them kept going back over and over to make certain they had gotten every spot. No one wanted to mess up and be responsible for leaving Zale and Rainier in a possible compromising situation. In the end, Raine was the one to call it.

"I'll follow you to the rental agency," Stella said. "It's actually on the way to the Airbnb. We won't have to backtrack at all. I think it will be faster to just follow behind you."

"I'll ride with you, Vienna," Raine said. "That will give them more room in the 4Runner."

"Are you kidding, Raine? You're the smallest." Harlow laughed. "Well, besides Zahra. And she's, um, curvier."

Zahra rolled her eyes. "My hips are bigger. Just say it. And my butt."

"Are you making fun of my butt?" Raine demanded.

"What butt?" they all asked simultaneously and then burst out laughing.

Raine craned her neck as if she could see. "Maybe that's why I despise riding a bike so much. No padding."

"Nope, none," Vienna confirmed. "You have to have the fastest metabolism in town. I've seen you put away an entire pizza by yourself."

Zahra groaned. "Don't remind me. She does that. She doesn't even notice either. I *love* food. She barely notices food. I have to chew slowly and savor, and she *works* while she eats. She doesn't pay attention to her food. That's so wrong of you, Raine."

"I pay attention to what I drink," Raine said. "Especially Moscow mules."

"The three times a year you actually have a drink," Stella pointed out.

Another round of laughter went up. Vienna slipped into the driver's seat of the truck. Raine and Shabina both got in the truck with her to give the others more room in the 4Runner at least as far as the rental agency.

The engine turned over immediately as if eager to go. There was no having to warm it up or let it run, although she waited to make sure Stella and the others were good to go in their vehicle before she pulled out of the lot onto the road to head back toward Vegas and the rental agency.

Partway down the road, the headlights flickered for a moment. A tingle of awareness went down her spine, that first unpleasant warning she sometimes got when her radar went off that something wasn't right. She flexed her fingers on the steering wheel and breathed evenly, checking the instruments. Everything *seemed* fine.

"Did you notice the headlights?" She threw the question out to both women because that nagging little red flag wouldn't go away now that it had waved at her.

Nothing else happened as she drove down the road, and she should have dismissed that one little flicker, but instead, little knots began to tighten in her belly.

"I noticed it," Shabina said.

"Me too," Raine chimed in.

"A short?" Vienna asked. No way was it a short. Zale would have mentioned if there was a short in the headlights. She didn't believe that for a minute. It hadn't happened again, so why was her uneasiness increasing instead of decreasing?

Raine leaned forward as if peering at the road in front of her. "Are the headlights dimmer?"

Vienna couldn't honestly say. She was almost afraid to touch the high beams. She kept up her even breathing, staying strictly to the speed limit if a little under. Because Stella was behind her and luckily no other cars had come up on them, she was even traveling below the speed limit for the most part. Once on the main highway, she knew she would have to decide to either pull over and have the truck towed, just on her intuition that something was wrong, or drive at full speed. If she did that, she didn't want the others in the car with her.

"I don't know. I just have a bad feeling. Maybe I should pull over and have the two of you ride with Stella."

"No." Shabina was firm. "If you think something is wrong, we pull over and all of us get out, not just the two of us. We're in this together."

"I'm most likely paranoid after all the stories of dead bodies in the desert and seeing Zale and Rainier injured and then the blood in the truck."

"You don't get spooked," Raine said calmly. "I think the lights are dimmer. How is the truck handling?"

"Sluggish. That's the other thing. You said the truck handled so well. This feels like a big slug. It feels almost as if it's fighting me every little bend we go around. We're coming up on the first really big turn." She slowed even more.

"Is it the tires? Maybe the tire pressure is too low," Shabina said. "Can't that be a factor? I don't really know anything about cars, but I've heard Stella and Raine talk about tire pressure."

Vienna considered that for a moment. Could the tires be so low that the truck wasn't responding? Wouldn't she have noticed? Raine would have. Stella would have. And no, this had a different feel to it. Something else, then. Her radar was screaming now. Something was very, very wrong. She didn't want to go into the turn that was coming up fast.

She slowed more—or tried to. Her foot went all the way to the floor. Immediately, she dropped her hand to the emergency brake.

"Oh, hell no," she said softly. "Not both." There was no

way to make the turn. She wasn't going that fast, but still too fast for the turn. She could take both lanes, but naturally, after no car had been anywhere close, bright lights were sweeping around the turn. "We're going off-road. We're not taking a chance of hitting someone."

Raine had already calmly texted Stella, and Stella pulled over immediately, leaving them to their fate. Shabina didn't make a sound. Vienna fought the steering. It was gone, almost nonexistent. Someone had done a very good job of getting rid of the brakes, the lights and the ability to steer properly. Unless Zale and Rainier were trying to kill her, this truck had been rigged to finish the job of murdering the two agents. It was just her bad luck that she'd been asked to take it to the rental agency for them.

Vienna wasn't certain she could manage to maneuver the truck off the road and onto the dirt and sand. The steering refused to cooperate. For a moment, it looked as if they would plow straight ahead into the oncoming car as it swept around the curve right toward them. Vienna fought the wheel, using every bit of strength she had. She put her arms, shoulders and back into it. The truck plunged off the road, the tires hitting the dirt and rocks. The left side came down on two higher boulders, lifting that side so the truck rocked hard, throwing them back and forth as it settled with a jarring bounce into the sandy, rock-covered soil.

Vienna, heart pounding, switched off the key and sat for a moment, assessing the damage to the other two. Both women were locked tight against their seats, but strangely, none of the airbags had deployed to help lessen the impact.

"Is anyone hurt?"

"I don't know yet," Shabina admitted. "I think I'm in shock."

"Raine?" Vienna insisted on an answer. Raine appeared to be texting again.

"I'm okay. A little shaken. What about you?"

"You're bleeding. You have a cut on your head."

"Do I?" Raine touched her forehead and looked at her fingers when they came away smeared with blood. "It doesn't hurt. I didn't even know I hit my head."

"Damn it, we're going to have to call the police and report this accident," Vienna said.

"Not necessarily," Raine denied. "I'm required to report any accident I get into. I immediately sent the details to my field office, and they'll send their nearest people to take care of it for us. They'll want to process the truck, which means they'll tow it to their site and take care of the rental agency and make it right with Zale's people."

"Are you certain? Zale's people might not like that," Vienna said.

Raine shrugged as she pressed her palm to the cut on her forehead. "I learned a long time ago to let the higher-ups fight it out. I stay out of everything. We were in an accident. Someone sabotaged the truck. I did exactly what I was told and reported it, and I'm waiting for instructions. When they come, we'll follow those instructions."

"You make it sound so simple."

"It is that simple."

The passenger door was flung open and Harlow's frightened face appeared. "Oh my God, is everyone all right? That was so terrifying. Raine. Let me look at you." Harlow looked in the back at Shabina and then at Vienna. "Any broken bones? Concussions? Vienna? Injuries?"

"Shabina hasn't said much." Vienna was worried about her friend.

"I'm really okay. Shaken up. Scared. Someone really wanted Rainier and Zale dead. If they were driving full speed instead of slowly like you were, Vienna, they might not have made it." She sounded as if she was crying.

"I'm getting a reply now. They're on the way. We're to walk away. They're coming with a tow truck and will bring the truck back to their garage. We need to leave now. Don't worry about our fingerprints. Just go."

"Wouldn't this be considered leaving the scene of an accident?" Vienna asked as she unsnapped her seatbelt. She felt unsteady, her insides jarred and still settling into place. She looked over at Raine.

Harlow was wiping the cut with antibiotic wipes to examine how deep it was.

"We have to go now," Raine reiterated. "I don't know how fast they'll get here, or if someone will come along and see us. Harlow, you can do this in the 4Runner." There was a note of anxiety in her usually calm voice.

"Someone will have to help me out," Shabina said. "I'm a little shaken up. Not hurt, but just unsteady."

Zahra and Stella both helped unclip Shabina's seatbelt and once she was out of the truck, wrapped their arms around her and escorted her to the 4Runner. Harlow helped Raine from the passenger side.

"Don't move, Vienna. I'll be right back to help you. I mean it. You're probably in shock. I don't want you falling down and hitting your head on top of everything else." Harlow sounded very authoritative, just as she did at work at the hospital. In her studio or the gallery, she was professional but very soft-spoken and tended to stay in the background.

Vienna didn't want to move anyway. The thought of standing up made her feel sick. If Zale had been driving, he would have been going much faster—probably. Unless he had noticed that first little flicker of the headlights. Would he have? He was wounded. Both men were. She sent up a silent plea to the universe that they were safe.

She put her head down on the steering wheel. This would be her life for the next year or longer if she truly committed to Zale. She would be waiting alone for him, worried sick that he wasn't somewhere wounded, bleeding to death, hunted by men who wanted him dead. It took a strong person to live that kind of life, knowing their partner was in danger but having no idea where they were or when or if they would return.

"Let's go, Vienna."

Harlow's voice startled her. She'd been that deep in thought. She leaned on her friend, assessing the damage to her body as they crossed the uneven ground to the 4Runner. She might have a few bruises later on, but she had no real injuries.

Stella immediately drove away from the wrecked Ford Ranger. Vienna felt very guilty. She'd been told never to do such a thing, and it felt wrong. She glanced at Raine. Harlow was using little butterfly stitches to close the small cut on her forehead.

"Are you okay, Raine?"

"Yes. Whoever is after Zale and Rainier means business. I hope now they'll realize their cover is blown and get out of Vegas. Someone else can take over for them."

Vienna knew Wilder was still undercover in the casino. Was he now completely alone? Had she gotten that name wrong? She hadn't had a chance to ask Zale if Wilder was a part of his team or if it was a coincidence that his name was the same as one Zale had mentioned to her.

"I don't like to think of any of them taking risks," Shabina said. "Why do they do it?"

"There's something in these men that drives them," Raine said. "Just the way we almost need to climb or hike, they need to take on these risks."

Raine sounded a little shaky, but her eyes were clear when she looked at Vienna. A tow truck and two vehicles that looked official passed the 4Runner, heading toward the wreck. That made Vienna feel a little better. At least Raine's people were going to get the evidence out of the way before the police came. She closed her eyes and rested until Stella got them to the Airbnb.

CHAPTER ELEVEN

〰〰〰〰〰〰〰〰〰〰〰〰〰〰〰〰〰〰〰〰〰

Someone's inside the house," Raine warned softly. "At least they opened the front door. Keep talking, all of you. Vienna, put the code in and step back out of the way." She slid a Sig Sauer micro-compact handgun from inside her shirt, where none of her friends had had any idea it had been concealed.

Vienna only recognized the handgun because at one time, she'd taken lessons and considered getting that same gun. She was at the hospital late at night and was called out for emergency surgeries so often that she sometimes felt it would be a good idea to have some protection. In the end, she decided against it. She wanted something a little more solid. She had a bigger hand and wanted to feel the grip in her fist.

Vienna did as Raine said. Raine might have been slight, but she was a force to be reckoned with when she became this serious.

"Should I call the cops?" Vienna whispered as she stepped back.

"I think it's your Zale, but I have to be sure. You stay out here. If anything happens, call the cops and get out of here. Don't try to help." Raine didn't wait for an answer. She went through the door, stepping to one side, making it difficult for Vienna to see her. "I'm armed and I'm a very good shot. If you make one move, I *will* kill you."

Vienna heard that very clearly. Raine sounded as though she meant it, and Vienna had no doubt that she did mean it.

"My name is Zale Vizzini. You met me before briefly when I brought Vienna to Shabina Foster's house a few months ago when all of you were in danger."

"What are you doing here?"

"My partner and I are both wounded. Vienna is a nurse, and as we both require medical attention and can't go to the hospital, we made the decision to come here for her help."

Shabina clapped a hand over her mouth to stifle a sound that threatened to escape. Harlow and Zahra immediately stepped closer to comfort her.

Zale sounded the same, completely in control, but then so did Raine. Vienna was always a bit surprised when quiet Raine suddenly took charge and exhibited very lethal behavior.

Raine stepped back into the doorway. "Vienna? Is this your Zale?"

Vienna had already identified him just by his voice. She nodded. The gun disappeared and Raine stepped aside to allow the others into the house. Vienna went in first, her gaze moving over first Zale, inspecting for damage, and then Rainier. Both looked fit and neither had blood on their clothes, but they would have cleaned themselves up before going out in public. Rainier was no longer playing the part of an older man. He looked to be in his mid to late thirties. There were lines in Zale's face that she wouldn't have noticed if she hadn't known him so well.

"For heaven's sake, Zale. Not again." Vienna didn't know whether to run to him or throw something at his head.

Rainier looked very pale, almost gray. The lines in his face were much more pronounced. He had looked younger the few times she'd seen him without his mask as Wayne Forsyne. Shabina stood uncertainly inside the doorway, leaning against the wall while the other women began to bring in the gear from the 4Runner. Vienna noted that it was unlike her to just stand in one place when there was work to be done. Shabina was usually the first one to volunteer or just dig in. Vienna feared the situation was too overwhelming to her. Harlow immediately went to the master bath to retrieve the large medical kit she'd brought along.

"What are the injuries and who is the worst?" Vienna asked briskly. She refused to run to Zale and throw her arms around him. She felt awkward, not completely certain of the status of their relationship. She knew that was her issue, but what if all the little vibes that last day together and the way things were worded really reflected how Zale felt? She was very aware that men like Zale became restless easily.

"Snowflake, what are you doing way over there?" Zale's voice held that low, dangerous purr. She often wanted to kick him when he used that voice, even though her body reacted to it, but right now, she was grateful that it gave her an excuse to go to him.

Still, she was a nurse and she gave him her professional once-over. "I need to know what's going on with you two."

"No one followed us here," Zale assured, as if that would be her main concern. "We took extra precautions. We were ambushed after we checked out of the Northern Lights. Rainier found a tracker in the luggage. We'd gone over it but we failed to find it the first time around." He began unbuttoning his shirt while he talked to her.

Her breath hitched when she saw the thick bandages across his chest. "You were *shot*? With a bullet? Someone shot you and you're just sitting there like nothing happened?"

"Take a look at Rainier. Mine's a scratch. Rainier took a slug and went down. He's acting all heroic, but he could be in trouble."

Shabina slid down the wall, jamming her knuckles into her mouth and biting down hard. After the revelations she'd given the women earlier, Vienna was worried about her. PTSD was a real problem and could lead to panic attacks and even cause individuals to slip into an alternate reality if things became bad enough.

She glanced at Zahra and indicated Shabina with a slight nod of her head. She couldn't be in two places at one time and needed someone looking after Shabina. Zahra wouldn't leave Shabina's side once she was close to her. Zahra immediately set a backpack down and sat on the floor next to her.

Rainier frowned, watching the interaction with interest. He noted the cut on Raine's forehead and the way Shabina's hands were shaking. Before he could speak, Vienna did.

"I need to take a look at your leg, Rainier."

"It's a through and through. I bandaged it." He sounded gruff. He wasn't looking at her, but his shrewd, assessing gaze kept moving back and forth between Raine and Shabina.

"Nevertheless, since you aren't a doctor . . . You aren't a doctor, are you?" Vienna asked. Who knew what kinds of letters these men had in front of or behind their names? "Don't tell me. I don't even care. I'm going to look at the wound and assess for myself whether or not you need further attention. Do you want to go to one of the bedrooms or do it right here?"

They were in *her* Airbnb, invading *her* space. They'd cut into Stella's bridal shower, and they'd almost gotten Raine, Shabina and her killed just by association. The hell with them dictating to her. She would not be intimidated just because Rainier suddenly turned his intense steel-gray eyes on her. She put her chin up and refused to look away.

"Give up, Rainier. She's got that stubborn look. She isn't going to back down. When she gets that look, you know she'll charge Hell with a bucket of water. Just show her your owie and let her decide whether or not she has to rip your Band-Aid off and start all over." Zale sounded amused.

Rainier's gaze didn't so much as flick toward Zale, but he did sigh a capitulation. "I suppose you feel you have no choice. It is a through and through."

He stood up, a fluid motion in spite of the injury, but she

could see it hurt. His face turned just a little grayer. Obviously, they'd explored the house, because he walked unerringly to one of the bedrooms, opened the door and went right inside.

"Make yourself at home." Vienna couldn't keep the bite of sarcasm out of her voice as she closed the door and leaned against it, keeping the medical kit in front of her with both hands.

She looked around the room, anywhere but at Rainier as he eased the soft jeans over his hips and the pad on his thigh. He sank down onto the bed and actually lay on his stomach, dragging the throw loosely over him so he was partially covered. She appreciated his attempt to be modest on her account.

"The exit hurts like a mother," he admitted. "I couldn't see to take care of it the way I should have and Zale had to keep us covered, so I just slapped antibiotic ointment into it and gauze over it."

She could see that Rainier had covered the wound with a thick pad of gauze. The tear in his flesh was large, raw, the edges ragged and ugly, creating a wide hole in the muscle. Vienna shook her head. "Were you going to ask Zale to sew this up for you?"

"Eventually. I wanted to ensure you women were safe first."

The pain had to be sawing at him, but he was stoic as she gave him a shot of antibiotics and then took her time cleaning and sewing the wound. She was meticulous, making certain the bullet hadn't nicked anything vital. He would be feeling this one for a long time, but he'd recover. He was lucky.

"Were you worried about us returning the truck?"

"I had a bad feeling. When I get bad feelings, I pay attention to them," Rainier said.

"Was that before or after you dropped off the truck?" she asked, more to distract him than for any other reason. He was holding still as she took those small little stitches in the back of his thigh, but she felt the tremors in his body. She'd tried to numb the wound, but she didn't have anything that was really adequate to numb the entire injury. She felt a little as if she were torturing him.

There was a small silence. He wiped his forehead on the pillow. "A while after. It didn't seem as if it would be a big deal to ask you to take the truck back for us. As time went by, I had second thoughts about you going anywhere near that truck. Any of you women going near the truck."

"That's so interesting that you didn't feel any alarm right away." It actually was. "Did you see who shot you?"

"Three of Daniel Wallin's security guards tailed us when we left the hotel. We didn't want them to make their try with civilians around, so Zale, who was driving, led them into the desert. He acted as if he were making a run for it. We didn't want them to shoot into the truck, so we got far enough ahead to get out and acted like we were looking for a place to hide in the boulders out in the desert. There was a narrow passage where they would have had to come at us one at a time. We'd scouted it out a few days earlier as one of the places we might use if necessary."

That fascinated her. She planned ahead for every type of rescue situation she could think of and went over and over it with her crew. She had the gear, knew the terrain, and each member knew exactly what they were responsible for if they were ever in the situation. Apparently, the missions Rainier and Zale planned were similar in that they planned ahead for every contingency.

"What went wrong?" She was nearly finished. A good thing. He was a big man with a lot of muscle, and he needed stitches inside as well as out, just as Zale had on his bicep. She hadn't realized how sore her arms were. She still had to check Zale's injuries and make certain he didn't need to be sewn up.

"A couple of their buddies followed in a second car. They came over the rocks instead of straight at us."

"Five of them?" Vienna straightened wearily and shook

out her arms. Rainier was older than Zale. Not by much, but he was still older and he hadn't slowed down at all. According to Zale, Rainier was used to working alone. It was abundantly clear he was an authority and didn't take orders. He was used to giving them.

"We're alive, Vienna. Zale is alive. That's how the game works."

She gathered up the bloody bandages, dragging everything into a bag and then peeling off her gloves. "That's just it, Rainier. It isn't a game. Zale's asking me to commit my life to his. If he wants that, he can't treat his work as if it's some kind of game, because if you lose, it's permanent, isn't it?" She didn't look at him, she just took her medical kit, the used instruments and the bag of garbage to dispose of properly as she left the room.

The moment she entered the large living room, she felt everyone's eyes on her. Shabina was no longer sitting on the floor. She'd gone into the kitchen with Zahra. Vienna could see them easily through the large, open archways. The equipment had been put away, other than Shabina's, which was sitting against the wall just outside the room Vienna had been treating Rainier in. Zale narrowed his eyes, his gaze jumping to hers, but she ignored him and went straight to the guest bath to wash her hands.

Every single bone in her body ached. She wondered if Raine and Shabina felt the same way. When she emerged, Raine had curled up in one of the more comfortable chairs in the living room, but she didn't have her ever-present computer on her lap, which worried Vienna. She went to her.

"How are you feeling, honey?"

Raine looked up and gave her a wan smile. "My head is killing me. You know I tend to get migraines sometimes, and right now one is pushing at me." She glanced at Stella, who was carrying on an animated conversation with Harlow as they mixed a large salad together. "I'm not going to ruin Stella's bridal party. She never asks for anything."

"You need to go lie down. I know you have medication for that. We have a day tomorrow to do nothing but relax before we go kayaking. If you take care of it now, that gives you plenty of time for it to go away."

"I thought I should eat before I take the meds. They're heavy duty, but I'm feeling sick."

Instant alarm bells went off. "You could have a concussion. We should take you to the hospital as a precaution, Raine."

She glanced over her shoulder. Rainier was back in the room, seated in a chair where he could watch those working in the kitchen as well as Raine, the front entrance and anyone moving around through most of the open floor plan. Both men were listening to her conversation with Raine.

"What happened, Vienna?" Zale demanded. This time he used that low, commanding, no-nonsense purr. He wanted to know, and he expected her to tell him. "Raine is obviously injured. I can see that you're hurt."

"And so is Shabina," Rainier added. "Just like you, she's moving gingerly. And when she came in, she was very distraught. All of you were, but she's very controlled. She acted out of character."

Shabina looked up swiftly from where she was preparing the meal in the Instant Pot. Her eyes met his. Shabina had unusually colored blue eyes. Right now, liquid made them even more royal blue than usual. Her long lashes feathered down, covering the brightness, and she looked down again.

Vienna wanted to strangle Rainier and his cold observations. "Don't think you know us because you read about us in some report," she snapped. She did hurt all over. She was at her limit trying to be nice to the two of them. "Zale, how bad is your wound, and tell me the truth. Don't be stoic, because I'm not in the mood."

"I told you I took care of it, and I did." His eyes narrowed on her. "Snowflake, tell us what happened."

"Whoever tried to kill you kept coming after you. They

rigged your truck," she said tersely, and turned her back on him. "Raine, are you certain you don't need to go to the hospital?"

"No, I don't have a concussion. I wasn't feeling sick until the headache started becoming worse. I have all the signs of one of my migraines. I'll take the meds to stop it. It's just missing out on Shabina's cooking." She gave an exaggerated sigh.

Shabina glanced up with a small smile and continued her prep.

"Rigged the truck how?" Zale persisted.

"No brakes, no steering, lights going out. Pretty much making certain if you were driving the speed limit you were going to get in a nasty accident. We crashed. Fortunately, we weren't going very fast. As it was, we didn't roll the truck. The airbags didn't deploy either. Raine and Shabina were with me. Stella and the others were behind us. We'd alerted them to back off when we realized something was wrong."

There was a long silence. Vienna knew Zale willed her to look at him, but she refused, instead once more examining Raine's face. There was bruising around the cut. "Harlow did a good job with the butterfly stitches."

"Where's the truck?" Zale asked. "We need to have someone take care of it. Your fingerprints are in that truck, Vienna."

"Raine has to report any accident she's in to her people." Vienna refused to turn around. "They told us to get out of there and they'd have the truck towed. We saw the tow truck as we were driving away."

"Her people?" Rainier echoed. "A computer analyst, an independent contractor for the government, has the kind of clout to call in that kind of cleanup crew that fast?" There was total disbelief in his voice.

Vienna did turn. She couldn't push down the flash of temper. "Yes, Rainier. Her people. Zale said someone had to take care of the truck. I presume he meant *your* people. In this case, it was our good luck that when Raine reported she'd been in an accident, *her* people took care of the truck.

If *your* people and *her* people want to sort that out between them and gather the evidence to see who wants you dead, it's all right by me. I just don't want to hear your take-charge voice in our house when we did you favors, and now, you're sitting in our Airbnb and probably expect to eat Shabina's excellent meal."

"Vienna, honey, come here." Zale's voice was gentle.

She felt the burn of tears behind her eyes. She knew she was too tired and her body ached. She was still in mild shock from the accident. She swallowed the lump in her throat and forced herself to look at Zale. Really look at him. That first look always took her breath away. Always. It wasn't that he was so incredibly gorgeous—and to her, he was—it was the way he appeared so invincible. He looked as if he could handle anything, no matter how difficult. Even more than that, it was the look on his face. His expressionless mask disappeared, his cold eyes softened and he looked at her with such raw intensity she didn't know what to do with it. There was just a glimpse. Just a moment, and then it was gone, but in that moment, she felt as if she belonged.

"I'm going to check that wound, Zale." Pride kicked in, mostly because Rainier was watching her and she had to put her anger somewhere. She *was* angry. At Rainier because he was still working in a field he should have gotten out of a long time ago. He was an intelligent man. He didn't need to stay in it unless he was an adrenaline junkie, and what did that say about Zale?

"Snowflake . . ."

She glared at him. "Just don't say anything for a minute. No one talk until I can breathe again. It was terrifying to have Shabina and Raine in the truck with me and know I had no control. It was terrifying to know you and Rainier were wounded. Rainier's side of the truck had far too much blood on it. You may think only you two worry, but all of us do as well."

She caught up the medical kit and stalked over to him,

trying not to breathe him into her lungs. The moment she got close enough to him, Zale reached out and shackled her wrist, gently pulling her between his thighs.

"I have to know if you were injured."

"Just knocked around. A few bruises. I don't have a cut on my head like Raine does." She tugged at his shirt until he obliged and took it off. The wound was lower this time—not his biceps, his actual chest. He was lucky the bullet didn't hit a bone or an artery. She sighed and removed the bandage to take a closer look.

"What about you, Shabina?" Rainier prompted. "Are you injured?"

She glanced up from where she was working in the kitchen. "Nothing significant."

He frowned. "That tells me nothing." There was a distinct warning in his voice.

Vienna paused cleaning Zale's wound and turned slightly to view Rainier. He did sound concerned. She shouldn't be so upset with Rainier simply because he was still working at his chosen profession and she didn't want Zale to make that same choice. That wouldn't be Rainier's fault. She knew she had to come to terms with her emotions. She wasn't the kind of woman to believe a man—or a woman—should have to change to be in a relationship. She'd fallen for Zale because of his character. Rainier was very much like him.

"I didn't hit my head, so no concussion." Shabina was matter-of-fact. The Instant Pot was already on and she had prepared something else to slide into the oven. Vienna couldn't see what it was on the flat tray, but the aromas coming from the kitchen were adding hunger to her already frayed nerves.

"I was thrown around, although the seatbelt did its job. I have quite a bruise across my body where it locked up on me and some bruising on my arm where the door crushed in a little bit. My neck hurts. That's about it. I imagine I'll feel it more tomorrow."

"Shabina."

Rainier's voice was low. Quiet. Something in the way he said Shabina's name made Vienna turn around fully and look at him. His entire focus seemed to be on Shabina. She kept her back to him. That was unlike Shabina. Her shoulders were straight, but her head was down. The other women in the room went silent at his tone as well.

"Where is your security team?"

The ticking of the grandfather clock could be heard in the silence of the room.

"I don't see the dogs. Vienna treated my wound in the room you're staying in, and they weren't in there."

Rainier's tone was very low now, so low Vienna found herself straining to hear him, yet his voice easily carried. A frisson of fear crept down her spine. Rainier hadn't moved from his chair. He was wounded and she knew he couldn't move fast, but he exuded danger, a lethal energy that surrounded him, and even in his stillness made it clear to everyone that he was in charge and no one better cross him or they could be risking their life.

Shabina finally turned to face Rainier. "I decided to come with just my friends." Her eyes didn't meet his.

Vienna couldn't quite understand how he knew Shabina had a security team around her all the time. Well, mostly it was her three Dobermans. As guard dogs went, they were very well trained, and Vienna never doubted for a minute that they would protect Shabina with their lives.

"You didn't even bring the dogs?" There was an underlying hint of disbelief, as if Rainier couldn't conceive of Shabina going somewhere on her own.

"No one brought their dogs on this trip."

"It doesn't matter what others do. It matters that you're safe. That security team is in place for a reason. You have the dogs for a reason."

There was no reprimand in his voice, but Rainier conveyed some kind of hard authority. Rainier had no authority over Shabina as far as Vienna knew. How did he know the first thing about what went on in Shabina's life? Vienna had known her for years and yet she'd just found out the revelation that Shabina had been kidnapped in her teens.

Vienna glanced up at Zale. Zale was looking at his friend with that same mask he always wore, but she knew him better now. He was as puzzled as she was. It was clear Shabina and Rainier had a past relationship, but when? It couldn't have been that brief time when they'd all been sequestered in Shabina's house. She'd barely spoken to him—to any of the security personnel—other than to feed them.

"I feel perfectly safe, thank you, Rainier," Shabina said.

"You aren't safe and you know it. Thankfully Raine had threads on the windows and doors, so I wasn't worried, but when we didn't encounter your dogs inside, I thought you had taken them with you, although you should have left at least one behind in the house." Rainier didn't let the subject drop, and he sounded very stern. "I intended to talk to you about the need for doing that."

Vienna turned back to finish cleaning Zale's wound, but her mind went over what Rainier said. Shabina wasn't safe? Safe from what? She did have security at her house, a high fence with a guard at her gate. Others patrolling the grounds. Was that all the time? Vienna wasn't there that often. Shabina brought her dogs with her everywhere—even to work—but then, all of her friends brought their dogs with them when they could most of the time.

She looked across at Raine. If anyone knew what Rainier was referring to, it would be Raine. If Shabina was in danger—and it certainly sounded as if she was—they all needed to protect her. Raine watched Rainier carefully, one hand pressed against the side of her head, indicating she was still having trouble.

"Raine, go take your migraine meds right now." She used her authoritative nurse voice. "If you don't, I'm going to get your shot and give it to you right here."

Raine gave her a look that said "back off," but she slid off the chair on shaky legs and disappeared down the hall.

Vienna turned her attention back to Zale's wound. Now that it was cleaned, she could see how truly lucky he'd been. She looked up at his face, her eyes meeting his just for a moment. "Another inch, Zale."

"It didn't happen. Missed bone. It skimmed across my chest. Burned like hell. Didn't go in."

"It took a chunk of flesh."

"It didn't go in," he reiterated.

She shook her head. "There's no way to stitch this up. Too much skin missing."

"Yeah, I got that, Snowflake. Put your magic glue on it and call it good."

Behind her, she heard Rainier shift in his chair, easing his weight off, or maybe onto, the leg where the wound was. Vienna turned again, a little frown on her face. He needed to be careful and at least give his body twenty-four hours to recuperate.

"Shabina." Rainier was persistent. "You don't get to leave your dogs or your personal protectors behind."

Shabina closed her fingers into two fists and rested them on the center island in the kitchen. "Actually, Rainier, I not only can, but I did. Fortunately, it's my call to decide whether or not to use the security team or to take my dogs with me."

She sounded serene, but when Vienna looked at her, she could read the tension in her body.

"Actually, it isn't," Rainier disagreed.

Shabina looked up quickly from where she had begun scrubbing the center island. She watched as Rainier took out his phone and began texting. "What are you doing?"

"Ensuring you're safe."

"Are you talking to my father? I'm not sixteen. He isn't in control of my life."

Vienna couldn't hear even a small shimmer of anger in Shabina's voice. She glanced at Harlow. She didn't like what was going on. When she looked around the room, she could see none of the others did either.

"No, your father doesn't control your life, Shabina. No one does that. But someone has to take your safety seriously if you don't."

There it was again, that shadow of doubt that Vienna didn't like. If Shabina really was in trouble, why hadn't she said anything to any of her friends? They would never have minded if she brought the dogs. This particular Airbnb was convenient because it was close to Red Rock, but it didn't take pets. They would have kept looking until they found another house that would have allowed them to bring Shabina's Dobermans.

"Shabina?" Stella asked.

Shabina shook her head and turned away from them, walked to the sink to wash her hands a second time and then went to the back door and stepped outside. Rainier swore under his breath and stood up immediately, holding one hand to his hip as he limped after her.

There was silence after Rainier followed Shabina into the backyard, closing the kitchen door behind him.

"Do you think one of us should go out there and rescue her?" Harlow asked.

"Do you think he's going to shoot her?" Zale countered.

"More like strangle her," Zahra said. "What was that all about? Shabina is careful. She's more careful than any of us." She looked at Harlow. "With the exception of Raine. She put threads on the windows and doors? When did she do that? And why?"

There was a small silence. Raine was in her bedroom, lying down in the dark with a migraine. Vienna knew she'd taken her medication in order to short-circuit the massive headache.

"Zale?" Vienna used the glue to cover the wound. "Do you know why Raine would put threads on the windows or doors? And how would you notice?"

"Raine is interesting to Sam, Rainier and me. She claims to be a computer analyst but she has a very high clearance, so much so that we can't touch her."

"I don't know what that means."

"It means we have high clearances and should be able to get the dirt on anyone we want to look into. Once Sam fell like a ton of bricks for Stella, he was determined to keep her safe."

"Which means you pried into our lives." She felt some resentment toward him. "What happened to getting to know someone naturally?"

"Snowflake, really? That nasty little temper of yours flares up at the most unexpected times." Zale put his hand over his heart and looked pious. "*I* didn't look into you. That was Sam. He didn't share with us either, in case you wanted to know, but when he called on us for help to protect all of you, he did mention that some of you had troubled pasts. At that time, he disclosed that Raine's clearance protected her from his ability to check into her past. Just so you know, Shabina's past is a mystery as well."

Zale fell silent for a moment, staring at the kitchen door toward the backyard. "Apparently not to Rainier. In any case, getting back to Raine and the threads. It's an old trick. If she's gone from her home for any length of time and she's been taught that certain men can get around a security camera or even multiple security cameras, then she might use the old-fashioned alarm system of placing a piece of thread that blends in with the door and window frames. If someone opens the door or the window, the thread will fall to the ground. The chances of an intruder noticing a single very small piece of thread floating to the ground would be almost zero. Your Raine is smart."

"She is away from home for long periods of time," Vienna confirmed. "She has alarms on her windows and cameras everywhere. She has a little Jack Russell she adores and she takes that dog with her when she goes. They almost always send a helicopter for her."

Vienna peered into the large medical bag Harlow had brought with her. "That thread trick didn't work on Rainier or you. I don't see that it did Raine much good."

"Only because we were looking for any security measures. Rainier knew Shabina was here, and he expected the dogs and at least one man left behind," Zale supplied. "Remember, he thought Shabina's personal security team was with her. Rainier doesn't get upset, or at least he doesn't show it, but I could tell he wasn't happy when there wasn't a dog or a man left behind in this house. Ow, are you trying to stab me with a needle?" He glared at Vienna. "I thought you didn't have any antibiotics."

"That was in my little medical bag. Harlow brought the much larger one. I told her we might need it. Stop being such a baby."

"If you quit waving the needle around, I'll stop."

Stella burst out laughing. "He sounds like Sam. What is it with these big, bad men when they see a needle? You were shot, Zale. Did you act like a baby when you were shot? I'll bet you didn't. You acted all stoic and manly, didn't you?"

"I am stoic and manly. Vienna, get that damn needle away from me. And stop wiping my arm with alcohol."

"If you don't stop acting like a child, I'm going to give you the shot in your butt, Zale."

"You don't have a very good bedside manner."

"I don't do that kind of work. I've told you that before. I'm a surgical nurse. I can crack open your chest if you need that done. And I can give you a shot of antibiotics with no problem. Do you want Stella or Harlow to hold you down? Would that help?"

Zale glared at her when both women snickered. "I think getting in that accident made you mean."

She straddled his thighs and bent her head. "Close your eyes and look away, you big baby."

He wrapped one arm around her waist. "I'm not that much of a baby, not with you sitting on me."

She gave him the shot and then leaned in to brush a kiss, featherlight, across his lips. "I was afraid for you."

"I know, Vienna. I'm sorry. It's not what I wanted for you. We had the opportunity to disappear and we took it, but that meant using you to get rid of the truck for us. It was the wrong decision."

Before he could tighten his hold on her, Vienna slipped off his lap and began to clean up the gauze and empty wrappers. "What is it with Rainier bossing Shabina around?"

"I honestly don't know."

"Dinner's ready," Zahra said. "I've set out plates buffet style so everyone can take what they want. I even rescued the dishes from the oven," she added.

"Shabina will be so proud of you," Harlow said.

"If Rainier wants food, he'd better come in," Vienna said. "No one passes up a meal Shabina puts together."

She was certain Zale would be whipping out his phone and texting his partner to come in right away, and Shabina would be saved from having whatever lecture Rainier was in the middle of giving her.

Glaring at her, he pulled out his cell. "You're exasperating, Snowflake."

She dumped the stained gauze and wrappers in the kitchen garbage can and cleaned the instruments she'd used with alcohol. "Only you think so, Zale. Everyone else thinks I'm always reasonable."

"It's not being reasonable when you won't let me comfort you."

She supposed he had a point. "Dinner is ready. Comfort can come later."

CHAPTER TWELVE

~~~~~~

Melancholy or dark moods never sat well on Vienna. She was by nature an optimistic person. When there was a problem, she faced it head-on. She knew she wanted to be with Zale. She'd never felt such a tremendous drive to be with any other man the way she did with him, and yet she continued to put up roadblock after roadblock. She didn't know why, but she needed to find out. It wasn't fair to either of them. She knew what Zale did. She didn't want to change him or dictate to him. She wouldn't want him to ask her to change her life for him.

She was aware of him sitting close to her through dinner. He took part in the conversation with the others far more than she did. At no time did he try to draw her out or even tease her. In his Zale way he seemed to know she needed space. It was strange how he always seemed to know what she needed, as if he had a special gift.

Rainier had followed Shabina inside. She looked as if she'd been crying. He looked grim, his skin gray, as if the pain of his injury was getting to him. He didn't sit at the table but chose the longer couch, where he could stretch his leg out. He made no move to make himself a plate of food. Zale got up to fix him a plate and take it to him. Shabina disappeared for several minutes, presumably to wash her face, and came back looking a little better. She flicked a quick glance at Rainier to make certain he had everything he needed and then she sat with them at the table. That was Shabina. No matter how upset she might be, she would see to their guests first.

"What's the plan?" Stella asked Zale. "Neither one of you look like you're in great shape. We have room here if you need to lay low."

Zale flashed her a brief smile. "That was the original plan, but after hearing what happened with the truck, it might put you in more danger."

"That's one way to look at it," Harlow agreed. "Or we have more protection. Do you think you were followed?"

"No. No one knows we're here." He said it with certainty, glancing across the room at his partner. "Rainier? You have an opinion?"

"It might be better if we stay. They're only going to be here another couple of days. Tomorrow they're staying in, and then they have a kayak trip before they head home. They'll be safer with us looking after them."

"Are you coming to Knightly or up to Sunrise Lake right away?" Stella asked.

"We have to wrap things up here," Zale said.

Vienna's heart jumped in her chest. That meant the two men were going to put themselves in harm's way again. She looked up at him. "Wrap things up?" she echoed. "Are you any closer to finding out what's going on? Who wants Wallin dead?"

"If Zale would stop being a pansy and give me an hour or two with one of these assholes we'd be out of here in no time," Rainier snapped. He put the dinner plate on the coffee table.

"What does that mean?" Harlow asked.

"It means Rainier has seen things no one should ever have to see and he's tired, a grump and in pain right now. Go to bed, Rainier," Zale instructed.

"Not without dessert. Shabina just put together a fantastic

dinner and there's no way she didn't whip up some kind of great dessert to go with it." Rainier put his hands behind his head and smiled at Shabina. "I won't say another word, I promise, *qadri*."

Shabina stood very still and then she began to gather the plates. Zahra and Harlow leapt up to help just as Raine came into the room.

"Don't tell me I missed out on dinner."

"I saved yours for you," Shabina said immediately. "Are you feeling any better?"

"The shot always works," Raine conceded. "But it does make me sick if I haven't eaten."

She looked very pale. Vienna went to her and indicated a chair close to Rainier. There was a shared end table she could use when Shabina brought her a plate of food.

"Sit down, honey. We're about to start on dessert." While she helped Raine into the chair, she assessed the bruising on her forehead. The bump was larger than she would have liked, and the bruise was dark and angry-looking.

Rainier's dark eyebrows drew together. "Raine, I'm sorry you were hurt. We would never have asked Vienna to take the truck back to the rental if we thought it would put any of you in danger."

"I don't understand," Stella said. "No matter what, whoever wants Daniel Wallin dead must know you're agents here to protect him or they wouldn't be trying to kill you. They missed you once, so naturally they'd keep coming after you. Sabotaging your truck doesn't seem like a huge jump to me."

There was a small silence broken only by the clock and the sound of Zahra and Shabina rattling crockery as they scooped up the berry crisp and ice cream into bowls.

"You didn't think we would be in danger because you killed them all," Raine guessed softly.

Again, there was a telling silence. Vienna glanced at Zale. His hard features gave nothing away. Shabina and

Zahra handed out the dessert dishes and spoons to everyone. Harlow brought Raine her dinner on a separate plate.

"Are you certain these people after you didn't follow you here?" Vienna asked. "I would much prefer if you stayed at least another day so I could keep an eye on Rainier's wound. I want to make sure infection doesn't set in."

Shabina spoke up. "I think that would be best, Vienna. I don't mind giving up my room. They can stay in that one. It has two beds in it."

"Mine has two beds," Harlow said. "You can stay with me, Shabina."

"That's settled," Raine declared.

"Do you know why someone wants Wallin dead?" Stella asked. "We've been putting together all kinds of theories."

"So have we," Zale answered. "But so far, we have theories and no real facts."

"Well, if we're going to talk theories," Raine ventured, "I've got one. There is another possibility that none of us have considered. At least in all the theories we tossed around we didn't. Maybe the two of you did."

"That would be?" Zale prompted.

"Daniel Wallin may have a grudge against your boss and want to shut down your organization. All of you work in the shadows. No one knows about you. He calls this friend of his who knows your boss and suddenly you lose two agents when no one knows they're supposed to be working at the casino but him. You and Rainier are compromised, and he isn't in the know. If he had eyes on you and connected you with Vienna, he might think she works for your boss as well."

There was a long, stunned silence. The women looked at one another and then at Raine almost accusingly.

Zahra sighed. "There goes my romantic theory. And it really was romantic. Poor Daniel, we were all feeling sorry for him. Now he's the villain again."

"I'm just playing the devil's advocate," Raine said. "It's

one more possibility to consider. The cameras in Vienna's room really bother me. They don't make sense unless Daniel is involved in some way."

Vienna had to agree with her. She wanted to believe that Daniel Wallin was a victim because if he was threatening her, it was a huge threat—but what would be the reason? Someone had tried to kill her before she had won the last hand of cards. The cameras had been installed before the game she played with him. Yet he hadn't been in the crowd when she'd felt an overwhelming threat. That didn't mean anything. He could hire accomplices. She doubted if he would get his hands dirty and do the killing himself.

Raine was an analyst and a darn good one. Vienna knew her very well. When she came up with an idea, it wasn't an idle one. She looked at her theory from every possible angle before she shared. Usually, Raine was fairly certain she was onto something before she actually expressed what she was thinking.

Rainier sank all the way back on the couch, his focused gaze on Raine's face. "Interesting idea you've come up with, although he's had a couple of attempts on his life."

"Anyone can arrange a couple of near misses." Unexpectedly, it was Zahra who answered Rainier, not Raine. "It would give Daniel a great excuse to go into seclusion and surround himself with his own security force."

"He knows that," Raine said. "And the two of them have already considered the idea that Daniel Wallin set this entire thing up."

"True," Zale admitted. "But we didn't consider that he had a grudge against our boss."

"Why does a computer analyst have a team that would immediately come to her rescue and grab a truck out from under the hands of our people?" Rainier asked. "That isn't logical."

Raine lifted an eyebrow and winced, putting one hand to her head, covering her expression as she did so. "Don't pretend you didn't run a background check on all of us, Rainier. You know I have a high security clearance."

"You're practically a national treasure the way they guard you." Zale made it a joke, but his tone wasn't joking.

"Funny, I thought the same of all of you."

"We're open books," Rainier countered.

"Are you?" Raine fired back. "I suppose you could say that if one believed the carefully crafted bios put out about each of you."

"Carefully crafted?" Zale echoed. "You don't think Rainier is a doctor? Or that I have a legal degree?"

"I believe the details of your education and your military careers are the only real things in your bios," Raine said with a little shrug. "Not that it matters any more than what you couldn't find on me. I don't ask questions because I don't think the answers are necessary. As far as the truck goes and any information it might reveal, I'm sure your agency and the people I work with can work out the details of sharing without us."

"I'm sure you're right," Zale agreed. "So, let's get back to Daniel Wallin. He's an interesting man with quite the history. He's the grandson of Angelo Bottaro, who was head of the notorious crime family in Vegas for years. Bottaro had a stranglehold on quite a few of the businesses in Vegas. His daughter, Isabella, gave birth to Daniel. Daniel was raised by his father, Norman, not Isabella, and no one knew he was Angelo's grandson, although his father hung around the crime family for years."

"That matches with what Raine found on Wallin," Harlow said. It was clear she didn't want either of the men to think they had more on the casino owner than Raine did.

Vienna didn't want her to say anything at all. It was better to pretend ignorance and let the two men give them as much information as possible.

"Raine, you were using your skills to find out about Wallin?" Rainier asked.

"Naturally. Vienna told us about the men coming to her suite in an attempt to kill her and then Wallin's strange story about no one ever winning at cards with him when it counted until Liam Gram did." Raine kept her attention on her food. "Shabina, this is delicious as usual. Thank you for saving me some. I'll bet there wasn't anything left."

"You would be correct," Shabina agreed, amusement tingeing her tone. "Plenty of dessert though."

"There won't be," Zale assured. "This crisp is terrific, Shabina. I wasn't kidding about those cooking lessons."

"Everything Shabina cooks or bakes is terrific," Rainier said unexpectedly. He eased his body into another position. "Even when she first started learning, she pretty much cooked rings around all her instructors."

Shabina shook her head, color tingeing her cheeks. "That's not true, but thank you."

"I don't say personal things unless they're true." Rainier's voice was gruff. "You know that about me."

Vienna wondered more than ever when the two had known each other. Shabina rarely volunteered information about her past, now that Vienna thought about it. Rainier was a hard man, and he definitely felt he had the right to look after Shabina's safety. Vienna had always made it a policy not to pry into her friends' lives. She felt if they wanted to disclose any secrets to her, they would. She'd never been more curious in her life. To keep from asking questions, she turned the spotlight back on Daniel Wallin.

"You said you hadn't explored the possibility that Wallin had a grudge against your boss and was killing his agents, but you must have discussed some kind of similar scenario with him. Did he know Wallin?"

"No," Zale answered before Rainier could tell her that was information they couldn't disclose. "He's never met the man. Wallin called in a favor from a friend, and a guard detail was sent to him. Those agents were killed. Our boss wasn't too happy. He's no fool. Immediately suspicion fell on

Wallin's security detail. We went around that detail and another agent was killed. That made no sense."

"No," Raine said softly. "That wasn't in the least bit logical."

Vienna couldn't help watching Rainier. He appeared to be enjoying the dessert, but his gaze was sharp each time it rested on Raine. A part of her wanted to stand between them. She didn't know why. He didn't feel as if he were a direct threat—and yet he did. Zale was a scary, dangerous man and gave off that vibe, but Rainier, now that he was revealed, more and more, seemed to really show what a truly dangerous man could be.

Rainier seemed as if he were cool and still, just like Zale, blending into the background when he wanted. Taking part in a discussion if he desired. Becoming very protective or in charge, taking over without hesitation. Then there was a side of him that suddenly came out that made Vienna think he could pull out a gun and shoot everyone in the room without hesitation. Did Zale have that same side? Did Stella's Sam? Had she deliberately not seen that trait in them?

"It's possible you're onto something, Raine," Zale said. "Wallin might be behind the attacks on the agents for some reason of his own. We haven't uncovered what that reason would be, and our investigators have dug deep. Have you?"

Both men were watching Raine very closely. Tension slowly filled the room. Now it did feel as if a threat might be creeping into the air. Why that would be, Vienna didn't know, but even Zale's dark eyes were flat and cold, giving off that intense, focused attention that was just this side of terrifying.

Raine didn't appear in the least fazed by the intensity of the gathering tension. She ate her dinner slowly while she contemplated the question. Waving her fork in the air after she swallowed her food, she gave them a small frown. "It's impossible to know whether or not I uncovered an actual reason. Everything is speculation at this point. I don't have the romantic views the others have, and it's easier for me to take a different spin on Wallin. For instance, I didn't buy the car accident that killed his son's mother, Miriam."

"We didn't like that either," Zale admitted. "It felt too convenient."

"Exactly. Daniel Wallin likes control, and he didn't have complete control of Miriam and Axel. He had to get rid of Miriam in order to train Axel the way he wanted him brought up. Vienna told us Wallin has a psychic gift he uses to persuade others in his business deals and when he plays cards. It's one of the many reasons his casino has profited. It's also the reason he doesn't want to build a second one. He hasn't disclosed that gift to the crime side of his family. I'm willing to bet his son has it as well, and he's working with him in order to expand."

Raine sent the two men a serene smile that told them nothing. "Of course, again, this is pure speculation on my part. Other than looking at the official reports on the accident, which were pure bullshit and clearly the result of Daniel or his grandfather, Angelo, bribing the officials to make it look as if they believed Miriam's death was an accident." She fell silent and put her fork and knife down, indicating she was finished with her food.

Immediately, Shabina stood. "Would you care for dessert?"

Raine nodded. "I've been thinking about it all day, Shabina."

Vienna wished she could be more like Raine, not allowing the strain in the room to get to her, but the more she tried to breathe away the gathering tension, the more darkness coiled in her like a snake waiting to strike. In the back of her mind, just out of reach, there was something very important she kept reaching for. She needed to remember it. Until she did, she wouldn't understand why she kept pushing Zale away.

Zale and Rainier wanted Raine's input, that was very clear. She didn't blame them. Raine could step back and look at puzzles, and pieces clicked right into place for her. At the same time, the two men feared what she might disclose in front of her friends. She didn't know what it was Zale and Rainier didn't want them to know. She could see it was like they were walking through a minefield. They didn't want to give Raine information, but they wanted her to tell them everything she knew. She could have told them Raine was far too intelligent to fall into their trap. If she disclosed anything to them, it was because she knew their investigators had to have already discovered it or she had a reason for telling them.

"Vienna."

She tried not to react to Zale's soft, compelling voice. She needed to remember and she was so close. The door was right in front of her. She just had to find a way to open it. Zale stood squarely in front of it. If she was too close to him, she might never be able to open that door. Just like with her mother, should she just let it go? But if she did, how many times would her issues derail them? She needed to figure out what it was that was nagging at her. She gave a little shake of her head, denying Zale. Denying herself.

"Did your investigators uncover what exactly the bet was that Daniel made with Liam Gram in that last poker game between them?" Raine asked as Shabina put a bowl on the coffee table beside her. Her question sounded casual enough, but she was looking directly at Rainier.

Vienna chose to look at Zale. If Rainier appeared even half as intimidating as Zale, Vienna was sure that question was the last one either of the two men wanted asked. Her breath caught in her throat and her hand crept up protectively. Zale wasn't looking at her—he was looking at Raine.

"The bet?" Rainier repeated. "That seems to be a difficult question to answer. So far, there isn't a definitive answer."

He was lying. He hadn't hesitated, and his tone wasn't off, but Vienna was certain he knew what Daniel and Liam had bet on that last hand. Zale's expression hadn't changed in the least. He hadn't blinked, but he knew as well. She flicked her gaze from Zale to Rainier. The man had a stone face.

Vienna took a deep breath and looked at Raine. She looked serene, but she hadn't taken her eyes from Rainier's. They were locked together in a weird, silent battle no one else was involved in. Raine didn't so much as blink. She looked so young—like a teenager. Her youthful appearance was one of the reasons so many people underestimated her. Vienna knew Rainier wasn't in the least fooled anymore. He was well aware that Raine O'Mallory was incredibly intelligent and more than a worthy opponent. Vienna flicked her gaze to Zale. Evidently, he did as well. There was something both men wanted from Raine, but it was imperative she not reveal information to the rest of them. They were trying to make that clear to her.

Raine shrugged her shoulders. "That's too bad. I think if we knew the answer to that question, things would be clear."

"What does that mean?" Rainier prompted. "You're an analyst. You must have ideas. So far, I think you're coming closer than anything our people have come up with."

A faint smile touched Raine's mouth but didn't light her eyes. "Seriously, Rainier? Do you actually think flattering me is going to work? The truth is, you both are worried I'm going to get the answer to that question. I'm already suspicious of the answer and what that would mean." She glanced at Zale.

Vienna caught that look, and the knot in the pit of her stomach tightened. She followed Raine's gaze to Zale and saw his eyes go glacier cold. Her heart stuttered. Whatever Raine suspected, Zale and Rainier *really* didn't want it exposed to the light of day. She knew, just by the look in Zale's eyes, that whatever that was had something to do with her.

They can't be trusted. The voice was very clear in her mind. Not Mitzi's voice. Vienna frowned, trying to hold on to that sound. She rocked back and forth, wrapping her arms around her middle. *Do you hear me, baby? They can't ever be trusted.* That door began to creak open. Just the slightest crack. Her heart began to pound in alarm. In anticipation. She was close. So close.

"Fortunately, you understand classified information," Zale said.

There was a definite warning in his tone. That warning sent a shiver creeping down Vienna's spine. It didn't seem to have the same effect on Raine. Her blue-gray eyes went steel-gray.

The images in Vienna's mind shattered. The door slammed closed and once more Zale stood firmly in front of it. Her head hurt. Blood thundered in her ears, pounded behind her eyes.

"What I'm researching right now isn't classified. I'm not working for anyone other than for my friends, particularly Vienna. If you have something you need to say to her, say it and get it done before I find what I'm looking for, because I will find it."

"What are you looking for?" Vienna asked, rubbing at her temples in an effort to calm the storm the memory had created. That voice. Where had she heard it? Why was it familiar and yet not?

"The bet between Liam and Daniel," Raine said. "My gut tells me Daniel is behind the attacks on the agents. Nothing else makes sense. I don't know why he wants to lure them to the casino and have them killed, but he's behind it."

"There's no way to be certain," Zale said.

"No, there isn't," Raine agreed. "But I'm rarely wrong when I have this strong of a feeling. Everything I've uncovered about Daniel Wallin and his son, Axel, leads me to the conclusion that they have a vendetta against the—for lack of a better term—operators or ghosts."

Vienna looked around the room at her other friends. None of them had weighed in on the discussion between

Raine and the two agents. They were all intelligent women and were used to having lengthy and very lively debates on every subject. They enjoyed coming at a variety of topics from different points of view, yet not one of them had said anything at all. Like Vienna, they appeared mesmerized by the battle between their friend and the two men.

There was silence. Harlow and Stella stood to collect the dessert dishes. "Sounds to me like Daniel and Axel Wallin aren't to be trusted," Zahra said. "Not that we trust that many men."

They can't be trusted. Vienna's heart pounded too hard and she chewed on the inside of her lip, trying to grasp on to an elusive memory from her childhood. That voice. Where had she heard it? *Do you hear me, baby? They can't ever be trusted.* The voice whispered to her over and over. There were tears dripping on Vienna's face. Not her own. Real tears of anguish. Vienna felt each one like the cut of a knife. The voice was female and she was talking about men. Cautioning Vienna not to trust them. There was the sensation of rocking, of arms around her, as if she were being held and tears were falling on her face from above her.

"Vienna, are you all right?" Zahra asked, coming up behind her chair and wrapping an arm around her shoulders. "Do you want to go out to the hot tub? You're pretty banged up. It might be good for you."

Zahra was offering her an escape, a way out. Zale wouldn't come out to the hot tub with the other women, not with open wounds. He would remain inside with Rainier and their secrets. She'd have time to think about what it was he was hiding. She could ask Raine to clarify. Raine would never disclose anything classified, but as she said, she wasn't working on anything for the military at the moment. She was on her own time.

"I think that's exactly what I need, Zahra," Vienna agreed, rising immediately. "Shabina? Raine? We should soak in the hot tub. That will help with the sore muscles. Otherwise, we'll never get to sleep tonight."

Harlow looked up from where she was putting dishes in the dishwasher. "That's a great idea. I'll get Shabina's room ready for Rainier and Zale and then I'll join you."

Vienna avoided looking at Zale. He was holding information back from her. She was positive that he was, and she resented it. It was work related, and it shouldn't have mattered, but that death stare he'd given Raine had made her think he knew she wouldn't like whatever it was. Taking deep, meditative breaths, she changed into her swimsuit in her bathroom.

She shouldn't have been surprised to nearly run right into Zale when she stepped into her bedroom, but she was. He stood almost in the doorway of the bathroom, so it was impossible to get around him.

"You're avoiding me."

She blinked up at him and nodded slowly. "For the moment. I've got a few things I have to work out, and it's difficult when I'm close to you."

"I thought we made a pact that we'd talk things out together."

"We did, didn't we? But you aren't telling me everything. In fact, you aren't telling the truth. I already have a difficult time trusting relationships and men, and I know you and Rainier are avoiding telling us the truth, if not outright lying. That doesn't make me believe everything you've said to me, Zale. I'm trying, but it's difficult. It's been a long day. I'm tired and I hurt like hell. I just want to relax and not think about anything but having fun with Stella and the others. This was my time with them, remember? You and Rainier intruded on that."

"We did, didn't we?"

She noticed he didn't deny that he was avoiding telling the truth to her. That hurt. She wasn't going to bring it up again. This was Stella's bridal shower. She'd been so patient and kind, allowing the men to disrupt her schedule time and again. The Airbnb had been rented in order for the women to have fun in the pool together and not feel self-conscious. With the two men there, that wouldn't be easy to do. Certainly, they wouldn't have their normal, hilarious discussions about men.

She noticed Shabina, in particular, had gone very quiet. Rainier seemed to intimidate her. Stella easily could have asked them to leave, but she hadn't. None of the women had, and Vienna was proud of them for that. At the same time, it wasn't fair that they were intruding on the bridal shower, and she wasn't going to let Zale forget that was exactly what they were doing.

Vienna nodded. "Yes. This is what Stella asked for. She rarely takes time off for herself. She wanted to climb, get some biking in, and kayak, as well as just have time with us together here at the house. When we get back to Knightly, we've got a hike planned together right before the wedding. We're looking forward to that trip as well. Hopefully, you and Rainier will have completed whatever it is you're doing and can be at the wedding so Sam won't have to replace you."

"We'll be there," he assured.

Zale tucked a stray strand of hair behind her ear. She'd braided her hair and put it up on her head as she normally did when she was going into water that had chemicals in it. Her hair was so naturally blonde it was nearly white, and she didn't want it turning green. She'd saturated it with conditioner before she braided it just in case. She didn't intend to get it wet, but there was always the possibility of an accident.

"That's good, since Sam is counting on you." She knew her voice was stilted, but she couldn't help it. He was standing right in front of her, knowing he was lying to her, or at least withholding something terribly important, but it didn't matter.

They can't be trusted. That voice. Where had she heard it? Why did it sound so familiar? It wasn't Mitzi's voice. The register was a little lower. Softer.

Zale cupped her chin. His thumb slid along her cheek. "Don't pull so far away from me, Snowflake. You know the kind of job I have. I can't tell you everything I want to. Some of the information I gave you I shouldn't have. I did because I put you in a dangerous position and I felt you needed to know in order to better protect yourself. Not to mention, you brought a different perspective."

He avoided saying "like Raine," which would have been natural, because he didn't want to bring her into the conversation. Vienna kept her eyes fixed on his. She simply nodded. He was telling her the truth—and yet there was more to it. She was becoming so much more adept at reading him now that she'd been with him.

"The fact that two men entered your suite with the intention of killing you terrified me. I thought Rainier and I controlled the security cameras in the hallway and no one saw me coming and going from your room, but I must have screwed up and put you in danger."

She had to quickly veil her eyes with her lashes. They *had* controlled the security cameras in the hallway, and he knew they had. No one had seen him coming or going from her room. He had been terrified for her. That much was true. Why was he lying to her, and over what exactly? He was mixing truth with lies, and he was really skillful at it. An expert. How did one enter into a relationship with someone with an expertise like that?

She rubbed her temples. "I need some space, Zale."

She didn't mean to tip him off with sheer despair in her voice, but she didn't have the same skills he did.

He framed her face with his hands. "I can give you space, Vienna, but don't pull away from me, not until this is all resolved and I can speak freely. Can you at least do that for me?"

She hoped she could do that for him, but she honestly didn't know, and she didn't make promises she couldn't keep.

"I'll do my best, Zale."

He bent his head to brush her lips with his. Her stomach somersaulted in spite of every resolve to be strong. His palm slid around the nape of her neck and he rested his forehead against hers.

"I know we interrupted your time together and all of this looks bad. It has to feel that way too, Vienna. I just want you to know I'm trying to keep you safe."

That did ring true, and she believed him. There was a raw ache in his voice that hadn't been there before. Unfortunately for her, the sound slipped past her every defense. She didn't dare raise her eyes to his. That would be a disaster for her. Instead, she nodded to indicate she heard him.

To her relief, Zale stepped back, giving her the ability to breathe again. She hadn't realized she'd been breathing shallowly in order not to draw him into her lungs. She still had the spa towel in her hand, and she stepped around him and went to join Shabina and Raine outside on the deck.

Shabina hadn't turned on any lights other than the LED lights that wound around the covered part of the deck and the colored lights in the spa itself. Steam rose from the surface of the water, shrouding the two in the hot tub in mystery. Vienna went up the two steps and swung her long legs over the rim to settle into the hot water.

"This is heaven," she admitted. "I should have done this first thing."

"Right?" Shabina agreed. "I brought out water for all of us. Hydrate, hydrate, hydrate."

The three laughed together.

"If one of us was going to remember that important detail," Raine observed, "it was going to be you, Shabina."

Shabina tipped her head back and rested her neck in the padded slot so she could look up at the stars. "I was in that desert a long time. Water became very important to me. I would think about it constantly. Dream about it. After a while it was difficult to think about anything else if we were traveling. I watched them to see where the water supply was and where they would get it. From plants. Where they created holes. How far down. Rocks. It became an obsession, I suppose. Now I make sure I always carry a filtration system and enough water with me at all times. More than enough."

Vienna found every single tiny detail Shabina was willing to share of her past very interesting. "It's very clear that you know Rainier from somewhere other than when Sam had his friends help him keep all of us safe while he hunted for the serial killer. Would you mind telling us where you met Rainier and why he feels he can tell you what to do?"

Shabina sighed, but didn't take her gaze from the stars. "He was the operative they sent to rescue me. He got past all the guards and came into the camp where they were holding me. I was in bad shape. The worst. I didn't think I was going to live very much longer. I believe his intention was to get me out of there without any of them being aware I was gone until the changing of the guard."

She fell silent. The sound of the bubbles filled the quiet. Vienna could feel the froth bursting against her legs, arms and back, massaging the sorest spots where she'd been so shaken by being thrown around in the truck.

"I think seeing what they did to me, seeing the condition I was in, triggered something in Rainier. I was sixteen. He didn't expect to feel anything at all. He was doing his job." She tapped her fingers on the surface of the water. "He killed them all. Every single one of them. There were quite a few of them. He wiped out the entire cell. He was fast too, without hesitation. He unlocked the chains on me and whispered to me to look away. I didn't. He didn't make a sound, but he went from cot to cot after he killed the guards. He left that room and went to other rooms. When there was no one left alive, he treated as many of my wounds as possible and then he carried me out of there. First, we rendezvoused with a vehicle and then a helicopter. He never left my side. He was definitely in charge."

"Why is he so concerned that you have security around you at all times, Shabina?" Vienna persisted, trying to be gentle. "Should we be concerned for your safety?"

"I don't think so. It's been years. I think he's just worried is all."

Raine made a small sound of denial. "Those men in that particular cell had very connected families, Shabina. They live for feuds and Rainier knows that. Your father is very well known. It's very easy to keep track of him. The moment you decided to strike out on your own had to be a nightmare for everyone who loves you."

"And yet there's never been a hint of retaliation against me," Shabina pointed out.

"That's true," Raine said. "But you can't blame Rainier for being worried."

"I suppose not, but I wish he wouldn't. He's very intense, and it can be very difficult for someone like me to deal with," Shabina admitted.

"They'll be gone after the wedding," Vienna said. "Speaking of gone, Raine, what is it Zale doesn't want you to tell me?"

"I don't know for sure." Raine sounded reluctant to discuss the subject. "Believe me, Vienna, the moment I do know, I'll tell you. I don't like the way any of this is playing out. I could be way off base, and I hope I am. Until I know anything for certain, I'm not going to give misinformation and take a chance on hurting any of my friends or their relationships."

"I think Zale and Rainier are hurting those relationships all by themselves by not telling us the truth," Vienna said.

"If they're given orders not to reveal certain details of a mission, they can't," Raine pointed out.

Vienna sighed. That was more or less exactly what Zale had said to her.

CHAPTER THIRTEEN

$\wedge$s they always did, the women prepped breakfast together,
Shabina and Zahra doing the actual cooking while the
others set the table and squeezed oranges for orange juice.
The men insisted they could eat on the deck but the women
told them that was silly, they could all eat together.

Vienna knew Zale had talked with Rainier and persuaded
him that they were there for Stella's bridal shower and should
be left alone as much as possible. She knew she should feel
guilty, but she didn't. It was the simple truth.

Fortunately, the talk swirled around hiking and climbing
rather than anything controversial, so that made for a pleasant breakfast filled with laughter as they told stories of having to leap over snakes on the trail and finding a place to dig
a hole to go to the bathroom, only to find another person ten
feet away when they thought they had the entire forest to
themselves.

Zale and Rainier contributed a couple of equally funny
stories, laughing at themselves, and after breakfast, helped
to clear the table. Shabina ordered Rainier away from the
kitchen when it became clear he was limping and his wound
was not cooperating. Both Harlow and Vienna insisted on
looking at it.

Vienna was certain he would have ignored them, but Shabina put both fists on her hips and stared him down until he

complied. The wound looked swollen and ugly, and they gave him another injection of antibiotics after a consultation with Raine.

"I could call the doctor here on the local staff and have him drop by just to be certain," Raine offered.

"That's not necessary," Rainier protested.

"It isn't if you don't care if you lose your leg," Vienna pointed out, not looking at him. "That might be a good idea, Raine, unless you have someone your people can send?" She turned fully to him and lifted an eyebrow.

"I am a doctor," he reminded.

Vienna rolled her eyes. "Doctors are notoriously the worst patients, and they always misdiagnose themselves. Call for a doc and have him come by. We can say one of us cut ourselves while preparing food."

"Shabina." There was distinct amusement in Rainier's voice.

It was the first time there was real humor that lit his face and eyes and made his eyes appear almost an icy blue.

Shabina feigned outrage. "*Not* Shabina. I would never cut myself chopping anything. You are deliberately insulting me, and if you keep it up, you will not be eating any of my delicious meals for however long you're here. You'll be sending for take-out pizza."

Rainier actually shuddered. "Not pizza." He held up both hands. "I surrender. Not you, Shabina. Someone else. Who is most likely to cut themselves in the kitchen?" He looked around at the women.

"That would be more Zahra's department." Stella threw her best friend under the bus.

Zahra lifted an eyebrow, looking bored. "I doubt it. Harlow was raised with the silver spoon. She was never in the kitchen."

"That's unfortunately the truth," Harlow agreed. "Although, I am a nurse, so I don't exactly hack myself up by slipping up when I'm wielding instruments."

Zahra gave an exaggerated sigh. "Raine?"

"Not only do I cook, which you do as well, but I took multiple types of self-defense lessons, including weapons. I doubt I'd hurt myself with a knife while chopping up veggies."

Zale burst out laughing. "There are some very healthy egos among you ladies."

"I suppose it has to be me," Zahra said. "I don't mind at all. Hopefully the doctor is young and good-looking. If he is, all of you remember you didn't want to be the one he looks after. You can just go into another room while he treats my laceration."

"Zahra, you don't have a laceration," Stella pointed out. "The doctor is coming to treat Rainier's wound, not your mythical one."

"Well, jeez." Zahra flung herself on the couch across from Rainier. "Do you see what I have to put up with? I sacrifice my reputation in the kitchen and I don't even reap rewards."

"The doctor is most likely an old man with fourteen children and twice that number of grandchildren," Zale assured. "These military stations like the ones Raine tapped into, out in the middle of nowhere, they're occupied by the has-beens. These guys haven't moved in years."

"Just my luck," Zahra complained. "I'm never going to find a hot billionaire to rescue me from the perils of working behind a desk."

"You love your work," Stella reminded.

"That's true, until there's all this wedding nonsense, and then I feel left out," Zahra said, although she didn't sound as if she felt left out. She gave them a faint grin. Vienna wasn't altogether certain Zahra planned to give anyone a fair chance at dating her. She'd considered Bruce, one of the businessmen in Knightly, but he was so shy he couldn't even manage to ask her out. He stayed in the group, danced with Zahra and made it known to others that he considered her off-limits to everyone, but he never actually made a move.

Vienna had never understood why Zahra let the flirtation with Bruce go on for so long when it obviously wasn't going to go anywhere. In a way, Zahra was protected from other men asking her out, and that might have been the answer right there. Zahra was fond of Bruce, but she wasn't in love with him. How could she be, when Bruce just wouldn't commit to even so much as an actual date with her?

"I'm sure Raine's doctor is an old man, Zahra," Zale reiterated. "So, you're not losing out. These military types tend to just sit around and vegetate."

Raine coughed behind her hand. "I believe my people beat your people to the truck."

"Only because my people didn't know about the truck," Zale pointed out.

A ghost of a smile touched Raine's mouth. "That could be true."

"It would be kind of funny to have seen a standoff between the two factions," Vienna said. "Both trying to be the first to tow the truck away."

"Unless they decided to shoot at each other," Harlow ventured. "Guys are kind of trigger-happy. They don't make any kind of sense at all."

"I do want to point out one thing, Zale," Raine added. "You were in the military for years. Technically, you're still there. Operative. Ghost. SAG. Whatever branch you're serving under, it's in the military. So, you're one of those military types who tend to sit around and vegetate."

His eyebrow shot up. "Your point being?"

Vienna's heart stuttered the way it did whenever she looked at Zale and saw that sweet, vulnerable side of him. It was impossible to think he could laugh at himself when one looked at his stony, expressionless face, and then he gave them his mischievous grin. It didn't even matter that it failed to light his eyes, or that she knew he was skilled at playing people.

The women laughed. Even Raine. Zahra shook her head.

"I suppose we can't hope that Raine's people will have equally hot men for us to ogle."

"I don't think it's necessary for all of you to ogle hot men," Zale said.

"Don't be a tattletale and text Sam. Stella's the worst when it comes to ogling," Zahra confided. "She can't help herself if she's drinking. But he knows because he's always the sober driver."

"I'm ogling *Sam*, you monster," Stella corrected.

"That's true," Zahra said, in no way repentant. "Long before you and Sam were a thing, you were terrible the way you made eyes at him and commented on how hot he was when he was driving us home from the Grill."

"You said I didn't make the comments where he could hear me."

"How could you believe anything I said when I was every bit as drunk as you were? He wasn't suddenly struck deaf. He was just too much of a gentleman to take advantage of the fact that you were always throwing yourself at him."

Stella buried her face in her hands. "If you weren't my best friend, I'd strangle you. I still might."

"Sam doesn't mind that you think he's hot," Zahra pointed out. "Although, he has a big head now. His ego is totally out of control."

"Sam doesn't have an ego. He's zen."

"Sam's zen?" Zale repeated.

Stella glared at him. "You know very well Sam is zen. Don't pretend you aren't aware he's zen, unlike the two of you."

"What's not zen about us?" Zale demanded.

"Rainier isn't zen," Shabina ventured.

Rainier looked up, his eyes capturing Shabina's. "You once told me I have a stone face. There's an affiliation between stones and zen," he said, without any expression whatsoever.

Shabina burst out laughing. "Only you would make that association count."

"But it does count," Rainier insisted. He waved dismissively. "Poor Zale. Nothing zen about him."

"My name starts with the letter 'Z,'" Zale defended himself.

That made Vienna laugh. "You're really grasping at straws."

"I can't let Rainier outdo me in the zen area. Especially when all of you think Sam is so perfect."

"He is." There was a chorus of female voices instantaneously rising together. They looked at one another and burst into laughter again.

Rainier groaned and covered his face with his hand. "How did Sam manage to pull the wool over your eyes? Raine? You too?"

"He's our sober driver and keeper of all our secrets." Again, they looked at one another and burst out laughing. "He has the patience of a saint."

"Well," Zale conceded, "Sam does have patience. There's no doubt about that. He likes the mountains. Once he's in them, you never see him. It's impossible. He blends in and can be so still I swear he becomes part of the terrain. I used to go with him and I could never spot him, even when I knew where he had gone. That was part of the game, trying to find him."

That little piece of information fascinated Vienna. There was admiration in Zale's tone. She knew he was good at his job. He didn't take the kind of work he had been doing in the casino often. Mostly, he worked alone in foreign countries, so he had to be as skilled as Sam, yet he was openly admiring Sam for his expertise. She liked that about Zale. He wasn't so egotistical that he couldn't show respect for another man's abilities.

"And Rainier?" Shabina asked. "Is he like Sam?"

"I'm right here, Shabina," Rainier pointed out. "It would be difficult to say anything either way."

"Not if Zale was going to be truthful," she said, lifting her chin stubbornly.

"I doubt if Zale or Rainier would be able to tell the entire truth without lightning striking them." Vienna couldn't help her honest opinion from tumbling out. She clapped a hand over her mouth, but it was too late.

Zale raised an eyebrow. "You don't think I tell the truth?" He put a hand over his heart. "You make my heart hurt."

"Car just pulled up in front of the house," Harlow observed. "If you're about to have a heart attack, now might be the perfect time. This could be the doctor. Zahra, you're the one with the laceration."

"Rainier and Zale, you need to get out of sight. Two men walking up to the door," Raine reported as she moved quickly toward the front foyer. She pulled out her compact rose-handled Sig Sauer, concealing the gun behind her back. "Spread out, everyone. Be somewhere you can get to cover fast."

Zale didn't wait for Vienna to find a spot in the spacious living room. He caught her arm and took her with him to the shadowy alcove just to the right of Shabina's bedroom. There was a massive cabinet in the alcove there. He placed her beside the cabinet as he stepped inside the bedroom, leaving the door ajar so he could cover the front door with his drawn weapon. Rainier had chosen to go to the opposite side of the room, indicating for Shabina and Harlow to accompany him. He concealed himself in the shadow of the doorway to Stella's bedroom while Harlow leaned against the wall close to the guest bathroom door. Shabina was beside Stella's bedroom door.

Zahra stood in the kitchen with a tea towel wrapped around her hand as though she were injured. She could easily dive behind the center island if necessary. Raine's phone pinged once and then there was a firm knock on the door. Raine glanced at her phone just to make certain before she opened the door. Still, even with the information stating the doctor had arrived, she kept her grip on the gun behind her back.

"I need to see your ID." She was very firm about that.

Both men had their IDs out and ready to show her. She looked them over thoroughly. Raine was good at spotting fakes. "Thanks for coming." She stepped back and allowed them entry, closing the door and taking up a position behind them.

"You're the legendary Raine O'Mallory. Dr. Briac Brannan. Please call me Briac. This is my colleague Gage Barrington."

"Lovely to meet you, Briac. Gage." Raine indicated Zahra. "My friend Zahra isn't your patient. I'm afraid I had to be a little inventive. Two operatives are here and were wounded. Our nurses fixed them up, but one of the wounds is worrisome. We hoped you'd take a look at it for us." Raine gave him her winning smile. "I asked that a formal request be put in just to make it all legit, but I wasn't certain there was time for it to go through all the channels."

Briac shrugged. "We don't need to wait. Where's my patient?"

"Most likely holding a gun on you," Raine said in a flirty, teasing voice Vienna rarely heard her use.

Vienna took another look at Briac. Irish. In his late thirties. Early forties. No ring on his finger. Very attractive with thick, dark hair that had a bit of a reddish tint to it when the light hit it. He was a doctor, so intelligent, which Raine needed to keep up with her super-smarts. He also looked as if he was the athletic type, which would be good because Raine was all about the outdoors on her days off.

Vienna looked at Zahra and mouthed, *"Hot."*

Zale leaned out of the doorway and bit her neck. "I saw that," he hissed.

"Well, he is." She wasn't in the least repentant. "For Raine. He's looking at Raine and she's looking back."

"He can stop looking at Raine. She's ours, not theirs." Zale was decisive.

Vienna narrowed her gaze as she looked at him over her shoulder. "What does that mean? Supposedly she's an independent contractor, but she works exclusively for the military. That would make her theirs."

"Nope. She's your best friend. She belongs to Sam. Sam's with us. That makes her ours. They don't get to claim her."

"You're being totally serious." Vienna could tell he was.

Zale scowled at the doctor and his companion as Rainier limped toward them. Evidently, Rainier decided that he would be treated in Shabina's bedroom. It made sense as both men had slept there the night before. Like Zale, he was eyeing the doctor and Gage Barrington as if they were enemies and needed watching at all times. Vienna decided she would never understand men in a million years. They'd regarded Raine with suspicion, and now they were acting as if she were a national treasure they had to guard.

Zale stepped back farther into the room and indicated for Vienna to follow him. "Come inside, Vienna."

She frowned at him. "They don't need me."

"You're a nurse." He reached out and caught her wrist before she could elude him and drew her into the bedroom.

Shabina had always kept her home immaculate. The room she stayed in was no exception. There was no evidence that either man had stayed the night there. In fact, the room held a faint fragrance that was definitely all Shabina.

"I need you to be visible." Zale's voice was low. "Stay close to Rainier but out of my line of a shot at Barrington. And stay out of reach of Barrington."

He stepped away from her and then disappeared. Vanished. Like a ghost. Vienna blinked. How the hell was she supposed to stay out of his line of a shot at Barrington if she didn't even know where he went? It was too late to ask the question because Rainier had stalked into the room.

Even with his limp, the man managed to stalk and look menacing.

"Vienna, good. Come to the side of the bed." He went straight to the bed as if he and Zale had mapped out a plan beforehand. It had been impossible. How could they have known Harlow and Vienna would insist on a doctor looking at Rainier's wound?

Rainier slid down his pants, and she realized he was wearing soft drawstring sweats. She had known, of course, but it hadn't really registered with her. She was so used to him being so impeccably dressed. He stretched out on the bed, facedown, sliding his hand under the pillow as he rested his head on it. It seemed a natural gesture to put his hand there, but she knew, now, there was a weapon stashed under the pillow.

So, the two men had known all along that the two nurses would insist on Rainier being seen by a doctor, and they'd prepared in advance. She didn't make the mistake of scowling toward shadows or closets, but she wanted to.

This is what I'd have to live with. Zale always being one step ahead.

She felt a faint stroke, like a caress along her nerve endings, but she didn't find it soothing in the least. She found it annoying, mostly because, in spite of everything, her body reacted to his touch. He would be *hell* to live with.

Gage followed Briac into the bedroom, shutting the door behind them. The bedroom was actually quite spacious, but the moment the door was closed, Vienna felt as if the space were very small. The doctor came straight to the side of the bed and put his medical bag on the end table.

"I'm Vienna." She thought it best to introduce herself. "I'm a surgical nurse and thought in case you needed anything, I could assist you."

She glanced at his companion. He hadn't approached the bed or patient. He walked around it, but kept his distance.

She could see that he had noted Rainier's hand under the pillow and he had assessed her.

"Do you have any weapons on you?" Gage asked her abruptly.

"No."

"You aren't needed. I can assist him if he needs help," Gage said.

"There's no need to be rude to her," Rainier said very, very softly. "She stays. You talk to her like that again and you're the one who leaves the room."

"Briac doesn't have to help you," Gage said.

Briac glanced at what clearly was his personal protector. "Leave it alone. We're on the same side, remember? Vienna, would you cut away the bandage, please?"

She took the scissors and did as the doctor asked, ignoring the man pacing behind her. She decided everyone in their business had to be a little paranoid.

"Have you known Raine long?" Briac asked.

"Several years. The six of us live in a small town, and all of us like the same things. Well, Stella lives about an hour from us, but essentially, we all live close. We like climbing, hiking, skiing, dancing, that sort of thing."

"Stella is the one getting married," Briac qualified.

"Yes. Did Raine tell you that?"

"When she reported there was an accident, she said she was here in Vegas for a bridal shower. I believe it was mentioned that Stella was the bride." Briac studied the wound. "Who initially cleaned this?"

"I believe Rainier did. He's a doctor."

Briac straightened. "We do make the worst patients."

"I couldn't go to a hospital," Rainier explained without lifting his head. "Did I leave something behind?"

"I believe so."

Rainier swore under his breath. "I was afraid of that."

Vienna had been just as afraid. "We'll have a little chat

about that later, Rainier, considering all the crap you gave me about calling a doctor."

"They always bring muscle along," he answered, unrepentant.

She couldn't exactly fault him on his tone. It was as flat and expressionless as ever, yet somehow, even lying on his belly with his pants around his ankles, when he should have felt vulnerable, Rainier managed to give off the feeling of being superior. Of being in complete control. She didn't see how he could be so sure of himself, not with Gage prowling around the room, making her feel nervous in spite of her determination not to notice him.

"I don't understand why, when you're on the same side, you have to act like enemies," Vienna said, automatically laying out the doctor's instruments on the small tray he had in the very large medical bag he'd brought with him. "It's just plain ludicrous."

Briac laughed. "I agree wholeheartedly. We'll just ignore them. I'm going to numb this, Rainier," he added. "It will take a few shots to get the entire site numb, and it's going to be very uncomfortable. Don't shoot me."

"Vienna can stand between you," Gage suggested helpfully. "It would be easier for her to hand the doc instruments."

"Vienna can stay right where she is," Rainier said. "She has the tray of instruments and can hand them across my body."

Vienna sighed. "If you two keep it up, I'm going to have the doctor give you a shot of something to knock you out, Rainier, and I'll have you leave the room, Mr. Barrington."

"I'm not allowed to leave Doc." There was amusement for the first time in Gage's voice. "I'm not opposed to you having Briac knock out his patient. It would save me a lot of work. I could sit down and relax for a change."

The admission told Vienna that Gage had no idea Zale was in the room looking out for Rainier.

"He's lazy," Briac said.

Vienna prepared four long needles where Rainier could see what she was doing to assure him he would be getting the proper dosage and it would be numbing the site, not putting him out as she had threatened. Deliberately, she showed him the vials she drew from and where she laid each syringe on the tray for the doctor to use. Rainier's gaze flicked up to her once and he barely nodded, an almost imperceptible acknowledgment, but she felt connected to him for the first time since they'd left the hotel.

Briac picked up the first syringe in his gloved hand. "I'm injecting now, Rainier."

Rainier didn't respond. He made no sound as, one after another, Briac injected the syringes full of numbing agent into the wound. Little beads of sweat formed on Rainier's forehead, but he wiped them on the pillowcase with a small turn of his head and then settled again.

"Is Raine seeing anyone?" Briac asked casually.

Rainier frowned. "What the hell kind of question is that?"

"A personal one," Briac responded. "I understand she enjoys hiking. I do as well. I have some time off coming and always wanted to see Yosemite. I thought . . ."

"Well, whatever you're thinking, don't," Rainier said. "You mess with that girl, do you have any idea what kind of hell you'll bring down on your head? It's best just to leave her alone."

"Is she yours?" Briac asked.

Vienna couldn't help laughing. She tried to cover it up, but was unsuccessful. "I'm sorry." She knew her voice gave it away that she wasn't. "Raine might shoot Rainier in the middle of the night if he bossed her around the way he does everyone, although I don't know. Maybe not. It's difficult to predict what she'll do in any given situation."

"It isn't just my people, Doc," Rainier said. "Yours as well. She stubs her toe and there's going to be hell to pay from both sides."

Vienna sobered immediately. She hadn't thought of that. What did that mean for Raine's dating life? What man would risk bodily harm trying to date her? It would be difficult enough just trying to keep up with her intellect and outdoor skills, let alone worrying about her military connections. Vienna hadn't thought of the problems Raine's dates might encounter, but no doubt Raine had.

Briac shrugged, although Rainier couldn't see him. "Who Raine chooses to hike with isn't anyone's business but hers. You might consider that I'm about to dig into your leg with a really sharp instrument before you reply to me."

Vienna liked not only his sense of humor but also the fact that he wasn't intimidated by the warning. She watched him work. She'd worked with a good many doctors, both in emergency rooms and in surgery rooms, and recognized that he was very good. The military had sent one of the best they had to help out.

It took some time to find the tiny piece of rock left behind in Rainier's leg. Briac triumphantly pulled the bloody sliver out and dropped it into the tray. "It always amazes me how much damage a tiny foreign object can do to our bodies when the initial bullet wouldn't have caused that much of a problem. You were lucky, Rainier. This is actually a piece of rock."

"Yeah, the bullet was a through and through and didn't hit anything vital, but it ricocheted off the boulders we were in. Two of them maybe before it actually hit me. Hurt like a mother. I had quite a few pieces of rock embedded in the back of my leg. We weren't going to come here to the women, but then we needed Vienna to check the damn thing."

Vienna watched as Briac closed the wound with tiny, precise stitches. She didn't know why, because she did trust the doctor, but she felt responsible for Rainier. Zale had to keep his eye on the biggest threat—Gage—and he wouldn't know exactly what Briac was doing. She would be able to see if Briac attempted to introduce anything out of the ordinary to the wound. He did give him a hefty shot of antibiotics and placed a bottle of pills on the end table.

"Take all of them. You know the drill."

Rainier made noises that could have meant anything.

Vienna cleaned up, gathering all the used bandages and gauze, putting them in the hazmat bag the doctor had with him. He would carry it out of the Airbnb so there was no evidence left behind.

Briac stood up and stretched. "Be a little careful with that, Rainier. Don't just jump back into action right away."

Vienna pulled a sheet over Rainier and followed Gage and Briac out of the room, uncaring whether or not Zale would be upset with her. The doctor had done a really stellar job, and if he wanted to talk to Raine for a moment before he left, she was going to see to it that he was able to do so.

"How is Rainier?" Harlow asked as Vienna emerged.

"He's doing fine. He did have a sliver of rock in him. The doc found it and thankfully removed it, otherwise that infection would only have gotten worse."

Shabina's brows drew together. "Is he supposed to take antibiotics?"

"Yes," Briac answered. "I gave him a shot and left pills on the nightstand. He has to finish all of them."

Harlow heaved an exaggerated sigh. "You know those doctors. They never do anything they're supposed to."

Briac laughed, his gaze fixed on Raine. "I've never been hiking in the Sierras before. I've hiked in Europe and managed Shasta but haven't had the opportunity to do any hiking in the Sierras. I've been hoping to get out that way soon."

Gage edged toward the door, but had to stop when the doctor didn't follow him out.

"The Sierras are beautiful," Raine said. "Absolutely beautiful. I could email you some of our favorite trails to hike if you'd like."

Zale came up behind Vienna. She knew he was there without him saying a single word. There was a powerful energy he exuded. He stood close enough that she felt his body heat. "She walked right into his trap," he whispered against her ear.

She glanced at him over her shoulder and knew immediately it was a mistake to look at him. He was too close. His eyes too dark brown and focused on her with that look he reserved only for her. Her heart skipped a beat and her body reacted.

"You need to go away," she whispered. "Stand across the room. Or better yet, in the other room."

He bent his head the scant two inches to touch his lips against her ear. "Why do I need to do that, Snowflake?"

"You know why. I can't think straight when you're around."

"You aren't thinking straight unless I am around," he corrected, his breath warm in her ear, his lips sliding against the sensitive skin. "The minute I leave you alone for any length of time, you start overthinking things."

Goose bumps rose in reaction. His knuckles slid up and down her back. She couldn't help herself. She leaned into his fist. It was true that she overthought everything. There was no question about it.

Zale managed to guide her away from the others as Gage urged the doctor toward the front door. Raine and Harlow escorted the two men out, chatting away with them.

Zale threaded his fingers through Vienna's and walked her through the kitchen and out the door to the backyard so they could have privacy.

"I missed you last night. I gave you the space you asked for, Vienna, but it wasn't easy. Being with a man like me is never going to be like the relationships your friends have. Even after I retire, it won't be the same. Our life will always be different, and hopefully you'll be okay with that."

"I do want a partnership, Zale. I want communication. I don't like being left in the dark. I know that when you go off on your missions or whatever you call it now, you can't exactly give me details, but there should be a way to let me know you're alive if I need to know. You talk to Sam. That means you can set up a way to talk to me."

He remained silent, but his fingers went to the nape of her neck, stroking, kneading, easing the tension out of her.

Vienna decided she might as well take the plunge and tell him the real issue. "And maybe I haven't caught you in an outright lie, but you certainly aren't telling me the entire truth. That doesn't make me trust you. In a relationship where you're going to be gone for weeks, maybe months, without communication, I have to be able to trust you implicitly. I have to be able to believe everything you say to me. I have to come first, and that means you don't go behind my back with half-truths that your buddies understand but I don't."

Zale continued to remain silent, allowing her to express her concerns for their relationship. Or was that what he was doing? That was the problem. She didn't know. When she looked at his face, it was impossible to read him.

"Is that what you're afraid of, Vienna? That my friends know things you don't?"

His voice was so quiet, velvet soft. His hand never stopped that gentle glide down her back. She knew she should stop him. It was seduction at its worst. Not open. Not sexual. But intimate, tying them together in a way that twisted him deeper around her bones until he was branded there.

"Is that what your takeaway is from what I just told you, Zale? Do you really believe that I'd worry you would tell all your buddies things you don't tell me? I'm not sixteen years old and in a schoolyard. I don't look at you and your friends standing by your cars whispering together. You don't get to reduce what I'm afraid of to something that small-minded."

"I'm sorry if you took what I said that way. In this case, Rainier is privy to certain aspects of our missions that I can't disclose to anyone else, no matter how much I might want to. I'm not always going to be at liberty to tell you the things you might want to know, Vienna, and you have to be able to live with that. Most of the time, I work alone. Sam has the ability to read code we use. I'll do my best to get permission to teach it to you, but because often what is said on those loops is classified, the answer is most likely going to be no."

"I don't want to be on a loop where everyone can hear what is said. I just want the ability to communicate in case of an emergency. What if I'm pregnant and I go into labor early? There's a problem with the baby? With me? Wouldn't you want to know?"

Mostly, she would want to know if he was injured. Shot. Stabbed. She saw the scars on his body. On Rainier's. Those were very real.

With the gentleness that got to her heart every time, Zale turned her to him and lifted her chin. "Snowflake, I know you'll be worried about me when I have to leave. I'll be worried about you. We'll find a way to make it work. We'll have to." The pad of his thumb slid gently over the curve of her bottom lip. "I'm not willing to go without news of you and how you're doing, and I won't want you worried. If I'm injured, I'll get word to you somehow. Those are things we can work out."

"Are you really going to retire when your contract's up, or are you going to be like Rainier?" That was another burning question. In her opinion, Rainier, as gifted and experienced as he was, shouldn't remain in the field. She wondered if he was looking to die that way. Or if he wanted to climb up a political ladder. Was there one in their field? She didn't know or even care.

"We've gone over this, Vienna. Where is this coming from? Why are you suddenly doubting us all over again? I told you I would get out . . ."

"Yes." She pounced on that. "You said you would get out, but not that you wanted out. There's a difference. A huge difference. Sam was ready to get out. He'd made that decision on his own. I don't want you to leave a career you love for me. Eventually you would resent me. You know you would."

"Snowflake, stop. I don't do anything I don't want to do. I wouldn't get out if I didn't want to. You'll learn that about me, but for now, you'll just have to take my word. I know you're worried I'll get bored. I've looked Yosemite over and there are all kinds of things to do there. It's the kind of country I need to live in. I don't foresee a problem living there with you and raising a family. If something comes up that I didn't foresee, we'll cross that bridge when we come to it."

She heard the sincerity in his voice, and it settled the fears that kept blindsiding her. "I don't know why I can't stop this issue from coming up."

"You warned me it would, and I'm okay with reassuring you as long as you always give me the chance."

LATE THAT NIGHT, after the most relaxing day swimming in the pool, laughing with her friends, eating the best meals, staying up late drinking just a little too much although they had to get up early, Zale snuck into her room and crawled into bed with her. He was voracious, the way he always seemed to be with her. Vienna was equally as demanding, and he was receptive every single time.

The dream woke her, her breath catching in her lungs, the memories pouring in. *You can never trust them, Vienna. They'll lie to you every time to get what they want and then they'll walk away, leaving you shattered and broken.*

Don't tell her that, Avril.

It's true. You know it's true. I thought he loved me. He said he didn't do babies and he'd pay for me to get rid of her. That we could still see each other after if I wanted, but he was working on his career. He thought I understood that. We never even discussed his career. When I said I wouldn't consider abortion, he said I was on my own.

He wasn't the right one, Avril. Not all men are like that.

They are. Every single one of them. I don't want her to ever feel like this. Not ever. Look at me now. Broken and alone. If I didn't have you, Mitzi, what would happen to her? I'd die and she'd go into the system.

I love her. You know I do. I'll take care of her. I want it to be legal, though, so he can never come back on me.

I have an insurance policy. It isn't much, but it will help for a while. He'll send money if you ask for it.

I don't want anything from him. He didn't want her. Just get him to sign his rights away.

I asked the lawyer to do that a long time ago.

Vienna closed her eyes. Her birth mother. Avril. She remembered her vaguely. How old had she been when Avril had passed away? Avril had whispered her mantra to her over and over for years. *They can't be trusted. They lie to you. They'll say anything they think you want to hear in order to get their way.*

It had been her birth mother instilling her deep fear of a real relationship, rocking her as an infant and toddler, whispering what she believed to be a truth to protect her daughter. Mitzi had tried to stop her, so she'd just stopped doing it in front of her. Vienna knew that kind of indoctrination at such an early age could be extremely difficult to overcome.

She turned over and snuggled closer to Zale instead of turning away from him the way she normally did. She would talk to Mitzi about her memories of Avril and then let Zale know what she'd remembered. It was such a relief to finally get to the bottom of her fears.

CHAPTER FOURTEEN

F our thirty in the morning came early, especially since Vienna had spent most of the night making love with Zale. The Airbnb they'd rented was about twenty minutes from Red Rock because they planned to climb and bike as well as visit the coffee shops. Unfortunately, that put them nearly an hour from the Hoover Dam Lodge and Casino, where they were to check in with their guides, who would shuttle them in vans to the launch area with the others coming on the kayak trip on the Colorado River.

The guide company had all the necessary permits and was responsible for checking their IDs to take them out to the Hoover Dam. Vienna thought it was so cool that on part of the trip, one shore of the river would be in Arizona and one side Nevada and yet they would be traveling on the Colorado River toward Lake Mead.

Vienna waited until they were on the road before she brought up her nightmare. These were her best friends. "I honestly didn't remember my birth mother, although I should have. It's weird how I remember everything else so easily, yet it's almost as if I blocked her out. Her name was Avril, and I didn't even remember that."

"It's possible the memories of losing her were too painful," Harlow suggested.

"Maybe," Vienna mused. "I don't know. But I even suppressed the way she would tell me men aren't to be trusted and that they are liars. She would whisper that to me every time she held me. It's like a subconscious suggestion I can't seem to overcome. I can accept Zale's work and his being gone for long periods of time, but I have this doubt that he'll stay with me, that what he says is real. These men are so good at saying or doing whatever they need to in order to get what they want if they're on a mission."

"But you aren't a mission," Stella pointed out.

Vienna chewed on the side of her lip for a minute and then rubbed at her eyebrow to smooth her frown away. "I wish Mitzi had talked to me about Avril. It would have made it so much easier for me to understand things. I don't know why she didn't." Her eyes met Raine's. "I know you had to do background checks on all of us. Do you have any information on Avril and Mitzi? Anything at all?"

Raine looked uncomfortable. "Mitzi was friends with Avril. They grew up together. I don't know a lot, honestly, which is surprising, although I'm working on it. Avril apparently came to Mitzi sick and pregnant and Mitzi took her in. You said you remembered Avril saying the father had signed away his rights, allowing Mitzi to formally adopt you. That wasn't true. The father hadn't signed his rights away. Avril lied to Mitzi and then lied to the authorities and said she didn't know who the father was when she turned you over to Mitzi to be raised after her death."

Vienna realized at once the mess Mitzi would have found herself in. It wouldn't have been so easy for a single woman, especially a lesbian, to adopt a child. She would have to try to track down the father and then free her of his parental rights in court if he continued to refuse to give up his rights to her.

"It's possible your father doesn't know you even exist," Zahra ventured.

"Maybe," Vienna conceded. She went over her birth

mother's voice when she spoke to Mitzi about the man whom she'd loved—the one who'd wanted her to have an abortion. She didn't sound as if she were lying. She sounded completely brokenhearted. Shattered. "I think Avril did tell him. I believe he was focused on his career and told her to have an abortion. She refused and went to Mitzi. Why she made up the rest about signing away his rights, I don't know, but I can understand why Mitzi wouldn't want to open that can of worms when she realized Avril had lied."

Harlow nodded in agreement. "Mitzi would have been so afraid of losing you. She had the legal right to raise you and that had to be good enough, even though she was never able to formally adopt you."

"How old was I when Avril died?" Vienna asked Raine.

"Avril died when you were five. The cancer had slowly spread through her body and Mitzi took care of her mostly at home, with the help of friends who were nurses. Mitzi had a circle of friends in her community who were very supportive of her throughout Avril's illness, and they helped her care for her—and you."

Vienna rubbed at her eyebrow again. "Those days are so vague to me. I remember so many things with Mitzi and even her friends. Playing board games, cards, learning to knit or crochet. Their cats. I really loved their cats. But I can't recall Avril. That really bothers me. I should be able to when I remember details so clearly."

"Trauma is a funny thing," Shabina said. "I have periods of time completely gone from my memory. Not during the time I was with my captors, but after, when I was back home with my parents. I would be talking to them and suddenly realize I didn't have a clue what we were talking about."

Zahra nodded in agreement. "I think it can be normal to close the door, especially when you're a young child, on a very frightening event or illness you don't understand."

Harlow sighed. "I'm sorry to have to point this out to you, Vienna, but you're a nurse. You know the cancer could have spread to Avril's brain. Your mother sounds as if she was grieving and sometimes even a little out of her mind. Mitzi might not have recognized the signs. She wouldn't have known to protect a child from the things Avril would say or do that seemed quite reasonable to her."

Vienna knew there was every possibility Harlow had hit on the truth. Depending on where the tumors were, Avril could have been suffering all kinds of delusions.

"You know I've never once had a problem with self-confidence," she confided to her friends. "I've never cared one way or the other whether I was in a relationship with someone until I met Zale. I fell pretty hard for him. When he left and didn't contact me, I was far more devastated than I thought possible. I accepted it, because I'm not the kind of woman to chase after a man, and I wasn't about to repeat the experience even after I met him again in Vegas."

"But you did repeat the experience after all," Harlow pointed out.

Vienna nodded. "We talked and he explained what happened, and I believe him. He had planned to contact me after his mission. He had to work out how he was going to keep me safe. Unlike Sam, he will still be working."

"And that's okay with you?" Zahra asked.

"He'll be gone for weeks or possibly months with no communication," Shabina said.

"I'm aware of that. It's not like I go out on dates or have anyone as it is now," Vienna said. "I'll worry about him. I can't help that, but he's my choice. I've never been with anyone else who interests me the way he does. He makes me laugh. He loves the outdoors the way I do. He listens to me when I give my opinion on any subject and actually hears what I say and doesn't treat me like I'm not quite bright because of the way I look. I love being with him."

"You're certain he was coming to you after this assignment?" Raine asked.

Vienna nodded. "Yes. It took quite a bit of convincing. I

didn't believe him at first, but he managed to convince me that he had been trying to find a way to make it all work. He told me quite a bit about his past. We talked for hours. I didn't just fall into his arms, although to be honest, I wanted to. I made it clear it wasn't going to happen. I was honest with him and told him I had been really hurt and didn't want to go through that again. I told him there was an entire hotel full of women who would be willing and to find one of them."

"Ouch," Zahra said. "That must have hurt you even to suggest that."

"It did. I know it would have killed me to see him with another woman, but I couldn't have gone there again with him and have him leave me like he did. I had to really think a long time before I made the decision to start all over again with him. He made it clear he wanted to make it a permanent relationship."

She had braided her hair and wound the thick braid up on top of her head for the kayaking trip, but out of habit, she pushed at the sides as if she could shove hair behind her ears. "I still hear Avril's voice warning me that men say whatever a woman wants to hear in order to get their way, but that they're lying. I wanted him to tell me he wanted to be with me permanently, but then I'd get squirrelly on him, thinking he's just saying that to appease me. It's my issue and I've been honest with him about it. I'm fortunate in that he's extremely patient with me."

"I'm happy for you, Vienna," Harlow said. "Especially that he's patient. Have you told him about your birth mother?"

She shook her head. "Not yet, but I will."

"Raine, you haven't found anything at all on Vienna's father?" Shabina asked.

Raine frowned. "In my original search, nothing showed up at all. He was the big mystery man. I'm not surprised. Avril clearly didn't want Mitzi or the authorities to identify him. She also didn't want him to find Mitzi. Mitzi was a school friend but didn't run in the same social circle. She didn't have money, and the kids at school suspected her of being a lesbian. They were rather cruel. Avril was gorgeous and popular. She was also very compassionate and sweet. She stood up for Mitzi, befriending her. That friendship was genuine. She didn't ask anything in return."

Vienna liked hearing that about her birth mother. It also explained quite a bit about why Mitzi was so fiercely loyal to Avril.

"Avril clearly liked Mitzi and hung out with her, uncaring that anyone might think she preferred women to men. Since Avril was so popular, eventually Mitzi was accepted in her circle of friends as well, and no one dared say anything cruel to Mitzi, or they liked her once they got to know her, just as Avril did."

"That makes me happy," Vienna said. "Mitzi doesn't have a mean bone in her body. I hate the idea that anyone would be cruel to her. I'm grateful Avril made her childhood easier."

"It only seems fair that Mitzi made Avril's life easier at the end," Harlow said.

"It's funny how life can come full circle," Zahra agreed.

Vienna stifled a yawn and Stella laughed, catching it as she glanced in the rearview mirror. "Don't think I didn't see Zale sneaking out of your room this morning."

"Is that why she keeps yawning?" Zahra demanded. "I can't believe you, you little hussy."

"That's exactly why she keeps yawning," Stella said. "And she's your partner on the river. She's riding tandem with you in the kayak."

"What? I thought you were my partner, Stella," Zahra protested.

"Not on your life. I'm not that good, and neither are you. We'd be so far behind everyone else we'd get lost."

Zahra laughed. "That's probably true. I paddle in circles and Stella's worse. She paddles backward."

"That was only after you bashed me in the head with the paddle because I didn't pass you back the chocolate bar."

"That was an accident and you know it. I was trying to reach the dry pack and the dumb paddle kind of got away from me and swung around and smacked you in the head. You should have just given me a chocolate bar instead of hogging them all for yourself."

"Did you swing that paddle or let go of it and it swung on its own?" Stella posed the question in a demanding voice.

"You'll never know for certain, will you?" Zahra asked, her nose in the air.

"Yikes," Vienna said. "I'm not certain I want you in the kayak behind me. You probably should be up front, where I can keep an eye on you at all times."

"That's the only place for her," Stella said. "Right where you can see her."

"Clearly, that bash in the head wasn't nearly as hard as you pretended." Zahra's dark eyes narrowed. "All this time you've made me feel guilty and you weren't that hurt at all."

"It did allow me to go first and pick my favorite person every time we played Clue," Stella said.

"Is that why you always got to go first and we didn't roll to see who would go first?" Harlow asked. "Zahra always backed you no matter what."

Stella laughed. "Guilt. Better than blackmail."

"Lovely," Harlow said. "So, you're with me, Stella. And Raine and Shabina are together. Raine has tons of experience and Shabina is strong. They'll do well together."

"The Hoover Dam Lodge and Casino is coming up," Stella announced. "Everyone had better have their IDs with them. The vans won't wait. Apparently, there are two companies taking out groups today on the river, so there will be one launching right behind us. They want us to hustle."

Vienna was shocked to see Benny Dobsin checking everyone in. He was clearly marked as the guide for their group, along with another man identified as Clay Fontaine for River Adventures, the company they had booked. Benny had a clipboard and was meticulously checking every ID. The second guide was clearly handling all the gear.

Just the sight of Benny put Vienna on edge. First, she'd seen him at the Blue Diamond overnight parking lot where Zale's rental truck had been left before they had started out on the biking trail. Now he was here at the lot where they would be leaving Stella's 4Runner. That seemed like a huge coincidence to her.

She caught up her small pack, shrugged into it and slid her sun hat between the straps. She had very fair skin and needed the wide brim to keep the sun off or she'd be a lobster by midmorning. They joined the other tourists, mostly dressed in shorts and tank tops like them. Some wore light jackets, but most just wore tanks in preparation for the sunny day.

Benny grinned at her when she handed over her ID. "I recognized your name and gave your group a discount, Vienna. I own the company as well as the bike rental and tour company. I grew up here and started both businesses years ago."

Even as he talked to her, she could see he was very thoroughly checking her ID.

"I had no idea the businesses, something I love to do so much, would take off the way they did. You're good to go." He waved her forward and reached for the next ID.

It made sense that he would have businesses, she had to admit. If Benny was local, had grown up in Vegas, he would have climbed, biked and run the river, even played cards, for most of his life. A lot of owners worked their own businesses, particularly guides. Still, it made her incredibly nervous to know that Stella's 4Runner would sit unguarded in the parking lot all day and they would be on the river, where anything could happen.

They were being urged into the van, as time was of the

essence. Another guide company was behind theirs, and they had to launch immediately and couldn't miss their window. That meant she didn't have time to gather her friends and warn them that Benny had been one of the men she'd gambled with and that he'd lost immediately. She had been the one to put him out of the running for the final win. He'd been gracious enough, but that might not matter, not after the warning she'd received. But then, she'd been warned about all the players.

Vienna sighed as she took her seat on the van. Her friends were all around her, but so were the others going on the kayaking adventure with them. It was too close quarters to attempt a private conversation.

Raine caught her eye. "I had no idea Benny Dobsin owned River Adventures." She just came out and said it in a casual voice, as if Benny were an old friend of theirs and they were just discovering he owned the business.

Vienna followed her lead. "It was a surprise to me as well. He didn't say a thing to me, about River Adventures or Desert Biking Rentals and Tours."

"Both businesses are huge. He's so modest," Raine continued.

"He's lived here all his life and knows the river like the back of his hand," Vienna improvised. "Benny told me he's been riding in the desert since he was a little kid."

"Doesn't he play cards with all the top celebrities too?" Raine asked.

"I think so. He's really good." Vienna kept her head down, partially hiding behind Harlow in case anyone else in the van might recognize her from the obnoxious digital pictures displayed on the casino walls, both outside and inside during the tournament. The tournament had been televised for days. Hopefully, no one in the van was a huge poker fan. She slouched in the seat even more.

Benny got behind the wheel, and the doors of the van closed. As he took them toward Hoover Dam, he told them once they were actually at the launch point they would have to move very fast. There was a Porta-Potty. If you had to go, do it fast. If not, skip it because the other company would be coming behind them and want to launch quickly. They would have to carry the kayaks down steep stairs to the river.

The van paused at the Hoover Dam security checkpoint and Benny showed the permits and IDs before taking them through to the launch area. The other van was already there with the kayaks. Benny gave them instructions on the basics of paddling a kayak and water safety as well as making it very clear that everyone was to wear a life jacket at all times. He showed them how to keep things dry, pointed out the line in the water where the serious border alarm was and said no one was to approach it. Once in the water, they were to wait so that everyone launched at the same time. That was one of the reasons it was important to stay together if possible and out of the Porta-Potty.

Vienna and Zahra started down the very steep stairs with their kayak. She was a little surprised that the narrow steps were as difficult as they were. She was used to navigating slate and granite and other kinds of rocks when climbing or hiking, but it did make it awkward with a kayak over her head. As expected, Zahra complained the entire time but never once faltered. She was much shorter than Vienna, and Vienna put her on the high side in order to keep the weight from coming down on her.

Once they placed their kayak, Vienna looked back up and noticed two of the older women who had come together. One had silvery hair wound around her head in a braided figure eight. She wore a tank top and shorts and looked fit. Her companion was a bit shorter, with darker hair streaked with silver cut short in a bob. She wore a light sweater over her tank, but also wore shorts. The two obviously struggled with their kayak as they tried to take it down the narrow, steep staircase leading to the launch.

"Harlow," Vienna called, and jerked her chin toward the two older women.

Harlow followed her without hesitation back up the stairs. Vienna smiled at the two women. "I'm Vienna, this is my friend Harlow. Would you like help? The stairs are extremely steep. We don't mind carrying your kayak for you."

"Would you? I'm Elsa Robinson," the one with the silvery hair said. "This is my friend Verma Shaley. I had no idea it would be so difficult. I do know how to use a kayak. We're both looking forward to seeing the Emerald Cave."

Vienna and Harlow took the kayak, aware that Benny and the other guide, Clay Fontaine, were waiting. As they approached the others with the two older women trailing behind, Vienna became aware of Zahra holding court. The two men, Benny in particular, seemed completely enamored with her. It wasn't unusual. Zahra didn't do anything more than smile her mysterious smile and men seemed to fall at her feet. She had an accent that managed to sound sultry, and her eyes were so dark they were almost black. In this case, Vienna knew she was deliberately distracting the two men so they wouldn't be impatient with the older women.

She flashed a grin at Zahra as Benny helped her into the kayak. No one was going to help Vienna, or the two older women, that was for certain. Zahra took it as her just due, looking up at Benny with her dark eyes and soft, mysterious smile. Harlow got into her seat behind Stella. Everyone else was in the water and ready to go, just waiting on them.

They set out for Sauna Cave, their first stop, which was less than a mile from the dam. Vienna hung back to allow Elsa and Verma to stay ahead of her kayak, just to ensure that they knew what they were doing. Surprisingly, they were extremely good at maneuvering their kayak through the water together, perfectly in sync. They hadn't been exaggerating when they said they were experienced. The paddles cut smoothly through the water.

Vienna knew she didn't have to worry about the two older ladies at all. On the other hand, there were two young men—brothers, if she remembered correctly from the van, Burt and Blane Watson—celebrating Blane's graduation from glass-blowing school. They seemed to be turning their kayak in circles and whooping and hollering every few minutes. Blane, in the front of the kayak, continually threw water at his brother, who retaliated.

Vienna didn't mind anyone having fun, and the two boys seemed to keep up, but there was a young woman by the name of Liza Fremont who had assured everyone over and over that she was very experienced. She was in a kayak by herself. She didn't appear to be very strong to Vienna, and Benny dropped back several times to check on her when she lagged behind the others.

They parked their kayaks, pulling them onto the bank, until everyone was there with the exception of Liza. She couldn't seem to dock. No matter how hard she tried, she couldn't angle in against the current. She paddled and paddled, and her kayak would go backward, not forward. Benny went out to tow her in, but Vienna could see Liza was more of a hindrance than a help. Benny had to give up trying to pull her kayak straight through the current. He circled around her and tried a different angle. This time, Liza put a little more effort into paddling, but the current defeated them.

Without Liza being able to dock, the rest of them couldn't explore Sauna Cave. They had to stick together. No one expressed disappointment, they simply got back into their kayaks and joined Liza and Benny in the water and began paddling toward their next destination—Goldstrike Canyon.

The morning was already very warm, with sun hitting the water and bouncing off the rock walls rising on one side or the other. Vienna was grateful she'd thought to wear her sun hat. It had a very wide brim that shaded not only her face but her shoulders and chest. She knew she'd have to eventually pull on her swim shirt, the one that protected her arms, back and neck as well, but for now, she appreciated the breeze and the cool air coming off the water, and the sun wasn't that high yet.

In spite of the antics of Burt and Blane, the river was peaceful. She enjoyed the fact that Arizona was on one side and Nevada on the other. It seemed such a strange phenomenon.

"You do realize that Goldstrike Canyon has been known to kill people, right, Vienna?" Zahra asked, turning to look back at her. "I read about all the various stops last night. Aside from the fact that Liam Gram was buried feetfirst in the desert so he was like some weird statue, did you know that Lake Mead actually has more dead bodies than any other national park, including Yosemite?"

Vienna stared at her for a moment, resisting the urge to throw water at her with the paddle. "You stayed up last night reading about all the places we'd visit and this is what you're suddenly telling me now? When it's too late and we're already on the water?"

Zahra nodded complacently. "Yep. Someone needed to find out all the facts about the places we'll be visiting today and the risks involved. I wondered if Sam deliberately directed Stella here because secretly, he doesn't really want to get married. Or maybe he has an insurance policy on her."

Vienna frowned at her, not that Zahra could see because she'd already turned around to face front again as she paddled. "Why in the world would you really look up horror stories on all the places we're going, Zahra? You get nightmares over anything remotely scary. You don't read horror and you don't watch scary movies. Why would you have stayed up last night reading about finding dead bodies at these places?"

Zahra really did have an aversion to anything frightening or bloody, even if it was supposed to be funny-scary. She never would watch horror films, even if they were the old ones that were classics. She might have tried to play off the story about Liam Gram being found buried upright in the desert with the cards wired into his teeth, but even that most likely had given her nightmares.

Zahra paddled several strokes, putting muscle into it. She was small, but there was no question that she was an athlete. She might appear lazy to an outsider, and she liked to complain, but she could run circles around them when she made an effort. Sometimes she didn't even have to make much of an effort. Her body was efficient when it came to running, climbing, skiing or just about any sport. The one thing she couldn't do, surprisingly, was swim. She sank like a stone. She kayaked with them, but she was never without her life jacket, and she practiced going underwater all the time so she could hold her breath if she got dunked.

"Zahra. Honey, why would you research any actual deaths occurring at these sites?" Vienna pushed, keeping her tone gentle. There had to be a reason. Zahra wasn't a masochist. She wouldn't give herself several sleepless nights just for the thrill of learning lives had been lost at each of the stops along the river kayaking tour. She was anxious enough being on the water.

Zahra glanced over her shoulder again. "I was worried about you," she admitted.

She rubbed her chin with her forearm and the paddle swung wildly. Vienna ducked. She could see how Stella might get bashed in the head.

"You were worried about me why?"

"I know it sounds silly, but sometimes I get very strong feelings about things. Ever since I heard how Wallin told you the story about Liam Gram being found buried upright in the desert with the cards in his mouth, I've had this feeling that you aren't safe. I know everyone will say it's just because I get freaked out about scary stories, but it's more than that."

Zahra's very expressive face twisted into a cute, but very concerned countenance. "I think that man was threatening you because you bested him at cards and his fragile little ego couldn't take it. That can happen, Vienna. It can really be that simple. Some men have egos so big, if you step on them, they will start some horrible vendetta and won't stop until they think they've won."

Zahra swung back around again, dipping her paddle in the water with a powerful stroke that turned the kayak nearly sideways. Vienna corrected automatically. Was Zahra talking about her life or Vienna's? Or both? Zahra was definitely worried, but how did that fit into researching stories of deaths at the various stops they would be going to? Vienna believed in instincts and following them. She wasn't going to make fun of Zahra because she had a strong feeling that Vienna was in danger.

She let the peace of the river sink into both of them, watching until Zahra's shoulders came back down and her tension seemed to melt away.

"We're coming up on the shore of Goldstrike Canyon now, Zahra. I'll be especially careful," she promised.

Benny stood waiting as Vienna hopped out of the kayak to run it up on shore. He barely managed to nod at her in greeting, too busy helping Zahra out of the kayak.

Zahra smiled up at him, her long dark lashes veiling her eyes. "I was just telling Vienna to be careful. I read that several people have died here. Is that true?"

Vienna stopped in her tracks. Zahra was a natural flirt in that she sounded flirty with her accent. She looked adorable, but she wasn't a woman who ever led men on intentionally. She was looking up at Benny as if he were her hero. She even let him help her over the uneven ground.

"There have been a number of fatalities," Benny agreed, "due to heat exposure, but the trail is closed now during the summer months. Tourists used to hike in without realizing just what they were getting into with the kinds of heat we get here. These are geothermal pools. The waterfalls are even hot. When you wade through the water, you'll feel how warm it is."

He indicated for Vienna to walk ahead of him, but he retained possession of Zahra's arm as if she might not be able to make it over the ground by herself. Liza hurried up to him and began to pepper him with questions, bouncing around him in her very small one-piece that looked as if it might fall off of her.

Benny sighed and looked down at Zahra, who looked up at him more amused than anything else. Vienna had seen her charm everyone male from two-year-olds to ninety-year-olds with just that little lift of her dark eyebrow and twisted enigmatic smile. Benny looked as if he might heave Liza right back into the Colorado, although Vienna doubted it was a possibility. The woman was sticking to him like glue.

She left them to vie for the guide's attention and joined Harlow, Stella, Elsa and Verma as they explored. Raine and Shabina waded through the warm, shallow pools and then came back to their little group.

"What is going on over there? What in the world is Zahra doing?"

"Trying to get away from Benny," Harlow said. "At least she's pretending she's going to leave him. Liza is doing her best to drag Benny away from Zahra, and Benny is holding on to Zahra for dear life. I think the shark is circling and he doesn't want his lifeline to get away."

"She's having way too much fun scaring him like that," Shabina observed.

Behind them, just emerging from the narrow passage, Clay Fontaine and Burt and Blane waded through the shallow warm water to the rocky path that brought them back to the shore.

"Look at that," Clay said, his voice a little overloud. "Benny's got all the luck."

They watched as Liza gripped Benny's arm and pretended to hop around on one foot as if she might have hurt her ankle. Zahra stepped back again to give Benny and Liza room, but Benny caught at her wrist and reeled her in like a fish.

"That's what he gets for being stinking rich and being good-looking. I want a piece of that tail," Clay said, "but you don't see women like that falling all over me."

Burt whistled low. "Some guys get all the luck. I want a piece of that too."

Blane studied the two women with the guide. "Guess we're going to have to make a lot more money, Burt."

"I don't know, some women fall for the cute-boy act," Burt said.

"You'll have to teach that one to me," Clay said. "I have to get them drunk. Works every time."

Harlow and Vienna exchanged a long, mischievous look and then gazed around their circle of friends. Elsa and Verma were already on the move. Elsa slithered up beside Clay, running a hand up his arm to his shoulder.

"I don't think you'd have to get me drunk, Clay, I'd fall all over you," Elsa decreed in a sultry, southern voice. "Verma? Honey? What do you think? Should we take him home to the others? They've been looking for a really hot man. He's a river guide. I think he'd qualify."

Clay's laughter was gruff, but he looked a little alarmed as the women circled around the three men.

"I don't know, Elsa, he's looking pretty hot to me too," Harlow said. "Stella's getting married, but the rest of us are just looking for a good time. These boys qualify. We just want a piece of tail. I like looking at fox tails."

"You and your fox tails, Harlow," Vienna said with disdain. She rubbed Blane's boyish cheeks, which were now bright red. "Have you ever done pony play? You'd look divine with a bit in your mouth." Her thumb ran over his lips.

The three men, mouths open, stared at the women, shock on their faces. Elsa and Verma stroked Clay's arms, shoulders and back, murmuring to each other as if he were just an object, what fun the other women would have with him. All the while, Vienna, Shabina, Harlow, Stella and Raine discussed how the two brothers would look so cute dressed up in various forms of kinky play.

By the time the three men managed to break free from the circle, they were bright red and not from the heat or the sun. The women burst out laughing.

"That should teach those boys not to make objects of women," Elsa said. "Where in the world did you learn all that, dear?"

"I do all sorts of research," Raine answered. "I pass interesting things on to my friends. You never know when it will come in handy."

"He said he wanted a piece of tail," Vienna said. "Perhaps he shouldn't use that specific language."

"Let's go rescue Zahra and see what she's really up to," Stella said. "Not that I'd put it past her to do anything to get out of exploring in this kind of heat."

"It isn't that hot yet," Vienna pointed out. "The water isn't even that hot. We have hot springs where we live. She goes there with us all the time."

"True," Stella said. "But she doesn't actually get in the hot springs. She waits until we go to Shabina's or up to my resort or anywhere there is an indoor jacuzzi or hot tub. She's certain there is some kind of bug that will kill us all if we get inside an outdoor hot spring. Not to mention she is certain a volcano will erupt and we'll die that way."

"Did one of you insist she watch *Dante's Peak*?" Vienna asked.

"Action-adventure night," Harlow and Shabina said together.

"There you go," Vienna said, throwing her hands into the air. "All of you know Zahra can't watch movies like that. Now she'll never go in the hot springs again."

They reached Benny, who had managed to untangle himself from Liza. "We've got to load up fast, ladies," he greeted them. "The other company is right behind us, and we want to be able to spend time at Boy Scout Canyon."

"I might need help into my kayak, Benny," Liza wheedled.

Elsa raised an eyebrow. "Is something wrong with you? I'm sixty-three, and I have no problem getting myself in. I can help you."

Liza glared at her. "I'm perfectly fine, thank you."

"Clay is free," Benny said. "I've got to check and make certain everyone gets back safely. Clay." He raised his voice. "Liza needs a hand."

"Oh, never mind," Liza snapped, and turned toward the line of kayaks.

Elsa put her arm through Verma's as they trailed behind Liza. "I just don't understand why Clay insists on working for Benny when his family comes from old money. He inherited the entire fortune."

"Maybe that's it, dear," Verma went right along with it. "He probably gets tired of women chasing him for his money. On the river, you can tell the fortune-hunters. They go after the owner of the company and never look his way."

It was all Vienna could do not to laugh as Liza lingered behind and then went back to Benny to ask if he would call Clay to assist her into her kayak.

CHAPTER FIFTEEN

▃▃▃▃▃▃▃▃▃▃▃▃▃▃▃▃▃▃▃▃▃▃▃▃▃▃▃▃▃▃▃▃▃▃

Boy Scout Canyon was on the Nevada side of the river and had a sandy shore. Zahra commented on the sand as she helped to dock the kayak with the others.

"So much nicer than all those nasty rocks," she told Vienna.

Vienna shook her head. "You aren't getting out of coming exploring with us this time. No watching the kayaks or building sand castles. No saving the guides from barracudas. Or me from potential killers. You're here to have a good time."

Zahra looked up at the mountain looming over them. "It's hot now, Vienna, and I read about this place. You use ropes to climb up and down rock with water pouring over you."

"Zahra, you're a climber. That's what you do. This isn't a big deal to you."

Zahra made a face.

"Elsa and Verma probably will need help. Liza might need help. You know what you're doing, so you need to come just in case."

Zahra heaved an exaggerated sigh. "Fine. But those ropes are going to be sketch. And they'll be covered in algae, so slimy." She shuddered.

Still, she crossed the sand to join their group just as Vienna knew she would. Elsa and Verma were with them. Elsa applied more sunscreen to her arms, shoulders and face. Vienna didn't think it was doing her much good; her skin had taken on a reddish glow. She took the tube from her and applied a thicker coat to her shoulders and back of her neck before turning to Verma.

"I don't ever burn," Verma assured. "Not like Elsa does. I have this complexion. She's white as snow and turns into a lobster. I just get darker."

"And more beautiful," Elsa assured.

Verma laughed. "You've always said that to me."

"Because it's the truth."

Vienna thought it was so sweet that their friendship had lasted so many years. She hoped her friendships with the women she had now would stand the test of time as well. They followed Benny as he led the kayakers into the narrow passages where water ran over eroded fragments and shot out of the sides of the rock face.

Zahra was absolutely correct when she guessed the ropes would be slimy and green. They were in poor shape as well, an accident just waiting to happen. Used as they were to climbing and depending on rope to keep them alive, the six of them looked at one another before Vienna took the rope in her hands and followed Benny up the narrow passage. Water raced down as she climbed, using her feet and hands to pull herself up.

The rope was old but it held, and she nodded to Zahra, who stepped aside and placed it in Elsa's hands. She stood beside the woman, giving her instructions on how to climb up with the water pouring down on her. It wouldn't get into her face, but still, it was a nuisance and distraction if one wasn't used to climbing. Looking down at her, Vienna could see the determination on Elsa's face. The moment she neared the top, she broke out in a smile and Vienna reached for her, dragging her to the flat surface, where she stepped aside and peered down at Verma and gave her the thumbs-up.

Verma struggled a little bit more than Elsa did. Liza's

sighs could be heard above the roaring of the water falling. Vienna helped Verma onto the top of the rock and then everyone waited for Liza to make it up the rope. She slid down twice the first time she tried. Zahra rolled her eyes and put a hand on her hip, but no one sighed or made a comment the way Liza had. Cursing, Liza fought her way up until she got to the top and dragged herself over the rim, where she sat for a minute catching her breath.

Zahra caught the rope and easily climbed, Stella and Shabina following. Harlow and Raine waited to ensure the rest of their kayaking group made it up without incident. There were two more ropes and then they were in between two large boulders. Evidently, Benny expected a ladder to lead to the top of the boulder, but the ladder was missing. Instead, two men seemed to be camping in the nest at the top of the boulder. They had camping chairs set up and had laid out their personal gear.

One man stood up. "Hello, ladies," he greeted. He was an older gentleman with a long graying beard and a good body, and he was wearing absolutely no clothing. "I'm Rick. This is Morty."

Morty remained seated in his camp chair.

Zahra's eyes went wide and she put her fingers over them but splayed them wide so she could still see. "Oh my. Definitely not PG in here, Benny."

"Merciful heavens," Verma said, fanning herself. "Benny, you need to charge more."

"Where did you find him? He's rather well put together," Elsa added. "I agree with Verma, you aren't paying him enough."

"How did you get here?" Benny asked.

"We hiked in from the trail," Rick supplied. "We're camping."

"I can see that," Benny said.

Rick seemed very comfortable in his nudity, but then he had every reason to be, Vienna decided. He folded his arms across his chest and leaned one hip nonchalantly against the rock as if he owned the place. "Don't have a lot of extra, but if you ladies want to join us . . ."

Two of the younger women who had come with their mothers giggled. Benny glanced over at them. They were underage. The mothers didn't know whether to laugh or be outraged.

"Sorry, this hasn't happened before," he mumbled. "Let's keep moving. Lunch is at our next stop. No one needs to join them."

"That's disappointing," Rick said, winking at Zahra.

Benny scowled at him. "This is a family event, Rick." He began to usher his group of kayakers away from the tall double boulders.

Vienna exchanged a smirk with the others. He hadn't seemed that upset until Rick singled Zahra out. Zahra had that little mysterious smile she sometimes got that no one seemed to be able to interpret but drove men crazy. Liza stayed very close to Clay, much to the amusement of Elsa and Verma. Burt and Blane kept a distance from the group of women, preferring to keep the mothers and teenage girls in between them.

The paddling to the next stop, Arizona Hot Springs, was easy enough, with Zahra putting her core behind each stroke. When she wanted to get somewhere, she was good at any sport. She might not be able to swim and she might even give them all a hard time and say she was going to fall asleep in the kayak, but she would never leave all the work to Vienna.

"What's up with you hanging with Benny so much, Zahra? And don't give me a bunch of crap about finding him attractive. Or that you're saving him from Liza. Especially now that Liza's zeroed in on Clay. As long as Clay doesn't let it drop that he isn't from one of the wealthiest families on the planet, he'll get very lucky."

Zahra gave one of her very charming giggles and sent

Vienna a quick look over her shoulder. "I wish I'd thought of that one. Elsa and Verma are wonderful. I really like them."

"I do too, but that isn't going to stop me from wondering about Benny."

Zahra sighed again as she turned back toward the front. "As long as I'm with him, he can't arrange any accidents for you. Don't think I'm paranoid. I still have this feeling of dread. It's getting stronger, not going away. Do you know Benny has four brothers? He's the oldest."

Vienna hadn't known. She wasn't certain where Zahra was going with that information, so she remained silent.

"His father passed away when he was fourteen, and he took over providing for his family. He wanted his brothers to go to college. In some ways, he's really to be admired."

"Why do you have that hesitancy in your voice, Zahra? Looking after his family and starting several businesses that became so successful is admirable."

"Yes. At the same time, if his brothers didn't or don't meet his standards, if they don't do what he wants them to do, he cuts them out of his businesses. He dictates what he believes is best for them and they have to do as he says. It doesn't matter if it isn't their dream. One wanted to become a surgeon, but he thought it would take too long. He said it would be better if he settled for being an accountant. He actually told me he made fun of him, and pointed out how blood used to make him queasy when he was in grammar school."

"I can't imagine you staying quiet about your opinion."

"Liza laughed her head off and was very snarky. I waited until she was finished before I gave him the eyebrow and told him some of the best surgeons started off that way. I told him I certainly hoped he changed his mind and fully supported his brother's dream. I didn't stop looking him straight in the eye until he squirmed away."

Zahra looked over her shoulder, frowning again. "He's very much a dictator, and he definitely has a bad temper. I think he's used to his brothers falling in line with whatever he wants. If you notice, Clay does his job but keeps his distance."

Vienna hadn't noticed. She'd been having fun. "Benny seemed to take the naked men in stride until Rick invited you up to share his lunch."

"That bothered me because he should have been looking out for the underaged kids." Zahra glanced over her shoulder again. "I don't know, I wish I could shake this feeling, Vienna. You usually get this feeling before any of the rest of us."

She sounded so hopeful that Vienna wished she could tell her she had a growing feeling of dread, but she didn't. She had enjoyed every moment of being outdoors and on the water, and of exploring the various places they'd stopped. She felt guilty that Zahra had spent time watching Benny so she would be safe.

"Benny said something that upset you, and you clearly said something that upset him." Vienna was very careful.

Zahra went silent again, paddling strongly through the water toward Arizona Hot Springs. "I should have kept my mouth shut, Vienna. I don't know what possessed me to tell him anything. I don't even talk to my best friends about my life, but I just blurted out things I shouldn't have because he was so certain he had the right to dictate his brother's life. He was also sure his brother would just fall in line and stay quiet and grateful."

Zahra wasn't someone who cried. Shabina could cry once in a while. Harlow was known to cry over a sad movie. Stella definitely did. Vienna was known to be a sympathy crier if it was someone she loved who was crying. Zahra remained stoic. Vienna would have bet her last dollar that Zahra was crying at that moment, but she was in the front of the kayak and it was impossible to see her face.

"Benny was so pompous, saying how he told his brother not to go to med school. It really bothered me. When we were alone, he brought up the subject again. He was upset that I didn't see his point of view and he wanted to convince me that he was right. He told me how childish his brother was being. That rather than take the college money set aside for him—that Benny had dictated could only be used for accounting classes—his brother had left home and was working his way through pre-med."

"Good for him."

"That's what I said. Benny nearly exploded with anger. He said his brother wouldn't even talk to him, but that he'd come around when it got too rough. He'd come crawling back. I told him not to bet on it. That I hadn't."

Vienna went very still. Zahra never talked about her family because it was such a painful subject. To have her talk about her family to a complete stranger was shocking no matter the circumstances.

"He asked me what I meant, and I told him I came from a small village where arranged marriages were common and women had no rights. My brother and older sister had both been married in that way, but my parents had promised me I wouldn't have to be. They allowed me to attend schools outside of our village. In return, I promised to send them money. I went to visit them and a man saw me, one of the very important men in our village. I told Benny when that kind of man offers marriage for your daughter, you don't decline."

For a moment Zahra rubbed her face on her arm, but then she squared her shoulders and continued rowing. "I didn't give him details, but I said I refused. They all thought I'd come around if it meant I'd never see my family again. I never relented and I told him I never saw my parents again. They refused to even FaceTime with me when that became available. I did send them money and they accepted it, but they never spoke to me. I told him it would be terrible if he never spoke to his brother, that my parents were dead and we were never able to heal that wound. I pointed out anything could happen, car accidents, anything at all. Did pride matter so much? Dictating what his brother did? Was it so terrible to support his brother's dream whether he succeeded or failed? Wasn't he proud of him for just trying?"

Vienna definitely heard a quiet little sob in Zahra's voice and a lump formed in her throat. "Honey, I'm sorry this brought up sad memories when it was supposed to be fun for you. Not everyone understands that family is more important than anything. I almost lost sight of that when I got into that terrible fight with Mitzi. I don't even understand why I was so angry with her. Jealousy, I guess, that she found Ellen and I was alone."

"You don't? It wasn't jealousy, Vienna. You wanted her to be happy. You never once expressed jealousy that Mitzi found Ellen. Not one single time. In fact, you often said you regretted not knowing Ellen. You were hurt that Mitzi said she wasted her life raising you when you weren't even hers. That was the real reason."

Vienna contemplated the truth of that while they docked their kayak alongside Stella and Harlow's kayak. The shore was sandy, and Clay announced there were pit toilet bathrooms nearby. Immediately there was a rush in the direction he had indicated. Liza glared at Zahra, seeming reluctant, but in the end, nature won out, and she hurried off with another warning glare.

"You're such a man-stealer," Raine accused, nudging Zahra with her shoulder.

They pulled out their packs and settled together to eat. Vienna found she was very hungry after using so much energy to paddle all morning. Paddling a kayak used nearly all the muscles in the body, including back, shoulders, arms, abs and core muscles if one paddled correctly. Elsa and Verma joined them, and they simply widened their circle. Benny and Clay and the mothers with the teens joined, bringing their lunches. Surrounding them came the others.

"What are all those walkways built into the rocks we hear about above Emerald Cave?" Burt asked.

"The catwalks," Benny said. "River workers had to measure the depth of the water in two locations daily. They'd walk along the catwalk to get to a steel wire system that held a pulley cart. The steel wire was suspended across the river."

The entire group surrounding Benny looked out over the wide expanse of the river. Right now, the banks were full and the current was strong.

"There were two gauging stations where the water was measured, and one still can be seen. You can access it from the water by climbing up to it. It's really cool. The second gauging station was also perched along the cliffs downstream, but it no longer exists."

"Why would they need to measure the water?" one of the teenage girls asked.

"That's a good question," Benny said, shooting her a quick smile. "When Hoover Dam was being built, two engineers were given the huge responsibility of collecting data on things such as silt content, flow, depth and even temperature of the water. That information was critical in order for the dam to be able to carry out its main purpose of flood control."

"That catwalk is pretty cool," Blane said. "Burt and I want to take a walk on it. I'm not afraid of heights, which is a good thing."

"Yeah, but take a good look as you paddle under it. You can see the wood is rotted in places. The catwalk is pretty unstable, and the rangers discourage visitors from using it," Benny said. "And it's a big no to try to use technical gear to cross on the steel wire to the catwalk. The wire is extremely unstable now."

"I'll bet you've done it," Blane said.

Benny looked up from his sandwich, a small grin on his face. "When I was young and stupid. I have younger brothers, and we used to come here nearly every day with my dad. He'd tell us all the rules and then he'd go to work and we'd proceed to break every single rule he'd given us. We didn't understand the danger, we were just kids and we thought we were invincible. We ran along that catwalk back in the day and challenged each other to do the stupidest things, but we had so much fun."

Vienna exchanged a quick look with Zahra. There was joy in Benny's voice at the memories, and his face had lit up, easing some of the serious lines.

"Did your father catch you?"

"He knew," Benny said. "Dad wasn't the kind of man to get upset with us. He just would shake his head and tell us if he came home without one of us, Mom would likely do him in. He made sure we were safe by teaching us how to be safe on the river. He worked on our skills all the time, but he made everything fun."

"Wish my dad was like that," Burt said. "He's all about responsibility and 'Do what I say or you're going to be kicked out of the house.' That's the threat all the time."

Blane gave a little snort. "He was ready to boot us out when we were three. We didn't clean our room or pick up our toys." He deepened his voice. "'You're out of here, boys.'"

"You're lucky, man," Burt reiterated. "What's he doing now? Does he help you guide?"

A shadow crossed Benny's face. "We lost him when I was a teenager. He was in a freak accident, had a ruptured spleen, needed an operation and they couldn't get a surgeon in time." He trailed off and suddenly looked at Zahra as comprehension set in. "Guess that's why my younger brother is studying to be a surgeon. He'll make a good one."

He stood up abruptly. "I have to check with the other guides and companies and see if they're on time. It can get stacked around Emerald Cave. We want to hit Willow Beach Marina around four thirty or five o'clock at the latest. Clay will get you to Emerald Cave and then take you to the marina. I'll have everything ready for us to shuttle you back to your vehicles."

He sounded gruff. Vienna didn't blame him. He'd just

gone down memory lane and most likely realized his father had made life fun for his brothers and him. He'd taken on the responsibilities of a man at a young age. Losing his father to an accident had most likely scared him and he wanted to keep his brothers safe, so he'd gotten overprotective. That trait had worsened in him over the years until he didn't remember why he was that way.

Vienna watched Benny expertly launch his kayak into the river. He did it smoothly and paddled as if born on the river. Remembering his father's death and the need for a surgeon when they'd been unable to get to one in time had made him realize his brother's determination to become a doctor stemmed from that loss. Benny had a lot to think about.

"Elsa, you're really burned. I don't think your sunscreen is really working," Verma said, sounding worried.

Vienna turned to look. "Oh no, Elsa, she's right. Your skin is fried. Do you have a shirt or something you can wear?"

"No, but I'll be all right. It isn't that much longer. I'll put more sunscreen on," Elsa promised.

Vienna would have offered her swim shirt, but she knew it wouldn't fit the older woman. It was long sleeved and Vienna planned to put it on. She was getting burned in spite of using sunscreen.

"Take my sun hat at least. It will really keep the sun off your neck and shoulders. The brim is so wide it shades your body."

"No, you're very fair, Vienna, but I appreciate it," Elsa refused.

"I've got a ball cap in my pack."

"I can wear the ball cap," Elsa said.

"It's grungy or I'd have you wear it. I have a shirt as well, so I'll be fine." Vienna passed her the wide-brimmed sun hat. "It has a string to wear under the neck so it won't fly off in the wind. Trust me, the brim is so wide, it occasionally acts like a sail."

Vienna fished around in her small daypack and came up

with her swim shirt, pulling it on over her sunburned arms.
She really should have put it on much earlier. She wasn't as
burned as Elsa, but she hadn't done her skin any favors, and
she knew better. The ball cap really had seen better days.
She wore it often and it looked it. Normally, she would have
pulled her hair—either a braid or a ponytail—through the
hole in the back of the cap, but she left it pinned on top of
her head.

They meticulously picked up their litter and were back in
the kayaks heading to Emerald Cave. The cave had been on
Stella's list of things to see for a long time. Emerald Cave
was located on the Arizona side of the river. Vienna still got
a kick out of thinking there was an Arizona side and a Nevada side of the Colorado River.

From the outside, the cave didn't look like much. They
had to line up with quite a few other kayakers waiting to go
inside before it was actually their turn. Vienna found herself
looking up at the rising canyon walls and the catwalks
Benny had told them about. On the side of the river up high
was the gauging station, a boxy building jutting out from the
side of the cliff. She was glad she hadn't been the one to take
the measurements. The river rocked the kayak. Peace settled
over her. She loved the outdoors.

"I really detested being inside that hotel, Zahra," she con-
fessed. "This is so much better, being out here on the river.
I know you don't like to swim, but are you enjoying it at
all?"

Zahra laid her head on her arm. "It isn't that I don't like
to swim, Vienna. I sink like a stone. I can go underwater and
hold my breath. I'm not afraid of the water going over my
head or anything like that. I just can't float or swim. I sink."

Vienna couldn't imagine not knowing how to swim.
Mitzi had been terrified of Vienna drowning and had her
take swim lessons every summer, all summer long. She
wouldn't accept excuses from Vienna on not attending either. Consequently, Vienna was a very strong swimmer.

She'd learned to dive as well as rescue in the water, and eventually she became certified in CPR.

"I could teach you. We could use Shabina's pool."

There was a small silence. "I'll think about it. I do want to learn. It's just that when you get to be old, learning seems to take longer. The things you could have learned that seemed no big deal now look dangerous."

"That's true, but I'd never let anything happen to you."

Zahra didn't lift her head, but she turned it so she was looking at Vienna. "I feel so lucky that I found this group of women. Most times we're lucky to find one really great friend in our lifetime, but I've got five and they're the best."

"You're not wrong," Vienna agreed. She picked up the paddle. "I think it's our turn to go in. You get ready with your camera. You're really good at taking photographs."

"If I remember to turn the camera on." Zahra giggled and sat up straight again, pulling out her cell phone and getting it ready. "What makes the water in the cave so green? I know Benny must have told us, but I was sleepy and I took a nap during some of his stories."

That made Vienna laugh. She lined up her kayak behind Stella and Harlow. "It has the deepest and cleanest water from Lake Mead. There was something about the hot springs dumping hot mineral water into the river. The explanation of volcanic activity beneath the surface creating the hot springs. Then that water evaporating and condensing into rainwater, giving the Colorado the cleanest water ever. Don't ask me to explain the process, I wasn't listening either."

"What?" Zahra turned around again.

Vienna laughed. "Before you look outraged, I do know the sun has to shine to the bottom of the water just right to give you the full effect of that brilliant emerald green. It glows and can make you glow as well. Some say the sun hits the cavern walls and produces the light, but it's really the sun piercing the water and hitting the floor from above."

"You could have been a scientist."

"Not really. If I pay attention, I can pick things up. Stella told me Emerald Cave is gorgeous, so I kind of wanted to learn a little bit about it."

Vienna paddled slowly into the cave. Her breath caught in her throat as at once there seemed to be a brilliant strobe effect as green danced over their bodies. The emerald was brilliantly green, bright and vivid, more than she ever expected, even after seeing photographs others had taken. She knew the color depended on time of day and even the river itself and fluctuations, rain and lack of it. She hadn't expected to see the intensity of color displayed. Just coming into the cave was worth feeling the animosity she'd felt from so many players when she'd worked her way up to the final table in the tournament. The cave was that beautiful.

They couldn't stay, there were too many kayaks lined up behind them. Vienna and Zahra paddled out and set their way to go down the river toward Willow Beach Marina. Most of the others were ahead of them. Vienna had kept in the rear of their group to ensure everyone was safe. Harlow tended to lead the way while Vienna stayed for the rear guard.

She could see the catwalk built around the canyon and, looking up, saw that some of the boards did appear to be rotting.

Zahra turned her head. "I have to pee."

"No, you don't," Vienna said firmly.

"I do. Really bad. We have to find a place to dock the kayak. It will only take me a minute, and it isn't like we're going to get lost."

"Why didn't you go at lunch? There were those outhouses."

Zahra wrinkled her nose. "Seriously? And stand in line to go to a smelly outhouse? I'd rather dig a hole in nature. Come on, Vienna."

"You were planning this all along."

"Maybe," Zahra conceded.

"It's only a couple of miles to the marina, and there are bathrooms."

"No, Benny will say we have to hurry and get on the shuttle or we'll be left behind. Please, Vienna. I really have to go."

Vienna looked toward the heavens. It wasn't as if they were going to get lost. "You are such a pain in the butt, Zahra."

Zahra flashed her a grin. "I know, but you're so sweet you love me anyway."

Vienna looked the bank over. Most of it wasn't very approachable. The current was getting stronger and the wind was picking up. She didn't want to fight her way back to the marina.

"If you see somewhere, give me the heads-up. The current's pulling at us."

"Just ahead, it's a small sandy spot. I know they said to be careful where you pull up your kayak, that the river fluctuates fast, but I won't be a minute and if you stay with it, we won't lose it."

"That's all we'd need," Vienna groused, but she really didn't care. They were fairly close to the finish of the trip, and she was enjoying every second on the water. The slight delay was only going to allow her to be on the river longer.

It did take some strength to fight the current in order to get to the little beach Zahra had spotted, reminding Vienna of Liza's inability to manage to dock at Sauna Cave. Zahra hopped out, caught up her daypack and raced to an outcropping of boulders a short distance away. Vienna found herself laughing and looking up at the sky where a couple of birds circled lazily. This was so Zahra. She marched to her own beat. Quirky. Funny. Giving. She was her own person all the way.

True to her word, Zahra was back in the kayak within minutes and they were once more paddling down the river toward the marina.

"I noticed you managed to get into the kayak all by yourself," Vienna observed. "I wasn't certain you could take a step without support."

"If I was good at wielding these paddles, I'd smack you the way Stella is always saying I smacked her. I sacrificed for you."

The sound of terrified screams was loud, reverberating off the canyon walls. The screams came from multiple sources and went on and on, seemingly increasing in volume. Vienna poured strength into her paddle, Zahra adding her muscle so that the kayak shot through the water.

Just up ahead they saw their group of kayakers gathered around two of the kayaks. Clay was fastening a tow rope to both kayaks. He tossed one to Harlow as Vienna and Zahra swept in close to them.

"You sure you can do this?" Clay called to Harlow.

"Yes, just go. You called ahead for ambulances?"

There was no place to stabilize the wounded. Vienna could see splashes of bright red. One was Burt's kayak, the other Elsa's. She pulled her kayak close to Elsa's. The older woman was slumped over, unconscious. Verma cried piteously and called out to her.

"Keep paddling, Zahra," Vienna instructed. She reached for the first aid kit. It would be difficult to try to assess and treat Elsa on the water in a moving kayak, but she didn't want her to bleed out if that was a possibility. "Stay at the exact pace with Elsa's kayak." That wouldn't be easy either, not with the wind and current.

She waited until Zahra had lined up their kayak, bringing Vienna opposite Elsa. Vienna leaned carefully over until she could gently move Elsa back to examine her. One bullet had skimmed her forehead. That had taken a chunk of skin. The bleeding was severe, but head wounds often were. The one that looked gruesome was the one up high in her shoulder, close to her neck. That had to have shattered her shoulder.

Hopefully, it hadn't severed an artery. If that had happened, there was nothing Vienna could do.

She searched for the entry and exit wound. Once she found both she was fairly certain the artery had been missed by a hairsbreadth. Her kayak bumped the other one and bounced off, jerking her and throwing the unconscious older woman sideways in her seat.

"I'm sorry, Vienna, I'm trying," Zahra said.

"You're doing great. Clay's towing Elsa's kayak and he's having trouble as well," Vienna soothed her. "Verma, honey, please stop crying so loud." She didn't want to say the woman was getting on her nerves, but she was. If it was bothering her, she couldn't imagine what the noise was doing to Zahra, who wasn't used to kayaking and had to be afraid. "I need you to try to help steady the kayak. Clay's strong, but he's fighting the wind, paddling for his kayak and yours. Zahra has never really done this before. You're far more experienced than she is. Can you help out so I can take care of Elsa?"

Verma hiccuped and nodded her head wildly. She dipped her paddle in the water and steadied the kayak, her gaze fixed on Clay, suddenly matching the way he pushed the paddle through the water. Zahra lined up Vienna with Elsa and guided their kayak alongside.

Vienna had used the time to make up several sterilized gauze pads so she could pack the wound front and back to try to stem the bleeding. Thankful Elsa was unconscious, she did her best to stabilize the shoulder so if she did wake while they were still on the water, the bones might not grind together so horribly.

"That's the best I can do for her, Verma. I'm going to try to go to the other kayak and see how bad those boys were wounded. You want her to remain unconscious. This wound is serious and would hurt like hell if she woke. Paddle and help Clay as much as possible. We're not that far out now and they'll have ambulances waiting."

Vienna signaled to Zahra and they pulled away from

Elsa's kayak and stalled to wait for Harlow and Stella, who were towing Burt and Blane.

"How bad is she?" Zahra asked.

"I don't know," Vienna answered honestly. "Who would shoot at a bunch of innocent kayakers?" She tried to push away the nagging thought that she'd switched hats with Elsa and it was entirely possible that someone had shot the older woman thinking she was Vienna. That didn't explain the two brothers being shot, but she still couldn't push the thought away entirely.

Both brothers had been wounded. Neither could paddle, leaving Harlow and Stella to do the work of towing them against the wind. Fortunately, they were closing in on the marina. It looked to Vienna as if the two boys had been clipped and little damage had been done. She frowned as she assessed the damage. How had they escaped with minor injuries from what was obviously a high-powered rifle? Probably a sniper rifle of some sort. Yet Elsa had nearly been killed. Most likely she would have been killed, but the kayak was on rough water and had fortunately lurched, saving her life—at least Vienna guessed that was what happened.

Had the brothers been wounded just so it appeared as if Elsa was a random target, not the central one? And why hadn't anyone heard the shots? They were on open water. The shots from a rifle should have been loud. Even suppressors were somewhat loud. The back of her neck tingled.

"Zahra, you don't have that feeling, do you? The one that told you I was in trouble?"

Zahra gave her a look over her shoulder as they swept into the Willow Beach Marina and what looked like a military operation. There were men with guns on the beach. There was a helicopter in the distance. Ambulances. Clay looked haggard as he dragged Elsa's kayak onto the shore with Verma's help.

Vienna and Zahra raced to help him, but instantly they were surrounded by grim-faced men with guns.

"Vienna Mortenson?" one man said. "Zahra Metcalf? You both need to come with me now."

"I need to see to my patient." Vienna indicated Elsa.

Two EMTs had raced down to the kayak. Shabina and Raine pulled their kayak onto the shore and immediately they were surrounded by the armed men as well, almost before they could take a step. The moment Harlow and Stella had gotten the two brothers in close, the men with guns waded into the water to help pull the kayak onto the beach.

Stella protested the order to go with the men. "I have to take the shuttle to my 4Runner."

"No, ma'am. You have to come with us now."

Vienna continued to protest as well until a hard hand gripped her arm. She looked up to see Zale. He'd never looked so dangerous or grim-faced in his life. He appeared— terrifying.

"Get in the helicopter now, Vienna. All of you."

It was a clear order. Stella looked from him to the others and she marched to the helicopter, leading the way.

CHAPTER SIXTEEN

〰〰〰〰〰〰〰〰〰〰〰〰〰〰〰〰〰〰

Pack fast," Zale said. "Your flight leaves in two hours."

"My 4Runner . . ." Stella protested.

"Will be driven back to your home. Sam's got it covered. You can text him," Rainier replied. "We're not taking chances with any of you."

"You think whoever shot Elsa was really trying to kill me," Vienna said. "That's why you were so fast to come after us."

"I don't know, Vienna," Zale admitted. "But I'm not willing to take chances with your life. It's best you're back home, where this nutcase has to come onto your turf if he's really after you."

"Why would he be after Vienna?" Raine asked.

"Get packed," Rainier interrupted. "We need everything out of here. For once, Raine, your people and my people agree. They want you gone and we'll divide the cleaning work."

Vienna had brought very little with her in the way of personal items, so it wasn't that difficult to put everything into her pack when it came to clothes. Gear was another matter altogether. She'd brought hiking, climbing, kayaking, and biking gear. The women piled their packs near the front entrance in record time, going over their lists to ensure they didn't leave anything behind.

Shabina and Harlow made them hot chocolate with

whipped cream and they gathered in the living room together once they had everything ready to go.

"Have you heard how Elsa and the two brothers are doing?" Vienna asked Zale.

"Elsa is still in surgery. The brothers are both fine. The wounds were no more than superficial at best."

Raine had her laptop out. She sat on the love seat seemingly caught up in what she was reading, but glanced up sharply when she heard the report. "That sounds deliberate to me. And as if the shooter is a marksman. He knew exactly what he was doing."

Vienna's heart sank. Raine's assessment went along with what she'd been thinking. She looked to Zale, but he was wearing his stone face and didn't comment.

"Raine, do you think Elsa was shot because I gave her my hat to wear? I put on a long-sleeved swim shirt and ball cap and she put on my wide-brimmed sun hat." There was no way to keep her voice from trembling. She pressed her fingers over her lips. If Elsa died because she'd given her the hat, she would never be able to forgive herself.

"This isn't your fault, Vienna. Even if the shooter was after you, it wouldn't be your fault." Raine frowned at the two men. "Do either of you have any thoughts on this?" Raine asked Rainier but looked at Zale.

When neither reacted, she sighed. "The problem with being an analyst is my brain won't turn off. For instance, I couldn't stop thinking about why two very experienced operatives would insist on remaining in roles that clearly had been blown. No operative would do that, not if they knew what they were doing, not unless they had a very good reason to want to remain in that hotel where anyone could be an enemy. Security had keys to the rooms. It just didn't make sense."

"You're getting way off track, Raine," Zale cautioned. "What we were doing at the hotel has nothing to do with what happened on the river."

"Oh, but I think it does," Raine contradicted.

Vienna wasn't sure how the two were connected, but she had thought it odd that the two men had stayed at the hotel after their cover had been blown. It didn't seem a reasonable thing for any experienced operative to do. She had let Zale convince her it was Rainier who was insisting on staying. Rainier, who was older and even more experienced. He wasn't a man who lost his temper. He would pull out a gun and shoot someone but he would do it coldly. Why hadn't the two men left?

"Vienna said she thought there was another agent in the hotel somewhere. One of yours."

Vienna ducked her head. "I did. I'm sorry. I thought he might be a double agent trying to kill you both. I didn't name him." Now Zale would never trust her.

"How the hell would she know that?" Rainier demanded.

"Let's not get off track here," Raine said smoothly. "As much as I'm sure you both would prefer that. If another agent had the mission you claimed to have, what were you really doing there?"

Vienna froze, her breath catching in her throat. Where was Raine going with this?

"What we're sent out on is not anyone's business, and you more than anyone else know that, Raine," Rainier cautioned. "You need to stop right there."

Vienna moistened her lips. "Are you confirming that Raine was correct when she said you weren't there to find out who was trying to kill Daniel Wallin? Or who had killed those agents?" She didn't take her eyes from Zale. Pleading with him to deny what Raine was intimating.

"Are you certain you don't want to do any talking?" Raine repeated to the two agents.

"I'm certain you shouldn't divulge classified information." Zale definitely sounded threatening.

"I have no intention of doing anything like that. I know better. I've discovered what the original bet between Daniel

Wallin and Liam Gram was. I believe you both knew what that was all along."

"Maybe you should talk to the two of us in private before you disclose any information that has the possibility of being classified to anyone else, Raine," Rainier cautioned.

"Nothing I've uncovered involves secrets that have to do with the military," Raine replied. "This has to do with Liam's son. I'm certain you're very aware of who he is and why Daniel Wallin wants him dead." Raine lifted her gaze from her laptop screen and gave them both an accusatory glare. "You've had this information all along and could have disclosed it at any time. You simply chose not to."

Neither man denied her statement. Vienna avoided Zale's eyes when it was so obvious he wanted her to look at him. The women gathered around Raine and looked at her expectantly. She always came through for them. As tired as they were from the day on the river, as much packing as they had done, they wanted answers, especially Vienna. Vienna sat next to Raine when she scooted over to make room for her on the love seat.

"Liam Gram had one son, Elliot. Elliot never lived with Liam, and few people knew of him. He didn't have Liam's last name because Liam and his mother, Astrid Blom, had never married. The bet between Daniel Wallin and Liam Gram was for half of Wallin's stock in the Northern Lights Hotel and Casino. That would give Liam thirty-seven-and-a-half percent, or equal the shares as Daniel. Daniel wouldn't like that, nor would his grandfather. The entire point of allowing Daniel the seventy-five percent was to have a legal business the Bottaro family could still control. Angelo was a very shrewd man. No doubt he saw the handwriting on the wall and knew the Feds were going to be cracking down in Las Vegas. Daniel was making a fortune for them. The last thing they would want was for him to lose his shares to an outsider."

"Wow, Daniel must have been very sure of himself to make a bet like that," Harlow said.

"He was," Vienna said. "Just the way he was with me. He relied on his psychic gift to always win the big hands. My guess is his voice didn't work on Liam any more than it did on me."

Raine looked at Zale and Rainier again. She waited a few moments while the clock ticked, filling the silence with the rhythmic sound. Vienna glanced up at her and then followed her gaze to Zale and Rainier. They appeared to be wearing expressionless masks. The tension in the room wound tighter. Both stared at Raine as if they might really pull out their guns and shoot her at any moment. Vienna felt that the danger to her friend was so real she shifted position to put her body between Raine and Rainier, believing, at first, that he might be the bigger threat.

"Liam apparently went directly from the casino to a young lawyer who was a junior partner in a rising firm in Vegas," Raine continued. "He had his will drawn up, leaving his shares in the casino to his son and any heirs his son might have. He instructed the lawyer to file the will and also his share in the casino immediately. Liam then disappeared, which scared the junior lawyer. He did, in fact, file the document proclaiming Liam was a shareholder, but it wasn't the original. He had that as well as Liam's will locked away in a safe in the law offices."

Vienna's heart began to pound. Zale's eyes had gone very dark. His gaze narrowed until his eyes were twin laser beams, deadly and lethal. There was no doubt that he was warning Raine to stop the flow of information. Vienna had shifted her body to block the wrong man from her friend.

"Wallin owned someone who intercepted Liam's claim and he destroyed it. He was certain that was done. There were no more filings and as far as Wallin knew, when Liam turned up dead, that was the end of it. The junior lawyer was terrified after Liam's body was found. He didn't want to end up the same way, and he knew that the Bottaro family had to be involved, so he simply wrote a letter to be opened in case of his death and put it with the original document containing the shares and Liam's will. That lawyer died recently and his firm opened the letter."

"Raine, enough," Zale said quietly. The purr of menace was in his voice.

"You had every chance to come clean," Raine said. "Both of you."

There was no fear in her voice, but Vienna knew there should have been. The tension in the room was coiled so tight she expected the room itself to shatter at any moment. Her chest hurt. The pressure felt enormous. She lifted a hand to her heart and pressed hard. Tiny beads of sweat trickled between her breasts and her palms felt clammy.

"I'm telling you to stop," Zale commanded. "You're walking the edge of classified information."

"None of this is classified. Do you think I don't know the difference? This is information certain parties don't want known and you didn't disclose but know you should have."

For the first time, Vienna could see that Raine was angry. She rarely lost her temper but when she did, the explosion was like a bomb going off. She was extremely angry at Zale and Rainier—and that didn't bode well for Vienna. Whatever Raine had discovered neither man wanted disclosed, but more than that, Raine knew it was going to really hurt her friend. Raine only got angry when someone harmed her friends.

"Liam's son, Elliot Blom, was raised by his mother, unaware that he owned shares in a very lucrative casino. His mother passed away right before he turned eighteen and he joined the service and made that his career. He was extremely intelligent and while in the military pursued college. Eventually, he became an officer, got his degree—several degrees, in fact—and joined special ops, where he had an exemplary career."

Vienna glanced at Raine's face because she stopped speaking and was looking at Vienna with sympathy. The tightness in her chest increased. The pounding of her heart accelerated. This definitely had something to do with her. Elliot Blom. She didn't know that name. The connection couldn't be through that name. She flicked another quick look at Zale. His dark eyes focused on her intently.

This was going to be bad. Very bad. She heard Avril's voice. *They can't be trusted. They lie to you. They'll say anything they think you want to hear in order to get their way.* Elliot Blom. A special ops soldier choosing his career. She pressed a hand to her stomach. She had a psychic gift. Daniel Wallin had gone so far as to have the doctor take her blood. Why? Not to see the alcohol content in case she tried to sue him but for DNA purposes. Had she been invited to the casino because Wallin was certain she was Blom's daughter? Was that what Raine had discovered?

"No." She whispered the denial aloud. She didn't want Raine to confirm it. If she did, that meant that everything Zale had told her was most likely a lie. But it made sense. It fit. She was sweating. Barely able to breathe. "Just wait a minute, Raine. Give me a minute. Don't tell me yet."

"Vienna," Zale started.

His voice. That voice. She wanted to drown him out. Put her hands over her ears like a small child might. She shook her head. "Don't, Zale. Not now. I think it's a little too late for explanations, don't you?"

"I'm sorry, Vienna," Raine said gently. "Do you want to stop until we're on the plane?"

If she said yes, did that make her a coward? She wouldn't have to face Zale. On the floor, her back to the love seat but facing the two men, Shabina stared at them both.

"What I'm getting out of this conversation, Raine, is that neither Rainier or Zale were actually in Vegas for the purpose they said they were here for. Rainier, we just had a conversation yesterday, out in the backyard. Was a single thing you said to me the truth?" Shabina asked.

Rainier didn't answer her. He kept his gaze fixed on her

face. She shook her head. "I should have known. You're so good at telling lies. I don't know why I ever believe a single word that comes out of your mouth. I want to believe you, I suppose."

Vienna heard the raw hurt in her voice. Shabina wasn't good at deception. She'd sacrificed to draw attention away from Vienna.

"The limousine is here to take us to the airport," Harlow reported.

Vienna all but jumped up, reaching down to help Shabina up. She looked straight at Zale. "If you weren't there to find out who was killing agents, what were you doing at that hotel, Zale?"

He didn't answer her. She shook her head and walked past his outstretched hand without looking at him again. Bending down, she shouldered her pack and picked up as much of her gear as she could carry. Ignoring the men guarding the walkway, she went to the limousine's open trunk and placed her baggage on the ground just outside of it. The guards urged her to get inside the vehicle. She complied, mostly because she knew Zale would come outside to insist if she didn't do what she was told.

No one spoke on the ride to the airport or boarding the private jet. They waited until the plane was in the air and they could gather together again. On the plane was a small dining table and they sat around it, all of them looking at Raine expectantly.

"I'm really sorry, Vienna. I suspected something wasn't right almost immediately. I couldn't understand why Zale and Rainier stayed at the hotel after their cover was blown. That made no sense. I tried to come up with reasonable explanations that might fit, but there just weren't any, not when they were agents of that caliber. And then there was the taking of your blood over that little assault in the hotel. That didn't seem right either."

Raine put her head back on the seat. "I hate being the one

to make you so miserable. They knew what that bet was between Daniel and Liam. They could have told you. They knew that Liam had a son, Elliot."

Vienna sighed. "Elliot Blom is their boss, isn't he?"

Raine nodded. "Yes, he is."

"Blom had an affair with Avril. He's the man she was so upset over when she went to Mitzi. He's my father." Vienna forced herself to state the truth aloud. "He rejected me and ultimately her because of me."

"We don't really know that," Raine cautioned. "But he does know you're his daughter."

"That's why Zale and Rainier were at the hotel. They weren't there to look after Daniel Wallin. They were there because Blom wanted them to look after me," Vienna said. "That was why Zale got close to me again."

They can't be trusted. They lie to you. They'll say anything they think you want to hear in order to get their way.

The pain was so much worse than the last time. Far worse. She couldn't look at her friends. She got up and paced away from them, refusing to cry. She'd already shed far too many tears for Zale Vizzini. She just needed time to come to terms with his betrayal. They were going on a four-day hike, so there would be no chance of seeing him until the actual wedding. She could get through the wedding.

"Wallin invited me to the tournament in order to see if I really was Blom's daughter," she mused aloud. "He must have been looking for me."

"I suspect he wanted both you and Blom dead," Raine said. "With both of you dead, no one would be the wiser and the shares would revert to him. His son stands to inherit a tremendous amount of money if anything happens to him. They want to open a second casino, at least the other investors do."

Vienna turned that information over and over in her mind. It fit, but that meant that Zale already had those facts. He was aware that Daniel Wallin had a reason to want her dead and he hadn't told her. She pulled up the memory of the two men coming into her room, the security detail she absolutely knew were there to kill her, and how terrified she'd been. Zale had soothed her, stayed with her, made her feel grateful to him.

"Why wouldn't Zale just tell me the truth? I can handle the truth. So Blom doesn't want to admit he's my father, big deal. I'm all grown up. He doesn't have to tell the world. He doesn't have to be in my life. Zale didn't have to pretend he wanted to be with me long-term." But she knew why. Her mother had told her long ago, many, many times.

They can't be trusted. They lie to you. They'll say anything they think you want to hear in order to get their way.

She'd been so easy. Falling right back into his arms. Making such a fool of herself again. He was able to get close to her and she didn't question him. She made his job easy.

Her throat closed and she had to stop talking. She kept her back to the others because she knew if she saw sympathy on their faces, she'd break down completely.

"They can't think he'll stop coming after you and Blom just because you're no longer in Vegas," Stella said.

"I think Blom believes it will be that much more difficult for Wallin to get to you. Blom and his people can keep track of Wallin's men's movement," Raine said. "In Vegas, Wallin had the advantage."

"I'm the bait," Vienna said. "Run, little rabbit." There wasn't any bitterness in her voice because she wasn't bitter. Just sad. Brokenhearted. Humiliated perhaps, but mostly sad. Zale could have been honest with her. She was an adult. She didn't have daddy issues. She would have cooperated, especially knowing that Wallin had killed good men in order to lure her father out into the open, where he could have him killed.

"I'm really sorry," Raine said again. "I feel like I'm always that one that has to tell my friends the worst possible news."

Vienna did turn around then at the sheer sadness in

Raine's voice. "Please don't feel like that. If I didn't have you, I'd still be being played. I'm grateful to you."

"We don't know for certain that Zale's feelings for you aren't genuine," Raine cautioned. "If his boss told him he wasn't to tell you that he was your father, what could he do? He's under orders and has to comply."

"That's bullshit and you know it, Raine," Vienna disagreed. "He didn't want to tell me or he would have. He broke the rules several times. Zale isn't a rule follower, as much as I'd love to give him that excuse. I want to say I'm going to be like Stella and get a happy ever after, but I don't think that's in the cards for me. Suffice to say, I cheat when I win big, so maybe I don't deserve the big happy ever after."

Shabina shook her head. "It's them. The way they think, Vienna. We have all these issues from our childhood traumas or whatever it is that happened to us along the way, so we blame ourselves, but really, it's them. Look at Blom, your birth father. He decided to sleep with a beautiful woman, carry on with her to the point that she believed he loved her. She gets pregnant and he doesn't say he wants to dump *her*. He tells her he isn't ready to be a father. They can still get together whenever he has time for her, but she should get rid of the baby. Do you see how selfish that is? It's all about him. His career. What he needs. What he wants. It still is. Blom sent his men to protect you—yes. But he dictated the terms to them. They couldn't tell you. He didn't want you to know about him for whatever reason."

Vienna crossed back over to the little table and sat down. Her legs were shaky. She was exhausted, but not sleepy tired.

"Some would say he was being very honest with her," Harlow pointed out. "Better that than lying."

"True," Zahra agreed. "But did he lead her on in the first place? Or did he commit the sin of omission and let her believe they were going to have a future when he knew they weren't?"

Vienna frowned. "Zale over and over has insisted he

wants a future with me. He told me he'd marry me right now. He said he'd be happy if I was pregnant with his child. He also was up-front that he had a commitment for another year but after that he would get out. Each time I said I was worried he would find life boring, he pointed out all the things one can do in the Sierras and said he would have no problems living there with me and starting a family."

There was a long silence. Vienna heard her heart thudding. She didn't want to hope. She didn't want to be that woman who kept going back and getting kicked in the teeth. No matter how much she thought that, she had to admit there was a small part of her that couldn't help hoping Zale hadn't lied to her about wanting to share his life with her. Maybe he hadn't told her the truth about why he was in Vegas, but surely, he wouldn't sleep with her to keep her close to him for his job. That just didn't make sense.

They can't be trusted. They lie to you. They'll say anything they think you want to hear in order to get their way.

She *detested* Avril's voice creeping into her head every time. She had enough demons.

"Vienna," Harlow began slowly. "That doesn't sound like a man lying to get you in bed. He wouldn't have to go that far."

Stella shook her head. "Sam would kill him for saying something like that to you and then walking away. Zale has to know that. These men play for keeps."

"I agree with Stella," Raine said. "Sam's so quiet, but underneath, he's a volcano. You're family to him. If someone messes with his family, he'd go after them. Leading you on qualifies as messing with you. Zale knows Sam and he would never violate a code they have."

Zahra frowned. "I don't know Zale at all, but I do know Sam. He lives his entire life by a code of honor. If Zale is anything like him, if he told you he wanted to marry you and have children with you, Vienna, I can't imagine that's a lie. Why go that far?"

That was a good question. It made no sense at all. Zale would have known he could have seduced her back into his bed. She was extremely susceptible to him, and she wanted to be with him in spite of telling him to leave her alone if he didn't mean the things he said. She had to decide whether or not she believed he was an honorable man.

Her gaze dropped to Shabina. Shabina hadn't really weighed in with an opinion once they'd all started talking about what Zale had said to her. She sat very still, her face pale, her large eyes very blue, her dark lashes veiling her expression.

"Shabina, what do you think?"

Shabina shrugged without looking up. "I'm not someone you can ask. I don't know the first thing about men. I stay away from them and if I get too close, I nearly always misread every single thing I think they mean."

"You're upset over something Rainier said to you." Vienna made it a statement.

"I'm always upset over anything Rainier says to me. Anytime he comes around. He sometimes shows up in the middle of the night to check on things. To see to my security, he says. He treats me like I'm still a child. No matter how hard I try to overcome the things that happened to me, he throws me right back to that girl that can't breathe or think. I panic when I'm around him. It's pathetic. He has a way of being so superior, almost amused and above it all, while I'm struggling just to maintain my equilibrium."

Raine, the closest to her, put a gentle hand on her shoulder. "I doubt Rainier tries to make you feel that way, Shabina. He was there when those terrible things happened to you. He saw you at your worst. That's bound to bring the memories too close. He can't help that."

Shabina nodded. "I tell myself that all the time. I think he tells himself that as well. He goes really blank when he's around me. Impossible to read, you know, but sometimes I think I hurt him. He thinks I can't stand for him to be around me. I don't blame him for what happened to me, and I'm not afraid of him because I saw him kill all those men. If I could have done it myself, I would have." She bowed her head at the confession.

"Why are you afraid of him?" Vienna asked gently. Shabina seemed the most fragile of all of her friends. She'd fought hard to overcome her past. She'd opened up her own café and made a success of it. She lived on her own with her protection dogs, although she did have security, but that was mandated by her father. Vienna didn't blame him after hearing what had happened, and she knew Shabina had downplayed her experience, given them just the bare bones. The fact that an experienced operative had lost his sanity and killed everyone in the camp rather than get her out without anyone the wiser was testimony to what he must have found.

"You see him. Aren't you a little afraid? I saw him in action. I know what he's capable of. He did that for me and he'd do it again."

"So, you are afraid of him because you saw him killing all those men," Raine clarified.

Shabina shook her head. "Not exactly. Not that he did it or could do it. That he did it because of me. Because of what he saw they did to me. He's very controlled. Extremely controlled and disciplined. He doesn't make mistakes. He doesn't do anything without purpose, and he doesn't screw up. That was a major screwup. What he did could have ended his career. He made enemies that to this day have put bounties on his head."

Raine nodded. "That's true. Rainier has the largest bounties on his head I've ever seen of any operative. He's definitely the most-wanted man any of the high-profile terrorist cells are looking for. Not only that, but they have vowed to pay any mercenary who brings them his head."

Shabina rubbed her temple as if she was getting a headache. "I didn't know that."

"Fortunately, they don't have good photos of him, but

they keep the chatter going on their news channels. He's considered one of their greatest enemies."

"Because of what he did when he rescued me?" Shabina asked.

Raine started to reply and then hesitated. "Rainier is wanted for a lot of reasons, Shabina. I'll have to leave it at that. He's a very active operative."

"Do you believe Wallin will send his assassins after me to Knightly?" Vienna changed the subject. Shabina looked mutinous, and if Raine was getting into classified information, she would never give up the data. Vienna didn't want the friends upset with one another.

"Assuming we're correct about Wallin," Harlow clarified. "If we're wrong and he's really a good guy, then I don't have a clue who wants you dead, Vienna."

"Maybe Elsa stepped on someone's toes and she was the true target all along," Zahra said.

"She's such a firecracker." Vienna hated that Elsa had been shot, especially since she was certain she was the cause. "I'm going to ask Mom and Ellen to visit her. If Verma needs a place to stay, maybe they can put her up. Their apartment is large and it's near the hospital. Elsa will be there for a little while, I'm afraid."

"That would be good," Zahra said.

"If I am the real target, and you all know most likely I am, then it isn't safe to be around me," Vienna pointed out.

Stella glared at her. "Don't be silly. We're all in this together. In any case, in Vegas Wallin could have you followed, but in Knightly a stranger would stand out. We're going on our hike, and if we leave tomorrow morning there's no chance anyone will have time to find you. We can ask our friends in town to keep an eye out for strangers. I'll talk to Sam before we leave."

"Do you really think it's a good idea to stick with the plan, Stella? We'll be four days off hiking on our own," Vienna said. She really wanted to go. She didn't see how a city boy like Wallin could find her, but she didn't want to endanger her friends.

"Of course we have to stick to the plan, Vienna. If we leave at first light, how would anyone from Wallin's camp know where we're going? We're in a private jet. We'll meet at first light, park at the meadow and take the shuttle to White Wolf Trailhead. Even if they manage to get to Knightly by private plane tomorrow, we'll be gone. Sam will hear they've arrived and he'll be all over them."

Vienna knew that much was true. Sam would be watching for anyone suspicious coming to town, in particular hanging around looking for Vienna. Still, she was a little anxious about endangering her friends.

The pilot told them they would be landing soon. To get seated and put on their seatbelts. Vienna snapped her seatbelt around her while she contemplated everything that Raine had discovered. Elliot Blom was her birth father. He was Zale and Rainier's boss. He'd once been Sam's boss. Had he known about her since Sam had come to live in Knightly? She didn't think so. He had been lied to by Avril just as Mitzi had been. Still, when he had discovered the truth, rather than talk to her himself he'd simply sent a couple of his men to keep her safe while using her as bait to draw out his enemy.

She sat up very straight. That was what Blom had been doing. He'd known Wallin wanted to kill her, and he'd used her in order to try to get criminal evidence on Wallin and his son. Rainier and Zale both had known what he was doing. They might not have liked it, but they knew. She glanced at Raine. Their eyes met and her heart dropped. Raine was so damn intelligent. She had already figured that out.

The reason Zale hadn't answered her questions or given her explanations was because he didn't want to admit they'd used her as bait to draw out Wallin and his son. How would that go over? *I love you so much but I'm setting you up to lure a killer out. Oh, and I'm not telling you.* That was bound to go over well. If he'd told her, she would have accepted it. She wasn't the fainthearted type. She would have preferred to be told what was going on.

She dropped her head in her hands and rubbed her forehead. How did people work these kinds of problems out? She doubted if most people had problems of this nature. She didn't want them. They seemed endless to her. One thing after another. She'd come to Knightly for peace. It seemed Zale brought chaos to her. Things should be easy at this stage, not so difficult. She did her best to keep her mind blank until the plane landed. Raine and Shabina had driven their vehicles to the airport, so they had transportation. Harlow and Zahra caught a ride with them and Vienna was about to when Sam stopped her.

"I'll take you, Vienna." He took her gear from her and stowed it in the back before she could protest.

She stood next to Stella a little reluctantly. Clearly, Sam had a few things he wanted to say to her, and she was certain Zale's name would come up. She so didn't want to keep talking about him, not until she was home and had a little time to curl up in her house alone with her cat and think things through.

"Get in." Sam held the door.

Stella rolled her eyes. "Be still my heart."

"You could kiss me," Sam pointed out.

"I suppose. If I must," Stella said and proceeded to do a thorough job of it.

Vienna couldn't help but laugh. Stella was seriously gone on Sam. She was much more likely to swoop on him and demand kisses than the other way around. Vienna loved their relationship and was so happy her friend had found someone so perfect for her. She got into the 4Runner, sliding onto the backseat. Sam's SUV wasn't as tricked out as Stella's was, but it was really nice.

"We had such a good time," Stella enthused. "Until someone shot up the kayakers."

Sam shot a quick glance at Vienna through the rearview mirror. "I understand you're aware Elliot Blom is your birth father."

"Yep." She kept her answer short, trying to convey she didn't want to talk about it.

He set a course for her home in Knightly. Vienna looked out the window. She loved the Sierras. This was her place, and it always would be. She always reset when she came home, no matter how terrible things had gotten for her—and this time they were pretty terrible. Well, maybe not as bad as she thought. She'd made headway with her mother and Ellen, and that was very important to her. And she'd won a ton of money for the hospital and for the rescue equipment they desperately needed to update. She would be able to add to the scholarship fund for single moms to go to college.

"Zale is a good man, Vienna. When he's working a job, he's under certain restrictions."

"It might be better not to discuss this right now." She tried to be careful, knowing Zale was his friend. She didn't want to say anything one way or another. "I process things, Sam. He used me as bait to bring a killer and his son out into the open. He may have been under orders, but he knowingly did that and never said a word to me. He risked my life, and believe me, more than once I came close to dying. Elsa only escaped death by a fluke, but that should have been me. Then there was the time in my hotel room. That behavior may be okay with you, but I'm not certain it is with me."

Vienna heard Stella's breath catch in her throat. She shook her head. "I had no idea. It isn't okay with me either."

"Put like that, it does sound terrible, Vienna."

"How else does one put it?" Vienna knew better than to ask. She shouldn't have. She should have just left it alone. She didn't want to know, but then—she did. She wanted Sam's take on it.

He sighed. "We're wired differently, hon. We take risks all the time. We don't think twice about it. And maybe we grow arrogant thinking we can control every situation. If Blom gives an order and tells us to say silent, we do. That just goes with the territory. As for setting you up, Zale wouldn't consider you as bait. He would consider himself as your personal protector. It's a different mindset. Rainier more than likely has filled him in on the way you will view this."

"You honestly don't think he would see it that way?"

"No. You're Elliot Blom's daughter. Wallin was trying to decide if you were or not. As far as Zale was concerned, he was there to make sure if Wallin did figure it out, he could keep you alive and get you out of there."

"But they didn't leave right away when Wallin did figure it out." She was silent for a moment, putting it together. "Blom ordered them to stay, and Rainier had already guessed what he was doing. Using me to draw them out, right?"

"Right."

"Why didn't Zale tell me at that point?"

"You'll have to ask him."

CHAPTER SEVENTEEN

ⵡⵡⵡⵡⵡⵡⵡⵡⵡⵡⵡⵡⵡⵡⵡⵡⵡⵡⵡⵡⵡⵡⵡⵡⵡⵡⵡ

The women were able to leave their vehicle in the valley and take the shuttle bus to the White Wolf Trailhead. The snowpack had been especially high, so the river was really flowing and the waterfalls, even this time of year, were full and powerful.

They intended to hike a little over ten miles the first day. Most of the trail wove in and out of forestry land. Rocks sometimes rose up, flat or jagged, but for the most part, trees dominated the scenery. Meadows were normally filled with beautiful wildflowers, but they'd missed the explosions of colors due to the time of year. The grass was drier and brown in color rather than the various shades of green normally found earlier in the year, but it was gorgeous terrain.

The hiking was downhill, and the roar of the river became a constant sound as they approached the bridge. The year before they'd been warned it was impossible to cross, as the bridge was in ruins, but obviously it had been rebuilt. They had no problems crossing at all. Still, they could feel the power of the river as they went over the bridge, the water hitting the beams and supports.

They met a couple coming the opposite way on the trail and stopped to talk to them briefly. They'd camped for two days and had run across two rattlesnakes on the trail the day before on the rocky switchbacks. The ranger had warned

Vienna's party of a bear that had suspicious behavior. It took three incidents coming in contact with humans before a bear was removed, and this bear had only one. It hadn't actually attacked anyone, but they were told to watch out for it. The couple had avoided the campsite where the bear was reputed to have been seen.

They continued on downhill, the grade much steeper now. Vienna loved hiking. It didn't matter how hard the trail was, there was something about being in the open air surrounded by rock and trees, the meadows, grasses and wildflowers that reset her every time. Even if it happened to rain, which it didn't, she loved it. The day was clear and actually hot. The skies were cloudless and a perfect pale blue.

A very large downed tree hung partially across the path and partially over the river. They could detour around it or scoot over it. Looking at each other with big grins, they immediately made the decision to go over it, using it like they would a bridge, although they weren't going to walk on it.

Vienna found herself laughing and talking about Stella's upcoming wedding and the past antics of their animals—whether or not she should have all of them present when she walked down the aisle. The hike was strenuous but exhilarating and just what she needed, resetting her. She didn't once think negative thoughts. The scent of the pines and redwoods, the various grasses and flowers, even the churning river and slabs of rock, were all so familiar and felt like home to her.

Her heart was much lighter by the time they reached the campground. All the pressure in her chest was gone. She was exhausted, but it was the kind of exhaustion that was good. The problem was, the bear had claimed the campground before them, and it was adamant that it wanted to stay. The six women looked at one another and decided none of them were in any condition to take on the bear.

"Backtrack," whispered Stella. "Let's camp by the river. There was that one little spot that looked sandy."

They backed away and began walking very fast in the direction they had come. "That's right," Shabina said. "It was a swimming hole. I noticed because I was so hot and thought it was a good place to cool off, but we were so close to the campground and I was tired and hungry."

"Water was calm there, cut off from the current," Raine agreed. "Nice little cove."

They made it back to the sandy beach in record time. No one else had claimed it for a camping spot. They set up their individual tents and ate. There was no campfire, but they were used to that. The evening was warm and they spread a ground sheet and made drinks, mixing the vodka with various flavors that were usually poured into water. Raine was the only one not drinking, and Vienna only drank a couple of the drinks because most of them were pretty bad. All food was put in a bear container just in case they received a visit from the resident bear.

It was still warm, and Vienna stripped down to her panties and bra after everyone had retired to their personal tents. She went back outside to the groundsheet to lie down and look up at the stars. The sky was particularly beautiful and very clear. She tried finding the various constellations and then counting the stars.

"*Bear. Bear.* Don't you come around our camp, you cranky old bear. I'll punch you if you try to take over this campsite."

Stella's belligerent voice jerked Vienna awake. Vienna jumped to her feet, looking wildly around for the bear, but she didn't see the animal anywhere. Stella was also in her underwear, and she had her fists raised as if she were ready to punch the bear just like she'd claimed.

The other women raced out of their tents dressed similarly, with the exception of Raine, who had thrown on a light, unbuttoned shirt. She looked calm and ready for business.

"No bear that I can see," Vienna hastily informed her.

Harlow showed her fist. "That old bear better not come around. I'll fight him off."

"I've taken plenty of self-defense lessons," Shabina said. "I know exactly where to place a good kick to send that bear flying. He wouldn't come back to our neck of the woods."

"I think I'd be the one to fight him off," Stella said. "I saw him first. I think he ran when he saw how big my fist was."

Zahra made a sound between a laugh and a snort of derision. "Seriously, Stella? Your fist wouldn't hurt a fly."

Stella looked at both her fists. "I beg to differ with you. I have big fists. Hammer fists."

Raine and Vienna exchanged a long look. Sometimes when they got together and were alone, they did drink a bit too much because it was such a rare occasion. Stella was funny when she drank, but she did have a wild imagination and the others tended to egg her on in whatever she was pursuing. They weren't going back to bed anytime soon.

"Do you know how utterly hot Sam is? How utterly hot and truly dreamy he is? Have I ever told you I think he's both?" Stella asked.

"Only when you're incredibly drunk," Zahra confirmed.

"Well, he is," Stella continued. "But don't ever tell him I think so. I wouldn't want him to get a big head. He's perfect the way he is. If he knew what I thought, he'd be so arrogant. You'll have to go to your graves with this secret. Swear it. All of you."

"Do you have any idea how many times we've had to swear to take this to our graves?" Vienna asked.

"Do you have any idea how many times *Sam's* had to swear right along with us to take this to his grave?" Zahra asked. "Anytime you've had too much to drink in the last two years, we've heard about Sam's hotness and his dreamboat status. He's heard about it too."

"He has not," Stella denied.

"Stella, he's our sober driver, and you go on and on about him and how you want to 'do' him and kiss him all over," Zahra pointed out. "You whisper in a loud voice all the way home."

"I most certainly do *not*." Stella glared at her. "I know I don't. You know how I know? Because I *always* ask you if I said anything like that in front of Sam and you always reassure me I didn't."

Zahra burst out laughing. "Honey, we'd all been drinking every time. That's why Sam's the sober driver. How would I know if Sam heard or not?"

"He heard," Harlow said, nodding wisely.

"Oh, yeah, he heard," Shabina confirmed. "You were pretty loud and you were always in the front, turning around to talk to us. How could he not hear you?"

Stella turned to Raine as if she would save her. "He didn't."

"He did. Every single time."

Stella fell over backward, groaning, a palm to her forehead. "He never said a word. Not a single word."

"Now we have to hear how he's *such* a gentleman."

Stella sat back up. "He *is* a gentleman, Zahra Metcalf. A hot, dreamy gentleman, and I'm *so* going to marry him."

"Yes, you are," Harlow said very solemnly. "We'll all be there to witness it too, so if you ever decide you want to kick him out, it isn't going to happen. We won't let you."

"Nope," Vienna agreed. "We're going to remind you how hot and dreamy he is."

"We'll get you drunk," Zahra said. "That's all it would take for you to be all over him."

Stella laughed. "Sam isn't the type of man to let me get so upset with him that I'd want to kick him out, but thanks for wanting to support us in our marriage. That's why I love all of you so much. I know you'll stick by us. You let Sam be part of us, and that means so much to me."

"We love Sam, Stella," Shabina reassured. "He wormed

his way into our affections very early on. He's a man of few words, but he's someone we know we can always count on."

Vienna realized that was true. Sam had a quiet strength about him. He didn't talk much, in fact sometimes he went hours without saying a word, but he was a man of action. If something needed doing, he just did it without any fanfare. He didn't wait to see if anyone was paying attention. He didn't want accolades. He just got the job done. That was Sam. And he always watched over them.

"Most importantly," Raine contributed, "he loves animals. Especially dogs."

"Hey," Vienna protested. "He loves cats too."

"He *used* to love cats," Zahra corrected. "Until your haughty high-and-mighty Princess raked all the skin from his arms when he had to rescue her out of the tree she was clinging to after she escaped the leash on one of your nonsense walks."

Vienna groaned and threw herself sideways, lying down on the groundsheet to look up at the stars. That had been a *terrible* day. Princess had refused to walk on the leash. Vienna was trying to train her by taking her out daily. She allowed Princess to lead and sort of amble around while she followed behind, keeping the leash loose, but the Persian cat despised the entire idea and wasn't in the least bit shy about letting Vienna know. The cat had persisted in lying down and when Vienna would go to pick her up in surrender, Princess would hiss her displeasure and show her claws and teeth.

"Don't remind me. And the walks weren't nonsense. I read all about training the cat to enjoy walks with their person. I thought if I could get her to like that, she could be outdoors a bit. Cats are supposed to want to be outdoors. She was deeply offended every time I took her outside."

"Your cat is not normal, Vienna," Shabina said. "You know I love you, but it has to be said. Princess is a devil cat. She's of the devil."

Harlow nodded her agreement. "At least a demon."

"Sadly, I have to agree," Raine said. "Her eyes even glow red, and she takes on a demonic appearance when a dog gets into the house. She chased poor Daisy around the house until Daisy nearly died from exhaustion and fright. She's a Jack Russell, for heaven's sake. Nothing can wear out a Jack Russell."

"With the exception of my naughty little Persian cat." Vienna sounded more proud than embarrassed.

"You weren't thinking she was so great when she bolted up the tree and then clung to the peeling bark and cried pitifully," Stella pointed out.

"Who you gonna call?" the women shouted out in perfect harmony.

"Sam Rossi!" they all answered together.

"Poor Sam," Stella said. "It's a wonder he even wants to stick around. He came right away and got torn up like you wouldn't believe. Even his manly chest."

There was a collective groan.

"That's it, Stella," Vienna said. "Go to bed. We have to break camp super early and hike our butts off tomorrow. It's going to be a long, hot day. Just sleep and don't dream about punching bears."

Stella looked a little embarrassed. "He wanted our campsite, and I wasn't going to let him have it," she muttered as she stood.

All of them laughed. "You weren't alone," Raine pointed out. "Everyone joined in. It was a regular MMA fight against the nonexistent bear."

THE SECOND DAY the women expected to hike around nine miles. Quite a lot of the trail, with switchbacks going up steep, was exposed rock. The highlights were the breathtaking views of the river on one side. It was far hotter than expected this time of year, and they encountered only one other group of hikers heading back toward White Wolf Trailhead in the first two hours.

The little family stopped to talk to them. The father was worried because they had left their car on the side of the road without a permit and hiked in the evening before. They were hurrying back down to the beginning of the trail in order to make sure their car wasn't towed. Vienna didn't point out it was clear he knew he wasn't supposed to park there without a permit and more than likely the car was gone.

They also mentioned they hadn't seen any other hikers. That did surprise Vienna. This was late in the year, and most people would expect that the falls weren't at their height of glory, but the weather was warm, the views were beautiful, and the trail was popular.

They took a break to hike down to a swimming hole before starting up the switchbacks, which would be blazing in the heat. As they lay out in the sun, Harlow tossed a small stone in Vienna's direction to get her attention.

"We've got to talk about what we're going to do about Wallin. If everything Raine found out is the truth and you really are Elliot Blom's daughter, Wallin won't stop coming after you. Not if you're in line to inherit a good portion of his hotel and casino."

Vienna had been enjoying her time outdoors without thinking about Wallin or whether or not she had been a fool over Zale. At the simple statement, instead of being upset, she found herself feeling overwhelmed that she had friends that would stand by her no matter what the circumstances or even the danger to them.

"Is there any way to prove that he's making threats against Blom and Vienna?" Zahra asked.

"If Rainier had answered questions instead of deciding to be a clam, we might know," Shabina said. "Once he makes up his mind to something, like not talking, it would take a miracle to change it."

"What about Sam, Stella? Would he know?" Zahra asked.

Stella looked uncomfortable. "When we get back, I'll ask him, but if he can't talk to me about it, I'm not going to push him. I don't want a big fight before the wedding."

Vienna sat up straight. "No, don't do that. I would hate that, Stella. If Zale comes around again, and I know he's in the wedding party, I'll ask him myself. If he still refuses to talk to me, we'll just figure another way." Just saying his name hurt. She wasn't expecting the emotional response.

"I'm really sorry," Raine murmured again. "I wish I hadn't been so angry with those two for withholding the information about Blom. And also the bet between Liam and Wallin. I have such a bad temper. I could have maybe been a little more careful in the way I handled that. If I'd gone to the two of them first and talked to them . . ." She trailed off.

"In the end, Raine, the point is they not only withheld the information, but Zale lied to me about why he was there," Vienna said. "My life was in danger and I didn't know."

"Because they're so arrogant they think they can outwit everyone, even killers." Shabina didn't sound as disgusted as she did worried.

"What about reaching out to Elliot Blom?" Stella suggested. "Would that really be so terrible, Vienna? You could ask him for the information."

"If he didn't want Zale and Rainier to even share the information they had on the bet between Liam and Wallin, and he was willing to use me as bait, I don't think he would suddenly be all that forthcoming. In any case, I don't particularly want to talk to a man who was willing to throw me to the sharks just to further his cause. Whatever that was. Saving his own life maybe? Making certain he inherits the shares in the casino? Who knows?"

"More than likely, it was to find out who was killing his operatives," Raine ventured.

Vienna sighed. "I honestly don't care what his reason was; he was willing to hang me out there, putting my life in jeopardy. Why didn't he check in to the hotel and have his agents protect him? He was safe somewhere behind a desk while Zale and Rainier took the risk to protect me. I just don't think I'd trust any information coming from him."

"I think it's safe to say the two of you aren't going to be friends," Harlow said. "That's what I'm hearing."

"I believe you're reading me correctly," Vienna said.

Stella glanced at her watch. "We'd better get on the trail. I told Sam we were taking four days to hike this trail. You know how he is. If we take five, he'll send every branch of the military after us."

"Did he put a tracking device on you?" Raine asked as they dressed in their hiking clothes and gathered up their gear.

Stella scowled at her. "I said no. The most I did was set up my mini Garmin to send him an alert at night when we camped so he'd have our location. And that was grudging. Before I left, I did set up the Garmin to send to Zahra's phone every half hour just in case she gets lost." She held up her mini Garmin and then pushed it into the inside zippered flap of her pack. "That way, she can follow the GPS right back to us, or we can find her. I put an app on her phone."

"I don't get lost," Zahra denied, shouldering her pack.

"You get lost in a parking lot at the mall," Harlow told her.

Zahra's dark brows drew together. "Those parking lots are huge. Why do they even have malls that size? No one can find their way out of them. Everyone gets turned around, it's not just me."

"Yosemite is bigger than a mall parking lot," Stella pointed out. "And I don't want to lose my best friend."

The narrow trail was stony with loose rock everywhere. The sun reflected off the rock on one side of them and off the churning water below as they began the climb.

Zahra laughed. "I suppose I do get turned around. I did learn after the last time not to go alone at night to find a place to pee. And this time I have a whistle."

"Good to know," Vienna said. "You need realistic survival gear, even if it's the minimal gear."

Zahra rolled her eyes. "You always tell me that. I do carry a water filtration system. If I get lost, I plan on sitting in one place until all of you find me."

Vienna had drilled it into her enough times that she needed survival gear when they hiked, even with all of them together. It didn't matter that she didn't plan on being separated. No one ever planned to get lost, but it happened all the time. Each time Vienna had organized a rescue and brought home a dead body or bodies, she had more talks with her friends about necessary survival gear and what to do in circumstances based on the time of year.

Zahra listened to her, and she was carrying more gear, but sometimes Vienna felt as if it was pulling teeth to get her to do it. Vienna knew part of Zahra's resistance was fear. She told herself she wouldn't ever get separated because the thought of being lost and alone in the forest was terrifying to her.

The views were gorgeous, and no matter how uncomfortable the heat was, it was well worth it to see the amazing panoramas. Vienna looked out over the cliff edges as she walked up the steep slope and immediately set her foot down on an unstable rock. It rolled out from under her foot and she went down. As she did, what seemed like a series of angry bees struck the rock face where her head had been, sending splinters of granite bursting back at them. The sound of gunshots followed as the shards cut into packs, hair and skin.

Shabina screamed. Raine shoved her forward. "Run. Run to the bend. We're sitting ducks out here. Pull out mirrors and reflect them back on the shooters, they're on the ridge."

Stella crouched down to help Vienna, who was trying to scramble on her hands and knees. The next bullet hit the granite above them and sent rocks sliding down on top of them. Raine rushed to help Stella and Vienna as the others fled upward.

Vienna's ankle was twisted, but she did her best to push up into a crouch as Raine came around to assist her. A bullet caught Raine and slammed her into Vienna so that they both hit the slab of granite hard and slid to the trail floor. Stella dropped her pack instantly, screaming at Vienna to get up.

With her ears ringing so loud they hurt, Vienna still heard Stella's voice in the distance calling her name. Vienna forced her body to roll over and found herself almost on top of Raine. There was blood on Raine's face and leg. She wasn't moving.

"Is she alive?" She might have yelled it. Her ears weren't working very well.

Stella dragged Raine's pack off in order to lay her flat so she could check to see if she was breathing.

"Get out of here, Stella," Vienna said. "If they shoot you too, none of us will get out of this. Go, I'll try to get her to you. I can carry her." She didn't know if that was the truth. Her ankle was definitely twisted. Adrenaline and need made up for a lot.

"She's alive," Stella said with obvious relief, waiting until Vienna reached down to lift Raine's slight body into her arms. Raine's head lolled back against her shoulder. Seeing her leg, Vienna was grateful she was unconscious.

She hobbled toward the bend that would take them out of sight of the rifle. She couldn't imagine what was stopping him from shooting until she saw the rest of the women holding mirrors and reflecting the sun back at the shooter.

"How bad is it?" Harlow asked as Vienna lowered Raine to the ground.

"I don't know yet. I didn't have time to assess." Vienna did her best not to snap the answer. What had they expected? That she would keep Raine exposed so the shooter could kill Stella, Raine and her?

"That came out wrong," Harlow said, flinging her pack on the ground and ripping it open. She took up the position at Raine's head, leaving her leg to Vienna.

Vienna could see the leg was in bad shape. The bone hadn't just been cleanly broken, but clearly the bullet had torn through with such force it had done major damage. She didn't have to worry that the bullet was still inside. The exit wound was large. When she wiped the blood, she could see parts of the bone, and her heart dropped. They needed an orthopedic surgeon immediately.

"We've got to call in Search and Rescue," she whispered to Harlow. "She's only got hours before it will be too late to save the leg. And I'm being generous with the time."

Harlow swore under her breath. "The head wound looks as if it's from the granite, not a bullet."

Vienna continued to work as fast as possible to stabilize Raine's leg.

"There's two shooters," Shabina said. "I know because at one point they fired almost simultaneously. We've got to get out of here. We can't stay on the trail either. We'll have to get into the forest and try for a meadow where a helicopter can set down for Raine."

Vienna tried to stay calm and breathe deep to clear her mind. She needed to figure this out and not move until they had a plan. "They're across the ridge," she reminded calmly. "Even if one stays up there with his rifle, the other has to hike to us. That's most likely what they'll try. We'll be exposed the moment we move around this bend. We'll send out an alert to Raine's people, Sam and Search and Rescue. For one thing, we don't want any innocent day hikers caught up in this."

Vienna continued to work on Raine's leg while she assessed their situation. The only real thing she could do was try to minimize the bleeding and stabilize it for travel. It would hurt unlike anything Raine had ever felt if she woke before they got her to the hospital.

"Oh no. I was the one tasked with bringing the GPS," Stella said, panic in her voice. "I dropped my pack on the trail when I went to push the slab off Vienna. Raine's is there as well and she's got the most weapons and all those fancy things to call in the military."

"Don't worry about that right now," Vienna said. "If someone did try to come hiking up that trail, we'd be able to hold them off."

"With what? I just said Raine's pack is on the ledge with the gun in it," Stella challenged.

"She's not the only one with a gun," Vienna admitted. "At the moment we're as safe as we can be unless they go all the way around to the other side of the trail. That's not going to be easy for them. The first thing we need to do is to get word out we need help. Get into my pack, Stella, there's a small plastic case I keep for emergencies. I have the larger version of the Garmin in there as well as my gun. The other case holds more ammo. I want both cases."

She kept her voice quiet and soothing but absolutely firm, letting them all know she was in charge. She *had* to find a way to turn the hunt back on the hunters. If she didn't, it wouldn't matter how many helicopters they brought in. By that time, Raine was going to lose her leg. They wouldn't be able to move her to a meadow where the helicopter could land.

"Make a gurney. Use your jackets. Be aware of any angle the shooter might get on you. You'll need a couple of poles to put the sleeves through." She had no idea what they were going to use, but her friends were an ingenious bunch.

The moment Stella handed her the Garmin, she got it up and running and sent the signal for help. Within seconds a text message came back asking if she needed help or if her device was accidentally triggered. She replied quickly, texting, Two snipers active in the White Wolf Trail at this location. One member of our party in bad condition. She wrote out what Raine would need and told them the trail should be cleared of any day hikers from either end. If there were campers, try to remove them if possible.

"In the inside pocket of my pack there's a small laminated card with a number on it. I need that card." It was difficult for

Vienna to keep pressure on the leg with the wraps they had. Harlow had brought a medical kit, but it wasn't a full-size one. They were traveling light.

Stella handed her the card. She texted again. You need to call this number immediately. When open line answers punch in this code. 4780981. You can't make a mistake. Make certain you punch in those numbers. A person will pick up the line. You tell them who you are and that Vienna Mortenson has activated the call code for Raine O'Mallory. Raine has been shot and her life is in jeopardy. Tell them active shooters, at least two with sniper rifles, are present and we're pinned down.

"I need more gauze and something stronger to put pressure on the wound," she said aloud. She could only hope her lifeline, the man or woman on the other end of the Garmin, was taking everything she said seriously.

Supervisor. I have this correct. Active shooters. Trail to Pate. Switchbacks. One wounded. Military personnel.

Correct. Call this number as well. She gave them Sam's number. Advise of situation. I will find a way to clear the shooters if possible to put helicopter down in nearest open terrain available.

"Vienna, someone's moving on the trail. I can hear them coming," Harlow said.

"I need you here with Raine, Harlow," Vienna said decisively. "If anything happens to me, you take charge. Stella, you're going to have to do the updates. I sent them Sam's number and told them to advise."

She took gauze from the outstretched hands of Shabina and Zahra. Both women had packed small medical kits. She wrapped Raine's wound tighter and used the tape they gave her.

"As soon as you can finish stabilizing the leg for travel, get something together to carry her out of here."

She took the gun and ammo, attaching the ammunition to the vest, and scooted on her hands and knees to the very edge of the bend where she could see their back trail. She could hear the sound of boots on rock. Shabina flattened herself against the rock and then held up two fingers.

Vienna gestured behind her toward the other women. "Tell them to get ready to leave as fast as possible. If necessary, you and Harlow can take turns carrying Raine."

Shabina nodded and slipped back as quietly as possible. Vienna stretched her body out so she lay on her belly. Digging the toes of her hiking boots into the ground, she waited, gun ready. Her hands covered the grip of the pistol, stabilizing the weapon as she'd been taught so there was little recoil.

Small rocks slid, displaced by someone hiking the trail. The sound of male voices whispering was carried on the slight breeze fanning her face. Vienna took slow even breaths. She'd practiced hundreds of hours on a range, shooting at targets, never a human being. She was a nurse, pledging her life to saving others, and yet she was here, lying on the ground, ready to kill someone, something innately abhorrent to her. The terrible feeling of wrong didn't lessen her resolve.

She caught a glimpse of a man as he rounded the bend of the switchback below the area where they'd been shot. He was medium build and was wearing a ball cap and hiking clothes. He looked familiar to her. She knew she'd seen him before. She studied the confident way he walked up the narrow trail of rock. Something about the way he moved caught her attention.

He turned his head to look back at someone just out of her sight. Again, she heard the low whisper of words, but couldn't quite catch what was being said. The two men were still a distance away. But that movement, that head turn and the confident way he seemed to flow over the uneven rocks, triggered her memory.

Vienna knew she *had* seen him before. Not once, but twice. He had come into the coffee shop and sat behind them when her friends had discussed this very trip. He had also walked right on past the boulder the women were climbing.

He'd been with another man, and neither had been friendly when she'd called out a hello. Not only hadn't they answered, but they barely glanced her way. Their reaction had triggered a little red flag that noted the odd behavior in an otherwise friendly community.

The second man came into sight and she recognized him immediately as Axel Wallin, Daniel Wallin's son. He had no backpack and sweat poured off him, darkening his shirt. He also wore a ball cap to shade his face, but there was no mistaking his features, even with the dark sunglasses.

Her heart began to pound and her mouth went dry. This was really happening. These men had come to kill her.

"Damned hot, Larsen," Axel commented.

Larsen didn't turn around to look back this time. They rounded the switchback, coming to the spot where Raine had been shot. Larsen took a long look upward, toward where the women had disappeared, before he proceeded forward until he reached the precise location.

Axel broke into a huge smile. "Yeah, you got her. There's too much blood for it not to be a kill shot. Look, they dropped their packs and ran like rabbits."

Larsen examined the ground carefully. "How many times have I told you to look at everything before you make up your mind? We've gone over this a million times, Axel. You didn't wait to take the shot when I told you to. You were so afraid I'd kill her instead of you."

Axel shrugged. "So, I wanted the bragging rights when we went back to Dad." When Larsen continued to stare at him, he nodded. "You're right, I shouldn't have taken the shot. It doesn't matter now, you got her. We can pack up and go home."

Larsen shook his head. "No, read the signs, Axel. I had her in my sights and then another woman stepped in front of her. This is her blood. We've still got it to do. Your father made that clear. Don't come home until she's dead. You don't want to piss him off."

Axel wiped his forehead with his forearm and swore softly as he jerked his chin toward the two packs lying on the trail. "They did run like the little scared bitches they are." He stalked over to Stella's pack and lifted it as if to hurl it over the edge of the cliff.

"We need that. Do you ever listen to me? Before you get rid of it, look inside and see who she is and what she is to Mortenson. You always want to know everything you can about your enemies."

Vienna could hear the irritation and growing contempt in Larsen's voice. He had Raine's pack in his hands and he jerked it open.

"This is bullshit, Larsen, and you know it," Axel snapped back, grabbing at Raine's pack and yanking it out of Larsen's hands. For the first time he sounded as if he was in charge and not Larsen. "I shouldn't be out here. I send men out to do whatever I want done and to kill who needs killing. I'm too valuable to be running around in the heat after a bunch of whiny little girls and you know it. Dear old Dad wants to prove some point to me."

Larsen reached for Stella's pack and drew it to him. He sighed and turned to look back up the trail straight at Vienna. She was low to the ground, in the shadow and staying very still, but he paused all the same.

Should she call out to them before she fired? If she did and she didn't kill both men, they would be pinned down for certain. Raine didn't have time for negotiations. Shabina had heard two rifles firing simultaneously, but that didn't mean there wasn't a third man. She didn't just want to kill the men in cold blood. Was this considered self-defense? A million questions ran through her mind. All the while her heart went wild, but her grip on the gun never once wavered.

"I don't think they ran, Axel," Larsen said softly. "I think they're right up there because their little friend is still alive and they're bleeding hearts and won't leave her behind." He shouldered Stella's pack. "Walk back to the nearest bend,

Axel. I think Mortenson has balls after all and she's got the drop on us."

Axel threw Raine's pack onto the trail behind him and whipped out a semiautomatic pistol, lifting it and spewing bullets at the rock sheltering Vienna. She squeezed the trigger without hesitation as Axel stepped back, tripped on Raine's pack and staggered dangerously close to the edge. The bullet caught him just to the left of his heart. He screamed and staggered back, a look of shock and horror on his face. One foot went off into empty air.

Larsen made a lunge toward Axel in an attempt to stop him from falling just as Vienna pulled the trigger a second time, switching her aim to Larsen. Larsen abandoned his attempt to save Wallin's son and Axel fell, screaming, bouncing off rocks to the churning river below.

CHAPTER EIGHTEEN

//

Larsen rolled over toward the rock side of the trail, dragging packs around him for protection even as he scooted backward toward the safety of the bend. He didn't return fire. There was no wild shooting. He just kept moving on his belly as Vienna tried to find a target. He scraped Raine's pack back and forth over the trail to kick up dirt and dust as he fishtailed his legs, kicking rocks and debris into the air as he scrambled for the safety of the bend.

Vienna took her time, concentrating on his motion, and then rapidly firing three bullets at his scissoring legs. She knew one bullet splintered rock, but there was a distinct possibility that one or both of the others scored. When the dust and dirt settled, there appeared to be splashes of blood on the trail.

"I'm going to hunt you down," Larsen called. There was no anger in his voice, only a quiet menace. A promise. "I will hunt you to the ends of the earth. There is nowhere that you can go that I won't find you. And your little friends? I'll kill every single one of them. The woman you call mother? She's dead."

Vienna remained silent, waiting to see what he would do or say next. He had both Stella's and Raine's packs. She couldn't leave him out there to keep the helicopter from coming to get Raine or to get to her mother.

She shifted position slightly and instantly splinters of rock showered down on her head as he fired at her. She didn't have tons of ammunition and no clear shot at him, so she scooted all the way back and rested against the other side of the thick rock wall rising between them. There was blood on her arms and one cheek from the splinters of granite.

"Wallin's going to be really angry with you, isn't he?" she asked. She needed to give the other women as big a head start as possible. Hopefully when Shabina told them to go, they did exactly what she'd said. The moment she could, she would go after the women and retrieve the rest of the ammunition she had in her backpack.

"I'm a dead man," he agreed, his tone amicable, as if they were friends discussing the weather. "My one hope is to kill all of you and hope he's appeased."

"I can't wait for you to look in Raine's backpack. It's the larger of the two." She matched his tone. Just as amicable. Friends talking on a hot afternoon with a body turning the river below them red. "She's the one you shot, in case it matters to you. It might not now, but look in her pack and tell me if it matters when you see who she is and what you're now in possession of."

Vienna wiped the small beads of sweat from her face and concentrated on listening. There was no way he could move back up the trail without her hearing him, even though the river sounded like thunder, as if it were yelling to the world that she had killed a man.

She heard the rustle of what she presumed was Larsen searching Raine's backpack. Then he erupted into a string of low curses. There was some satisfaction in knowing he wasn't quite as happy with himself as he'd been a few minutes earlier.

"What is she? A damned government agent? If I touch any of these little locked cases, I have the feeling they might explode in my face."

"Probably. Raine is like that. As for what she is, I don't actually know. Only that they send helicopters for her, and the moment she was shot I sent her people the message she told me to give them if anything ever happened to her. They will be coming, Larsen. And they will hunt you to the ends of the earth. It won't matter if you get me, or every single one of my friends. It won't matter if you get my mother. It definitely won't matter if Wallin thinks you're the best security man he has, because they will hunt you and never stop until you're dead."

"Well, you're just painting a rosy picture of my future."

She smiled in spite of the fear gripping her. If he had gotten angry and gone ballistic, she wouldn't be so afraid, but he was too calm in the situation. She feared that meant he knew what he was doing. He'd faced combat. He was good in the terrain. He knew and had weapons she didn't. Wallin had sent him along with Axel to teach him how to survive.

"Sorry, but then you painted a similar picture of mine. I'd ask how bad your wounds are—after all, I'm a nurse—but I get the feeling you're not so bad at putting on a field dressing."

"It isn't my first time," he admitted.

She glanced at her watch. If she could just keep him there a little longer, it would give the women time to get Raine to the rendezvous point with the helicopter. Search and Rescue wouldn't risk coming in with an active shooter, but Raine's people would. And Sam's people would. Nothing would stop Sam from coming after Stella. *Nothing.* And if Larsen managed to kill Stella, he would have another powerful enemy hunting him to the ends of the earth.

She thought about whether Zale would hunt Larsen if he managed to kill her. She considered the odds. Yeah. Larsen was going to kill her. At least the odds were high in his favor.

"Are you married, Larsen?"

"No. I tried it once. Didn't have whatever it took to keep it going."

Vienna gave that consideration. He sounded sincere enough. He also sounded a little farther away. Not a lot. Just a little.

"Have you ever really loved someone? A woman, I mean. Someone you wanted to keep."

"If I wanted to keep a woman, I would keep her."

There was that same firm decisiveness in his tone that he had used when telling her he was going to kill her. The voice was also a distance away. He was on the move.

She stretched her legs out slowly, moving her injured ankle around. It was swollen, confined in her hiking boot. She hoped that would give it enough stability to support her when she took off after the other women. She wanted to ensure she could cover them as best she could when they brought in the helicopter.

With infinite care, she rose to her feet. The ankle was very painful, enough that she bent over for a moment, breathing deeply to acclimate herself to it. She couldn't think about anything but getting Raine help. There was no room for anything else in her mind. A rock rolled down the trail in front of her, not behind her, and her heart accelerated. She once more covered the grip in a two-handed fist, ready in case an enemy emerged. All the while she concentrated on listening in case Larsen was coming up behind her. Had there been a third enemy she hadn't realized?

A bird sang a cheerful melody. Vienna nearly missed the notes drifting to her on the shifting breeze because her heart thundered so loud in her ears she could barely hear anything. Listening so intently for Larsen didn't reduce the noise but rather made it louder. The bird sang again, uncaring that life or death was being played out right there on the trail.

"You still with me, Mortenson?"

Not close, she decided. If he was creeping up the trail behind her, she would have known. His voice was too far away.

"Yes."

"I took his money for a lot of years. I take the job, I finish it, you understand? It's a job." If there was regret in his voice, she didn't hear it. He was matter-of-fact.

"I'm sure Raine's people are going to understand."

"I know I'm a dead man. I accepted that fact when I couldn't save Axel. At least I'll have the satisfaction of knowing I completed my job when you're dead. It's always mattered to me that when I give my word, I follow through."

Her heart squeezed down hard in her chest. The pain felt like a heart attack. Her mouth went dry and her palms damp. She waited several heartbeats until she knew she could control the tremor in her voice.

"Good to hear you care so much about your work, Larsen. I know whether I live or die, if Raine dies or if you manage to kill me, I'll have the satisfaction of knowing you'll never have a single moment's peace until you're dead."

The moment she issued the statement, she realized how true it was. Zale would come for her. He would come and he would never stop hunting if he found her dead. Never. She had wondered if she could count on him—now she fully comprehended just how much. It mattered little if he returned the feelings she had for him. He would still come. He had his own code. In his way, for whatever reason, she belonged to him. He would come and he would never stop. The satisfaction was overpowering.

She heard small rocks rolling down the trail as Larsen was up and hobbling away from her. She continued to face forward, her feet shoulder width apart, front foot under her elbows, her back foot with the ball of the foot pressing into the ground. She kept her knees slightly bent for even more stability. Never once did her pistol waver.

The bird continued to sing, a happy melody. It took a moment to hit her, to make her understand—that songbird wasn't an avian at all. Shabina was an avid birdwatcher, and she knew how to call to nearly every species in the vicinity, male or female. Vienna had no idea how to sing like Shabina had, but she could make a chicken sound. The idea had her grinning. She answered the beautiful songbird with her very poor imitation of a chicken. Let Larsen think she was taunting him.

Shabina and Zahra came into view, hurrying toward her. Both had their backpacks on, and as Shabina came up to her, she stretched out her arm toward her. The satellite phone was on her palm.

"They want to talk to you," Shabina explained, sounding apologetic.

Zahra looked anxious, but she held out the small plastic container that held the last clip of bullets. It didn't look like nearly enough, but it would have to do. Frowning, she glanced down at the last text sent.

Get the phone to Vienna. A clear order. The text looked angry even though it wasn't in caps.

Vienna here. I don't have a lot of time. Neither do you. Bring in the helicopter before Larsen gets to a place where he can pick off anyone helping. I'll try to keep the pressure on him. He's very experienced.

There was a slight delay and then the text came back looking bold and decisive. Helicopter on way. ETA five minutes. Will medevac patient. Second helicopter to follow first. All of you are to get aboard. Everyone.

Vienna studied the text. Sam? Zale? Rainier? Or were all three behind that order? She couldn't obey it. They didn't understand the situation there on the ground, or how dangerous Larsen really was.

"Zahra, didn't Stella tell me she preprogrammed her mini Garmin to send the Garmin's location to your phone every fifteen or twenty minutes? That way, if you got lost, you could track us on your phone?"

Zahra nodded and set her pack down, immediately pulling her cell out of the side zipper pocket. "You should just come with us, Vienna. Get on the helicopter."

"I can't. He's going to kill everyone. He told me. It was a vow. He knew he was dead the minute Axel Wallin fell."

She bit her lip and then texted again. Can't delay. One shooter dead, need to go after last shooter. First name Larsen. He's in Wallin's employ. Knows what he's doing. I have to keep pressure on him or he'll stop the helicopter from taking Raine.

Snowflake. For me. Get on the helicopter. We'll go after Larsen. We have a file on him and he'll be like tracking a wounded cougar. He's got military training. Get out of there.

You'll be too late to keep him from stopping the helicopter evac Raine. She doesn't have time to wait. Can't argue. She contemplated sending a heart to him, hoping he'd understand what she was trying to convey. It might be the last time she ever spoke to him. Instead, she just wrote it out for everyone to see. Know you were loved.

Wait then. Stay where you are. I'm coming to you.

There was no use in arguing. She handed the satphone to Zahra. "Go, hon, fast. Get moving so you can get on that helicopter."

She knew Zahra's code and enabled it so she could find the app on the phone for the mini Garmin. If Larsen had ignored the mini Garmin in Stella's pack and he left it there, she could follow him using the app on Zahra's phone. She shoved the pistol into her vest and hooked the ammo clip to the bag at her waist. She had two full clips and the rest of the bullets in her pistol. She would need to make every shot count. No more trying to warn him off or scare him off.

"Shabina, what are you doing? Go with Zahra."

Shabina stubbornly shook her head. "I'm going with you. I might not be able to boulder like you, Vienna, but I can shoot a gun. In fact, I'm very good with one." She lifted the corner of her vest and showed Vienna a small gun with a cherrywood grip. It appeared to be a work of art, a masterpiece, not a lowly firearm that would barely penetrate skin.

Shabina dropped her vest into place and gestured toward the narrow trail.

"Let's go if you're willing to die, because this man is really good in the woods. I shot him and he not only treated his own wound but was as calm as heck when he told me he was going to kill me, my mother and all of you."

"He isn't better than you out here, Vienna. This is your backyard. He might be trained by all kinds of specialists, but you know this terrain. You've been organizing searches for missing campers for the last few years. I'm putting my money on you."

Vienna tested her weight on her ankle. Yeah, that wasn't going to feel any better now than it had a few minutes ago. She took several tentative steps toward the bend and then took a cautious look. She knew he was gone. She felt it. She'd heard him leaving. Rounding the bend, she took lead. She didn't have time to argue with Shabina, so maybe that absolved her of responsibility, and Shabina was an adult, able to make up her own mind about the danger.

"You're a nutcase for making that foolish bet, but I love you all the same." She knew there was a note of relief in her voice. Not just relief, but happiness. She had good friends. She shouldn't want Shabina with her because it was dangerous going after Larsen. On the other hand, she was elated she didn't have to go by herself. "I hope you really are good with that gun."

"I am." Shabina kept her voice low. "I spent hundreds of hours practicing self-defense and learning to shoot. I didn't want to become paranoid after what happened to me, but I am."

Vienna glanced over her shoulder to take in Shabina's determined expression. "Why didn't you insist on all of us getting an Airbnb that allowed dogs?"

She turned back toward the trail, placing her feet cautiously. At the next bend she was going to check the app on Zahra's phone to see when it would next send out a location.

If Larsen kept the mini Garmin inside the pack where Stella had it, he wouldn't see the screen light up with an alert that the location had been sent and he wouldn't toss the Garmin.

Shabina remained silent for several steps, keeping pace behind Vienna, but staying far enough away to allow for sudden retreat. They were nearing the middle of the trail between the two switchbacks. That left them very exposed on the rock, and Vienna picked up the speed in order to make it to the next bend faster.

"When I'm with all of you, I do feel safer," Shabina admitted with reluctance. "And I try to be as normal as possible. I want to *feel* normal. I keep waiting for that to happen. Maybe it never will, but I keep hoping I'll have moments where I'll forget."

Vienna knew that wasn't going to happen easily. "You do go to a counselor, don't you?" It wasn't like she saw or heard that Shabina had a counselor there in Knightly.

"I've been seeing one for a long time. Mostly I talk to her online."

Was there a note of despair in Shabina's voice?

"It takes time, maybe a lifetime, to get over what you went through."

"It wasn't just my life affected, Vienna. My parents will never be the same, and neither will Rainier. I think I cost him his career, and I know I cost him the woman he loved."

Vienna once again stopped to look at her friend. There had been so much guilt and regret in Shabina's voice. "How do you know that?"

"I heard him talking once a few years ago. He said his actions cost him the one woman he loved. His friend told him there were plenty of women in the world and he just said no, not for him. He only loved once, and she was lost to him. I know that's why he stays in the field. A part of me thinks he has a death wish. I'm responsible for that."

"No, you're not. He had choices, just as those who kidnapped you had choices. You were the only one who *didn't* have a choice," Vienna whispered decisively. "You can't take on that responsibility." But she knew if she survived and Raine didn't, or Raine lost her leg, she would always feel guilt. How could she pontificate to Shabina when she would feel exactly the same? Just because one knew something intellectually didn't mean their emotions agreed.

Shabina sent her a faint smile. "Rainier feels responsible for me, like I'm his child or something. Maybe because he thinks he'll never have any. That's another reason I try so hard to stand on my own two feet, so he'll realize I'm okay and he doesn't have to keep checking on me." She shrugged. "Not that I think he'll ever view me any other way but that terrified sixteen-year-old he rescued."

"That's on him, Shabina, not you." Vienna turned back toward their destination and began the approach to the blind bend in the trail warily, holding up one hand to caution Shabina.

Shabina froze in place, but her pistol was rock-steady. Vienna moved as silently as she could, placing each foot carefully so as not to disturb any loose rocks. Half expecting to get shot, she forced her body to keep going, rounding the sweep of trail, frantically searching for signs of Larsen. There was blood on the rocks in several places, but there was no Larsen.

She studied the drag marks where he had scooted to safety, using the backpack to keep her from getting a clear target. Along one side of the trail was a small steady stream of blood. She crouched down to examine it. The bullet hit the rock right above her, showering her with granite splinters. The sound of the gun being fired reverberated against the towering rock.

Shabina returned fire instantly, the first bullet hitting the barrel of Larsen's gun and the second two bouncing off the granite to spray rock all over his face and arm. Shabina's cover fire gave Vienna the time to scramble on hands and knees to the safety of the other side of the rock face. She threw herself forward onto her belly once she was behind the rock wall, just lying there, hugging the rock trail, her heart pounding loudly.

There was silence when Shabina stepped back behind the rock. She'd been careful, only using three bullets to spare their short supply of ammunition. She didn't say anything to Vienna, but she touched the back of her calf gently in camaraderie. She knew that fear could be tasted, could roll and churn in the stomach until bile built up and wanted to come out. Vienna sat up slowly, her heart still pounding.

"Never saw anyone with your kind of luck, Vienna," Larsen said. "Just like Lady Luck favored you in the cards, she does here as well. I should have bagged you several times by now, but you just keep slipping out from under my kill shot."

"Bagged me?" Vienna forced a laugh. Maybe if she pretended to laugh, she'd actually find humor in the situation. She doubted it. She might be closer to hysteria than humor. "Is that how you regard your human victims? Like you would an animal you hunt for food?"

"No, I have little regard for humans, but I like animals. I don't hunt animals for food. I wouldn't eat one unless I was starving and it was a last resort."

His declaration was unexpected. Vienna and Shabina exchanged a look of surprise.

"Which of your friends handles a gun like that? She nearly took off my arm. You said Raine's the one shot. I can't imagine the senator's daughter knowing how to shoot like that."

Vienna put her finger to her lips to caution Shabina. "He's fishing," she mouthed. She didn't want Larsen to know who was with her. Maybe, in the end, if he managed to kill Vienna, he'd let the others go free.

Shabina nodded her understanding. She stayed alert, her attention on the trail.

"Might be that dinky one from Russia."

Zahra would have exploded if she had heard him. She wasn't Russian. She was from Azerbaijan but had been raised in Uzbekistan. Vienna didn't respond.

"Could be the little gorgeous one, daddy's little darling, mommy from Saudi Arabia, although I can't imagine her doing anything more than ordering her maid to help her dress."

Shabina lifted an eyebrow and then covered her mouth, her eyes dancing with laughter. That allowed Vienna to remember her sense of humor. If Shabina could find amusement in the disastrous situation after all she'd been through, Vienna certainly could.

"Could have been the blushing bride. We do know Stella Harrison is getting married in a few days. My condolences to the groom."

"Don't count your chickens, Larsen," Vienna said.

"It's one of the three of them," Larsen continued, ignoring her comment. "Unless you lied about Raine being the one shot earlier. Just because she dropped her pack doesn't mean you were telling the truth about which of the women was hit."

Vienna strained toward the sounds coming a distance from them. This was just a bit longer stretch of trail. Still, she heard him tear off something.

"There should be a medical kit in Raine's backpack. A good one," Vienna said. "Your arm is probably numb and you can't use it very effectively at the moment . . ."

"Don't you worry, honey," he snapped, his normal calm disappearing for just a moment. "I can defend myself against amateurs like the two of you."

Larsen was hurting all right. She'd scored two hits on him. They weren't lethal and probably no more than a couple of flesh wounds. Shabina's shot had torn the gun from his hand and most likely left him with a broken hand and possibly wrist. His arm had to be numb, and like Vienna, those splinters of rock embedded in the skin had to have stung like hot, angry bees. They might not be scoring a kill shot, but they were picking him apart.

"I was more concerned with you being able to treat your wound. I'm a nurse, remember?"

There was a short silence and then he laughed. His laughter was genuine. Like Shabina and Vienna, he had suddenly found humor in the situation.

"What were you going to suggest? That we call a truce so you could treat my wounds? I suppose you don't want me to get infected."

"Sepsis is a nasty way to die, but no, even if you gave me your word that I'd be safe, I wouldn't trust you. I do have some self-preservation left."

"Good for you," Larsen praised. "In another life, Vienna Mortenson, I think I would have gone out of my way to protect you. It's rare that I wasn't happy with my boss's order of who to kill. Don't worry though, I won't hesitate. If I have the shot, I'll take it. I've never been much of a bleeding heart."

"I wasn't worried, Larsen. I expect you to follow the plan." She glanced at her watch. The forest seemed eerily silent, but in the distance she heard the sound of helicopters.

Larsen swore. "The cavalry is coming. I see now why you persisted in following me when you're really too intelligent for such a stupid move. I actually do admire your courage, Mortenson. You're sacrificing yourself for nothing though. Sooner or later, I'm going to kill all of them."

"There's that possibility," Vienna agreed. "But I could always get you first."

He gave a snort of derision. "Don't fool yourself into thinking you've got a chance. This isn't Vegas and a card game. It isn't a game of chance. This is all about experience, lady."

She could hear again that he was backing away from them. He would have to get out of the open if the military ended up dropping soldiers into the area to hunt him. Even if the helicopters flew overhead, the soldiers manning their guns would be able to kill him as soon as they spotted him. It wasn't as if there was adequate cover. His only real chance was to get to the forest and stay out of sight.

She reached out a hand to Shabina and indicated she needed to get on her feet. Her ankle was throbbing with pain, but once she put her weight on it, that pain exploded into agony. She forced air through her lungs and breathed away the worst of it, willing what felt like torture to settle back to the throbbing she'd thought was bad before. She would welcome that kind of pain now that she knew the difference.

"Maybe, Larsen. One never knows. You have some experience, but this is my backyard." She hoped he wouldn't be able to resist answering her and she could get a better idea of where he was.

He gave another snort of derision. "You think highly of yourself."

The voice was coming from even farther away. Quickly taking Zahra's phone out, she opened the app installed for the mini Garmin to communicate to. Sure enough, it pinpointed Larsen's location right there on the switchback trail now a few yards from her. It looked to her as if he was approaching the next bend. There would be forest for him to disappear into if she didn't get him before he got to his destination.

She indicated for Shabina to be as silent as possible and once again began stalking Larsen, only this time, Vienna hurried. She still tried to be as quiet as possible, but she ran toward the curving trail, her weapon in hand.

The moment she got to the center of the curve, she stepped out as far as possible in order to catch a glimpse of Larsen as he ran toward the forest just as she knew he would. Her finger squeezed the trigger without hesitation. She had to make every bullet count, so she didn't just spray the entire area around him when he dove into the higher grass and sapling trees.

Larsen returned fire, driving her back into the shelter of

the switchback. Now she didn't have eyes on him, and he could just wait until she came at him again. He would be taking a chance that the soldiers hadn't been put into the field already and were hunting him. The intelligent move would be to make his run for it, but she had a feeling his desire to get his job done might make him stay right on the edge of the forest where he could hide from the helicopters but still kill her if she came after him.

She waited, her heart in her throat, for any kind of indication of where he was. The breeze fanned the sweat beading on her forehead. "We'll be sitting ducks for him if we go out into the open and he's still there, Shabina."

"He heard the helicopters. He has to know they'll be flying overhead in order to check on his whereabouts. Don't you think he's smart enough to get out of here? They'll lock down the trails and move all the civilians. He won't have very much time in order to leave the area before they send in soldiers to make a sweep. You know they will because of Raine."

"I think he isn't worried about getting out of Yosemite. He can live off the land, and he's probably really good at surviving in the woods. He has Raine's backpack. She carries survival gear even if he didn't bring his own."

Shabina glanced at her watch. "By now, they had to have picked up Raine and are flying her to a hospital. If they listened to you, they'll have an orthopedic surgeon on standby. You've done what you set out to do. You wanted to keep him from having an opportunity to shoot at anyone trying to load her into the helicopter. We can wait here and let the military get him."

Vienna wanted nothing more than to do exactly as Shabina said. "He said he'd kill all of you and my mother."

The sound of a bird singing had both of them turning to look up the trail. Shabina sang a few notes as if another songbird answered the first. "That's Rainier. I'm sure of it." Even so, she took a stable stance and extended her arms in line with her shoulders, pistol in her hands.

"Shabina, stay behind me," Vienna pleaded. She was slower trying to move around Shabina.

Shabina refused to give way. She stayed where she was and when the bird sang again, she answered a second time.

Rainier came into view and he looked as if he was heading into a combat zone. He wore a vest and a belt, both dripping with weapons. Zale was behind him, wearing the same type of gear. Both looked grim, and neither even tried to appear as if they were anything but there to hunt and kill a man.

Rainier's penetrating gaze slid over Shabina as she lowered her weapon. "You injured?" he hissed as he came straight up to her. His long strides indicated he'd shot his leg full of some kind of numbing agent so he didn't feel the wound he'd had no time to heal from.

Vienna wished her ankle had that same numbing agent injected into it. Then Zale all but yanked her into his arms, holding her hard for a brief moment before he tipped her face up to study the scratches and lacerations from the splinters of rock.

"Where are you injured, Vienna?" His voice was harsh.

"My ankle. I turned it, but I'm able to walk on it." She tried not to devour him with her gaze, or give in to the sudden weakness she felt. She wanted to fling herself back into his arms, where she felt safe.

"What the hell were you two thinking?" Rainier demanded. His voice was low and sounded like the crack of a whip.

Shabina flinched visibly, but her voice was steady when she answered. "We were thinking Raine needed surgery and every single minute counted if she was going to keep her leg. That meant putting pressure on Larsen so he couldn't target the medevac team."

"We would have located him and dropped enough firepower on him that he would have made a run for it." Rainier gave Shabina the smallest shake and then tucked a stray strand of hair behind her ear, his fingers gentle. "You might take a look at how gray I'm getting. You're doing that to me."

She gave him a shaky smile. "I'm so relieved you're here, although I hate that you're going to have to go after Larsen. That's what you're doing, right?"

Vienna looked up at Zale. "He's wounded in a couple of places. Shabina shot the gun right out of his hand. We managed to harass him, but he's determined to kill me and every single one of my friends and then he said he was going to kill my mother too. He meant it, Zale. He said that was the only way Wallin would be appeased over the death of his son, and even then, it might not work. Once he found Raine's pack and realized she was important to the government, he figured he was a dead man no matter what, and he wanted to finish his job right."

Zale indicated for her to sit down. "I want to look at your ankle."

"Everyone will think he's making a run for it." Vienna sat down on the rocky trail. "Don't take my boot off. I'll never get it back on and I have to walk out of here."

"Sounds to me like you had a conversation with Larsen."

"I thought the longer I kept him talking the more time it gave for everyone to get here," Vienna said. "He hasn't run, Zale. He's lying out in the forest right now waiting for me to take a step out into the open. I know he hasn't run."

"Anything give you that indication?" Rainier said.

"I just have this feeling about him. He's sure of himself. Really sure of himself." She pulled out Zahra's cell. "Look. I have his location on the app. The mini Garmin sends an alert to Zahra's phone in case she gets lost." She held it out to Zale, who took the cell.

Zale handed the cell to Rainier after glancing at it. "Very clever, Vienna," Rainier praised. "This was smart."

"We've got a ride out of here for you and Shabina," Zale said. "If you say Larsen's waiting right out there on the edge of the forest, I believe you, Snowflake. We'll take every precaution. This is what we do."

His hands were gentle on her ankle but she still winced. Her ankle was swollen over the top of her hiking boot, and when he rolled the top of her sock down, her skin was black and blue.

"Let's get them out of here," Rainier said. He indicated to Shabina to follow him back up the trail.

Zale handed Rainier his pack and the rifle slung around his neck by a strap and simply lifted Vienna. She had no choice but to put her arms around his neck. "You can't carry me to the meadow," she whispered.

He didn't answer but followed Shabina.

IT WAS HOTTER than hell and his skin itched and burned. Larsen wiped the sweat from his eyes with his sleeve. No way would those women have the kind of patience it would take to allow so much time to pass. They were stalling him again for some reason. Whatever the reason, he wasn't going to wait and find out.

Staying low in the grass and weeds, he crawled on his belly, using fingers and toes to move his way into the thicker trees. He just needed to find the best place to set up a base. He had survival gear with him, and Raine's pack contained several items he could use. He had a good water filtration system. He could stay out in the forest until the heat died down and then go after Vienna Mortenson and her friends.

Once in the trees, he jogged toward the heavier growth where he could erase his tracks on the forest floor and go high. Very few people thought to look up into the trees. He had to find a very sturdy tree that had branches large enough to support his weight as he made his climb.

Once he found his tree, he was careful to make his way up into the heavier canopy. After securing the packs, he went back down to make himself a ghillie suit. It was a hasty job, but it would do, helping to hide him from anyone who came to look. Once back in the tree, he placed his weapons around him, securing them to the branches, and figured out several ways to exit the tree if necessary. The last thing he did, before closing his eyes to nap, was pull out his favorite rifle from his pack.

Zale studied his prey from the flat boulder he lay on. Larsen had made himself a cozy little den up in the tree. Even without Vienna giving him the phone with the locator on it, that particular tree would have been one of the first places Zale would have suspected Larsen would have decided on retreating to.

He indicated to Rainier. "He's there. Sitting up all pretty like he owns the place."

"Let him sit. He'll get tired enough. The soldiers will make the sweep. We can protect them from here. If he makes a move to leave his little den, he's dead. If they spot him, he's dead. We'll fade away and no one will be the wiser."

The forest came alive with soldiers moving slowly, examining the ground and rocks. Going over the trail. They found the blood on the trail. Raine's. Vienna's from the spray of granite. Larsen's. Eventually the soldiers continued their sweep away from Larsen's tree and disappeared into the woods. Larsen didn't move for a long time, proving he was well trained and had patience, but as no more soldiers came near, he sat up and drank from his water and ate an energy bar, all without the knowledge that they had him in their sights.

Quiet descended with the night. An owl hooted. Bats took to the air, wheeling and dipping to find every insect over the rushing water in the distance. Zale slipped off the boulder and circled around into the heavier forest, coming close to Larsen's tree. Eventually, he would climb down and stretch his legs. He was feeling confident if his smug expression was anything to go by.

It took another hour before Larsen moved, making his way down the tree, using the branches, avoiding the trunk as often as possible in order to keep from scraping bark and leaving evidence. He jumped the last few feet, landing in a crouch. He wore a tactical vest and his weapons were close.

Zale emerged out of the shadowy darkness behind him. "You're military, Larsen. Do you know what a ghost is, when someone in the military refers to one?"

He spoke low, so low Larsen wasn't certain he actually heard a voice at first, but then he froze. "Ghosts never speak. They just make the kill and walk away."

"True, unless it's personal. This is very personal. Vienna's mine. You shouldn't have come after her."

Larsen swore under his breath. "I knew almost from the beginning that I should walk away. Wallin isn't a man who ever lets anything go. He's got the backing of the Bottaro family. He carries weight, a lot of it with his kind of money and power." His hand inched toward the pistol in his side holster. It was the hand in front of him, the one he was certain the "ghost" couldn't see.

"Consider him already dead," Zale said softly. This time he was only inches behind Larsen and whispering in his ear. "Because he's going to die too."

Larsen felt the bite of the knife in his left kidney as it went in, twisted and came out. Then the blade was at his throat and he felt the incredible sharpness slicing through his skin and artery. His knees went weak and his legs went out from under him. He fell forward, facedown onto the forest floor. Leaves, twigs and dirt met his eyes and nose. He opened his mouth to speak. He didn't remember what he was going to say. The last thing he saw was the ants coming for him.

CHAPTER NINETEEN

Vienna stroked her cat's soft white fur as she sat in the dark on top of her bed. Princess purred her approval of Vienna's attention. The Persian had always demanded to be number one in the household, and when Vienna wasn't giving her the devotion she felt she deserved, she turned up her little snub nose in pure disdain. Sometimes she would turn her back on Vienna and refuse to associate with her in retaliation.

"My ankle is very sore, Princess," she told the cat, massaging the small, round-tipped ears. "I'm not certain I'll be doing much dancing at Stella's wedding."

For the hundredth time she looked at the clock on her nightstand. She tried not to worry about Zale and Rainier, but it was impossible given that she knew Larsen was trained in survival. Most likely he'd received that training from the military.

"I should have just told him. I don't know why I didn't. You would have advised me to just come clean, wouldn't you, Princess? Because you're so wise."

The cat tilted her head and looked lovingly at Vienna with her soft, wide gaze, purring her answer and tucking in closer.

"Larsen could be every bit as good in the woods as Zale," she said aloud to the cat. "We don't know. Maybe he was trained just like Rainier and Zale. I should have insisted on staying instead of letting them load me onto a helicopter with Shabina."

The cat suddenly mewled a protest and leapt off her just as a voice came from the doorway. "Larsen wasn't nearly as good as he thought he was."

Vienna's heart jumped and then began to pound. Zale stood framed in the doorway looking even better than she remembered. His shoulders were wide, and he looked as if he took up the entire doorframe. He had a way of filling the room with his presence. Just knowing he was alive made her feel weak.

"I was worried about you, Zale."

"I'm sorry, Snowflake. I don't want you to be afraid for me. I know what I'm doing when I go after someone. You aren't going to be looking over your shoulder for the rest of your life. I'm cleaning this mess up."

That told her exactly nothing about the way he felt about her. She knew she loved him and that she'd much rather live alone waiting for him to return to her than be without him. But she wasn't certain of his feelings. Had he just been doing his job? She didn't think he would ever lie just to get a woman in bed. He wouldn't have to—certainly not her. Eventually, she would have been seduced by him and he had to know that. There was no need to tell her he wanted to be with her permanently.

He came all the way into the room, tossed a duffel bag into the corner and sat on the edge of her bed, bending down to take off his boots. "When we're given orders, Vienna, we have to follow them. This assignment convinced me I really did want to get out. You're so damn smart, and I kept giving you as many clues as possible, skating very close to getting myself in trouble, but you trusted me so much it didn't occur to you that I could be misleading you."

She swallowed the sudden lump blocking her throat. "Misleading me?"

He turned his head slightly, his dark brown eyes meeting her gaze unflinchingly. His thick dark hair fell across his forehead, giving him more of an untamed look. Normally, the short sides gave him the appearance of a very groomed man. She could see the unruly waves now that he was bent over and the longer hair on the top was revealed. She had spent so many nights with her fingers buried in his hair and the memories welled up.

"Yeah, baby, misleading you. I couldn't tell you Rainier and I were there specifically to protect you from any threats. Elliot forbade us to talk to you about him being your father, or a possible inheritance, later, when he learned of it. Almost from the beginning, Elliot was certain it was Wallin having the agents killed, but he didn't know the reason. And then you were invited to the tournament. Eventually, the terms of the bet were uncovered and then it all made sense. Elliot inherited his father's shares in the hotel and casino. If Wallin could draw him out, he could be killed. Then you would inherit. If you died before Elliot, all to the good."

She pressed her lips together and continued to watch him remove his boots and socks. He crossed the room and placed his boots beside his duffel bag before turning back to face her. She could see lines of strain on his usually expressionless features.

"I'm going to be as straight and direct with you as possible, Vienna. I'm not willing to give you up, so we're talking this out once and for all. That will be the end of it. I mean what I say. I know you're in love with me. I absolutely know that or I wouldn't be acting like you have no choice here. Obviously, you do."

She blinked up at him, a little shocked. "Don't you think it should be easier than this? I'm not trying to throw up roadblocks, and I'm not denying my feelings for you, but at the beginning of a relationship, shouldn't it be easier?"

"It is whatever it is," Zale said, coming to sit on the edge of the bed again. His palm slid gently over her bruised and swollen ankle. "Difficult, easy, it doesn't matter, Vienna, because we're supposed to be together. You scared the crap out of me, going after Larsen. I had his entire history right in front of me and he was someone pretty damn scary when he served. The thought of you going after him was enough to take ten years or more off my life."

She plucked at the comforter with nervous fingers. "I had to make certain Raine was able to be put on the helicopter. That meant keeping pressure on him so he couldn't lie up in a tree somewhere and shoot anyone trying to help her."

"I'm going to admit I admire you for your choice, but I didn't like it. And I want you to agree with me that from this time forward, you'll leave going after killers to me."

She studied his tough features from under her lashes. A few clouds drifted in front of the moon, throwing shadows across his face. "I can safely say chasing after Larsen terrified me. I don't see that I'll be taking that up as a career. I've crossed it off my list."

"This gambling in tournaments seems a risky business as well," he added.

"I prefer to play online. Having my picture plastered everywhere was disconcerting."

His eyebrow shot up. "Snowflake. Really? Having people see your picture was the one thing you didn't like about playing in that tournament? How about Wallin deliberately inviting you to set you up to be murdered? That might be a reason to stay away from those tournaments."

She pretended to contemplate. "I doubt anyone else wants to kill me because I'm Blom's daughter, although Blom might. He didn't seem too excited that I might find out. In any case, Wallin really wanted to play against me. I think in some way he felt if he won, it would vindicate his loss against Liam Gram."

"Blom doesn't want you dead, Vienna. I'm sorry he's not the ideal father."

She shrugged. "I've gone all these years without a father, Zale. I know there are some people who really want and need to know their birth father and mother, but I feel as if I had a wonderful childhood with Mitzi. She's my mother and she'll always be my mother. She was my father when I needed it as well. I'm old enough now that I understand some people just aren't born to be parents. He's got his life and I have mine. I don't need anyone to make me happy. I am happy."

His dark eyes moved over her face. "I don't have anyone in my life and haven't for a long time, not since Sophia Vizzini took me in. We may have had a strange relationship, but she was all I had—until I found you. I want you in my life, Vienna. I might not need you in it in order to live, but I'd end up like Rainier—waiting for a bullet to end my misery."

Her heart clenched hard at the image he created. The idea of Zale staying in his current job endlessly, just waiting for death, was too much for her. On the other hand, she didn't want to be blackmailed emotionally into an unhealthy relationship.

"Zale, only you can be responsible for your life choices and your own happiness. Another person can't provide that for you."

Those dark eyes of his seemed to pierce right through her soul. "I'm not making you responsible, Vienna, although I can see where it sounds like that. I was coming back for you on my own. You don't have to believe that, but it's true. I thought about you day and night and the problems we'd face together. I thought about the risks to your life because of enemies I may have made along the way. I still had another year on my contract. Through all of it, I knew I was going back to you because there was no staying away."

The sincerity in his voice, in his eyes, convinced her he was speaking the truth. What reason did he have to lie to her anymore? She already knew about Blom. Zale was never going to be hard up when it came to finding a woman who would want to have sex with him. The things he said lightened some of the terrible heartache she had been feeling since she found out his assignment had been to guard her.

"I kept tabs on you through Sam. Maybe if you'd found another man I would have stayed away, but most likely I would have come immediately."

"How could you do that if you were on an assignment?" There was more curiosity than challenge.

His strong fingers began to massage her calf. It felt like heaven when her ankle was still throbbing with pain if she moved it too much.

"All of us have favors owed to us. I would have called in as many as I needed to. I want you to know I was already completely gone on you. I knew you had to be in my life. I just didn't know how to safely get you there."

"Did you tell Blom about us when he gave you the assignment to protect me?"

"The original assignment was to back up our other agents in the hotel. We had three placed in various positions. Wilder managed to get onto the security team assigned to Wallin, and there was never any suspicion falling on him. We have two other agents placed on hotel staff, not quite as effective, but they're backup. I was telling you the truth when I said we were trying to find out who was killing our agents. I just didn't give you the entire story."

That reminder upset her more than she wanted to admit. "I don't like lies, Zale. If you're going to be half a world away where I can't even reach you to talk to you, I have to be able to trust you implicitly. Lying about anything erodes trust, and I already have too many trust issues."

"I realize that," he agreed. "I knew it every single time I talked with you about what I was doing in Vegas. Elliot gave us the assignment once you made it into the semifinals and your picture was everywhere. He told us about the bet between Liam Gram, his father, and Daniel Wallin. He said he believed Wallin was trying to determine if you were Gram's granddaughter and possible heir. At that point, he admitted to us that you are his daughter and he wanted you protected. When I told him I was involved with you, he absolutely forbade either of us to tell you the truth about who he was or that he wanted us protecting you."

There was a tinge of anger in his voice, something she didn't associate with him when it came to his work. Vienna fought back the urge to soothe him. She needed to hear what he had to say. It was important, and both of them were easily sidetracked because they weren't used to having to explain their actions.

"I explained to him that my omitting information and keeping it from you could very well put my relationship with you in jeopardy. He was adamant and said then we didn't have a very strong bond if it could be broken so easily. He's never been in a real relationship and has no idea how difficult it can be when you're someone like me with no background in relationships."

"Partners don't lie to one another, Zale," she said. "Having been lied to for my entire life, it's even more distasteful to think my chosen partner would choose to lie to me."

"Lying is a part of our job. Misleading and misdirecting. That's how we stay alive, Vienna, so Elliot acted like it was no big deal." He ran his fingers through his hair and looked at her with his dark eyes filled with trepidation. "I knew it was. I didn't want to deceive you, but we were under orders, and the one thing you don't do is disobey a direct order from Elliot unless it's a matter of life or death."

"Lying can't be part of our relationship, Zale."

"There will be things I can't tell you about my work when I'm going out," he said.

Vienna nodded. "I can accept that. Just don't lie to me. Tell me what you can and say up front that you're not allowed to divulge anything else. I'll understand." She was silent for a moment, biting down on the corner of her lower lip. "Are you ever involved with other women as part of your job?"

His dark eyes jumped to her face. "As in sleeping with a woman? Or having a female partner? What do you mean?"

"You have female partners?"

"There are a few female operatives. I've never partnered with any of them. Rainier has. I think Rush may have. We didn't have any at the hotel, although I think we could have used one. But no, Vienna, I don't sleep with women as part of my job, and if Elliot ever asked that of me, I'd break my contract."

"Was he using me as bait to draw out Wallin?" She paid close attention to Zale's eyes. They narrowed, and for a fleeting moment she could see the killer in him blazing back at her.

"Had I thought he was deliberately using you as bait, that would have been an issue that he wouldn't have overcome. I would have stashed you somewhere safe and hunted him down. He may have known all along that you were his daughter, but I'm not certain he ever looked that hard for you. When it became apparent Wallin was hunting for you, you were already entrenched in that tournament. Elliot didn't think Wallin would make a real attempt to murder you because he had to establish beyond a shadow of a doubt that you were one of Liam's heirs."

"So, he really did change his orders from finding out who was killing the agents to guarding me?"

"Yes. Although the original order stood. We thought only Rainier and I were at high risk, not you. Not until those men showed up in your room posing as security. That's when we realized you were in real danger. Rainier and I both talked to Elliot about getting you out of there. In the end, he said to try to see it through until the end of the tournament. He knew Wallin would play cards with you if you won—and you won."

Vienna nodded. "I did win, and a great deal of money our Search and Rescue team needs, as well as our hospital."

"The bottom line to all of this is simple." Zale slipped around the side of the bed so he was sitting close. "I love you. I don't want to be with anyone else. It won't be easy learning to live together, but I don't make the same mistake twice. You want children, we'll have them. I'll get out when my contract is up. Those are things I can promise you. I'll stick with you to the end of our days and work hard to keep you happy. I want you to make that same commitment to me, Vienna."

"I know I love you, Zale," she admitted. "And I realized I didn't want to live without you. If you can put up with my trust issues, which I promise I'll work very hard on, I can put up with you. I do want children, and I want you out of that business. Having said that, if you aren't happy here in Knightly and you need to go back to it, I'll do my best to support your decision."

He pulled a small jewelry box from his pocket. "I want it official." He snapped open the lid with a push of his thumb, revealing a blue diamond in a princess cut. It was small and simple, nothing showy, but it was exactly what Vienna would have chosen for herself. "Marry me, Vienna. I'm done with worrying about losing you every time I make a mistake. I'm going to make a lot of them. I need to know you'll stick with me. The one absolute I know about you is your unwavering loyalty."

She looked at the ring and then up at his face. There was sincerity there. Love. She saw it smoldering in his eyes. She nodded, her heart nearly bursting with both trepidation and absolute, overwhelming love for him. "I'll marry you, Zale."

He pushed the ring on her finger and then kissed it. "We may be in for a rocky roller-coaster ride, but we'll make it."

She believed him.

STELLA LOOKED GORGEOUS in her wedding gown. Absolutely gorgeous. Vienna and Zahra fussed over her train to make certain it was perfect before they stepped away and took their places to go down the aisle with their partners. Zale was best man. He was escorting Zahra. Vienna recognized Wilder, who was partnered with Harlow. There was a man named Rush who would be escorting Vienna. She liked him. He was very quiet but had that same edge of power and danger clinging to him that Sam and Zale had. Vienna thought Rainier would be escorting Shabina, but he was nowhere to be seen. Instead, a compact, broad-shouldered man with a thick chest, shaggy black hair and startling green eyes accompanied Shabina. He was called Zyair, but she didn't know if that was his last name or first.

As she waited to go down the aisle where Sam was standing, she noted his father's woman, Charlene Bartolomeo, sitting up front, but the seats beside her reserved for Marco Rossi and Luciano Vitale were noticeably empty. She was pleased to see her mother and Ellen had made it and were seated where they could see Stella as she started down the aisle toward Sam. Most of the town of Knightly was there, including some members that were not always so nice, but that was Stella, including everyone.

There was a flurry of movement behind her and her escort, Rush, immediately thrust her behind him and produced a semi-automatic from somewhere in his immaculate suit. She had to admit, he looked extremely intimidating. There was no give to his broad body. None at all. He was built like a solid oak tree, although he could have blended easily into any group. His face was arresting, with a bluish-black shadow on his chiseled jaw and deep blue eyes.

Heart pounding, Vienna peeked around him. Several strangers in suits were surrounded by armed men. The strangers placed their weapons very carefully on the ground. Marco Rossi and Luciano Vitale walked confidently through the line of men surrounding the strangers. Rainier was with them.

"In case you aren't aware of who I am," Rossi began, "my name is Marco Rossi, and you're interrupting my son's wedding." He pulled out his cell phone. "Let me just have a word with your boss."

He spoke amicably enough, but a chill went down Vienna's spine. Then Sam and Zale were standing beside Rossi. She didn't like them so exposed. If this turned into a bloodbath, they would be the first ones hit. She also noticed that Sam had positioned his body slightly in front of his father. Although he had been estranged from his father and they were barely getting their relationship on track, Sam was the kind of man to protect family.

Rush leaned down to whisper into Vienna's ear. "Zale wants you to step back even more. I don't think there's going to be trouble, but it would be a good idea to slide into the shadows close to the flower garden over there." He indicated Stella's garden, where the archway began the walk to the aisle. He really didn't give Vienna much of a choice, crowding her with his larger body until she had to move back into the position the men wanted her. She noticed the other men were doing the same, maneuvering the wedding attendants out of harm's way.

"If there's a problem, run for the shelter of the reception building. The outdoor kitchen is better than nothing," he added.

Vienna nodded, but her attention was on Marco Rossi, who had the phone to his ear. "Fredrick. Marco Rossi here." His hand came up and gestured, indicating for the man on the other end of the phone to hurry up. "Yes. It is a surprise. The biggest surprise is I'm here at my son's wedding and we have unexpected visitors. That's what I'm calling about. The visitors showed up with weapons and have every intention of gunning down my son, his bride and all of her friends. Needless to say, I'm not too happy about that. My men aren't too happy either. Did I miss something? Has your family declared war on mine?"

His voice had gone from friendly to deadly in the matter

of seconds. Vienna's heart began to pound. This really could turn bad, and Zale and Sam were front and center.

"The wedding is taking place right now, Bottaro. I was sitting in my chair waiting to see my son married when the call came that we had visitors. Their orders are to kill the entire wedding party. That's plain enough. Stella Harrison is my son's bride. Every member of the wedding party is under my protection. It's bad enough that our little Raine is lying in a hospital at the moment and may still lose her leg. Incidentally, that won't make me happy."

There was more listening and more of Marco Rossi's hand gestures. It was clear he was very used to instant compliance from those around him.

"Yes, Fredrick. I see where the confusion is. Let me explain this to you as plainly as I can. If one more member of my family—and that includes Vienna Mortenson—is threatened by your family or is injured or, God forbid, killed, I will take that as a declaration of war. If you have men going after Raine, they won't get through her guards. Nevertheless, call them off. If that bastard Daniel Wallin puts out a hit on any of these women, you cancel it and him. A contract with any of their names on it will be considered a declaration of war. Have I made myself clear?"

More talking. This time Marco was nodding his head. "Yes. Thank you." Now his voice was back to friendly. "I'll make certain to get to Vegas. Lovely place. I'm going to put you on speaker so you can direct your men. Hopefully, they understand just how much trouble they were in and how badly this could have ended for them. Make them understand that they had better return immediately to Vegas."

He put his phone on speaker and held it out for the strangers to hear. "This was a mistake, Andre. We don't touch other families. Make your apologies and come on home."

Marco cut off the call abruptly. "There it is, gentlemen. You have your orders. Get the hell off the property. If you're seen again, you'll be going home in a body bag." Curtly, he turned on the heels of his elegant, highly polished Italian leather shoes and started toward the wedding venue. Luciano Vitale mirrored his movements, shielding his body from the others.

Sam and Zale walked close to Marco. "Thought you said you were finished with being head of the Rossi family," Sam said, his voice tinged with amusement. "You even bought a house for your lady."

Vienna could tell just from his voice that Sam had never believed his father's declaration to step down.

"It isn't that easy," Marco said. "Let's get you married."

Sam and Zale went on down the aisle to take their places again. Marco and Luciano seated themselves, Marco taking the hand of Charlene. Rush offered his arm to Vienna. She placed her hand in the crook of his arm, but watched the strangers being escorted off the property by those surrounding them. She was pretty certain the men guarding the wedding were Elliot Blom's men as much as Marco's.

The music started and she followed Harlow and Wilder. Her gaze went to Zale, standing beside Sam. Zale Vizzini belonged with her and someday she was going to marry him. His eyes met hers and he smiled. Just that smile, reserved for her alone, sent an overwhelming wave of love for him through her. Maybe theirs wasn't going to be the easygoing relationship that Stella and Sam had, but it would be unique and they'd learn along the way.

Zale put his hand over his heart. She put her hand over hers and then Rush was leaving her to stand with the men and she moved to take her place beside her friends.

"GOOD EVENING, DANIEL," a male voice greeted.

Daniel Wallin spun around in his chair, one hand automatically reaching to press the panic button to call in his security. He didn't see anyone. Shadows moved in the room, and his heart accelerated to the point he heard it thundering in his ears. He whipped his head from left to right, back and forth for a terrible moment, wondering if he was hearing things. If he was finally really going crazy.

His son was dead. Axel. The only human being that had ever truly loved him. Why had he sent him off with Larsen? Why did he think Axel needed toughening up? Because Axel had feelings and sometimes acted emotionally instead of logically. He'd wanted to stamp that out of him. Instead, Axel was dead and he was losing his mind.

He looked down at his desk. It had no sentimental photographs on it. The walls of his office didn't have pictures hanging of his son. He hadn't wanted to give away how he felt to anyone. He refused to be vulnerable in any way. Now, Axel was dead along with Larsen, the one man he'd counted on for years to watch out for Axel.

He swore. "Don't worry," he whispered aloud. "I'll get that bitch for you. All of them. Every single one of them is going to die. No one can escape me, Axel, least of all Liam Gram's bastard heirs."

"You do think a lot of yourself, Daniel." The voice came again, smooth and taunting him with amusement.

He stabbed his finger into the panic button, once more twisting his head frantically from side to side in an effort to see who was speaking to him. The panic button disengaged the locks on his office door, allowing his security team entrance.

"Press away. It's disabled," a second voice informed him.

Daniel breathed deep and settled in his chair. He wasn't going insane—not yet. He wasn't alone in his enormous office with its private bathroom and bedroom. Sometimes, when he was in the mood, he called down to one of the many women working in various capacities for him to come upstairs and accommodate him.

A few of the women in his employ were paid to entertain his high-end guests or business clients who wanted a female companion for a weekend. The woman had to be discreet because many—or most—of his guests were married and didn't want the hassle of a wife finding out.

Very slowly, Wallin moved his hand away from beneath his desk. He put his fingers on the edge of the desk, but close to his buttoned suit jacket. These men intruding into his office could be in any of the other rooms. He had an extraordinary talent few knew of. His son, Axel, was the only one he'd voluntarily shared the information with. Axel had a similar talent but it hadn't been as developed. Daniel needed him to work harder at it if they really were going to build another casino and run it. He would have had to rely on Axel to pull his weight.

His partners—his cousins in the Bottaro family—didn't know that was why the hotel had been so successful so quickly. Daniel had used his voice to get everything he wanted. The building going up faster. The first-class materials, deliveries when no one else could get them. Daniel had managed it all. Angelo Bottaro, his grandfather, had immediately seen the wisdom of keeping all illegal business out of the casino. He had come to admire and trust Daniel to run things.

Angelo Bottaro was dead and now his son Fredrick ran things. Daniel detested having to answer to a man who continually questioned everything. It wasn't like Fredrick had fought to bring their family out of the mud and claim territory the way Angelo had.

Daniel was well aware Fredrick had ordered Daniel's father killed when, as always, in his drunken state, he'd threatened the Bottaros that he'd tell the world Daniel was Angelo's grandson. He was always asking for money, from Angelo and Daniel. It had been Fredrick who had killed him and left his body beside the dumpster where he always rummaged for food. Daniel was certain Fredrick's contempt of his father was carried over to him. Still, when he wanted vengeance for Axel, Fredrick had come through, sending a crew to kill Vienna Mortenson and her friends at the Harrison wedding. There was great satisfaction in knowing all the women would be killed and hopefully their relatives as well.

"What do you want? If you're looking for jobs, you'll have to apply like everyone else. I'm well aware Larsen's death left a large hole and opportunity for you men. I admire your ingenuity, but . . ." He lowered his voice an octave and tried to match the flow of the pattern of the voices he'd heard, although it was very little to go on. "You should leave these rooms immediately."

Daniel waited for a reaction. None came. His heart accelerated. Surely, he wasn't really losing his mind. Someone was there.

"There's no need to be afraid. I told you, I do admire ingenuity. It's how one gets ahead in this world. I'll put in a good word for you with the security company, that much I can promise you."

"I haven't come looking for a job, Wallin," the first voice said. "What about you?"

The second voice answered, "Don't like his line of work."

Wallin cocked his head to one side. The second voice sounded closer to him, maybe in the same room now.

"You don't like my hotel? The casino? Why wouldn't you?" He just needed them to talk a little more so he could find the exact rhythm he needed to coerce them into doing his bidding. Sometimes he felt a little like a god. He'd tried to tell Axel that he'd be able to get anything he wanted, from women to money to power. He just had to practice.

"Your hotel is just fine," the first one said. "The fact that you murder women, including the mother of your son, disturbs us both immensely."

Daniel stiffened. How could these men possibly know Miriam's death wasn't an accident? He'd managed to get rid of the three people who had known for certain.

"My son's mother died in a car accident." He feigned outrage. The triumph he felt when he had his son with him exclusively, with no input from Axel's bleeding-heart mother, swept over him. Maybe she was the reason he had been so hard on Axel, trying to stamp out the worst of her influence and character flaws.

"No, she didn't, Wallin," the first voice concluded. "You had her killed so you could raise your son yourself."

Now he recognized the voices. He'd heard them talking several times when his security team brought him tapes of men they suspected were agents for Blom. A bodyguard and an older man who had taken the suite next to Vienna Mortenson.

Wallin's private detectives had uncovered three women they believed might be Blom's daughter. The other two women had no indicators at all that they were in any way related to Liam Gram. Vienna had his DNA. She had his mysterious talent at cards. She had roots in Sweden. He had seen it in her photographs. And those eyes. They were a dead giveaway.

"Zale Vizzini and his older friend, although I'm certain you're agents of Blom's."

"Name's Rainier," the other voice introduced himself.

It most likely wasn't a good sign that neither man cared he knew their names. But he wasn't that concerned. He had his voice and he had more money than either man could possibly dream of. Everyone had a price. He just had to find theirs. If he was really lucky, he could use his voice to get them to kill each other.

"How did you get in?" He kept his tone friendly and without the least alarm, but he was certain he knew the answer. The men must have entered through the vent system—somehow—and they would leave the same way. The large system had been a security concern he'd dismissed because of the miles of vents throughout the hotel and the obstructions built in.

"We're not here to pass the time with you," Zale said.

"You should have known better than to go after Elliot or Vienna. You're supposed to be a very intelligent man, but that was on the stupid side."

Wallin could hear little noises behind his chair, but couldn't see what was happening. His office was soundproof. All the yelling in the world wouldn't bring his security team. The door was locked from the inside—he'd locked it himself. A hand came into view, slid inside his jacket and removed his gun and cell phone. Wallin noted the hand—a man's—wore a thin glove. For some reason, the sight of that glove made his situation seem even worse.

"You need to understand," Wallin began.

He didn't like talking to someone he couldn't see. Deliberately, he spun his chair back around to face his desk. One man lounged on the corner of his desk. Daniel didn't recognize him but he looked as hard as nails. There was no mercy on his face and he had the eyes of a killer. His arms were folded across his chest as he leveled his piercing gaze on Wallin.

"I have more money than you could possibly imagine, enough to make your every dream come true." He opened negotiations. Money settled everything. It was just a matter of how much. "I can pay you both millions. I could use a couple of good men like you working for me. Whatever Blom pays you is scraps. Nothing. I can transfer the money to your accounts right now."

He made a movement toward his keyboard to awaken his computer. He could send out an SOS if he could just get to his messages.

An arm reached over his shoulder and pushed the keyboard away, using the same gloved hand. This time, he felt something drop over his head and snake around his neck. He gasped as the noose pulled tight.

"Wait. Wait. You have to listen to me." He leapt out of his chair, knocking it backward. "I can pay you. Blom will just use you up and then discard you. At the end of it all, what do you have? A little pension? You can name your price. I'll pay you whatever you like."

The noose tightened even more, cutting off his air. Looking up, he could see a rope suspended over one of the many thick open beams he'd admired so much. They were white oak and sanded and oiled to perfection. Now, the huge beams seemed ominous and sinister. He knew he'd never be able to look at them again without remembering this frightening moment. He caught at the rope and tried to yank it down. The rope tightened just enough that he was fighting to breathe. Part of that, he acknowledged to himself, was panic.

"You might want to step up onto your chair there and relieve some of the pressure. I wouldn't move around too much because the chair rolls." The bodyguard, Zale had been his name, spoke matter-of-factly.

The pressure of the noose didn't let up at all. Wallin caught at the arms of his office chair in desperation. Shoving the back of the chair against the desk to stabilize it, he carefully stepped onto the seat. No one helped him. They just watched dispassionately as he put one knee in the chair and tried to pull himself up. All the while the noose grew tighter, cutting off his air.

"I'm trying." He practically sobbed it. His voice came out a hoarse whisper. The rope hurt. Stung his skin. "You don't have to do this. We can make a deal."

"The noose will keep tightening unless you stand up, Wallin." Zale's voice was implacable.

"Why are you doing this?" Wallin demanded, trying to take some control back. "Don't you know who I am? The kind of money I have?" His legs shook terribly and felt like rubber. He actually feared he would embarrass himself by wetting his ten-thousand-dollar suit.

The two men remained silent, just watching him with their cold, merciless eyes. The noose seemed to have a mind of its own, pulling tighter—or maybe he was imagining it. He forced himself to struggle into a standing position, balancing precariously on the seat. The chair wobbled, but it held against his desk. Although the noose constricted his air, it had stopped cinching tighter.

"Vienna belongs to me," Zale said softly. "I would have been here just for the agents you had killed. They were friends of mine. Friends of Rainier's. But then you decided it wasn't enough for you. You got greedy and went after Vienna."

"You killed my only son, Axel. And you killed Larsen," Wallin retaliated. He just needed to look at this as a business deal. Use his voice. He could persuade anyone with his voice. Normally, he would have been able to get their rhythm and twist their thinking into doing his bidding, but these men with their cold-blooded demeanors had thrown him.

"Actually, Vienna killed Axel," Zale clarified. "I did kill Larsen. He was very persistent about carrying out your orders."

"We're even. I'll rescind the order to have her killed. I can call off my cousins, the Bottaro family. They would never let this go, but I can dissuade them." Daniel threw out the name of his relatives. Few knew he was related to the notorious family, but now was a good time to point out they would have relentless enemies.

Zale's dark eyes moved over his face. He looked for all the world like the grim reaper. "They've been dissuaded. Vienna's part of Sam Rossi's family. You must have heard of the Rossi family out of New York. They're powerful and very well-connected."

Daniel's heart dropped. His connection to the Bottaro family had always been his last resort and one he thought guaranteed to keep him safe.

Rainier was the one to inform him. "Sam's father was at the wedding when Bottaro's men showed up. We were waiting for just such a move. Personally, I wanted to kill them all. We had them surrounded and could have picked them off easily, but Marco Rossi had other ideas. He called Fredrick Bottaro and they had quite a little chat. Apparently,

Fredrick wanted a truce with the Rossi family more than he wanted to exact revenge for Axel."

That would be like Fredrick. He was nothing like his father. And he'd never liked Axel or Daniel in spite of all the money that poured in from the Northern Lights.

Okay, he had to put a stop to this before it was entirely out of hand. Grasping at the rope with the tips of his fingers in an effort to loosen it, he pitched his voice low, attempting to use the hypnotic, mesmerizing tones he knew could crawl into a man's mind and turn them to his bidding.

"You want to release me and take the jobs I've offered you. The money sounds good to you."

Rainier shook his head and slid off the edge of his desk. "He's trying that heebie-jeebie garbage Vienna told us about with his voice. I can hear it trying to get into my head."

"Same here," Zale said. "Good thing we listened to her. We're wearing ear distortion plugs to keep your voice from affecting us in any way. So, no, we're not taking your jobs and we don't want your money. We're not going to shoot each other either."

He shoved the chair with his foot as Rainier used the mechanical pulley to raise the rope higher into the air, leaving Daniel Wallin dangling. His legs kicked uselessly and his hands tore at the rope that had tightened so that he was dizzy and seeing black spots. It happened so fast there was nothing he could do to combat it.

"So sad that you became so despondent that you committed suicide rather than face the charges of murder that you knew were going to be coming your way once the law firm brought everything out into the open," Zale said.

Daniel tried to tell them he'd never take his own life. He didn't believe in that.

"We'll leave the remote in your hand, Wallin, so you can lower the rope when we're gone," Rainier said. He reached up with an outstretched gloved hand. "Elliot sends his regards."

Daniel did his best to take the remote from him. He felt it in his hand and he tried to find the button that would lower the rope. He moved his fingers everywhere over the surface of the thing, but his strength was failing and the remote slipped to the floor. He heard it, but he couldn't see. His lungs burned for air.

There was no way to scream his defiance. This wasn't right. This couldn't be happening. Not to him. It couldn't be. Not Daniel Wallin. No one had ever caught him no matter how many lives he'd ended. He wouldn't accept this even as his brain refused to function any longer.

CHAPTER TWENTY

~~~~~~

Good grief, Raine, you have more guards at your door than a military prisoner would have," Vienna greeted. She looked around the large room that held only Raine. "No roommate, and enough flowers and plants to start your own flower shop."

Raine looked pale and very small in the bed. Her injured leg was stretched out with blocks wedged all along it. Raine waved toward the chairs in the room. They were really nice, comfortable leather chairs.

Rush sat in a chair in the corner of Raine's room, almost obscured by all the flowers. Vienna gave him a cheery wave, a little shocked to see him there. "Rush. Nice to see you again. Have you been regaling Raine with all the details of the wedding?"

"No, he hasn't," Raine said, sounding a little miffed. "He doesn't talk. He just pulls out the chess board and sets it up. I think he's taking advantage of the fact that they have me on painkillers." She glared through the huge bouquets at her guard.

Rush raised an eyebrow, but he didn't reply.

"Sometimes he changes it up and plays Go instead of chess. And he won't give me my laptop." Raine's eyebrows came together.

"Rush, that's just a sacrilege," Vienna said.

"It's right over there, Vienna," Raine said in her sweetest tone. She pointed through the jungle of flowers and plants to the briefcase sitting against the wall, very close to the silent operative. "Would you mind getting it for me?"

"No problem." Vienna took two steps toward the briefcase, but Rush's hand caught the handle before she could.

He shook his head. "The doctor said absolutely not. In fact, he's going to cut down on her visitors soon too. She has an endless parade of male visitors traipsing through here. Doc wants her resting. She doesn't seem to know what that word means. I handed her a dictionary since she can't seem to understand half of what he says to her."

Vienna was stuck back on the endless parade of male visitors traipsing through Raine's hospital room. "She has guards with guns at her door. It isn't like you can just walk in. How many men? Raine? Who are these men visiting you? How come I don't know about them?"

Vienna turned to look at Harlow, Shabina and Zahra, who had accompanied her to visit Raine. "Did any of you know about Raine's secret stash of hot men?"

"No one used the word *hot*," Rush objected.

Raine shifted her position in the bed and a low sound escaped, somewhere between a moan and a whimper, sounding too much like an animal in pain. Rush was up and at her side instantly.

"What did I tell you about trying to change positions without asking me for help? Damn, woman, you're stubborn." Even as he was chastising her, Rush was gently guiding her body into a more comfortable position and placing the multitude of pillows around her to keep her upright. "Is that better?"

Raine's breathing had turned ragged. She nodded, her hands still gripping his shoulders, her head down as she tried to let pain wash over and through her.

Vienna could visibly see Rush's reaction. He stabbed at the button, calling the nurse.

"Rush, no. I can get on top of this," Raine protested.

He didn't answer. The nurse entered the room so fast Vienna thought she might have been a private nurse. She hurried over to the bed and stood looking at Rush, not Raine, for instructions. Immediately, Vienna wondered if Rush, like Rainier, was actually a doctor.

"She needs pain medication. She isn't taking it the way she should. We may have to put her on a regular time schedule." His voice was hard with authority.

"Rush, no. Seriously. I'll take the meds."

"You're supposed to take them before the pain gets to this point, Raine, but you're too damn stubborn. Your body won't heal. I've explained that to you. Your doctor has." He suddenly turned to Vienna, narrowing his eyes. "You're a nurse and Raine's friend. Am I bullshitting her?"

Vienna ignored the fact that Rush was scary as hell and went to Raine's bedside, pushing right past him to lean toward Raine. "Honey, as bossy and annoying as Rush sounds, he's right about this. The injury to your leg was extremely severe. You nearly lost it."

"She still could," Rush put in.

Vienna resisted the urge to kick him. She glared at him over her shoulder and then turned back to Raine. She could see on Raine's face that she was entirely aware of how bad her leg was, and she was scared. Maybe if someone didn't know her, they couldn't see her fear, but Vienna knew her very well. She smoothed back her hair with gentle fingers.

"You have to stay on top of the pain, honey. I know you're tough, but in this instance, it really is better for you to keep up with the medication. I know you're aware you should. Why aren't you?" Because that was the real question. Not whether or not Raine understood the dire circumstances. She did.

The nurse had already adjusted the pump to push morphine into Raine's veins, and the medication was beginning to ease the worst of the pain. Vienna took the cool washcloth

Rush passed to her and pressed it to Raine's forehead, wiping away the little beads of sweat.

"I can't think straight," Raine admitted. Her voice trembled, and for a moment her gaze shifted to Rush and then she looked toward the door as if someone might come through it at any moment with guns blazing. "I feel like I can't defend myself if I needed to."

Beside her, Rush froze. Before Vienna could stop him, he leaned around her and put his hand on Raine's. "*Taku kairangi*, do you think I would ever hurt you? Is it me you're afraid of? I can ask Elliot to have another guard assigned to you if you prefer. You have to take those meds. I'd defend you with my life, Raine, and I prefer to stay, but if you're afraid of me, I'll step aside."

Vienna kept her gaze glued to Raine's face. Normally, Raine could be difficult to read, but it was impossible for her to guard her expression. She shook her head, color moving up her neck to her face. Vienna had no idea what language he spoke or what he'd called Raine, but obviously she did. He'd also used a velvety tone when he'd called her whatever he had.

"Not you, Rush." A ghost of a smile curved her lips. "You're just a pain bossing me around. I've stirred up a hornet's nest . . ." She hesitated and then added, "Now and then. There are a lot of people who wouldn't mind seeing me dead."

"You didn't share that with me," Rush said, his voice once more intimidating.

"I didn't know I was supposed to share things like that with anyone. It's very personal."

The moment the information escaped, Raine pressed her fingers over her mouth as if she'd disclosed a national secret. Vienna's heart skipped a beat. Personal? *Very* personal? Vienna would have thought Raine had stirred up a hornet's nest in some military covert operation she'd helped with, not that she was afraid because of something personal.

"Does this have something to do with Luciano Vitale?"

Rush demanded, now sounding lethal, as if he would march out of the room and gun down Vitale the moment he encountered him. "Every time that man comes to visit you get tense as all get-out."

Luciano Vitale visited Raine? Vienna sent a quick look to Harlow, Zahra and Shabina. Were they aware that Vitale knew Raine? Vitale was Sam Rossi's father's enforcer. Or his bodyguard. Or something of significance. She didn't really know, only that he looked mean and tough. Why would he visit Raine?

"Talk to me, Raine," Rush insisted when Raine didn't speak.

"Stop trying to intimidate her," Vienna snapped. "What is it with all of you? Does Elliot have a special school he requires all of you to go to in order to work for him?" She still hadn't heard from her birth father. She didn't want to, and the longer he went without contacting her, the more she was certain she didn't want anything to do with him.

For the first time Rush's features seemed to soften. "It would be impossible to intimidate Raine, wouldn't it, *e te paruhi?*"

Now Rush's voice was back to that brush of velvet. Was he flirting with Raine? Sam's friends were just plain scary in that they seemed capable of getting their way by any means.

Raine gave a little shrug, the blush back. Vienna didn't know the language, or what Rush was calling her, but Raine did.

"My family is Irish, Rush. My father was involved in some shady deals and ended up dead because of it. I started poking around, trying to find out who might have killed him. Our family had moved from New York to California and he was out of the business. He shouldn't have been touched."

Rush studied her face for a few moments before retreating to his comfortable spot behind the forest of plants and flowers. "We can talk about that later. Enjoy your company. Be sure to fill them in on all your male visitors."

Vienna knew he'd said the last deliberately in order to lighten the mood. She took her cue. "Yes, Raine. I think all of us would like to know about your male visitors."

Raine heaved a sigh. "He's exaggerating."

Rush made a noise somewhere between a cough that sounded suspiciously like "bullshit" and the sound of a frog croaking. Raine laughed. Her first real laugh. She rolled her eyes.

"Briac came to visit me. You remember him, Vienna. The doctor who treated Rainier in Vegas. He's come three times and he brought me a plant each time."

"Did his bodyguard, Gage, come with him?" Vienna asked curiously.

"Yes. He stood up against the door, glaring at Rush. Rush paid no attention to him, which made Gage act even sillier. Is Zale with you? I was hoping the two of you might patch things up. And did your mother come for the wedding? Sam's father came to see me, so I know he was there."

Vienna found herself laughing with the other women. As a rule, Raine was quiet, but sitting in the hospital room with no one but Rush to talk to and no laptop to get her information had to be driving her crazy.

"Zale and I did patch things up and he's here, just outside your room talking to Rainier, who came as well."

Rush stood up. "Why didn't you say so. I'll just step outside and leave you women to it." He reached down and picked up Raine's briefcase. "Just in case one of you gives in to temptation."

"Don't you dare take that out of this room. That's my personal property, Rush," Raine objected.

He ignored her and sauntered out.

Vienna burst out laughing. "I can see you two get along just fine."

"He's an arrogant ass, but at least he has a brain."

"What language is he speaking when he calls you something in that soft velvety tone, the one that makes you blush?" Vienna asked.

"I don't blush," Raine objected.

"You blush," all the women said simultaneously, and then laughed.

Raine joined in. "He does make me blush sometimes and I don't even know why, except that he can get intense all of a sudden, especially when he's speaking Maori. He's fifty percent Maori. His mother was from New Zealand, his father from Maryland."

"So, you have Dr. Briac coming to see you. Luciano Vitale as well. Who else?" Zahra asked. "I'm getting jealous."

Raine waved her hand in the air dismissively. "Don't be. There's just one or two friends from work that have dropped by to make sure I'm doing okay."

Harlow's eyebrow shot up. "Is it one? Or two?"

"Or more?" Zahra asked.

Raine's freckles had been standing out starkly against her pale skin, but now a wave of color once more crept up her neck into her face. "Stop teasing me. You're as bad as Rush. The general came to see me, and after he left, Rush was relentless. He barely acknowledged the general and wouldn't leave the room, acting as if the man might take my pillow and try to smother me."

They all started laughing. Vienna could barely breathe, she was laughing so hard. "He must have been jealous."

"No, I think he dreams about smothering me himself, so he puts that on everyone who walks through the door. He's assigned to keep me alive. If he thinks everyone's out to kill me because *he'd* like to, that's his problem."

Vienna held up her left hand and waved it around. "What do you think of this?"

"Come here. Let me see."

Raine looked as if she might throw herself off the bed, so Vienna hastened to her side so she could see the engagement ring close up.

"He picked it out himself and it's perfect for me."

"It is. He knows you so well." Raine subsided against the pillows, looking lost. "I don't think I'm ever going to have that—someone really knowing me. I confuse men." She gave her friends a smile that didn't reach her eyes. "I think I confuse myself."

"What do you mean?" Harlow asked.

Raine shrugged. "I'm a contradiction. Most brainiacs are gamers on their downtime. They don't hike and climb. I'm an avid hiker and climber. Most hikers and climbers don't have the kind of job I do. And they aren't all girlie." She looked down at her perfectly manicured fingernails. "They don't have gorgeous boots in their closets they can't wait to wear with darling little swing dresses they're addicted to. They don't dream about owning a gift shop instead of dealing with classified material."

"Raine, you'll find someone." Vienna's heart ached for her.

"I want someone who knows all of me. Not just one side of me. And I have such a bad temper. I really try to get that under control, but you know how mean I can get under the right circumstances. That doesn't help. I try not to be the smartest person in the room, but when men get all superior and start talking down to me, I can't help putting them in their place, and I'm not subtle about it."

Vienna knew Raine had had her heart broken once. She'd been shattered, and the effects had been long-lasting. She didn't trust herself anymore. She didn't trust the men vying for her attention. She never let them in.

"You'll find someone," she reiterated. "When you least expect it. I did. Zale was persistent when I kept shoving him away." She had the feeling that if a man really wanted Raine, he would have to pursue her and knock her over with a bowling ball.

Raine smiled at her. "I'm glad you all came to see me. What other news do you have for me? I can't look anything up on my laptop and they've disconnected my television set."

"That's so mean," Shabina said. "What is the point of isolating you?"

"They want my brain to rest. And they want me to learn to meditate and slow down."

There was a small silence. "Does your brain slow down?" Vienna asked carefully.

"No," Raine answered honestly.

"Did you explain that to them?" Vienna pursued.

Raine shrugged. "What's the use? I did to Rush when he kept asking me what was wrong. I hated that he knew something was wrong. No one ever knows, but he seems to be able to read me when no one else can. It's disconcerting."

"What did Rush say when you told him you can't turn off your brain?"

Raine rubbed her temple. That small gesture alarmed Vienna. Raine only did that when she had the beginnings of one of her headaches. "He said he understood because he had the same problem. He told me his mother used to say his brain was too big for his head and there was no off switch. He told me his mother would massage his scalp when he would get headaches, although that would make his father angry because men don't get headaches."

The women gave a collective gasp of exasperation. "I thought that bull had been put to bed a long time ago," Harlow said.

Shabina shook her head. "It's alive and well."

"It's awful," Zahra said. "I know my brother was expected to live up to a very high standard and never complain about anything. I thought I had it bad, but he had it worse in many ways."

Zahra rarely talked about the family she no longer was allowed to see or interact with. Vienna's heart ached for her. More than ever, she was grateful she had Mitzi and Ellen back in her life. "I forgot to tell you, Mom and Ellen said to say hello and they hope you get better soon. They would have come to visit you, but they couldn't get their names put on the visitor list. We were lucky to get ours on there."

Raine's golden-red eyebrows nearly met as she frowned. "I have a visitor list? And only a certain number of visitors can be put on there? Are you serious? People like Luciano Vitale are making the cut but your mother and Ellen aren't?" She sounded outraged. "Who is making the decisions on who can see me and who can't?"

She threw back the covers and looked as if she might leap from the bed. Vienna caught her hand to stay her actions. "What are you doing?"

"I have to get out of here, Vienna. I'm going crazy. I really am. I can't stay in this place another minute. Now they're telling me who I can see?"

Vienna put her arms around Raine and held her. She felt thin. So small. Her body trembled and she was shaking as if she was silently crying. The other women crowded close, murmuring softly to console her, putting their hands on her shoulders. The slight twisting wasn't good for her leg and had to hurt, but Vienna decided Raine needed comforting more than a lecture on keeping her leg exactly in a certain position.

"I'm all right," Raine assured after a couple of minutes. She hiccuped and pulled away, looking sheepish. Her face was red and splotchy. Both hands went to her thigh. "I think I did something I shouldn't have, Vienna."

"Let me help you. You just sit straight. I take it you can't get up to go to the bathroom." Vienna eased her twisted thigh back into a straight position.

Instantly there was relief on Raine's face. "No, and that's so embarrassing. I have to let Rush know. I mean, I buzz for the nurse, but he says it's silly not to just let him help me when he's a doctor. That's *not* happening. I think he regards me as a child."

Shabina burst out laughing. "That's exactly how Rainier views me. Like a little kid. He's the calm one, and I can't stop having panic attacks around him. I'm sure he causes them."

Raine joined her, laughing. "It's the same here. Rush absolutely causes me to have panic attacks. And he's so superior sometimes, always in control. I'll bet he's the one deciding who's on my visitor list."

"No way," Vienna objected. "Dr. Briac would be off that list so fast. I think Luciano would be as well. It isn't Rush controlling that list."

"All right, tell me more news."

"Daniel Wallin committed suicide," Vienna announced. "He was alone in his office and he hanged himself. He must have been afraid it would come out that he had tried to have Elliot and me killed."

Raine shook her head slowly. "No way did he kill himself, Vienna. Elliot's men got to him."

"He was alone in a locked office," Vienna reiterated.

"It was Zale and Rainier or some other of Elliot's men," Raine said. "If you're going to spend the rest of your life with Zale, you had better know who he is."

"You think he really killed Daniel?" Vienna sank into the chair Rush had vacated.

"Yes." Raine glanced at Shabina. "There's no doubt in my mind that Rainier was with him. He tried to kill you. He threatened to kill all of you. He would have done it, too. Daniel Wallin believed he could do whatever he wanted. There was no way Zale or Rainier would leave a threat like that hanging over any of your heads."

In the back of her mind, Vienna had feared there was a possibility that Zale had something to do with Daniel's death. She hadn't asked him because she wasn't certain she wanted to know. She looked at Shabina to see how she was taking the news. Shabina didn't look surprised, more like resigned.

She shrugged. "I tried to talk to Rainier about Daniel Wallin, but as usual, he wouldn't listen to me. He just said that he wasn't going to have the man put a bounty on my head." There was a hint of despair in her voice. "I wrecked his career. Lost him his woman. I think he stays in that life because he has a death wish. I think eventually someone is going to kill him, and that's going to be on me as well."

"Shabina." Raine's voice was gentle but persuasive. "Rainier is a grown man. Every single decision that he makes is his own. His choices. He isn't your responsibility. What he chooses to do on your behalf isn't your responsibility. You don't ask him to take on those tasks. In fact, you try to stop him."

Shabina looked down at her hands. "I don't have any influence at all on him."

"That's my point, Shabina," Raine said. "You can't take responsibility when Rainier refuses to consider anything you say."

Vienna took one look at Shabina's expression and wanted to hug her. Shabina had never been good at hiding her emotions. She might logically understand what Raine said, but that didn't mean her feelings didn't tell her something different.

"You know what, Shabina? I understand perfectly. I think all of us do. We all have issues. Poor Zale is going to spend the rest of his life reassuring me. He doesn't even know it yet, but that's what he's signed up for." She poured cheer into her voice. "I feel guilt over it, and my birth mother was the one to whisper how men lie all the time. My birth father, who just happens to be his boss and hung me out to dry, left her for his big career. I shouldn't feel guilt but I do. Just like you. I'm sure every woman here feels guilty over something they shouldn't, because that's what we do."

They all nodded solemnly. "And we're really good at it too," Zahra said. "Take for instance the fact that I brought along contraband. Smuggled it right past those guards with guns. I just looked at them and batted my eyelashes. They looked in my backpack and purse, but didn't *really* look."

Raine gasped. Clapped her hands. "Zahra. You wonderful, amazing, astonishing woman. You have superpowers. I love you beyond anything. What did you bring me?"

"Only your favorites." Zahra got up and approached the bed, looking around the room, up at the walls and corners. "Are there cameras? Do they have you under surveillance? I brought a little locked case for you to keep them in. That way you can have them on the bed with you and no one can get to them."

She flipped open the lid of the small pale mint green box. It had a lock on it that could only be opened if one knew the long row of numbers to put in the correct order. The box contained several chocolate bars with nuts, and salted caramel, Raine's favorite.

Raine caught up one of the salted caramels and opened it immediately. "You have no idea how much I love you right now, Zahra. I'd share, but they'd all be gone and I really, truly need them."

"Zahra brought them so you could have them when you need one," Vienna said.

"I'll just have to hide them from Rush."

"We've got that covered," Vienna assured. "We brought letters. You can put the letters in the box so if he sees you open and close the box one or two times, he'll think it contains private letters."

"That's perfect." Raine beamed at them. "You all are the best."

Vienna looked around at her circle of friends. "I agree wholeheartedly, Raine. We are the best together."

GLOSSARIES

⁄⁄⁄⁄⁄⁄⁄⁄⁄⁄⁄⁄⁄⁄⁄⁄⁄⁄⁄⁄⁄⁄⁄⁄⁄⁄⁄⁄⁄⁄⁄

CLIMBING TERMS

anchor: A point of attachment for a climbing rope.

belt line: The belt placed at the waistline.

beta: Information about a climb.

bouldering: Free climbing without ropes or harnesses on boulders or relatively small rock faces.

chalk: Soft limestone used to keep a climber's hands dry.

chalk bag: A small pouch that holds a climber's chalk.

climber: Someone who participates in climbing.

climbing: Movement on rock, snow, ice or a mix.

crash pad: A small foam pad used for protection and safety. Also called a bouldering mat.

crimp: A technique of gripping small edges with fingertips flat on the surface while fingers arch above their tips.

crux: The most difficult position of a climb.

downclimb: Descending by climbing downward.

flag: When a leg is held in a position to maintain balance rather than to support weight.

heel hook: Using the back of the heel to hold for balance or leverage.

highball: A tall and potentially dangerous boulder problem.

hiking: A walk or trek through the wilderness on a path.

hold: A place to temporarily grip, hold, stand or otherwise stabilize during the process of climbing.

jug: Short for jug hold, which is a large, easily held place to grip or otherwise hold.

overhang: A section of rock that is angled beyond vertical.

project: A bouldering problem that is repeatedly attempted over time, but has not been successfully completed.

rope climbing: Use of rope while climbing.

spotter: The person who stands below the climber ready to absorb the energy of a potential fall.

VB: V-scale for beginner bouldering problems.

V-scale: Grading scale that defines difficulty starting from a V0 (v-zero) to a V17.

POKER TERMS

all in: Pushing all of your chips into the middle of the table to bet on your current hand.

ante: A forced bet that must be made by all players at the table prior to cards being dealt.

bet: A wager during the play of a hand.

big blind: The larger of the two forced blind bets. This is the first full bet in a hand of Texas Hold'em.

blinds: Forced bets players make before the cards are dealt in a new hand. They are called blinds because the player places a bet without seeing the cards first.

bluff: Playing and betting when you know you have a weaker hand than another player, with the intention of getting them to fold.

burn card: A card removed from the deal to prevent cheating.

bust: When a player loses all their chips; an uncompleted hand.

buy-in: The cost to enter a tournament, or the minimum amount needed to join a game.

call: Matching or raising another player's bet.

check: Choosing not to bet and to pass the action to the next player if there is no bet to you.

chips: Small discs that are used in poker to represent cash.

dealer: The person dealing the cards.

draw: Taking a card from the deck or dealer.

flop: The first three community cards that are dealt on the table.

flush: A hand with five cards all of the same suit.

fold: Discarding a hand and ending your participation and ability to win the pot. Also called laydown.

four of a kind: Four of the same ranked cards.

full house: A five-card hand consisting of three of a kind and a pair.

hand: Five cards, the player's pocket (hole) cards and the community cards.

hole cards: The two cards each player holds facedown, also known as pocket cards.

odds: The chance of a particular outcome, represented by a ratio in most cases.

pair: Two cards of the same rank.

pot: The place in the middle of the table that is made up of chips that have been bet.

push: To go all in. Bet all in.

raise: Betting more in addition to another player's bet.

river: The final card dealt in a poker hand, to be followed by a final round of betting. The river is the fifth and last card to be dealt to the community card board, after the flop and turn.

royal flush: The best possible hand in poker, a straight from ten to ace, all of the same suit. "Royal" because it includes all the face cards.

straight: Five cards in sequence but not in the same suit.

straight flush: A straight that is also all of the same suit.

tell: A detectable change in a player's behavior or demeanor that gives clues to that player's assessment of their hand.

three of a kind: Three cards of the same rank.

top kicker: The best possible side card in a given hand. A card that doesn't add to the rank of a hand but can be used in a tie with the highest card, helping determine the winner.

top pair: The best two possible pairs based on the community cards and what a player holds.

KEEP READING FOR AN EXCERPT FROM

SHADOW DANCE

THE NEXT SHADOW RIDERS
NOVEL BY CHRISTINE FEEHAN

Geno Ferraro leaned one hip against the wall as he looked through the two-way mirror at the prisoner seated very uncomfortably in the metal chair in the middle of the interrogation room. The room was all about efficiency. Drains, overhead sprays and hooks, long counters laid out with power tools and instruments one could use to help the prisoner regain their memory very quickly if they'd mysteriously lost it. A shower. A toilet. A sink. Even a tub. Just about anything one needed for a successful interrogation if one was serious. He was *very* serious. Murder was a serious crime—doubly so if the victims were one's parents.

"Something's wrong, Stefano. I can feel it," he said, never once taking his gaze from the prisoner. "I don't want her to see you or my brothers. No one else. Fiero and Donte Lantini, my main personal protectors, picked her up and brought her here. It couldn't be helped that she saw their faces, but I don't want her to see anyone else until I know what's going on. I sent for you because I need someone I can trust implicitly to help me figure this out."

Geno had been head of the Ferraro family in New York for years. The Ferraro territory was a crime-free safe place for those who lived and worked in the neighborhood. *His* neighborhood. He knew every shop owner. Every resident. This was his community, and he was responsible for it. He took that responsibility very seriously. Ferraro territory started right on the edge of Little Italy and ran all the way west through Tribeca to the Hudson River.

"I don't just know every one of the businesses and those living in my territory, Stefano. I know most of those in Little Italy. They know me and my brothers and our *famiglia*. They know they can count on us if there's need. Mama was raised with her second cousins, Viola and Noemi. Both married and became nurses. When they retired, they went to work in their husbands' shops. Viola's husband, Marcelle, had a hat store. Noemi's husband, Caio, had a very high-end watch shop."

Stefano Ferraro regarded the prisoner with shrewd, assessing eyes. He ran the Ferraro territory in Chicago and had interrogated many prisoners under tough circumstances. He turned that piercing gaze from the prisoner to his cousin.

"There have always been petty crimes, thefts, tourists getting pockets picked, I was told, but our family was never asked to help," Geno continued. "Mama would visit her cousins and come home at times and tell us that the thefts were becoming more frequent, but no one thought to come to us. A few months ago, I could see concern on her face and strain on Papa's. He's always been distant, but he became even more so. I wondered why they didn't insist on investigating."

Geno pulled his gaze away from the prisoner to look at his cousin. Although they were somewhat close in age, he'd always looked up to Stefano.

"I rarely questioned my parents. Once they turned over the reins of the business to me, they no longer gave advice to me on any subject, including parenting. They made it clear they would only do their job and nothing more. My brothers, Salvatore and Lucca, don't remember them any other way, but I do. Not even concerning themselves with the escalating problems in Little Italy, with their friends and even *famiglia's* livelihoods and safety, made no sense to me."

Geno shoved a hand through his hair. "Granted, in the beginning the crimes were petty. Stolen merchandise. Tourists being robbed with more frequency. But the thefts became more violent over a period of months."

"I take it your parents refused to turn the series of crimes over to investigators," Stefano ventured. His voice was low.

Geno sighed. "They wouldn't discuss the subject, not even when many of the business owners began to look on the Ferraros with suspicion."

"Why would that be?" Stefano's expression didn't change.

"Many of the robberies occurred after hours. The safes were locked. There was no evidence of a break-in. No images were caught on surveillance tapes in the store or outside of it. Those who knew of our reputation began to worry that one of us was stealing and the others were protecting a family member."

"And yet your parents refused to order an investigation."

Geno nodded slowly.

"You could have ordered one."

"I could have, but I was gone more than I was home. We're short of riders and I was continually taking rotations. I had hoped my parents would step up and see that there was a problem, especially as the robberies began to spill over into our territory. Not only did that not happen, but when I insisted we investigate, they threw roadblocks in the way of the investigation."

"That makes no sense."

"Nothing my parents have done has made sense since the night my mother woke me up and took me into their suite in the dead of night. Their private surgeon, Dr. Mortan, was there, along with Dr. Vargas, an anesthesiologist, Viola, Noemi, and my parents' bodyguards. Blood was everywhere and IVs were hooked up to my father with fluids and blood draining into him."

"You never really talked about that night, Geno."

"There was no explanation. His leg was amputated, but I

don't know how he was injured. He never said. Neither would my mother. For one year, we weren't allowed into their suite. There was no contact with either of them. That night, my father gripped my shoulder with merciless fingers and stared at me with hard, pitiless eyes. I'll never forget the way his fingers dug into my shoulder or how his eyes stared into me. He looked wild and not at all like my father. It was the first time in my life I was ever really afraid of him. He looked like a demon."

"He must have been in tremendous pain. You were thirteen. Your father was being prepped to have his leg amputated." As always, Stefano's voice was low and steady.

Geno nodded. "I know that now, but then it was terrifying. He said 'You're a man now, Geno. You'll lead the family. You will guide the riders and protect the people in our territory. There can be no mistakes. None. All deaths will be on your shoulders. Yours alone. Do you understand? We look to you now.' Of course, I didn't understand. How could I? I was thirteen fucking years old. He wasn't making any sense. No one would answer any questions. His bodyguard grabbed me by my arm and hustled me out of the room. He threw me out and slammed the door shut. That was the last time I saw my father or mother for over a year. I was left to try to explain things to my two younger brothers when there was little or no explanation to give them."

Along with being head of his family, Geno had become leader of the Shadow Riders of New York, and it was an immense responsibility. A rider was able to slip through one shadow to the next, finding portals to travel unseen anywhere he wanted to go. There was a terrible toll on the body. The rider trained from the age of two to be able to withstand the pull of the tunnels. They could tear him apart. More than once he'd had to carry a dead rider from the shadows. The riders were required to always keep maps of cities in their heads because the shadows were so fast it was easy to get turned around, and again, once one was lost, there was no getting out. Shadow riding was extremely dangerous. Riders were tasked with the job of bringing justice to those who couldn't be dealt with through regular law enforcement.

"A series of trainers arrived from France," Geno continued. The Archambaults were considered the fastest shadow riders in the world. They policed all shadow riders and were the only riders who could investigate and assassinate a rider. "They trained me from morning until night on every aspect of riding and leadership. I was required to learn languages and interrogation. I was barely allowed to see my younger brothers and often heard the riders from France speaking in harsh voices to them. That was the only time I stopped what I was doing and intervened. I didn't care if I got in trouble with my trainers, and I would. They would be furious that I would dare to reprimand them for being so ugly with Salvatore and Lucca. I didn't have our father or mother to guide me, and my two brothers were so much younger. They were left alone and were grieving for our parents. I didn't want strangers treating them so harshly. I understood they had to be trained to ride shadows and to pay attention to their other studies, but I wasn't going to allow anyone to be ugly to them. I just wasn't."

"That's why you called me," Stefano said. "And asked me all those questions about the way I balanced raising my siblings and training them to ride in the shadows."

"Yes. You had to raise your brothers and sister from a very early age, and you're the only person I've ever trusted with my brothers. I needed advice, so I called you. You'd been looking after your siblings since they were born."

The two men looked at one another, understanding and deep affection in their eyes for just one moment, and then movement inside the interrogation room drew their attention. The prisoner didn't turn her head, but she lifted it slightly, just enough that she could shift her gaze around the room. They studied the prisoner through the glass.

It was extremely rare for a woman to be held in that room.

In fact, Geno couldn't remember the last time it had ever happened. She had her head down, partially lying on her forearm where it was tied to the arm of the chair. She looked tiny, so slender, she could have been a child.

"Who is she?" Stefano asked.

"Her name is Amaranthe Aubert. She arrived in the country five months ago from a region in the South of France. She dances and teaches ballet at the Ferraro Performing Arts Theatre Company. She is also working in Little Italy at the Performing Arts Center. From all accounts, she's an excellent dancer."

"I take it your investigators have checked up on her in the short time they've had?"

Geno nodded. "She's danced all over the world. I've got a file on her, but nothing about her makes the slightest sense. There's no reason she should be sitting in a chair waiting to be taken apart by a man willing to be as brutal and as disconnected to emotion as I can be. I had even planned to ask Dario for help if need be."

"You changed your mind." Like Geno, Stefano hadn't taken his gaze from the prisoner.

"Something is very off here, Stefano. This is the third time she's done what she's doing. That stealthy scan of her surroundings. I don't go to the ballet. I've never had the time or the inclination to go until just now, just watching her, and that's a huge red flag, given the circumstances."

Both watched as Amaranthe's dark eyes slowly moved around the room, taking in everything from the ceiling to the walls to the floor.

"I guarantee she knows the exact position of every single tool in that room. She'll be able to tell you the distance to every exit. She probably knows *our* escape routes," Geno said. "No ballet dancer would be sitting there that cool after being dragged into a basement by two bodyguards and tied to a chair with torture instruments surrounding her. She may be trying to look scared and intimidated, but she's not afraid in the least. Her brain is working on something all the time."

Stefano considered the various possibilities, just as Geno knew he would. "You're keeping everyone away from her because you believe she's an assassin."

Geno's nod was slow in coming because he didn't want to believe it. She looked the least likely person in the world to be an assassin.

"The first murders were Viola and Marcelle. The hat shop was robbed, and both were stabbed repeatedly. Brutally. In fact, each had twelve stab wounds. It appeared personal to me, Stefano. Viola was seventy-two, Marcelle seventy-five. There was no need to kill them. Marcelle would have turned over the cash. The police were called. Naturally, our family was approached. For me, that was a relief, although I would have insisted we investigate anyway. Viola and Marcelle were family."

The moment the murders had been reported to the police, he knew friends from Little Italy would end up in the parlor of his parents' home.

The way their family business worked was simple—yet not. Anyone could ask for a meeting with his parents. In their world—the Ferraros' world known as Shadow Riders—his parents were described as "greeters." They had a psychic gift, were able to discern whether someone they spoke with was lying. Former shadow riders often took the job of greeters because every rider had to be able to detect a lie. Geno knew the gift was also aided by the casual conversation they had with the petitioner in the beginning of the interview, establishing breathing patterns, heart rate, and inflection in the voice.

No cell phones were allowed. No recording. Those asking for a visit were treated as an invited guest or guests, simply having tea or coffee and telling his parents what crime had occurred, what evidence they had and any suspicion they had of who might have done it.

The greeters listened but didn't participate in that part of the conversation, never taking part in discussions of crimes and never making any promises. That way, if a policeman slipped through their precautions, there was no chance of being trapped. If the greeters believed a crime had been committed and were willing to have the Ferraro family investigate, they never said so.

The greeters never indicated in any way that they were going to help. They simply inclined their heads, gathered whatever evidence had been brought to them and murmured their sympathies. They made polite conversation and then indicated the meeting was over, adding that someone from the family would check in with them occasionally to see if they needed anything.

At that point, all evidence was turned over to the investigators. The New York Ferraro family had two sets of investigators. Usually, one team investigated the petitioner and the other the suspect. Geno's cousins, Lanz and Deangelo Rossi, were exceptional investigators. There was very little they couldn't do on a keyboard. Team two was also cousins, Beniamino and Davide Latini, and they were equally as skilled. Geno relied on them not only for their skills as investigators but also for their accounting skills as well.

"In this case, there was very little evidence left behind. Anyone killing with a knife, particularly when stabbing that many times, usually will cut themselves and leave traces of their own blood behind, but they didn't. There wasn't so much as a hair. No fingerprints, no partial sole print of a shoe despite all the blood."

"A pro," Stefano said.

"A professional wouldn't stab someone that many times. He would kill quickly and cleanly. He'd get the job done and leave."

Gino took another long look at the woman slumped in the chair, looking fragile and defeated other than those eyes. Her eyes were dark brown, so dark they were nearly black.

They didn't seem to miss much at all. Her lashes were thick and long, very feminine, adding to the dramatic sweep around her large eyes. Already, the lashes were falling, and she once again appeared to be that shaken prisoner, the epitome of a defenseless woman terrified of her captors.

"The second murder victims were Noemi and Caio. It was an exact match of the first one, right down to the number of stab wounds, and it occurred thirty days after the first. Like clockwork, if you will excuse the pun, since it was a clock shop they robbed. No watches or clocks were taken, only the money in the safe. Although, I'm not convinced there was money in the safe to take. The safe was open, but that doesn't mean Caio and Noemi had money in it," Geno said. "That was the conclusion the police came to."

"What makes you think it wasn't a robbery?"

"I think these are revenge killings, Stefano. And I'm beginning to believe another shadow rider family is involved."

Stefano sighed. "I was afraid you were going to say that."

"It's the only way they could get to my parents. *Both* of them." Geno indicated the woman slumped in the chair. "I came up with a trap to catch a thief. I believe whoever has been doing the petty crimes is helping the one doing the murders. The petty crimes are being committed to spread dissension and cast suspicion on our family. Unfortunately, I think I may have been outsmarted and brought the assassin right into my home, where she wanted to be all along. She was able to get to my parents, but she couldn't get to me."

Stefano studied the woman with his piercing eyes. Unlike Geno, he could step back from the situation and be completely unemotional. "I'm not in the least affected by the woman, where it is very clear to me that you are. Have you heard her speak?"

"Not yet. Nor have I seen her shadow."

"Yet you're convinced she's a shadow rider."

"I think she is, yes," Geno agreed. "And elite. Cool under fire. She'd have to be to stick her head in the lion's den. If she came here without backup, without a way to send her family members the coordinates to aid her, she has to believe she can kill me and escape."

"It's good you aren't underestimating her, as most men would. It might be a better idea to have someone else interrogate her, Geno. If you're the target, it would be better not to give her access to you. We need the information she has. Dario can extract it without danger to himself."

Dario Bosco was one of the few nonriders in existence who knew of the shadow riders and lived. He was also a powerful crime lord holding a vast territory in Chicago for the Saldi family. The Saldi family was reputed to be the number one enemy of the Ferraro family. Emmanuelle Ferraro, youngest of the Chicago Ferraros and Stefano's sister, was wife to Valentino Saldi, who happened to be head of the Chicago Saldi family. Dario had been Valentino's enforcer for years and had a reputation for being vicious as well as able to get information from any prisoner.

Geno shook his head; his entire body rejected the idea. Every single cell in his body. He had such a visceral reaction to the idea of Dario interrogating Amaranthe that he knew he was in trouble. Had it been anyone other than Stefano with him, he wouldn't have said a word, but his uneasiness was the very reason he'd sent for his cousin. Stefano was the one person he trusted.

"I can't let Dario take her apart, Stefano. I haven't heard her voice. My shadow hasn't connected with hers. I don't even know if she's a shadow rider, but somehow there's a connection between us. I don't know what it is, but as much as I know she's a definite threat and she has information I need, there is a part of me that feels as if I need to protect her."

"You know it's too dangerous for you to be in there with her."

"I can't allow anyone else to take a chance. I do know without a doubt that she's lethal. She may look like a fragile little dancer, but I know in my gut she's anything but." Geno was certain he was right.

"Let's take this back to the house," Stefano said. He didn't wait for Geno's agreement, he simply stepped into a shadow and disappeared.

Geno watched the woman for a few more minutes, wondering if it would be better to simply kill her than to take a chance on her killing anyone else he loved. Shadow riders executed criminals—men and women who had committed heinous crimes. Those criminals had somehow managed to escape justice and the riders had been called in as a last resort. He didn't know for absolute certain Amaranthe was guilty of any crime. He couldn't sentence her to death.

Swearing under his breath, he stepped into the nearest shadow and allowed the familiar wrenching pain to tear him apart, take his mind from the puzzle of the woman to be replaced by a grid of the city as he made his way home.

Stefano waited for him in a chair in front of the fireplace in one of his three libraries. Geno preferred open spaces as a rule, but this library appeared small, mostly because of the tall walls of books surrounding him on every side. Geno liked real books. He had one wall that was enclosed and temperature-controlled so the vintage books were preserved carefully from the sun and no further damage could be done to them. He preferred to read them in the language in which they were originally written, and went to great lengths to acquire them.

"Tell me about the night your parents were murdered," Stefano said.

Geno poured two small glasses of scotch and handed one to his cousin. "We'd taken an assignment in San Francisco. I was the primary rider. Salvatore and Lucca were the alibis with our cousins there."

Shadow riders rarely meted out justice in their own cities. They investigated and brought riders in from another city to do the actual assassination. If Stefano came in from Chicago to do the actual assassination, he would do so with his brothers on a private jet. Several family members would come to party. One member would ride the shadows to the jet and board unseen. While the others partied in front of the paparazzi all night, with the cousins in that city in front of cameras, the one in the shadows would dispense justice to the criminal. No one would ever know the Ferraros had anything to do with the death. They simply looked like they had too much money and too many toys.

"I appeared to stay home that night. Our parents always visited their friends and the priest in the evenings and took a walk around the neighborhood. Papa had a prosthetic leg, but at night he often used a wheelchair. He was doing so that night. They liked to go to the park after they visited the priest. That's where the killer caught up with them."

"Even at their age, and with your father in a wheelchair, he still had to be dangerous," Stefano pointed out. "Your mother was a rider as well, Geno. I don't care if this killer surprised them. How was he or she able to kill both? You had to have seen the reports. You know the sequence of events."

"Just as with the first two murders, Papa was killed first with a slash to the throat from behind. He was jabbed twice more, once to the jugular and once under his arm. That attack took seconds."

"In those seconds, your mother had to have been alerted."

Geno nodded, swirling the scotch. "I've thought of this a hundred times. The killer rode a shadow right up behind my father's chair. That's the only explanation or he would have known. My mother was facing my father."

"There was a second killer," Stefano concluded. "He or she came out of the shadows behind your mother."

"It had to have happened that way. The police had no idea my parents had the skills they did. If Mama was facing Papa and the killer emerged from the shadows to cut his throat . . ."

"He would have had to carry a knife through the shadows,

Geno," Stefano said. "That would have been impossible. How would he have been able to do that? What composition would that have been?"

"It is possible. You know there are ways to make weapons out of natural materials. Damian Ferraro has done it," Geno objected.

"He's a jeweler," Stefano said. "And yes, he does experiment for us. Another cousin, a good man."

"He can't be the only one able to come up with ideas. Your own brothers experiment."

Stefano took a drink of the scotch. "Suppose they managed to come up with a way to take a knife through the shadows, and there are two of them. One emerges behind your mother. She's facing your father. How is it the police have no inkling there's a second killer?"

"Every stab wound was in the front and the pattern is exactly the same as on Viola and Noemi. It appeared as if the killer went straight from murdering Papa to stabbing Mama, and he stabbed her twelve times, just as he had stabbed Viola and Noemi. In fact, there was a transfer of Papa's blood to Mama."

"So, the same knife was used on her." Stefano frowned. "If there were two people, what did the second killer do?"

"Inject my mother with a drug to prevent her from fending them off." That was the only conclusion Geno could come up with. "It had to be fast acting and had to leave her system quickly for it not to show up when a tox screen was run. The ME didn't find an injection site either."

It wasn't easy to calmly discuss the murder of his parents, but over the years, as head of his family and the shadow riders, Geno had learned to compartmentalize. He needed a cool head and to be able to think quickly. While he had initially disliked what he considered the overbearing and exacting Archambaults when they had arrived to take over his life, they had trained him in every aspect of leadership.

They worked day and night with him on every type of

self-defense and fighting technique they could teach him. They were never satisfied with his speed or reaction time. The Archambaults were the fastest in the world, and training with them brought his speed up, improving his reflexes and forcing his body into becoming a machine it would never have been without them. Not only his body but his mind as well.

The Archambaults had rotated trainers and stayed throughout the years until he was of age, even after his parents opened the doors to their rooms. They never once consulted with his parents, only him. Every decision he made was his alone, but they asked him why he made the decision and afterward discussed the consequences with him.

They insisted on talking to him in various languages and corrected him on accents. He didn't have tutors the way his brothers did—the Archambaults tutored him while they worked out. He was forced to do several assignments at the same time to keep his mind working while his body did other things. They wanted certain muscle memory to be automatic, and eventually, even though Geno despised every single Archambault in his teenage years, he had to admit, they knew what they were doing. His brain worked at a high rate of speed even while he was in a fight for his life. He didn't have to plan his moves ahead of time; his body worked smoothly and efficiently. He still trained every day and left nothing to chance. He paid attention to instincts and every gut feeling. He might have an occasional drink of scotch, but it was rare.

Geno found, as he grew older, he was grateful for the men and women who had given up so much of their time to come and train him. In turn, he had trained his brothers and knew they were as safe as he could make them in the shadows. As suspicious as he had become when his parents had been murdered, he acted on his instincts as the Archambaults had taught him.

"You're worried these killers aren't just targeting your family," Stefano suddenly guessed, leaning forward. "That's why you held a private service for your parents and didn't even allow me to attend, isn't it?"

Geno nodded.

His parents were entitled to a show of respect from other riders. Normally, representatives from around the world would come to their funeral. Geno and his brothers held a private closed service, sending out word that they would hold a memorial service later.

"I couldn't take a chance with other riders. Certainly not with you or your *famiglia*. You are like my own. The same with our cousins in LA and San Francisco. I wouldn't risk you. I worry for Salvatore and Lucca all the time. Someone is behind this."

"The kills are not the signature kills of a trained rider," Stefano said.

Geno watched him closely. He always felt like he could learn from his cousin. Stefano was a shrewd man and very analytical. Not only was he a family man, but as head of the riders in Chicago, like Geno, he had carried responsibility from a very young age. He took that responsibility seriously and never stopped trying to do the best for his family. No one would ever have thought a Ferraro would have formed a partnership with a Saldi, and yet Stefano had made it work. He changed with the times, but always kept his family safe. He played his hands close to his chest, not always consulting the council for the riders.

The Ferraro cousins were close. LA, San Francisco, Chicago, New York. They relied on one another because they were cut off from the other riders for the most part. Until Stefano had found his wife, Francesca, the others didn't believe they had a chance of finding a partner they could love and raise a family with. He had given them all hope. Now his siblings were married. His family had taken in Elie Archambault, and Elie was happily married as well.

"Why do you think they started here, with your family, if

you believe their ultimate goal is to draw the other riders in and kill as many as possible?"

This was where Geno was on shaky ground, and he knew it. He didn't have much to go on, only the observations of a scared thirteen-year-old boy. But this was Stefano. Over their years together, they'd come to respect one another. If anyone would listen to him, it would be his cousin.

"I think these killings have to do with whatever happened the night my father lost his leg. I know everyone was told he was in an automobile accident, but that wasn't true. He was wearing his rider clothes. So was my mother. I watched my parents all the time. I was very good at observation; in fact, it was one of the things my father always encouraged. They had been acting strange for a few weeks. They had meetings with other riders, but always denied anyone had come to see them. I heard the lies. I never saw the other riders, but I knew they were there in the shadows. That night, other riders were in the room. Someone had carried my father into his room. My father was a big man. My mother couldn't have carried him."

"You didn't see anyone else?"

Geno took another sip of scotch. "No, but they were there. And I believe my father had gone into the shadows with a horrendous wound knowing he was risking losing his leg. He didn't want to be seen. To him, keeping the secret was worth losing his leg or even his life."

Going into a shadow tube with even a small wound was taking a terrible chance. The force generated by the speed in the shadows could tear open any laceration and pump blood into the tube at a furious rate. If Geno was correct about his speculation, whatever secrets his parents shared with the hidden shadow riders had been worth his father's life—at least that is what they all believed.

"How would our enemy find out who was in the room that night other than your parents?" Stefano asked. "If you didn't know? You said the surgeon, an anesthesiologist, the two nurses, their bodyguards. Anyone else?"

"I know the riders hidden in the shadows were there. The priest. He was giving him the last rites as I was escorted out of the room."

"No one else?"

"Viola and Noemi had no knowledge of shadow riding. They only knew we had several successful businesses and our *famiglia* made a great deal of money. Most of the family doesn't have a clue about what we do, Stefano. My best guess would be the two of them told their friends about the hasty operation they attended at the home of a very wealthy man related to them, particularly after they had retired. Once they were working in their shops, they most likely got comfortable around their friends and began regaling them with amusing or exciting tales of their time as nurses. They wouldn't leave out going to the Ferraros' home for surgery."

Stefano let his breath out in a long sigh and then finished off the scotch. "If you're right about this, Geno—and you've rarely been wrong with your gut feeling—whoever is behind this has been planning their revenge for a number of years. They've had ears and eyes in our territories and in Little Italy. Who knows where else."

"That's what I'm afraid of. I set a trap for a petty thief. I didn't expect to catch an assassin," Geno reiterated. "Now I have to figure out how to interrogate her without getting killed."

"You're absolutely set on doing this yourself." Stefano made it a statement.

"I refuse to put anyone else in jeopardy."

"I think there's more to it than that."

Geno shoved his hand through his hair. "Unfortunately, you could be right. I'll know when I get in there. If I'm right about her, and she's a shadow rider, I intend to compromise her shadow as fast as possible."

"Geno, that's dangerous to you," Stefano cautioned. "By compromising her shadow, you're jeopardizing your own."

"I'm aware of the risks."

Stefano studied his set features for a long time. "If you're determined, Geno—and I know how fucking stubborn you are—then you're going to do it my way. You called me here for a reason; that's to ensure your safety. That means you do what I say. Agreed?"

Geno hesitated. Stefano wouldn't have a qualm about taking out a gun and shooting their captive if she threatened Geno's life in any way.

"You aren't going into that room unless it's my way," Stefano said, absolutely no compromise in his voice.

Geno knew he needed that assurance from Stefano. He just didn't know why.

The House of Dies Drear

An ALA Notable Children's Book
Edgar Allen Poe Award Winner

Other books by Virginia Hamilton

M.C. Higgins, the Great
The Planet of Junior Brown
Zeely

VIRGINIA HAMILTON

The House of Dies Drear

Aladdin Paperbacks
New York   London   Toronto   Sydney

This book is a work of fiction. Any references to historical events, real people, or real locales are used fictitiously. Other names, characters, places, and incidents are the product of the author's imagination, and any resemblance to actual events or locales or persons, living or dead, is entirely coincidental.

The excerpt on page 174 from Paul Laurence Dunbar's "We Wear the Mask" is quoted with the permission of Dodd, Mead & Company, publishers of *The Complete Poems of Paul Laurence Dunbar.*

ALADDIN PAPERBACKS
An imprint of Simon & Schuster Children's Publishing Division
1230 Avenue of the Americas, New York, NY 10020
Copyright © 1968 by Virginia Hamilton
Copyright renewed © 1996 by Virginia Hamilton
All rights reserved, including the right of reproduction
in whole or in part in any form.
ALADDIN PAPERBACKS and colophon are
trademarks of Simon & Schuster, Inc.
Also available in a Simon & Schuster Books
for Young Readers hardcover edition and a Simon Pulse
paperback edition.
Designed by Debra Sfetsios
The text of this book was set in font Galliard.
Manufactured in the United States of America
First paperback edition 1970; reissued 1984
This Aladdin Paperbacks edition January 2006
4 6 8 10 9 7 5 3
The Library of Congress has cataloged the
hardcover edition as follows:
Hamilton, Virginia.
The house of Dies Drear.
Originally published: New York: Macmillan, 1968.
Summary: A black family tries to unravel the secrets of their new home
which was once a stop on the Underground Railroad.
ISBN-13: 978-0-02-742500-0 (hc.)
ISBN-10: 0-02-742500-2 (hc.)
1. Children's stories, American. [1. Mystery and detective stories. 2.
Afro-Americans—Fiction. 3. Underground railroad—Fiction.] I. Title.
PZ7.H1828Ho [Fic] 68023059
ISBN-13: 978-1-4169-1405-1 (pbk.)
ISBN-10: 1-4169-1405-6 (pbk.)

For Arnold,
who loves mystery most of all

1

Thomas dreamed he walked a familiar forest, following a time-worn path of the Tuscaroras. The trail seemed the same as he had known it all his life. The way he walked it, without making any sound, was true to the way ancient Indian braves had walked it. But now the once familiar evergreens on either side were gigantic. Their needles were as large as railroad spikes. He had no trouble accepting the great new height of the trees or the long, smooth size of the needles. It was the awful smell of resin and oil over everything that upset him. The odor nearly choked him; the trees gave it off, as though they were raining turpentine. He seemed to feel it on his hair and on his hands. His palms itched and his eyes burned. He tried to get the smell out of his mind and stopped on the path to cut an enormous branch from a fallen pine.

He made tiny marks on the bark with one of his whittling tools, and he didn't find it unusual to be using so small an instrument for such hard work. He'd always used whittling tools to cut branches. He had started whistling to himself when a man swung down from a mile-high spruce.

"Stay back," the man said. He lifted the huge branch Thomas wanted and flung it away as if it were nothing.

Thomas stood still. He began to feel small. "Papa says you will do," he told the man, "but I don't say it. We are going anyway."

"Carolina is for you," the man said. "Stay back." He reached for Thomas with arms covered with curls of white hair. His eyes glowed red and then spewed fire.

Thomas leaped for a tall pair of stilts against a tree. Fastening them to his legs, he turned around on the path.

"I'm running," he said. But when he moved, the stilts sank into the bed of oversized pine needles covering the ground.

The man grabbed Thomas' ankles. Thomas fell slowly forward from a long way up. He could hear the wind whistling by his ears as he fell.

I'll never reach the end of the trail, he thought. And for the first time, he was afraid.

Thomas Small lurched out of his dream, waking his twin brothers at the same time. The boys leaned against him and looked at him with wide, senseless eyes. Thomas didn't dare move. His heart pounded as the dream fear moved up and down his back. He couldn't think where he was.

In a few minutes, the twins were sleeping again. Thomas could rearrange them and rest his arms.

That was a good dream. Good and scary, he

thought. I was in the trees at home and the man was somebody I should know. I can't place him right now, but I do know him.

He glanced out of the car window and smiled. He knew where he was now and everything was fine. The day was a dismal Saturday; the month was March. All around were heavy patches of mist, and there was a steady rain. His papa's sedan with the red trailer attached was the lone automobile on the Blue Ridge Mountain Highway. Thomas was thirteen years old today and never in his life had he been so far from home.

Home, he thought. Well, I'm sorry.

He and his family were leaving an old house and folks who were mostly relatives. He had known the old house and the old people forever.

"Like Great-grandmother Jeffers," he said to himself. His papa had asked Great-grandmother to come with them to live. Thomas recalled how she'd been leaning on her bright blue gate at the time.

No longer was there a fence around Great-grandmother Jeffers' house. Its blue pickets had long since fallen and rotted back into the ground. But the gate continued to stand, and Thomas, since the age of ten, had painted it bright blue every spring.

Great-grandmother had laughed when his father asked her to come with them. Her hand was propped under her chin as she leaned heavily on that old gate.

"You go look at the North two, three times," she

had said to his papa. "Then come back here one day and tell me if it is better."

"I'll tell you now," his papa had said. "It won't be worse." He had smiled and kissed Great-grandmother. No need to tell her to take care of herself. She always had. He turned and walked swiftly away.

Thomas had stayed a moment. "Who will keep your gate?" he had asked her. "Who will paint it each spring?"

"You think you are the only boy in all these parts that can paint my gate?" she had asked him.

"I'm the only one who ever has," Thomas had said.

"Well, that's so," she had answered. She looked at Thomas hard. "You can trot back here next spring and paint it again, if you've a mind to. Spring," she said softly. "That's a long row to hoe."

Thomas saw something in her eyes that made him feel sad. But then whatever it had been was gone. She'd looked at him with that mean expression she used only with him and the bobwhite quail that lived off her handouts. He had to smile, for he knew she liked him even better than the bobwhite.

"I've got to go now," she had said. "No telling what fool thought took hold of your papa to leave these hills to go live in some craven house. I'm going to fix my chicory. I expect I'll roast it all night and all day tomorrow. Maybe then your papa will get you all there in one piece." She believed roasting chicory was the best power to ward off calamity. Thomas accepted the fact and was comforted.

Great-grandmother had turned and, not looking back, slowly walked to her house. At the steps, she held up her arm in a wave. Thomas hadn't needed to say anything. Within the wave was everything between them.

Thomas had few children to play with in those mountains he and his family were leaving. Homes were sometimes foothills apart. Most of the families with boys Thomas' age had already gone North. No one heard from them again and old people like Great-grandmother Jeffers took this to be a sign that the North was a place of sorrow. Still Thomas hadn't minded being alone most of the time. There had been the forest to walk and there had been Great-grandmother to talk to.

He stared out of the car window and thought about the trees spreading up and over the hills behind his old home. There were times when he had sensed a coming rain and raced it to the pines. Diving under heavy branches, he had watched the rain slant into the forest. It never reached where he lay sheltered, but from the tree's farthest boughs made a silver circle around him.

"I won't think about it again," he promised himself. "It'll be fun living somewhere in Ohio." They were to live in a big house, and only his father had seen it.

Thomas sat wondering why it was taking them so long to get there.

Maybe an axle will break, he thought. Maybe

we'll run out of gas in the night, with woods on both sides of the road!

If that happened, he would creep through the darkness in search of a house. And at last he would see ghostly lights flickering through the trees.

If it's going to take forever, we might as well have some excitement, he thought.

"Papa," he said suddenly, "tell about the new house again."

His father drove hunched over the steering wheel of the car. When Thomas broke the silence, Mr. Small took up a cloth to wipe the windshield. Then he rubbed the cloth on the back of his neck. He was tired of driving and tired of the rain that had stayed with them since morning. Yet he hadn't changed his plan to reach the new house by this afternoon at the latest.

"How many times must I tell it to you before you get it all?" he asked Thomas.

"Just once more, Papa," said Thomas. He had the story straight after the first time he heard it. He simply liked the tone of his papa's voice whenever he spoke about anything so full of history as the new house in Ohio.

"Well," his father began, "it has gables and eaves and pillars. It's large, quite large. There are many windows from floor to ceiling and there's a veranda all the way around on the outside."

"It must look like a plantation house," Thomas said. He pictured a gold mansion with green trim and a lawn as long as forever.

"No, not *quite* like that," said Mr. Small, smiling. "Not that stately. Our place is more . . . more . . . well . . ." he hesitated.

". . . more sinister," Mrs. Small finished for him.

Neither Thomas nor his father had realized that Mrs. Small was awake. For most of the morning's journey, she'd slept in the front seat with her head cradled on a pillow. Now she shivered and sighed. "How I could let myself get talked into this!" she said. "Going off to live somewhere I've never seen. Rattling around in a big old place!"

"You're just as excited about going as Papa and me," Thomas said. He leaned forward against the front seat and looked sideways at his mother. He liked the way she almost smiled when he teased her. "I don't think she'll like walking in the rain much anymore though, Papa," he said.

His father laughed, and his mother had to laugh, too. No, she didn't like so much rain. That was why she'd slept so long. She didn't like thinking about a big Civil War house she had never laid eyes on. It had been an important station on the Underground Railroad, and Thomas still wanted to hear about it, even if his mother didn't.

"Does the house look haunted?" he asked.

Mr. Small was a long time answering. He finally shrugged. "It's a handsome place, once you get used to it," he said. "A fine period piece. It will be the talk of the whole town once I have it painted and landscaped properly."

"What's the town like?" Thomas asked.

"Oh, it's like any small village," Mr. Small said. "And like most Ohio towns, it has a good college at one end of it. But our house isn't in the town, Thomas."

"I thought it was," said Thomas.

"No, it sits alone on a rise in a kind of wilderness." His father spoke then to Mrs. Small. "I believe the townspeople thought I was out of my mind when I finally signed that lease."

Thomas heard caution come into his father's voice. "I never did get the complete floor plans from the real estate people—did I tell you that? They said the plans have been missing for years. They've no idea how many hidden rooms and such the house has. We do have the partial plans though. I should be able to puzzle the whole of it out from them. But it's odd, don't you think, that all the complete plans should be gone?"

"That should tell you there's something funny about that house and anything to do with it," Mrs. Small said.

Thomas' father cleared his throat loudly and gave Mrs. Small a warning glance. But Thomas had heard what she said and he let his mother's words pass into his mind in a neat line. He would think about them some other time. Right now, he was thinking about the new house sitting alone.

"I do wish the rain would stop before we reach that place," Mrs. Small said. She shivered again and tied her scarf tighter about her neck.

"Papa . . ." Thomas said, "does 'wilderness' mean the soil is dead and trees can't grow? Does it mean there's no hope left in the land?"

"What a funny thing to think of!" said Mrs. Small.

"I did say the house stood alone," Mr. Small said. "Thomas was thinking of that."

"No, I was thinking about North Carolina and Great-grandmother," said Thomas. "I was thinking that Great-grandmother and all the other old people had lived in wilderness just forever almost. Maybe that's why she wouldn't come with us. Maybe she thought she was only changing one wilderness for another."

Mr. Small was silent for a time. "Some folks might think a hundred-mile stretch of pine was wilderness," he said, "although you wouldn't, Thomas, because you grew up in pine country. And some might call the prairie wilderness, but I suspect it must have looked pretty good to the pioneer. No, I meant by 'wilderness' that the house itself has about it an atmosphere of desolation."

"But you say it's by a town," said Thomas.

"Yes," Mr. Small said.

"And you say it sits alone."

"Absolutely alone," Mr. Small answered. "There's no way to describe the feel of it or its relation to the town. You have to see it and know about it that way."

"I wish we'd hurry and get there," Thomas said. "It feels like we've been riding forever."

They lapsed into silence. Thomas could think of

no better birthday present than to have the new house suit him. He wanted to like it the same way he liked the masses of clouds in front of a storm or the dark wood of the pine forest back home.

His father had given him a book for his birthday. It was a volume, bound in real leather, about the Civil War, the Underground Railroad and slaves. Thomas loved the smell of real leather, and he rubbed the book lightly back and forth beneath his nose. Then he leaned back, flipping idly through the pages. In a moment his brothers were nestled against him, but Thomas did not even notice.

He had come across a curious piece of information earlier. Of the one hundred thousand slaves who fled from the South to Canada between 1810 and 1850, forty thousand of them had passed through Ohio. Thomas didn't know why this fact surprised him, yet it did. He knew a lot about slaves. His father had taught Civil War history in North Carolina. He would be teaching it in Ohio in the very town in which they were going to live. He had taught Thomas even more history than Thomas cared to know. Thomas knew that Elijah Anderson had been the "superintendent" of the Underground Railroad in Ohio and that he had finally died in prison in Kentucky. He knew that in the space of seven years, one thousand slaves had died in Kentucky. But the fact that forty thousand escaping slaves had fled through Ohio started him thinking.

Ohio will be my new home, he thought. A lot of those slaves must have stayed in Ohio because

Canada was farther than they could have believed. Or they had liked Elijah Anderson so much, they'd just stayed with him. Or maybe once they saw the Ohio River, they thought it was the Jordan and that the Promised Land lay on the other side.

The idea of exhausted slaves finding the Promised Land on the banks of the Ohio River pleased Thomas. He'd never seen the Ohio River, but he could clearly imagine freed slaves riding horses up and down its slopes. He pictured the slaves living in great communities as had the Iroquois, and they had brave leaders like old Elijah Anderson.

"Papa . . ." Thomas said.

"Yes, Thomas," said Mr. Small.

"Do you ever wonder if any runaway slaves from North Carolina went to Ohio?"

Mr. Small was startled by the question. He laughed and said, "You've been reading the book I gave you. I'm glad, it's a good book. I'm sure some slaves fled from North Carolina. They escaped from all over the South, and it's likely that half of them passed through Ohio on their way to Canada."

Thomas sank back into his seat, arranging his sprawling brothers against him. He smoothed his hand over the book and had half a mind to read it from cover to cover. He would wake the twins and read it all to them. They loved for him to read aloud, even though they couldn't understand very much.

No, thought Thomas. They are tired from being up late last night. They will only cry.

Thomas' brothers were named Billy and Buster and they knew all sorts of things. Once Thomas had taken up a cotton ball just to show them about it. They understood right away what it was. They had turned toward Great-grandmother Jeffers' house. She had a patch of cotton in her garden, and they must have seen her chopping it.

They loved pine, as Thomas did, although they couldn't whittle it. Thomas' papa said the boys probably never would be as good at whittling as he was. Thomas had a talent for wood sculpture, so his father said. There were always folks coming from distances offering Thomas money for what he had carved. But Thomas kept most of his carvings for himself. He had a whole box of figures tied up in the trailer attached to the car. He intended placing them on the counters and mantles all over the new house.

Thomas could sit in front of his brothers, carving an image out of pine, and they would jump and roll all around him. When the carving was finished, the twin for whom it was made would grab it and crawl off with it. Thomas never need say, and never once were the twins wrong in knowing what carving was for which boy.

They were fine brothers, Thomas knew.

If the new house is haunted, he thought, the twins will tell me!

2

The sedan headed through the Pisgah National Forest in the Blue Ridge Mountains, and then out of North Carolina. Thomas had seen a sign and knew exactly when they entered Virginia.

"That's done with," he said to himself.

If Mr. Small noticed they had left their home state, he gave no hint. Mrs. Small slept or at least kept her eyes closed. The twins awoke, and Mr. Small told Thomas to give them their lunch. Soon the boys were subdued, staring out the windows and eating, looking far below at the bank upon bank of mist nestled in the deep valleys of the Blue Ridge.

Thomas was thinking about the new house in Ohio. The house was a relic with secret passages and rooms. In Civil War times it had been one of the houses on the Underground Railroad system, which was a resting and hiding place for slaves fleeing through the North to Canada. Such houses had been secretly called "stations."

When Thomas' father read about the station house for rent in Ohio, he had written to the foundation that owned it for a full report. For years he had hoped to explore and possibly live in a house on the

Underground Railroad. Now was his chance. But not until he saw the report did he find out how important the Ohio station had been. Those who ran the house in Ohio had an even greater task than the care and concealment of running slaves. They actually encouraged the slaves to let themselves be caught and returned to slavery!

Thomas hadn't believed slaves went willingly back into slavery until his father had explained it to him.

"If you'll recall your history, Thomas, you'll remember that the incredible history of the Underground Railroad actually began in Canada," his father had told him. Slaves who had reached Canada in the very early 1800s and established settlements there returned by the thousands to this country in order to free others. They came back for their families; they became secret "conductors" on the Underground Railroad system. And they returned to bondage hoping to free masses of slaves.

"But slaves continued to flee by whatever means," Mr. Small had said, "with or without help. Upon reaching the Railroad, they might hide in our house in Ohio, where they would rest for as little as a week. Some of them were given rather large sums of money and returned again to slavery."

"What would slaves need with money?" Thomas had wanted to know.

"Even a fleeing slave needs maneuvering money," his father had said. "He would need food and shelter and the best and safest way for him to get it was to buy it from freed Negroes."

"But the slaves connected with the house in Ohio were going back *into* slavery," Thomas had said.

"Yes," said Mr. Small. "And after they were caught and went back, they passed the hidden money on to other slaves, who would attempt to escape."

Still Thomas couldn't believe slaves could successfully hide money on themselves without having it found.

Some slaves did have their money found and taken away, his father said. It was dangerous work they were involved in. But others managed to return to bondage with the money still in their possession.

"Remember," his father had told him, "the slaves we're talking about weren't ordinary folks out for a peaceful stroll. Many had run for their lives for weeks from the Deep South. They had no idea how far they had to travel and they were armed with little more than the knowledge that moss grew only on the northern side of trees. Any who managed to get as far as Ohio and the Underground Railroad had to be pretty brave and strong, and very clever. Most of them were young, with a wonderful, fierce desire to free themselves as well as others. It was the best of these who volunteered to return to slavery. They were hand-picked by Dies Drear himself, the abolitionist who built our house in Ohio. He alone conceived of the daring plan of returning numbers of slaves to the South with sizable amounts of money hidden on them."

"He must have been something!" Thomas had said.

"He was a New Englander," Mr. Small said, "so independent and eccentric, most Ohio abolitionists thought him crazy. He came from an enormously wealthy family of shipbuilders, and yet his house in Ohio was fairly modest. To give you an idea how odd he was," said Mr. Small, "his house was over-flowing with fine antiques, which he neither took any interest in nor sold for profit. All the furniture remained in great piles, with just enough space to get through from room to room, until the house was plundered and Drear was killed.

"But when his plan to send slaves back to slavery worked," said Mr. Small, "there grew among freemen and slaves an enormous respect for him. You know, they never called him by his name, partly because they feared he might be caught, but also because they were in awe of him. They called him Selah. Selah, which is no more than a musical direc-tion to raise the voice. And yet, Selah he was. *Selah,* a desperate, running slave might sigh, and the name—the man—gave him the strength to go on."

Selah. Freedom.

Thomas sat so quietly in the car with his eyes closed, he appeared to be sleeping. But his mind was full of thoughts about what else his father had told him was in the report from the Ohio foundation. The report went on to say that three slaves whom

Dies Drear had hidden for a time were caught in an attempt to reach Canada. In truth, they were headed south again, but because they were captured on the northern side of the Ohio River they were believed to be fleeing to Canada. Their hidden money was discovered. Two of the slaves were killed by the bounty hunters who caught them. That same week, Dies Drear was murdered.

There had been pages and pages of the report from the foundation. Thomas recalled his father poring over it until very late at night, often jumping up and stalking about the room with obvious excitement. Then his father had made a trip to Ohio. He was gone three weeks, nearly ten days longer than he had intended. While he was gone, Thomas found the report and read it.

Thomas smiled to himself, his eyes still closed. He had discovered something in the report that his father hadn't mentioned. There was a legend that came with the house of Dies Drear. The report made light of the legend, but when Thomas read it he was at once frightened and pleased. The legend was that two slave ghosts and the ghost of Dies Drear haunted the house to this very day.

Right away Thomas had made up his mind that the two ghosts had to be the two slaves killed by bounty hunters. And the two ghosts had then killed Drear in revenge for their own deaths. But if all this were true, Thomas was faced with a problem.

Why would two slave ghosts haunt a house

owned by the man they had murdered, who himself haunted the very same house?

Deep down, Thomas didn't believe in ghosts. But when night fell, when he was alone in the dark, he feared he might see one. And if there were haunts in the new house, he wanted to be sure he had everything straight in his mind about them.

That way they won't ever scare me, he thought, sitting in the car. That way I'll know how not to get in their way.

When Mr. Small returned from his trip to Ohio, he wouldn't talk to Thomas about the house.

"Is the house really haunted?" Thomas had asked. "Did you hear the noises and see the flashing lights?"

"I thought I told you to stay out of my study!" his father had fumed. "I didn't give you permission to read that report. Besides, there are no such things as haunts."

"But is it true no one has lived in the house for more than three months in the last hundred years?" Thomas had asked.

"It's true," his father had to admit. "The house hasn't been lived in for very long at any time."

"Well, if the house isn't haunted," Thomas said, "who or what was it caused people to run away? And why would two slave ghosts stay in that house with the ghost of the man they had murdered?"

Thomas' father had become furious. His voice had been quiet, but filled with rage. "People are so full of superstition, they aren't able to see the truth when it practically stares them in the face!" he had said. "Quit talking about ghosts. Don't ask so many fool questions. All old houses have ghost legends, and they are all poppycock!" He had retreated to his study, slamming the door behind him.

Mr. Small made a second trip to Ohio, still not sure if he would rent the house of Dies Drear. This time he was gone five days. When he returned, he had the lease in his hand. He was in high spirits. He hoped someday to buy the house, he told Thomas and Mrs. Small. At last, he made them a full account of his trip, the house and all its history.

"No," whispered Thomas. No, his father hadn't mentioned the legend.

Now why didn't he tell the legend to Mama? he wondered. Or does she know about it, and he didn't mention it in front of me, hoping I'd forget about it?

Thomas stared out at the steady rain and the mountains, which were no longer familiar. Again he smiled to himself. His father had to be hiding something.

There's something in the legend I've missed, Thomas told himself. At least there's something more to the story of the two slaves killed by bounty hunters, and Dies Drear's murder. Papa meant to hide it from me by not letting me get at that report. But I know I remember most of what there was in it. It must be that whatever Papa means to hide from me isn't written down. It's something you would have to put together from what *is* written down. When he got mad at me and slammed the door, I must have been close to finding out. I just didn't ask the right question."

"Papa," Thomas said. "Papa." He propped his brothers one against the other behind him as he once again leaned forward on the front seat. "Tell me again about Mr. Pluto, Papa," he said.

Thomas was interrupted by Mrs. Small awaking and stretching. "Where are we now?" she asked.

"Getting closer," Mr. Small said. "Outside of Bluefield."

"You mean Bluefield, West Virginia?" Thomas asked. "How many more hours until we reach the Ohio River?"

"Just be patient," Mr. Small told him. "You'll see the Ohio River in about three hours if we don't stop too long."

In Bluefield they stopped twenty-five minutes for lunch. Once they were on their way again, Thomas leaned forward to talk to his father.

"We were going to talk about Mr. Pluto," he said.

"Now, Thomas, he's told you enough about him," said his mother.

Mrs. Small didn't like hearing about Mr. Pluto. No matter how often Thomas and his father kidded her, she really didn't like hearing about anything that had to do with the house of Dies Drear.

She won't like it, Thomas thought. She hasn't seen it, but she doesn't like it at all.

"I want to be sure I know what Mr. Pluto looks like before I run into him," Thomas said. He had tried making up a picture of Mr. Pluto from what his father had told him. But that was hard; never had Thomas heard about anyone quite like Pluto.

Thomas' shoulders jerked nervously; he cocked his head to one side as he did always when he was about to listen hard. "Please, Papa," he said, "tell about him."

Mr. Small sighed. "I might as well," he said. "We still have a long ride ahead of us."

Mr. Small started talking and Thomas listened, letting his long arms dangle over the front seat.

"As I've told you, he's the caretaker of the new house," Mr. Small said. "Pluto isn't his real name, but another name for Hades, the Lord of the Underworld. Well, Hades had cloven hooves."

"I know that," Thomas said.

"Mr. Pluto has been lame in one leg for as long as anyone can remember," Mr. Small said. "I have no idea how old he is. Neither does the foundation, which hired him years ago. He's spry, although that isn't quite the right word to describe the way he gets around. He's a big man, with white hair and a beard. I believe he has the most piercing green eyes I've ever seen. With that beard and hair and those eyes, it's no wonder he's known as Pluto. Otherwise," Mr.

Small added, "he's harmless enough, and takes fine care of the place."

"The dream!" shouted Thomas. "It was him!"

"Thomas, please!" said Mrs. Small, holding her ears.

The twins began yelling too, and Thomas had to hold them for a moment before they calmed down.

"I had this dream," Thomas told his mother and father. "Mr. Pluto was in it, but I didn't know it was him until just now!"

"Pluto knows many of the secret recesses of the house," his father was saying to Mrs. Small. "He was kind enough to show them to me. I'm glad we're keeping him on as caretaker—Thomas, I want you to be nice to him, no funny business. He's an old man with quiet ways about him. You could even say he's a bit secretive and strange. He rides around in a two-wheeled buggy drawn by two horses, one bay and one roan. He has a black, too, that he switches off with the other two. He's lived all alone on that property for such a long time, I'm sure he wouldn't know what to do without it."

"Does he live in our new house?" Thomas asked.

"No," said Mr. Small. "No, he lives on the other side of the hill from us. You'll be surprised by his house and the way he lives." He was about to say more, but seemed to change his mind.

"I'll warn you though," he said. "Pluto walks as agile as a cat. He came upon me while I was in the cellar. I hadn't heard him or seen him coming, and I nearly jumped out of my skin."

"Does he really look like the devil?" Thomas asked.

"Oh, anyone can startle you in a house as old as that," said Mr. Small. "I don't think there's a straight angle in the whole place. All the ceilings are amazingly high. But Pluto's no devil. He did try to convince me not to live in that house. He was serious about it, too. He knows the legend, and I'm sure by now he believes it."

"Are there a lot of old people?" asked Thomas. "I mean in the town—old ones who remember everything and talk a lot, like Great-grandmother always did?"

Mr. Small was silent a moment. "You are going to miss her, aren't you?" he said.

"Yes," said Thomas, "I guess I will miss her."

"I'm sorry she wouldn't come with us," said Mr. Small, "but she has that right to end where she began. Anyway, it's time you learned about young people. You are already wise in the ways of the old."

"I like old people," said Thomas. "They never need to know what you are carving out of wood or even why. They just wait until it's done and then they say it's good."

Mr. Small had to laugh. "You don't like to be bothered, do you? You have to be free. Well, there was a freemen's community in the town even during slavery. Many slaves probably settled there. There are young people and there are old ones who remember things."

Thomas had a jumble of thoughts he couldn't quite make come clear, so he began to ask question after question about the town. They had driven a long way before he did catch hold of what he was after.

"Papa!" he said suddenly. Mrs. Small raised her head from her pillow and looked around at him.

"Papa," Thomas said, "whatever became of that third slave?"

Mr. Small stiffened over the steering wheel. He looked straight ahead, gripping the wheel with both hands.

Thomas held his breath for a second, then blew a silent whistle through his teeth.

His father began speaking so gravely and in such a low voice, Thomas had to lean very close to hear. "When we get where we're going. . . . Now listen closely," his father said, "because I don't want to tell you again. You are to speak to no one about the foundation's report on the house of Dies Drear, do you understand? And nothing about the three slaves. Don't even think about it, and speak of it to no one!"

Thomas sat back with his brothers, watching the bleak West Virginia landscape through the rain that right-flanked them in dull, white sheets across the highway.

So the third slave is the question, Thomas thought. I have found that much out.

Thomas' eyes grew heavy with fatigue. His brothers played happily around him. As he fell asleep, his mind curled around one thought.

But what is it? What is the answer?

3

Thomas did not wake in time to see the Ohio River. Mr. Small was glad he didn't, for through the gloom of mist and heavy rain, most of its expanse was hidden. What was visible looked much like a thick mud path, as the sedan crossed over it at Huntington.

Thomas lurched awake a long time after. The car went slowly; there was hardly any rain now. His mother spoke excitedly, and Thomas had to shake his head rapidly in order to understand what she was saying.

"Oh dear! My heavens!" Mrs. Small said. "Why it's huge!"

Mr. Small broke in eagerly, turning around to face Thomas. "You've waited a long time," he said. "Take a good look, son. There's our new house!"

Thomas looked carefully out of his window. He opened the car door for a few seconds to see better, but found the moist air too warm and soft. The feel of it was not nice at all, and he quickly closed the door. He could see well enough out of the window, and what he saw made everything inside him grow quiet for the first time in weeks. It was more than he could have dreamed.

The house of Dies Drear loomed out of mist and

murky sky, not only gray and formless, but huge and unnatural. It seemed to crouch on the side of a hill high above the highway. And it had a dark, isolated look about it that set it at odds with all that was living.

A chill passed over Thomas. He sighed with satisfaction. The house of Dies Drear was a haunted place, of that he was certain.

"Well," Mr. Small said, "what do you think of it, Thomas?"

"It must be the biggest house anyone ever built," Thomas said at last. "And to think—it's our new house! Papa, let's get closer, let's go inside!"

Smiling, Mr. Small kept the car on the highway that now curved up closer toward the house. In a short time they were quite near.

At the base of the hill on which the house sat, a stream ran parallel to the highway. It was muddy and swollen by rain; between it and the hill lay a reach of fertile land, lushly tangled with mullein weed and gold wildflower. The hill itself was rocky and mostly bare, although a thaw had come to the rest of the land and countryside. At the very top of the hill Thomas noticed a grove of trees, which looked like either pine or spruce.

The house of Dies Drear sat on an outcropping, much like a ledge, on the side of the hill. The face of the ledge was rock, from which gushed mineral springs. And these came together at the fertile land, making a narrow groove through it before emptying into the stream. Running down the face of the ledge, the springs coated the rock in their path with red and yellow rust.

Thomas stared so long at the ledge and springs, his eyes began to play tricks on him. It seemed as if the rust moved along with the spring waters.

"It's bleeding," he said softly. "It looks just like somebody cut the house open underneath and let its blood run out! That's a nice hill though," he added. He looked at the clumps of skinny trees at each side of the house. Their branches were bare and twisted by wind.

Thomas cleared his throat. "I bet you can see a lot from the top of that hill." He felt he ought to say this. The hill was hardly anything compared to the mountains at home. Otherwise the land in every direction was mostly flat.

"You can see the college from the top of the hill," Mr. Small said. "And you can see the town. It's quite a view. On a clear day those springs and colored rock make the hill and house look like a fairyland."

"All those springs!" Thomas said. He shook his head. "Where do they come from? I've never seen anything like them."

"You'll get used to the look of the land," Mr. Small said. "This is limestone country, and always with limestone in this formation you'll find the water table percolating through rock into springs. There are caves, lakes and marshes all around us, all because of the rock formations and the way they fault."

Mrs. Small kept her eye on the house. It was her nature to concentrate on that which there was a chance of her changing.

"No, it's not," she said softly. "Oh, dear, no, it will never be pretty!"

"Everything is seeping with rain," Mr. Small said to her. "Just try to imagine those rocks, that stream and the springs on a bright, sunny day. Then it's really something to see."

Thomas could imagine how everything looked on a day such as his father described. His eyes shone as he said, "It must look just about perfect!"

They drove nearer. Thomas could see that the house lay far back from the highway. There was a gravel road branching from the highway and leading to the house. A weathered covered bridge crossed the stream at the base of the hill. Mr. Small turned off the highway and stopped the car.

"There's been quite a rain," he said, "I'd better check the bridge."

Now Thomas sat with his hands folded tightly beneath his chin, with his elbows on his knees. He had a moment to look at the house of Dies Drear, the hill and the stream all at once. He stared long and hard. By the time his father returned, he had everything figured out.

They continued up the winding road, the house with its opaque, watching windows drawing ever nearer.

The stream is the moat. The covered planks over

it are the drawbridge, Thomas thought. And the house of Dies Drear is the castle.

But who is the king of all this? Who will win the war?

There was a war and there was a king. Thomas was as sure of this as he was certain the house was haunted, for the hill and house were bitten and frozen. They were separated from the rest of the land by something unkind.

"Oh dear," Mrs. Small was saying. "Oh dear. Dear!"

Suddenly the twins were scrambling over Thomas, wide awake and watching the house get closer. By some unspoken agreement, they set up a loud, pathetic wail at the same time.

"Look!" Thomas whispered to them. "See, over there is clear sky. All this mist will rise and get blown away soon. Then you'll feel better."

Sure enough, above the dark trees at the top of the hill was deep, clear sky. Thomas gently cradled the boys. "There are new kinds of trees here," he told them. "There will be nights with stars above trees like you've never known!" The twins hushed, as Thomas knew they would.

Up close the house seemed to Thomas even more huge, if that were possible. There were three floors. Above the top floor was a mansard roof with dormer windows jutting from its steep lower slopes. Eaves overhanging the second story dripped moisture to the ground in splattering beats. There was a veranda surrounding the ground floor, with pillars that rose to the eaves.

Thomas liked the house. But the chill he had felt on seeing it from the highway was still with him. Now he knew why.

It's not the gray day, he thought. It's not mist and damp that sets it off. There are things beyond weather. The house has secrets!

Thomas admired the house for keeping them so long.

But I'm here now, he thought happily. It won't keep anything from me.

The twins refused to get out of the car, so Thomas had to carry one while his mother carried the other. They cried loudly as soon as they were set on the veranda.

"They don't like the eaves dripping so close," Mr. Small said. "Move them back, Thomas."

Thomas placed the boys close to the oak door and then joined Mrs. Small in front of the house. His father was already busy unloading the trailer. The heavy furniture and trunks had come by van a week earlier. Thomas guessed all of it would be piled high in the foyer.

"It's old," Mrs. Small remarked, looking up at the dormers of the house. "Maybe when the sun comes out . . ." Her voice trailed off.

Thomas placed his arm through hers. "Mama, it must be the biggest house for miles. And all the land! We can plant corn . . . we can have horses! Mama, it will be our own farm!"

"Oh, it's big," Mrs. Small said. "Big to clean and

big to keep an eye on. How will I ever know where to find the boys?"

"I'll watch them," said Thomas. "Wait until it's warm weather for sure. They'll be with me all the time."

"Let's go inside now," Mr. Small said to them. He had unloaded cartons beside the twins on the veranda. "Thomas and I will have to set up the beds the first thing."

"And I'll have to get the kitchen ready," said Mrs. Small, "and you'll have to drive into town for food. Goodness, there's so much to do, I won't have time to look around." Then she smiled, as though relieved.

Mr. Small went first, and Mrs. Small held the door for the twins and Thomas. At once the boys began to cry. Thomas watched them, noticing that they avoided touching the house, especially the oak door trimmed with carved quatrefoils. Mrs. Small hadn't noticed, and Thomas said nothing. He scooped up the boys and carried them inside.

When the heavy door closed behind them, they were instantly within a place of twilight and stillness.

Thomas couldn't recall having been in a more shadowy place, nor had he ever felt such a silence that seemed to wait. There was no small entrance room, as Thomas had imagined, but a long, wide hall. One part of the hall was cut by stairs, which rose in a curve to disappear somewhere above. Beyond where Thomas' father stood, there was a wide doorway leading to another room. Thomas could make out cupboards there. It was the kitchen and it seemed to be very large. On either side of the hall were closed doors, which he guessed led into sitting rooms.

"Papa," Thomas said. He was growing uneasy just standing there. Mrs. Small motioned him to be quiet.

"What is it?" she whispered to Thomas' father. "What *is* it?"

Mr. Small softly cleared his throat. "Nothing," he said, "but I had expected the furniture from the van to be piled up in this hall."

The twins grew heavy in Thomas' arms. He found that he was leaning against a table. He had been for some time. "Here's some of the furniture," he said.

Billy turned to see and caught his ghostly reflection in a mirror by the table at the same moment as did Thomas. Billy screamed and cried. Thomas was so startled, he nearly dropped the boys. Mr. Small quickly found a light switch. Now they saw a grand, gilded mirror, on either side of which were two familiar end tables.

"Why, that looks beautiful!" said Mrs. Small. "Those are my tables, but whose mirror is it?"

"That mirror was there the first time I saw the place," Mr. Small said. "If you like it, I guess we can keep it."

He opened one of the doors off the hall, paused, and then beckoned them to come. He switched on a light inside. They saw that their livingroom furniture had been cleverly arranged to fit a much larger room.

"Who did all this?" Mrs. Small said. "How did they know I'd want it like this—it's just beautiful!"

"I don't know for certain who did it," said Mr. Small, "but I suspect it was Pluto. He's the only one who would think to do it."

They looked at the room. The two oversized easy chairs which Thomas had known for so long were placed side by side with a mahogany lamp table between them. No longer were they catercornered on either side of the couch, familiar, as they had been at home. They sat like soldiers on their guard.

The couch was placed across the room from the chairs. And between two of the floor to ceiling windows stood Mrs. Small's kitchen worktable.

Thomas gave Buster to Mrs. Small to hold. He went up to the worktable holding Billy, patting the boy, who still cried. The top of the table had been sanded smooth and rubbed with linseed oil. All the old nicks and gashes from all the meats his mother had prepared on it had been worked away. And placed at either end of the table were plants of ivy in the white china tureens his mother had never favored.

"Who would have dreamed my old table could look like that?" Mrs. Small said. "And I never would have thought to use those tureens that way."

"It makes a nice decoration," Mr. Small said. "The table and tureens belong to another time. Mr. Pluto saw that."

Thomas turned slowly around. At the far end of the room was a massive fireplace. Old Mr. Pluto hadn't thought to build a fire there. But on either side of the hearth he had arranged Billy's and Buster's little rocking chairs.

Mrs. Small laughed on seeing the chairs, and Mr. Small smiled.

"Look, boys, there's your chairs," said Mrs. Small. The boys looked and then turned to Thomas. Thomas was still wary, so the boys refused to sit just yet.

As soon as Thomas had entered the room, he understood what old Pluto had tried to do. He had arranged the furniture in a rigid progression, with the two long windows, not the open fireplace, as its focus. Thomas' eyes swept from the fireplace to the windows, then out into the gray day, on and on, until he could see no farther.

It's his warning, thought Thomas. He means for us to flee.

"I don't like it," Thomas said. "I don't like it at all. And who is this Mr. Pluto to work out the cuts in Mama's table? He's sure taken a lot on himself. He's got no business in our new house!"

"I would have placed that table in some corner of the kitchen," said Mrs. Small. "I don't know why I ever bothered to bring it, it's so old. Thomas, I'm surprised at you."

"It was thoughtful of Mr. Pluto to put the house in order for us," said Mr. Small. "I certainly hadn't expected him to."

But Mr. Small would not meet Thomas' questioning gaze.

He doesn't like Mr. Pluto doing this any more than I do, Thomas thought. I know he doesn't. He just doesn't want to upset Mama.

"Come, let's take a look upstairs," Mr. Small said. "I would guess Mr. Pluto put the beds up. It will be interesting to see what rooms he chose."

"Papa, are you going to let him take over?" Thomas said. "How does he know what room I want?"

"We can change your room if you don't like it," said Mrs. Small. "But if Mr. Pluto took as much time with the bedrooms as he did with this room, they will do just fine."

Thomas was shocked. His mother and father were allowing a stranger, and a man who looked like the devil besides, to walk right in their house and fix it to suit himself. He wasn't even a relative. He wasn't anybody!

"I don't want to see any more right now," Thomas said glumly. "I think I'll go out and look at the rocks and springs."

He sat Billy down in his rocking chair. At once Billy began to cry, clinging to Thomas' leg. Buster, still cradled in his mother's arms, began to cry too.

"Well then," Mrs. Small said, "you go with Thomas. I don't know what's got into you."

"I think they're just tired out," said Mr. Small.

"Thomas, you keep an eye on them," Mrs. Small

said. "I don't think you'll have much trouble if you sit them far back on the veranda."

Once outside, Thomas placed the boys on the dry veranda and squatted between them. He put an arm around each one until they hushed crying. After they had quieted, he stroked them gently.

"What do you suppose that old Pluto is up to?" Thomas said in a low voice. "Fixing things and arranging things. Maybe he hopes to get Papa to like him a lot . . . then he can rule everything. Well, he didn't count on us, did he? He's the devil and he won't be king!"

"Now," he said to the boys, "Mama and Papa are upstairs. We're all alone here. Tell me what it was about this door that caused you not to touch that pretty design. Remember? We came in the house through this door, and there was something about it you didn't like."

The twins stayed quiet. Thomas knew they couldn't tell him anything. But he was used to questioning them and finding answers in himself.

Thomas got up to examine the front steps. They were weathered but recently painted white as was the rest of the house. He examined the oak door and saw nothing unusual. He bent close to study the quatre-foil designs that were carved on the doorframe. They were shaped like petals. He was ready to turn away, when he found something. One petal, on a line with the doorknob, had a tiny, wood button in its center. Thomas checked, but not one of the other petals had such a button. He wouldn't have found this one if he hadn't been looking hard for something.

"So that's it," he said, "but how in the world did you all know?"

He took each twin by the hand, and led them up to the button. They bobbed from side to side, whimpering as if something hurt them. Thomas released them and let them sit on the veranda facing the barren lawn.

Cautiously he waved his hand over the button. There was a stream of cold air coming from around it. He glanced at the twins. When they stood, the air just about hit them in the face.

"It was chilly and you didn't like it," he said to them.

Carefully, and with a hand that was shaking, Thomas pushed the button. He pulled, he jerked, but nothing at all happened.

The twins fell into tantrums unlike anything Thomas had ever seen. They kicked their legs and flailed their arms wildly. They jumped up high and sat down hard, at the same time screaming at the tops of their lungs.

"You'll hurt yourselves!" Thomas warned them. He didn't touch them. He feared he might make matters worse. So he just stood there, looking down at them with his eyes darting all around.

"Quiet, kids! You'll have Mama come get you!"

It seemed that was exactly what they wanted, for they kept up the screaming.

"So you saw something!" Thomas whispered.

His eyes were wide. "Something scary? Something I didn't see and couldn't take care of?"

Thomas thought of ghosts. Suddenly he was afraid, not for himself but for the twins, who could see but not say.

"Not very nice ghosts," he said, "if they have to go around scaring babies."

Thomas picked the boys up, balancing one on each hip. "But why would ghosts come just because I pushed a button?" he wondered out loud. "Ghosts?" he asked them. They whimpered and nestled against him.

"No," Thomas decided. "Something else a little more real." He hadn't the time to think what that might be, for his mother came then to see what was causing the twins to scream.

"They're just hungry, I guess," Thomas told her. "They were sitting there and then they started to cry."

"They're tired, too," Mrs. Small said. She took them from Thomas. "Now don't be long," she told him. "I'll have supper ready early. Mr. Pluto filled the refrigerator with food!"

Thomas held the door for his mother. He waited until she was in the kitchen with the twins before he closed the door hard.

Mr. Pluto, he thought. Always Mr. Pluto!

He stood on the veranda with his back to the oak door; he took in all there was to see—the grand pillars, eaves dripping wet onto the barren ground, and the circle of gray mist beyond the lawn.

When he looked carefully, Thomas was able to see through the mist. He could make out the downward slope of the hill, with its rocks and springs, and the fertile land lying along the stream. He thought he could see the bridge and the muddy roadbed that crossed over it. Somewhere beyond that lay the highway. He listened, but he could hear no traffic. All was silent. The only movement was the stream, rapid and swollen with the long rain, and the springs rushing into it.

Thomas was satisfied that no one watched him. He turned around to face the oak door and pushed the button in the quatrefoil. Nothing happened. He looked left and right and, at last, craned his head to see behind him. At once he saw what must have caused the twins' tantrum. The front steps were poised about a foot off the ground and wide to the left of their proper place. Where the steps should have been was a black and jagged hole about three feet around.

Thomas stood as still as one of his wood carvings. With his back pressed against the oak door, he faced the steps and waited for whatever it was—ghosts, demons—that would rise up from the hole to challenge him. Instead, the sudden shock came from the side of the house.

He fell to his knees instinctively to hide himself. Coming forth now was the queerest sight he'd seen in all his life.

4

Out of the trees on the right side of the house came walking the blackest, biggest horse Thomas could remember seeing. Maybe it was not as huge as he thought at first, but he was closer to it than he had ever been to a horse. Riding on it was a tiny girl, sitting straight and tall. She had a white, frilly nightcap on her head and she wore red flannel pajamas with lace at the neck and sleeves. She had no shoes on her feet and she sat well forward, her toes clasped in the horse's mane. With her arms folded across her chest, she stared into the distance. She was serene and happy and seemed not to notice Thomas.

Following the horse was a big boy about Thomas' age. He was stronger and heavier than Thomas, and his arm muscles bulged as he pulled back on the horse's tail.

"Whoa, you black!" he said in a loud whisper. "You mean old devil! Let my Pesty off, you hear, before I break off your tailbone! Pesty, you get down off of him. Please? Come on, make him stop, I've got to get my supper before it's all gone!"

The little girl paid no attention to him. Once she laughed and then turned the horse with just her toes.

She circled the lawn, with the big boy pulling hard on the horse's tail. The horse didn't seem to care. Soon they came toward the house again, right for the steps and Thomas.

Thomas felt for the wood button, but he couldn't find it unless he took his eyes off the little girl, the horse and the boy. They were very close, almost to the steps, and the boy was yelling for the girl to stop that horse.

"You want him to fall down under them steps? You going to walk him right through that door?"

But the child knew what she was doing. She gently nudged the horse; it stopped in front of the hole. She looked at Thomas as though she'd known he was there all the time, and smiled very sweetly at him.

Coming around the horse's flank, the boy bent delicately to look into the hole. He was aware of Thomas. Thomas could tell. Both children were playing a game with him, and he could not figure out the rules.

"Anybody go foolin' around down there maybe will get lost forever," the boy said. "Maybe get lost in one of Mr. Pluto's tunnels and never get found again."

"Nothing down there," said the child. "Nothing but sounds."

"Now how do you know that?" asked the boy. "I bet there's plenty down there nobody's run into yet."

"Mr. Pluto let me walk it," said the child, "and I know there is nothing."

"Pesty, how many times must I tell you not to get too close to Mr. Pluto? He's going to make you disappear one of these times, and then how will I ever get you home to supper?"

"I'll tell him to tie you up," said the child. "Leave you in one of those tunnels for the ghosts to play with."

"Do you intend to go down under there?" asked the boy. "You planning on finding out how quick you can get scared in the dark?"

A few seconds passed before Thomas realized the boy was speaking to him. The boy still wouldn't look at Thomas, but pretended to be concerned with the hole.

"Who *are* you?" asked Thomas, still afraid and not at all eager to move from the safety of the door. "Who *are* you!"

The boy looked up at the child on the horse in mock amazement, then he quickly turned a polite, smiling face on Thomas.

"Well, how you been! How you feeling?" he said.

Now anger began slowly to take the place of Thomas' fear.

Then the boy said, "We are Darrow's children. I mean, I'm Mr. Darrow's youngest son, and that girl there, she follows me around so my Mama lets her stay. I call this girl Pesty. My Daddy calls her Sarah, and Mama calls her Sooky. Mr. Pluto, he calls her Little Miss Bee, and I guess you can make up a name, too, it won't matter to her."

"You mean to say she lives with you," Thomas said, slowly, "and follows you around—you all call her different names, but she isn't your sister?"

"I just have brothers," said the boy. He looked

carefully at the child on the horse. "Still, she's as close to a sister as I guess I'll ever get."

"But where did she come from?" asked Thomas. Still on his knees, he had crawled out as far as the steps now, close to the boy and close to the horse. He didn't realize he had moved.

The child kicked the boy in the chest playfully and laughed.

"She came in a new tin tub," said the boy. "It was night, and I was sleeping. I was five and I don't remember it. But they say that Mama brought her in to show her off to Daddy. And the next day I saw her and I've been seeing her ever since."

Thomas wanted to ask more questions, but now the child was asking him a question.

"What you doing on Mr. Pluto's porch? He'll snatch you baldheaded if he finds you."

"He's liable to turn Pesty on you, too, and that's the worse thing could happen," said the boy.

"Mr. Pluto just works here," said Thomas angrily. "This is my father's house. We are going to live in it, and old Pluto is going to work for us."

The boy fell into a fit of laughter calculated to make Thomas even madder. He slithered on the wet ground and pounded his fists silently. Even Pesty was giggling softly into the horse's mane.

"I think you children just better get off my father's land," said Thomas. He stepped off the porch. "Part of the Underground Railroad must be under these steps. I've got work to do."

"There's no train tracks down there," said Pesty. "There never was none that I ever seen."

But Thomas was not stopping for them. The boy stood up, eyeing Thomas seriously now. Pesty backed the horse off so Thomas could kneel down by the hole.

"You fixing to go down under there? You want some company?" asked the boy.

"You'd just better get out of here," said Thomas, not looking at him. "I don't need any of your help."

"Well, I reckon that's true as far as it goes," said the boy. "But I suspect you'll be needing me later."

"We'll come back after a while to see how you come out," said the child on the horse. And then she and the boy fell into more laughter.

"Naw," said the boy laughing. "Naw, Pesty, you can't come back today. You are all ready for bed in your pajamas, and after supper I'm going to lock you up so you can't bother this here new boy. How you like Pesty's pretty night clothes, new boy? She likes to wear red because Mr. Pluto told her red was the best color. Mr. Pluto likes red because it is the color of fire, and he is the keeper of fire. Pesty is the keeper's helper!" The boy laughed and laughed.

Thomas was excited at having met such odd children. But he hid his feelings from them by turning calmly away. "You get out of here," he said, "before I call my father!"

"Oh, we're going," said the boy. "And I'm M. C. Darrow, the youngest."

"I don't really care who you are," said Thomas

right back at him. "I am Thomas Small, the oldest son of my father."

"But you can just call me Mac," said M. C. Darrow. "Everybody calls me Mac, even Mr. Pluto, when I let him get close enough."

Thomas didn't say anything. Lying flat on his stomach, he looked into the hole; his head and shoulders disappeared inside. It was then he lost his grip and fell head first into thin, black air. He landed some five feet down, on damp sod that smelled like a mixture of yellow grass and mildew. All the breath was knocked out of him. He lay there unable to move or think for at least ten seconds, until air seeped back into his lungs. Otherwise he seemed not to have hurt himself. He could hear Pesty and M. C. Darrow going away. Mac was talking quietly to the child. Then Thomas couldn't hear them anymore.

There was gray light filtering down from the opening of the steps to where Thomas lay, and he could see that he was at the edge of a steep stairway cut out of rock. The stairs were wet; he could hear water dripping down on them from somewhere.

"I could have rolled down those steps," he whispered. Mac Darrow and Pesty must have known there was a drop down to where Thomas now lay. But they hadn't told him. "They are not friends then," said Thomas softly. He cautioned himself to be more careful.

I was showing off, he thought. I hurried and I fell. That was just what they'd wanted.

"Move slowly. Think fast," Thomas whispered. "Keep in mind what's behind and look closely at what's in front."

Thomas always carried a pencil-thin flashlight, which he sometimes used for reading in the car. He sat up suddenly and pulled out the flashlight. It wasn't broken from the fall, and he clicked it on. He sat in a kind of circle enclosed by brick walls. In some places, the brick had crumbled into powder, which was slowly filling up the circle of sod.

That will take a long time, thought Thomas. He looked up at the underside of the veranda steps.

Thomas got to his feet and made his way down the rock stairway into darkness. At the foot of the stairs was a path with walls of dirt and rock on either side of it. The walls were so close, Thomas could touch them by extending his arms a few inches. Above his head was a low ceiling carved out of rock. Such cramped space made him uneasy. The foundation of the house had to be somewhere above the natural rock. The idea of the whole three-story house of Dies Drear pressing down on him caused him to stop a moment on the path. Since he had fallen, he hadn't had time to be afraid. He wasn't now, but he did begin to worry a little about where the path led. He thought of ghosts, and yet he did not seriously believe in them. "No," he told himself, "not with the flashlight. Not when I can turn back . . . when I can run."

And besides, he thought, I'm strong. I can take care of myself.

Thomas continued along the path, flickering his tiny beam of light this way and that. Pools of water stood in some places. He felt a coldness, like the stream of air that came from around the button on the oak doorframe. His shoes were soon soaked. His socks grew cold and wet, and he thought about taking them off. He could hear water running a long way off. He stopped again to listen, but he couldn't tell from what direction the sound came.

"It's just one of the springs," he said. His voice bounced off the walls strangely.

Better not speak. There could be tunnels leading off this one. You can't tell what might hear you in a place like this.

Thomas was scaring himself. He decided not to think again about other tunnels or ghosts. He did think for the first time of how he would get out of this tunnel. He had fallen five feet, and he wasn't sure he would be able to climb back up the crumbling brick walls. Still, the path he walked had to lead somewhere. There had to be another way out.

Thomas felt his feet begin to climb; the path was slanting up. He walked slowly on the slippery rock; then suddenly the path was very wide. The walls were four feet away on either side, and there were long stone slabs against each wall. Thomas sat down on one of the slabs. It was wet, but he didn't even notice.

"Why these slabs?" he asked himself. "For the slaves, hiding and running?"

He opened and closed a moist hand around the

flashlight. The light beam could not keep back the dark. Thomas had a lonely feeling, the kind of feeling running slaves must have had.

And they dared not use light, he thought. How long would they have to hide down here? How could they stand it?

Thomas got up and went on. He placed one foot carefully in front of the other on the path, which had narrowed again. He heard the faint sound of movement somewhere. Maybe it was a voice he heard, he couldn't be sure. He swirled the light around over the damp walls, and fumbled it. The flashlight slid out of his hand. For a long moment, he caught and held it between his knees before finally dropping it. He bent quickly to pick it up and stepped down on it. Then he accidentally kicked it with his heel, and it went rattling somewhere over the path. It hit the wall, but it had gone out before then. Now all was very dark.

"It's not far," Thomas said. "All I have to do is feel around."

He felt around with his hands over smooth, moist rock; his hands grew cold. He felt water, and it was icy, slimy. His hands trembled, they ached, feeling in the dark, but he could not find the flashlight.

"I couldn't have kicked it far because I wasn't moving." His voice bounced in a whisper off the walls. He tried crawling backward, hoping to hit the flashlight with his heels.

"It's got to be here . . . Papa?" Thomas stood,

turning the way he had come, the way he had been crawling backward. He didn't at all like walking in the pitch blackness of the tunnel.

"I'll go on back," he said. "I'll just walk back as quick as I can. There'll be light coming from the veranda steps. I'll climb up that wall and then I'll be out of this. I'll get Papa and we'll do it together."

He went quickly now, with his hands extended to keep himself from hitting the close walls. But then something happened that caused him to stop in his tracks. He stood still, with his whole body tense and alert, the way he could be when he sensed a storm before there was any sign of it in the air or sky.

Thomas had the queerest notion that he was not alone. In front of him, between him and the steps of the veranda, something waited.

"Papa?" he said. He heard something.

The sound went, "Ahhh, ahhh, ahhh." It was not moaning, nor crying. It wasn't laughter, but something forlorn and lost and old.

Thomas backed away. "No," he said. "Oh please!"

"Ahhh, ahhh," something said. It was closer to him now. Thomas could hear no footsteps on the path. He could see nothing in the darkness.

He opened his mouth to yell, but his voice wouldn't come. Fear rose in him; he was cold, freezing, as though he had rolled in snow.

"Papa!" he managed to say. His voice was a whisper. "Papa, come get me . . . Papa!"

"Ahhhh." Whatever it was, was quite close now. Thomas still backed away from it, then he turned around, away from the direction of the veranda. He started running up the path, with his arms outstretched in front of him. He ran and ran, his eyes wide in the darkness. At any moment, the thing would grab him and smother his face. At any time, the thing would paralyze him with cold. It would take him away. It would tie him in one of the tunnels, and no one would ever find him.

"Don't let it touch me! Don't let it catch me!"

Thomas ran smack into a wall. His arms and hands hit first; then, his head and chest. The impact jarred him from head to foot. He thought his wrists were broken, but ever so slowly, painful feeling flowed back into his hands. The ache moved dully up to the sockets of his shoulders. He opened and closed his hands. They hurt so much, his eyes began to tear, but he didn't seem to have broken anything.

Thomas felt frantically along the wall. The wall was wood. He knew the feel of it right away. It was heavy wood, perhaps oak, and it was man made, man hewn. Thomas pounded on it, hurting himself more, causing his head to spin. He kept on, because he knew he was about to be taken from behind by something ghostly and cold.

"Help me! It's going to get me!" he called. "Help me!"

Thomas heard a high, clear scream on the other

side of the wall. Next came the sound of feet scurrying, and then the wall slid silently up.

"Thomas Small!" his mother said. "What in heaven's name do you think you are doing inside that wall!"

5

"I see you've found yourself a secret passage," said Mr. Small. "I hadn't thought you'd find that button by the front door so soon."

Mr. Small, with Billy and Buster, was seated at the kitchen table. They were finishing supper. Mr. Small smiled at Thomas, while the twins stared at him with solemn eyes.

Mrs. Small stood directly in front of Thomas and then stepped aside so that he could take a few steps into the kitchen. Thomas glanced behind him at the tunnel, a gaping space carved out of the comfortable kitchen. He saw nothing at all on the path.

He sat down beside his father. There was the good smell of food hanging in the air. The twins seemed full and content.

"You knew about that tunnel, Papa?" Thomas said. He felt discouraged, as though he'd been tricked.

"If anyone came unexpectedly to the front door," said Mr. Small, "the slaves could hide in the tunnel until whoever it was had gone. Or, if and when the callers began a search, the slaves could escape through the kitchen or by way of the veranda steps."

It's not any fun, Thomas thought. Not if he already knows about it.

"Thomas, you frightened me!" Mrs. Small said. She had recovered enough to take her eyes from the tunnel and sit down beside Thomas at the table.

"Goodness, yelling like that all of a sudden," she said, "I didn't know what it was." She jumped up, remembering Thomas hadn't eaten, and quickly fixed his plate. Then she seated herself as before.

"Yes, why were you calling for help, Thomas?" asked Mr. Small. "You really made your mama scream."

Thomas bent down to take off his shoes and socks. A pool of water stood dark and brackish on the linoleum. "There was something down there," he said.

Mrs. Small looked at him hard. Without a word, she got up and disappeared down the long hall from the kitchen toward the front of the house. When she returned, she carried a pair of Mr. Small's socks and Thomas' old tennis shoes.

"This is all I could find," she said to Thomas. She fairly flung the shoes and socks into his lap. Then she cleaned up the pool of water.

"There was something on that path," Thomas said. "It was coming after me as sure as I'm sitting here."

"You shouldn't make up stories like that," his mother said, "not even as a joke."

"There was something there." His voice quivered

slightly, and the sound of that was enough to tell Mr. Small that Thomas wasn't joking.

"Then what was it?" asked Mr. Small. He watched Thomas closely.

"I don't know," Thomas said. "I didn't see anything."

His father smiled. "It was probably no more than your fear of the dark and strange surroundings getting the best of you."

"I heard something though," Thomas said. "It went 'ahhh, ahhh' at me and it came closer and closer."

Mrs. Small sucked in her breath. She looked all around the kitchen, at the gaping hole and quickly away from it. The kitchen was large, with a single lamp of varicolored glass hanging from the ceiling on a heavy, black chain. Her shadow, along with Thomas', loomed long and thin on a far wall.

"Thomas, don't make things up!" his father said sternly.

"I'm not, Papa!" There was a lump in Thomas' throat. He gripped the table and swallowed a few times. He had to find just the right words if ever his father was to believe him.

His hands rose in the air. They began to shape the air, to carve it, as though it were a pretty piece of pine. "It was like no other voice," he began. "It wasn't a high voice or a low voice, or even a man's voice. It didn't have anything bad in it or anything. I was just in its way, that's all. It had to get by me and it would have done anything to get around me along that path."

"I forbid you to go into that tunnel again!" whispered Mrs. Small. She was afraid now, and even Mr. Small stared at Thomas.

Mr. Small seemed to be thinking beyond what Thomas had told them. "You say you saw nothing?" he asked.

"I thought I heard somebody moving around," Thomas said, "but that could have been you all in here. Or maybe it was the kids, come back to scare me."

"Kids?" said Mr. Small.

"The Darrow children," Thomas said. "I mean that youngest Darrow boy and that little girl he calls Pesty, who lives with them although she doesn't really belong to them. She came riding around the house in her pajamas on this big horse, and M. C. Darrow was hanging on the horse's tail. He was trying to get the horse to stop, but it wouldn't. Only Pesty could stop that big horse, and she was so little, too."

"What in the world . . . ?" said his father.

"Thomas, if you don't stop it!" warned Mrs. Small.

"Mama, it's the truth!" said Thomas. "There were these children, I'm not making it up! I can't help it if this is the craziest place we've ever lived in!"

"All right now," said Mr. Small. "Start over and take it slowly. You say there were children here?"

"Yes, they came from around the house just after I found the button and moved the steps." Then Thomas told all about Pesty, the horse and Mac Darrow. He even managed to make his father and mother understand that the children had been playing with him, toying with him, as if he were the object of a game.

"They were not friends," Thomas said finally. "They let me fall under those steps."

"No, they weren't if they did let you fall," said his mother, "but maybe they didn't know about that drop down."

"No," said Mr. Small, "they probably knew, but I would guess they had no real intention of causing Thomas harm. It was their joke on the 'new boy.' It wasn't a very nice joke and it was a joke that might have not worked at all. They were playing with you, Thomas, to find out what you knew. They must have thought you knew more than they did. After all, you came from far away to live in a house that no child in his right mind in these parts would dare enter. I would think that by now you are pretty famous all over town."

"I see," said Thomas. "Because I dared go into 'Mr. Pluto's tunnel'!"

"Yes," his father said.

"It wasn't a human voice I heard," Thomas said. "It wasn't alive."

They all fell silent for a moment. Then Mr. Small asked, "And you're sure you heard nothing more than that sighing?"

"That's all," Thomas said. "It just kept coming at me, getting closer."

Mr. Small got up and stood at the tunnel opening. He went into the long hall after a few seconds and came back with a flashlight. "I'll go with you," Thomas said.

"I'd rather you stayed here. I'll only be a minute," said his father.

Mr. Small was gone less than a minute. Thomas and his mother waited, staring into the tunnel opening, flooded with the light from the kitchen. A few feet beyond the opening, the kitchen light ended in a wall of blackness. They could see the light from Mr. Small's flashlight darting here and there along the ceiling of the tunnel until the path descended.

Mr. Small returned by way of the veranda steps. His white shirt was soiled from scaling the brick wall. As he came into the kitchen, muddying the floor as Thomas had, he was thoughtful, but not at all afraid.

He walked over to a high cabinet on the opposite wall from the tunnel. Beneath it, a small panel in the wall slid open at his touch. The panel had been invisible to the eye, but now revealed what seemed to be a jumble of miniature machinery. Mr. Small released a lever. The tunnel door slid silently down, and the patterned wallpaper of the kitchen showed no trace of what lay hidden behind it. Lastly, Mr. Small removed a mechanism of some kind from the panel and put it in his pocket.

"Did you see anything?" Thomas asked him. "Did you find my flashlight?"

"I didn't see anything," Mr. Small said, "and I didn't hear any sighing."

"Well that's a relief," said Mrs. Small. "Goodness,

if you'd found somebody . . . I'm sure my nerves would just give way."

"Your flashlight must have fallen in a crack," said Mr. Small. "I couldn't find it. Oh, yes, I removed the control from the panel. Without it, a giant couldn't raise that tunnel door."

"But you said there wasn't anything in the tunnel," said Thomas.

"That's so, but I don't want you wandering around in there," his father said. "The walls and ceilings are dirt and rock. There hasn't been a cave-in that I know of in a century, yet I think it best we don't take chances. I also removed the gears that control the front steps."

All he had to do was tell me not to go into the tunnel, Thomas thought. Give me a good reason and I wouldn't go . . . he knows that's all he has to do. He saw something or he heard something, and he's not going to tell anybody!

The twins had sat calmly through the commotion of Thomas' coming through the wall and their father going back through it again. Now they scrambled down from their chairs and slapped the wall with their hands. When the wall didn't move, they kicked it. They were crestfallen when the wall wouldn't slide up, as it had for Thomas.

Thomas had to laugh at them. "See? It's just a wall," he told them. They shook their heads.

"It's just a wallpapered wall with a pretty design to look at."

"I'd better get them ready for bed," Mrs. Small said. "They'll make themselves sick trying to get through the wall the way you did.

"Why is it you have to do just like Thomas?" she asked, teasing them. "Are you going to get into everything, just like Thomas, and cause me trouble?"

The twins laughed. Mrs. Small swept them into her arms and carried them out of the room.

Thomas sat at the table. He didn't look around the kitchen. He still wasn't ready to see the inside of the house, for he hoped to get the outside fixed in his mind first. When he heard his mother upstairs with the boys, he ate quickly. He glanced at his father, who sat across from him filling his pipe.

"It's still light out," Thomas said.

Mr. Small paused with the pipe. Thomas hadn't needed to say anything more for his father to understand his wish.

"Maybe you'd better wait until tomorrow," Mr. Small said. He glanced out of the window. There was still no clear sign of dusk in the sky.

Thomas picked at his food. He would not look arond at the kitchen. The twins were making a lot of noise upstairs.

"Do I get to have a big bedroom for myself?" asked Thomas.

Mr. Small nodded. "Your room overlooks the front lawn," he said.

"Does it have a secret door?"

"We thought it best that you and the boys have

good, solid rooms. Mr. Pluto chose rooms that I would have chosen," his father said. "Better not tamper with the walls until you see how the tunnels and passages fit together."

He could at least let me have a secret closet, Thomas thought.

Still, he was eager to see the room, to put his possessions in order.

He thought, If that Satan, Mr. Pluto, has made it stiff and cold, I won't sleep there until it's fixed the way I want it.

Thomas' anger at old Pluto flared up and cooled. His thought shifted to what his father had said a moment before about the secret tunnels and passages.

"Papa, how *do* the tunnels fit together?"

His father explained that they were all of a plan. "Eventually, they lead in the same direction, to the same place," he said.

"But what if an enemy of the slaves knew that?" Thomas said. "He could just wait at that place, because sooner or later he was bound to catch somebody."

"No, Dies Drear knew what he was doing," said Mr. Small. "Let the tunnels meander like a maze, with subpassages and dead ends. Have the same sign or symbol marking the main passages, a sign that only the slaves would understand. And let the slaves reach that one place where there would be people waiting to carry them quickly in many direction going farther north. No, it wasn't likely that at the time anyone knew for sure what was going on inside this house."

"Papa," Thomas said. He gulped down his milk to show that he had eaten. "It's still light out. I just want to see how the house looks all the way around. I won't go far."

His father smiled and said, "What is it you're looking for and why are you in such a hurry?"

Thomas wanted to tell his father exactly how he felt, but how could he say it? He didn't want to pry.

Papa, I feel you are keeping something from me. Could he say that?

Papa, I see on your face that you are worried. You didn't like it, either, that Mr. Pluto arranged our house.

"I'm not looking for anything," Thomas said at last. "I just want to try to figure out which rooms have the passages, after I've seen the outside. Like now, I know this kitchen isn't right. I haven't looked at it good, but I can tell something's wrong.

"Please, Papa," he said. "When it gets dark, I'll come inside."

Mr. Small took a deep breath. "You have perhaps an hour," he said. "Darkness has a way of falling down on you around here. It doesn't give you time to wander home, as it will in the South."

Thomas sat still for a second. He had a quiet vision of home. Springtime would be everywhere, and black crows sat all day, thick and shiny, in the fresh furrows of the fields. Just as the last sun slid out of the foothills, when you couldn't tell the crows from the earth, the birds flew in a mass into the air. The tips of their feathers caught the last sun, Thomas remembered. Their wings were blue and silver sails, like pinwheels. Then, the crows grew quickly smaller. The light slipped off them; the sound of them slid out of the sky. And the coolness of dark flowed over the hills. Thomas would walk from the pines to home with the night coming like liquid behind him.

He left the kitchen without another word to his father. Outside, he felt ready to explore. But he was unsure of the night that could trap him, and he was sad that he would never again walk those hills of home.

6

The gray-painted veranda closed in the house on all sides. As Thomas crossed it, back and forth, he felt it separate him and the house from everything beyond it. Many times he walked the veranda, looking for loose or trigger planks. He did find a few creaking boards. Stepping on them hard, pulling at them, jerking at them, he at last decided they concealed nothing.

Whoever old Pluto is, he thought, he sure takes good care of things.

Thomas made his way around the house. He took notice of every window, flower bed and what few bad pieces of siding there were. He missed nothing of what there was to see. There were fifteen windows on the first floor, and five of them were floor to ceiling. He counted six 5-foot window boxes loosely packed with fresh earth and seeded already.

What do you suppose he planted in them? Thomas wondered. He leaned over one of the boxes. He could see shoots of some kind, perhaps summer and autumn blooms, but he didn't know much about flowers. He tried smelling the soil.

It smells sweet, he thought. Why did he have to *do* everything!

Thomas would have liked planting the boxes himself, carefully seeding them in evening, when soil seemed most fresh. He would have planted them with hyacinth, maybe, and pale green fern.

He might've planted them with poison, that Mr. Pluto, Thomas thought. Just a good-smelling poison. When you leaned over a box to see what was growing, you would get a whiff of it and that would be the end of *you*!

"Then he could be king," Thomas said out loud. "That's what he thinks he's going to be."

There were five entrances to the house. There was the front entrance, with the oak door and the steps with the tunnel beneath. There was one on either side of the house and two in the rear. One rear door led to the kitchen. The other looked quite old, was boarded up, and had been replaced by the newer one. Thomas examined the rear of the house more carefully. He had the feeling that there was something odd about it.

He backed away from the house to get a clearer view. Behind him, the land rose to the top of the hill.

There were trees up there—big, ancient trees, dense and wet with rain.

Just trees, he thought. If I climb one, I can see how the house looks from the roof down.

Thomas worked his way up the hill. Closer to the trees, he saw that they were a variety he didn't know.

"Won't be able to climb those," he said, eyeing the sharp needles. He looked behind him down the hill and was surprised to find he could see beyond the house to the stream below it. He saw that the house hadn't been built directly facing the stream, but at an angle to it.

It looks like you're facing the stream when you're standing down there, he thought.

Thomas squatted down to study what lay before him. Then he stretched out on the damp ground with his head propped on his elbow. Slowly he grew calm and tired. After what had happened under the house, he was content to be where he was.

"The house doesn't look so scary from up here," he said. "It's not pretty though, but that flat roof makes it look more graceful."

Thomas stared a long time at the house and landscape, thinking of nothing in particular. He must have dozed. When at last he started and sat up, his legs were stiff. He got up, and his arms and face were cool.

He felt strange all of a sudden. He looked around him. The trees held darkness; below him, lights were on in the house. It seemed as though night had risen from the earth.

Thomas was ready to start down the hill as fast as he could go, when something rooted him where he was. He must have been hearing the sound for some time.

He couldn't move now if he tried, for the sound was dreadful, there in the dark trees.

"Ahhh, ahhh, ahhh, ahhh."

It came from behind Thomas. The night was still;

he could hear the sound clearly. Moving ever so slowly, he turned toward the trees. He listened for a long time, and, standing there, he became hidden by night.

Thomas was afraid, but it wasn't the first time today he had been afraid.

It's my birthday, he thought.

Papa, don't turn out the lights. Please don't.

He slipped through the trees, so used to walking in woods he could calculate where the pine boughs would touch him and have his hands in position to push them away. He walked on his toes, with one foot in front of the other. Indian scouts had walked that way so they could be ready to run in an instant if they had to.

Thomas followed that steady sound. His eyes darted blindly. Soon he was over the crest of the hill and moving downward on the other side. He didn't look back. He knew that by now the trees and hill blotted out the lights of the house.

"Papa, just keep them on," he said to himself. "I don't need to see them."

"Ahhh, ahhh," the thing went.

Thomas was getting closer to it. It was louder; there was something else—a crackling, sighing sound running beneath the ahhhing. The new sound was like dry leaves breaking under foot.

A lot of leaves, Thomas thought. A lot of them breaking together, with a wind coming up to blow them away.

The trees grew thicker. Thomas used his shoulders to get through them. He had the feeling he was moving too fast, and he tried to slow himself down.

You won't see anything quicker if you hurry than if you don't. You can't see anything anyhow.

His heart beat hard. As long as he didn't allow himself to think what the ahhhing might be, he could keep moving. Holding his mind as blank as possible made him less afraid. Finally he was able to slow himself down, but by then he had made his mistake.

The springy, slippery bed of pine needles Thomas had been walking on was no longer beneath his feet. His shoes clomped loudly before he could silence them.

"Boards!" he said. He was walking on wood. He still couldn't see anything.

The wood moved. Thomas began to slide. He was standing on a platform of some kind and the thing was rising. With his body off-balance, he had no chance to run.

Thomas slid to the ground in a crouch. He could see light coming from below the platform. The ahhhing had grown loud, with the crackling, sighing, under it, trying to catch it.

Then there was no sound. The light from the platform reflected an eerie red and orange in the trees. There was the smell of smoke. Thomas hugged the earth.

Ever so slowly, two doors in the platform opened.

Thomas saw two hands and bright fire, which turned the trees a slippery gold. Out of fire and out of the ground rose a huge head, huge shoulders. Up and up the thing rose, with a head full of hair that was red and yellow with light. The hair hanging mosslike from its jowls bristled and tumbled gold and orange.

"Who's that! What's that!" called a harsh, loud voice.

The frightful head looked down. Thomas saw its angry face. The eyes of it caught the firelight and glinted emerald and wet. The eyes of it found Thomas holding on to the earth.

"What demon walks on Pluto's house!"

"Devvvvil!" Thomas cried out shrilly.

He was breaking through the trees.

Devil!

Branches whipped at him; needles stung him. He fell twice. Once he got turned around, heading toward the fiery light again. He tripped and somersaulted, barely missing a tree. But he picked himself up and ran again toward his own house, up and over the hill. He was sure that the devil waited for him somewhere in the trees ahead.

"I've got to run," he told himself. "It's the nightmare! It's just like the dream in the car!"

It seemed to him he was moving ever so slowly. "I've got to run and hit it hard!"

When he ran into it, he would hit it with his full force. That way, he would cause it to pause long enough so that he could get around it and away.

But the man or devil, that Pluto, whatever he was, had fooled Thomas. He had not moved fast enough to get in front of Thomas. He caught up with him from behind.

He caught Thomas in mid-stride. Thomas' legs were still running when Pluto's arms tightened around his chest and, with ease, swung him into the air.

It happened so suddenly, Thomas had the notion that time had stopped. His mind went blank. Then it began to function almost reluctantly again, as did his struggle to free himself. One endless thought clawed its way into and out of his head: No old man who was lame, who was like any old man anywhere, even if he weren't lame, could ever catch him from behind. No, nor lift him off that ground and hold onto him.

Devil! Devil!

"Let go! Let me go!" Thomas whispered.

The man, that Pluto, heard Thomas and laughed. It was a mean laugh, like a snarl.

"You rounders," he said, "think you can come scare me out of my wits! You want to know? I have found it before you, and you ought to see it!"

Something bright exploded inside Thomas. He had no time to put away carefully and remember what Pluto had said. Now he was awake, when a moment ago he had felt inside a dream. He lashed back with his elbows, in a motion that was swift and unexpected. Pluto let out a grunt, and his body sagged just enough for his arms to relax.

Thomas ran free.

That devil was coming also. Thomas could hear him, and he was not running, but striding swiftly through the trees.

Thomas was over the crest of the hill. Below him were lights in the new house. The house was sweet to see. Thomas laughed—it was no better than a cry—and he ran faster once he had cleared the trees.

Thomas burst open the kitchen door, tripped over the threshold and slid across the linoleum on his stomach. He hit the table; dishes crashed to the floor. He lay there, trying to breathe. Someone bounded down the stairs. It was his papa. He heard his mother calling, "What is it? What's happening?" Somewhere above, the twins let out a tired wail.

Mr. Small was shocked by the scene that greeted him. Thomas lay sprawled half under the kitchen table, with broken dishes around him. There was mud on his trousers and a lone, dirt skid mark across the linoleum. The kitchen-door lock had been pulled completely out of the molding and hung, useless, by one screw. Mr. Small couldn't think why he had locked the door in the first place, since he knew Thomas would be returning by way of it. But he had, and now he couldn't imagine what force had pulled out the lock.

Mr. Small kneeled beside Thomas. "Thomas. Son," he whispered. He didn't touch the boy, but absently picked away bits of splintered glass from Thomas' shirt.

Mrs. Small came in and kneeled down. "Who did

this? she said. "Is he bleeding? Thomas! Please get up!"

"Lock." Thomas managed to say. He tried to keep his voice from trembling.

"It's . . . he's coming . . . lock." He was too tired to bother with making sentences. All he wanted his mother to do was lock the back door so Pluto—that devil, whatever he was—wouldn't be able to get him.

There was the sound of heavy feet on the rear veranda. A loud knock on the door caused it to slowly swing open. And framed by night stood that massive, black and bearded man some souls called Pluto.

7

A movement of cool air from the open door fanned springy curls tucked behind Mrs. Small's ears. She'd never seen old Pluto. Her hands clenched, as some instinct to defend her family made her stand boldly in front of him. When the loud knocking started, she had moved forward. She stood there, not menacing but watchful and strong.

Pluto stepped over the threshold in a direct but courteous manner. He had thick, white hair and a full white beard, just as Mr. Small had described. And he was tall, taller than any elderly man Mrs. Small had ever seen. His broad shoulders drooped forward with age, causing his huge head to seem as untamed as that of a white gerfalcon.

What Mr. Small hadn't done was put the whole picture of Pluto together for Mrs. Small—his beard and hair against the dark brown skin of his face, out of which peered glassy, green eyes. He was somehow larger than dream or nightmare. She studied him from head to foot and did not think about him being lame. It was something other than his fearful head that caused her face to tighten. The way Mr. Pluto dressed seemed out of place and out of season, although there was no one thing that was wrong.

Too well ordered, Mrs. Small thought. Yes! Just too well groomed for a country man!

The idea came to her that maybe Mr. Pluto had planned with great care some particular effect.

But why? She wondered. She carefully wiped her damp palms on her apron and extended her hand to this stranger.

"You are Mr. Pluto." Her voice was uncertain. "I shouldn't stare . . . my, gracious, I *was* staring at you. I'm awfully sorry!"

Mr. Pluto walked near and politely took her hand. He wore heavy hide gloves; they looked new, and he did not remove them. He said nothing. He retreated to a place just within the open door, where there was least light.

"This is Thomas, my son," Mrs. Small said. She turned slightly in Thomas' direction, where he still lay half beneath the kitchen table. There was an awkward silence in which Mrs. Small tried not to notice the mess Thomas had made. For it was Thomas alone who had caused the dishes to crash down upon his head. Mrs. Small slowly freed herself from the shock of Mr. Pluto, and, in the silence of the kitchen, she understood clearly what must have befallen her son.

Quickly Mrs. Small spoke again. "And this is my husband. I believe you two already know one another." Looking at Pluto, her features tensed. Her eyes darkened, as though shadow passed over her vision.

"Pleased to meet you, Mrs. Small," Pluto said. He was boldly cordial. "I'm afraid I mistook your boy." He cleared his throat.

Thomas, still shivering, watched Mr. Pluto secretly from beneath his arm.

"There are strangers . . . every once in a while . . ." Pluto said darkly. "They come out here and they mean no good. I chase 'em off. I thought your boy was one. . . ." He nodded at Thomas by way of apology. His eyes flicked toward Mr. Small and quickly away before they could make contact. He did this several times.

Now why is he shifty? Thomas wondered. And he's a speechmaker, but he doesn't seem to know his speech, or else he hasn't written all of it yet.

Thomas shot a glance at his father. He couldn't have been more surprised by the look on his face.

Mr. Small stood stock still, in a pose of deep concentration. His arms were rigid at his sides. He stared so hard at old Pluto, his whole face seemed caught in a terrible spasm.

Thomas whistled silently through his teeth. Secretly he looked at old Pluto to see if he had noticed. But Pluto was staring into some neutral space above the table, as if waiting agreeably for what was to come next. Thomas had another look at his father, only to find him his usual self. Whatever had caused him to become upset no longer showed in his expression, nor in the way he stood there.

Was I seeing things? Thomas asked himself.

"Nice to see you again," Mr. Small said. He picked up his pipe and walked around the table to shake hands with Mr. Pluto. "I want to thank you for taking care of things. You did well putting the rooms in order—saves me a lot of time and energy. You'll work yourself too hard though."

"Why, the big moving van came at the beginning of the week. I took my time," said Pluto. "I hope it's all right."

"Couldn't be better," said Mr. Small. "Everything is fine just the way you arranged it." He watched Pluto as though he had been struck, suddenly, by some new and strange idea of him. Again Pluto would not meet his eyes, but appeared to pull back from him as far as he could without moving physically.

Mr. Small took a step toward Pluto and shifted the conversation without warning.

"How's the black doing, and the bay?" he said matter-of-factly. "I remember you were working on their shoes."

The question startled Pluto; there was no place for him to back up to without going out the door. "Oh . . ." he stammered. Mr. Small took another step forward. Yes . . . yes, sir!

"The bay is fine, just fine." Pluto was talking fast, and Mr. Small did not move. "But I had to hobble that black," Pluto said. "He's got the chill, but he won't stay still. He tries to run all night to get away from it. I had to hobble him, had to tie his feet to keep him from bursting his heart."

"Horses?" said Thomas. "Papa, horses?" He was on his feet, forgetting his fear of Pluto. He thought of Pesty and that Darrow boy, and the black horse they had with them.

"Mr. Pluto has three horses, son," said Mr. Small. "I told you he uses two at a time for the buggy he gets around in. At night, he keeps them in the cave on the other side of the hill from here. The black has simple fever, which is odd, isn't it, Mr. Pluto, in a horse of such dark color? I thought simple fever hit horses with lighter coats, such as the whites and grays."

"Yes . . . well." Mr. Pluto thought for awhile. He seemed to struggle with his memory, and Thomas watched him. Indeed they all watched him, as though he were not just strange, someone they'd only heard of, but a man beyond their knowledge.

"If it was just a heat problem," Mr. Pluto began, "say heat like they have in India, it wouldn't have hurt the black. It wasn't the heat though, it was nervous shock."

"I had no idea nervousness could act on a horse's heat centers," Mr. Small said. He had taken another step forward, and Pluto became agitated.

"Not nervousness," Pluto said. He squeezed his gloved hands together. "Nervous shock. Nervous shock! By haunted things nothing living should have the unhappiness to see!"

At once Thomas had a vision of night and Mr. Pluto's black horse grazing the hillside. A specter floated slowly nearer, until it was beside the horse. The horse lifted his head, standing there for a second before falling with a thud to the ground.

"Papa, ghosts!" Thomas whispered. "He's talking about ghosts!"

Mr. Small looked sternly at Thomas; after that Thomas stayed quiet. Then Mr. Small looked hard at Pluto. At that moment, Thomas saw the faintest trace of amusement on Pluto's face. His father didn't seem to notice it.

"You have a sick quarter horse on your hands," said Mr. Small. "This is a lonely stretch of country. I'm sure the town boys like fooling around along the stream. Thomas, didn't you tell us you met two children out here today? One of them was a little girl called Pesty. She was riding a black horse, Mr. Pluto, and I believe she left the impression the horse belonged to you."

They all stood still in the room, with the quiet slowly closing in on them. Mr. Small's meaning had been clear to Mrs. Small and clear to Thomas. But if he had meant to startle Mr. Pluto with his knowledge of an unhobbled, seemingly well horse, he had been mistaken.

When Pluto started speaking, he didn't even bother to lift his voice above that hostile silence; he seemed not to consider that Mr. Small had raised the possibility he might be lying. Now he kept his eyes on Mr. Small's feet moving steadily forward.

"That Pesty!" Mr. Pluto said, fondly it seemed to Thomas. "She can do more with a wild animal than any small child should be able to do with anything!"

"You mean to say a child could unhobble a full-grown quarter horse suffering from simple fever?" Mr. Small's voice was angry now.

"No," said Mr. Pluto quietly. "No, I mean to say that Pesty can ride that black anytime. Anytime at all, as long as it's day. But once night hits, that horse has the fever of nervous shock. And I have to hobble him so he won't burst his heart with running."

"You're not talking sense, man!" said Mr. Small. He was well on Pluto now and with a few more steps, he would be able to see whatever it was he was obviously looking for.

"Sense!" The word hissed around them, stopping Mr. Small's forward movement. There was a twisted smile on Pluto's face. Thomas still couldn't see that face as well as he had when the firelight had played on it.

"Sense," Pluto said again, less in anger than with sadness.

He looked gently at Mrs. Small. He looked at Mr. Small with that odd trace of amusement on his face. He stared vacantly at Thomas, then up at the ceiling. And he spoke a kind of chant that sounded old and worn, like history.

"When hoot owl screeching, westward
    flies,
Gauge the sun . . .
Look to Dies,
And Run."

Mr. Small stepped forward. Pluto moved into the frame of the gaping door. Like fluid, the tall figure of him flowed out and was the same as darkness. Thomas didn't even hear his feet on the veranda. But he was gone, leaving them free for awhile of whatever it was had possessed them.

8

"It will just have to hold until morning. I can get into town then and buy a new lock . . . maybe two or three locks, the way things look here. India! Can you beat it? That's the puzzle!"

Mr. Small was speaking to himself. He wasn't aware that Mrs. Small and Thomas listened to him, so intent was he on his work at the kitchen door. He had been working on the door for the past ten minutes. He had looked out once, right after Mr. Pluto had disappeared into darkness, and then had spent a few minutes trying to slam the door shut. But without the spring lock, the door wouldn't stay closed. He had taken two dinner knives and slid them in the groove of the doorframe. One knife he placed by the lock and the other just below the doorknob. He then slid the latch in place.

"No. No," Mr. Small muttered to himself. "Something else. Something different. Was it about the head? No, that was all right . . . perhaps the neck? The shoulders? If I could have just realized the difference when I shook his hand! If I could put my finger on it . . . *that's* what it was. The gloves! He's trying to conceal his hands. He might have burned himself badly. I've told him the kind of work he does is too hard for a man his age. And being the superstitious man he is, he will be afraid to see a doctor. He will suffer with pain as best he knows how, because a doctor has supernatural power the same as a ghost!"

Thomas and Mrs. Small listened. They understood that something had to be haunting Mr. Pluto. Whatever it was, part of it had taken hold of Mr. Small. Although he was finished with the door, he still stood before it, talking to it as if it were alive.

"Good Lord!" he was saying. "The man is history! He doesn't have to leave this land, that other side of the hill. And yet he is running just as hard as the slaves had to run, as if he were one! He stays here, colliding with the past on the one hand and the present on the other. But does he mean to run with the one and away from the other? Or run to both and pull them together? Here he stays . . . now why! Why does he stay?"

Finally Mr. Small sat down glumly at the kitchen table, with one hand cupped over his mouth. Thomas, after taking in the large, lopsided kitchen, sat down beside him.

Mrs. Small busied herself by cleaning off the table and sweeping up all the broken dishes. She didn't utter a word to Thomas or his father. When she had finished, she deposited all the trash in an empty carton as quietly as she could.

"I think I could do with more coffee," Mr. Small

said finally. His voice no longer held that feverish, crazy sound, Thomas noticed.

If he goes around talking to some more doors, Thomas thought, I'm just going to have Mama take him to a hospital.

"It's still good and hot," Mrs. Small said. "Thomas, will you have your coffee black, too?"

Thomas was so surprised he couldn't think of anything to say. His mother never allowed him black coffee. What small amount of coffee she would permit him to have came only at Christmas or Thanksgiving, and then it was mostly cream and sugar with a dash of cinnamon.

"Oh, I know," Mrs. Small said to him, "but you know you'd dearly love to have it strong and black, the way your papa does. And since you're sitting here . . . well, it's your birthday."

She poured two full cups of black coffee, placing one cup in front of Thomas and one in front of Mr. Small. She then poured a half cup for herself and sat down between them.

The smell of coffee filled the room. It flooded Thomas' mind with kitchen and coffee memories of long ago.

Mr. Small raised his cup. "Happy birthday, Thomas," he said quietly.

"Yes," Mrs. Small said, "happy birthday!"

So it was that Thomas had his first full cup of bittersweet, black, black coffee. He felt so good sitting there in the new kitchen, in the new house, with his mother and father. He felt as though he were at the center of whatever would happen next. Talk would happen next. He could tell that by his mother's excited face and his father's solemn one. They would talk things out the way they always had. Late at night, he'd often heard them in the kitchen talking things out, with that pure, hot smell of coffee filtering up to his room.

"Mama," Thomas said after a while. He had taken a few sips of coffee. ". . . do you think now you are here and have seen everything that you'll ever want to go back home?"

Mrs. Small sat very still. Thomas thought she looked tired. He knew he was tired—all of them were. But he had to know right now how she felt about staying in the new house. And he knew none of them wanted to think about Mr. Pluto just yet.

"No, Thomas," said Mrs. Small. "I don't think so. Your father and I have moved around quite a bit, it's true. We travelled this whole country in a camper we made ourselves."

"Looking . . . looking," Mr. Small said quietly.

"We finally settled in North Carolina," said Mrs. Small, "and we stayed there a good long while. But it was never right for us. No. No, never go back."

"And you won't be afraid of Mr. Pluto?" Thomas couldn't help asking.

"Thomas!" Mr. Small spoke sharply. "Nobody talking about ghosts and chanting verse is going to scare us out of this house. Nobody is going to take it away from us."

"Do you think he will try?" Thomas said.

His father was silent. He rubbed his jaw thoughtfully, but said nothing.

"Well," said Mrs. Small, as though to answer Thomas and clear their thinking at the same time. She looked searchingly at Mr. Small.

"Mr. Pluto *is* the strangest man, isn't he? I mean, you never told me he was such a huge man and such an odd-acting man."

"Well, he didn't seem . . ." began Mr. Small. "I mean to say, he wasn't at all . . ."

For the second time this night, Thomas watched his father become rigid, his face controlled by an instant spasm. Mr. Small rose swiftly from the table.

"We won't talk anymore about Pluto tonight," he said.

"But, Papa," Thomas protested, "we just got going on him."

"Tomorrow is Sunday, Thomas," Mr. Small said sternly.

Mrs. Small sucked in her breath. "Sunday," she said. "My goodness, how in the world did I forget! I don't have our clothes unpacked!" She looked worried. "I can't remember where I put my hatboxes!"

"Oh, for heaven's sakes," said Mr. Small. "There will be plenty of time for your hatbox search in the morning if we all get to bed now. Thomas, you go ahead. Your room is at the end of the hall, on the right side as you go down the hall. Get your pajamas out of the suitcase and your towel, too. Don't forget your toothbrush."

"It's going to be Sunday all right," Thomas said. "We'll probably meet just everybody!"

"I don't doubt that," said Mr. Small.

"I did want to see the house tonight though," Thomas said. He looked around at the lopsided kitchen. "I can tell straight off this room is smaller than it should be."

"That's because you've had time to see the house from the outside," Mr. Small said.

"Let me see if I can figure it out," said Thomas.

"I want you to go to bed. Here," his father said, "I'll show you myself to save time."

On either side of the kitchen door there were sliding panels, which vanished into the wall at Mr. Small's touch. Within were arched cubicles, large enough for a man stooping to hide.

"Why, I wouldn't have imagined!" said Mrs. Small.

"That's great!" Thomas said. "Boy, I wouldn't have thought they were there either."

"A very temporary measure," Mr. Small said. "Slaves might be hidden in these walls for a short time, until the trapdoor could be raised so they could escape through the tunnel."

"Old Dies Drear thought of everything," said Thomas, clearly impressed.

"Now go upstairs," Mr. Small said. "The twins

have the room across from yours, so be quiet. We'll be up shortly."

"Papa, you won't be able to get locks tomorrow," Thomas said, "because it's going to be Sunday."

"Maybe I can find out where a locksmith lives," Mr. Small answered. "I did forget for a minute that it would be Sunday. You go on up. Good night."

Thomas went up to his room, treading softly down the carpeted hallway. The hall was not well lighted, and the ceiling was very high. There were closed, varnished doors on either side. Tall and dark, they didn't seem at all friendly.

Why do I have to be so far away from the stairs? Thomas wondered. I'll never be able to hear a sound back here!

He stopped long enough to find out if he could hear his mother and father talking. The silence made him feel he was smothering.

"That proves it," he said. "You wouldn't be able to hear anything coming *or* going. You'd just be a sitting duck!"

He thought of looking in all the rooms before going into his own bedroom. And he did march up to one door about halfway down the hall. For some reason, he couldn't bring himself to turn the knob.

"Better wait until tomorrow," he told himself and backed away from the door.

At his own door, at the end of the hall, he held on tightly to the doorknob but didn't turn it. It was a brass knob. It felt cold. He looked across the hall, seeing the twins' room. Their door was open, and a yellow nightlight shone through the darkness.

Gathering his courage, Thomas opened the door to his room and was at once blinded by the bright light. There was a clear, glass globe suspended by a chain from the ceiling. The room was larger than he could have hoped, with a narrow fireplace to his left at the far end. There were two long windows across from him; his bed had been placed between them, facing the door. There were smaller garret windows on each side of the fireplace. Directly in front of the fireplace was a large, old-fashioned captain's chair. It was a ghostly chair, with its back to the room; it faced the bare, charred insides of the cold hearth. Thomas had the awful notion that someone he couldn't see was sitting in it.

"Hello," he said. "Who do you think you are?"

He hoped to startle anyone who might be there into some sudden movement. He still held onto the doorknob, half in and half out of the room. He could yell and run fast down the hall if he had to.

There was no movement from the chair. There was no sound of any kind in the room except his own breathing. He came cautiously inside, leaving the door slightly ajar. Going up to the chair at an angle, he saw that it was empty. At the same moment, he noticed that he was cold and clammy.

"Whose old chair is it anyway?" he said out loud.

The chair wasn't one that had come from their home in North Carolina. Its cumbersome, hard seat and back were upholstered with faded leather. The flat, wood armrests were not even carved, and the base of it, made from the same hardwood, sat squarely on the floor.

"I've got to move it," Thomas told himself. "I'll never get to sleep if I don't turn it around."

As he struggled to move the heavy chair, he thought of fifty ways to get even with old Pluto for putting the chair with its back to the room.

He did it just to scare me. He's just a mean old man! Thomas thought.

But he couldn't move the chair no matter how hard he tried. He couldn't slide it on the gray, musty carpet and he could not tilt it and swivel it the way his mother did when she had to move furniture.

Mr. Pluto had arranged the room with the same plan in mind as he must have had when he'd arranged the front parlor. Thomas began to form a plan of his own as he went about getting ready for bed. He wasn't going to sleep in the room, that was for certain.

Not until I change everything. Not until I get that chair into some corner.

Thomas' old bookcase stood next to his bed, blocking the view from the lower half of the windows. On the other side of his bed, a crate of his books had been placed with great care. On top of that, his father had flung the smaller carton full of his carvings. There was a note attached to it as a reminder for him to put the contents away.

He took a few of his best carvings and grouped them at one end of the fireplace. That made things a little better, he thought. The view from the bed to the mantel of the fireplace was less balanced. Then Thomas opened his suitcase at the foot of the bed and got into his pajamas. He threw his clothes over the back of the chair. That made the room look almost messy. He smiled, relaxing a little. After that he lay down on his bed and stared up into the light.

The ceiling of the room was painted the dullest gray Thomas had ever seen. The color of it was worse than the carpet, which was dimmer still. The walls were papered in a pale blue flower pattern with loops of brownish leaves. Automatically, Thomas let his mind redo the walls and ceiling in bright earth colors.

Windowframes and baseboards were trimmed a dark mahogany. The floor where the carpet ended was the same mahogany.

I'll let the floor stay dark, Thomas thought. But all the trim he allowed his mind to paint pure white.

There were two more mahogany doors in the wall across from him. Thomas leaped up from the bed and snatched one of them open.

"Only an old, empty closet," he said. "I knew it."

It was not a large closet; it had a few hangers spaced about two inches apart along one wood pole. Thomas hung his Sunday suit in the closet and left the closet door open.

Treading barefoot, he went to the next door and flung it open. There was a tiny room with a sink and a three-paneled mirror above it. Thomas was pleased, and he remembered to brush his teeth. He even washed his face, eyeing himself in the three mirrors. After that he gave one last look around the room, especially at the chair, and turned out the light.

Lying with his arms over his eyes, Thomas tried not to think about anything. He didn't want to scare himself about what he planned to do. Soon he heard a door open and close down the hall; then the voices of his mother and father. He'd wait about an hour and then he would take the sheets from the bed and carry them downstairs to the front parlor. He was going to sleep all night on the couch, where he could see anything coming up on the front porch and where he might hear something coming through the kitchen.

Thomas was tired, but he did stay awake. When he thought an hour had passed, he did as he had planned. He made a ball of his bedding and stealthily headed down the hall. Thank goodness there was a runner on the hall and stairs. His mother had helpfully left the dim hall light on.

Once downstairs, Thomas felt a lot better. He looked at himself in the ornate mirror just beyond the oak door, right next to the parlor. He couldn't see himself well, but he was sure he must look brave. He went right into the parlor.

Without any light save what night glow came through the windows, he made his bed on the sofa. He felt almost calm as he settled down. Quickly he lapsed into semisleep, before going off altogether.

Once he thought he heard water running some-where, but that was an ordinary sound and he didn't bother to wake himself. Vaguely, he heard the slight-est movement, not far away. But he was too tired, to deeply gone. He had not even bothered to close the parlor door.

Thomas was asleep when suddenly the upstairs hall light went off. Awhile after that, there was again the sound of running water. Then the hall mirror near the oak door swung silently open. And through it all Thomas slept.

Soundlessly the mirror closed. Whatever stood there in front of it gave back no reflection in the totally dark house. The thing was not the same as night. It was darkness detached from the black of the entranceway. It was solid, but it could move, and it did not hesitate. It went directly to the stairs and up them, a mass of shadow-black that knew its way. At the top of the stairs, it paused as though listening. All remained silent. The thing, as it stopped before each closed door, was once more a part of the black house.

It pressed itself against each doorjamb, on the right side, but did not try to enter any room. Near the twins' room, where the yellow light still glowed, it became more visible. Now it was massive, bold. Not vapor, not blackness, it was not ghostly at all. It was a thing become manlike.

It moved across to the twins' room, skirting the light, where it placed something dimly metallic in the doorframe. It crossed back to Thomas' room, doing the same. It did not move; it listened a long while. Then it crossed over to Mr. and Mrs. Small's room, where it again placed something in the doorframe. After that it went down the hall and down the stairs.

Whatever it was did not bother looking at Thomas asleep in the parlor. Perhaps it didn't know he was there. It vanished behind the mirror, the way it had come. All was still once more. The night passed, as dawn came creeping into the house through the parlor windows.

9

Thomas was talking to himself in his sleep. He could hear himself; he could feel the shape of words in his mouth. He became half conscious and recognized the sounds of birds singing in the trees outside the house. They were so many and so loud, they were noisy. But sleep overcame him again. He dreamed of trees and the danger of Mr. Pluto.

Later he awoke with a start and sat up on the couch. Clear morning sunlight filled the parlor. Whatever he'd said in his sleep, he couldn't remember now.

Was it a dream? he wondered. I've forgotten something. Was it a dream I've forgotten?

Across the foot of the couch lay his new suit and fresh underwear. There was a note pinned to his shirt from his mother. Thomas read it and laughed. It said, "Thomas you are to wear these clothes."

He recalled the day was Sunday and jumped up to get dressed.

"Anyhow," he said out loud, "I can't remember if it was a dream or not. I've got to think about what it is I've forgotten. But not today. No, not today!"

He hurried to the kitchen, still fumbling with his

tie. The table was set; there were glasses filled with juice. But there was no one about, not even his mother. The oven was on. Thomas peeked inside.

"Good!" he said. "Good hoecakes just waiting. Mama must be missing Great-grandmother. It's Sunday for sure!"

In sunlight, the kitchen looked much like any big kitchen anywhere. There were no shadowed angles to bring out its lopsidedness.

It looks almost friendly, Thomas thought. But I know there's the tunnel. I know about slaves hiding and running.

He went toward the staircase. There was not a sound from up above, although his mother had to be up, probably his father, too. The twins would be sleeping, or he would have heard them.

He paused at the mirror next to the front parlor and carefully surveyed himself.

My head is too big, he thought. But the suit is all right. Everybody will know it is a new suit. I will tell them I got it for my birthday.

He straightened his tie.

Maybe we'll bring some folks home with us. They will sit in the parlor with Papa. They won't like him at first because he's a teacher. But they'll come because they'll want to know why we are here and living in this house. They'll like him once they hear him talk.

It seemed to Thomas that his father talked best on Sunday. He always spoke of history—not only the history of black people, but American Indian history and the history of the Hebrew tribes. Once, when they had a minister back home, he would often stop by on Sunday to listen to Thomas' father and to have a cup of coffee. Thomas felt very proud at those times. But usually, there were just ordinary people in their house on Sunday.

Some neighbors. Or his two uncles and their families, who would come one Sunday a month for talk, all the way from Tennessee.

"There's no minister anymore," he whispered. "I said I wasn't going to think about home. I said I wouldn't."

Folks will come to visit here just like they did at home, he told himself. I'll have friends like I never had before, you wait and see.

At the top of the stairs, Thomas couldn't have been more startled by what he saw. His father sat in his best suit, cross-legged on the floor in the middle of the hallway. His mother kneeled beside him in her gray wool suit and her brand-new, white-and-black straw hat. They were completely silent, and Thomas' father was examining something he held in his palm.

Thomas tiptoed up to them and knelt down. "What have you got there?" he asked his father.

Mr. Small had three metallic objects spread out on his hand. He didn't answer Thomas; instead, he carefully placed the objects one by one on the floor.

"Triangles!" Thomas said.

"Three of them," said Mrs. Small softly, "and they're exactly alike."

"Yes, three right triangles," said Mr. Small, as though talking to himself. "Thomas, go to my room, fetch me my pen on the dresser and a sheet of paper from my briefcase. I have an idea we might be able to understand them better if we diagram them."

Thomas went and returned almost at once.

Mr. Small laid out the paper beside the triangles. Then he drew on the paper a large triangle that looked the same as those in front of him.

"The two legs of the triangle which make the right angle are wood," he said. "Probably a hardwood, like oak." He drew on the paper, marking each leg of the right angle with a capital W.

"The surface of the triangle, between the legs, must be tin. In any case, it's lightweight and coated with silver paint."

He drew the line to mark the hypotenuse—the side opposite the right angle. He then shaded the space between the hypotenuse and the angle and marked it with a capital S to show that it was painted silver.

"The angle seems to be real gold, I can't tell for sure." Mr. Small marked it with a G for gold, and seemed to be finished. "Wait," he said.

Next to the triangle he had drawn he wrote down each letter, and beside each letter he wrote an explanation of what the letter represented.

"Now let's see what we have," he said.

"You forgot something," Thomas said. He picked up one triangle to show his father. Hardly noticeable was a circle of metal in the wood, where the legs of the triangle joined. Thomas turned the triangle on its opposite side. Protruding was a metal peg about a half an inch long.

"Ah, you're pretty good, Thomas," said Mr. Small. "I'll show the peg with a black dot." He made a dot on the paper. The completed triangle looked like part of a puzzle:

W   legs of wood, forming right angle
G   90° angle of gold
S   area between right angle and
     hypotenuse: metal coated with
     silver paint metal peg

Mr. Small began to arrange the three triangles on the floor to see if they fit together in any way. He thought of taking one and laying it over the diagram he had drawn.

Thomas picked up one of the other triangles and fitted it next to the one on the diagram, with the wood sides next to each other and the wood angles touching.

Then Mr. Small picked up the third triangle they had found. He fitted it next to the one Thomas had placed down, so that all three wood angles were touching.

"If it's a square, there's one missing," Mr. Small said. "The top one."

"Any one of them is missing," said Thomas. "I mean, you can move them so that there is always one missing, since they are three triangles just alike."

"It doesn't make any kind of sense," Mr. Small said. "Why did they leave just three triangles if they are meant to make a square? Clearly, there's a triangle missing."

"Where did you get these three?" Thomas wanted to know.

"They were stuck in the doorframes on the outside of the three bedrooms we occupy," Mrs. Small said.

To Thomas, his mother's voice sounded breathless. She's frightened, he thought. She's just scared to death.

"They weren't there last night. I would have seen them," Thomas said.

Then Thomas sat quite still. It struck him why his mother was so afraid. His eyes grew wide and searching.

"Yes," said Mr. Small, reading his thoughts. "Someone walked right in, not making a sound. While we slept, he, or they, came through our locked doors to place these triangles in the walls."

"A warning!" Thomas managed to say. "Mr. Pluto's second warning!"

"Warning? Mr. Pluto?" his mother said.

"The first warning was the way he arranged that parlor downstairs," Thomas said. "He made it so it was a progression going out the windows and on and on."

"You are letting your imagination get the best of you, Thomas," she said. "You don't know that it was Mr. Pluto who was here last night."

"It's a warning, I tell you!" Thomas said. "He means for us to flee. To flee south!"

All at once Mr. Small leaned very close to the paper on which he and Thomas had fitted together the three triangles. "Thomas!" he said. He began to move around the paper, looking at it from all sides. "It's an optical illusion. It's a box, true, but the wood legs form a cross . . . a Greek cross!"

"What in the world?" said Mrs. Small.

"Son, you are pretty good," said his father. "I don't know about that parlor, the way it was arranged, being a sign. That might be too much for a man like Mr. Pluto to think up. But this triangle is definitely a warning, and it could be a warning to flee. And now, all we need to do is wait."

"For Mr. Pluto," Thomas said.

Mr. Small spoke quietly. "We may not see anyone. But you can be sure there will be another triangle sometime, somewhere, and that we will find it."

"Papa, what is a Greek cross? You said the triangles made a Greek cross," Thomas said.

"I meant that we will have a Greek cross when we fit together all the triangles." He drew a Greek cross next to the diagram of the triangle and placed the three triangles on it. The top right triangle was missing.

He explained to them what a Greek cross was.

"It's also known as a St. George's cross," he told them, "the cross used on the flag of Great Britain. It differs from our familiar Christian cross, or cross of

The Greek Cross

The Greek Cross

Calvary, in that if you connect the points you have four triangles exactly the same."

Mr. Small hesitated. "And why a Greek cross," he said, "where any one of the triangles can be moved to fit the place of any other?

"It's confusing," he added softly to himself. "If it's a warning, it surely says nothing to me at the moment."

"We'd better get the twins up," Mrs. Small said. "We're going to be late if we don't get out of here soon."

"I nearly forgot it was Sunday," Mr. Small said.

Mrs. Small hurried to wake the twins and to dress them.

Thomas and Mr. Small went outside. They looked the car over; it was quite dirty from the trip, and they took cloths and cleaned it as best they could. Then they cleaned out the inside of all the candy wrappers and potato chip bags that had accumulated over the trip. They pulled the trailer off the road onto the lawn. It was then Thomas asked his father about the intruders.

"How do you suppose they got into the house, Papa?"

"I don't know," said Mr. Small. "There are corridors I assume I don't know about. We'll have to take care." He looked cautiously at his son. "You had no business wandering about the house in the dead of night. You could have run into someone. Why did you move down into that parlor?"

"Well, because . . ." answered Thomas. He remembered the captain's chair facing the fireplace in his room. He couldn't let his father know he had been afraid of an empty chair. "Because I thought I would be able to hear somebody if they came in the front or back doors."

"Anybody stealing into a house in the dead of night isn't going to use the main entrances," said Mr. Small.

"I suppose not," said Thomas. He felt foolish. "I guess I didn't think."

Mr. Small drew Thomas aside, as though the lawn, the very trees, pressed close to the house might hear. "Can I confide in you, son?" he asked. "May I trust you with something and have you stay silent about it? I won't want to worry your mother."

A chill ran down Thomas' back. He was surprised by the seriousness of his father's tone. "Yes! Sure,

Papa—what is it we've gotten ourselves into!"

"Trust me with that," said Mr. Small. "It may not be anything at all. And then again, it might be. I don't know for sure what's at stake. I really don't want to involve the police. . . ."

"The police!" Thomas broke in on him. He fairly shouted, and Mr. Small had to tell him to keep quiet.

"We'll have to set up a watch," Mr. Small said. "Probably from midnight until dawn, until about five o'clock. You'll take two hours and I'll have three."

"I can take three, Papa," said Thomas. "I'm strong. I can stay awake."

"I hope we won't have to do it," his father said. "If things continue to happen as fast as they have been, there may not be any need for a watch."

"Papa, do you think that in the next day or two . . ." Thomas couldn't finish the thought. He couldn't get beyond the idea of having to call the police. Who was Mr. Pluto anyway, and what did he have to do with those funny triangles?

"Before this day is over, I think we'll know a lot more than we do now," said Mr. Small. "And if we do have to set up a watch, you'll patrol the upstairs. No matter what happens, no matter what you hear or see, you're not to leave that upstairs hall. Just give out a whoop and I'll come running."

"Yes, sir," Thomas said. "I'll yell like the devil!"

Somewhere there was the sound of horses' hooves. There was a whinnying nearby.

Mr. Small went quickly across the lawn to where

the springs rushed down to the stream. Thomas followed close behind.

Thomas looked down on the stream and the springs running over the rocks. The stream sparkled in the morning sun, and the rocks were gold and rust where the water ran over them.

"Oh, that's about the prettiest sight I've seen," Thomas said.

"Look there," said Mr. Small. "You can see the spires of the college."

"You'll be teaching there," Thomas said, "and I can come on my bike every day."

"Would you do that?" asked Mr. Small. "We could have lunch together with the students in the dining hall." He looked fondly at Thomas. "That is, until you have so many friends you won't have time to take lunch with your father." He watched Thomas closely, for he knew his son would be most unsure of himself when it came to making new friends.

"Maybe I'll bring a friend or two along," said Thomas. "Maybe not every day because there'll be so much to do. But we'll come once a week for sure."

"I'll look forward to that," Mr. Small said.

Bursting from around a bend in the stream came a buggy drawn by two horses.

"Papa, look! It's the black—the black that was here yesterday!" There was a lighter horse hitched up with the black. It was the bay Mr. Small had mentioned before. "And Papa, Mr. Pluto's driving. And there's that child with him, that Pesty I told you about!"

The driver was indeed Mr. Pluto. He had a black cape draped over his shoulders. It was held with an enormous safety pin across his chest. The cape was old and misshapen; it appeared he had made it himself, out of material such as monk's cloth. Although it was clean, it looked the worse for wear. He wore on his head a stovepipe hat, which tipped crazily back and forth as the buggy bounced along.

Pluto drove with one hand, holding the reins wrapped around his palm. He held a black and shiny whip in the same hand. The lash dangled from the whip in a curious, sideways S. In the crook of his free arm leaned the child called Pesty. She was dressed in pink tulle and a blue, polka-dot bonnet. Below pink silk stockings she wore white, high-button shoes. There were the queerest shoes Thomas had ever seen.

"Where are his gloves?" whispered Mr. Small. "I thought surely he had burned himself . . . but look at the child. A bonnet no less! And high-button shoes. That stovepipe is a knockout. History, I tell you, living history! Out of time!"

"Papa, he sees us," said Thomas. "He's slowing."

At the sight of Mr. Small and Thomas, Pluto brought the buggy nearly to a stop.

"Good morning to you," he shouted, smiling broadly. "The bad weather has made its getaway, and I'm feeling good." He laughed loudly. "I see you all be going to Sunday, all dressed up."

"Good morning to you," Mr. Small said. He was somewhat taken aback by the friendliness of this odd-acting stranger of the night before. But quickly he fell into the spirit of Pluto's good humor. "We are going to Sunday for sure—all of us, even my two little boys."

"That so?" said Mr. Pluto. "It's a long spell for the little ones. Preacher likes the sound of his own voice." He laughed again.

"Well, they will endure it," said Mr. Small.

"I reckon we all will," Mr. Pluto said. "Glad to see you folks are fine," he added. "Did you have a good night—sleep well there in the big house?"

There was a pause in which Mr. Small studied Pluto without blinking. If the old man had meant anything sinister by the remark, there was no trace of it in his eyes.

"We slept fine," said Mr. Small. "Couldn't have been better."

"Well, we'll see you there," said Mr. Pluto. "Glad you folks arrived and are feeling good."

He had moved off with the buggy when the child Pesty piped up. "Mr. Thomas," she called, "how do you like my pretty new shoes?"

Thomas didn't know quite what to say. "They are nice, Miss Pesty . . . where did you get them?" he did manage to call back.

Mr. Pluto gave a whip to the bay. The buggy leaped forward, drowning out Pesty's tiny voice. But Thomas saw the shape of what she spoke.

"Mr. Pluto got them for me . . ." The last was something Thomas couldn't make out.

At the foot of the bridge, Mr. Pluto turned his buggy into the stream. On the opposite bank, he took with ease the incline to the gravel road and disappeared down toward the highway.

"If they aren't a pair!" said Mr. Small. "I bet they dress up like that every Sunday, just to get the goat of Sunday folks, the ones who believe Pluto is at least part devil. But what did he mean by the other, that's a puzzle too."

"By the other what?" Thomas wanted to know. Mr. Small had spoken almost to himself. Now he turned on Thomas a brooding look.

"Why, the part about being glad we folks arrived," said Mr. Small.

"I thought it sounded funny when he said it," Thomas said. "Maybe he was just apologizing for being so scared of the dark and ghosts and everything."

"Maybe," Mr. Small said. "Perhaps he was ashamed of himself for mistaking you for someone else in the dark. By the way, we never did find out why you were running in the first place. What happened out there to cause you to break open the door and upset Mama's dishes?"

Thomas felt ashamed. All around them was peace and quiet. Even the house did not look ugly in the clear sunlight. There was nothing at all to be afraid of now.

"It was spooky on top of the hill last night," he said. "I went up there to see the house from above. I was just going to come back, when it got dark and

I heard that ahhhing sound. Papa, it had a funny sighing that went right along with it. I just had to follow that sound and I was going fast because I was kind of scared. I got going too fast and I was standing on this big wood platform or something before I knew it."

"Oh, I see," said Mr. Small. "So that's what happened."

"Then the platform started to move," Thomas said. "I slid on it. Next there was fire coming up from under it, and Mr. Pluto yelling at me . . ."

Mr. Small threw back his head and laughed. "The ahhhing sound, you say, led you to the platform?"

"I guess it did," said Thomas. "It had to be coming from there . . . what's so funny?"

"And it was the same sound you heard in the tunnel under the steps?"

"Yes, the same sound," Thomas said. He looked doubtfully at his father.

"Thomas, I should have told you about that place before now, but I suspected you would enjoy discovering it for yourself. I never thought you would find it at night. You see," said Mr. Small, "that platform is one of the two openings in the cave in which Mr. Pluto lives."

"He lives in a real cave?" Thomas said.

"It's dry and clean," said Mr. Small. "It's as good a house as any above ground. It might even be better, because it stays fairly dry. I haven't seen it, but I've heard a good deal about it.

"Mr. Pluto is a blacksmith, son," continued Mr. Small. "At least, that's what he did for a living a long time ago, when there were enough horses in these parts to make his line of work worth doing. That ahhhing sound you heard along with the sighing couldn't have been anything more than his bellows working. I didn't hear it when I went to see if there was anyone in the tunnel under the steps. I suppose that's why I didn't guess before now what that sound was. Pluto must have heard you walking on the roof of his house. . . . Tell me, did you hear that sighing once the doors in the platform had opened?"

"I don't believe I heard it after that," Thomas said.

"That's it, then," said Mr. Small. "When Pluto heard you, he thought you were one of the town boys who like to fool with him. He climbed up out of that opening to scare the wits out of anyone out there, and he sure did."

"I see," Thomas said sheepishly. "But I still don't understand how that sound could've been in the trees and in the tunnel under the house too."

"That's not hard," said Mr. Small. "Air currents caused it. This whole place is crisscrossed with tunnels and caves. Sound might travel a long way on a current of air. Mr. Pluto's bellows is a huge thing that can produce a mighty draft of air and the sound to go with it."

"Just an old bellows," Thomas said glumly. They were hurrying back across the lawn toward the house. Mrs. Small was standing in the doorway waving to them to come even faster.

"We're going to be late if we sit down to breakfast," Mr. Small said.

"But I saw hoecakes, Papa, a mess of them!"

"So did I, Thomas," said Mr. Small. "So did I!" He began to run. Thomas sprinted along with him, letting out a whoop loud enough to be heard for a month of Sundays.

10

"It's the same," Thomas said. "I knew it would be. I knew it had to be the same." Standing in the vestibule, he felt so glad it hadn't changed.

He recalled a time not too long ago when he and his father had spent a quiet, talking week together, camping in the hills and pines back home. He could remember details of the nights and days of that week, how the woods had seemed smoky and close because there had been so little rain. When they were not hunting for their food, he and his father lay low under the pines, where the air was almost pure. Close to the ground, where the earth smelled so sweet, Thomas never wanted to let go of the fallen pine needles. His father had talked and talked. Later, when Thomas tried to recall what his father had said, he couldn't. But now it came to him in snatches.

". . . may I talk to you about it, son? Our African church? The Negro church! . . . I can yield to its separateness when I realize that without it segregated, there would be no story of the Underground Railroad. There could be no sure refuge for the exhausted, runaway slave."

"That's the past," Thomas had told him. "That's no reason for the way it is now."

". . . through part of history, behind time or ahead of its time, it always reveals men strong enough to lead us out of the trap of any time. 'Go Down, Moses' . . . the singing of that was once forbidden. Think of it! Then it was sung by a whole nation!"

"Who sings it today?" Thomas had said. "Nobody listens. Great-grandmother stopped going to church even before the last minister left us. It's all over, Papa."

"You can argue, Thomas, I don't blame you. You young get stifled by its lecture and runagate Jesus. I won't deny its narrowness . . . but do you remember the Sunday school?"

"I don't remember any of it."

"The boys and girls?"

"Oh, yes, I remember how we would laugh, how we would cut up when we got tired of the lecture. And, yes, I remember the ladies."

"Those ladies in white, who would always volunteer to teach you," his father had said. "They could talk so about Jesus, until he never *was* a man."

". . . and the moonlight picnics. I remember them, Papa. And the hayrides. Why did they have to stop? Where did they go to?"

"Yes, you remember, Thomas. That's all I mean. The church is our treasure, son, our own true chance. And we are all the luck it has."

Maybe so, thought Thomas. The far-off voice faded out of his mind. Maybe not. He stood calmly, waiting to enter the small and stifling church. "It sure does feel good to be here though. It sure feels like home."

Mac Darrow was seated at the piano, playing quiet chords as the church members entered. Thomas wasn't surprised at all on seeing him there at the piano. Maybe it was true what his father had said about remembering the church, for slowly he recalled there had been a boy about the manner and size of Mac Darrow a long time ago.

He came when the last preacher came, Thomas thought. Yes, he was the preacher's own boy. He had a big, new piano and he didn't like us little kids touching it. But we would sneak into the church and touch it, we loved it so. I remember, I did that. He caught me and he told Papa and he never spoke to me after that.

Why is it bad boys bigger than me always play the piano so well? Thomas wondered. Why can't they sit back and be content with being bad? And big?

Like Thomas, Mac Darrow wore a dark suit. It wasn't a new suit, Thomas could tell, but it was a good suit and quite all right for Sunday.

Darrow wore a black tie. He had on black shoes that had a hard, high gloss.

He doesn't look like the same boy, Thomas thought. No, not at all like that boy hanging onto the black's tail.

As though sensing some stir in the congregation, Mac Darrow turned away from the piano toward the vestibule. He didn't look at Mr. and Mrs. Small nor at the twins. He looked at Thomas, and his hands never stopped moving over the piano keys. There was a playful flicker in his eyes as he recognized Thomas. Next he looked almost afraid of something, but then, that, too, was gone.

That's all right, Thomas thought.

He accepted the fact that there were certain things you didn't do in church. Even the most comic boy wouldn't laugh or make fun of it. Even the worst boy would not set flame to it, as some white boys had done at home, when the last preacher and his son began holding night meetings. To his mind, making fun and setting flame were degrees of the same evil.

Mac Darrow's hands were soft and sure over the keys. He looked at Thomas and through Thomas all at the same moment. He saw Thomas, but denied him.

I'm like that, thought Thomas. When I'm carving something from wood, I'll all by myself too. Mac Darrow could be my friend if he wanted to be, even if he is big.

The congregation had turned around to see. Thomas had known they would do that. The church was more than two-thirds full, and folks had turned around to look at Thomas and his family standing in the vestibule. Mr. Small searched out a pew empty enough to hold them all and far enough away from the pulpit so as not to take seats from the regular members.

Thomas waited to see if all those looks would be not unkind. He wanted to find out if the boys sitting like a rook of hawks close to the exit would lift their faces with some comment.

Their eyes flicked innocently over at Mac Darrow, but Darrow kept his mind on the hymns at his fingertips. He would not tell them how to behave, his bowed head seemed to say.

So they know about me, Thomas thought. They know about the house and that M. C. Darrow was fooling with me. But do they know we had a visitor last night?

The boys couldn't keep their curiosity hidden. They looked at Thomas with half-concealed excitement; Thomas was pleased by it. He tried standing straighter. He made himself look at them coolly, keeping his mind as empty of emotion as he could.

The women of the congregation—those ladies in white who would forever keep faith with picnics and Sunday schools—smiled fondly on the twins. Thomas had known they would. It wouldn't be anytime before they were asking to hold the boys or to sit with them on a Saturday. But it was those folks between age and youth that worried Thomas most.

They'll want to know what Papa has to offer them and what he intends to take away. They'll wonder what he's doing coming to their small church, because they won't know that the Black church, large or small, is all the same to him.

And they'll want to know if Mama is going to be

just as regular as everyday or whether she will pretend she is too good for them. Mama is so pretty besides. She always will have the trouble.

The mothers and fathers of those boys sitting hawk-eyed and shrewd in the far corner stared at Mr. and Mrs. Small. Mr. Small nodded to them while going down the aisle. He had spied seats about halfway to the pulpit, but at an angle from it, near one of the squat, stained-glass windows. His nod was a polite greeting and a gentle probe to see if they would allow strangers among them.

Some folks nodded slightly. Others looked long and hard. Thomas and his family passed one pew where four big men were sitting. Something about them made Thomas check them in his mind. They looked alike, that was it, and they did not wear suit jackets. They were somewhat light of skin, with the burnt look on their necks and cheekbones that spoke of country and sun.

Farmers, Thomas thought. Maybe barn builders. Why are they here today, without their jackets?

They didn't look at Mr. and Mrs. Small nor at Thomas or the twins. Their faces feigned disinterest.

Thomas gave a silent whistle through his teeth. By the time he sat down in the pew Mr. Small had found for them, his hands were sweating.

Thomas sat next to his papa. The twins sat between Thomas and his mother. Save for Mac Darrow playing the piano, there had been almost a hush until Thomas and his family sat down. Now people were again talking in church; women were fanning themselves, for it was very warm. Thomas whispered nervously to his father.

"Did you see them, Papa? Did you see the four men?"

"Yes, I saw them," said Mr. Small. And understanding Thomas so well, he added, "Don't make too much of it. Don't let your imagination play with your sense."

"They wouldn't even look at us," said Thomas. "They were pretending we weren't even here!"

Mr. Small looked around. Folks were still staring at them while talking quietly. "That boy at the pinao," Mr. Small said to Thomas, "he must be of the same family as the four men."

Thomas couldn't believe he had heard right.

"He's got the same head and the same build," continued Mr. Small. "Yes, they are of a family, five of them. One of the four is the father."

"But that's Mac Darrow at the piano," Thomas whispered. "That's the boy with Pesty and the horse yesterday!"

Mr. Small had been taking in and gauging the feelings of the people around him. He had expected people to be standoffish at first. You could assume that of country people in the North, he told himself. He knew about their clannish history, which gave little room to strangers. But he hadn't expected folks to be as cold as they appeared to be today in church. When Thomas told him the boy at the piano was Mac

Darrow, he at once sensed a hostility in the crowd. A moment before, he had dismissed it as a product of his own frayed nerves.

Now the minister entered and walked to the pulpit. After him came the young people's choir, taking their position behind and to his right.

He was a short man, the minister. He was thin and not unpleasant-looking, Thomas thought. The choir looked nice in blue robes. They saw Thomas and his family right away and they stared with simple curiosity.

The church grew still. There was the sound of horses' hooves in the distance. A lazy breeze filtered through the open window to the Smalls' pew. It hardly touched Thomas before it died. The horses' hooves were closer, pounding forward.

Something buzzed in Thomas' head; he was watching the minister and the choir. The minister seemed to be waiting. Looking down at his Bible, he seemed to be listening.

The horses came to a halt at the side of the church.

A horse? Thomas thought. Horses? Here?

Not more than half a minute passed, while all remained still in the church. The elderly women in the front row seemed to fan themselves harder. People looked down at their hands or their hymnals, but no one spoke.

What's he waiting for? Thomas wondered, staring at the minister. Why doesn't the choir begin?

There were noises in the vestibule. Thomas

turned around, but no one else did, and he was embarrassed. The twins smiled up at him. They were settled and happy to be where they were, between Thomas and Mrs. Small. They were lulled into a pleasant frame of mind by the heat and stillness of this new place.

Down the aisle, past the Smalls in their pew, came Pesty in her outrageous pink-and-white costume and Mr. Pluto in his black cape and high hat. They made their way to the very first pew. Even though Thomas had known they were coming, he couldn't believe he was really seeing them.

Pluto seemed tired. Pesty led him along; his hand rested heavily on her shoulder.

There was a murmur, which ran from the back of the church forward. Folks around the Smalls' pew grunted to themselves angrily. The minister looked hard at them, and they quieted. He followed the progress of Mr. Pluto easing himself slowly into that first pew—the old ladies there had moved far over to make room for him and to avoid him at the same time.

They don't like him, but the minister says it's all right, Thomas thought. The minister is going to preach to the devil, and the folks don't like it one bit!

Pesty did not sit down. She went around the pulpit, all daintiness, gathered a robe folded on a chair and slipped the robe on. Then she took her place in the very front of the choir in the middle.

Why do they let her be in the choir—she's too small, Thomas thought.

"Two hundred eighty-five," the minister said. His voice was a startling, deep bass.

People stood up with opened hymnals. Thomas grabbed a hymnal from the basket attached to the seat back in front of him. He gave it to his father. Mrs. Small had taken another one for herself. They stood. The whole congregation was standing, except for the twins and old Mr. Pluto. Pluto was bent over in his seat. From the rear, he looked as though he might be sleeping. He appeared tired out, not at all the man of the night before or even this morning.

Mac Darrow played beautifully. Thomas recognized the hymn at once and smiled. He didn't have to look at the words. Neither did Mr. Small. They closed the hymnal, and then they knew why Pesty was in the choir.

It seemed to Thomas that Pesty's voice slid down from the ceiling, down the hot walls and into Mac Darrow's hands. It seemed to him that Mac Darrow's hands were inside the sound of the choir, holding on to Pesty's voice and then letting go of it when it became too strong for them. Her voice was like no other Thomas could remember hearing. It was pure and strong, not like a child's, and it was sweet and good, like a girl's.

"Over my head, I hear music in the air
Up above my head, I see trouble in the air."

The congregation joined Pesty and the choir in a surge of new strength:

"There must be a God somewhere!"

The hymn went on and on. The minister sang part of it alone, with the choir and congregation humming softly. It was enough to cause chills to run down Thomas' spine. The minister had a voice finer than Pesty's, better than any voice outside of the stage.

Mama is sure to come every Sunday, Thomas thought. She will say Preacher has a voice good enough to speak with the Lord.

Through it all, Mr. Pluto sat hunched over as though not listening. He didn't move the whole time.

Thomas only half realized when the song ended, there was so much to watch and remember. He found himself sitting down and shushing the twins. They wanted more music. He promised them if they'd be still, there might be more in a few minutes. The choir had sat down. Pesty looked like a big doll in her long robe. Her bonnet looked pretty and not out of place. She was serious and sweet, sitting there in the midst of the older boys and girls.

The minister spoke solemnly of a God somewhere. Thomas listened for awhile. He talked about the Christian need to search out an invisible God in all things.

"Go to the rock," the minister said. "Tell the sinner who hides his face on the rock that he need not.

No, he need not! Tell him that he is God. Say to him that the rock is God. Tell him to love himself and the rock and you, for God is with you. I say, inside of you there is God. Inside all of us, in all things, you will find God."

Thomas stared at the still form of Mr. Pluto. Mr. Pluto's head nodded, and his high hat rolled from his lap into the aisle. The minister paused. A man got up and gingerly returned the hat to Pluto. He did not smile at the still form nor touch it. The still form did not react as if anything out of the ordinary had occurred.

Is he sleeping there? Thomas wondered. Does Preacher mean to find God in old Pluto?

The minister droned on. Thomas stopped listening. He glanced out of the window. He could hear children playing somewhere down the street. They would be noisy until the church service was over, at which time they'd go home for dinner and more play.

Is that all they knew how to do?

Thomas felt a little tired. The excitement of the new church, the new minister, was wearing off. Somehow it was becoming confused with past Sundays in church. Irresistibly his eyes were starting to close.

"Four hundred seventy-one."

Thomas woke up with a start. He couldn't tell how much time had passed, but automatically he stood up.

Why is church always the same? Awhile ago, I was glad it was the same.

Sleepily he tried to appear interested.
But why must it be so slow and boring!

Preacher walk, Preacher talk
Preacher eat with a knife and a fork.

The rhyme came to Thomas out of some mean memory of a long morning.

I got a ticket to raffle
I got two tickets to sell
I got three pastors a-waiting
To preach down in hell.

Let the devil get ready
Tell the devil his fate
I got three pastors a-coming
To pass him the plate.

Pesty's voice quivered high above the choir,

"King Jesus lit the candle by the water side
So all the little children could be truly baptized . . ."

Mr. Pluto got on his knees in the aisle beside his pew. Thomas nearly choked. One of the ladies in the front row stared at Pluto with sheer malice. Mr. Small watched him with grave concern. There was an angry stirring in the congregation.

"Honor, honor, unto the dying day . . ."

One of those big men who must have been a brother to Mac Darrow came forward and tried, without touching him, to get old Pluto to get up.

"Darrow, sit down!" the preacher commanded.

"This isn't no Baptist place! Carrying on in the aisle," Darrow said. "We're Methodist here!"

"I said sit down! Mr. Pluto wants to kneel, let him kneel!" the minister said.

"So come along children and be baptized,
All the little children will be truly baptized,
Honor, honor, unto the dying day!"

When the hymn ended, the choir filed out. Pesty came forward and helped Mr. Pluto back into his seat. She squeezed in beside him and then watched the minister.

The minister was clearly upset. Thomas hoped he would forget his lecture and maybe preach around what had just happened. He didn't much care for old Mr. Pluto, but he decided he liked that Darrow man even less. Somehow he wanted the preacher to put the Darrow man in his place.

Instead, the minister turned to his Bible again. He grew calm and he read for a long time, hardly noticing the people looking out the windows.

Thomas looked up at his father. Mr. Small's face was bemused. Becoming aware of Thomas staring, he gently patted Thomas' knee.

All at once, Thomas felt totally let down. Everything had come to a standstill for some reason, he felt. All the hope of a new place—a new beginning and a new happiness—went out of him.

Nobody will come home with us. No one will laugh and talk with Papa. I won't have anyone to show my carvings to.

The church service was coming to an end. The collection plate was being passed around. They all stood to say the words that meant a parting.

"May the Lord watch between me and thee
While we are absent, one from another,
Amen!"

Mac Darrow disappeared through a rear door, the way the choir had gone, before Thomas had a chance to catch his eye. All those boys in the corner milled around their parents before they all filed out.

Thomas held one of the twins, while Mrs. Small held the other. The minister had not even welcomed them from the pulpit. Perhaps he had forgotten, Thomas thought.

But the ministser did come forward to shake hands with Mr. Small. He was Reverend Breckenridge, he told them, and he was pleased to have them come.

"You are a historian, I hear," he said to Mr. Small.

"Yes, I'll be working here for a time," said Mr. Small.

Folks were coming over to say a few words to their

minister. In doing so, they were introduced to Mr. and Mrs. Small and Thomas. There were Henrys and Davises; there were Harrises and Browns. But that was all. If any of them had the least curiosity about Mr. Small leasing the house of Dies Drear, he said nothing about it. The four big men, those Darrows, filed silently out without a word even to the minister.

"You have yourself a good slice of history in that big house," the minister was saying to Mr. Small. "I've always admired it. I don't have a family, however, and I can't say I would care to live in it alone." He smiled pleasantly.

A warning? Thomas wondered.

"We had a good turnout this Sunday," the minister went on. "I haven't seen some folks who were here today in quite awhile. Mr. Darrow and his sons I haven't seen in a few months, although the one son, McDonald, plays piano for me each Sunday. It always surprises me how good weather will bring folks out more than anything I have to say." He laughed, amused at himself.

Mr. Small watched him closely. "I don't believe I've met the Darrows you speak of. . . ."

"Oh, you will meet them. You will get to know everyone—we are a small community here. Folks are a little shy at first, but they are good-hearted people. Awfully glad to have you among us."

"Thank you so much," said Mr. Small.

"Good luck to you all, and I do hope to see you next Sunday," the minister said.

Mr. Small told him he would surely see them.

Outside some of the congregation were still gathered, talking with one another. As the Smalls emerged from the church, folks looked down at their feet or away to the street, as people will do when they are shy and cannot think of what to say. Mr. Pluto was just climbing into his buggy. He favored his lame leg considerably and fell heavily into his seat. Beside him was Pesty, and she smiled at Thomas. On seeing Mr. Small, Pluto touched his fingers to his high hat. His mind seemed to be on something other than passing the time of day with strangers. He went off the way he had come, with Pesty in the crook of his arms.

I'll not wave to them, Thomas thought to himself. I'll not wave at the devil, nor the devil's disciple!

Folks moved away, got into cars and went home. Mr. and Mrs. Small and Thomas, carrying the twins, walked slowly to their own car.

No one to come home with us, not even Pesty! No one to listen to Papa and hear about all the lives of history. What kind of place is this North anyway? What kind of no-account place!

11

Mr. Small decided they would combine lunch with dinner in the college dining room.

"It will be a Sunday treat for everyone," he said cheerfully. "Afterward, we'll still have time to find a locksmith."

He looked anxiously at Thomas. The boy wanted to meet young people, and there seemed to be no easy way to go about it. Thomas would need time to become adjusted; he would have to take things easy until the town had got used to them.

Mr. Small said nothing to Mrs. Small or to Thomas about the aloofness of the church members. He occupied them with talk about the college. Thomas forgot for a while the mystery of the new house.

Mrs. Small was interested first in walking the college campus and hearing about its century-old history. They made their way to the campus, and Thomas enjoyed walking under the great oak trees. The trees made the grounds dark with shade. Mrs. Small liked the stone benches placed over the whole all of the campus, for she could rest often and allow the twins to play in the grass.

"That's the main building," said Mr. Small, pointing

out the twin towers of the oldest college building. "All the business offices are there, and a few of the class- rooms. I have my office in the left tower—would you care to see it? You'll have to walk up. There are no elevators."

Mrs. Small declined to climb so many stairs. But Thomas wanted to find out what it was like to sit in a tower. He and Mr. Small climbed up and up. Finally they entered a corridor where Mr. Small opened one of the closed doors with a skeleton key.

"This will be a cool place in summer," he said to Thomas. "Ivy covers the windows, keeping moisture close. Not much sunlight can penetrate. But come the winter, I'll probably freeze here."

"Isn't there any heat?" Thomas asked. He had not much heart for talk. The climb up to the tower had tired him; he wanted no more than to go home to rest in his room.

"No heat that I know of," Mr. Small said.

"I thought colleges were supposed to be mod- ern," said Thomas. "I thought up North they'd at least be heated."

Mr. Small had to laugh. "Now don't blame the North for everything," he said. "This isn't your state university with new buildings, sleek offices and cen- tral heating. Why this is history, son. Many of the buildings are much the same as they were a century ago. And if you don't mind, I'll dispense with heat any day for some good atmosphere."

I wish history would just die, thought Thomas.

Why must Papa have it clutter up everything?

Mr. Small's office was not like any office Thomas had seen. It was like a watchtower, with garret windows and a musty smell. There were books piled everywhere, and bookcases lined the curved walls. An ancient desk by one narrow window had a small table on wheels next to it. Resting on the table was a typewriter that looked like an antique. The room was chilly, with a faint scent of cigar smoke.

"Nothing much ever changes in places like these," said Mr. Small. "Here there will be time to think, and time even to be bored."

"Papa, how is it you always know where to go so you don't ever have to change?" Thomas said glumly. He went behind the desk to see out of the windows.

Uncomfortably Mr. Small watched him, for Thomas had spoken in anger.

"I've had to adjust myself, too, to these new surroundings," Mr. Small said. He came quietly to the window. "It's not always easy at my age to begin life all over again in a strange place."

"Then why do it?" whispered Thomas. "Why bother when it's all the same anyway?"

Out of the window, Thomas could see clear to the other side of town. "There are farms way out there, Papa. Look at that big one over there. They are plowing, even on Sunday."

A haze hung over the town and farms. If he stared a long time, the town would get smaller and smaller and then would jump back again in focus. Thomas tried to make it stay in place, but it kept on moving farther away and then back again.

He rubbed his eyes. "It keeps jumping at me," he said. "The whole town just keeps jumping around!"

"That's because you don't have a point of view," Mr. Small said. "Pick out a landmark and it won't happen."

"No, it'll happen if I was to pick out a landmark. I don't want to . . . it just doesn't like me looking at it. It just doesn't want me!"

"Thomas, that's childish," Mr. Small said. "You're tired. Things have happened too fast. Just hold on to yourself. Give the town time."

"I don't care anything for it," Thomas said. "You can keep it!" He spoke bitterly, and Mr. Small saw that he was close to tears.

"What is it, Thomas? What have I done to make you so mad?"

"I'm tired of everything being always just the same," Thomas couldn't help saying. He felt a sudden relief, as though somewhere inside him he had let fly a rock. "Always colored churches! Always white churches somewhere hidden! Why is it folks never get together? We didn't have to leave home at all. We could've stayed with Great-grandmother and had the very same change. We wouldn't even have to go to church, because there isn't any church left to go to!"

"Oh, I see," said Mr. Small. He looked out over the town. "I do see. . . . But you can walk any part of that town down there and nobody will stop you. A few folks might look at you hard, but no one will be vicious with you. No one will call you names."

"How do you know?" asked Thomas. "As long as there are hidden churches, how can you be so sure?"

Mr. Small was silent. He knew this town. He knew that Thomas, his whole family, was safe in it.

But for how long? he wondered. And what about all the other towns, everywhere?

"You will have to try it," said Mr. Small. He knew what he said was not good enough. "You will have to walk it and see what happens." Nothing he could say would ever be good enough.

"Thomas, I wanted to take you to that church this morning because I thought it would be familiar. I thought it would be a good place to start to meet people and to make friends. You will have to give it time."

"Let's go eat now," Thomas said. "I'm hungry, I don't want to do anything but eat." He could not look at his father.

Thomas had turned from the window away from his father, when his eyes fell on something below one bookcase, where there was wood paneling. The thing glinted, and Thomas thought it no more than a pinpoint reflection when it jumped at him the way the town had seemed to. He sucked in his breath and stared. A cold fright passed over him.

"Papa," he said softy, "Papa, look there . . ."

Mr. Small looked and saw. He reached around Thomas for the object stuck in the wood.

"They are bold, aren't they, coming here like that through my locked door?" said Mr. Small.

"Another triangle!" Thomas said.

"And they knew we would come here," said Mr. Small. "They knew I would show you my office."

"They who, Papa?"

"Whoever knows what I'm going to do before I do it. Whoever it is that has figured out my moves as though we, all of us, were pieces in a game of chess!"

"They could've been watching us for a long time," Thomas said. "Anyone hanging around up here in these towers could see anybody coming or going almost forever. It wouldn't take an awful lot to jimmy that door."

"You're right, of course," said Mr. Small. "I let the atmosphere, this whole morning, carry me off a little. Probably they have watched us from the time we left church. They may be close by even now."

"I don't like them," Thomas said. "I don't like them at all!" But his spirits lifted. At least folks cared enough about them to try to warn them out of town.

"Let's look at the triangle," Mr. Small said. He held it in his left hand while taking from his pocket one of the three they had found in the house.

Moving the new triangle around, Mr. Small fitted it above the triangle he had taken from his pocket. Then he took from his pocket the last two triangles and fitted them to the first two.

"Papa, now we have all of it," Thomas said. "We

have all four triangles and it's a Greek cross! But what kind of warning . . . what kind?"

"What kind indeed," Mr. Small said. "A cross made from four interchangeable triangles."

"Do you think there is danger?" Thomas asked.

"I have no idea," said Mr. Small. "In any case, danger usually doesn't come in the light of day. We won't worry about danger until nightfall." His manner was confident, and this pleased Thomas.

Mr. Small spoke matter-of-factly to Thomas. "Let's eat now and then find a locksmith," he said. "I don't like leaving that house all by itself for too long."

They ate, speaking not of the triangles or of anything that had to do with crosses or church or the house of Dies Drear. They'd eaten in the large, college dining hall. The hall had screened-in porches at either end, and they sat at a big, round table on the porch. There had been a pitcher of ice water on every table; Thomas had poured water for them all, even the twins. The twins had high chairs to sit in. The waitress had brought the chairs. She even brought the twins wood dolls to play with, since the hall was crowded with Sunday diners, and there might be a long wait for food.

It was the first time Thomas had sat down in a private room such as this, where there were white families eating just like his family. No one seemed to pay much attention at all.

Thomas felt so good he couldn't speak. Mr. Small watched him anxiously, and Thomas grew shy. After awhile, he looked up at his father, giving him a big grin. Mr. Small cleared his throat, chuckled to himself, and studied the menu.

But they never found a locksmith. After a fine Sunday dinner of turkey with good dressing and gravy—Thomas had topped it off with Boston cream pie—they'd got into their car to begin the search.

"We'll go into the main part of town first," said Mr. Small. "See if anything is open."

They turned onto an avenue lined with trees. Xenia Avenue it was called. It extended from the college all the way through town.

"There's a library," said Thomas as they drove. He cradled the twins, one in each arm. They were tired now, hungry for the warmth of their bottles and their cribs.

"There's a drugstore and, look, a big church," Thomas said.

"That's the white Presbyterian church," said Mr. Small. "I know the pastor. He teaches a seminar on religion at the college."

"Can I go to that church sometime, Papa?" asked Thomas.

"You can go anytime you want," Mr. Small said. "We'll all go."

"Are Presbyterians like Methodists?" asked Thomas, eager to talk.

"They are okay," said Mrs. Small, "but they aren't quite as good as Methodists."

"Mama!" said Thomas.

Mr. Small laughed. "Your mother's a Methodist from way back, Thomas. You'll have to forgive it. She can't help it if she's prejudiced."

"I'm not prejudiced," said Mrs. Small. "I simply have good taste."

Mr. Small threw back his head and laughed.

"I just want to try it," said Thomas, looking at the enormous, granite church. "Just to see what it's like inside."

Mr. Small stopped at the drugstore to get a Sunday paper. He made Thomas stay in the car so the twins would not want to get out. Mrs. Small stayed in the car also. He came back with candy and news that there was no locksmith in the town. There *was* the hardware store, which sold locks, but it was closed on Sundays. You might try the filling station, the druggist had said. All the Carr boys, who owned it, were handy with all sorts of things.

"It's surely a small town," Mr. Small said. "I love the flat way folks say things — not unfriendly but just flat, like maybe they all walked in from northern Kentucky in one big bunch."

"Where is the filling station?" asked Thomas. "I don't see it."

"No, it's on Highway 68 near the high school, the druggist told me," Mr. Small said. "We'll have to go out there and talk to the Carr boys, whoever they are. Thomas, you'll get to see the high school, if it's that close by."

School, Thomas thought. I forgot all about it.

"Do I have to go to school tomorrow, Papa? Can I wait a few days until we get more settled?"

"They are still having Easter vacation here," Mr. Small said. "You have a few more days."

They drove a short distance out of town, away from the college on Highway 68. They passed a police station. To Thomas, it looked like a cramped chicken coop. There was one light-blue patrol car parked in front of it, with one policeman, who leaned against the car and looked sleepily across the highway. He checked their license plate as they passed and stared after them down the highway.

They found the filling station easily enough, for it was a large, well-attended and modern place. Mr. Small eased the car up close to the office. He didn't have to get out, for a big man came forward to see what he wanted.

"Afternoon," said Mr. Small. "Walter Small's the name—we've just moved here, in the old Drear place outside town. I need some locks and someone to install them. Can you help me out? Druggist said you might."

"I'm Carr," the man said. "The oldest boy. I have a few locks I can give you at a good price. Can't put them in until Monday though. All the boys is home with their families. Will that do . . . Monday?"

"Monday will have to do then," said Mr. Small. "Monday early morning, if it's all the same to you."

"All the same by me," said the man. "You have

some vandalism out there?" he wanted to know. He was curious about them. His broad, white face was serious and intent on them.

"No," said Mr. Small. "No, nothing like that. My son didn't realize the kitchen door was locked when he stormed through it. While I'm at it, I thought I might as well change a few other locks."

"You intend to stay awhile then?" the man said. "The place has been empty for such a long time . . . I mean except for the old one called Pluto."

Mr. Small was cautious. He didn't want to tell the man too much. News spread like wildfire in a town such as this one. At the same time, he didn't want to give the impression he was hiding anything.

When he did speak, his manner was casual. "I'll be teaching at the college," he said. "We wanted space for the children. I thought I might do some farming on the side."

The man seemed to become more friendly. "You picked yourself a good piece of land for farming," Carr said. "Along that stream, the soil is rich as can be. I know, because the same stream meanders onto my father's land. Do you know his farm?"

Mr. Small said he didn't.

Carr continued. "Well, you can recognize it by the catalpa trees. There's a whole woods of them. Lots of berry patches in between them. Kids like to pick the berries. Get a good price for them, too, these days." He smiled at Thomas. "I know, I picked the same bushes when I was a boy."

"That right?" said Mr. Small. He started up the car, hoping to ease away without appearing impolite.

"Oh sure," said the man. "Kids love playing there in the trees. My father, he's old now, and he never did mind them, except for the Darrow boys."

Mr. Small switched off the ignition. Thomas leaned forward.

"Darrow, did you say?" Mr. Small said. He tried to appear only slightly interested.

"Do you know them?" asked Carr. "They have the closest spread to my father's. They're all around you out there. Mean ones, sometimes. Use' to bother that other old man—Pluto he's called. That Pluto and my father were young about the same time. My father, he was born in a log cabin in this town. But Pluto, he come here as a boy from somewheres. Seems to me I heard something about there being bad blood between the old man Darrow, the grandfather, and Pluto when they was young." Carr looked pleasantly at Mr. Small, pleased to talk on this slow Sunday. What he had to say appeared innocent enough. Of course, you never could tell about strangers, Thomas thought.

"The grandfather still living?" asked Mr. Small. He took out his handkerchief and wiped perspiration from his neck, then folded it neatly and returned it to his breast pocket. The gesture was slow and easy, giving the impression that he was tired and willing to sit a moment and talk.

"Oh no, indeed," Carr said. "He's been gone now,

oh, seven, eight, maybe ten years. But he was a mean one. I know, I use' to play with one of the older boys. Old Wilbur Darrow. Haven't seen him in a couple of months though. They can stay out on that farm of theirs for six months at a time without folks seeing them. Always digging up trees and putting them back. When the grandpaw was living—he was River Swift Darrow—they moved the whole house a few feet to one side, looked around under it for about a week and then moved it back again where it was in the first place." He chuckled to himself, looking off down the highway.

"Sure, me and Wilbur Darrow were all right. The father, he was River Lewis, didn't seem to mind me. But the old grandpaw didn't like it. No sir, he didn't like me hanging around one bit. He'd come tearing out of that house calling me all kinds of rednecks. Now you know that can't be right. My family, we was always the same with everybody. We played no favorites and saw no difference."

"That's the best way," said Mr. Small.

"That's the truth, as I see it," said Carr. "No, they don't like folks hanging around. Real secret they are. Always have been. They have a boy about your son's age. He doesn't seem to be as tough and sour as the rest. Maybe they're changing." He chuckled again. "Better watch 'em though. They got something in for that Pluto." Carr's eyes flicked away from Mr. Small's. "They're close by you, and I give you honest warning."

"Thank you kindly," said Mr. Small. He started the car.

"Got plenty good tires here anytime you need them," Carr said. "Plenty of good gas."

"I'll be coming back soon," said Mr. Small. Without effort, he imitated the flat, hill speech of the man.

"My young brothers like as not can fix most any busted thing. You let me know. They paint houses real well, folks say. We got a few tractors for plowing. The price of a field ain't high either."

"I'll be calling again," said Mr. Small as he drove out of the filling station.

12

"Well then," said Mr. Small, "we know a little more than we did an hour ago." He headed the car back toward town, the way they had come.

"Carr people, Darrow people," Mrs. Small said, "I wonder what Mr. Pluto's family name is."

"Skinner," said Mr. Small.

"Who? How do you know that?" asked Thomas.

"I found out from the foundation, the first trip I made here—didn't I tell you?" Mr. Small said. "They told me his name is Henry Skinner."

"But is he the only Skinner?" Mrs. Small wanted to know. "Does he have family here?"

"I never thought to ask," said Mr. Small. "I suspect the Carr man would have said something if Pluto had family here."

"You could find out," Thomas said. "You could go to the county seat maybe. They keep records."

"I don't care to find out," Mr. Small said. "Besides, Carr said Pluto came from somewhere else as a boy."

"And that there was bad blood between the old grandfather Darrow and him. I wonder why," Thomas said.

"Time may tell," Mr. Small said. "Let's take things easy and wait awhile."

"Look," said Mrs. Small. "Look there, isn't that a school?" There was a drive off Highway 68 leading into an expanse of land, on which sat a sprawling, ivy-covered school. Mr. Small drove down.

"Oh, that's a pretty school!" said Thomas. It was called Washington Junior High and High School. It had a smooth lawn and a large playing field. To the right of it was a wide stream called the Little Miami River.

"Miami!" Thomas said. "That's in Florida."

"This whole area, both the town and country, is known as the Miami Valley," Mr. Small told him. "Some comical folks like to call it the Sinus Valley because it has so much rain and snow."

"Boy, I bet there will be lots of sledding," said Thomas. "I'm going to get me a big sled and whomp down every hill."

Mr. Small turned the car around and went back to the highway.

"I want to see the rest of it," said Thomas. "Please, Papa, I want to see the whole town."

The twins were quiet, almost asleep. Mrs. Small said they could drive around for awhile.

Mr. Small chose a street at random. On one side of the street was a white house the size of a mansion, with black trim. There was a huge lawn full of trees; there were swings and slides on both sides of the house.

"That's the grade school," said Mr. Small.

"What a lovely place for children to play," said Mrs. Small.

Thomas could see paper cutouts of Easter rabbits in many of the school's windows. He felt happy. Everything seemed normal again. He didn't even feel very tired. He looked at all there was to see and kept on feeling so good, he thought he would burst.

It was a pretty town. People lived in nice houses, large and small. Some of the houses were quite old. but well taken care of. They passed through what looked like a new section of town. Outside playing were many children still dressed in their Sunday clothes. Some houses had swings and slides in their backyards. Thomas thought they must be kindergartens, but, no, Mr. Small said, they were homes. People could afford good playthings for their children, he said. People made good money.

Thomas saw homes side by side where white and colored children played on the lawns together. And he saw houses on streets where you couldn't tell what kind of people might live in them.

They turned onto a back road leading through farmland. They traveled the road for some time. There were many barns with cows. There were fenced-in areas with hogpens and hog houses. Fields were plowed. Large pools of water stood like silver ponds along fence lines. The sun made them sparkle. The gentle wind made shallow waves over their surfaces. The air was so pure, Thomas could have laughed out loud. He poked his head out of the window, letting his face brush the leaves of trees by the road.

You could live here forever, he thought. Forever and forever. You could get a bicycle and let all kinds of dogs chase after you down these roads.

Soon they found themselves on the divided highway that passed by the house of Dies Drear.

"Time to get home," said Mr. Small. He looked at his watch. "Why, it's almost five-thirty! We've been fooling around almost the whole afternoon."

"I want to get to my room," Thomas said. "I want to take off these shoes and unpack my school clothes. I've got to register for school next week, don't I, Papa? I've got to get me my school supplies."

"I'll need to buy curtain material," Mrs. Small said to no one in particular. "Goodness, I'll need a lot of it for all those high windows."

"Buy. Buy," said Mr. Small. "All you think about is buying. Wait until I see some salary before you two start to buy."

"You're always crying 'dollar poor,'" said Mrs. Small to him. "I know how much is in the bank."

"But you don't know which bank," said Mr. Small smiling. "I bet you don't know that."

"I do," said Thomas. "I saw the bank book on your dresser. The Miami Savings and Loan Bank, that's the name!"

"You're supposed to be on my side," Mr. Small told him.

"I have to get my school supplies," Thomas said. "I've got to be on Mama's side!"

Mr. Small turned the car onto the road leading up to the house of Dies Drear. The road had dried somewhat from the sun; in another day, it would be completely dried out. The sun lay above the trees on top of the hill behind the house. The sky was almost clear blue, with only the slightest sign of night in it.

They grew quiet in the car. The twins were sleeping.

"Poor dears," Mrs. Small said. "They can't imagine what's happening to them."

They crossed over the bridge. Almost at once, Thomas felt their isolation from all things ordinary. They were so cut off from the highway, from the town, from all life that was normal, they might as well have been locked in a closet. The dark and silent house looming over them had already reached out for them and was pulling them in.

Thomas could feel it turning him cold all over.

You've got to fight back at it, he told himself. You've just got to keep being warm inside and not let it get through you.

Like intruders, they went silently into the house. The house seemed to listen to their uncertain tread. It seemed to watch them, pressing close as if trying to overhear. But they were silent. Thomas and Mrs. Small tiptoed upstairs with the twins. The nightlight still burned in their room.

"Just take off their coats," whispered Mrs. Small, "and their stockings and shoes."

"These are their Sunday clothes, Mama!" Thomas whispered back.

"Do as I say," said Mrs. Small. "I don't want to disturb them by taking clothes off and putting clothes on."

Thomas did as he was told, although he didn't like it one bit.

Babies shouldn't have to go to bed in their Sunday suits, he thought. It's like they're ready to run away in case something bad happens—like they didn't belong here. This old house thinks it's going to get them—it thinks it's got us all on the run. I'll be patrolling this hall tonight. No sir, this old house will be sorry if it tries to scare my babies!

One of the twins whimpered in his sleep and shivered as with a chill. Quickly Thomas leaned over him. He covered Buster, putting his arm around him. Thomas stayed close until the child breathed silently, until the bedding was warm. Then he and Mrs. Small left the room, tiptoeing down the hall and down the stairs. They had looked from one closed door to the other going down the hall. They were on their guard.

Mr. Small stood in the doorway of the kitchen. The way he stood, so still there, caused Thomas and Mrs. Small to come quickly. He let Thomas through, but tried to bar Mrs. Small's way.

"You let me through," she told him. "Let me by."

"Don't look," Mr. Small said. "Please, let Thomas and me . . ." But Mrs. Small pushed by him. What she saw caused her to cover her face with her hands. A choked cry came from deep inside her. But that was all. She stood there without saying a word, with her eyes tight closed and her hands covering them.

Nothing Thomas could imagine, not all the devilment of strangers, of bad boys older and more daring than himself, could have prepared him for the sight of the kitchen. Looking at it, he was overcome with dread and loneliness. He reached out for his mother and put his arm around her. Mrs. Small swayed and leaned against Thomas.

The large sack of flour Mr. Pluto had bought for them had been emptied over the entire kitchen floor. It had been spread evenly in a layer, and over the layer had been poured water and apple juice. The whole mess had been mixed into a sticky, brown paste, which was spread over the kitchen table, over the stove and sink counters, over all the chairs and over part of the walls. The door of the Frigidaire hung open, and all the food there had been removed. Whatever could be squeezed had been squeezed onto the floor. What could be poured had been poured out in swirls on the floor. What dishes had remained after Thomas' fall of the night before were broken in the sink with the same sticky paste covering them. The whole room, the windows, everything, glistened with this unspeakable icing. Over it all was a warm odor of rotting food. The only canned goods that had not been punctured and emptied into the sink were the cans of evaporated milk used for the babies' bottles.

Thomas let go of his mother and took a step into the room.

"No," said Mr. Small, "leave it be." His voice was low, with an edge to it rough as jagged rock. Thomas didn't have to turn around to know what his face looked like.

"They mean to make us run with this," Mr. Small said. "They thought to terrify you so," he said to Mrs. Small, "that there would be nothing for us to do but run!"

"Oh, Walter," Mrs. Small whispered, "we could move into town. We would be safe . . ."

"Is that all we're made of?" he said. "Are we to let fools run us out of this historic house, our home? We're better than that, oh yes! Whoever thought to make us run doesn't know what we are made of!"

"Thomas," he said, "you come with me. Martha, you go up with the twins. Make bottles for them. Turn on the light up there if you want. Lock yourself in with them, but stay there until we get back. I'm going to get to the bottom of this right now. And before this night is done, somebody, some fool, is going to catch it!"

Mr. Small and Thomas saw her to the room. They made her lock the door from the inside before they left her. They had given her a small table lamp, which would give her light to see the whole room without disturbing the twins.

"All right now?" Mr. Small called through the door.

"Yes," she said whispering. "Yes, you can go."

"We're going. Don't be afraid. I don't think they will come back."

"Oh, I'm sure of that," she whispered.

She heard them leave. She wasn't sure of anything. But she took a deep breath and smoothed her hair behind her ears.

"All right, ghosts," she whispered, "come right on in! If you can work over my kitchen, I can surely work over your head!" She sat down to wait, with Thomas' baseball bat resting delicately across her knees.

13

Behind the house, Mr. Small slipped through the trees on the hill, much the same way Thomas had the night before. Darkness had fallen; there was no moon, nor any starlight to speak of. Instead of going up and over the hill as Thomas would have, he went around it from left to right. He moved swiftly, making hardly a sound. Thomas followed him closely. He couldn't see his father, but he could sense his movement through the stillness; he could feel the boughs settle back after his father passed.

We are Tuscaroras. He is my chief and I am his brave son.

Thomas had these thoughts and at once felt foolish for having them. Here they were about to fight off whoever it was had come to destroy Mama's kitchen, and all he could do was imagine he was an Indian brave.

"Thomas, are you with me?" Mr. Small called softly.

"I'm right behind," Thomas answered. "Keep going."

"Wait. Shhh!" Mr. Small had stopped. Thomas came up to him, not even panting, although it was tiring keeping up with his father and walking silently at the same time. But he stood still and straight; he was invisible there in the dark, as was his father. Relaxed in the manner of the sprinter, his muscles were attuned for action.

Thomas listened. Always he had found it strange that sound could become caught within the random growth of trees. He could hear a truck on the highway. If he were standing on the veranda of the house, he might not hear it. When the truck sound disappeared, he listened again. Trapped there in the trees was the sound of someone walking. It was a soft sound of feet going back and forth and around, back and forth and around.

Whoever it was walking was not in the trees with them. The bed of pine needles would have deadened the footsteps. The sound was ahead of them and not at all muffled.

Is there an opening in these trees? Thomas wondered. An open place where they can ambush us?

Mr. Small had started again.

Thomas knew where to follow. Moving blindly, he would suddenly have the sensation that his father had left behind part of his spirit like a handprint in the air. Thomas would stumble upon this unsettled space and would know his father had passed there.

He had no idea where they were headed; he'd never been around the hill the way they went. He assumed his father had some plan and he hadn't thought to question what it might be.

They went down into what must have been a dried-up gully and then back up the other side. They went over a hillock that had a barren outcropping like a bridge. Covered with wet moss and fern, it was quite slippery. Once Thomas fell. There in the dark, he had the feeling he might slide forever.

Will they ambush us here?

When he scrambled to his feet again, they were back on the hill, with trees all around. A pale-yellow glow outlined pine boughs and tree trunks. It was enough light for Thomas to see the shape of his father a few paces in front of him. Mr. Small stopped again. This time he raised his arm motioning Thomas to stand where he was.

Thomas' muscles jumped and jerked beneath his skin. He was wet with the slime of moss and with his own perspiration. It was almost impossible for him to stand still, so ready was he for whatever lay before them.

If they ambush us, I'll swing up into the trees and jump down on them. I can do that a couple of times before they realize there are only two of us.

Then Mr. Small and Thomas were moving. They had walked a short distance when, without warning, the pale glow grew bright. The dense covering of trees gave way suddenly. They were indeed in open space.

They found themselves at the edge of a natural clearing and blinded momentarily by bright light.

There lay before them a bed of flat rock, rectangular in shape, at the end of which was a cave. The cave mouth had heavy, plank doors. On either side of them were sconces, which held burning torches. The torches flared violently, sending smoke and a yellow glow up into the surrounding trees.

In the midst of it, pacing back and forth like a falcon tired of his perch, was Mr. Pluto. He seemed in thought, and wasn't aware of them watching. He rubbed the back of his neck with one hand; the other was hooked in his belt.

Thomas couldn't quite believe he was seeing Pluto, the cave and those eerie torches, he had so prepared himself for danger and ambush. And something else, Thomas thought. The whole scene was suited for another place and time. Mr. Pluto should have fitted right in, like a bearded pirate perhaps, left in the wilderness by his fellow scoundrels. He should have been a part of these surroundings, Thomas thought. Only he wasn't.

Thomas couldn't quite catch on to what was wrong, but there was something about Pluto that kept jarring Thomas' mind.

Mr. Small started around the clearing toward Pluto.

"Mr. Pluto?" he called. "Pluto? I want a word with you!"

Pluto swung around, taking in the whole of the clearing. He must have seen Thomas and Mr. Small coming at him. His own face was in shadow caused by the torches above his head. But the rest of him was clearly visible. He looked massive, powerful, in the yellow light. Every inch of him recoiled in surprise. Still recoiling, he shrank toward the cave.

"Wait!" said Mr. Small. "You wait!"

But Pluto was gone. It wasn't possible a man his age and size could move so quickly, and yet he had. Like fluid pouring itself away, he was gone, leaving only the gaping doorway.

Thomas remembered the night before, and the way Pluto had lifted him off the ground. Again he thought what he had thought then: No old man anywhere, lame or not, could catch him from behind, let alone swing him off the ground.

Then Thomas was on to something. He didn't know what, but he knew what had been wrong with Pluto's pacing back and forth a moment ago.

"Papa, he wasn't sick at all. He was strong, did you see it? Papa, he was smoking . . . he had a cigarette!"

"I saw," said Mr. Small. His voice had that hard edge, the way it had when he had seen the mess in the kitchen. "And he wore new hide gloves like the first time. You bet I saw!"

Mr. Small tore one of the torches from its sconce and thrust it in the opening to the cave. He went inside, and Thomas followed. They were in a tunnel similar to the one under the house of Dies Drear. It ended some thirty feet ahead, in what appeared to be a room. Mr. Small threw the torch out of the door, since the room ahead of them was lit. They went cautiously forward. And once inside the room, they stood against the wall next to the tunnel, looking all around.

"This is where he lives," Mr. Small said. "I've never been inside it, but there's his forge. And over there must be where he sleeps. The other tunnel entrance to the right must lead to the place where he keeps his horses. I do remember, he mentioned to me that there was an inner tunnel leading from this main room."

The cave was perhaps twenty-five feet wide and thirty feet long. The ceiling of rough and jagged stone was fifteen feet high. Thomas hadn't ever seen anything like it. One portion of the room was carpeted, with a large, worn armchair and a table for eating. There were photographs on the wall nearest to the table, and many yellowed calendars. On the other side of the room was a simple, brass bed. There was a pair of slippers placed neatly beside the bed, and flung across it was a robe.

What light there was in the room came from Mr. Pluto's forge. There was a fire burning, and his bellows rested on a tree stump next to the forge.

This was the first bellows Thomas had seen. He stared at it for a long time. He had known it would be large, but he had no idea it was such an awesome, strange instrument. A mighty bellows it was, old as an old man and tough and weathered as old Pluto himself had to be.

"Where the devil is he?" Mr. Small said. "He

didn't come out the way we came in . . . so that leaves just two ways he could have gone."

Mr. Small crossed the room. There against the far wall was a ladder. Above the ladder in the ceiling, Thomas noticed for the first time, were two wood doors.

"Papa! Look!" Thomas said.

"Yes, I know," said Mr. Small. "On the other side of those doors is the platform you stumbled upon last night. It's a trap, you see. He built that platform just so he would know when folks were approaching. You always run into it before you expect to, even when you know where it is. That's why I came around the hill, so as not to be found out before I was ready."

Mr. Small climbed part way up the ladder. The doors were locked from the inside. "He didn't leave from up here."

"How about the tunnel leading to the horses?" Thomas said.

"You stay here," said Mr. Small, coming down the ladder. "If I find him, I'll bring him back with me."

He left the main cave and was back again in a minute without Mr. Pluto. "Looks like he has vanished into thin air," he said. "Maybe he is the devil, like you thought."

Thomas' father stood by the forge, with his hands deep in his pockets. Thomas knew he hadn't been serious about old Pluto being the devil. But where *was* Pluto? And what did he mean by running away from them?

"So there's another way," Mr. Small said. "There has to be another way out."

"A secret way?" Thomas wanted to know.

"At least one he never let on to me about," Mr. Small said.

Thomas walked around the room. In back of the table in the corner was a woodburning cooking stove. The stovepipe went through a metal plate attached to the wall above the stove. There was more than likely a natural opening to the surface ground, Thomas decided, that would allow the smoke to escape. He put his hand gingerly on one round, iron cooking unit in the stove. It was cold. There was no fire at all.

"We'll wait for him," Mr. Small said. "He has to come back. This is his home."

Thomas walked around and around. He let into his mind everything he saw in the room. He didn't touch anything there, but he saw all there was to see, and closing his eyes, he remembered where most things were placed. Then, he stood still in the room.

That's not it, he thought. You can hide something pretty well by putting an object in front of it. You have to know what you're doing though. Most of the time, you'll just attract attention. The best way is to leave it out in the open. Leave what?

He spun around the room, taking in the bare part of the floor, that space between the table and bed. He scanned the walls where the calendars and photographs left off. On the wall opposite, there were many harnesses, many lengths of rope, and some chain. There were clothing hooks. And on the wall nearest to the entrance, there were cooking utensils by the stove; below that Thomas saw a pile of firewood.

On the far wall, above which were the trapdoors in the ceiling, there was nothing save that ladder. And one, single length of rope almost hidden by shadow in the corner.

"Papa . . ." Thomas started across the room.

Mr. Small had no intention of waiting all night for Pluto. He remembered his wife alone, locked in the big house. His anger came back, flowing into him cool as night air. He'd been looking the room over all the time. He had just come to focus on that blank wall, just as Thomas had.

They both started toward the rope at the same time. It hung from a hook of some kind. Indeed, it was looped somehow, loosely, around an old clothes hook. Mr. Small moved the ladder over to it and climbed up, so that his eye was on a level with the hook. Just above the hook was a smooth hole. Mr. Small saw that the rope came out of the hole. And looped around the hook, it hid the hole entirely. You wouldn't see it unless you had a chance to stand, as Mr. Small was now, looking sideways at it.

"This is it, Thomas," Mr. Small said. Carefully he climbed down the ladder and returned it to its position against the wall. He then took hold of the rope. Slowly he pulled down and down, like a bell rope. When he let go of it, it returned to its former position.

Between the ladder and the rope, the wall began to slide. Thomas heard a grating sound. It wasn't loud, but it was unpleasant, the way the sound of rock rubbing against rock can be. When it stopped, after a moment, that wall had slid back completely. And what now lay before them was far beyond dream, or even nightmare.

Mr. Small took hold of Thomas' arm. No matter how hard Thomas tried to pull away, his father held onto him and dragged him down.

"Lord!" Mr. Small whispered. "My Lord in heaven, look at that! Look at it! *Look* at it!"

14

They had to walk down into it. Considering that they were underground to begin with, they had to walk down into it from an unbelievable height. They had to walk down a wet, slippery ramp of chalk-white limestone, with enormous stalactites hanging just above their heads.

Mr. Small had to drag his son along. Thomas gaped at the stalactites, fearful that one might fall on him. He was terrified of the stalagmites that they had to walk through. He kept jumping away from them as though they were creatures from another world.

"You've seen them before, Thomas," Mr. Small said. "Get hold of yourself!"

All Thomas could think about was a fragmentary bit of information from an earth-studies class, which he had somehow filed away in his mind: *Stalagmite: a calcium carbonate deposit shaped like an icicle and formed by the dripping of percolating calcareous water . . . Stalagmite: dripping of percolating calcareous . . .*

But he could not connect the phrases with the monstrous forms around him. They stood like sentinels guarding what had to be one of the most stupendous caverns anyone had ever seen.

Only no one had ever seen it, thought Mr. Small. No one besides himself and Thomas, and Mr. Pluto and Pesty, who sat down there watching them come, waiting for them to get there and to get on with it.

They took their time, Thomas and Mr. Small. The knowledge that all of it had remained down there for a century or more was almost more than Mr. Small's mind could take at one time. So it was that he literally carried Thomas forward while, at the same time, trying to hold himself back.

Once they had cleared the stalactites and stalagmites, Thomas and Mr. Small were well into the cavern. But they still had to go down. They had reached a place much like a rampart arch in a staircase. They could stand almost level; the limestone beneath their feet was completely dry. But they still had more of the ramp to walk to reach where Pluto sat, behind a massively constructed desk.

It's Renaissance, Mr. Small thought, staring at the desk. The desk was dark, and elaborately veneered with fine woods. And it was decorated with the usual metal ornamentation of the period, although this decoration was far superior to anything Mr. Small had ever seen in a museum.

It has to be French Renaissance. Where the devil did old man Drear get hold of such an incredible work?

Mr. Pluto sat behind the desk with his profile toward them. He had propped one elbow on the desk with the hand under his chin and the index finger extended to his cheek. A brown woolen throw covered his shoulders like a cloak of gloom. It wasn't so much that he watched Mr. Small and Thomas come slowly forward, it was more that he listened and dreaded for them to come.

There is no war, Thomas thought. Mr. Pluto is the king!

The Lord of the Underworld! thought Mr. Small. This is a dream, I tell you. It has to be!

But it was no dream. Where the ramp became dry, the cavern grew warm. Mr. Small and Thomas felt it at once, and it was a dry heat.

A uniform temperature, thought Mr. Small. A heat coming from the depths of the earth. Just warm enough, dry enough for all this . . . this . . . wealth to maintain itself. It's unbelievable!

At the end of the ramp, Mr. Small and Thomas were in the midst of the cavern. Barrel-shaped, the cavern rolled up and up over them into an immense, vaulted ceiling. Hanging on all sides were tapestries and Persian carpets reaching almost to the floor. There were row upon row of them, with colors that leaped and glowed in the light of torches grouped in the center of the cavern.

Mr. Small recognized in the carpets a color massing and texture, and particularly fine dye tones that one could find only in museums. He could believe easily enough that an eccentric man such as Dies Drear had to have been would possess them. What was astounding was that because of the constant climate in the cavern they were close to their original colors and textures.

But why did he have them here? wondered Mr. Small fleetingly. A source of sure and easy money?

Whatever the reason, Dies Drear had amassed and saved what was perhaps as fine and complete a collection of decorative art to be seen anywhere.

And that wasn't all. Between the rows of hanging carpets and tapestries were whole canoes, a few as long as forty feet, and whole, richly painted, beautifully crafted totem poles. Interspersed among these were carved and painted wood chests. They were Indian also. They had to be, Mr. Small thought. And piled atop them were blankets with similar designs.

He wondered what Indian people had painstakingly crafted such work. He didn't recognize any of it, although its value was obvious.

There were barrels upon barrels of silks and embroidered materials, which burst from the barrels and spilled out onto the floor. Mr. Small noticed some jewelry, pairs of shoes, watches, and chains of gold.

And there was more. One section of one huge wall was covered with glassware. Thomas stared it. It was like a prism, for the glass came in colors ranging from aqua to deep brown and nearly black.

Thomas stood there next to Mr. Small at the end of the ramp, trembling all over. From the time they passed through the stalagmites, he realized they had discovered a place of great importance. Like his father, he had guessed rightly that they had stumbled upon the treasure house of Dies Drear.

The carpeting and tapestries were finer than anything Thomas could have imagined. They were hung very high up from oak cylinders, which had been polished a smooth, pale white. The cylinders were hung on chains, which were suspended from hooks sunk into the vaulted ceiling. The rugs and tapestries were of varying lengths and sizes, and they divided the cavern into corridors of rich hues. In one shadowy depth of the cavern, Thomas noticed for a moment an enormous chain with links the width of three fingers. Some of the chain was wound around a winch, which had a lever attached to it. The rest of the chain rose up between tapestries to disappear in the murky darkness. With so much else to take in all at once, Thomas forgot all about it.

It was the glass that he couldn't take his eyes off.

"There must be a million bottles," he whispered to his father. His voice made echoing sounds, like many praying voices in a cathedral. He had to knot his hands at his sides to keep his arms from jerking convulsively. "Look at all the dishes and bowls and things. Why aren't they dusty? Look how they glow!"

It was true, the glass shone and sparkled.

"Some of it is as old as time!" whispered Mr. Small. "See how misshapen some of it is. Probably the earliest hand-blown glass you'll see anywhere."

Pesty, who all this time had been sitting on the arm of Mr. Pluto's great, carved chair, now rose and walked toward the ledges of glass. Suddenly there were hundreds of Pestys reflected in the glass. The sight of Pesty so perfectly reflected in so many different colors and shapes made Thomas dizzy.

There was a sliding ladder. Pesty hooked it into a groove on the wall above the glass. By climbing the ladder and pushing herself against a ledge, she could maneuver anywhere she wanted along the rows of glass. She demonstrated this for them now. She had taken up a cloth, and, ever so carefully, began to polish one thin-necked bottle.

Be careful! thought Mr. Small. Break that and you have smashed hundreds of dollars, you have let a part of history die.

No need for Mr. Small to worry. No curator anywhere could have handled the old and valuable glass with such delicate care. She looked over her shoulder at Thomas and smiled proudly at him.

"Mr. Thomas," she said. "This is my job to do." Then she placed the bottle back and came down the ladder. She took her position beside Mr. Pluto again. He had turned around to the desk to face Thomas and Mr. Small.

For the first time, Mr. Small was aware of the books in great glass-doored cases to one side of the desk. Some, oblong and yellowed, lay on the desk. Old Pluto had folded his hands lightly on top of them. Mr. Small stared at them, his eyes feverish with wonder, for he understood what they were. He stared at Pluto and then again at the ledgers; and he thanked the Lord that this old man, like Dies Drear before him and like himself, too, was a keeper of history.

Gently Mr. Pluto drew one of the ledgers close to him.

"An accounting," he said softly, his voice no better than a cry. He looked worn out—too tired, Thomas thought, to have had strength enough to mess up his Mama's kitchen.

"The day by day barter of black people," said Pluto. Sadly he smiled. "They weren't Mr. Drear's accounts . . . don't know where he got them. But they tell a tale or two. They show how mean folks had to be to buy and sell our people."

He stared dumbly at Mr. Small for a moment. Then he said, "I'm awful sorry I didn't stop to speak with your wife at church this day. But I felt so low there for awhile. I felt just like I was going to lay myself down and not get up. I've been sick you see. Yes . . . yes."

Vaguely Pluto looked around him. His old mind seemed to shift to something else. "I see you've found us out. I knew, oh yes. I knew you would when first you come over to see that house. Knew I hadn't long . . . all these many years, no one. And then Pesty. Old Little Miss Bee!" He laughed and folded the child in his shawl.

"Ain't it funny though, of all people, you can trust a child? Never knew I could until one day she followed me in here. I didn't know she had until I saw her perched upon that ladder. I was so sure she would then tell Mr. River Lewis Darrow. I was sure of it, and that him and his boys would clear me out and clean this hall out. But no. I guess it is her plaything. I never know why she won't tell. But she likes to come here and I let her keep the glass. It is written down in the books that Mr. Drear was most fond of his glassware. Oh, Little Miss Bee and I can spend hours not even talking. Sometimes, I tell her stories about long ago, and she will fall asleep right in my arms."

Again Pluto's mind shifted. His eyes became frightened. He clutched at the ledgers on the desk. Pesty rubbed her head against his shoulder and put her hands up on his hands until he had calmed.

"They think because you're old, they can walk in and take over," Pluto said. "Isn't that right? They come around a-howlin' and pretending they're the ghosts. But they don't know, do you see? Little Miss Bee knows, don't you, my babe?" The child nodded. "Yes!" said Pluto. "Some night them Darrows forgets about me, but there will still be signs of the old man and the slaves. I've seen him! I've seen them! Then my black horse, he will run with the wind, those spirits bother him so. I reckon they want to ride him, but he won't have nothing to do with 'em."

"Mr. Pluto," Mr. Small said softly. "Mr. Skinner. It will be all right."

Thomas felt awful inside. Looking at Pluto so old, so afraid, he thought suddenly of Great-grandmother Jeffers.

Why do they have to grow sick and weak? Why must it end like that for them?

He was filled with sadness. It was evil of him to have thought such a tired old man could be the devil. He could no longer see Pluto as king. And there *was* a war, but it was Pluto's with himself.

"We are sorry," said Pluto. "I mean I . . . we . . . hadn't ought to have fooled with you like that. Carrying on. Tricking you with stage magic . . ."

"Mr. Skinner, I wish you'd try very hard to make yourself clear," said Mr. Small. "Tricked us? You couldn't have had anything to do with what was done to the kitchen."

"No," Pesty said. "He means the other. He means about . . ."

But Pluto stopped her. "It was that I was afraid, that's why we tricked you, don't you see?" he said.

"I thought sure them Darrows would just walk in and clean this place out if they knew how sick I was. They would find that sliding wall the way I found it, oh, years, years ago. . . . What would it mean to them that slaves walked here, lived here peaceful, content no one was sure to find them? Here they were taught, the slaves were . . . yes, taught all the tricks and ruses old Mr. Drear could think up for them. And the good Jesus in heaven, he sure could think them up . . . the books tell it all! And they were taught the cross reading. They were taught . . ." he gazed around the cavern, "what wonder there is when men are free to see.

"It was all right when I was strong," Pluto went on. "They were always halfways scared of me. Their grandaddy, he was a boy with me. He was River Swift Arrow. He always said *his* grandaddy was a Mohegan by the name of River Thames. River Thames was supposed to have come down with Dies Drear from up East. And River Swift always said whatever was hidden when we hunted that house was his by legacy. I never said nothing when he said that, because I knew whatever it was was mine. I *knew* it. How did I know?"

Mr. Pluto laughed silently.

"Because what I hunted I couldn't put a name to. I couldn't have told you what it was I hunted, except it was inside me. And I knew that house would bring it out of me and show it to me.

"River Swift, he hunted treasure. Sure that's all he knew to be legacy. But he was afraid of it, of that house," said Pluto. "So was his son and his son's son. He was scared to death, because the spirits knew he was evil and knew his sons was evil. But I wasn't afraid.

"No, not I," Pluto continued. "I grew to love that house. I got so I could walk it blind. All the tunnels. All the caves. But they was afraid, those Darrows. So the years passed, and they were afraid of me.

"I meant not to trick you, sir," Pluto said. His voice rasped, making a dried-up sound all about the room.

"It was just that if they were ever to know I be sick, they'd walk in out of the open. They wouldn't be halfways afraid of me being the devil at night.

"I see you are a historical man, an educated man," Pluto went on. He looked around him as though it was difficult for him to remember where he was. "I had no chance for education, but I do know hard thought in another. I am so sorry we had to fool you."

Mr. Small heaved a deep sigh. He could make little sense of what Pluto was talking about. He had so many questions, there was so much he needed to know. Gently he started to probe.

"Mr. Skinner, sir," he said. "I know you're tired, but just a little longer. Try to think about what I'm going to say. Can you tell me . . . is this the last unknown cavern? Is this the last uncharted hiding place?"

For a moment Pluto stared at Mr. Small and, then, looked beyond him. He bowed his head on his arms on the table. "We shouldn't have fooled you like that," he whispered. "It wasn't a proper thing to do. No. No. We had no right. No business!"

Pesty stood up straight, alert, also looking beyond Mr. Small and Thomas.

"Then again, as a historical man, perhaps you are not so all-fired proper," said a fierce, withering voice.

Mr. Small stood stock-still. Thomas couldn't have moved if he'd tried. It was River Lewis Darrow, it had to be. He must have followed them, waiting all this time.

Ambush, Thomas thought. How many sons with him? How many to handle at the same time?

"You just might be another branch of that Mohegan bunch, come here to steal from the storehouse and drive an old man half out of his mind!"

Mr. Small spun around. Thomas turned around ever so slowly. But what he saw was too much for him. The strength seemed to drain from his arms. No longer could his legs hold his weight. Not uttering a sound, he fell to his knees, unable to comprehend the phantasm before them.

For it was Pluto standing there. It was Pluto, who still sat slumped at his desk mumbling sorrowfully to the air, who, at the same time, stood in front of Mr. Small and Thomas.

"You!" hissed Mr. Small. "I knew there had to be another one of you!"

The Pluto who stood nodded in recognition to Mr. Small. His beard and wild hair were golden in the torchlight. His eyes were wet and emerald green, flecked with gold sparks. He threw back his head and laughed and laughed.

No, thought Thomas. It wasn't fair to be a devil, to be able to divide one's self and have power over human beings. Now he understood everything. Pluto had spun all the tapestries, those carpets, himself. Pluto had blown all the hundreds of bottles, just by multiplying himself until he had enough Plutos to do the job. No wonder he was so worn out.

"No!" screamed Thomas. So terrified was he that in another minute there might be a thousand Plutos, he began to sob.

"You devil! You hairy, green-eyed devil!"

He leaped on this second Pluto. He leaped high, before his father could stop him, catching the man about the neck. He wrapped his legs around the man's body and twined his fingers in that long, white beard. But Pluto was strong. He shook Thomas off like a lion shaking off ticks.

Suddenly Thomas flew through the air and hit the floor. By the time he pulled himself up to a sitting position, he was staring at his hands. His hands were gold and orange. His hands were covered with hunks of Pluto's beard.

"Get away!" he yelled. "Papa, it's stuck, it won't get away . . . Papa!"

Mr. Small tried to get hold of Thomas. "Son! Son!" he kept repeating. But Thomas was scooting all over the floor, trying to get away from his hands covered with the white beard. Some of it now seemed to be sprouting on his arms.

"He's turning me into a devil. Oh, Papa!" cried Thomas.

"Thomas Small!" The voice of the second Pluto boomed through the cavern like a hundred rushing voices.

Abruptly Thomas sat still. He looked up at the strong, powerful Pluto towering above him.

Ever so slowly, the Pluto raised his hands to his face. He wore the now familiar hide gloves, though only Mr. Small noticed them. The Pluto began to speak, his hands still poised there, near his cheekbones.

"We wear the mask that grins and lies,
It hides our cheeks and shades our eyes . . .
With torn and bleeding hearts we smile . . .
We wear the mask!"

With the most delicate motion, he peeled away the corners of his face just below the ear and let it hang in shreds around his mouth.

15

"Thomas, don't be afraid," said Mr. Small. "It's only a false face. Look. Look at it."

"It's stage makeup. You see, Thomas?" said the man. "There's a half-mask with the beard attached, which fits around my ears. There's the white wig and a dyed plastic substance that looks like skin. I had to add more beard with paste to make the mask fuller. That's why it came off in your hand."

"You could have got away with just the beard and the hair, you look so much like Pluto anyway," said Mr. Small. "Why did you bother with such difficult makeup? With the same green eyes, anyone would have been fooled."

"Yes, lucky for me my eyes are the same color as his," the man said. "I really didn't think you would be easy to convince. If I had to face you in the daytime, I wanted to resemble him as closely as possible. But you were on to me from the first, weren't you?"

"You said a few things out of place," Mr. Small said modestly. "Something about India in a way I'm certain Mr. Pluto wouldn't have said. And you wore those new, expensive gloves—they were a mistake, you see."

The man had to smile. "Yes, the gloves were wrong," he said. "I know that now. And when I saw you all there in the kitchen that night for the first time, I couldn't resist a bit of overacting. You were all so stunned, you see. But it was never my plan to terrify your son, then or now. Thomas, are you all right?"

Thomas had sat unbelieving through the conversation between his father and the man. Slowly he came to his senses. Not looking at the man, he rubbed the wetness of tears from his face.

"I knew no man as old as Mr. Pluto could catch me from behind."

"As it was, I had a hard time catching you myself," said the man.

Thomas was pleased by this. "Who are you anyway?"

"I'm Mayhew Skinner. I'm my father's only son."

Thomas slowly shook his head, forcing himself to understand that old Pluto had a son who looked just like him. "But why . . . why did you have to pretend like that?" he asked.

Mayhew had been kneeling in front of Thomas. He got up and walked over to the desk where Mr. Pluto now sat holding on to the ledgers. When Mayhew put his strong hands on his father's shoulders, Pluto looked up at him with all the hope he had left in him in his eyes.

"How were we to know what type of strangers you folks would be?" asked Mayhew. "My father became quite ill in January. He's had this running battle with the Darrows for as long as I can remember. But he was always strong, he could take it. I do believe he enjoyed the fight with them, since he alone knew about this cavern. He was certain they would never set foot into his cave, where he lived, as long as he could frighten them by being devilish. And he was right, they never did dare come too close. But when he grew ill, that all changed. He was desperate with the fear they might see how weak and sick he was. And when the foundation told him you folks would be moving in, he was terrified of what the Darrows might do to you."

"Then it wasn't Mr. Pluto who considered we might be an enemy," said Mr. Small.

"It was I," Mayhew said. He smiled grimly to himself.

"Calling my father the devil," he said. "As if being lame was a crime. Folks around here have been cruel to him for years—not only the Darrows. At least River Lewis believed he had a reason for *his* crime. Full of greed, he thought my father stood in the way of his legacy, which he believed was a treasure in gold." He looked around at the cavern. "I guess it is treasure of a kind." Sadly he smiled. "But not to my father, not to Drear.

"But let's get back to the nice Sunday-moaning church folks who never once cared whether my father lived or died. No, you can have them. They're the reason I left town. Even when I was small, I always hated them for their stupid ways. I guess I hated you folks before I saw you because I figured you would be no better than the rest."

Mr. Small glanced at Thomas, who stared at Mayhew Skinner with something close to awe. Thomas had never heard anyone talk the way Mayhew talked, at least not in front of his father.

"You shouldn't hate," Mr. Small said. "It will destroy you."

"That's a well-meaning lie," said Mayhew. "Folks have hated other folks for centuries, and the same business is still with us."

"Son," said Mr. Pluto, "please to tell him how it had to be."

"Don't worry, Father, I'm telling him," said Mayhew.

"You see, it was Carr who contacted me when my father fell ill," Mayhew was saying. "I live away from here. I'm an actor. I've lived away and worked since a long time ago, when my mother and I left this town for good. We had lived on that Drear property until my mother could no longer stand seeing the house *or* the town folk who thought we were strange. She loved that cave we lived in though. Odd isn't it, Mr. Small, that a son and daughter of slaves would find peace in the very sort of cave running slaves hid in?"

Mayhew didn't wait for Mr. Small to answer; he went on, his eyes seeming to go back to that long-ago time.

"You see," Mayhew said, "we lived on this land

not conscious of the reason for our peace with it. We lived with a legacy we weren't aware we had. And yet we had a nameless knowledge of it, as my father has tried to tell you.

"We left it finally," Mayhew said, "but my father wouldn't leave. I blame him for that. I still blame him for forcing us to leave. He had grown obsessed with the tunnels, with the haunting figure of Dies Drear. He became fanatical about protecting the house and its history, and even its legend. I would say he is like you, Mr. Small, in his taste for what he calls our heritage."

"Indeed," said Mr. Small softly. "We always tend to belittle that heritage in our zeal to be free."

"I'll take freedom any day over all the romantic nonsense about slavery," said Mayhew.

"I mean not to glorify it," said Mr. Small. "I simply want people to know about it. It's a part of our history, and yet no one tells the truth about it."

Uneasily Thomas watched his father and this strange Mayhew. He couldn't take his eyes off him.

Uncomfortably Mr. Small and Mayhew Skinner glanced at Thomas. For his sake, they would let their argument go, for another day perhaps. Pesty sat down next to Thomas, as though to say that whatever sides there might be, she would take the one closest to Thomas.

"But to get on," said Mayhew, "Carr, the father, called me on the telephone. He said I'd better get back here, that new folks were moving into the big house. He said it looked serious—that you had obtained a job at the college."

"Serious in what way?" asked Mr. Small. "He didn't know about the cavern."

"No, of course not," said Mayhew. "And yet, he knew something . . . how can I tell you! He knew and respected my father. He knew the Darrows were after something to steal and he knew my father was hiding something from them. When Father became ill, and you folks were to arrive, he was worried. He understood that if my father was keeping something from the Darrows, it had to stay kept from them and possibly you, too."

"I see," said Mr. Small. "So we were suspect even before we arrived."

"Carr was afraid Father would have worse trouble if you folks turned out to be like the Darrows. I arrived here about three weeks ago. Then your furniture arrived. Father had made up his mind to trust you folks and decided to unload the furniture and place it in the rooms. I tried to tell him it was none of his affair, that he wasn't strong enough for it. He wouldn't listen. He never does. So me and the Carr boys fixed things up a bit."

"So then," said Mr. Small.

"You have to understand," said Mayhew, "we had more than one consideration. There was the foundation to think about also. They knew people searched for treasure on this property, but they had no idea why, or that the searchers were all one family. They knew the legend, that the house was supposed to be haunted. But they are sane people. How could they possibly understand the meaning of the legend to my father? To him, Dies Drear *lives!*"

"Did you know about this cavern?" asked Mr. Small.

"No, never," said Mayhew. "Not until a week ago, when my father decided he was mortal, like all of us, and thought it was time to tell me."

"Do you blame me, son?" asked Pluto. Sadly he looked up at Mayhew and Mayhew turned way.

"All these years," Mayhew whispered, "all this time, when there was this much wealth . . ."

"It wasn't mine to touch, it wasn't mine!" cried Pluto.

"You say it is our heritage!" Mayhew's voice burst around them. "When all these years you've struggled and I've struggled. Yes, I blame you!"

"It was ours to hold, to take care of just the way the old man had," said Pluto. "But not to plunder, no, not to touch!"

Mayhew laughed without smiling. "How foolish, that history could be more important than men! No, of course not to touch," he said. "Father, do you have any idea how close you and Drear have become? He collected all this perhaps as a whim and he put it here, again perhaps, to save for slaves a portion of life which had been denied them. And you, Father, still save it, for, like a slave, you are bound to it simply because a troublemaker called Dies Drear says you are!"

"The man was more than just a troublemaker," said Mr. Small.

"To you, maybe," Mayhew said. "To me he was a troublemaker, who thought himself a prophet."

Mr. Small started to say more, but then seemed to change his mind.

After a time Thomas spoke up. "What will you do now?" he asked of Mayhew. "Will you tell the foundation about the treasure? Will you let them take it?"

Mr. Small waited. Mayhew looked at him, his eyes as cold and clear as glass. Then he looked down at his father.

"We could talk about it," said Mr. Small quietly, "if you'll allow me to become involved in the decision."

Mayhew nodded. "It's late," he said. "I'd better get Pesty back to the house, or they just might send Macky out looking for her. Pesty, are you ready?"

"I'm ready," she said.

"Then say good night to Father," Mayhew said.

Pesty went to old Pluto and threw her arms around his neck.

"Child!" Pluto whispered happily. "You'll come tomorrow, and maybe I'll feel like riding in the buggy. You want to still ride with a poor old soul?"

"I do!" she said.

"And remember," Pluto said, "not a word!" He put his fingers to his lips.

"No, never a word," she said. Sleepily she turned to Mayhew and held out her tiny arms to him.

Mayhew swung her onto his shoulders. "I'll take

you as far as the yard," he told her. "I don't dare come closer. If they spy me, they'll think I'm Father."

Mr. Small looked at his watch. "Lord, it's late," he said, "and my wife is there, locked in the twins' room! I forgot all about her! Oh, I hope she didn't turn brave and venture out to clean up the mess they made in the kitchen."

"Something happened?" Mayhew asked. "What brought you all here so unexpectedly in the first place?"

"We came here, I guess, to accuse your father of trying to run us out of the house," Mr. Small said. "I was just so mad, I didn't think much about it. I just got over here as fast as I could." Then he explained what had been done to the kitchen.

"What a bad thing, a sinful thing!" said Pluto. "They'll stop at nothing. Nothing!"

Trembling he tried to stand and nearly fell. Mr. Small caught him in time and braced him in his arms.

"Father, you're ill," Mayhew said.

"Let's get him out of the heat of this place," Mr. Small said. He helped Pluto up the ramp and out of the cavern.

In the cave, Mr. Pluto lay down heavily upon his bed.

"Ahh," he said, "I am tired tonight."

"You stay right here until I get back from taking Pesty home," Mayhew said to him. Pesty still rode on Mayhew's shoulders.

"Oh, son, I'll be all right," said Pluto. "I feel so

much better just having Mr. Small know about the cavern. You see, he is a historical man, an educated man. He will know what to do with it all, Mayhew."

"Don't worry anymore about it," said Mr. Small. "Your son and I will take care of things."

Outside they slipped through the trees on the hill.

"It was them that did it to the kitchen," said Pesty to Mayhew.

"Which ones?" he asked her. "River Lewis, too?"

"No, not him," said Pesty. "After he seen Mr. Small at church, he told them to leave off. But they wouldn't listen. They was afraid that because he was a historical man, he would find the treasure before them. They think to scare Mrs. Small so she'd want to move into town. But not Macky."

"No? Macky wouldn't do it?" asked Mayhew.

"No," she said. "Macky, he told them he was tired and then he said to them that he was going to make a friend out of Thomas. He got slapped down for it, too."

Thomas was pleased to hear that Mac Darrow liked him. He was almost sorry the boy had got slapped for wanting to be friends.

But maybe it serves him right, Thomas thought. He did let me fall in the hole under the front steps.

He thought to himself that maybe Mac Darrow had a bicycle. If he did, they could ride around and have dogs bark at their wheels. He sure hoped Mac Darrow had a bicycle.

"So it was just the three of them," said Mayhew. "Wilbur and Russell and River Ross. They should be ashamed of themselves, acting like vandals on Halloween."

"You have any ideas on how to handle them?" asked Mr. Small.

"Call the police," said Thomas. "Just call the law and have them put away!"

Mayhew laughed to himself. "That would give me great pleasure," he said, "but taking care of them is easier than that. If their level is that of overgrown boys making mischief, then that is the way we'll have to treat them."

"How so?" asked Mr. Small.

"Let me get Pesty home," Mayhew said.

"I want to hear!" cried Pesty. "I want to know what's to happen!"

"You'll be in on it, good girl," Mayhew said. "Right now, it's time to run you home." He began to trot through the trees. Then he stopped and called back to Mr. Small, "You folks going to be up awhile?"

"I expect we'll clean up the kitchen," Mr. Small called back. "I'm much too wound up to sleep."

"Then I'll come by for a while," Mayhew said. "I'll help you with the kitchen if you want."

"That's kind of you," said Mr. Small. "But hadn't you better get back to your father?"

"I won't stay long with you," said Mayhew. His voice was farther off. He was moving again. "I want to give you an idea of what I have in mind for the Darrow boys."

"Will you need our help?" called Thomas.

"Yes," Mayhew called back. "We're about to become a company of actors!"

16

"**Thomas, you and your** mother are staring at me again," said Mayhew Skinner. He did not look up at them. "Mr. Small, why do you suppose they keep on staring at me?"

"They've never seen anyone like you," Mr. Small said. "Anyway, neither one of them ever looks twice at anything they don't like."

"Well, my goodness!" said Mayhew. "I wonder what kind of a 'thing' I am."

Mrs. Small had to smile. So did Thomas. They looked shyly at Mayhew. Here Mrs. Small had known him for only a couple of hours, and he seemed like a close friend.

Thomas couldn't keep his eyes off him. He wanted to know what kind of person became an actor. And how it was an actor used makeup and played different parts.

They were all in the kitchen, Mr. and Mrs. Small, Thomas and Mayhew. It was one-thirty in the morning, and none of them felt actually tired. Mrs. Small and Thomas sat at the kitchen table. Only Mr. Small and Mayhew worked with the fury with which they'd started. Thomas was scraping the hardened paste off a chair, and Mrs. Small was wringing a hot, wet dish towel onto the tabletop.

Mayhew had organized them into two teams. They were to use hot water to loosen the caked flour and juice. Once it was loosened, it wasn't difficult to scrape and wipe it off the kitchen. Mayhew had the floor done already. Mr. Small cleaned the refrigerator and the stove. Mrs. Small and Thomas had done less because they had to watch Mayhew and they had to listen to what he was saying. He hadn't stopped talking since he'd come back from taking Pesty home. He still had a good part of the false beard hanging from his face. He had put the wig back on his head.

Looking at him covered with perspiration and dirt from all the mess, Mrs. Small couldn't help feeling sorry for him.

"Mayhew, why won't you take off your jacket—it'll be filthy! That wig must be terribly hot. Take a break, both of you, before you get sick."

"Listen to Mother," said Mayhew to Mr. Small. "There she goes, trying to change me already. Why do they always try to change us?"

"Because we're so perfect, naturally," said Mr. Small.

"That's right," said Mayhew. "No, they can't stand perfection, can they?"

"Both of you are just devilish," said Mrs. Small. Then she became serious suddenly. "Mayhew, how soon do you intend to leave here? Won't you stay awhile before going back to the city?"

Mayhew looked at her fondly and then turned away from her before he began to joke with her again. "There she goes," he said. "If I stay here one day too long, she'll have me enrolled in that college before I know what hit me."

"No, I wouldn't," she said. "Have you ever been to college, Mayhew? You might like it. I hear they have a fine drama department at the college."

Mr. Small laughed. "I suspect college drama would be like child's play to Mayhew," he said. "The only training he needs is good steady work."

"You're right about that," said Mayhew. "I'm up for a good part in a road company in another month."

"Then you'll stay here at least that long?" Thomas wanted to know. "You'll stay here for a month more?"

Mayhew smiled. "I'll have to stay awhile," he said. "We've got to get things straightened out here." He turned to Mr. Small. "I'll have to see what's to be done with my father."

Mr. Small stopped his work and sat down at the table on the chair Thomas had just finished cleaning. "Mayhew, take a break," he said. "Thomas, get him a chair from the parlor."

When Thomas came back with the chair, Mayhew sat down. Mrs. Small remembered she had half a jar of instant coffee packed somewhere in a carton. After a short search she found it. Quickly she made the coffee and they all drank it from paper cups, all that was left to drink from in the house.

They sipped the coffee, and Mayhew started talking again. "We have to decide a number of things," he said to Mr. Small. Mr. Small nodded. "But first we have to find out just how sick my father is," Mayhew said.

"He's an old man now," said Mrs. Small.

"Yes, but if he can get well," Mayhew said, "I mean, if there's nothing more wrong with him than fatigue and mental anguish—Lord, that's enough for an old man, surely! I have to get him to a doctor. Better yet, to a hospital and let them give him the once-over."

"Will he *go* to a hospital?" asked Mr. Small.

Mayhew was silent for a moment. "He's like all old people around here," he said. "Take them to a hospital, even mention that they have to go, and they're ready to lie down and die."

"Why is that?" asked Thomas. "Why would they be afraid of a place that can help them?"

"Understand," said Mayhew, "my father comes out of a time when people didn't have doctors. When there were no hospitals even halfway close-by. There weren't clinics. The only medicine people had they made themselves from alcohol and tree bark, roots and herb plants. And it was good enough. I don't remember him ever being sick, or my mother either. This is the first time in his life he can't take care of himself. It's killing him, knowing he has to depend on someone else."

Like Great-grandmother Jeffers, Thomas thought. She couldn't bear the sight of the traveling nurse who once tried to give her a hypodermic of penicillin. Great-grandmother had chased the woman out of the house, Thomas recalled, and had warned her not to come back soon.

How long has it been since we've been gone from there—two days? Just two days we've been here? It seems like a year.

"But you will have to get him to go," Mrs. Small was saying, speaking of Mr. Pluto. "If only to get him away from here so he can rest."

"Well, I have a plan," said Mayhew. "I'm chock full of plans." He laughed. "I'm going to tell him we've got to make the Darrow boys think he's so sick, he has to go into the hospital. Then they will make their move to find the treasure. It's not really a lie. Once they see him leave, they'll be over here under cover of darkness before you have time to blink.

"I'm going to call Carr as soon as it's morning," Mayhew said. "He'll have to make arrangements to put Father in the hospital." He glanced around at them sitting there. "You folks are going to have to do for Father, because no one can know that I'm here."

"What do you want us to do?" asked Thomas.

"Everything," said Mayhew. "I'm going to hole up in that treasure house of old Mr. Drear's until it's time to come out. First off, we will make a show of getting Father to a hospital. We could take him by car, but I think we'll call an ambulance. Then,

Thomas, you and Pesty will let it be known he is in the hospital for a week or so . . . or at least until tomorrow, depending on what's wrong with him."

"I get it!" said Thomas. "You want them to think they've got to move tonight, I mean the night that's coming, because they can't be sure Mr. Pluto will be in the hospital more than twenty-four hours."

"Right," said Mayhew. "I want to get the Darrows over here fast, before they have time to think too much about it. And I'm going to have Pesty let them know Father became very excited, making himself sick over something Mr. Small found belonging to old Dies Drear."

"Oh, I don't know," Mrs. Small said pensively. "Are you sure we're doing the right thing? Shouldn't we just call the police on them, have the law reprimand them good, and leave it at that?"

Mayhew glanced at Mr. Small, and Mr. Small nodded ever so slightly. "Martha, there's more to it," Mr. Small said. "There are things you don't know about . . . let Mayhew do it his way."

Thomas was about to ask what it was they didn't know about. So was Mrs. Small. But Mayhew turned away from them in that sad, alone way he had. In the last couple of hours, Mrs. Small had seen him do this many times, as though there was something weighing heavily upon him. Whatever it was, she knew it was not her business to speak of it.

Thomas understood this too. There was some secret, he imagined, that involved Mr. Pluto,

Mayhew and the Darrows. His father knew about it.

How was it his father always knew more than everybody else, he wondered. Mayhew couldn't have told him anything more than what he had told all of them, because they'd been together, all of them, from the time Mayhew returned from taking Pesty home.

So then, Thomas thought, it's something Papa has figured out from what has already happened. I'll have to wait to find out, if I'm ever to find out.

"It won't be easy getting Father to go to the hospital," said Mayhew, "but I think Mr. Small and I can convince him. We'll make excitement out of it. We'll tell him we can't work the stage magic on the Darrows until he is gone."

"Whatever you plan on doing," Mr. Small said, "please don't use this house to do it in. I don't want the Darrows here or near my little boys."

"No, of course not," said Mayhew. "You needn't worry about them getting in here anymore. There's only one way they could have got in to do their work on this kitchen. Why is it Father never told you about that hall mirror?"

"What?" said Mr. Small.

"You mean the mirror right out there beside the parlor door?" said Thomas.

"There's a tunnel behind it," Mayhew said.

"How is that possible?" asked Mr. Small. "The mirror hangs between the parlor door and the front door."

Mayhew explained that the parlor wall was a false

wall, about a foot and a half short of the outer wall of the house.

"The corridor between the false wall and the outer wall leads down to the tunnel," Mayhew explained. "That tunnel is parallel to, and to the right of, the tunnel under the front steps."

"Are the two tunnels connected?" Thomas wanted to know.

"I believe they are," Mayhew said. "At least they used to be. The tunnel behind the mirror has several branches, while the one beneath the steps connects only with the kitchen, for the purpose of hasty concealment. The mirror tunnel goes under the stream at the foot of this property, onto the Darrow property and the Carr property. I would guess a long time ago, nature started the tunnel. But then men, probably slaves helping Dies Drear, expanded it to the two properties, where there were farmers friendly to runaway slaves."

Thomas shivered. To think he had slept in that parlor because he thought it would be safer than his room upstairs! He could have been carried off by them and hidden in the tunnel!

"My goodness!" said Mrs. Small. "That handsome mirror . . . all the time . . ." She couldn't finish the thought. She, too, shivered as with a chill.

"Yes, and you'd better remove the mechanism," said Mayhew. "It's at the base of the mirror—here, I'll show you, Mr. Small, because if your twin boys like to crawl around, they might find it and easily get into the tunnel."

They all went with Mayhew to the hall. There he kneeled down and felt around the bottom frame of the mirror. "Here it is," he said. Mr. Small bent down to get a close look. Then Mayhew released a lever, and the mirror swung gently out.

In front of them was a dark, narrow corridor, which slanted steeply down below the foundation of the house. Thomas could clearly hear running water.

"Whoever came here last night most surely removed his shoes," said Mr. Small. Squeezing himself sideways, he made his way down the corridor and peered into the tunnel.

"He had to," said Mayhew, "else your carpet would have been soaking wet.

"This tunnel is never dry," he said. "There have been several cave-ins below the stream, and I would suggest you not allow Thomas ever to walk around in here."

He closed the mirror, and he and Mr. Small worked on the mechanism until they had removed it.

"That's a relief," said Mrs. Small. "Goodness knows, I don't think I'll ever be able to look into that mirror without feeling a bit strange."

They returned to the kitchen but Mayhew declined to sit down. "I'd best be going now," he said. "You folks ought to get to bed, get as much sleep as you can."

"Yes," said Mr. Small.

"I'll come back here early," Mayhew said, "dressed like my father, in case anyone is watching. I'll do business with Carr from here and then I'm going into hiding."

"But what is it we are going to do with the Darrows?" Thomas asked. "When will we begin our show?"

"Once we get Father in the hospital, we'll have the whole day to get ready for them. You're going to do some shopping for me, Thomas. Mr. Small, you might have to take him to Columbus. It's the only city close-by that I know has a theater supplies store large enough to have what we are going to need."

"I'll be glad to," said Mr. Small.

"Do I get to wear a costume?" Thomas wanted to know.

"I'm afraid you'll be wearing mostly rags and chains, Thomas," said Mayhew. "I'm sorry to say slaves were never very keen dressers." He grinned.

Thomas was awfully disappointed. "Not even a false face?" he asked Mayhew.

"Oh sure, you can have a false face and a false head of hair, if you like," Mayhew said.

Thomas felt better and he smiled.

"What do I get to wear?" asked Mr. Small.

"You're going to look swell," laughed Mayhew. "I've got you all set for a black fire-and-brimstone suit and shoulder-length, gray-blond hair."

"I can hardly wait," said Mr. Small smiling.

Mrs. Small looked at bit peeved, but she didn't say anything. Mayhew, noticing her expression, winked at Mr. Small.

"Now what is it, Mother? Are you feeling left out?"

Mrs. Small wouldn't say anything.

"You want to be an actor, too?" Mayhew said.

Mrs. Small's face lit up. They all burst out laughing.

"I'll have to get one of the Carr girls to look after your little boys," Mayhew told her. "Will that be all right?"

"Oh, that will be fine!" said Mrs. Small breathlessly. "What . . . I mean . . . who do I play?"

"Well, there's nothing that says one of those slave ghosts couldn't have been a woman!"

"Oh no, really!" said Mr. Small.

Mrs. Small covered her face and giggled into her hands.

"You can't do that," Thomas said. "Old Dies Drear wouldn't have sent a woman back into slavery."

"Sure he would have," said Mayhew.

"And he probably did too," said Mr. Small. "Many times women slaves could pretend they were house servants out on an errand, when actually they were running away."

"But the Darrows would never believe it," said Thomas. "I mean, I bet they think of ghosts like I do—that they are men."

"Maybe you're right about that," said Mayhew. "We could shave her head perhaps."

Mrs. Small gasped. Mayhew and Thomas laughed uproariously. "No," said Mayhew, "we can do better than that. We'll make you a man, like Thomas. We'll have to build you both up with muscles. Tell me, Mrs. Small, do you think you could manage a pair of men's shoes with wood blocks attached to them?"

"Do I have to?" she asked.

"If you want to be a ghost, you'll have to do what Mayhew says," said Mr. Small.

She thought a moment. She, like Thomas, had an urge to act. "I rather fancy myself more of the lace and satin ghost-type," she said. "However, I will wear men's shoes and muscles if you all promise never to tell anyone!"

"We *don't* promise!" they all said in unison.

And then Mayhew Skinner took his leave of them. Mr. Small let him out of the kitchen door. Mayhew paused there a moment before leaving. That look of sadness, of loneliness, they'd all seen before passed over him. He looked at each of them in turn, his fierce, green eyes turning suddenly soft.

"I adopt you as my family of rascals," he told them. "I adopt you, each and every one." And with a flourish of his arm, he disappeared into the night. Without a sound, he went and was a part of it.

Now how do you suppose he does that? thought Thomas. I wonder if before he goes away, I could get him to maybe teach me how to melt away like that!

17

"I have lived these caves for fifty years. I have lived them when no one cared but the damp and dark. And now you come here telling me how to be and how to die. No, I'll not let them steal. I'll not leave. I'll not go to any hospital!"

So old Pluto spoke. They all stood around his elaborate desk, Mr. Small, Thomas and Mayhew, watching him clutch at his ledgers. It was splendid night in the cavern of Dies Drear, although it was nearly midday outside. The burning sconces, grouped like a fiery bouquet in the center of the cavern, flared high. The rugs and tapestries leaped and glowed in a fury of color. Mr. Pluto's green eyes were alive and dreadful, with pinpoints of light. His great black cloak fell around him like a shroud. No one of them dared come too near him, for, at the moment, he was almost mad with fear.

"Father," said Mayhew softly, "Father, listen, I have been trying all morning to tell you."

"You be still!" screamed Pluto. "You just keep yourself still! I allow you to come here—you think on that! I allow you here, all of you. This is *my* house to hold and to keep as long as I live. And no tribe of thieves, whether they be educated or fools, is going to steal it!"

"No. No, this time you are wrong." Mr. Small spoke evenly, hardly letting his voice rise above a whisper.

"You!" hissed Pluto. "You are a thief after all. You thought to fool me to get at this storehouse, but you'll not do it. No, it's mine to hold and to keep!"

"No, not yours," said Mr. Small. "If any one of us were to tell, the foundation could come claim it at any time. They own all this land and these caves, too. It's not ours, it's no man's."

Mr. Pluto seemed to shrink down into his shroud. He was still, breathing heavily. Mr. Small thought to walk near, to see if he was all right. He hoped the old man was right; he gambled on the strength and will of decades to come hold the old man up now. He had no intention of destroying Pluto. He had meant only to somehow bring an end to his utter fear and dread. It was cruel, what he had said, for the cavern of Dies Drear should have belonged to Pluto, since Pluto alone had cherished it for so long.

"We mean not to steal one thing in the cavern," said Mr. Small. "I mean that we want nothing here for ourselves. All we want to be sure of is that the Darrows or anyone else should never waste it. What would become of the fine tapestries, the great goblets and bottles, if one day some men bought this property and decided to dig deep for wells or what have you? Anything at all could cause all of this to be destroyed. Do you understand what I'm saying? At any moment, at any time, all of this could be buried forever!"

Slowly Pluto raised his head. "Buried?" he whispered. "Sell this . . . my land?"

"Not your land," Mr. Small said. He held himself tight inside. He made his heart cold so he might speak what he felt he had to. "You are a squatter here, old man. You have been paid to be a groundskeeper, and that is all you are here. You have no right whatsoever."

"No, not true," said Mayhew. He came around Mr. Small and walked behind the desk where Pluto sat. He went to one of the cases that held the ledgers and old, rare books. Carefully he pulled down one large book, in which there was much handwriting on paper that was thick and deep brown.

"Here we have the last will and testament of Dies Drear," he said. "Care to look at it, Mr. Small? Well, no need for you to. The man had some kind of premonition—like a prophet, he knew his time was near. And he willed this cavern and whatever was found in it to the first son of slaves that was able to find it. He knew no bounty hunters, nor any other white men, would ever find this cavern. For the one who found it would have to have been cut off from his past, his history, as were the slaves. He would have to find that past in order to find himself. It took my father some thirty years, but he found it."

There was silence in which Mayhew handed the book to his father. Ever so carefully, old Pluto laid it atop the pile of ledgers on his desk.

"I wasn't looking for this place, nor no treasure," Pluto began. "You see, Mr. Drear built another wall in my cave where I live. Not the wall you see now, with the ladder and the rope hanging down. No, not *that* easy to find this. But he built a wall to look like any cave wall, with a bit of dye like a covering of seeping dirt, or maybe just a little grayness for to make it seem ordinary. How many years I stared at it because I had nothing else to look at! It was my picture screen, on which I placed my dream of finding something . . . I didn't know what. Then I began to dream of finding something belonging to those who were sold and those who were brave and sold all the same."

"Because your ancestor was one of the two slaves who died the week Dies Drear was killed—is that it?" asked Thomas.

"No," said Mayhew.

"No, not the two slaves that was hunted and killed just the same as the old man," said Pluto.

"But the one mentioned just once in all the history and the legend told of the house," Mr. Small said. "There were *three* slaves caught the night two of them were killed."

"The third slave!" said Thomas. "He got clean away!"

"He got away," said Mayhew, "and he went far

north, reaching Canada, where he lived and prospered until he died."

"And his great-great-grandsom came one day to claim all this," Mr. Small said quietly. "Maybe he had heard some ancient tale about something hidden in this house. A tale that had been passed on from generation to generation, each time becoming less clear and more mysterious."

"Yes," Mayhew said, "but the slave who ran free wasn't the only slave who ran free the time the house of Drear fell silent as a tomb. This cavern had at least once slave still resting within it. He could have been Mohegan, as the Darrows say. The bounty hunters who caught and killed two of the three running slaves and killed old Drear never had an inkling of this cavern. They never even found that first cave. But at least one slave had to be in here. When he, too, ran free, he told a tale of hidden wealth, which, as you say, Mr. Small, became distorted through generations of telling. By the time River Swift hunted the house of Dies Drear, what he looked for was hardly more than a wish."

"You've got to try to understand," said Pluto. "River Swift, he wasn't so awful bad. He was my companion when we were young. We shared the dark and dank of the tunnels—our footsteps together made hardly a sound on those ghostly paths. I suppose in the beginning he hunted for himself, the same as I did. But he always was a greedy boy, greedy to have and greedy to take. I reckon he got to thinking hard about old Mr. Drear dying wealthy as a king. So over the years, what he hunted got changed into a stake of glitter all for himself. By the time his manhood came, he knew there was a treasure of gold some place. He would have laid out his footsteps on my back to get to it, too. But you shouldn't blame him to his soul. We both lost, he and I. We both did lose . . ."

"So then," said Mr. Small, "we have all of it now."

"But listen," Mayhew said softly, "let him tell it—it has been so long that he couldn't tell it."

And Pluto told them, his voice going back to that hopeless time.

"After the boy and his mother had picked up and gone," Pluto said, "I had nothing to look at but that wall, night after night and year after year. Until one time, I got so I couldn't stand to look at it. So I got me some paint and I was going to paint the whole cave white. I started with that wall. I painted the whole wall that night and then I went to sleep, glad I had done something to take my mind off the tunnels. I had walked them so often, finding things—clues, bits and pieces of the cross. . . ."

"Like this cross?" said Mr. Small. He produced the four triangles he and Thomas had fitted into a Greek cross. Very carefully, he put the cross in Pluto's palm.

Pluto stared at it. "It's just a one they will make to pretend with," he said. "Them fool Darrows. The cross was handed down to them just like the tale of the Mohegan was. But they don't know how to read it . . . they don't know what it's for. Just mindless, they will make the cross and stick around the triangles."

"How do you read it?" asked Mr. Small. "How can you read from four triangles that are exactly alike, that can be moved to fit any angle of the cross?"

There was a pause in which Mr. Pluto's fingers moved over the cross. He looked up after a moment and smiled at Mr. Small. "Old Mr. Drear surely did fool you with this one!" he said. He chuckled. "First, before I read it, you must tell me how you found it, Mr. Small."

Mr. Small explained how he had found three triangles stuck in the doorframes inside the house and the last one in his office in the college tower.

"Thomas and I found that by moving them around, we could make a Greek cross out of them."

"Surely you did," said Pluto, "and that was your first mistake. Now wouldn't you know Mr. Drear would figure out that folks, not knowing what they saw, would move a triangle when they came upon one? Wouldn't you know he knew folks well enough to figure they would have to touch it, turn it over, hold it up to the light and turn it around? Yes! And he counted on them doing that.

"You can't move a triangle from where you find it! You can't move it if you want to *read* it!"

"So, not moving it, how do you read it?" asked Mr. Small.

"This was a cross reading for fleeing slaves," Pluto

said. "It was Mr. Drear's own creation. It's all written down and diagrammed in one of his books. He gave the crosses to the people who helped slaves from one hiding place to another. They were called the Conductors, I believe, and it was rare that a slave ever saw them. But a slave would find their crosses. And what he found weren't fancy crosses like this one and others Darrow will make. Those a slave found might be twigs tied together and nailed up. Or even dead animals fixed on a tree trunk.

"The first thing a slave was taught about the cross reading was that he would never find a triangle laid flat—not on the ground or anywhere else flat. It wouldn't read, because you could move it around, and if you could move it around, you couldn't get the sense of it.

"The second thing a slave knew was that a triangle could be found on any object perpendicular to the ground—a cliff wall, a riverbank, a tunnel wall, a tree. Anything at all, as long as it was upright and stayed put. Then, when he found a triangle, he had to stand directly in front of it.

"The third thing a slave learned was never to touch a triangle he found. He was to stand directly in front of it, but never to touch it. If he touched it, he might change its position in some way and upset the reading.

"Next, he would imagine he could make two lines leading from the two legs where they made a right angle. And with his finger he would lengthen these lines until he had himself a cross. The place where the triangle he found fit on this cross would tell him where to go next."

Mr. Small pulled out the paper on which he had drawn his first diagram of a triangle. With dotted lines, he extended the two legs of the angle until he had made a perfect cross.

"That's it," said Pluto. "That is how it was done."

After a moment he continued. "The last thing a slave was taught was never ever tell the cross reading. Not to another slave, not to a freeman, not even to his kin. That's why so few people ever heard about it. Slaves took the reading to their graves. That's why, whenever I chance to pass a graveyard and see all them crosses, I can't help but pause awhile, just looking."

After a time Mr. Small spoke. "Please read for me

now, Mr. Skinner, the metal and wood cross the Darrows made."

Pluto held out the cross in his palm. "This way, with the four triangles in place," he said, "the cross reads nothing. But pull the cross apart and look at one triangle at a time . . . well then, each will read. Here."

He pulled apart the four triangles. Then, using Mr. Small's pen, he drew a cross on the side of one of the bookcases.

"Take the top triangle on the right side first," he said. He slapped one metal triangle in place on the bookcase. The peg sank deep into the wood. "One leg points north, the other to the east. That means flee east from where you found it.

"Take the second triangle, the one on the bottom right," he said. He slapped it in place. "One leg points south, the other to the east. Flight is south."

He placed the top left angle on the outline of the cross. "It points north and to the west. You must flee north.

"And the bottom left angle will point south and to the west." He placed it, completing the cross. "The flight is west."

Thomas and Mr. Small stared at the finished cross with eyes that could see it as running slaves must have seen it.

"What a wondrous thing," Mr. Small said, "to read freedom from so simple an object as a cross."

"Yes. Yes," said Pluto. "And a slave might find ten different triangles made from sticks, animals, even bits of rags, in one single night of running through woods, along streams, tunnels. Each time he came upon one, he would stand before it, make the outline of a cross and continue on."

"I can see how he would know east or west," said Thomas, "because that's the same as going left or right. But how is it he would know which was north or south? On a vertical surface north would be up and south would be down on the ground."

"Oh, Mr. Drear thought it all out," said Pluto. "Up meant for a slave to go straight forward from the place he stood. And down meant he should turn around and head straight away from the place he stood."

Pluto continued. "A slave might twist and turn, west, south, many times, but always heading for the same place. And it was the last hiding place after a slave left the Drear house."

"What place?" Thomas wanted to know. "What place would they all go to?"

Mr. Pluto stared at him. So did Mayhew.

"Why, the Negro church, son," said Mr. Small. "The freeman's church. A slave might hide among its congregation, and no hunter could find him.

Wherever the church was, the pieces of the cross would lead him to it."

"Father, it's getting late . . ." said Mayhew.

"You trying to hurry me?" Pluto said. He looked hard at Mayhew. The talk of the cross, and the fact that he could read its meaning when not even Mr. Small could, had seemed to strengthen Pluto.

"What was I talking about?" he asked them. "Where was I?"

"You were talking about painting that cave wall," said Thomas, "and then I think you said you lay down."

"That's right," Pluto said. "I did lay down and I did sleep. I don't think I dreamed about a thing that whole night. You don't know what rest that was for me—I was plagued by nightmares. Old Drear, he used to visit me there in my sleep. Sometimes, oh, in the dead of winter, sometimes he would come and even wake me up with his noise. Scare me so. But not lately. No, it's like he knows I am old and tired."

"Father . . ."

Pluto waved his hand impatiently at Mayhew. "So then I slept good that night and woke up the next morning ready to work with whatever came to my mind to do. Sometimes I had to make my own work. But the first thing I saw was that wall. It was like I never even painted it. The color, that grayness of dye the shade of shale or seeping limestone, it just bled right through my white paint. And then I knew. I touched the wall, and it came off gray, dirt colored, onto my hand.

"But there was no way to move that wall," Pluto said. "There was no trick to it. No. I had to build me a hammer made of iron and I had to pound that wall down. I pounded it down and carried its chunks and bits away by the bushel basket. And I buried that wall so no one would know. It took me a long time. I used to work at it only at night, only when I was sure I was safe. When it was done, I found that other wall where there was still a few strands of rope hanging in the corner. I fitted another rope in, oh, ever so carefully, and when that was done, I pulled down on it and I found all this."

"All this," Mayhew said quietly to Mr. Small. "And it *is* his. It is."

The splendor of the cavern made them remote and separate within it. Mr. Small gazed around, taking it all in as though he would breathe it into his lungs.

"You understand that you can never claim it," he said to Pluto and Mayhew. "You do know, don't you, that no court of law I know of would ever honor the last will and testament of a dead abolitionist to the great-grandson of an unnamed slave."

Mayhew smiled. There was that look of sadness, of loneliness absolute in his eyes. "We would fare worse than any Indian tribe trying to make honest claim to a legitimate treaty," he said.

"Oh yes, we know," said Pluto. "We know. We know."

Thomas couldn't translate all he felt now into any kind of thought. Standing there in the quiet, splendid beauty of the cavern, he was speechless. He was awe-struck by this old Pluto, who was king after all, who lived only to keep a treasure he couldn't bear to part with, which would never belong to him.

Mr. Small sighed. "I'm afraid I don't have much heart for scaring Darrows," he said. "It all seems so foolish now."

"Foolish?" said Mayhew. "No, not foolish. You feel that way because you have stood in this unreal place—this unnatural house which doesn't exist—listening to a story that shouldn't have happened, told by a man whose steadfastness is not believable."

"But we are here," said Mr. Small. "The story is true, and the man is true."

"It's all a dream," Mayhew said. There was a mocking look in his eyes, the look of stage magic. "The Darrows are the point, and fooling them is the game. Don't forget our actual world out there of silly deeds and simple wants."

"But does Mr. Pluto have to go to a hospital?" Thomas asked. "Can't he just stay right here where he is?"

"I'm not going to any hospital," Pluto said. "You can't make me go!"

"He could stay here," said Mr. Small, "right here. Sleep here until we are finished with the Darrows."

"Father, will you do it? Will you sleep here and not come out until we are finished with them?"

"Until you do the stage magic," said Mr. Pluto to his son. "Like you explained to me this morning."

"That's right," said Mayhew.

"Now why is it you think you can play me better than I can play myself?"

"Now, Father . . ."

"You answer me," Pluto said. "You just go ahead and tell me how it is. I been the devil Pluto for more years than I can remember, and you think you can do him better than me!"

"I don't want you to get sick," Mayhew said. "I know you can do it, but it will be dark—we might have to wait half the night."

"He's going to play me better than I can," mused Mr. Pluto. He turned his old, angry eyes on each one of them. "No, I won't do it. I'm going to sleep in my own bed tonight."

Mayhew heaved a deep sigh. Once he opened his mouth as though to argue further with his father. But then he shrugged and shook his head.

"You are stubborn, mean and the devil for sure," he said to Pluto. "All right. You play Pluto, but on one condition."

"What one?" asked Pluto.

"That you see a doctor as soon as this is over. This week for sure."

"I don't have to go to any hospital?"

"Not as long as you see a doctor, but you will do whatever the doctor says when you see him. Will you agree to that?"

"Oh, I don't suppose it will hurt," Pluto said. "There's nothing wrong with me that a little more rest won't cure. I've got some good medicine I fixed myself only last month. I'll go see some doctor, let me see, about Friday or maybe Saturday. Does that suit you, boy?"

"That will be fine," said Mayhew. "I'm going to tell Mrs. Small of your promise. She will see you get to the doctor on time."

"Now," said Mr. Small, "I would guess you will need to take my place in our play for the Darrows."

"I'd better," said Mayhew. "I'll have to be there to make sure Father doesn't terrify them too much. You can be a slave with Thomas, Mr. Small."

"What about my mother?" said Thomas. "She won't have a part."

"Maybe we can give her the job of getting us ready," said Mayhew. "Maybe that will satisfy her."

"It will have to," Mr. Small said. "I'm rather glad she's not going to be in it. If I know her, she'd give it all away."

"So then," said Mayhew, "we are ready to begin. It's almost afternoon. Father, we'll leave you for now. I have to get my stage magic together."

"What makes you so sure you can fool Darrow with it?" said Pluto. "You didn't much fool Mr. Small here."

"He fooled me for a longer time than we'll need to fool the Darrows," Mr. Small said.

"Anyway," added Thomas, "he didn't have me to help him, Mayhew didn't. With me to help him, we'll fool them good."

"Let's go to the cave," Mayhew told them. "I have some materials there. I'll tell you of my plan."

Thomas was so excited, he could hardly think. It was going to be scary, what they would do to the Darrows. He had no idea what the scaring of them would be like, what Mayhew had in mind.

But I'm going to be an actor, he thought. Maybe I'll be good at it, too!

18

It seemed to Thomas as though they had waited for hours. He couldn't see a foot in front of him where he lay in the trees surrounding the clearing. He was not to talk, nor could he move very much. This scaring of the Darrows wasn't at all like he had imagined it earlier, when it was still day. Now he was chilled through to the bone, lying low on his stomach in the pitch black night. He couldn't see his father where he, too, lay in wait, a short distance away. He couldn't see Mayhew or Mr. Pluto, nor hear them either. All was so silent, so mysterious, he had to clench his fists to keep his teeth from chattering.

Wy don't they come? he thought. What are the Darrows waiting for?

Thomas could feel small insects crawling over his ankles, where the chains were locked. He wanted to sit up and slap the bugs, but he dared not.

"Don't you think of moving," Mayhew had warned him. "They might wait in the trees for an hour or two just to make sure no one's around. If they spot us before they hit that clearing, the game will be over."

Thomas heard the slightest movement. He

buried his head in the pine needles. He had phosphorous tape over his eyebrows and around his eyes. The same tape outlined his jaw and cheekbones. He had to keep his head always down, so as not to glow there in the weeds and bushes.

He thought, I'm getting scared. I'm going to be just scared awful if one of them happens to step on me.

Think about something else, he told himself. Think about today.

Whatever sound Thomas had heard was no longer separate from the subtle sounds of night. Thomas let himself become full of the day and all the preparations they had made. They'd run into the Darrows once, Mr. Small and Thomas, and it had been a tense meeting. It had happened after Thomas and Mr. Small returned from Columbus, where they'd spent a lot of Mayhew's money in a theater supplies store. Never had Thomas been in such a place. There were costumes and masks, some of which they bought. There were trunks full of drapery material, and shelves of cosmetic paints and dyes. There were whole stage sets, with fake platters of food and crystal glasses painted to look as though they were filled with red wine. Mayhew had asked them to find gossamer wings. And they had been lucky to find a huge, feather-light pair, which they purchased at a fair price.

Thomas was still talking about the store when Mr. Small stopped the car downtown to do more shopping. They bought groceries and dishes to replace temporarily those which had been broken.

When later they were coming out of the hardware store, their arms full of paint-mixing pails and such, they saw three of the Darrows coming toward them.

Thomas stopped in his tracks.

"Keep yourself moving away from the car," Mr. Small had said out of the side of his mouth to Thomas. They had not bothered to cover up any of their purchases from the theater supplies store.

The Darrows appeared to be just as surprised to see Thomas and Mr. Small. One of them stopped in the street, looking around at the other two, but the two biggest ones came on ahead.

Mr. Small said good day to them in a matter-of-fact tone, since it was the custom always in a small town to speak to everyone. The Darrows looked hard at them, and then one said good day. He tried to smile and did manage a weak one.

"You be Mr. Small?" the one Darrow had said. Thomas remembered it all.

"That's right," said Mr. Small. "I don't believe I know your name."

But the Darrow man wouldn't say who he was. He went on talking, looking not at Thomas or Mr. Small but at the store wrapping paper that partially covered the paint pails and mixing sticks.

"Getting ready to paint things," Thomas couldn't help saying with a broad grin. "Going to paint the whole inside of the house."

Mr. Small had given him a sharp glance, telling him not to say anything else.

"Hear you folks had some excitement over there in the big house," said another one of the Darrows to no one in particular.

The Darrow who had spoken first looked menacingly at his brother.

Mr. Small smiled at them. "Oh, you mean old Pluto," he had said. "Yes, he took real sick in the night. We had to bring him to Columbus, where there is a good doctor I know. We left him there with a colleague of mine, since he wouldn't go into the hospital. He has to have a thorough going over, but I suspect he will be coming back home tomorrow morning."

Then Mr. Small avoided looking at them, giving the impression he was hiding something.

Thomas began to hum significantly.

The Darrows fidgeted nervously. "That's all?" one of them couldn't help asking.

"Why, what more could there be?" said Mr. Small. "Everything has been so peaceful and quiet, even with Mr. Pluto becoming ill." And then he bid them good-by. He and Thomas left the Darrow men gawking there in the middle of the street.

Now Thomas grinned at the dark, his mouth pressed against pine needles. He opened and closed his hands resting at his sides, trying not to rattle the chains attached to his wrists. By now, he was cold and stiff in every muscle. He shivered from head to foot, for he wore only a flimsy tatter of a shirt and trousers that were mostly rags. The fronts of both had been brushed with phosphorescent paint. He still lay in the position Mayhew had placed him a few hours before to hide the glow of his clothing.

I can't stand it much longer, he thought. I'm going to have to move in another five minutes, I can't help it. I just can't!

Mr. Small, close by Thomas, was having similar thoughts. They had waited three, maybe four hours. The time had to be well after midnight, and he wondered how Thomas was faring there, hidden in the weeds and bushes.

He won't be able to stay still much longer, Mr. Small thought. He must be cold with so little on. We'll all be at the doctor's before this is over.

Mr. Small was dressed much like Thomas, in tatters and rags, with chains about his wrists and ankles. The chains were real and quite heavy; Mr. Small hugged the ground in the way Thomas did. During the long period of time he lay there, he began to feel as though he *were* a slave hiding and running. Somewhere in the back of his mind was emptiness and fear; loneliness, the way a desperate slave would feel. At the same time, Mr. Small felt slightly ridiculous. The whole business of the night, having to lie so still, hardly breathing, was a bit mad. But Mayhew Skinner had a way of making the unreal and the unaccustomed seem normal.

He's a magician, pure and simple, thought Mr. Small. I wouldn't have believed a week ago that anyone could get me out here, catching pneumonia just to perform an elaborate joke. What have we come to, acting like fools!

But Mayhew had his mind on something entirely different. For one thing, he was burning hot. He could feel perspiration trickling down his neck onto his shoulders, then down his arms. He, too, lay on his stomach, hidden by trees and grass and bushes. He was dressed in a heavy, odd-fitting, old-fashioned suit. He wore a long, blondish wig streaked with white, which fell to his shoulders. The wig had been treated with a phosphorous spray paint, and the effect of it in the dark, when he removed his hat, was spectacular. His face and neck were covered by a cream-colored mask, fitting over his skull under the wig. Never had he imagined that one day he would play the part of a white abolitionist. He didn't find the prospect funny at all, however. He would play his role with all the grim skill he had. He fully intended to be the most superb apparition of all.

Slowly Mayhew lifted his head about an inch, just high enough for his eyes to scan the top of his father's cave across the clearing, directly above the wood doors in the cave mouth. Hidden there, among the trees, was Pesty.

Poor baby! he thought. Has she fallen asleep? I should have my head examined for letting her stay out here. They'll become suspicious.

He had tried to provide an alibi for Pesty staying out late this night. In his best feminine hand, he had written to Mr. Darrow, and had allowed Pesty to deliver the note saying that the child wished to stay in the big house until Mr. Pluto returned. The child was unusually upset over Mr. Pluto's sudden illness, the note said, and the Smalls would be pleased to have her stay the night, if Mr. Darrow did not object. Darrow had not replied, and Pesty had come anyway, since she always went where she wished and returned home when she felt like it.

If she falls asleep, we're sunk, thought Mayhew.

Lying the way they were, facing the clearing and the cave, neither Mr. Small nor Thomas, nor Mayhew either, had any way of knowing if the Darrows were creeping about among them. Pesty was to watch for them and give the signal because, being the kind of child she was, she knew enough about night and Darrows to know when they were moving.

Then Mayhew heard it. Just a soft sound it was, like a bird giving its last weak chirp before sleep overcame it. The sound came from above the cave. It was Pesty's signal.

Mayhew grinned uncontrollably.

Come on, Darrow. Come on in.

Mr. Pluto was calm and comfortable. He sat within the cave tunnel, just beyond the partly opened plank doors in the cave mouth. He rested in a cushioned chair Mayhew had provided for him. Wrapped snugly around his shoulders was his heavy brown throw. Upon his head was his black stovepipe hat. He played no man but himself and he was the same as always, except for Mayhew's warm, hide gloves on his hands and a wool blanket bunched around his legs.

Pluto could see the whole clearing and the trees surrounding it, without being seen himself. But he couldn't see Thomas or Mr. Small or Mayhew. He had stared at the clearing and trees for hours; he knew the three of them lay out there, but, after a time, he began to think maybe they'd gone and left him. Maybe they had tricked him, and an ambulance would burst suddenly into that clearing and take him away.

Halfway through the waiting, the staring, he had become afraid. The night settled around him; the minutes hung inside him in even lengths of cold. He felt his mind getting further away from him. He became frightened that he might see the real ghosts of old Mr. Drear and the two slaves, as he had seen them before when he was sick and tired with despair. There had been a time when what he saw was just the Darrows walking stealthily behind him, never too near and never too far away. They had followed him down the years, as had those ghosts, so that, oftentimes, he couldn't tell which he was seeing.

But now his mind settled back. He had caught hold of one thought he had tried earlier to fix in his mind. He could even doze off now and again, sitting in the chair with his chin resting in his beard. But always that one idea stayed close to his ear; that much of his mind was alert and ready.

He dozed.

If I do nothing more, the thought went, I'm going to fix up those Darrows once and for good!

He opened his eyes. He hadn't heard Pesty's signal. At least, he didn't know if he had. But darkness was moving ever so carefully back in the trees and from three directions. Darkness was making just the gentlest, swishing noises in the pine boughs.

Without effort, Pluto stood up. Straight and tall he was, easing the chair away from him with the calves of his legs. He placed his palms on each of the plank doors. There was no other thought in his head but the one thought he would never again, after this night, need to hold onto.

To Thomas, it had been years since Pesty had given the signal. His mind leaped and twisted. He tried to calculate how fast the Darrows were moving. He thought many times that they must have got by him. In another minute, he would have to yell out because of the exhaustion and excitement he felt. Then beside him stood a Darrow, when there had been nothing but trees a second before.

Thomas hadn't seen the Darrow come. He dared not move his head enough to see the man's trouser legs. But he knew the Darrow was there, standing in line with a tree. Standing so still, the Darrow could have been staring down at Thomas. Then he evaporated and went on. But this took minute upon minute. Thomas felt he would faint. He was suffocating, trying not to breathe out loud, when his insides ached for air and more air.

Once the Darrow had passed, Thomas couldn't help lifting his head and turning it quickly to the side. Fresh air hit him, cool and black. He breathed slowly and silently. He breathed so deeply, he thought he would explode.

There was another Darrow close to Thomas' father. Standing there, he was gone in a blink of Thomas' eye.

They are Mohegans, Thomas thought. We are Tuscaroras and they are Mohegans, not of our people.

He didn't see the third and last Darrow until the faint shape of him was in the clearing, close to where Mayhew lay. Next, all three forms were together and not moving. Thomas raised the lower part of his body upon his knees, keeping his head well down.

Darrows were whispering and looking around in all directions.

"I tell you he's gone, like they said," one was saying.

Another spoke quite clearly. "I don't like it—why ain't his torches burning on the cave?"

"Because he ain't here to light them, fool!"

"Mebbe so, but I can't see hardly a thing."

"When we get to the door, we can use the flashlight."

The forms moved slowly forward, ready to break away at the slightest sound. When they were about a foot in front of the cave, one of them turn on the flashlight.

Pluto slid himself out between the plank doors, blocking the Darrows before they had time to realize what had happened.

In the few minutes it had taken the Darrows to reach the cave, old Pluto had had an idea close to inspiration. Quickly bending down, he untied his shoes and removed the laces. Then, catching one end of his throw in his palm, he tied it to his wrist with a shoelace. When both ends of the throw were tied to both wrists, he pulled the neck of the throw behind his head, and fitted it over his top hat. What greeted the Darrows as they beamed their flashlight was a grotesque and chilling scene.

From the black mouth of the cave came an enormous bat with wings outstretched. By the time the Darrows realized it was Pluto, he was towering over them. With his arms held out to the height of his shoulders, he began to speak, his face turnd toward the heavens.

"Come, my winged bird, my glory, nightbird! Come, all ye demons three who walk with me forever. Come parade awhile with Pluto, who has missed ye so!" His voice roared through the clearing. The Darrow men ducked down. One of them dropped the flashlight. When it hit the ground, it broke and went out.

In the trees on top of Mr. Pluto's cave, Pesty let drop the canvas sheet that had hidden the painted brilliance of Mr. Pluto's bay horse. Already mounted on the horse, she took a sure hold on each of the gossamer wings attached to his withers. As she dug her bare toes into the bay's flanks, she began to work the wings up and down.

What the Darrows saw was a glowing giant of a thing, with wings as translucent as glimmering silk. The great wings brushed the air as lightly as feathers. The thing itself seemed to rise up and down, making only a muffled, soft sound.

There was a moan, as one Darrow sank down before the winged creature atop the cave.

Another one of them was yelling in a kind of strangled, husky scream.

The third and last began to jump up and down, first on one foot and then on the other.

The sight of the glowing bay with glimmering wings was indeed terrifying. Thomas, who was now supposed to come forward with Mr. Small and Mayhew, thus trapping the Darrows between ghosts and devils, was sagging down himself. He had not been prepared for the way Pluto looked, nor for the flashlight suddenly full on him. And no one had told him Pluto would say anything. Why had Pluto said what he had?

All at once Thomas was overcome with the night and with all the fear of Pluto that was buried deep inside him. He could not see Pesty on the bay's back. The reason he couldn't was that she was lying nearly flat, but Thomas didn't think of that. He simply saw that glowing devil of a horse and he began to sink down.

Mayhew grabbed hold of Thomas and carried him forward.

"Come to," he whispered. "We have got them. Stand up!"

Thomas stood, but barely. He and Mayhew and Mr. Small now spread themselves in a half circle behind the Darrows.

Just then, the Darrow who had fallen to his knees was lifted up by another Darrow and dragged away from the specter of Pluto and the winged demon, only to be dropped brutally at the sight of the three apparitions at the edge of the clearing. They shimmered so brightly that all three Darrows fell down.

All the Darrow men were yelling now. And Mayhew, as old Mr. Drear, was laughing in a most horrifying, crazed sound, screeching and groaning as he inched toward them. The laugh tore through what little courage Thomas had left, and he folded up again.

Mr. Small hissed at Thomas, rattling his chains and moaning so that Thomas would at least pump his arms, causing some of his own chains to clank.

The effect of Thomas' own fear was perhaps the most convincing to the Darrows, for it seemed to them that he was a slave ghost still driven by invisible tormentors.

"Let me out of here!" one Darrow screamed.

"Mr. Pluto, Lordy, call 'em off. Call 'em off! Please, let me go! I won't come back, oh please!"

Mr. Pluto commenced to laugh. It was a deep,

hateful sort of laugh, full of malice and memory of malice. He laughed and laughed. With his laughter, and Mayhew still screeching as Dies Drear, the whole hill rocked with earsplitting noise.

"Get them, my demons, get them!" cried Mr. Pluto.

Mr. Small raised his chains. So did Thomas. Mayhew folded his flowing arms around the closest Darrow.

Men were scrambling all over the clearing. Thomas got caught in his own chain and nearly broke his ankle; someone pulled him to his feet. He found himself face to face with a Darrow, and the Darrow was about ready to foam at the mouth. Suddenly all the Darrows broke away and were running free.

Mayhew began to laugh in his own voice. He slapped his hip and threw back his head and bellowed. One Darrow stopped dead in his tracks, just at the edge of the clearing where Thomas had been hiding. Mr. Pluto began to laugh too, like a man who had successfully played a wonderful joke on someone. His was now a pleasant, healthy sort of laugh; he put his arm around Mayhew, folding him tenderly inside his throw. The Darrow stared at the two of them for the longest moment, then walked away.

When the Darrows had gone for sure, Mr. Small said, "You laughed too soon. The last of them knew we were putting on for them."

"They would have figured it out, all of them, in

another minute anyhow," Mayhew said. "The point is that for about fifteen seconds, we scared the living daylights out of them. And to make it worse, we laughed at them to their face because they allowed themselves to be fooled."

"You have to know Darrows," said old Pluto to Mr. Small. "It's bad enough that anybody would dare trick them. But to get away with that and then to laugh at 'em right in front of 'em, why they'll never live it down!"

"And they'll be about ready to pray we won't spread it around how we made fools out of them," Mayhew said. "I'm going to have Pesty tell them we let all the Carr boys watch!"

Mr. Small had to smile. "You are surely something," he said.

Then Mayhew and Pluto laughed and laughed.

Gently Mr. Small led Thomas into the cave. The boy was trembling all over. Mr. Small tried not to let Thomas know he had noticed.

Thomas was so ashamed. He would never be an actor. Never in a million years.

19

In the cavern of Dies Drear, Mr. Pluto sat behind his elaborate desk with a most satisfied grin upon his face.

Mr. Small and Thomas were tired out. They had changed from their slave costumes into their regular clothes. They'd finished removing the makeup and had piled their chains, wigs and such into a heap.

Pesty came in with the gossamer wings, which she placed on the very top of the heap. "I put the bay back in his stall," she said to Mayhew. "I cleaned the paint off him, too."

"You are a good baby," Mayhew said. "Now you ought to go to bed."

"Come here, Miss Bee," Pluto said to her. "Come sit on my lap. You know, you handled that horse and those wings just about perfect." He folded the smiling child within his throw, so that only her head, with eyes black and bright, peeked out.

"That was about the best show I've ever seen," Pluto said. "And you all wanted to put me in a hospital!"

"My mistake, Father," said Mayhew. He hadn't felt so friendly toward his father in a long time.

"How in the name of heaven did you think of fixing that throw the way you did?"

"When you came out of that cave," said Mr. Small, "you looked like a huge, frightful bat."

"And what you said," Thomas said to old Pluto. He was still weak and trembling, and he wouldn't look at any of them. "You scared me, Mr. Pluto."

Mr. Pluto laughed softly. "It was a thrill for me," he said. "I had the best old time!"

Glancing at Thomas, Mayhew felt sorry for him. "Father did look pretty awful, what with that throw fixed the way it was. But being the way he is, I knew he would say something to terrify those Darrows. If I'm an actor at all, it's because he was one before me."

"I didn't do so well, did I?" Thomas said. "I guess I'm not too good as an actor." He couldn't find the words to apologize for his fear.

"You did just fine, son," said Mr. Small. "Having to lie there for so many hours—you did real well."

Thomas couldn't stand being treated so politely by them. He was growing angry at himself for being such a coward, and angry at them for being so nice about it.

"I think I'll go on home," he said. "See if Mama is sleeping."

"I'll walk over with you," Mayhew said. "Pesty, you ready to go over to Thomas' house and sleep?"

"She's asleep already," said Mr. Small. "Look."

It was true. Pesty had snuggled down against Mr. Pluto and was now fast asleep.

"Let her alone, Mayhew," Pluto said. "Mr. Small

can take her home when he goes along—you will stay awhile, won't you, Mr. Small?" Mr. Small and old Pluto silently surveyed one another. Mr. Small nodded that he would stay.

"Why do you have to stay?" Thomas asked his father. "Why won't you come on home now?"

"Never you mind," said Mayhew. "Let's get going, see if we can find any more Darrows in the trees."

"There won't be any more Darrows," Thomas told him, "and I don't need you to walk me home."

"I'm not walking you home," said Mayhew. "I'm just going to walk with you, that's all. You don't want to be friends with me?"

Without Thomas being aware of it, Mayhew was leading him up the ramp and out of the cavern.

"I don't mind being friends," Thomas said. Secretly he was pleased that Mayhew had thought to go with him. "But I don't need anyone to take me home."

"I'm not taking you home, for pity's sake!" Mayhew said. "Man, you sure are a tough one to handle. How come you are so hard on people?"

"Well, I've always been independent," Thomas said seriously. "I make wood sculpture. I'm an artist, some say, and you have to be pretty much by yourself to be able to carve well." He felt full of pride when Mayhew looked at him with real interest.

"Wood sculpture? No kidding?"

"Sure," said Thomas. "I have even sold pieces to strangers. But mostly I just keep the pieces for myself and my family. Papa says I have a real talent for wood sculpture."

They went into Mr. Pluto's cave. The wall of the cave slid across the opening, shutting off the cavern of Dies Drear.

In the cavern, Mr. Small stretched out on the floor to one side of Mr. Pluto's desk. He folded his arms across his chest and sighed deeply. Closing his tired eyes for a second, he opened them again to stare at the immense, vaulted ceiling far above his head.

"I think now you can tell me what this is all about," he said to Pluto. He was so tired, he would have no trouble falling asleep right where he was.

Mr. Pluto cleared his throat. "Mayhew said he would leave it to you," Pluto said. "Mayhew told me this morning, whatever you said to do with this cavern was all right by him. And so I leave it up to you. I will trust you to do the right thing." Pluto tried to keep his voice casual, but deep within it was all his hope and desire.

"I see," said Mr. Small. He sat up and fixed his gaze on the intricate, carved detail of the desk. "I was wondering a moment ago if anyone . . . Dies Drear, I mean, ever made a list of all the things in this cavern."

"No, not that I have found," Mr. Pluto said. "I have been through all the ledgers and books. I've found no list, nor no record of where he got any of it."

"Fascinating," said Mr. Small. "He never ever meant any of it to be sold. And what a job to inventory all this. But I think I should, don't you? Give each peace a number, a name and description, and try to fix a value for it. What do you think, Mr. Skinner?" Mr. Small deliberately kept from looking at Pluto or around the cavern.

And it was some time before Pluto spoke. Mr. Small was afraid he had fallen asleep, so still was he holding Pesty. But then Pluto breathed deeply.

"That will take as long as the rest of an old man's life," he said softly.

Mr. Small looked at him and smiled gently. "You know, sir, you have a way of saying things that I do admire," he said. "Your son, Mayhew, has the same gift with words. But just as you say, to inventory all this will take that long, at least."

"You will not turn this place over to the foundation right away?"

It was Mr. Small's turn to remain silent. When he did speak, it was with relief that at last he knew he had made up his mind. "All this has remained hidden for a century. Keeping it hidden awhile longer won't matter much." Saying this, Mr. Small felt peaceful inside.

Ever so carefully, Pluto got to his feet. "You take Miss Bee on home now," he said. His old eyes looked mistily at the child. "Just carry her like this, and she will sleep all the way."

Mr. Small did as he was told. "I will begin in the morning," he said. "I will inventory the books and ledgers first."

"They'll be ready," said Pluto. "Come as early as you will."

That was all then. Mr. Small left, carrying Pesty through the trees as carefully as old Pluto would have. Part way home, he passed close to someone he could but barely see. There was a laugh, a deep, sharp sound in the pine boughs. It was Mayhew coming back. He didn't stop to speak, nor did Mr. Small.

A half hour before, Thomas and Mayhew had gone through the trees all the way home. Thomas wouldn't have believed they could become friends so quickly.

"You can learn a lot about acting in the month I'll be here," Mayhew had said.

"You mean you will teach me?"

"I can teach you a good amount if you think you really want to learn," Mayhew said.

"I don't think I'd be much good at it," said Thomas. "But there's one thing I've seen you do that I'd like to learn."

"What's that?"

"How is it you can seem to flow out of doorways," Thomas asked, "like you were liquid spilling into the night? How do you do that, Mayhew?"

Mayhew laughed. "I'll have to think about that one. Maybe I can break it down and show you." He laughed again, and they walked without speaking.

"You know," Mayhew said suddenly, "I'm glad we did what we did tonight. Not so much scaring the Darrows. That was important, too, because now they know they can never fool with your father the way they did with mine. They'll fear your father in a way they never feared mine. They'll fear him not as a devil but as a man. He will have the right to say who can pass here and who cannot. Yes, they'll be afraid of him and the law he won't hesitate to use against them.

"But what I meant to say about being glad is that my father had such a good time with it. I felt closer to him tonight than I think I ever have."

"You never liked him much?" Thomas asked. He felt he could ask that. He felt Mayhew wouldn't mind talking about it.

"No, I never did," Mayhew said. "It's hard for a boy growing up without his father, not even able to wish for him since he didn't like him to begin with. You like your father though, don't you, Thomas?"

"Sometimes I get angry with him," Thomas said. "He always has to figure out everything before I do. Like in the house when we were planning to scare the Darrows."

Mayhew smiled. "Your father knew we were going to too much trouble to be scaring just plain people."

"No," said Thomas, "he had a report from the foundation about the whole history of the house, and from it he must have figured out that the third slave and you and your father and the Darrows were all mixed up together.

"But sure, I like him fine. He's pretty smart, you know. Folks always did say he had a powerful brain."

Mayhew laughed softly.

Then Thomas said, "Do you suppose I and that youngest Darrow, that Mac Darrow, do you think we could get to be friends?"

"Oh well," Mayhew said, "the Darrows aren't going to want him or Pesty fooling around here for a very long time. And you have to remember, Macky's a Darrow after all—we did fool his brothers pretty bad. He has to live it down, too, you know. But give it time. Anger might die down by the change of a couple of seasons. Wait for the winter. You'll most likely run into Macky here in these trees full of snow, when you both are out hunting rabbit."

"It will take that long a time?" Thomas said.

"That's not a long time. When you begin to think it is, just remember Father hunting thirty years for his legacy, which might have never existed. Yes, winter will be here before you have got to know this land properly. You will feel and breathe an air so cold that all things holding warmth will be your friend."

"You love it here," Thomas said. "How come you go away from it?"

"That's my secret, my friend," said Mayhew. "Not all questions can have answers to be said out loud."

They had entered Thomas' house. Mrs. Small was asleep on the couch in the parlor. On the floor beside the couch was Thomas' baseball bat.

"I'll be going," Mayhew whispered again. "I won't see you tomorrow. I have to take care of business in

Dayton. I'll see you the next day though, and we will maybe start your stage lessons."

Thomas said good night to him. He didn't wake Mrs. Small, but went up to his own room. He didn't even bother about the captain's chair, which still sat with its back to the room. There were his carvings, so familiar, grouped on the mantelpiece. Falling across his bed, he was instantly asleep.

Thomas awoke about ten o'clock the next morning. His clothing was hardly wrinkled, but he was stiff in every muscle. He washed his face, brushed his teeth and combed his hair. Not bothering to change his shirt, he went quickly down the hall and down the stairs. He found his mother busy with the twins in the kitchen. She looked tired, but she smiled at Thomas pleasantly and fixed him a heaping plate of ham and eggs with potatoes. Thomas ate all of it in a few minutes. He had two glasses of milk and two slices of toast besides.

"You were hungry, for sure," Mrs. Small said.

"Did Papa tell you about last night?" Thomas asked. "Did he tell you how we did it?"

"He told me," she said. "I'm glad I wasn't there. I wouldn't have been able to go through with it. Every time I think of you lying out there for so long, and little Pesty on that big horse, I can't believe it."

"It was really something," Thomas said. "We scared those Darrows half to death." He had forgotten about his own fear.

"Where is Papa anyway?" he asked. He didn't think to inquire after Pesty.

"Over at the cavern," Mrs. Small said.

Thomas kissed his brothers. "Boys, you like this big, old house of Smalls? You going to get lost in it and cause me worry? Maybe I'll take you hunting when winter snow falls, would you like that?"

The boys grinned happily at Thomas.

"I'm going to see Papa," said Thomas to Mrs. Small.

"Tell him I expect him back here about eleven," she said. "He went out after having only a half cup of coffee. And he will have to take you to register for school sometime. He's got an appointment at one to see someone at the college. And later on I would like to see that cavern myself. You tell him now, Thomas."

Thomas went. The morning was find and clear and the trees on the hill as he went through them were fresh with dew. In no time he was over the hill and in Mr. Pluto's cave. Inside the cave there was a ringing, pounding noise going on. It was a noise of metal beating against metal. Thomas walked the short tunnel to the main cave. A great fire roared in Mr. Pluto's forge. Every once in a while Mr. Pluto turned to work his bellows. Then Pluto would hammer on white-hot metal, held over the fire. He paused a moment as Thomas came close.

"What are you doing?" Thomas asked him. Mr. Pluto was dripping wet but otherwise looked strong and healthy.

"I'm making the biggest lock you ever did see," he said. "And good morning to you."

"Good morning," said Thomas. "What for?"

Pluto beat and turned the white-hot metal. "For to lock good those plank doors you just came through."

"You never locked them before," said Thomas.

"I know it," Pluto answered him.

"Well, you surely don't need to lock them now," Thomas said.

"I know that, too," old Pluto said, "but I think I will just the same. I haven't had something to do in so long!" He beat and turned the metal that now took shape. Thomas stared at him with his mouth open. A grin spread across his face. Then he asked if it were all right to go into the cavern. Mr. Pluto said for him to go right ahead.

Thomas walked to the wall where the rope was. He pulled down on that rope and watched the wall slide back.

Within the cavern the wall slid closed behind Thomas. He took his time going through the stalagmites. He walked around them to touch them, feeling the damp coolness of them. Far below sat his father at Mr. Pluto's desk. Mr. Small worked furiously on long sheets of yellow paper. He had books and ledgers from the cases piled on the floor around him. Thomas went down the ramp, taking his time. Finally he stood before his father.

Mr. Small sneezed and coughed. His nose was running. He glanced up at Thomas and nodded a hurried greeting. "Listing everything . . ." he said. He shook his head. "There is so much! This is only the beginning. And it makes fine reading . . . I have to read it, don't I? It will take me years!"

"Is that what you're going to do? List every bit and piece of it?" Thomas asked.

Mr. Small stopped long enough to blow his nose. "Well, we have to know how much there is," he said. "Since we don't know where Drear got it all, we can at least make a record of what it is. If the foundation is to have any order, if it should wish to start a museum . . ." He folded his handkerchief and began to read to himself from some volume that looked to Thomas as though it would fall into dust at any moment.

"Papa . . ." Thomas said.

"Shhh. Thomas, there is so much to do. Years!"

Thomas told him what Mrs. Small had said.

"Yes, yes," was all Mr. Small answered. Thomas couldn't tell if his father had listened or not.

Mr. Pluto's brown throw was lying on the floor by some books. Thomas went around, picked it up and carefully put it around his father's shoulders.

"You caught yourself a cold," he said softly. "You'd better take care."

Mr. Small continued reading. Once he smiled vaguely at Thomas, not unkindly. But his eyes were full of the eager concern he had for the work ahead of him.

It was then Thomas saw Pesty sitting at the very

top of the ladder, next to the shelves of bottles. She had a cloth in her hand; she smiled at Thomas and held out the cloth. Thomas placed a finger to his lips and shook his head. He held out his arms to her. Pesty came halfway down the ladder and Thomas lifted her the rest of the way. He went up the ladder and seated himself at the top. Again he held out his arms for Pesty. She climbed up and sat a few rungs below him.

"Papa's going to work himself until he catches the flu," he whispered in Pesty's ear.

"If he gets sick," she whispered back, "you'll have to give him the medicine, like I do for Mr. Pluto."

They sat for a long time then, without saying anything. Pesty was content to sit with Thomas, and Thomas by now was used to having her around.

Looking at the cavern from high up was different than seeing it down below. Suddenly Thomas saw the thick chain almost hidden by bright tapestries. He had noticed it the first time he and Mr. Small had entered the cavern. Now he could tell what was at the end of it. He pointed at it for Pesty. She nodded.

"It's been up there forever," she whispered.

High up, the chain was looped on a thick hook projected from the ceiling. Hanging from the end of the chain was a black trunk. It was quite a large trunk, which bulged with something that would one day burst its seams.

Thomas' curiosity was aroused. But then he leaned back. Slowly it came to him that he didn't care at all what was in the trunk. In the vastness of the cavern, one more item didn't seem to matter.

Let it stay a mystery, he thought. As long as the chain and hook can hold it, just let it stay there.

He didn't bother to look at it or to think about it again.

He and Pesty sat watching the still form of Mr. Small, almost hidden beneath Mr. Pluto's throw. They would wait for as long as they had to. They would wait on the ladder by the bottles as long as it would take Mr. Small to remind himself of them and need them to help. And they didn't mind the waiting, not this day nor the days to come. They had years.

About the Author

Virginia Hamilton grew up in Yellow Springs, Ohio, a southern Ohio community similar to the one Thomas moves to in *The House of Dies Drear*. This rural area of villages and farms was an important network on the Underground Railroad system to Canada during the Civil War era. As a child, Miss Hamilton was aware that many of the large old houses in her own community had once concealed running slaves. Her ancestors were among the one hundred thousand slaves who fled from the South in the first half of the nineteenth century, forty thousand of whom are said to have passed through Ohio.

Miss Hamilton believes her books grow out of her childhood wonder about these fleeing people. "I had a longing as a child," she has said. "I needed to know how men, women and children could travel hundreds of miles on foot through enemy land. I found out that they were brave and clever almost beyond belief. Perhaps with this book I have at last touched them the way they first touched me so long ago."

As far back as she can remember, Miss Hamilton says, she has wanted to be a writer. "I never thought seriously about any other career." She attended Antioch College and Ohio State University. After living in New York for many years, she recently moved back to Yellow Springs with her husband and children.

The House of Dies Drear
Reading Group Guide

About This Book
Thomas Small and his family are leaving their home in North Carolina to move north, to Ohio. Their new house was built by an abolitionist named Dies Drear and was once a station on the Underground Railroad. Will Thomas be able to unlock the mysterious old house's secrets? If he can, what will he discover?

Discussion Questions
Who was Dies Drear? What did slaves call him and why? What did he want escaped slaves to do?

What happened to Dies Drear and the slaves he had been hiding?

What does Thomas think about Dies Drear's house when he first sees it? What does he discover about it? Why does he think the house is haunted?

What is the meaning of the strange triangles Mr. Small and Thomas find around the house? How did runaway slaves use such triangles?

Who are Mr. Pluto and the Darrows? What are their secrets? What are their relationships to one another, to Dies Drear, and to the house?

Why is Thomas upset after the trick the Smalls and the Skinners play on the Darrows is over?

Explain the deal that Mr. Small and Mr. Pluto strike at the end of the novel. Is it a fair one?

Activities

The Small and Skinner families are fascinated by their families' histories and by the history of all African-American slaves. Research the history of your own family and ethnic group. What can you find that makes you proud? What can you find that surprises you?

The House of Dies Drear is fiction, but the Underground Railroad was real. Read more about the women and men who risked their lives running the Underground Railroad. You might start by reading more about the most famous conductor of the Underground Railroad, Harriet Tubman.

When the Smalls first arrive at Dies Drear's house, Mr. Pluto has unpacked for them and arranged their things in a way that makes Mrs. Small see her own belongings in a whole new light. Try arranging some of your things in a new way. Can you make familiar items seem new and strange?

When the Small family drives around town on Sunday, Thomas notices many ways in which Ohio is different from North Carolina; families are not as poor as they were in his hometown, and white and African-American children play together. Have you ever visited or moved to a new place where things were very different? What were the differences, and how did you feel about them?

Mr. Pluto is by turns frightening and fascinating to Thomas. Have you ever known someone who intimidated you but who also interested you? Who was it? Did you ever become friends with that person as Thomas becomes friends with Mr. Pluto?

Thomas wants to be an actor. Try acting yourself! Put on various costumes or disguises, use makeup and some props, and act out a story with friends or alone.

Read more about Thomas Small and Dies Drear's house in Virginia Hamilton's sequel, *The Mystery of Drear House: The Conclusion of the Dies Drear Chronicle*. Or try reading some other fictional works about the Underground Railroad, such as *The Secret Road*, by Robert Nordan; *Trouble Don't Last*, by Shelley Pearsall; or *The Slave Dancer*, by Paula Fox. Which do you like best and why?